The Clock

The Civilizations of the First and Second Man have been destroyed by the products of their own technology. Now the world is emerging from a new dark age into the dawn of a second Middle Ages. Britain is dominated by a Luddite Church and by the doctrine that all machines are evil. Into this strange world comes Kieron, an artist's apprentice who is inflamed by a forbidden dream – to construct a flying machine which will enable man to soar through the air like a bird.

All Fools' Day

Summer 1971. A marvellous spell of weather, idyllic in its warmth. But new sun-spots had appeared; and with their appearance came a significant increase in the suicide rate. The wonderful summer continued for a decade: simultaneously Radiant Suicide reached endemic proportions, the only people to escape its effects being the supposed transnormals, the obsessionals, the eccentrics and the psychopaths. These were to be the only remnants of the ancient 'homo sapiens' …

A Far Sunset

The year is AD 2032 The *Gloria Mundi*, a starship built and manned by the new United States of Europe, touches down on the planet, Alatair Five. Disaster strikes, leaving only one apparent survivor – an Englishman named Paul Marlow, whose adventures in the lair of the strange primeval race known as the Bayani leads him firstly to their God, the omnipotent and omniscient Oruri, and eventually to an unlimited power that is so great it must include an in-built death sentence …

Also by Edmund Cooper

Collections

Jupiter Laughs
Voices in the Dark
A World of Difference

Novels

All Fools' Day (1966)
The Cloud Walker (1973)
A Far Sunset (1967)
Five to Twelve (1968)
Kronk (1970) (aka Son of Kronk)
The Last Continent (1970)
Merry Christmas Ms Minerva (1978)
The Overman Culture (1971)
Prisoner of Fire (1974)
Seahorse in the Sky (1969)
Seed of Light (1959)
The Slaves of Heaven (1975)
The Tenth Planet (1973)
Transit (1964)
Uncertain Midnight (1958) (aka Deadly Image)
Who Needs Men? (1972)
Ferry Rocket (1954) (Writing as George Kinley)

The Expendables (Writing as Richard Avery)

1. The Expendables: The Deathworms of Kratos (1975)
2. The Expendables: The Rings of Tantalus (1975)
3. The Expendables: the Wargames of Zelos (1975)
4. The Expendables: The Venom of Argus (1976)

Edmund Cooper

SF GATEWAY OMNIBUS

THE CLOUD WALKER
ALL FOOLS' DAY
A FAR SUNSET

GOLLANCZ
LONDON

First published in Great Britain in 2014 by
Gollancz
An imprint of the Orion Publishing Group
Orion House, 5 Upper St Martin's Lane,
London, WC2H 9EA

An Hachette UK Company

A CIP catalogue record for this book is
available from the British Library

ISBN 978 0 575 11638 2

1 3 5 7 9 10 8 6 4 2

Typeset by Jouve (UK), Milton Keynes

Printed and bound by CPI Group (UK) Ltd, Croydon, CR0 4YY

The Orion Publishing Group's policy is to use papers
that are natural, renewable and recyclable products and
made from wood grown in sustainable forests. The logging
and manufacturing processes are expected to conform to
the environmental regulations of the country of origin.

www.orionbooks.co.uk
www.gollancz.co.uk

CONTENTS

ENTER THE SF GATEWAY . . .

Towards the end of 2011, in conjunction with the celebration of fifty years of coherent, continuous science fiction and fantasy publishing, Gollancz launched the SF Gateway.

Over a decade after launching the landmark SF Masterworks series, we realised that the realities of commercial publishing are such that even the Masterworks could only ever scratch the surface of an author's career. Vast troves of classic SF and fantasy were almost certainly destined never again to see print. Until very recently, this meant that anyone interested in reading any of those books would have been confined to scouring second-hand bookshops. The advent of digital publishing changed that paradigm for ever.

Embracing the future even as we honour the past, Gollancz launched the SF Gateway with a view to utilising the technology that now exists to make available, for the first time, the entire backlists of an incredibly wide range of classic and modern SF and fantasy authors. Our plan, at its simplest, was – and still is! – to use this technology to build on the success of the SF and Fantasy Masterworks series and to go even further.

The SF Gateway was designed to be the new home of classic science fiction and fantasy – the most comprehensive electronic library of classic SFF titles ever assembled. The programme has been extremely well received and we've been very happy with the results. So happy, in fact, that we've decided to complete the circle and return a selection of our titles to print, in these omnibus editions.

We hope you enjoy this selection. And we hope that you'll want to explore more of the classic SF and fantasy we have available. These are wonderful books you're holding in your hand, but you'll find much, much more … through the SF Gateway.

www.sfgateway.com

INTRODUCTION
from The Encyclopedia of Science Fiction

Edmund Cooper (1926–1982) was a UK editor and author who served in the British Merchant Navy 1944–1945. His literary career began soon after; he edited *Review Fifty* (three issues, Winter 1950–Spring 1951), contributing poems, fiction and nonfiction to that journal, and began to publish stories of genre interest with 'The Unicorn' for *Everybody's* in 1951. He produced a considerable amount of short fiction in the 1950s, much of it assembled (with considerable overlap) in his first three collections: *Tomorrow's Gift* (1958), *Voices in the Dark* (1960) and *Tomorrow Came* (1963). Most of his short work came early, perhaps his best known story being 'Invisible Boy' (23 June 1956 *Saturday Evening Post*), which was the basis of the film *The Invisible Boy* (1957). For longer works, Cooper's early pseudonyms included George Kinley, under which name he published his first sf novel, *Ferry Rocket* (1954), which speculated about Space Flight in near space; Martin Lester, the name he used for *The Black Phoenix* (1954), in which a Nazi cabal attempts to destabilize the Western world; and Broderick Quain. For the later Expendables sf adventure series, beginning with *The Deathworms of Kratos* (1975), he wrote as Richard Avery – the protagonist of an earlier novel under his own name, *Transit* (1964). From 1967 until his death, he was an influential reviewer of sf for *The Sunday Times* in London.

It was as a novelist, however, that Cooper was most highly regarded. Though it was for his earlier novels that he was most appreciated, the quality of his work held up until *Prisoner of Fire* (1974); his last novel, *Merry Christmas, Ms Minerva!* (1978), a Near Future tale set in a Britain dominated by trade unions, seemed less generous than his earlier speculations about the condition of the land. His first novels were clearly conceived within sf frames, but from the very first tended to focus in Satirical terms on the Near Future. His first novel under his own name, *Deadly Image* (1958; published as *The Uncertain Midnight* in the UK), vividly describes a post-holocaust world in which Androids are gradually threatening to supplant humankind; Cooper's vision of humanity, here and elsewhere, is acid-edged, as is his abiding sense (typical of the satirical mind) that we are all too capable of creating monsters in the name of Utopia; its bleak depiction of this android-threatened world hints at an underlying lack of trust in progress, a distrust of the new technophilic post-War milieu that – though increasingly acceptable for later readers – helps explain his lack of a wide and faithful readership. Several years later, in *The Overman Culture* (1971), he reversed field, with the androids seen as morally exemplary. Other tales with a refreshing sharp bite include *All Fools' Day* (1966) (see below), *The Last Continent* (1969), *The Tenth Planet* (1973) and *The Cloud Walker* (1973) (see below). These works incorporate, more or less fully, a basic premise that the planet has been rendered to a greater or lesser degree uninhabitable; a condition for which we must almost certainly take the blame.

Several of his better novels are set off-Earth, and tend to be more sanguine. *Seed of Light* (1959) is a relatively weak Generation-Starship tale in which a small group manages to escape from a devastated Earth. Stronger examples include *Transit* (1964) and *Sea-Horse in the Sky* (1969), in both of which Aliens conduct experiments on humans sequestered on strange planets. The best of these books is almost certainly *A Far Sunset* (1967) (see below).

There can be no real doubt that Cooper's later work struggles against a sense that the world was not improving, and that the inmates were running the asylum. This sense, that somehow we did not prosper from the experience of World War Two, is not surprising in an author who came to manhood in England of the late 1940s, and whose constant return to the theme of nuclear war amplifies the anxieties of his generation. Though some critics, who accused him of being anti-Feminist, may have taken his satirical thrusts too literally, it remains the case that his statement about women in a man's world – 'Let them compete against men, they'll see that they can't make it' – was perhaps injudicious in lacking a level playing field to test the hypothesis. A persistent edginess about women in power becomes explicit in *Five to Twelve* (1968) and *Who Needs Men?* (1972); but it would not be wise to suggest that this edginess did not also apply to men: there are no well-run worlds in Cooper's universe. In his last successful novel, *Prisoners of Fire* (1974), a group of people endowed with Psi Powers focus their energies on the assassination of the British political elite; who seem to deserve this comeuppance. Cooper died with his reputation at an unfairly low ebb; he was a competent and prolific author who amply rewards his readers, and deserves to gain more.

The three novels here selected argue strongly for Cooper's rejuvenation as a significant voice in British sf, as one of the relatively small cadre of authors who bore World War Two, and its aftermath, in their bones. *The Cloud Walker* may be his most successful work, and was so received on publication. Two nuclear Holocausts have transformed England into a medievalized Ruined Earth, but the Luddite response of a new church – Cooper was consistently acidulous about organized Religion – is stupefyingly oppressive, and the young protagonist properly wins the day with an Invention which he uses to defend his village from assailants. This invention allows him to fly. The march of history resumes; progress is possible. In *All Fools' Day, Homo sapiens* is murderously unbalanced by a change in solar radiation; the Near Future setting is rendered in vividly grim terms, and conveys as clearly as anything he wrote the characteristic Cooperian sense that given a chance we will fail in our duty to ourselves, our homes, our country, our world. The third novel here presented, *A Far Sunset* (1967), represents a welcome escape from the planet where we have behaved so badly. The protagonist has been stranded on a strange though seemingly Earthlike planet, where he is captured by Aliens, who demonstrate to him the narrowness of his human obsession with the benefits of Technology. These three novels are lessons in human nature. They are sharp-tongued, but winnowed with wit, and a love of story-telling. They are discoveries we should make.

For a more detailed version of the above, see Edmund Cooper's author entry in *The Encyclopedia of Science Fiction*: http://sf-encyclopedia.com/entry/cooper_edmund

Some terms above are capitalised when they would not normally be so rendered; this indicates that the terms represent discrete entries in *The Encyclopedia of Science Fiction.*

THE CLOUD WALKER

From 1811 to 1812 the Luddites destroyed stocking frames, steam power looms, and shearing machines throughout Nottinghamshire, Derbyshire, Leicestershire and Yorkshire, and their rioting broke out again in 1816. They derived their name from Ned Ludd, an idiot boy of Leicestershire, who, it is said, unable to catch someone who had been tormenting him, destroyed some stocking frames in a fit of temper (1779).

Everyman's Encyclopaedia
(1958 edition)

PART ONE

Earthbound

1

When Kieron was eight years old he was encouraged to spend much time in the company of his affianced bride, Petrina. Later, at the end of the age of innocence, they would not be permitted to be alone together until Kieron had attained his majority, had been released from his apprenticeship, and was thus able to fulfil his contractual obligations.

Kieron was apprenticed to Hobart, the painter. Already, the boy was allowed to clean brushes and to help with the stretching of canvas and the grinding of pigment. When he was ten years old he would go to live with Hobart so that he could attend upon his master at all times. Kieron looked forward to this time and also dreaded it. He was anxious to discover the mysteries of painting, the laws of perspective, the laws of harmony and the laws of proper representation; but he did not really want to be a painter. He wanted to fly. He wanted to fly through the air like a bird. And that was heresy.

He was old enough to understand about heresy, young enough not to be terrified by it. The dominie who taught him and the neddy who took care of his spiritual discipline had spent much time expounding the diabolical nature of unlawful machines. They had succeeded not in instilling Kieron with a proper dread of machines but only with a secret fascination. Even at the age of five, Kieron knew that some day he would have to construct an unlawful machine in order to fly like a bird.

Petrina was nice – for a girl. She was the daughter of Sholto, the smith. Because Kieron was affianced to Petrina, he was allowed to watch Sholto at the forge. It was a great privilege. Some day, Kieron realised, he, too, would have to be able to work metal. He would have to be able to work metal to make the necessary parts for a flying machine. He asked many questions of Sholto. The smith, a huge, gentle man who took great pleasure in his work, saw no harm in talking to a small boy – especially one who was contracted to his daughter – and did not regard it as a breach of the oath of secrecy imposed by the Guild of Smiths. Soon Kieron had picked up a little of the lore of the tempering of steel, the fastening of plates by rivets, the shaping of helms, clasps, pikes, ploughshares.

'Boy,' Sholto would say good-naturedly, 'you are nought but a loon, an idler. Your thoughts should be of draughting and colouring, not of beating metals to your will. Go now and think on how to hold a charred twig steady to your design, or Master Hobart will make your arse somewhat tender.'

Kieron was discreet. He knew when the smith joked or was earnest; and he knew also that it was wise not to mention his growing knowledge of the working of metals to anyone, and particularly his father.

The days of childhood are both long and short. Kieron would rise with his family at first light and, like them, carry out mechanically the routine tasks that were necessary before the real work of the day could begin. He would collect shavings and waste wood from his father's workshop for the fire, while his mother drew water from the well and set the porridge to boil, and while his father went out to seek game or to fell a tree to be stored against its seasoning. When the sun was its own width above the eastern rim of the world, the family would come together for breakfast. Porridge always, bread always, fat always, bacon sometimes, eggs sometimes – depending upon the state of the hens, the state of the pigs, the state of trade.

After breakfast, Kieron, along with a score of other children in the hill reaches of the seigneurie, would go to the dominie's house for an hour of instruction. After that, each boy would go to the house of his master, to serve at his apprenticeship until noon.

Kieron was luckier than most boys. Hobart was prosperous, having found much favour in the eyes of Fitzalan, Lord of the Seigneurie of Arundel. Hobart was strong on portraiture, and Fitzalan of Arundel was a vain man with a vain wife and three vain daughters. He still hoped for a son; but the daughters alone were more than enough to keep Hobart tolerably employed.

Hobart could afford to indulge Kieron, could afford to let the boy experiment with charcoal sticks and precious paper. Hobart had never married. Prosperous now, white-haired and lonely, he saw Kieron as the son he would have wished to beget had there been time. So the boy was indulged much and scolded little. Hobart discerned that he had a talent for line, but not as yet a great sense of colour. Well, perhaps it would come. Perhaps it would come. Hobart liked to think that his pictures and those of Kieron's would eventually hang side by side in the great hall of the castle, collecting the dust and the dignity of centuries …

The days of childhood are both long and short. In the afternoons, when Kieron had discharged his duties to Master Hobart, his time was his own. Such freedom was a luxury. It would end when he reached the age of ten and became a full apprentice. And after that, he realised, the freedom to do as he pleased would be gone from his life for ever. Unless he could change the destiny that had been chosen for him. He was young enough to believe that this was possible, old enough to realise that he would have to challenge established – almost sacred – traditions.

In the summer afternoons, he would go with Petrina to the woodlands of the downs – the ridge of hills that rose almost like a man-made barrier ten or twelve kilometres from the sea. There, on land that belonged to the roe deer, the pheasant and the rabbit, they would construct worlds of make-believe.

Petrina was a wide-eyed nervous girl, with hair the smokey colour of wheat that was overdue for harvesting. One day, Kieron would be her husband, the father of her children. Therefore she determined to learn about him. She already knew that he had a secret ambition; but she did not know what it was.

On a hot summer afternoon, partly by chance, partly by design, she learned what Kieron wanted to do most of all.

They had wearied of climbing trees, disturbing deer, picking wild flowers; and now they were resting on short, brilliantly green grass under an enormous beech tree, gazing up through its leaves at the sky.

'When you are a great painter,' said Petrina, 'I shall be able to buy beautiful fabrics and make dresses that will be the envy of every woman in the seigneurie.'

'I shall never be a great painter,' said Kieron without regret.

'You are apprenticed to Master Hobart. He is a great painter. You will learn his skills, and to them you will add your own.'

'I shall never be as great as Master Hobart. He gave his life to it. I cannot give mine.'

'Why?'

'Because, Petrina, there is something else I must do.'

'There is nothing else you can do, Kieron. You are apprenticed to Master Hobart, and you and I are contracted for marriage. Such is our destiny.'

'Such is our destiny,' mimicked Kieron. 'Stupid talk. The talk of a girl child. I want to fly.'

'Don't you want to marry me?'

'I want to fly.'

She sighed. 'We are to be married. We shall be married. You will be a grand master of your art. And we shall have three children. And your greatest painting will be of a terrible fish that destroys men by fire. It is foretold. And there is nothing to be done about it.'

Kieron was intrigued. 'It is foretold?'

Petrina smiled. 'Last summer, the astrologer, Marcus of London, was summoned to the castle. Seigneur Fitzalan wished to know if his lady would ever bring forth a son.'

'Well?'

'My father was commanded to repair the bearings of the stand for the astrologer's star glass. My mother persuaded Marcus to cast your horoscope in fee ... So Kieron, the future is settled. You will be a grand master, and I shall bear three children ... Listen to the bees! They dance mightily. If we can follow them, we can come back at dusk for the honey.'

'Hang the bees!' exploded Kieron. 'And hang the astrologer Marcus! I alone can decide my future. I shall complete my apprenticeship with Master Hobart. There is nothing I can do about that. Besides, he is a kind man, and a better master than most. Also, I like to draw. But when I am a man, things will be different. I shall be my own master. I shall choose my own future. And I choose to learn how to fly.'

'Will you sprout wings?'

'I shall construct a flying machine.'

Petrina turned pale. 'A flying machine. Kieron, be careful. It is all right to speak of such things to me. I shall be your wife. I shall bear your children. But do not talk of flying machines to anyone else, especially the dominie and the neddy.'

Kieron pressed her hand, and lay back on the bright green grass and stared upwards through the leaves of the beech tree. 'I am not a fool,' he said. 'The dominie is like the neddy, in that his mind is stiff with rules and habits. But the dominie is just a weak old man, whereas the neddy—'

'Whereas the neddy could have you burned at the stake,' cut in Petrina sharply.

'They don't burn children now. Even you should know that.'

'But they still burn men, and one day you will be a man. They burned a farmer at Chichester two summers ago for devising a machine to cut his wheat … Kieron, for my sake, try not to think about flying machines. Such thoughts are far too dangerous.'

Kieron let out a great sigh. 'All the exciting things are dangerous … Look at the sky through the leaves. So blue, so beautiful. And when the white clouds pass, don't you wish you could reach up and touch them? They are like islands, great islands in the sky. One day I shall journey among those islands. One day I shall reach out and touch the clouds as I pass by.'

Petrina shivered. 'You make me feel cold with this wild talk.'

'I make myself feel cold also. The First Men had flying machines, Petrina. Silver birds that roared like dragons and passed high over the clouds. The dominie says so. Even the neddy will admit to that. It is history.'

'The First Men destroyed themselves,' retorted Petrina.

'So did the Second Men,' said Kieron tranquilly. 'They also had flying machines; though not, perhaps, as good as those of the First Men. It must have been wonderful to pass across the skies at great speed, to look down upon the earth and see men go about their tasks like insects.'

'Men are not insects!'

'From a great height, all living things must seem like insects.'

'The First Men destroyed themselves. So did the Second Men. That, too, is history. The neddies are right. Machines are evil.'

Kieron laughed. 'Machines have no knowledge of good and evil. Machines cannot think. Only men can think.'

'Then,' said Petrina, 'too much thinking is evil – especially when it is about forbidden things.'

Suddenly Kieron felt strangely old, strangely protective. He said: 'Don't worry, little one. I shall not think too much. Very likely, you will have three children, as the astrologer says … I know where there is a plum tree. Shall we see if there are any ripe enough to eat?'

Petrina jumped up. 'I know where there is an apple tree. The high ones are already turning red.'

Kieron laughed. 'Plums and apples! Let us drive all gloomy thoughts away with plums and apples.'

Hand in hand, they walked out of the glade, out into the rich gold splendour of late summer sunshine.

2

On his tenth birthday, Kieron ate his farewell breakfast with all the solemnity required for the occasion. Then he shook hands with Gerard, his father, and kissed Kristen, his mother, once on each cheek. It was only a ritual farewell because they would still see each other frequently. But it was the symbolic end of Kieron's childhood. He would sleep no more in the house of his father.

Gerard said: 'Son, you will attend Master Hobart in all his needs. He will impart his skills to you. In years to come, your paintings will adorn the walls of the castle. Maybe, they will also hang in the great houses of London, Bristol, Brum. Then, perhaps, your mother and I will not have lived in vain.'

'Sir,' said Kieron, forcing back the tears that came to his eyes for no apparent reason, 'I will learn from Master Hobart all that I may. I will try to be worthy of you. I would have been a joiner like you, had it been your pleasure. But, since you wished me to make likenesses, I will paint portraits that will not shame the father of Kieron Joinerson.'

Kristen held him close and said: 'You have three shirts, three vests and two pair of leggings. You have a lambskin jacket and good boots. These I have packed in the deerhide bag. Keep warm, Kieron, eat well. We – we love you and shall watch your progress.'

He sensed that she, too, was miserable. He could not understand why. It was supposed to be an important and joyful occasion for all concerned.

'I will see you soon, mother.' He smiled, trying to cheer himself up as well.

'Ay, but you will not lie again in the bed your father made for you. You will not curl up under the sheets I wove and the down quilt I made before you were born.'

'Enough, Kristen,' said Gerard. 'You will have us all whimpering like babies.' He looked at his wife and was aware of the white streaks in her hair, the lines etched on her face. She was twenty-eight years old; but her back was still straight and her breasts were high. She had worn well.

Kieron picked up the deerhide bag. Suddenly, the sense of occasion was upon him, and he felt very formal. 'Good day to you, then, my parents. Thank you for giving me the breath of life. Thank you for filling my belly in summer and in winter. Ludd rest you both.'

Kristen fled into her kitchen, sobbing. Gerard raised a great hairy arm to his forehead, as he often did in his workshop, and wiped away sweat that did not exist.

'Ludd be with you, my son. Go now to Master Hobart. As I am the best joiner in fifty kilometres marching, so you will become the best painter within a thousand kilometres.'

'Father, I want to—' Kieron stopped. It had been on the tip of his tongue to say: I do not want to be a painter. I want to learn how to fly.

'Yes, Kieron?'

'I – I want to be worthy of you and to make you proud.'

Gerard laughed and slapped his shoulder playfully. 'Be off with you, changeling. From now on, you will eat better food than we have been able to give you.'

'I doubt that it will taste as good.' There was more he wanted to say. Much more. But the words stuck in his throat. Kieron went out of the cottage and began to walk along the track that led down to Arundel. He did not look back, but he knew that Gerard was standing at the door watching him. He did not look back because there was a disturbing impulse to run to his father and tell him what he really wanted to do.

It was a fine October morning. The sky was blue; but a thick carpet of mist lay over the low land stretching away to the sea. Arundel lay beneath the mist; but the castle, its grey stone wet with dew and shining in the morning light, sat on the hillside clear above the mist. A faerie castle, bright, mysterious, full of unseen power.

There was a saying: those who live in the shadow of the castle shall prosper or burn. Master Hobart had a house under the very battlements. He had prospered. Kieron hoped that he, too, would prosper. Only a fool would risk burning. Only a fool would want to build a flying machine.

High in the sky a buzzard circled gracefully. Kieron put down his bag and watched it. Such effortless movements, such freedom. He envied the bird. He envied its freedom, its effortless mastery of the air.

'Some day, buzzard,' said Kieron, 'I shall be up there with you. I shall be higher. I shall look down on you. You will know that a man has invaded your world. You will know that men have reconquered the sky.'

Still, this was no time to make speeches that no one would hear, and particularly speeches that no one should hear. Master Hobart, doubtless, would be waiting and impatient. Kieron bent down to pick up his bag.

He saw a dandelion, a dandelion clock. A stem with a head full of seeds. He plucked the stem, lifted the head and blew. Seeds drifted away in the still, morning air. Seeds supported by the gossamer threads that resisted their fall to earth.

Kieron watched, fascinated. A few of the seeds, caught by an undetectable current of warm air, rose high and were lost against the morning sunlight. Even dandelion seeds could dance in the air. It was humiliating that man should be earthbound.

Kieron remembered that, on this day of days, Hobart would be waiting to welcome him with some ceremony.

He sighed, picked up the deerhide bag and marched resolutely towards Arundel. Ahead of him there would be months and years wherein he would have to master all the secrets of Hobart's craft. But when he was a man, when the apprenticeship had been served with honour, that would be the time to learn to fly.

Meanwhile, there was always the time to dream.

3

Winter came, turning the land bleak, capping the downs with freezing mist, weaving a delicate tracery of frost over trees, grass, hedgerows and the walls of houses, bringing ice patches on the placid Arun river, making the air sharp as an English apple wine.

Hobart coughed much and painted little in the winter. The rawness ate into his bones, brought pains to his chest. He spent much time sitting by a log fire with a shawl or sheepskin round his shoulders, brooding upon projects that he would undertake in the spring. There was the mural for the great hall to consider; and Seigneur Fitzalan had commissioned a symbolic work, depicting the fall of the First Men, to the greater glory of Ludd, and for the Church of the Sacred Hammer.

Widow Thatcher, who cleaned house for Master Hobart and cooked for him, made many nourishing stews of rabbit or pheasant or lamb or venison with parsnips, mushrooms, carrots, potatoes, and the good black pepper for which Seigneur Fitzalan paid exorbitant sums to the skippers of windjammers that sailed as far as the Spice Islands.

Master Hobart would take but a few spoonfuls of the lovingly made stews. Then he would cough somewhat and draw shivering to the fire. Kieron, waiting properly until his master had finished eating, would gorge himself until his belly swelled and he felt the need to walk off his excess of eating in the frosty downs.

Though Hobart himself was idle during the dark months, he did not allow his young apprentice to remain idle. He instructed Kieron in the art of making fine charcoal sticks from straight twigs of willow, in the mysteries of fabric printing, in the newly fashionable art of collage, and in the ancient disciplines of colour binding and the preparation of a true canvas. He was even prepared to expend precious whale oil in the lamps so that on a dull afternoon Kieron would have enough light to sketch chairs, tables, bowls of fruit, hanging pheasants, and even the protesting Widow Thatcher.

Master Hobart was a white-haired old man, nearing his three score. The pains in his chest warned him that the summers left to him would not reach double figures. But he was stubbornly determined to live at least the eight years Kieron needed to complete his apprenticeship. Ludd permitting, he would see the boy established before he was lowered into the flinty earth of Sussex.

EDMUND COOPER

He permitted himself a small heresy – only a very small one, which surely Ludd would excuse. He permitted himself the secret delusion that Kieron was his natural son. Hobart had never lain with a woman. His art had been enough. But now he felt the need of a son; and Kieron, a boy with bright eyes and a quick mind, was all that a man could desire.

So Kieron escaped many of the usual rigours of apprenticeship. He was well fed, he had much freedom; and Hobart slipped many a silver penny into his purse.

Kieron understood the relationship very clearly. He loved the old man and did not object to the presumptions of a second father. Besides, Hobart was a great source of knowledge, and knowledge was what Kieron desired above everything.

In the evenings, before Hobart retired to an early bed, he and Kieron would sit, staring into the log fire, discerning images and fantasies, talking of many things. Hobart drank somewhat – to alleviate the pains and the coughing – of usquebaugh, or akvavit, or eau de vie, depending on which brigantines had recently traded with the seigneurie. In his cups at night, he was prepared to discuss that which he would shun sober in the morning. He was prepared to talk about the First Men and the Second Men. He was even prepared to talk about machines.

'Master Hobart, the dominie says that the First Men choked on their own cleverness. What does he mean by that?'

'Pah!' Hobart sipped his usquebaugh and felt the warmth tingle pleasantly through his limbs. 'Dominie Scrivener should teach you more of letters and the mysteries of nature and the casting of numbers than of the First Men.'

'Yesterday, when I was making a picture of this house as it stands below the castle, and represented the roughness of the flint walls, you said I was clever. Is cleverness a bad thing? Shall I, too, choke on it?'

'Peace, boy. Let me think. It seems I must not only instruct you in matters of art, but in matters of the world, and in proper thinking.' More usque-baugh. More warmth. More coughing. 'What the dominie says is true. The First Men did choke on their own cleverness. They made the air of their cities unfit to breathe, they made the waters of their rivers and lakes unfit to drink, they covered good farming land with stone and metal causeways, at times they even made the sea turn black. All this they did with the machines they worshipped insanely. And, as if that were not enough, they devised terrible machines whose sole purpose was to destroy people by the hundred, by the thousand, even by the ten thousand. Missiles, they were called: machines that leapt through the sky with their cargoes of death. Ay, the dominie was right. They choked on their own cleverness … But your cleverness, Kieron is something different. You are clever in an honest art, not in the love of mecha-nisms that destroy the hand that creates them.'

'Must all machines be bad?' asked Kieron.

'Yes, Kieron, all machines are evil. The Divine Boy understood that a thousand years ago, when machines first began to corrupt this fair land. That is why he attacked them with his hammer. But the people would not listen; and so he was taken and crucified.'

There was silence for a while; silence punctuated by the crackling of logs on the hearth, and by Master Hobart noisily sipping his usquebaugh.

At length, Kieron grew bold. 'It is said that Seigneur Fitzalan has a clock in the castle. A clock that goes tick-tock and tells the hours, minutes and very seconds of the day. A clock is a machine, isn't it, Master Hobart? Is a clock evil?'

The usquebaugh made Master Hobart splutter somewhat. It was a while before he could make his reply. 'I see that neither the dominie nor the neddy have shed as much light on this matter as they ought. It is true, Kieron, that a clock is a machine; but for the great ones of our world, who have many matters to attend to and little enough time to deal with their affairs, a clock is a *necessary* machine. Holy Church makes much distinction between necessary machines, which are proper, and unnecessary machines which are improper. So Seigneur Fitzalan's clock, which I have seen many times and which is a most marvellous thing – executed, so they say, by the best horologist in Paris – is a proper machine. There is no record that the Divine Boy ever attacked clocks.'

Kieron noted how much usquebaugh had been taken, and asked the question he would not have dared to ask in the light of a sober morning.

'Master Hobart, did the Divine Boy ever attack flying machines?'

'Flying machines?' Master Hobart was puzzled. 'There are no flying machines.'

'No, sir. But once there were.' Kieron was sweating. The fire, certainly, was warm; but his backside was cold. Nevertheless, Kieron was sweating. 'You, yourself, have told me of the missiles; and I have heard that once there were winged machines that transported people through the air, across the seas, from land to land, at great speed. That is why I ask if the Divine Boy ever attacked flying machines.'

'Ludd save us all!' Master Hobart scratched his head. 'Flying machines! My history serves me ill. But, Kieron, boy, I think they came long after Ned Ludd. I think they came when the First Men had utterly abandoned the ways of righteousness. I think they came but a hundred years, perhaps two hundred years, before the great destruction.'

Kieron gazed at the level of usquebaugh in the flask of green glass, and decided to press his luck. 'They say that even the Second Men had flying machines. Surely, if such machines were used not to destroy people but to take them wherever they wished to go, they could not be evil?'

Master Hobart rolled his eyes, tried to focus, took another drink and again failed to focus. He scratched his head. 'They were evil, Kieron. What is to prevent men walking or riding across the land? What is to prevent them from sailing across the oceans? Men do not need to take to the air. *Quod erat demonstrandum*. Therefore machines which lift men into the sky are evil.'

Kieron took a deep breath. 'Some day, I shall construct a flying machine. It will not be used for evil purposes, only for good.'

Master Hobart stood up, swayed a little, gazed down at his apprentice hazily. 'You will paint, Kieron. You will paint well. Ludd protect you from fantastic dreams. Help me to my chamber.'

4

At fifteen Kieron was a boy worth looking at. Master Hobart's spoiling and Widow Thatcher's prodigious cooking had given him height and broad shoulders and self-confidence. He looked more like a young farmer or hunter than a painter's apprentice. At Midsummer's Night Fair, he could run, jump, wrestle or hurl the javelin with the best of the young men in the seigneurie; though Master Hobart winced greatly and comforted himself with preach spirit when he saw Kieron leap seven metres along the sand pit and come down like a rolling ball, or when the boy's hand was held in a wrestler's lock and the joints could be heard to crack noisily under pressure. He was not afraid for Kieron's neck, only for his fingers. What kind of an artist would the boy become with broken fingers?

But Kieron was a golden boy and seemed to bear a charmed life. More than ever, Master Hobart thought of him as a blood son. Indeed, in a fit of stupidity, he had even gone to see Gerard the joiner and his wife Kristen, offering them one thousand schilling if they would surrender their blood claim for all time.

Gerard grew red in the face, and spoke more loudly and less courteously than he ought to one who had entry to the castle and the ear of the seigneur. Kristen, as was the way with women, wept somewhat, shrieked somewhat and uttered strange accusations for which Gerard promptly commanded her to apologise. Hobart was greatly embarrassed by the whole venture. He found himself apologising also, profusely and at some length. In the end, he managed to enjoin Gerard and Kristen good, honest people for whom he professed the greatest esteem et cetera – to say nothing of the matter to Kieron.

The next day, he sent Gerard a dagger of Spanish steel, and Kristen ten metres of Irish linen. He also sent them an imaginative picture of Ned Ludd raising his immortal hammer against the weaving machines. It was the first truly satisfactory composition in oils that Kieron had executed. It was signed Kieron app Hobart; and it was one of the most precious things that Hobart possessed.

Kieron's skill in art was now all that Hobart could desire in a boy of his age. His strength still lay in line – the master was amazed at the boldness and confidence of his strokes – but he had begun to develop the true, authentic feeling for colour and texture that is the hallmark of a great painter. Also, his mastery of the mechanics of his art was phenomenal. He could mix pigment and oil to achieve a true and beautiful primary. Also, without any help from Hobart, he had devised two methods of obtaining a purer flax seed oil. The first was elegantly simple: it consisted only of waiting. The oil was stored in jars until its impurities settled in a layer at the bottom. Then, not content with the purity achieved in this manner, Kieron would add caustic soda, which settled out any suspended matter still remaining. The result was a completely pure flax seed oil, clear, warm, golden. Perfect for the use of an artist.

Hobart was astounded by this. Previously he had used the oil as it came from the flax growers, with minute particles that muddied its translucence. But Kieron's refined oil, as he called it, was surely a gift of Ludd, in that it did not pollute the pigments or harden too quickly upon the canvas. Hobart was convinced that no painter in England could have a finer oil base than that discovered by Kieron.

He asked the boy how he had devised such methods of purification. The answer was not greatly enlightening.

'You always complained of the quality of the colours we use,' said Kieron: 'The pigments were true, so clearly the fault lay in the oil. I poured oil into a clear flask and gazed at it. I could see nothing wrong. But I let the oil stand and came back to it the following day. Still I could see nothing wrong. But on the second day, I discovered that the bottom of the flask was covered with fine particles. Again, I let it stand. Seven days later, there was a sediment, and the oil was more clear. Then I understood the need for patience.'

'But the caustic soda. How did you understand that the caustic soda would give yet greater clarity?'

'I didn't,' Kieron smiled. 'It seemed to me that the process of depositing impurities might not yet be over. So I experimented.'

'You experimented?' Hobart was shaken. Experiment was but a hair's breadth from heresy.

Kieron was unperturbed. 'I experimented with the addition of salt, with the addition of vinegar, with the addition of weak soda and with the addition of strong soda. I would have experimented with many other substances, too, had they been easy to obtain.'

'Boy,' said Hobart, 'you frighten me.'

Kieron laughed. 'Sometimes, sir, I frighten myself ... The flax seed oil is to your liking?'

'It is a great oil, Kieron. We could make a fortune by selling it to painters throughout the land.'

'Then, Master Hobart, do not sell my refined oil. Use it only yourself, and be the greatest painter of our time.'

Tears came to Hobart's eyes. He was not much given to weeping, except when the coughing spasms tore him apart. 'You truly wish to keep this clear oil for my use only?'

Kieron smiled. 'Sir, I could not wish for a better master. But is it not possible to establish both fame and fortune? If you use the refined oil until – until you no longer choose to paint, you will be known far and wide for the purity of your colour. Then would be the time to sell refined oil, when you are already too high to fear rivalry.'

Hobart induced a fit of coughing, as an excuse for the tears he could no longer conceal. 'Boy, I see that you love me, and I am proud. I see also that you are touched by greatness, and I am again proud, but also terrified … Kieron, humour an old man. The refined oil is truly marvellous. But do not experiment rashly. The church … The church likes new ideas little. I would commend discretion to you.'

'I think perhaps all experiment is rash,' answered Kieron, 'but my mind will not rest … However, I will be discreet. I would not wish to shame you or my parents.'

These days, Kieron did not see a great deal of Petrina. The times when they could go up on to the downs alone together seemed very long ago. Now, they met socially only in the company of their elders. They saw each other chiefly at the Church of the Sacred Hammer, at the fairs of the four seasons, and on holy days, when all work ceased and folk ventured out in their best clothes to visit relatives or friends or to promenade in the castle grounds listening to Seigneur Fitzalan's musicians.

Sometimes Kieron and Petrina met accidentally in the street, but they could not stay long to talk to each other for fear of the mischievous wagging of tongues. As Kieron had grown in stature, so Petrina had grown in beauty – or so it seemed. Her hair stretched below her waist in a long luxuriant plait. There was blue fire in her eyes, and her lips were hauntingly full. The freckles had gone, the boyish figure had gone, and the curves of a woman swelled pleasingly upon her. Kieron, normally full of confidence and self-assurance, became tongue-tied in her presence. But, without looking, he knew when she was watching him at the games; and her presence lent a curious strength. In three more years she would be his wife. Truly, his father had contracted well with Sholto the Smith.

Kieron made sketches from memory of Petrina, which he hung on the wall by his bed. Hobart inspected them and said nothing. The boy's artistic discipline went to pieces when he dealt with this particular subject. But the results were curiously exciting, enough to make the blood sing. There was one sketch of the girl climbing in what was, presumably, a beech tree. Somehow, Kieron had managed to make the girl look naked while being properly clothed. The technique was rough; but the sketch had great impact. It smacked of heresy. The church had never approved of nakedness. And yet she was fully clothed. And yet she seemed naked. Hobart hoped that the neddy would never see this sketch. He scratched his head and seriously wondered if he should summon an astrologer to conjure against daemons.

But preoccupation with dream images of Petrina did not distract Kieron unduly from his obsession with the conquest of the air. Over the years he had conscientiously studied all things – however great or small – that had some freedom of movement through the air: clouds, birds, insects, drifting seeds, even autumn leaves. On summer afternoons, when there was no great urgency of work and when Master Hobart was content to doze in the sun, Kieron would lie back on the sweet-smelling grass and feel the pull of earth, the flexible and invisible band that constantly tried to draw him to the centre of the world. And he would look up at white clouds drifting lazily across the sky, at larks soaring, at swallows cutting the air magically as with a knife, at butterflies that seemed to nervously jump across unseen stepping stones, at dragonflies hovering.

It seemed absurd that so great a creature as man was tied down. Once, so it was said, man had even ventured upon the surface of the moon. Kieron did not entirely believe the legend; but it was known beyond any shadow of doubt that men had once enjoyed the freedom of the sky. They would do so again, of that Kieron was sure – whatever the priests of Ludd might say.

Meanwhile, it was pleasant, if tantalising, to watch the great clouds scud, to know that they were made of water, which was heavier than air, and yet could still float high in the azure reaches. And it was pleasant, if tantalising, to watch a bird of prey hover, circle, and with little or no wing movement rise higher and higher until it became a speck.

Kieron contrasted such effortless movement with the frenetic motions of the bee, beating its wings so fast in order to stay aloft that they became invisible, though the sound of the tiny membranes was at times as he imagined that of a great engine of the old days.

Truly, the mysteries of being airborne were profound. Truly there must be many different ways of conquering the sky.

Kieron began to experiment with kites. Kites were permitted by the neddies. Kites were not defined as machines but as toys. Many of the children in the seigneurie flew kites. It was considered a harmless thing to do. But it was also considered eccentric in a young man of fifteen, with a bare three years of apprenticeship left; a young man whose mind should now be focussing on more serious matters.

Elders raised their eyebrows when they saw Kieron standing on the green on blustery autumn afternoons, solemnly reeling out string for a kite that climbed higher than any before it. They marvelled not at the height achieved by Kieron but at the indulgence of Master Hobart. Surely the old painter was in his dotage, or Seigneur Fitzalan was displeased with his work, else he would find much for idle young hands to do.

Kieron's contemporaries were less passive in their reaction. They made great fun of him, which he bore patiently. They thought him witless, and called him Kieron-head-in-the-air because he always seemed to be gazing upwards. Aylwin, apprenticed to the miller, went further.

Aylwin, a broad-set strong young man of Kieron's own age, had always envied him. For two reasons. Aylwin had never wanted to become a miller. From childhood he had been obsessed by drawing and painting. More than anything, he would have liked to be apprenticed to Master Hobart. Also, there was the matter of Petrina. Aylwin was contracted to Joan, daughter of Lodowick, the saddler. Joan, at best, was a dumpy girl, lacking grace. True, she would bear children well, and she was versed in the womanly arts. But she was not the kind of girl to make a young man's heart beat noisily inside his breast.

Aylwin could have forgiven Kieron for being apprenticed to Master Hobart. Or he could have forgiven him for being contracted to Petrina. But he could not forgive him for both. So, one afternoon when a kite newly designed by Kieron had risen exceedingly high, and when Kieron, impervious to the taunts of his fellows, continued to manoeuvre it yet higher, Aylwin threw discretion to the winds, rushed upon the green and cut the cord that held the kite. The wind was high. The kite swung crazily for a moment or two, then it drifted south towards the sea.

Kieron gazed at Aylwin in perplexity. 'Why did you do that?'

'Because you are a fool.'

'Do I not have a right to foolishness, if it is my pleasure?'

Aylwin was appalled at his own stupidity, but there was no going back.

'No. You should be as the rest of us. Kite-flying is for children. We are beyond childish things.'

'You are not beyond a beating,' said Kieron. 'There was much thought in the design of my kite. For that you shall pay.'

'Try me!' shouted Aylwin. 'Try me!' But he did not feel over confident. He had greater strength than Kieron. That he knew. But Kieron had suppleness of limbs and suppleness of mind. A formidable combination.

'Aylwin,' said Kieron quietly, 'you have earned some chastisement. I am sorry.'

The two young men faced each other; Aylwin confident of strength but not of tactics, Kieron confident of tactics but not of strength.

Aylwin rushed in. If he could come to close grips with Kieron, that would be an end of it.

He rushed in, but Kieron did not wait to receive him. He gave a mighty leap over Aylwin's head. Aylwin stopped his charge and turned round – only to receive both of Kieron's feet in his face – a magnificent flying kick to the jaw.

Aylwin saw stars. The world darkened, and he fell down. But sight returned, and he looked up to see Kieron waiting patiently for him. With a cry of rage Aylwin leaped to his feet. Again he rushed at Kieron, prepared this time for some evasive action. There was none. Kieron seemed determined to take the charge on his shoulder, a stupid thing to do in view of Aylwin's superior weight. But, at the last moment, with splendid timing, Kieron bent. Aylwin could not stop the charge and sprawled helplessly over Kieron's back. As he did so, Kieron straightened; and Aylwin executed a full turn high in the air then landed flat on his back with a jarring thud. He tried to get up, and could not. His head ached, there was a great roaring in his ears and pain in every part of his body.

Kieron stood above him. 'Are you sorry for cutting the cord, Aylwin?'

'Ludd damn you!' He snatched feebly at Kieron's leg.

Kieron trod on his arm, pinning it down. 'Are you sorry?'

Aylwin whimpered with pain. 'Damn you to hell and back. I will never be sorry. You have Master Hobart, and you will have Petrina. May Ludd strike me if ever …' Aylwin fainted.

When he returned to consciousness, he found that Kieron was gently slapping his face.

'Leave me alone, fellow. I am all right, and I will never be sorry. You may break my bones, Kieron-head-in-the-air, but I will never be sorry. I swear it.'

Kieron lifted him gently to a sitting position, then crouched by him. 'Why did you speak of Master Hobart and Petrina?'

Aylwin gazed up, white-faced. 'You have all that I ever wanted,' he sobbed. 'And yet you play like a child!'

Suddenly Kieron understood. 'You wanted to paint?'

'Yes! Ludd's death, I wanted to paint. But I shall only ever grind corn.'

'And you desire to be wed with Petrina?'

Aylwin grimaced. 'Be amused. You know I am contracted to Joan.'

Kieron said simply: 'Forgive me. I did not know the forces.'

'You did not know the forces?' Aylwin looked at him uncomprehendingly.

'I did not know the forces that drove you to cut the cord … There is nothing we can do about Petrina. I will wed with her. I love her. But, perhaps, there is something we can do about the other …'

'There is nothing to be done about it,' said Aylwin. 'A miller does not paint, a miller's apprentice does not paint. That is all there is to it.'

Kieron smiled. 'There is a law against it? Seigneur Fitzalan has proclaimed that all millers who daub canvas shall be put to death?'

Aylwin said: 'You mock me … Besides, who would instruct me? Who would give me canvas and paint?'

'I would.'

Aylwin's mouth fell open. He did not speak for fully a minute. 'You would! Why?'

'Is there cause for a feud between us, Aylwin? Must we be enemies because of decisions that were not of our taking?'

'No, but—'

'Hear me, then. I would have you as my friend. One day I may need such a friend. In the matter of Petrina, I can and will do nothing. But Master Hobart loves me, and I serve him well. He will give me canvas and pigments and will not ask questions that I do not wish to answer ... I will instruct you, Aylwin. I will pass on the skills that are passed on to me. Is that enough?'

Aylwin held out his hand and gripped Kieron's forearm. Kieron returned the gesture, thus sealing the ancient pact of mutual loyalty.

'It is enough,' said Aylwin. 'By the hammer of Ludd, it is more than enough. But why do you do this thing?'

'We have clasped each other, and so we are bound each to the other. It is agreed?'

'It is agreed.'

'Then I can tell you certain things, Aylwin. You wish to paint, but are destined to become a miller. I wish to construct flying machines, but I am destined to become a painter. Separately, we must accept our fates. Together we may overcome them. Are you truly with me?'

'To the death. But, as you say, it is not unlawful for a miller to paint. On the other hand, flying machines – machines of any kind – are unlawful. You have a bleak future, Kieron-head-in-the-air.'

Kieron smiled at the taunt, which now contained no malice. 'Men make laws. Men may change them ... The kite whose cord was cut was not just a childish toy, Aylwin. It was an experiment. It was an experimental design for a man-lifting kite.'

'Do not proceed. The neddies will burn you.'

'Hear me. I have discovered an idea, which, when the time is ripe, will prevent the neddies from doing anything.'

'What is the idea?'

'Historical necessity,' said Kieron. 'It will be necessary, sooner or later, for man to take to the air once more. Meanwhile, I must work secretly. I must be ready for that time.'

'I fear for you, Kieron.'

'I fear for myself, Aylwin. But, we have a bargain, you and I. I will share my skills with you, and you will be content.'

'What will you require of me, in exchange?'

'I don't know. Truly, I don't know. At some time, almost certainly, I shall require your help. The risks may be high. They may be high enough even to hazard your life. But I shall try to avoid that.'

Aylwin stood up. So did Kieron. They clasped forearms once again, in affirmation.

'Better a dead painter than a live miller,' joked Aylwin.

'Better by far a live painter and a live man of the air,' said Kieron.

5

Mistress Alyx Fitzalan was seventeen years old and the bane of Seigneur Fitzalan's life. Within the year, thank Ludd, she would be wed with the young Seigneur Talbot of Chichester. As far as Seigneur Fitzalan was concerned, it could not happen too soon. He wished Talbot joy of her, but doubted greatly that any joy would come of the union. Still, it was politically necessary for the Talbots and the Fitzalans to stand side by side. Between them, they controlled much of the southern coastline. Which was convenient in times of peace and doubly convenient in times of war. Which Ludd forbid.

Alyx knew that she was destined to be a sacrificial lamb and conducted herself accordingly. As Fitzalan's eldest daughter, she had many privileges. As the key to his control of a large segment of the coast, she realised that, until Fitzalan had a copy of the marriage vows in his strong box, she could demand anything within reason.

She did, frequently. She demanded entertainments, feasts, diversions. It was well known that Talbot of Chichester was a sickly young man who bled frequently from the nose. Alyx had spies who told her that he was not long for this world. Though she loathed him, she hoped he would live long enough to wed her and get a son. By this means, Alyx dreamed of equalling her father in his power.

Meanwhile, she held Fitzalan in thrall. He could not risk her rejection of the contract.

She was a great horsewoman. She loved horses, it seemed, more than anything else.

What more natural than that she should require a portrait of herself on horseback leaping a seven-bar gate?

Alyx already had five portraits of herself. Two hung in the castle, one had been sent to London, and two had been given to Talbot.

Master Hobart had painted all five portraits. At the suggestion of the sixth, he held up his shaking hands in horror.

'Seigneur Fitzalan, how shall I catch your daughter on horseback leaping a seven-bar gate?'

'I know not, Master Hobart, nor do I care,' retorted Seigneur Fitzalan calmly. 'But it is the price of peace – at least for a time – and I will have it done.'

'But, Seigneur—'

'No buts, master painter. See to it. And see to it also that the horse is no less graceful than its rider. I have a fine stable, and those who see your picture should know it.'

'Yes, Seigneur.'

'Be still, man! You shake like an autumn leaf. I trust you will not shake so when the brush is in your hand.'

'No, Seigneur,' assured Hobart hastily. 'It is but a tremor of agitation. When I hold the brush, my hand is rock steady.'

'If it be steady enough to make good likenesses of both horse and rider, I will put five hundred schilling into it.'

'Thank you, Seigneur.'

Fitzalan frowned and stared hard at the old man. 'But, if the canvas be not to my liking, you shall eat it.'

'Yes, Seigneur. Thank you.' Master Hobart retreated from the presence, bowing many times, his hands clasped tightly together (partly to stop them trembling) as if with intense gratitude, like one whose execution has just been stayed – if only temporarily.

'Hobart!'

'Seigneur?'

'A word. And stop bobbing up and down, man. You make me nervous.'

'Forgive me, Seigneur.' Hobart froze.

'This picture … Start soon, Master Hobart, but do not hurry. You follow me?'

'Yes, Seigneur,' said Hobart blindly. Though he did not.

Fitzalan explained. 'Mistress Alyx is a dutiful and loving daughter, but she is also – how shall I put it? – impetuous if not actually headstrong.'

'Just so, Seigneur.'

'No, not just so. Damnation! Don't you understand what I'm saying?'

'Yes, Seigneur. All in the seigneurie know that Mistress Alyx—'

'Hobart, you are a foolish old man, and you know nothing of womenfolk.'

'Yes, Seigneur.'

Suddenly, Fitzalan recalled that Hobart was indeed a foolish old man who knew nothing of womenfolk. 'Hobart, forgive me. I treat you ill, old friend.'

'You do me too much honour, Seigneur.'

Fitzalan smiled. 'Because we are friends, I will confide in you. Mistress Alyx, Ludd bless her, has curious notions. She needs interests, diversions. And for women, Hobart, diversions come costly. This picture, now. You could do it in a week, could you not?'

'Well, Seigneur, I—'

'Could you or could you not?'

'Yes, Seigneur.'

'The very point. You will not do it in a week, Master Hobart. You will not even do it in a month. You will take time, much time. You will require many sketches, many sittings or whatever. Many long sittings. I make myself clear?'

'Yes, Seigneur.'

'Mistress Alyx will scold you. I will scold you. But you will not hurry. I make myself clear?'

'Yes, Seigneur.'

'Mistress Alyx is burdened by time, Hobart. She does not know this, but it is so. Therefore you will consume as much of her time as possible, without appearing to so do … This prentice of yours – has he his wits about him?'

'Ay, Seigneur.' Here, Hobart felt on firm ground. 'A most intelligent and resourceful young man, and of great talent also with brush, chalk, pencil, crayon, char—'

'Enough. You need not declaim his battle honours. I have seen him about the castle, Hobart, and about the seigneurie. He is a pleasant young fellow … Yes, he is a pleasant young fellow. Have him attend Mistress Alyx, Hobart. Have him ride with her, have him walk with her. Have him make enough – what the devil do you call them?'

'Preliminary studies,' ventured Hobart.

'Have him make enough preliminary studies, sketches, or whatever the fellow does, to take up a full two-month of the wretched girl's forenoons, ay, and her afternoons also. Can this be done?'

'What of Mistress Alyx, Seigneur? She may weary—'

'Damn the Mistress Alyx! Women do not weary of being looked at nor of artists limning with devotion … Seven hundred and fifty schilling, Hobart, and not a penny more. You have heard my requirements. Go now.'

Hobart began his retreat once more, hands clasped tightly, the sweat dripping from his forehead.

Now he had two additional worries that would take much drowning in Scottish or French spirit. Mistress Alyx was a woman of some temperament. Also, Hobart realised with sad clarity that he had never been much good at horses.

6

Mistress Alyx drove Kieron to distraction. She was a wild young lady. Wild, beautiful, imperious, bored. Also intelligent. She was intelligent enough to realise that Kieron had been sent to her as a propitiatory sacrifice, a kind of whipping boy. Nevertheless, it amused her to apply the whip – verbally, emotionally, physically.

The first morning that Kieron presented himself with charcoal sticks, papers, drawing board, she allowed him to make a sketch while she offered barbed comment on his appearance, his dress, his accent, his ancestry, his lack of learning.

Kieron set up his drawing board and went to work. But after a few minutes, his hand was shaking, and the lines were terrible, and he knew it. So did Mistress Alyx.

Kieron's mission had been explained to him carefully and apologetically by Master Hobart.

'You see, my son,' Hobart had begun to lapse into this form of address more and more, 'there are diplomatic considerations in this commission. Seigneur Fitzalan was quite explicit. He requires Mistress Alyx to be distracted for a while. I am too old for such things. Therefore—'

'Therefore I must play the performing monkey,' said Kieron calmly.

'I would not have described your role as such.' Hobart tried to feign indignation, and failed. 'Your task is to make sketches which will be invaluable when we come to decide upon the final composition.'

'A monkey with a charcoal stick,' conceded Kieron. 'You yourself will execute the painting, Master Hobart. I am simply to delay matters until you and Seigneur Fitzalan judge that the time is ripe.'

'Not so, not so, not so!' protested Hobart. 'You will execute the portrait.'

'You would trust me with this matter?'

'Kieron, I would trust you with my life … Besides, look at my hands, boy. Look at them.'

Master Hobart held out his hands. Kieron looked. They were shaking badly. The veins stood out, the joints were swollen, the fingers were bent. Such hands would never draw a true circle again.

'Master Hobart, I am sorry. Truly, I am sorry.'

'No need for sorrow, Kieron, my son. No need. I have you. Seigneur Fitzalan does not know that I have finished with painting.'

'You have not finished with painting, Master.'

'Hear me. Hear me. The portrait will be signed Hobart. It is the last time I shall put my signature … But, when Seigneur Fitzalan has given his approval, I shall add to that signature. It shall read: Hobart app Kieron. Is that enough?'

Kieron was amazed to find himself weeping. 'Master Hobart, you cannot do this thing.'

'I can and will. Is it enough?'

'It is more than enough. Much more.'

'This once, and this once only, I require you to call me Father. And I require you to paint Mistress Alyx in such a fashion that it will add stature to us both.'

'Father, I will do my best,' said Kieron.

'I am content. Your best is good enough … Seigneur Fitzalan has undertaken to pay seven hundred and fifty schilling for a successful portrait.'

'Seven hundred and fifty schilling!' It was the first time Kieron had ever heard Master Hobart talk of money. The sum mentioned was enormous. Kieron's own official allowance was ten schilling a year.

'Mark you, the fee also includes the time that must be spent and the trouble taken to produce the preliminary sketches which will, with Ludd's help, take up many of Mistress Alyx's waking hours during the next eight-week.'

Kieron snorted. 'More a fee for the diversion than for the portrait, I'll wager.'

'My son, it is not for us to dissect Seigneur Fitzalan's generosity. Now, listen carefully. You have seen my hands. Also you must know by now that I paint horses less elegantly – shall we say – than I might … It is a strange thing, this matter of horses. But all artists have some weakness. No matter. I digress … The point is that you will execute the portrait. It will be a good one, that I already know. And in the matter of the signature, the world shall see that the master has been outstripped by the apprentice. But to return to the fee. Upon Seigneur Fitzalan's approval and payment, two hundred and fifty schilling shall be sent to Master Gerard, thus to recognise that the son of his flesh and the child of my spirit are formidably one person; two hundred and fifty schilling shall be held for you against your majority and the completion of your apprenticeship; and the remaining two hundred and fifty schilling I will keep, in fee for what I have taught you and to dispose of as I wish … Does this arrangement please you, Kieron?'

For a time, Kieron was at a loss for words. At length, he said: 'Master Hobart, you destroy me with kindness. I accept your generosity in all except one thing. The signature.'

'You have seen my hands. I will paint no more. It is true that I will attend to simple matters. My eye is good for design and composition. I can still produce schemes for good murals. But I will paint no more.'

'I will not have it so!' shouted Kieron.

Hobart was amazed. 'My son, these are facts.'

'Sir, you will sign the canvas Hobart, or I will void my apprenticeship and sell refined flax seed oil for a living.'

'But why? But why?' Hobart could not understand why Kieron could decline a sudden rise to fame.

Kieron could not find the right words. But the ones he had to manage with seemed good enough. 'Because, sir, I have the good fortune to serve and be instructed by a master painter. It is my pleasure to enjoy the privilege. I can say no more.'

Hobart promptly had a fit of coughing to conceal his emotions. Kieron brought him a flask of usquebaugh.

When he went up to the castle on that first morning of his attendance upon Mistress Alyx, it was raining heavily. Which was a good thing in some respects. Kieron wished to give some thought to the problems involved, before he attempted to limn a horse in motion.

Mistress Alyx, dressed in a morning gown of blue linen, cut a trifle high above the ankle and a trifle low above the breast, received him in a long room whose walls were covered with shelves on which lay many books. Kieron had never seen so many books. He stared at them openmouthed, a greedy look in his eyes.

Mistress Alyx, seated at a clavichord, stared at the damp young man with disdain.

'Well, boy, are you here to gawp at books or to begin making a likeness of me?'

'Your pardon, Mistress Alyx. Forgive me. I have never seen so many books.' Kieron advanced awkwardly across a rich Persian carpet, leaving behind him the wet imprint of his boots.

'You drip more than a washerwoman, bumpkin. I am minded to have my father's men put you out.'

'Then I shall drip even more, Mistress. It cannot have escaped your notice that the skies have opened.'

'Do not exercise your simple wit, prentice. Recollect that you are dealing with a high-born person.'

'Forgive me again, Mistress Alyx. I have yet to adjust to the importance of my task.'

'Then commence your task, boy, and say no more.'

'Yes, Mistress. Would you be gracious enough to remain still for a short time?' Kieron, not having been offered a chair, squatted on the carpet and pinned paper to his drawing board.

'If I choose to move, I shall move,' retorted Alyx 'Your hair is too long and you stink somewhat. I do not think I can bear your presence with great patience.'

Kieron bit his tongue and selected a piece of charcoal from his pouch. He began to sketch Mistress Alyx as he saw her.

'You are contracted to the slut Petrina, I understand.'

'Yes, Mistress.'

'She is quite pretty, but you are odious. Poor child. We women are rarely lucky in the men chosen for us.'

'Yes, Mistress.'

'Do not talk, bumpkin. Get on with your work.'

Kieron's hand was shaking badly. The lines he described were terrible, and he knew that this first sketch could be nothing less than grotesque.

'Let me see what you have done. Though you are ill-dressed and your conversation deformed, and though you are the son of a peasant, you may yet have talent.'

Mistress Alyx was enjoying herself. This one she would roast over a slow fire.

'Mistress, the sketch is but a trial,' said Kieron desperately. 'It is not worthy of your inspection.'

'Nevertheless, I would see it.' She rose from her seat at the clavichord, came to where Kieron sat and peered down at the sketch.

'Ludd have mercy! You draw like a dotard. Get from my presence, boy. I do not wish to see you again.'

'Yes, Mistress Alyx. I am sorry.' Kieron gathered up his papers and charcoal sticks and drawing board. It seemed to him that his best recourse was to leave the castle and quietly hang himself.

'Until tomorrow,' added Mistress Alyx in silky tones. 'Present yourself at this time tomorrow, boy. And pray for happier circumstances.'

Kieron fled sweating. He did not hang himself. But when it was time to go to his bed, he was greatly troubled by nightmares.

7

The following day it rained also. This time Kieron took precautions. He covered his head and shoulders with sackcloth and wrapped his drawing materials and a spare pair of boots in the same material. Then he trudged up to the castle. Before he was taken to Mistress Alyx, he begged leave to straighten his hair and change his boots.

She received him as before, seated at the clavichord in the long, book-lined room.

'So, boy, you keep time. That is something. And you contrive to appear less bedraggled. That, also, is something. Let us hope that this time you will not ruin good paper … Well, don't stand there like a scarecrow. Find somewhere to sit, and begin to prove that my dear father is not recklessly throwing away many a good schilling.'

Kieron felt the blood rush to his face. A volley of words struggled to burst from his throat, but he compressed his lips and stifled them. He stood rooted to the spot. There was no chair within reach, so he sat on the carpet.

'I hope your breeches are clean,' said Alyx. 'The carpet came from a far land, of which you are doubtless not aware, and cost more schilling than your poor talent is like to earn you in a lifetime.'

'Mistress,' he retorted softly, 'my breeches are clean, and I am aware that the carpet is of Persian style. Whether it came from Persia, I know not; though I am told that the Flemish weavers now make carpets in the Persian style, which are less costly than the originals and, therefore, of some convenience to the nobility.'

The carpet was Persian, as Kieron well knew. But some retaliation seemed necessary, and he chose the first that came to mind.

'Impudent peasant!' stormed Alyx. 'The carpet is truly Persian.'

'Mistress Alyx, I am indeed a peasant, and I doubt not your word,' said Kieron with every possible inference of doubting. 'May I commence?' He felt better.

'Yes, stupid one. Scratch the paper if you must. But let your representation be better than that of yesterday, else I swear my father's bailiff shall kick you all the way from the castle to Master Hobart's hovel. The poor man must be in his dotage to have taken such a prentice as you.'

'I may do him little credit,' said Kieron, 'but Master Hobart is the finest painter in the south country. The finished portrait will be to your liking, Mistress. That I can swear.'

For some minutes there was silence. Kieron sketched, Alyx fidgeted, but not too much.

Kieron felt he could get the measure of this young lady. She must be vulnerable. She must be vulnerable, as all women were, to flattery. So, his hand being steady now, he was able to flatter her. He made her eyes larger and more beautiful than they were, he narrowed her waist, he gave fullness to her breasts, he made her hair cascade luxuriantly round her shoulders.

Presently, curiosity overcame her. 'I would see your scribblings, boy.'

Kieron stood up; but, one leg being stiff and numb from sitting cross-legged to support his drawing board, he promptly fell down.

Alyx laughed. 'No doubt your legs give way with fear at my disapproval.'

Kieron said nothing. He picked up the drawing, hobbled to the clavichord, and laid the paper before her.

She studied it. 'My nose is not bent,' she said, 'and my ears are smaller. But you have improved somewhat since yesterday. Perhaps there is hope.'

'Thank you, Mistress.'

'I said perhaps,' she warned. 'Perhaps means only perhaps.' She glanced at one of the leaded windows. 'See. The rain has stopped. Now we shall ride.'

Kieron was nonplussed. 'Mistress, I do not ride. My commission is only to take your likeness in many attitudes and aspects.'

'Your commission, boy, is to attend me. It is agreed that Master Hobart shall depict me on horseback. In order for you to make studies of horses, you must be familiar with them – and with me when I ride. Therefore you will ride also. Wait here while I change.'

As Kieron waited, the books on the shelves became as magnets, drawing him. So many books! So many wonderful, glorious books. And they must be old, very old. The neddies, of necessity, permitted the use of printing machines – but only for the dissemination of approved sacred texts. Here were books that dealt not only with the works and life of Ned Ludd but also with all manner of recondite themes.

Mistress Alyx took much time to change into her riding apparel. While he was alone, Kieron began to examine the books. Many of them were immensely old, their bindings nibbled by mice, their papers brown and speckled with the ravages of time. There were works of biography – the lives of the seigneurs of Arundel, and many others – works of history, works concerning the skills of warfare, fanning, hunting; works concerning voyages of discovery, the establishment of trade with far countries; works concerning the study of the stars. And there was one thin, incredibly tattered, incredibly ancient book about the development of infernal machines – including flying machines.

Kieron pored over it greedily. Some of the words were hard, some incomprehensible. Nevertheless, it began to yield information – about people with strange names, who had accomplished strange things, such as the Brothers Montgolfier, Otto Lilienthal, Santos Dumont – until Mistress Alyx returned.

Guiltily, Kieron closed the book and pushed it back into its place on the shelves.

'Boy, did I give you permission to examine my father's books?'

'No, Mistress Alyx.'

'Then do not presume. Come, we will ride.'

'I cannot ride, Mistress.' Kieron had never felt less like attempting to mount a horse.

'You will ride, boy. It is my wish.' Alyx had the air of one anticipating much amusement.

The episode was doomed – as Mistress Alyx had intended. She had an old mare saddled for Kieron; so old and so gentle, she told him, that a child barely able to walk would be assured of a safe ride. For herself, Alyx chose a fine, spirited hunter.

Having had the grooms hoist Kieron more or less bodily into the saddle, Alyx led the way, allowing her horse to amble down the hill from the castle and among the cluster of houses that marked the growing township. Kieron followed as best he could, his teeth rattling somewhat in his head, and his bottom rising from the saddle and hitting it again somewhat heavily.

People looked up as Mistress Alyx rode by. Women curtsied, men touched their hats. They marvelled indeed to see that she was accompanied by Kieron the prentice boy, and were amused at his obvious discomfiture. Petrina saw him struggling anxiously to retain his seat, and could not repress a smile. Two or three idle apprentices made so bold as to cheer.

Once Arundel was behind, Alyx allowed her horse to canter. The open grazing land was still soggy from the rain, but the going was not too bad. Except for Kieron. Independent of anything he might do, the old mare seemed to take guidance from the hunter – or secretly from Mistress Alyx.

Soon Kieron had abandoned the reins and was hanging on desperately to his poor animal by its mane. Inevitably, he fell off.

Mistress Alyx had chosen to ride by the bank of the river Arun, now swollen with the rains. It was a cunning choice; for when Kieron became unseated there was an even chance that he would fall on the river side.

Ludd was not with him, and he did. He fell into a large patch of mud, taking much of the fall upon his shoulder and the rest upon his backside as he rolled over. It was worse than a body slam at wrestling on the green.

Alyx laughed heartily. 'So, prentice, your horsemanship is the equal of your limning. Mount again, boy. Do not look so dazed. I do not choose to wait here for ever.'

Kieron mounted, somehow. Aching and bruised, he managed to get back on to the mare. He did not stay in the saddle for long. The next time, however, he had the good sense to fall not on the river side but on the pasture side. It hurt more, but there was no mud. He got to his feet, shaking and aching. Blindly, he tried to get back into the saddle.

'Enough, boy. You have so terrified my gentle mare that she will throw you as soon as she feels your weight. Follow me back to the castle. I will go slow. Lead her carefully. She is not accustomed to boors.'

Alyx turned her horse round and, hardly glancing at Kieron, headed back through Arundel to the castle. Still showing extensive streaks of mud on his face and clothes, and visibly shaken, Kieron followed her, casting many nervous glances backwards at the docile mare he was leading.

The townsfolk who were about surveyed the spectacle and took care not to let Mistress Alyx see their amusement. However, they also took care that Kieron-head-in-the-air, whose muddy face was now downcast, should see. Worst of all, Petrina, having made purchases at the bakery, was now returning home with a basketful of fresh bread. At first, when she saw Kieron, her expression was one of horror; then slowly it changed, and she could not repress a smile. The smile hurt him as if it had been a blow.

At the castle, solemn-faced grooms relieved him of the mare. A lackey, commanded by Alyx, went through the motions of cleaning him up a little, with obvious distaste for the task. Kieron's clothes were of good, honest doeskin and wool. The lackey wore linen and velvet. Kieron thought it would be a heaven-sent convenience if he were suddenly to die.

Unfortunately, Ludd was not merciful. He remained alive. Mistress Alyx, with no expression at all on her face, directed him to attend her in the library. He followed submissively, resolving to gather up his materials and take leave of her as soon as possible.

His sketch and drawing board were on the Persian carpet where he had left them: Alyx seemed not to notice their existence. She went straight to the clavichord; and her riding boots, still wet and bearing traces of mud, left their imprint upon Kieron's sketch as she walked over it.

Suddenly he knew that he had reached the limits of endurance. To take more humiliation from this spoilt girl would be to accept more than his manhood could permit.

'Enough, bitch!' he cried. 'I have had more than enough of you!'

Alyx turned to him, affecting surprise, indignation. Cool and controlled indignation. 'Boy, you have exceeded yourself. You have used a certain word in my presence and directed at my person. For that I will have you whipped from the castle. Your apprenticeship will be dissolved and you will be sent forth to live as best you may on nuts in the woods.'

'Not before I have taught you a lesson,' retorted Kieron icily. 'Mistress, I am a freeborn man and I have dignity. Your blood may be noble, but your manners are exceedingly crude.'

And with that, he lifted her bodily, sat upon the stool by the clavichord and proceeded to spank her bottom with much vigour and enthusiasm.

Alyx screamed. Kieron enjoyed her screaming mightily. He was enjoying it so much that he was unaware of the doors of the library bursting open as servants rushed in. He was aware of nothing but the exquisite pleasure of spanking this spoilt child who presumed to be a woman. He was aware of nothing else until hands seized him and he was struck on the head and sank into oblivion.

8

He awoke to find himself in what seemed to be the castle donjon. He awoke because a pailful of cold water had been hurled at his face. He awoke to find himself hanging by his hands from manacles fastened into the stone wall. He awoke to find that his wrists ached, his arms ached, his shoulders ached, his head ached. He awoke to find that Seigneur Fitzalan, seated on a chair, was facing him. By Seigneur Fitzalan's side stood the castle gaoler. Behind his chair stood the Mistress Alyx.

They will kill me, thought Kieron hazily. I care not. Better to die like a man than live like a sheep.

'So, prentice, you are kind enough to rejoin us.' Seigneur Fitzalan's voice was pleasant, gentle, even. But his countenance was stern. Kieron saw no mercy in it.

'Forgive me, Seigneur,' said Kieron with accidental humour, 'I was not conscious of your presence.'

'Ha!' Seigneur Fitzalan permitted himself a thin smile. 'I will remember the jest … Well, boy, you struck the Mistress Alyx, repeatedly, in a place to which no gentleman cares to refer. Before I determine your fate, I would have you know that this is a precedent. Derive some satisfaction from it, if you may. Previous to your assault, no man – not even I – had ever laid hand upon my daughter in anger. What, then, have you to say?'

'Nothing, Seigneur,' said Kieron after a moment or two of reflection. It would be stupid to plead for mercy. It would be stupid to try to explain the provocation.

'So, boy, you are fairly condemned?'

'I struck Mistress Alyx, Seigneur. I intended no permanent damage. That is all.' He looked vaguely at Alyx. She was no longer the imperious young lady. She seemed white-faced, unhappy. Well, thought Kieron, let my death lie on her conscience for ever.

'That is all?' thundered Fitzalan. 'That is all?'

'Seigneur,' said the gaoler, 'allow me to encourage him.'

'Be silent, fellow,' snapped Fitzalan irritably. 'A knock on the head and his present situation ought to be sufficiently encouraging for the time being … Well, prentice, you have spoken. You have nothing further to add?'

Kieron thought for a moment. There was much that could be added, of course, but best keep it to essentials.

'I pray that my actions will not reflect upon Master Hobart, who is a kindly man and a great painter, and responsible for no actions but his own. I pray also that my parents be held free from blame. It was simply their misfortune to beget me. Already, they have their punishment.'

Seigneur Fitzalan made rumbling noises in his throat. His moustache quivered. Mistress Alyx leaned forward and, looking at Kieron, began to stroke her father's long silver hair.

'As to your punishment, prentice, I have given some thought to it. At first, I was minded to have your head struck off, as an example to all upstarts and mischief-makers, of which there are always a few in any domain. Then, since such a punishment was somewhat final and likely to be forgotten by many in a twelve-month, I was inclined to clemency, striking off only the offending hand and blinding the offending eyes.'

Kieron shuddered. Death was preferable to clemency.

'However,' continued Seigneur Fitzalan, 'my daughter Alyx, who is not without a mind of her own, suggested a more ingenious punishment.'

Kieron's mouth ran dry. The horrors already mentioned seemed bad enough. But, evidently, they were not sufficient to give Mistress Alyx the satisfaction she required.

'So, prentice, you will endure the punishment that Mistress Alyx has recommended, since she is the offended party.'

'Seigneur,' said Kieron quickly, 'I accept death by decapitation. It is just.'

'Do you, now? The choice lies not in your province, boy. Think yourself fortunate.'

Kieron did not think himself fortunate. The axe was quick, whereas whatever Mistress Alyx had devised was likely to be slow.

'I sentence you,' said Seigneur Fitzalan, smiling faintly, 'to attend Mistress Alyx upon her request, to execute such drawings as are necessary, and never again to raise your hand towards her in anger lest mine be raised fearfully against you … You are lucky, boy, that my daughter enjoys peculiar whims and also has womanly methods of twisting my resolution. Well, what say you?'

Kieron's mouth opened and closed, but no words would come.

'Loose him, father. The boy has suffered enough.' Alyx gazed compassionately at Kieron. It was the first time she had spoken.

Fitzalan cast a despairing glance at ceiling. 'When will I ever understand the ways of a woman?' Then he signalled to the gaoler, and Kieron was released from the manacles.

He found his tongue. 'I thank you, Seigneur, for the mercy you have shown.'

Fitzalan laughed. 'Mercy, by Ludd! Speak to me of mercy when Mistress Alyx has taken her vengeance. Now get from this place and pray somewhat.'

9

The following day, Kieron presented himself at the castle as usual; but Mistress Alyx chose not to receive him. He returned to Hobart's house dejected, convinced that Alyx had had time for reflection and that the commission was lost, seven hundred and fifty schilling and all. He supposed he ought to count himself lucky that he got out of the affair as lightly as he did. But he was truly mortified. He was mortified because he feared that his conduct might reflect upon Master Hobart, and that the old man might lose other commissions also.

He had related the entire story as accurately as he could, adding nothing, omitting nothing. He had expected that Hobart would be dismayed and also disgusted with him, would wish to beat him certainly, and quite likely would desire to end the apprenticeship.

He was right in that Hobart was dismayed. He was wrong in that Hobart would be disgusted.

'My son, I see that Mistress Alyx used you cruelly. Forgive me. I know that she is a wilful woman. I did not know that she would abuse her position. It matters not if we are out of favour at the castle. I liked this commission but little, anyway. What matters most is that you survived the incident.' He tried to laugh, but wound up with a fit of coughing that needed to be settled by usquebaugh. 'In any case, we have the refined flax seed oil, for which the demand will be prodigious.'

Kieron was amazed. 'You are not angry?'

'Yes, I am angry that talent should be impeded by temperament. What is Alyx Fitzalan? Nothing but the daughter of Seigneur Fitzalan. That is her sole significance. But you, Kieron, are an artist and quite possibly a man of genius. It is unfortunate that you beat her – though I rejoice in the thought, having had some temptation myself – yet it is not disastrous. Fitzalan was wise enough not to pursue the matter. We shall live.'

'Sir, I am grateful.'

'Say no more, Kieron. Tomorrow we will fish for trout.'

But, on the following day a lackey brought a summons. The Mistress Alyx Fitzalan desired that Kieron, apprentice of Hobart, attend her with his drawing materials.

'You will not go,' said Hobart. 'I will plead illness.'

'Sir, I must go,' said Kieron. 'It is part of the sentence.'

As before, Alyx was seated at the clavichord, waiting for him. A book rested on the music machine. Kieron recognised it.

'Good morning, Master Kieron.' He was taken aback at her civility. Besides, he was not a master, he was only an apprentice.

'Good morning, Mistress Alyx.'

She stood up and held out the book.

'You were interested in this volume, I recall. It is yours.'

Kieron was shaken. 'Mistress Alyx, you are most kind.' He took the book, fingered it lovingly. 'You are too kind. I—' He stopped.

Alyx smiled. 'Let us forget the past, Kieron. How would you like me to pose?'

'As you will, Mistress. As you will. I can take many sketches and compound them into something from which Master Hobart will discern the necessary form.'

'Kieron?'

'Mistress Alyx?'

'Call me Alyx.'

He was shaken even more. 'Yes – Alyx.'

'Kieron, no man ever before beat me.'

'I am sorry, Mistress – I am sorry, Alyx. I thought you commanded me to forget the –'

'Kieron?'

'Mistress – I mean Alyx?'

She rose from the clavichord and came close to him. Her gown rustled, and there was a fragrance about her, a redness in her cheeks, a softness in her eyes. She did not now look at all like the ice-cold girl who had goaded him beyond endurance. 'I treated you ill, and I am sorry. Yesterday, I cried into the night because I had been cruel and stupid, and I thought you would hate me. Do you hate me? If so, I must learn to bear it.'

Kieron knew not what to say or do. For reasons he could not understand, his heart seemed to be exploding in his chest. There was sweat on his forehead and a fire in his limbs. At length he found his tongue.

'Mistress, I do not hate you. Truly, I do not. Something has happened that ... Perhaps my mind is sick.'

She smiled. 'You forget. Say Alyx. My name is Alyx. You shall use it always when we are alone.'

'Alyx,' he said idiotically. 'Alyx.' He could think of nothing else to say. The word seemed both familiar and strange, a magic word. An incantation.

'Your mind is not sick, Kieron. At least, no more than mine ... We are friends, now?'

'We are friends,' Kieron was trembling. He seemed to be standing outside himself. He seemed to be listening to the voice of a stranger ... Why did she stand so close? Why was there a roaring in his head?

'We are close friends?'

'If it is your wish.'

'Is it not yours?'

'Alyx, I – I …' There was nothing to say. Nothing that made sense.

'Kiss me, Kieron. Your lips on mine.' The book dropped from Kieron's hand. He did not notice. Neither of them noticed.

'Kiss me,' she whispered. It was a whisper that drove all rational thought from Kieron's mind.

He held her in his arms. He felt the life in her. He felt her breasts against him, the liquid warmth of her belly. He felt her lips upon his.

This was like to earn him the donjon, the lash, the irons, the rack, all manner of tortures. He did not care. The taste of Alyx Fitzalan's lips, the touch of her body – he did not care.

Presently, they stood back from each other.

'No man ever beat me before. No man ever held me so before. No man ever kissed me so before.' Alyx seemed happy, even complacent. 'I love you, Kieron.'

'I am terrified of love,' said Kieron. 'It is a destroyer. But I love you also. I thought I hated you, but the hatred was a form of love.'

Alyx frowned as reality came back to her. 'It is but a short-lived bloom, Kieron. Let us enjoy it while we may. The child Petrina is your destiny. Talbot of Chichester – a pale, sad thing – is mine … Does Petrina kiss as I do?'

'Alyx, I know not, I do not – I have not …' He floundered.

'Hush, dear one. You gave me my answer … Until this time, you were but a prentice painter bullied by a thoughtless minx, taking advantage of her father's power. But love is dangerous, Kieron. It makes us equal in each other's sight; but in the eyes of the world the gulf between us is wide. Talbot and Petrina, and the customs of our people, hover about us like ghosts. We must be very careful, otherwise we shall be destroyed.'

Kieron managed to smile. 'I will be careful, Alyx, if only because I must. I am afraid for both of us.'

She took his hand. 'Be not too much afraid. If we keep our heads, all will be well.' She laughed. 'I surmise my father required Master Hobart to keep me distracted for at least a two-month. Is that not so? And you were to be the sacrificial lamb.'

Kieron shrugged. 'It is so, Alyx. Indeed, it is so.'

'Well, then,' she said gaily, 'who will protest if we stretch the two-month into a three-month? Not my father, not Master Hobart. Each would be delighted at the success of the stratagem. So, in public, I will be the haughty Alyx, whose aim is to humiliate you. And you will contrive to play the poor prentice who bears what he must for the sake of his master and his art and for the sake of his future. Can you bear this device?'

'I can bear it.'

'Good. Today, you will make sketches; but, tomorrow, we will ride again. Doubtless, you will fall off. The people will learn of it and be satisfied. Kieron-head-in-the-air – yes, I know what they call you – will be humiliated once more. Can you bear it?'

'I can bear deception only for the sake of truth.'

'Well spoken, my love.' She came close and kissed him. 'When we are alone – truly alone – you shall command me. I will kiss your feet, if it is your pleasure. I will stroke your hair and hold your body close to mine and rejoice in your touch.'

'Alyx, do not make me cry.'

'The tears will come later, Kieron – when I am taken to Talbot's bed, and Petrina comes to yours. How shall either of us bear it then?'

He held her tight. 'I do not know. I know only that we have a little time. For that I am grateful.'

'A little time,' sighed Alyx. 'Only a little time. So sad … I want to learn about you. I want to learn as much as I can. Do you truly want to be a painter like Master Hobart? Or is there something else.'

'Most of all,' said Kieron, caressing her, 'I want to fly. I want to conquer the air as the First Men and the Second Men did. I want to feel close to the stars.'

'Kieron-head-in-the-air,' she murmured, 'I love you. You are nothing but a fantasist, a cloud walker.'

10

Brother Sebastian gazed at Kieron, lying on his daybed, without any animosity or any attempt to inspire fear. Brother Sebastian, a pleasant-looking man of thirty years or so, concealed his ambition, his desire for power, beneath a benign exterior. He rarely bullied. He preferred to look sorrowful. People did not like to see Brother Sebastian unhappy.

Kieron's broken leg twitched abominably. It had been set by Seigneur Fitzalan's own surgeon. Nevertheless, Kieron remained convinced that the fellow knew little of his art. Already, when he stretched and measured his limbs, Kieron seemed to detect that the good leg was significantly longer. He would hate to exchange his present title for Kieron-game-leg. Besides, who would condescend to wrestle with a cripple?

Brother Sebastian was in a quandary. At the insistence of Mistress Alyx, Kieron had been removed temporarily from Hobart's house and given a room at the castle. Alyx had roundly condemned Kieron to her father, for indulging in childish pranks, and had implied that Kieron had broken his leg almost deliberately in order to avoid making the sketches and rough compositions that were necessary for the commissioned painting. Why, therefore, let the prentice have an easy time of it? Better, surely, to bring him to the castle so that he could continue his work without delay. That would teach him that he could not evade important affairs merely by breaking a leg.

Seigneur Fitzalan gave his daughter a curious look. He was an intelligent man. Intelligent enough to realise there were certain things it were better not to know. Besides, the boy was useful. Alyx had been relatively docile since she had had the prentice on whom to vent her feelings. So Kieron had been given a room in the castle while his leg mended.

Thus Brother Sebastian's quandary. Kieron, though a commoner, was now a person of some importance – temporarily, at least.

'Tell me, brother, how came you to break the limb?' This was a rhetorical question, because everyone in the seigneurie knew how Kieron had broken his leg.

'Brother Sebastian, I was but flying a kite,' said Kieron carefully.

'A kite? You were flying a kite. I have been misinformed, it seems. I had heard that you were flying *in* a kite.'

Kieron thought for a moment or two. Brother Sebastian had flung back his cowl. His head was clean-shaven; his face, totally visible, seemed totally innocent.

'It is true, brother,' amended Kieron. 'I was flying in a kite.'

'It must have been an exceptionally large kite.'

'It was, Brother Sebastian. It was a very large kite. I designed it.'

'And who aided you in this project, Kieron?'

Kieron thought carefully. If he admitted that Aylwin had obtained the sail canvas, that they had both cut the willow rods and that Sholto, the smith, had been persuaded to make fastenings for the harness, it could seem like conspiracy.

'No one, Brother Sebastian. It is true I coaxed the miller's prentice to hold the rope. He is but a stupid fellow and fit for nothing but the grinding of corn. However, dull though he is, it pleased me to make use of him. I little recked that he would take panic when I rose into the air.'

The neddy stroked his chin thoughtfully. 'That must indeed have been a sight.'

'Indeed it must, brother,' said Kieron with unguarded enthusiasm. 'There was a steady and strong offshore breeze, and I rose up from the beach, my legs dancing and seeking footholds where there were none. It was a wonderful feeling. I rose more than ten times the height of a man before the loop of cord was jerked from its hook.'

'You were lucky, Kieron, that the sea broke your fall.'

'That is why I waited for an offshore wind,' explained Kieron. 'That is why I chose to experiment on the beach.'

'Experiment?' Brother Sebastian raised his eyebrows. Experiment was a dangerous word. It smelled of fire.

'Experiment in the sense of finding out how to handle the kite,' amended Kieron hastily. 'Nothing more.'

Brother Sebastian stroked his chin slowly. At length, he said: 'The kite was made of sail-cloth and willow wands.'

'Yes, brother.'

'And the harness as you call it had metal fastenings which could only have been fashioned by the smith.'

'Yes, brother.'

'It was a very ambitious kite, Kieron.'

'Yes, Brother Sebastian. It was a very ambitious kite.'

'And you designed it alone?'

'I designed it alone.'

'Sholto did not know your purpose?'

'No, brother.'

'And the boy Aylwin helped you only by anchoring the cord and by moving as directed?'

'Yes, brother.'

'I am told you instructed him in the use of a pulley, by which means he could control the kite without great exertion to himself.'

'You are well informed.'

'Yes, Kieron. I am well informed.'

'The pulley. It is a very simple principle.'

'Simple principles can be dangerous, Kieron. You have been instructed in the Holy Scripture, have you not?'

'Yes, brother.'

'Men have burned for simple principles, Kieron. Remember that.'

Kieron wanted to rise from his bed and strangle this dull-witted neddy. But he had enough wit to say docilely: 'Yes, Brother Sebastian.'

'I have heard,' went on the neddy, 'that folk call you Kieron-head-in-the-air. Why should they call you that?'

Kieron thought quickly, gave a shrug, and laughed. 'Since I fell from Mistress Alyx Fitzalan's mare, they also call me Kieron-arse-in-the-muck. People amuse themselves as they wish.' It seemed as good a time as any to remind Brother Sebastian that Kieron was permitted to ride with Seigneur Fitzalan's daughter.

The neddy was not to be distracted. 'You do not know why they call you Kieron-head-in-the-air?'

'Brother, perhaps it is because I often look at the sky. The sky is a wonderful place. It is ever-changing. Its moods are always different.'

'You are fascinated by the sky?'

'Yes, Brother Sebastian, I am fascinated by the sky.'

'And you wish to voyage through it?'

Now, there was a dangerous question. Kieron was immediately alert to its implications.

'The sky, the firmament, is beautiful,' he said carefully. 'The artist in me is profoundly moved by its aspects, and by the subtle changes it undergoes throughout the seasons … To the greater glory of Ludd.'

Brother Sebastian crossed himself. 'To the greater glory of Ludd,' he echoed automatically. After a reverent pause, he continued: 'But do you wish to voyage through it?'

Kieron's leg was hurting, and sweat was forming on his forehead, and he did not know how long he could endure the damnable persistence of the neddy.

'I can admire the freedom of the bird without wishing to sprout feathers. I am a man, Brother Sebastian, accepting the freedom and the limitations of men. I rejoice in my human condition.'

'But, Kieron, my brother, do you wish to fly?'

'Brother Sebastian, I do not wish to be a bird.'

Brother Sebastian sighed, and looked unhappy. 'Your answers are less than direct.'

'I am sorry, brother. I thought my answers were accurate and truthful. This accursed leg gives me pain. Perhaps I do not think too clearly.'

'Perhaps so. I shall report our conversation to Holy Church, Kieron. Others, more competent than I, will consider it.'

'That is well, Brother Sebastian,' said Kieron, thinking it was far from well. 'Perhaps my childish adventure was ill-timed.'

'Kites are for children only, Kieron. Remember that. You are almost a man.'

'I will remember it.'

'Further, a kite is but a toy. But if a man should choose to ride a kite, it could be interpreted as a machine.'

'I will remember that also.'

'I shall pray for you,' said Brother Sebastian. 'You have a great future. Master Hobart tells me that you are gifted in your craft. Do not spoil that future, Kieron. Good painters are rare. Evil men are with us always.'

'I will remember your words, Brother Sebastian, and I shall dwell upon your wisdom.'

'Ludd be with you, my brother.'

'And with you also.'

'Farewell, then.' Brother Sebastian departed. Hardly had he gone, when Alyx came into the room.

'How went your discussion with Brother Sebastian?'

'He is a fool.'

'My love, I know that. But was he satisfied?'

'I don't know.'

'You should know. Why don't you know?'

'Because I too am a fool,' said Kieron irritably, 'and my leg twitches …' Then he smiled, and added: 'And it is a fine day, and I would be out walking in the woods with you.'

'This will teach you to try to walk upon air, when we have so little time.' She shuddered. 'You could have been killed. Promise me to be more careful, Kieron.'

He glanced at his leg. 'I can hardly be but careful, Alyx.'

'Not now, dolt. In the future, as. you well know.'

'I will be careful until you are carried off to Talbot's bed,' he promised rightly. 'Then I will construct a kite that shall raise me high above your father's castle. Then I will leap from it and dash myself to death before his eyes.'

Alyx pouted. 'I wish Talbot would die. I truly do, And I wish the plague or somesuch would carry off that dreadful Petrina, with her peasant breasts and a bottom like a cow's rump. Ludd forgive me, I pray for these things.'

'Petrina does not have a bottom like a cow's rump.'

'She does so. I have studied her.'

He laughed. 'Ah, you have studied her, Green Eyes.'

'I hate you! I hate you.'

'Come, let me sketch you while the fire still consumes you. I must earn my keep lest Seigneur Fitzalan and Master Hobart begin to imagine the absurdity that is the truth.'

'Peasant!' she stormed.

'Yes, I am a peasant,' he replied tranquilly. 'Be mindful that the gulf between us is great – with or without Talbot and Petrina.'

'I love you, and I would die for you. Is that not enough?'

'It is too much. I love you, as you know, Alyx, and we must both live in a world where such love is an affront to the minds of men … Besides, I have a destiny to fulfil.'

'I would not stop you painting.'

'You would stop me flying.'

She looked at him in amazement. 'Flying! Kieron, my love. You are mad. Men do not fly. Men will not fly.'

'Yes, I am mad – and I will fly. I will construct a machine that—'

'Do not speak of machines! Or, if you must, to me only. Machines are evil. That is the word of the Divine Boy, that is the teaching of Holy Church, that is what all men know.'

'And yet,' said Kieron, 'it is not true. Machines cannot be evil. Evil lies only with the human spirit … I will fly, I swear it. I will fly for the good of men. By the spirits of the Brothers Montgolfier, of Otto Lilienthal, of the great Santos Dumont, and of the Brothers Wright, I so swear.'

'Who are these creatures?'

'Nothing but ghosts. Great and friendly ghosts. Men who lived centuries ago upon earth and raised their eyes unto the stars … I read of them in the book you gave me.'

'I had done better to burn it. My father does not read, and therefore cannot have known that his library contained heresy.'

'Had you burned it, Alyx, I still would have lifted my eyes unto the stars. It is not in the nature of man to remain earthbound … Come, kiss me. Then I will try to be of some credit to Master Hobart.'

11

The days passed quickly. Kieron's leg mended and was not noticeably shorter. Spring deepened into summer – and brought a bloom to Mistress Alyx's face that did not pass unnoticed. She taught Kieron to ride – or, at least, not to fall off a horse when it was in motion. He made studies of horses. Horses grazing, horses ambling, galloping, jumping. The first time Alyx took her mount over a seven-bar gate for him, he was too terrified to put charcoal to paper.

'My love, never again! Don't do it. You are like to break your neck.'

'Poof! Thus speaks the cloud walker, who rose ten times the height of a man and fell into the sea.' And, to emphasise her point, she put her horse to the gate again; and rose, chestnut hair streaming in the sunlight, to ride like a goddess between sky and earth in a moment of infinite beauty.

Kieron worked like a demon, like one possessed. He made a hundred sketches and discarded ninety. This portrait of Alyx Fitzalan would be his sole claim to greatness as an artist. He knew it would be good, because it would be compounded of love, of beauty, of youth, and of joy in life.

Master Hobart coughed much and complained little. He complained little because Kieron had ceased to complain at all.

Hobart gazed at the sketches he brought back, and was filled with wonder. The boy had achieved rapport with his subject. There was elegance in his work and, yes, greatness. Hobart reached for the usquebaugh or the eau de vie and contemplated this greatness. Escapades with kites mattered little – indeed, were irrelevant – against such purity of line, such mastery of motion.

Soon, Kieron would begin to paint. Not at the castle, but in Hobart's studio. And the painting would be a masterpiece, signed Hobart. And when is was acclaimed a masterpiece, Hobart would add: app Kieron. Thus would his life's work be completed. Thus would Kieron be set upon the path to fame.

Kieron executed the painting in one day only. One day being a full twenty-four hours. During that time, he did not speak. He did not recognise Hobart. The old man hovered about the canvas, wringing his hands, and Kieron did not know him. The Widow Thatcher brought food. Kieron stared at her, uncomprehending, and the food was left untouched. As darkness fell, Hobart brought lamps, many lamps, and squandered whale oil prodigiously. Kieron muttered to himself at the change of light, but did not know what brought it about.

Once he fell to the floor, and was conscious of someone forcing a fluid that burned between his lips. He got up, and went back to the canvas. The rider was finished; but the fetlocks of the leaping horse were wrong. He scraped them away from the canvas and started again.

Now, what of that damned tail? And the nostrils? And, Ludd have mercy, the mane? And now the eyes were wrong. The creature should have great, proud eyes as it supported its glorious rider in that impossible leap. He looked at Alyx once more. Purgatory and damnation! The hair was wrong. That long, beautiful hair should flow with movement, be alive in this instant with a life of its own.

Master Hobart tended the oil lamps and drank usquebaugh and muttered plaintively to himself and gazed with awe at the young man who seemed to be engaged in a life or death battle with brushes and pigments as his weapons.

Who was the enemy? Hobart asked himself blearily, drunk with spirits and fatigue. Who was the enemy against which Kieron waged so ferocious a battle? It came to him that the enemy was time. Kieron was not only trying to paint a great portrait, he was challenging the Adversary, He was the Life Force incarnate; and every brush stroke was a sword thrust. He was declaring his bid for immortality.

The picture was finished shortly after daybreak. Hobart, who had dozed intermittently, drew back the curtains from the window but left the oil-lamps burning.

Kieron stood in front of the canvas. Brushes and palette had dropped from his exhausted hands.

Hobart gazed at the portrait and wept, knowing that he was in the presence of greatness.

Kieron looked at him, pale, drawn, red-eyed. 'I have done my best, Master Hobart. What say you?'

'My son, my son!' the old man was beside himself. 'You have joined the ranks of the immortals. I am a fool. I presumed to teach you. But now that it is too late, I know how much I had to learn.'

'If you love me,' said Kieron, 'you will sign it Hobart. You will add nothing.'

'Kieron, I am not worthy.'

'The style is yours. Had you been younger, the brush strokes would have been yours.'

'The brush strokes could never have been mine.'

'They are yours, because I was an extension of your will.' Kieron put his foot upon the fallen brushes. 'Sir, I will not paint like this again.'

'But why? Why, Kieron? You are a great artist. If you paint in this manner at the beginning of your career, who knows what we may see?'

'I will not paint like this again,' repeated Kieron. 'It was a work of love – doubly so.' He laughed. 'I may paint to live – though the work will be no more than adequate – if such is necessary. But I shall live to fly. That is my true destiny.'

Hobart could say nothing. The picture was magnificent. But the poor boy was clearly out of his mind.

12

Seigneur Fitzalan was pleased with the painting. He did not know that Kieron had executed every brush stroke, though he surmised that much of the fine work had been carried out by the prentice. Master Hobart's shaking had become more noticeable; and it was plain even to Fitzalan that the old painter's useful days were numbered. Fortunate indeed that the prentice showed signs of surpassing his master. There would be work enough for him in the years to come. Fitzalan liked to be surrounded by beautiful things – paintings he merely glanced at, books he did not read. A man's greatness was reflected in his deeds or his possessions. Time had not granted Seigneur Fitzalan the opportunity to perform great deeds, but it had allowed him to acquire many fine works of art from goldsmiths, silversmiths, armourers, scribes, painters. He would be remembered for his taste, if for nothing else.

The painting was to be called: *Mistress Fitzalan's Leap.* The signature was simply: Hobart.

But Alyx knew how the picture had been finished, and she wept somewhat that Kieron's name did not rest upon this painting that would hold the glow of her youth for ever. She wept also because of the grace and artistry she discerned, knowing that it was truly a work of love. And she wept because the dream-days were over. Henceforth, she would have to meet Kieron – if she met him at all – by 'accident' in some lonely or clandestine place. Soon, even that would not be possible because the wedding with Talbot was less than a month away.

Seigneur Fitzalan sent his bailiff with a chamois leather bag containing seven hundred and fifty silver schilling to the house of Hobart. The bailiff also conveyed Fitzalan's desire that Kieron should attend him. Hobart was apprehensive, recollecting the last interview Kieron had had with Seigneur Fitzalan. But Kieron did not seem perturbed. He put on his best leather and linen and followed the bailiff.

Seigneur Fitzalan received him in a room that Kieron had not seen before; a room that contained many weapons, a desk, a table, two chairs, a bearskin rug and little else.

Seigneur Fitzalan was seated at the desk, toying with a fine hunting knife.

'Well, prentice, are you satisfied with *Mistress Fitzalan's Leap*?' The tone was even, but the voice was ominous.

'Seigneur, I – I—' Kieron floundered, suddenly thinking of a hundred things that could be wrong with the canvas. 'It is as good, I think, as Master Hobart has ever done.'

Fitzalan gave him a faint smile. 'Ay, boy, that may be fairly said ... Since our last meeting, I have had reports of you. Both good and ill. Which would you hear first?'

Kieron began to sweat a little, but his wit did not desert him. 'The ill, Seigneur. Then I may console myself with the good.'

'The ill it is, then. Holy Church is interested in you, Kieron. I am told that you constructed a machine.'

'Seigneur, I did but fashion a large kite that—'

'Enough, I know the details. Holy Church ruled long ago that a kite is but a toy. However, if such a toy be used to elevate a man unnaturally from the earth, it becomes a machine. You know the history of our race. Machines have twice destroyed the greatness of man. The wisdom of the Divine Boy is apparent. Men can only survive if they reject the temptation of machines. Is this not so?'

Kieron swallowed. 'Seigneur, I must bow to the wisdom of Holy Church.'

'That you must, boy. Machines smell of burning. Have you ever seen a man burn, Kieron?'

'No, Seigneur.'

'I have,' said Fitzalan tranquilly. 'Holy Church is more powerful than all the lords of this island, and rightly so. For Holy Church guides us in the way we must live. I have seen a farmer burn for constructing a reaping machine. I have seen a smith burn for fashioning an engine driven by steam. I have seen a noble man burn for meddling with electrics and creating a light that was not born of fire. I have seen a poor washerwoman burn for devising a machine that would spin the water out of the clothes she washed. The stench of burnt flesh is not like the smell of roast pork, prentice. I make myself clear?'

'Seigneur, you make yourself excellently clear.'

'Then, Kieron, let there be no more meddling with machines. I have writ to Holy Church that you are aware of your folly. This time, my protection holds. Do not think it will hold a second time.'

'Seigneur, I am grateful.'

'So you should be. But I am grateful also. *Mistress Fitzalan's Leap* is a good painting. Further, the conditions I sought from your master were met in full – with a bonus.'

'I am happy, sir.'

'Do not be. The bonus gives me cause for unrest. I required the Mistress Alyx's spare time to be engaged for a two-month. You, sir, engaged it for a three-month.'

'There was the matter of my broken leg,' Kieron floundered. 'It took time to mend.'

Seigneur Fitzalan lifted the hunting knife with which he had been playing and pointed it at Kieron. 'My daughter, Alyx, was happy for a time. Now she weeps. Can you explain that?'

'Seigneur, I am at a loss.'

Fitzalan laughed, grimly. 'So, prentice, am I … With women, it is always the unexpected that a man should anticipate. Mistress Alyx spoke well of you – not too well, but well enough. She can be careful of her tongue, that one, when it suits her … Yet, now she weeps. She will wed with Talbot in a month. And yet, she weeps. Amazing, is it not?'

'Yes, Seigneur, it is amazing.' Kieron dreaded the way the conversation was turning.

'Know this, then. There are things better unsaid; for if said, they must be admitted or denied. And in certain matters, either course leads to danger. Now, boy, do not think to be clever, but tell me if your mind truly grasps that which I have left unsaid.'

Kieron swallowed, his eyes upon the hunting knife, which seemed to be pointing at his heart. 'Sir, I understand you.'

'So. I believe you.' Seigneur Fitzalan put the hunting knife down. He took up a small chamois sack and rattled its contents. 'The horse does not shame me, and I know that Master Hobart has no liking for horses. Also the rider is shown to be not without grace and distinction. At your art, boy, you may flourish. See that you flourish in nought else.' He threw the small sack to Kieron. 'These fifty schilling recognise that you have worked well under some difficulty. There are other gifts I could bestow for services that were not required. Be thankful that I do not.'

'Yes, Seigneur.'

'Go, then. And recollect that tears dry soon if more are not provoked.'

'Yes, Seigneur.' Feeling the sweat lie cold upon his forehead, Kieron left the chamber.

13

There was no longer any need for Kieron to visit the castle daily, and he did not. The warning given him by Seigneur Fitzalan had been clear enough. Besides, surely it was in Alyx's own interest that she and Kieron did not see each other again? As Fitzalan had said, tears dry soon if more are not provoked.

And yet it was hard, very hard, to face the whole of life without holding Alyx in his arms again. But he would love Petrina. It would not be difficult to love Petrina. She would lie by his side through ten thousand nights, and bear his children, and whiten and weaken as he whitened and weakened, Age might cool the passions of youth, but it could only add to the sharing of things known and loved.

Each man has but a single lifetime, thought Kieron. We are here but for a moment in history. There is so little time. So little time to lift man from the face of the earth and make him lord of the sky once more.

Master Hobart was more than content with *Mistress Fitzalan's Leap*. Much more than content. He was proud that his spiritual son had carried the day in such triumph. Contractually, Kieron's apprenticeship had several months to run; but Hobart knew that he no longer gave bed and food to an apprentice. He knew that he was privileged to enjoy the society of a genius. A genius who had insisted that his first great work be signed Hobart. So Hobart did not exercise the rights of a master. He was content to be a proud and a spiritual father. Which meant that Kieron now enjoyed absolute freedom. And this, in turn, meant that Hobart was prey to exquisite anxieties.

Kieron now possessed fifty schilling to do with as he wished. A veritable fortune. More money than he had ever handled in his seventeen years. How to use it? There were problems. Twenty schillings for Aylwin, who had served him well in the matter of the man-lifting kite. Twenty schilling would buy much canvas and pigment and flax seed oil for Aylwin. Add to this Kieron's instruction, and Aylwin would be well repaid for his friendship. He would become a master painter as well as a master miller. Aylwin would rejoice in, at least, a partial freedom from his destiny.

The remaining thirty schilling … Kieron had read the book given him by Alyx. He had read it many times. The conquest of the air had been carried out in steps. He would retrace those steps. And the next step was a hot-air balloon, such as had been fashioned by Joseph and Etienne Montgolfier many centuries ago.

For this, Kieron required much linen, and much paper to line the balloon that would be made of linen. Also, he required a small charcoal brazier. Also, he required again the help of Aylwin.

Mistress Alyx did not subscribe to the philosophy that tears dry soon if more are not provoked. Discreetly, she sent messages to Kieron. He did not dare reply. Then she took to riding daily through Arundel, pausing a while in front of Master Hobart's house. Kieron saw her and felt his heart leap, but he did not go forth to greet her. It was less fear of Seigneur Fitzalan's wrath that restrained him than the fear that her nearness would make him desire to be yet nearer and nearer, as the first cup of wine brings the desire for a second and a third.

Besides, even if Seigneur Fitzalan's anger could be avoided, the final parting was yet inevitable. And Alyx should surely take the more kindly to Talbot's bed if she were not still warmed by Kieron's touch.

So he watched her ride by and bit his lip and did nothing. And if, by chance, he should be abroad when she rode, he stood and lowered his head and bent a trifle from the waist, giving her courtesy as any man or prentice would.

For distraction, he busied himself with dangerous plans – the hot-air balloon. It was not to be a man-carrying balloon; for that would surely be defined as a machine by Holy Church. If, indeed, Holy Church should discover the matter. Which was not unlikely, for the Brothers of Ludd were feared as much as they were respected by the common folk; and many a man would inform against his neighbour if he thought that such action would improve his own prospects.

So a man-carrying balloon must not be attempted – yet. But a hot-air balloon that a prentice-boy could hold on the end of a cord – surely that could only be regarded as a toy? A clever toy, perhaps. But not a dangerous toy … Kieron was so obsessed by his need to experiment with airborne devices that he stupidly chose to ignore the fact that Holy Church was already interested in his activities …

At first, his design for the balloon was modest. It was to be no more than the height of a man, no wider than a wine cask; and it was to be constructed of four lengths of linen, cut to shape and sewn carefully over a light wooden frame. Where could all this be accomplished so that Master Hobart might remain in blessed ignorance and so that the curiosity of townsfolk would not be greatly tempted? Kieron consulted with Aylwin. Aylwin pondered the problem. It was similar to his own. He wished to be able to paint in freedom and seclusion without being scolded for wasting his time or jeered for attempting an art to which he was not contracted.

The solution was discovered by accident as Kieron and Aylwin walked together one day, discussing their projects, inland along the banks of the river Arun, far from the town that seemed, in the distance, to be squeezed between church and castle.

The solution to the problem was revealed in the form of a derelict windmill, unused for a century or more, that stood near the river. According to legend, the miller and his entire family had been put to the stake for misusing the power of the wind. According to legend the derelict mill was haunted by their ghosts.

Aylwin knew something of the story, and repeated what he knew to Kieron. The miller had been an ambitious and ingenious man who believed that the winds of heaven were given to mankind to be used for whatever purposes mankind could devise. Holy Church permitted the use of the wind for the grinding of corn – necessary for human survival; for the pumping of fresh water – also necessary for human survival; and for the propulsion of ships – again necessary for human survival. The Church admitted the use of machines for necessities: it did not admit the use of machines for luxuries.

But the miller had used wind power not only to grind corn but to turn a lathe that his son might fashion goblets, bowls, platters from seasoned wood, these to be sold to the nobility, who admired purity of shape in all things, whether glass, stone, metal or wood. And he had further permitted wind power to be used to operate weaving machines so that his wife and daughter could produce linen and silk cloth, the like of which could not be found in many days' travel.

Envious people betrayed him to Holy Church. The four of them – man, wife, son and daughter – were burned on the same day at the same time, so positioned that, smoke permitting, they would witness each other's agony.

And so the mill had been left to rot, and left also to the occupancy of ghosts. It was known as Weaver's Mill. Few people cared to visit it in daylight or in darkness. Besides, when the Arun flooded, the lower part of the mill came under water.

Kieron looked at the derelict windmill, and thought of its ghosts, and loved them. Here was the place to construct his hot-air balloon. Here was the place where Aylwin could paint in peace.

'This is our home,' he said. 'Among the rats and the memories, this is our home. Here I will show you something of the art of oil colour. Here I will construct my hot-air balloon.'

Aylwin was not happy. 'Kieron, it is far from the town.'

'That is good.'

'Also, the spirits may not welcome us.'

'You believe in spirits, Aylwin?'

Aylwin crossed himself. 'I believe that there are things in which it is dangerous not to believe.'

'Well, then, we are at one with the ghosts. They will be friendly to us, because we, too, rebel against our destinies.'

'I am afraid,' said Aylwin.

'So, also, am I. But is it not better to be filled with fear and do what one desires than to be filled with fear and achieve nothing?'

Aylwin had no answer. So Weaver's Mill became the refuge for a miller who wished to paint and for a painter who wished to fly.

14

It took Kieron many days to construct the hot-air balloon, which not only gave Alyx Fitzalan some moments of terror and brought Kieron himself to the brink of disaster but also changed the course of history.

Though Aylwin and Kieron were to share the derelict windmill for their separate purposes, Kieron was now resolved not to endanger his friend by involving him in this new project. Nor would he further endanger Sholto, though he would have been greatly glad of the smith's help in fashioning a small brazier. The message of Brother Sebastian had been clear. If anyone was to suffer because of Kieron's desire to reconquer the air, it must be himself alone.

He bought much coarse linen and quite astounded Master Hobart with his requirements of paper. The old man loved Kieron too well, and feared for his safety too much, to enquire closely into the reasons for his demands. Master Hobart chose to remind himself that Kieron was one of the great ones, that *Mistress Fitzalan's Leap* was a masterpiece by any standard, and that great ones were privileged to indulge their madnesses as best they may. Hobart drank more, coughed more and prayed more. But, otherwise, he did and said nothing.

So Kieron transported his linen and paper and needles and thread to the derelict mill; and he bought an old fire-basket from a tinker who was amazed to receive five silver pennies for a piece of useless iron. And Kieron went to work like a man possessed. He bound willow wands to make a frame – slender shoots whose suppleness was ideal for his purpose. Weight, Kieron had discerned, was all. The frame of the balloon must be so light that the hot air would triumph.

Meanwhile, Alyx rode daily, hoping to encounter Kieron at least once more before she was taken to Chichester to lie with a sad young man who was not long for this world. And meanwhile, Aylwin, whenever he was released from his duties, came to the mill to paint.

Kieron gave him instruction. Aylwin was a ready pupil: Kieron was a good teacher. Aylwin learned to paint land and sky with fire in his brush. His canvases became alive with colour and movement. Truly, Kieron saw, there was a great talent in the prentice miller. It was a pity that he was doomed to spend his life grinding corn.

Meanwhile, the construction of the hot-air balloon progressed. And Kieron's ambitions waxed bolder. The balloon would be twice the height of a man and twice the width of a wine cask. It would be a great balloon – no longer a toy but a declaration of intent.

Meanwhile, Mistress Alyx continued to ride. And one day she rode out along the bank of the river Arun, as far as Weaver's Mill, seeking the boy whose face haunted her dreams. And that was the day that the balloon was ready for its flight.

The balloon, slack and flapping, hung suspended from a wooden beam jutting out of a window in the mill until the heat rising from the glowing charcoal in the brazier should cause the air inside it to expand and become buoyant. When the balloon was extended and ready to rise, Kieron would release its fastenings and control its ascent by a long stout cord fastened to a length of metal wire, fastened in turn to the brazier suspended under the balloon.

Aylwin was busy sketching Kieron at work, as he checked the fastenings and blew the charcoal with bellows to a white heat. Neither of them noticed Alyx, as she rode along the bank of the Arun, until she had almost reached the mill.

'Ludd ha' mercy,' exclaimed Aylwin in fright. 'The seigneur's daughter is upon us.' He tried to conceal his drawing materials as if he had been detected in the commission of a serious crime.

'Rest easy, my friend,' said Kieron, glancing up. 'Mistress Alyx will cause us no difficulties, I promise.' He had not told Aylwin – indeed, he had not told anyone – of the intimacies that had passed between him and Alyx. These were matters best remembered – or forgot – only by those who had experienced them.

Alyx dismounted. 'Well, Kieron, I wondered where you hid yourself. What is this contraption that commands all your attention?'

'A hot-air balloon, Mistress Alyx.' His tone was deferential, as it always had been when others were present. 'A toy, a whim, nothing more.'

'So,' said Alyx, 'we have here a prentice painter who does not paint and a prentice miller who does not grind corn. Most curious.' She turned to Aylwin. 'Boy, walk my horse somewhat, then let him graze. I have ridden him passing hard.'

'Yes, Mistress.' Aylwin took the bridle and led the hunter away.

Alyx waited until he was out of earshot. 'Kieron, I have sought you for many days. Why do you humiliate me?'

'Beloved Alyx, I do not humiliate you.'

'You do not come to the castle.'

'I have no reason. Also, your father has commanded me.

'He knows about us?'

'I do not know how, but he knows about us.' Kieron smiled. 'He told me that you wept somewhat ...'

'It is a lie,' said Alyx fiercely. 'I would not weep for a prentice painter.'

'Of this I am convinced,' said Kieron tranquilly. 'Yet your father is an honest man. He must be mistaken.'

She flung her arms round him, not caring if Aylwin saw or saw not. 'Kieron, I love you.'

'Darling Alyx, I love you also. But our paths diverge. You wed with Talbot, I wed with Petrina. You are high born, I am low born. There is nothing we can do.'

'We will see about that,' said Alyx. 'Talbot will be dead within a year, that I promise.'

'You would kill him?'

'He will die, Kieron. That is all. He will die ... What of Petrina?'

Kieron kissed her and held her close. 'Alyx, we deal in idle dreams. You must know that.'

Alyx dabbed at her eyes. 'Yes, we must be what we are.' She stood back. 'The miller's boy – will he be a teller of tales?'

'Rest easy. He is my friend. I teach him a new art.'

Alyx tried to laugh. 'He is not the only one you have taught a new art, Kieron-head-in-the-air ... See, your balloon fills out like a fat marrow. It strains to rise.'

'Ludd's Grief! Excuse me, Alyx. I must cast loose up above.' He dashed into the mill, loosened the top of the balloon; and took the wood beam in from the window. Then he came down and regarded the balloon critically.

It was in truth like a huge marrow, bigger than he had imagined. The charcoal in the brazier suspended beneath it glowed brightly. The balloon swayed in a light breeze, straining at its mooring.

Alyx marvelled at the sight. 'How will you explain this toy to Holy Church, Kieron?'

'How should I need explain it?' he demanded bitterly. 'It is but a toy, and I am but a fool called Kieron-head-in-the-air.'

'The neddies might call it a machine. They might think you guilty of machinism.'

'Hang the stupid neddies!' Kieron carefully loosened the mooring, and the balloon rose. He paid out the cord that held it very cautiously, delighting in the strong pull on his arms. The balloon rose above the windmill. Aylwin had tethered Alyx's horse to a stunted thorn bush and stood hands on hips, mouth open, observing the wondrous sight.

Kieron felt the delicious pull of the cord – the pull that strove to free him from the confines of earth – and rejoiced in it. Impulsively, he jumped. The balloon instantly responded, lifting him over Alyx's head, gently returning him to the ground.

'Bravo! Bravo!' cried Alyx. 'What a toy we have here. Let me try, Kieron. Please let me try.'

'You will have to hold firmly,' he cautioned. 'The pull is stronger than you think … No, Alyx, perhaps it is best that you do not meddle with this thing.'

'Don't spoil the sport, Kieron. I must hold it. I shall. I am not a child.'

'Nor is it a toy for a child,' he warned. 'Well, hold the cord, so. And wrap it round your wrist, so.'

Carefully, he gave the cord to her, and made sure that she held it firmly. As she felt the pull, Alyx gave a cry of delight. Then she prepared to jump as Kieron had done. Unfortunately, as she jumped, there was a sudden gust of wind. The balloon responded to it. Also, Kieron had forgotten that Alyx was much lighter than he.

Hanging on to the cord for dear life, she rose majestically into the air – but did not come down. The balloon drifted smoothly over the grassland, rising a little.

Alyx screamed.

Kieron was horrified.

'Jump!' he called. 'Let go the cord! Let go!'

She either did not hear him or she was past hearing. She hung on desperately with both hands, kicking her legs frantically as if the very action would compel her return to earth.

Aylwin gazed at the scene petrified. Then he sank to his knees and began to pray.

Fortunately, the ascent of the balloon was very slow. It had risen no more than about three or four metres from the ground when Alyx either had the wit to let go or could hold on to the cord no longer. Kieron had been running after her, shouting his exhortations. Indeed, he leaped high, trying to grab her feet. When she fell, she landed almost in his arms, knocking him to the ground. Kieron was winded, but Alyx had hurt her ankle. She sat on the damp earth, whimpering a little, exploring the damage to her leg, and looked to Kieron for comfort.

He stroked her hair and mumbled words of comfort. But his eyes were on the balloon. Freed of its unwilling human ballast, the hot-air balloon rose majestically, trailing its cord like a long limp tail. The wind caused the charcoal in the brazier to burn more fiercely; and this, in turn, gave the balloon greater lift. It rose rapidly to about two hundred metres, then began to drift towards Arundel.

Kieron watched fascinated, full of pride. Truly, he had created a formidable thing. Had the balloon been only half as big again, he could have harnessed it to a basket in which he himself sat; and then he might have ridden through the sky like a god – or, at least, like one of the First Men.

'Kieron, my leg hurts.'

'Yes, love. I will attend to it.' But his eyes remained on the balloon.

'I'm wet, and there is mud on my clothes.'

'Yes, Alyx. Soon you will be warm and dry,' he soothed, 'and I will take you to the castle.' But his eyes remained on the balloon.

'I hate you!' she stormed.

'Yes, love. Most reasonable. I am a hateful person.' Still he watched the balloon.

'I love you! You are a fool but – Ludd help me – I love you.' She kissed him and held him close.

'Darling Alyx, indeed I am a fool. But I have achieved something this day.'

The balloon, having drifted over Arundel, now seemed to exhibit a will of its own. It changed direction and hovered over the castle. Then, apparently convinced that it had achieved its proper destination, it burst spectacularly into flame and fell in burning remnants upon the ancestral home of Seigneur Fitzalan.

Aylwin had recovered himself sufficiently to come running after Kieron. But when he saw what had happened to the balloon, he sank to his knees once more. 'Ludd ha' mercy! Ludd ha' mercy! Kieron, oh Kieron, you have done for us.'

Kieron smiled at him benignly. 'Aylwin, my friend, first collect your wits. Then collect your painting materials from the mill and return with some discretion to your master. You have not been here this day. You have not seen me or Mistress Alyx. You understand?'

'I understand, Kieron. But we are sworn in friendship.'

'Then let us maintain the bond. You shall not be put at risk for an accident such as this.' He turned to Alyx. 'Mistress Alyx, have you seen Aylwin, the miller's prentice, this day?' He was holding her in his arms, and he knew that Aylwin would see how he was holding her.

Alyx's cheeks became red. 'Not if you require it, Kieron,' she said softly. 'I have not seen the miller's prentice this day.'

'Well, Aylwin,' pursued Kieron, 'by the same token, you have not seen Mistress Alyx and myself. For if you claim that you have, I will surely kill you.'

Aylwin was offended. 'We are sworn. Was that necessary?'

'Forgive me, Aylwin. I do not think clearly. Events move too fast. Now go.'

Alyx tried to stand up, cried out with pain and fell down again. 'The ankle – it swells mightily, and the pain is worse ... What shall we do, Kieron? What shall we do?'

'If I were to put you on your horse, could you ride back?'

'Perhaps. I think so.'

He bent down and lifted her gently, then he carried her to where the horse was tethered. It was a greater distance than he had thought, and Alyx – though light – was still somewhat heavier than he had thought. The exertion strained his limbs and his lungs. He set Alyx down on the grass and waited to recover himself before lifting her on to the horse.

Alyx surveyed her swollen ankle, and her dirty clothes with a look of despair. 'How shall I explain all this?' she cried. 'What a state I am in!'

'You fell,' suggested Kieron. 'You fell from the horse.'

'I never fall,' she retorted regally. 'Is it not known that I am the best horse-woman in the south country?'

'Nevertheless, Alyx, today you fell. The truth will assist neither of us. Neither your father nor Talbot must ever learn that you rose perilously over the meadow on the end of a hot-air balloon.'

'What if I were seen?'

Kieron shrugged. 'The word of a commoner against the word of a Fitzalan? Besides, you could not have been seen, except with a spy-glass.'

'My father's watchman has a spy-glass. He reports on the arrival of vessels for trade.'

'Then he will not report on the antics of an unwilling aeronaut,' said Kieron patiently. 'Also, you were aloft so little time, and it would not be possible to discern your identity from such a distance.' He grinned. 'Particularly since you thrashed about so – behaviour which Mistress Alyx Fitzalan would never stoop, or rise, to … We must take some chance, Alyx. If, indeed, a figure were seen, I will plead guilty. It was, after all, my balloon … Come, I will lift you to the saddle.' He managed to get her seated in reasonable comfort on the horse without too much exertion.

She looked down at him unhappily. 'What will they do to you, my love?'

'I do not know,' he answered, affecting small concern. 'Likely there will be some tedious penance. But, swear that whatever happens, you will admit no knowledge of this matter.'

'Kieron, how can I so swear when I know not what they will do to you.'

'Because I require it, for your sake, for mine, and for that of poor Aylwin who is now half out of his mind with fright.'

She sighed. 'Then I so swear; but I am afraid.'

'Smile, Alyx. That is how I would always remember you.'

'Shall we meet again before – before I wed?'

'Ludd knows. I do not … Alyx, it is within the month is it not?'

'Seventeen days hence … I love you.'

'I love you also. Go now, and let us each remember the other's love with gladness.'

Sadly, Alyx turned her horse towards Arundel. Kieron watched her for a while, then returned to the mill. There were materials and tools to be put away and the place made tidy. And there was much thinking to be done. Was it better to go to the castle and confess to the balloon, or was it better to let Seigneur Fitzalan's men seek him out? It would not take them long. Such an adventure, everyone knew, could only be the work of Kieron-head-in-the-air. Therefore, better to make a virtue out of necessity and explain matters to Seigneur Fitzalan before the neddies intervened.

But Kieron was out of luck. The castle watchman was not the only man to use a spy-glass. Brother Sebastian possessed one, and frequently employed it from the cathedral tower to inform himself of the affairs of the world.

15

Kieron did not know how long he had been chained to the wall. He did not know whether it was night or day. He knew only that he was in a cell in the Luddite House of Correction and that his case might even merit the attention of the Inquisitor General. It was a long time, he had been told, since anyone had been charged with attempting to construct a flying machine. The matter, therefore, was of more than local interest.

On the day his hot-air balloon had lifted Mistress Alyx across the meadow and had then risen grandly only to descend in fiery fragments on the castle, Kieron had not managed to get as far as making his apologies and explanations to Seigneur Fitzalan. The neddies were waiting for him: Brother Sebastian and Brother Hildebrand and Brother Lemuel.

They charged him with heresy and arrested him in the name of the Divine Boy. He was marched ignominiously through Arundel at sword-point. And that was the last he saw of daylight.

Brothers Hildebrand and Lemuel would have been satisfied to frighten Kieron a little, considering his construction of the hot-air balloon to be hardly more than an ambitious prank. After all, the boy was almost a full year from his majority; and his transgression need not be regarded as a deliberate assault upon doctrine.

But Brother Sebastian was ambitious. It was his intention to rise high in the Luddite Church. And a man could not rise high unless he distinguished himself early. The way to advancement was by high connection – which Brother Sebastian did not possess – or by the revealing of significant heresy. Brother Sebastian prayed devoutly that Kieron would be revealed as a significant heretic.

True, Kieron was not yet a man. But heresy was no affliction of age. Brother Sebastian was aware that it was less than thirty years since a boy of thirteen had been burnt at the stake for harnessing the steam from a boiling kettle. The offence had been described by the Inquisitor General of the time as the attempted construction of a turbine, whatever that was.

Kieron's offence was more easy to define. He had attempted to construct a machine that would lift a man – or a woman – from the face of the earth. If that was not an heretical act, then Brother Sebastian would eat his habit. Already he was beginning to feel secure in his attitude. The spy-glass had revealed that it was not Kieron dangling from the infernal machine, but a woman.

Shortly after this observation, Brother Sebastian had noticed Mistress Alyx returning to the castle on horseback, but in a somewhat distressed condition.

She asserted that she had been thrown. But everyone knew that it was most unlikely for Mistress Alyx to be thrown. Brother Sebastian pondered the problem. Recently, Kieron had spent much time at the castle, executing studies for Master Hobart's brilliant painting of *Mistress Fitzalan's Leap*. Kieron and Mistress Alyx were almost of an age. Where there is smoke, it is hardly reckless to assume the presence of a fire.

Brother Sebastian had the wit to realise that Alyx Fitzalan was beyond his reach. Holy Church was not yet ready to directly challenge the feudal power of the seigneurs. But Kieron alone should be sufficient for Brother Sebastian's purpose. Having access to the castle and to the presence of Seigneur Fitzalan and Mistress Alyx, the boy could hardly be considered to be on the same level of insignificance as a common field labourer. Also, much could be made of his association with Mistress Alyx. Much could be made of it without much actually being said. Besides, if necessary, some importance could be attached to the matter of the book. At the very least, it was an effective means of silencing any protest from the Fitzalans.

After arresting Kieron, Brother Sebastian had speedily armed himself with a warrant for searching; and he had gone to Master Hobart's house, there to terrorise the old man somewhat in the hope that he might betray himself as a partner to the heresy, and also to search Kieron's chamber.

He succeeded in terrifying Master Hobart only into hysteria and a great fit of coughing. He did, however, find the book, hidden under Kieron's mattress. That the book concerned the history of forbidden machines was significant, that it was hidden, though badly, was of even greater significance, and that its leather cover bore the imprint of the Fitzalan device was of the greatest significance of all.

Let the seigneur beware, thought Brother Sebastian comfortably. If he attempted to interfere with divine justice in any way, he might find that he was in danger of scorching his noble fingers.

Brother Sebastian was tasting the heady delights of power. He had written an account of the affair to the office of the Inquisitor General in London and confidently expected that he would receive authorisation to proceed with a full trial for heresy.

Meanwhile, he had Kieron chained to the wall in the House of Correction. He did not relish the boy's discomfort. To do so would have been an unpardonable sin. Brother Sebastian convinced himself that he was concerned only with the salvation of Kieron's spirit. If Kieron should burn for his transgression – which Ludd forbid, if at all possible – it were better that he burned in enlightenment, in a proper state of mind, knowing that his sin would be forgiven if he showed true penitence.

So Brother Sebastian held much converse with his prisoner, seeking to distinguish diabolical intent from youthful indiscretion. Kieron was not entirely helpful. At least, he was not helpful to himself, though perhaps he furthered Brother Sebastian's unacknowledged aims.

'Do you resent me, Kieron?' Brother Sebastian asked the question while sitting on a stool, sipping from a glass of tea.

Kieron, who had survived on bread, offal and cold water for several days, still had his wits about him.

'Why should I resent you, Brother Sebastian? You do your duty, and in that you have my respect, even my admiration.'

'So. We understand each other. I do not wish to punish you. I wish to save you.'

'This, I perceive. You act from the best intentions.' Kieron smiled. 'I would much prefer to be saved rather than punished.'

'The hot-air balloon is a grievous sin. It is a machine, Kieron. A machine not authorised by Holy Church. You must see that it is the duty of the Church to protect the people from the wickedness and the temptation of machines. You know your history, boy. Machines have corrupted the world twice. They shall not do so a third time.' Brother Sebastian sipped his tea noisily.

Kieron licked his lips. He could not remember when he had last tasted anything warm. 'I was aware of no wickedness, Brother. The hot-air balloon was but a foolish toy which served to pass the time.'

'So?' Brother Sebastian looked at him coldly. 'There is also the matter of the book. Who gave it to you, Kieron? The book about flying machines.'

This was the first time Brother Sebastian had mentioned the book. Kieron, tired, cold, depressed, was taken by surprise. His mouth fell open. He thought of Alyx. Even she might not be safe from this black crow.

'You do not answer, Kieron. Do you wish to shield someone?'

'I wish to shield no one but myself. I borrowed the book. I – I intended to return it.'

'Seigneur Fitzalan gave you leave to take the book from his library?'

'No.'

'Someone else, then?'

'No.'

'Yet you say you borrowed the book.'

'Yes.'

'Without the owner's permission?'

'I intended to return it.'

'For that, I have only your word in these present sad circumstances. It is also possible to interpret such borrowing as stealing. A reasonable man might conclude that you had stolen the book with the intention of constructing one or more of the machines described therein.'

'Ludd damn you!' exploded Kieron. 'Destroy learning, if you must. Destroy progress, if you must. Burn me, if you must. But do not sicken me with words.'

Brother Sebastian emptied his glass of tea and looked sad. 'The damnation of Ludd is reserved only for those who construct machines with evil intent. Burn you may, Kieron. I will not deny the possibility. It would sadden me, but Ludd's will be done. However, I am your friend, your brother, and I shall save your soul. And in that, there will be some consolation.'

Whereupon, Brother Sebastian left Kieron to his thoughts.

16

The Inquisitor General found that there was a charge to answer and authorised a trial for heresy. The trial would begin, as was customary, on the first day of the next lunar month. If a verdict of guilty were given, the sentence would be carried out on the last day of the same lunar month.

Meanwhile, the conditions under which Kieron was held improved. He was no longer chained to the wall of his cell. He was given a bed of straw, a table and a chair. He was allowed one hot meal a day, and he was further allowed to have visitors and to call upon witnesses who might testify to his character. Holy Church allowed these things so that none might complain of partiality or impediment. It was true that few were ever acquitted of the charge of heresy. Holy Church rarely held such a public trial unless the facts were incontrovertible. Nevertheless, justice must be seen to be done.

Kieron's first visitors were his parents. Kristen came red-eyed with weeping. Gerard came full of hope, smelling of resin and wood shavings, convinced that too much had been made of a boyish prank.

'Kieron, child, how do they feed you?' sniffed Kristen. 'Do they feed you well?'

Kieron noticed that her hair was fully white, though she could be barely thirty-five years old. Yet there was beauty in her face and dignity in her carriage. He was immensely sorry for the pain he had caused.

'Yes, mother,' he lied. 'I eat excellently and want for nothing.'

'You are an artist,' exploded Gerard, 'a great artist. Master Hobart himself has said so.' He gazed at the straw bed and the bare walls of the cell. 'How dare they keep a man with a golden future in this place? Are you guilty of the charge, boy? Speak plainly. We who begot you have a right to know.'

'Sir,' said Kieron carefully, knowing that Brother Sebastian had his ear to the cell door, 'I constructed a toy for my amusement. A hot-air balloon. I did not know that Holy Church could be offended by so trivial a matter.'

Gerard stroked his chin thoughtfully. 'It was rash, boy. But it can hardly be sinful. The Church likes nothing new – quite rightly. The fault lies surely in those who have instructed you ... I have heard that *Mistress Fitzalan's Leap* is a masterpiece, though I know nought of such things. Master Hobart has said that it could not have been accomplished without you.'

'Master Hobart is generous,' said Kieron, 'but there may be a grain of truth in his words.'

Gerard held him close. 'Do not fear, boy. The charge will be dismissed, and those who brought it will suffer the consequences.'

'I bear no animosity to anyone,' said Kieron, chiefly for Brother Sebastian. 'My hope is that Holy Church will establish my innocence and permit me to continue my appointed work.'

Gerard clapped his shoulder. 'Well spoken! I knew! I knew! You are but a high-spirited lad, and it is all a great misunderstanding.'

But Kristen was wiser. She held Kieron close to her and stroked his hair. 'Are you afraid, little one?' she whispered.

'Yes, mother, I am afraid.'

'You know what they will do?'

'Yes, mother. I know what they will do.'

'Be at peace, Kieron. We will die together. And if there is another life, we will share it also.'

'Hold, woman!' stormed Gerard. 'Kieron will live.'

Kristen stood back, having achieved a strange serenity. 'Yes, Gerard, Kieron will live. Of that I am sure.'

'By the Hammer of Ludd, and by my hammer also he will indeed live,' swore Gerard. 'He will live to bury those who would besmirch his name.'

The gaoler rapped on the door.

'We will come again,' said Kristen. 'We will come tomorrow. I will bring scones and fresh butter and the blackberry preserve you like.'

When they had gone, Brother Sebastian entered the cell. 'Your father has a strong voice,' he said carefully.

Kieron smiled faintly. 'A strong mind and a strong right arm also. He is a good and simple man.'

'Yet he utters dangerous words.'

'My father is an honest man, as all in the seigneurie know,' retorted Kieron calmly. 'He deceives no one, commits no sins. His honesty is his armour.'

'What do you mean by that, boy?'

'Only, Brother Sebastian, that you have one bird in your trap. You will not snare another from the same nest.'

Petrina came to visit him also, accompanied by her father, which was proper.

Sholto, a huge man of few words and great good will, was tongue-tied. Petrina, buxom and ripe for the marriage that would only have been months away, did most of the talking.

'Kieron, you look dreadful pale. Do you have enough to eat?'

He smiled. 'Truly, women are alike. My mother's first thought was for my stomach.'

'There are certain differences,' flashed Petrina, 'which presently you will perceive.'

'I am sorry. I did not mean to rebuke you.' Kieron turned to the smith. 'Sholto, it was kind of you to come, and to bring Petrina. I am grateful. Neither I nor my father will be offended if you now wish to dissolve the contract.'

Sholto shuffled his feet awkwardly, and looked at the floor, at the walls, at the ceiling, as if seeking divine guidance. None came.

'Kieron, boy, I like you well. This is a sorry matter which, in truth, I do not understand. I understand how to work iron and steel, but not much else. Solvig, my wife, deals with other affairs.' He cast an anxious glance at his daughter. 'And now, alas, so does Petrina. At the forge, I am master.' He shrugged. 'But with women, who can argue?'

'Dissolve the contract!' exploded Petrina, tossing back her hair, thrusting out her firm breasts. 'Do you wish to dissolve the contract, Kieron-head-in-the-air?'

Kieron was baffled. The child he had known was now demonstrably a woman. He had assumed she would wish to be quit of a heretic, who would likely burn. But one should never assume with a woman.

'I did but think to save you some unpleasantness.'

'You think but little,' snapped Petrina. 'Otherwise, you would not have thought to construct stupid kites and hot-air balloons. And you would not have thought to embroil yourself with the Fitzalans.'

'Petrina, speak carefully,' said Kieron, mindful of Brother Sebastian's ear at the door. 'These walls are thin. Voices carry.'

'Poof!' said Petrina. 'So voices carry. Everyone knows that Alyx Fitzalan is besotted with you.' She gave a faint smile. 'Even Brother Sebastian has ears.'

'Brother Sebastian has excellent hearing,' confirmed Kieron. 'Even in this cell, I suspect, our conversation does not pass unheard.'

'No matter,' said Petrina calmly. 'There is nothing to be hid. Do you wish to be released from the contract?'

'No, by Ned Ludd. I would wed with you, Petrina. In happier circumstances, I would wed with you joyously.'

Petrina smiled. 'Then there is no problem, Kieron. I would wed with you. So be it.'

'You are still convinced that the astrologer Marcus foretold truly?'

'Yes, I am convinced. Besides, Kieron, whatever else Holy Church may do, it acknowledges the validity of contracts. This I have discovered, at some effort.'

'So?'

'So, Kieron, if we are both willing, the Inquisitor General may be petitioned to suspend punishment until I am with child – or until it is seen that I cannot conceive.'

Kieron was dumbfounded. 'You would do this for me?'

'You are my contracted husband. Could I do less?'

Kieron laughed. 'The astrologer Marcus may yet win the day.'

'Do not mock men of science.'

'But how do you know this – about punishment being suspended?'

'It does not matter how I know. Also the thing is not certain. Much depends upon the pleasure of the Inquisitor General. I know only that it has happened before.' She smiled grimly. 'Holy Church even has power to advance the con-tracted day of marriage so that the day of punishment shall not be over-delayed.'

'How, then?' Kieron was perplexed. 'I would be allowed my freedom until I had got you with child?'

'No, stupid. I would be allowed to share your cell. There are limits to benevolence.'

'You would wed with a heretic and live in a prison? You would be branded for ever.'

'I would also be widowed for ever. But that is my choice, Kieron. Do you complain of it?'

'No, I – that is, Petrina, my dear, it is too much to ask of you.'

'So. No one has asked it. Let your conscience rest easy.'

Shoko rubbed his hands nervously. 'Argue not with a female, Kieron. You will have the worst of it.'

'Do you still wish your daughter to wed with me?'

Sholto scratched his head. 'A contract is a contract, for good or ill.' He glanced at his daughter. 'What a woman wants, that she will get, as I know to my cost.'

Petrina said: 'Let us not waste time. It is settled. That is all there is to it … Kieron, many will speak for you; and it will carry weight that I am still willing to wed with you.' She moved close to him and whispered: 'Can you feign madness?'

He looked at her, aghast. 'Can I—' She placed a hand over his mouth. 'I am told,' she whispered, 'that a plea of temporary madness might be acceptable to Holy Church – particularly if there were those who testified to such fits.'

'You are well informed,' said Kieron softly. 'You are well informed about many things. Who has spoken to you, Petrina?'

She put her mouth to his ear. 'A lady came riding. Need I say more?'

Alyx! Alyx Fitzalan cared about him enough to persuade Petrina. His head was in a whirl.

The gaoler knocked on the door.

'We will come again, Kieron,' said Petrina. 'I am sure my father will wish to escort me here tomorrow. I will bring a bacon and egg pie, hot from the oven, and I will watch you eat it.'

'Petrina, I would kiss you.' Kieron glanced hesitantly at Sholto.

73

The smith laughed. 'Kiss her, then, boy. Kiss her well. It is the only way you will ever beat a woman.'

Somewhat later on the same day, Hobart came, a shawl round his shoulders, racked by coughing, clutching a flask of spirit.

'Kieron, my dear son, how do they treat you?'

'Well enough, Master Hobart. I am alive and healthy, as you see.'

'You are thinner. You are pale.'

'I do not crave for weight. My only lack is sunlight.'

'You shall have it, my dear son, you shall have it. I have signed a statement and had it witnessed that it was upon my insistence that you constructed the hot-air balloon. I required its construction for a painting, and that is the truth. I required to have a sketch of the castle from the air.'

Kieron was near to weeping. 'Father, you cannot do this thing. You shall not put yourself at risk in such a manner.'

With some effort, Hobart drew himself up straight. 'And who shall prevent me, boy? You have called me Father, of which I am proud. And is it not the duty of a father to protect his son, even if that son be not of the flesh but of the spirit?'

'A son – a spiritual son – also has a duty,' Kieron pointed out. 'I beg you to destroy the document. It is dangerous.'

'Dangerous! Poof!' Master Hobart took a sip of spirit. 'Forgive me, Kieron. This physic is necessary for an old man who has outlived his strengths and skills … All my life, Kieron, I have lived safely – and in fear. In fear of those who employ me, in fear of the loss of my poor talent. There comes a time when a man desires to rise above fear. Such a time is when he wishes to protect one he loves … Forgive me. I am not courageous. Forgive me for deriving courage from a flask … But, I have been in the presence of greatness. I am content. Do you understand? I have seen you make brush strokes that have a wild and savage beauty. I know that you will travel far … I wish you to paint, for in that you have a great gift. But if it is your pleasure to reach for the stars, I will accept it. I cannot understand it. I cannot say more. But I accept it. Do we understand each other?'

'We understand each other, my father.'

'Well, then, there is no more to be said.' Hobart took a deep draught of the spirit. 'I have outlived my strength and my skills, but I have not entirely outlived my usefulness. The document will stand, Kieron, though I fall.' Hobart smiled. 'Once I tried to buy you from your parents. You did not know that. Now, I do not wish to buy you. I am content only to pay a very small price for your freedom.'

Kieron could no longer hold back the tears. 'Sir, you destroy me with love.'

Hobart smiled. 'I have watched you grow with love. I have tutored you with love. I will not destroy you with love … Kieron, I doubt that I shall visit you again. My health, you understand?'

'I understand.'

'Therefore, kiss me, my son. It is but little to you. It means much to me, because I am a foolish old man.'

Kieron drew close and kissed him on the forehead.

'On the lips, my son.'

'So be it. On the lips.'

'Now we are truly united in resolve.' Hobart seemed happy. 'Farewell, Kieron. You will not burn. Rest easy.'

'Then I shall live to complete my apprenticeship,' said Kieron lightly.

Hobart gave a faint smile. 'Your apprenticeship ended with *Mistress Fitzalan's Leap*. It is a great painting. I can teach you no more.'

Master Hobart took some more spirit. Then he left the cell. Two days later he was discovered dead, hanging by the neck from a beam in his chamber.

17

In times to come, Kieron recalled the last few days he spent in the House of Correction almost with pleasure. They were the last days of the world he had known, the last days of order and security, the last days of peace.

Gerard and Kristen came to visit him again. So did Petrina and, with some apprehension, Aylwin the miller's apprentice.

Aylwin knew nothing of the measures being taken to defend Kieron. He looked upon his friend with much pity, as if the smell of smoke were already in his nostrils.

'So, Kieron, it is in a sorry condition that I find you.'

Kieron laughed. 'Not so sorry as all that. I have food, I sleep well, my friends and loved ones do not neglect me.'

Aylwin nodded towards the cell door, fully aware that there was a patient listener. 'I have not broken my bond word, Kieron.'

'Good, my friend. Neither have I. Nor will I. Let us each rest easy.'

Aylwin seemed relieved. He had no wish to be noticed in any way by Holy Church. 'Many will be willing to speak for you. I among them, if you require it.'

Kieron noted the unhappiness in Aylwin's eyes, and knew that it had cost him much to make the offer. 'Aylwin, I thank you. I do not despise your kindness, yet I think that stronger voices may be heard in my favour.'

'If the worst comes to the worst—' began Aylwin.

'It will not.' Kieron also nodded towards the cell door. Then he said prophetically: 'I will live to bury some who bear me small good will. This I swear.'

Aylwin shuffled his feet. 'I must go now.'

'Do not neglect the skills you have learned. You have some talent, as I know.'

Aylwin shrugged. Where now would he obtain the materials and instruction he needed? 'We are each called to our destiny, friend. I will come again.' He held out his hand. 'Also, I will think much upon you, Kieron. You are my true friend.'

But Aylwin did not come to the House of Correction again; and when Kieron next saw him, he was less a hand – the painting hand. And his black hair was streaked with white.

Alyx Fitzalan was the last visitor Kieron received. She was accompanied by her father's bailiff, who by his demeanour made plain his hearty disapproval of the encounter.

'Be upstanding in the presence of Mistress Alyx Fitzalan,' he intoned. An unnecessary command, since Kieron was already standing.

'Kentigern,' said Mistress Alyx with some tartness in her voice, 'go and keep company with the good Brother Sebastian, whose heavy breathing informs me of his nearness. Discuss with him whatever is dear to you, and benefit from his pure and learned mind.'

'But, Mistress, Seigneur Fitzalan commanded me to remain within your hearing.'

'Do that, then. My hearing is excellent. I can hear the good Brother Sebastian shaking like one afflicted. Perhaps he has received a vision. Enquire of him if this be the case.'

Kentigern retired, discomfited. For a moment or two, Kieron heard him exchanging words with Brother Sebastian on the other side of the cell door.

'Well, Kieron?'

'Well, Mistress Alyx?'

They gazed at each other, each resisting the impulse to come close and hold close. It would not do. The witnesses at the keyhole would report what they saw.

'So you stole a book from my father's library. At least, that is what I am told.' But her eyes said: Thank you, my love, for protecting me.

Kieron signified his understanding. 'I am bitterly sorry, Mistress Alyx. I intended to borrow it for a short time only.'

'Did you know that it contained heresy?'

'No, Mistress. Being simple, I thought only to take a book to read. I intended to restore it at the first opportunity.'

'My father thinks you are a fool, Kieron. A fool without malice.'

'So I am, Mistress. Definitely a fool. But I have no malice.'

'So I will testify,' said Alyx. 'You have a great talent for falling off gentle horses, Kieron. The talent of a fool. Nevertheless, I am capricious enough to defer my wedding so that I may speak for you. Perhaps I am foolish also.'

Kieron knelt and kissed her hand. He would have kissed her lips and felt her breasts against him. But he was mindful of the watchers and the listeners.

'Mistress, you are indeed foolish to concern yourself with my predicament. Though I am nothing to you, I am most grateful for your interest in my case.'

Alyx smiled sadly. 'Stand, Kieron. The artist knows his subject. The subject knows the artist. Between them, formality is tedious.'

'Mistress, I—' Kieron glanced at the cell door.

'Yes, I know. The ears flap. Master Kentigern grows red in the face, and the good Brother Sebastian breathes hard. It is of little importance … My father bids me thank you for removing the book from his library.'

'How so?'

'It is simple. He did not know that he possessed an heretical work. He is glad to be quit of it. Also, he, too, will speak for you. He bade me say that, while he supports Holy Church in the rooting out of heresy, fools are with us always and may be relied upon to accomplish their own destruction.'

'He is most kind.' Kieron, remembering his last encounter with Fitzalan, thought the seigneur was exceptionally kind.

'He is, above all, a practical man,' said Alyx enigmatically. 'He is prepared to pay a reasonable price to achieve his ends ... Kieron, I have news for you. It is both bad and good.'

Kieron knew before she told it. 'Master Hobart?'

'Is dead. He left a document.'

'I know. How did he die?'

'He hanged himself ... Holy Church will not burn you. The document absolves you from blame. Add to this those who will speak for you, and the Church is powerless.'

Kieron was weeping. He turned towards the cell door. 'Brother Sebastian,' he shouted, 'you hear me! Better for you to leave the seigneurie if I am acquitted. For if you do not—'

'Kieron!' Alyx spoke sharply. 'Indulge your grief, but do not undo the work for which a good man died.'

Kieron hid his face in his hands. 'Alyx, I am sorry. Hobart was as a father to me, and—'

'And,' said Alyx, 'he will be remembered for his last work, which was his greatest. You gave him some assistance, I recall. You are his monument, Kieron. Be worthy of him. That is all.'

Kieron looked at her, red-eyed, the tears streaming down his face. 'I will try to be worthy of him. But who can say if I succeed?'

'Time will reveal, Kieron. I must go now.' She smiled, and suddenly threw caution to the winds 'My father drives a close bargain ... But kiss me, so that I will remember it.'

Kieron was aghast 'But, Brother Sebastian?'

'Brother Sebastian is of little account, now. His days are numbered. And Kentigern is true to the house of Fitzalan. Kiss me. Indulge a woman's fancy. I have dreams, premonitions.' She shuddered. 'Kiss me.'

Kieron held her close, felt the warm young breasts against him, kissed her lips, her cheek, her ear, her neck. He, also, had premonitions, He knew that he would not hold the living Alyx Fitzalan again.

18

Kieron slept badly, tormented by dreams. He was a child, with Petrina, in late summer. There was some question of following bees to find their honey, or to seek apples and plums. Eventually, they decided on apples and plums.

The dream dissolved. Now it was a fine October morning, with the sky blue, and the castle rising out of the mist; and the boy Kieron, carrying a deerhide bag, was walking to Master Hobart's house. He saw a dandelion clock, plucked the stem and blew the seeds away through the still air.

A great voice that seemed to fill the world said: 'So you want to fly, do you?'

Kieron, terrified, looked all around him. There was no one to be seen. But it seemed advisable to make an answer. 'Yes, I want to fly.'

There was laughter. 'Birds fly. Men walk. Put away such dreams.'

Again he could see no one. Frightened, he continued on his way to the house of the painter.

Mist and darkness. Then more sunlight. He was riding through the sky, then falling, falling. The sea was cold and there was a sharp pain in his leg.

And suddenly, Brother Sebastian was looking at him. Brother Sebastian's face was as large as the castle. His eyes were cold. 'Heresy, Kieron! Men burn for heresy. Burn! Burn! Burn!'

Brother Sebastian's face became a black fog. No, not a fog. A column of smoke. Kieron could smell the smoke. It was choking him. He cried out, opened his eyes. But he could still smell the smoke, and the cell was entirely dark. Now he was aware of noises, shouts, screams, the sound of thunder. Or was it something other than thunder?

His mind would not work, but the smoke was real. In the darkness, he coughed agonisingly and his eyes streamed tears. He needed air; but there was no air. Only smoke, choking smoke.

The screams and the shouts and the thunder seemed not so near now. Everything was farther away. He was alone in the darkness, choking, choking.

He tried to shout, but there was only a pitiful rasping gurgle in his throat. He goaded his dulled mind, seeking an explanation. He found one.

'The trial is over,' he told himself calmly. 'The trial is over, and I was pronounced guilty. I am no longer in the cell. The smoke and heat have dulled my wits. I am at the stake, and I am burning. Why is everything so dark?

Perhaps my eyes were the first to suffer. Well, then, this is the end of Kieron-head-in-the-air. It is not so bad as I thought.'

He fell down, groping on the cell floor, coughing monstrously, but still conscious. 'I am in my cell,' he told himself. 'I am in my cell. No. It is an illusion.'

The stones of the cell floor were warm. He felt them against his face. 'It is an illusion. It must be an illusion. The dying man seeks to escape his fate. What a pity I cannot tell—'

He slumped unconscious.

Outside his cell, out in the streets of Arundel, the screaming and the shouting and the banging and the burning continued. But, mercifully, Kieron was oblivious of it all. He lay on the cell floor, his open mouth touching the stone, his lungs still pitifully striving to suck in what little air remained. He was like to have choked on the smoke, had not two things happened in rapid succession. A wild, bearded, blood-stained man with an axe battered down the smouldering door and thrust a blazing torch through the doorway so that he could see if the room contained anything of value. The torch flickered and died for lack of air; but before it died, the intruder was able to discern what appeared to be a dead man on the floor. Coughing and spluttering and cursing, the bearded man retreated. A corpse did not merit his attention.

Shortly after that, the wind changed, and the smoke was drawn out of the cell.

Kieron had been near to death; and it was many hours before he returned to conscious life.

There were blisters on his hands and feet and face. The pain was abominable. Every movement he made caused him to cough excruciatingly. But, somehow, he dragged himself to his feet and staggered out of the cell, out of the House of Correction. He trod, unheeding, on the body of Brother Sebastian. Brother Sebastian's throat had been cut. But Kieron did not notice.

It was shortly after daybreak.

He went out into the streets of Arundel.

It was a dead town. Dead, with the wreckage of its houses still smouldering. Apart from the crash of falling timbers, the crackle and spitting of charred wood, there was no sound. No sound of humanity. Arundel was deserted by the living, and the dead lay where they had fallen.

The nightmare that had followed the dreams was real.

PART TWO

Airborne

1

His conscious mind numbed by shock, and like one who had taken too much strong spirit, Kieron lurched towards the castle. The main gate hung in fragments, destroyed, apparently, by some explosion.

He clambered over the remains of the gate and the corpses of the men who had tried to defend it His mind refused to work. He tried to think. But his mind simply refused to work.

He followed his instincts only. And his instincts led him to seek out Alyx.

He found her.

And then he wished he had not found her.

She lay in the great hall, below the minstrel gallery. She lay on the floor of the great hall with her nightdress flung over her head and her legs wide apart. She lay with a sword that had passed through her navel pinning her to the wooden floor.

Kieron inflicted on himself the supreme punishment. He drew back her nightdress and looked upon her face. A pale, bruised stranger was revealed, her eyes wide with a horror now beginning to glaze in death, her mouth now open and slack, and the blood dried upon lips that she had bitten in her torment.

Kieron was man enough to understand the terrible fashion of her death, and boy enough to be shattered by grief. Letting out a great cry of anguish, he fell to his knees, and stooped to kiss the cold forehead. His tears fell upon her face and, half-crazed with grief and horror, it seemed to him that she wept also.

'Alyx! Alyx!' he sobbed. 'Would that I lay dead with you.' Then another thought pricked through his anguish, pricking deep like the thrust of a sword. 'No, by the hammer of Ludd, I will stay alive and seek those who have done this thing. And, if I find them, I will find a means to inflict a terrible punishment, or I will perish. This I swear.' Then he closed her eyes gently and eased the sword out of her body. It had a narrow blade. No blood came.

'I will keep this sword,' he said aloud, 'to return to those who have left it.' He straightened Alyx Fitzalan's limbs, smoothed her nightdress down decently over the outraged body. Then he stroked her hair a while. Presently, he murmured: 'Rest quiet now, my dear one. I must look to the living; though the dead shall never be forgot.'

Sword in hand, he moved cautiously through the castle. The devastation and carnage appalled him. Many of Seigneur Fitzalan's men lay dead, with weapons in their hands. Many strangers, also. Strangers in strange clothes, with black skins, white skins and brown.

Of the two younger Fitzalan daughters there was nothing to be seen. Perhaps they had been taken away, or had been killed elsewhere. Seigneur Fitzalan himself, Kieron soon discovered in one of the upper corridors. He lay on the floor, outside a chamber door, sword in one hand, dagger in the other, and with a great red stain on the fine linen that covered his breast, and a look of profound astonishment frozen on his face.

Inside the chamber, on a larger bed than Kieron had ever before seen, a bed whose fine silk coverings were now bloody and torn, lay the seigneur's lady. Her clothes had been ripped from her; and, by the look of it, she had suffered as Alyx had suffered, perhaps even more horribly.

Kieron could not bear to look long, could not even bear to decently enshroud the dead woman. He had had his fill of terror. He stumbled from the room, feeling foul juices rise from his stomach to his dry mouth. He was sick in the corridor, but there was none to remark his weakness.

After he had vomited, his head felt more clear. He felt better altogether. Weak, but definitely better. He began to think. The devastation was terrible. Arundel and its castle had been laid waste; but not everyone could have been killed. Some must have fled to the downs; and the downs folk themselves – including his father and mother – should have had ample warning of the attack. With luck, there would be many who had escaped the night of madness. He must find them. He must find his own people, and learn the nature of the catastrophe and what could be done about it.

Sword in hand, Kieron wandered down long, dark passageways, dully seeking his way out of the castle.

He heard a sound, a deep groaning. He stopped and listened. The groaning came again. He went towards it.

The sound led him back to the great hall. Not far from where Alyx lay, a stranger lay also, dressed in outlandish clothes. There was much blood upon his stomach, the evidence of good sword thrusts. Kieron could not understand why he had not noticed him before.

The stranger had brown skin, and eyes that rolled horribly. He mumbled something in a language that Kieron could not understand. His fingers fluttered, as if in supplication.

It came to Kieron, as he regarded the man, that he might well have been one of those who had outraged Alyx.

Kieron was glad of the thought. Here, at last, was someone from whom he could extract vengeance.

He raised the sword that he held, the sword that had transfixed Alyx.

'May Ludd have mercy upon you,' said Kieron. 'I will not.'

He thrust the sword home, once, twice, three times.

The brown-faced man grunted with each thrust. Then he uttered a great sigh and died.

Kieron exalted in his death. One blow for Alyx.

Then, hardly knowing where he was going or what he was doing, he somehow found his way out of the castle.

He was amazed to notice that it was a day of bright sunlight. Alyx and her parents lay dead in the castle, towns folk lay butchered in the streets and the remains of houses still smouldered. He gazed up at the blue sky incredulously and shielded his eyes from the glare. The sun was wrong. It should not have been a day for sunlight.

He tried to think what to do now. He must try to find Gerard and Kristen, anyone at all who remained alive. He must try to discover what had happened.

Wearily, still clutching the sword, he staggered away from the castle towards the downs. There had to be people left alive among the hills. Not everyone could have been killed.

He felt dreadfully thirsty. His throat was raw and sore, his lips blistered. Not fifty paces from the castle, he gave a despairing cry and fell on his face.

There had been sunlight, and now darkness was closing in. He was glad of the darkness. It came as a friend.

Kieron was near to his eighteenth birthday, the threshold of manhood; but the events of the last few hours had aged him greatly. Already he had seen much. More than a grown man might be expected to witness and yet retain his reason.

Kieron took refuge in the friendly darkness. It lay over him like a blanket of peace.

2

Sholto poured water between his lips. Petrina held his head. Someone was trying to take the sword from his hand but his fingers would not let go.

'Peace, boy,' said Sholto. 'You are safe. I have carried you on my back with that sword like to pierce my foot at every step. Let it go now. You are with friends.'

Kieron sat up, blinked his eyes, licked his lips, trying to comprehend where he was and what was happening. Petrina kissed him, and he let her take the sword from his hand. His fingers ached – how they ached! He must have been gripping the sword very tightly.

He looked around him. He was in a woodland clearing, presumably in the downs. The sun was still high. There were many people in the clearing: downs folk and towns folk. Strangers and friends. He did not see his parents.

'My father and mother?' They were his first words. He did not like the sound of his voice. It was rasping, shaky, like that of an old man. The smoke was still in his lungs. It made him cough when he spoke.

'Rest easy, lad,' said Sholto. 'There are misfortunes that must be borne.'

'Dead?'

'Ay, dead … Your father gave a good accounting. We found three dead men who would not dispute the claim.'

'My mother?'

Sholto said gently: 'My son, forgive me. There are things for which I cannot find the words. I am a simple man. Forgive me. Also, my own wife is dead, and my mind is not too clear … Your mother was a woman of great presence. She is dead. Let us say no more.'

Kieron digested this information. Sholto was right, he thought dully. Better not to enquire further.

Petrina said: 'Kieron, thank Ludd you are alive.'

'Alyx Fitzalan is dead,' he said. 'The sword you took from my hand is the one I plucked from her belly.'

Petrina kissed him once more. 'Ludd rest her. She was beautiful. I have no quarrel with the spirit of Mistress Fitzalan.'

'Well, then,' said Kieron, his voice rising. 'Who has destroyed us? What manner of men are they who came to destroy and pillage and ravish in the night?'

A strange face loomed before him. 'Sir, they are freebooters, scavengers, parasites. They came from the coast of North Africa. They have worked the Mediterranean coasts dry. Now they venture into Europe.'

Kieron looked up and saw a gaunt wild-eyed man in ragged clothes. A patch of blood showed through the rags on his shoulder. His weathered face and something about his manner suggested that he was a seaman.

'How do you know these things?'

'I have sailed with them.'

Automatically, Kieron felt for his sword. 'You have sailed with them!' He leaped to his feet. 'Then—'

'Peace, boy,' said Sholto. 'I do not wish to knock your head. The stranger comes as a friend.'

'I did not sail willingly. I was taken for a slave.'

'They take slaves?' Kieron was utterly appalled.

'Both male and female,' said the man sombrely. 'When the slave is strong and well, he is given food. When he falls ill or is no longer of use, he is thrown overboard. So, also, is it with women.'

'They cannot be human!'

The stranger gave a wintry smile. 'Human they may not be, but they are mortal. I have had little pleasure this past year; but one I savour is that I twisted chains about the necks of two of those who had set chains upon my wrists and ankles. Look, sir. It gave me pleasure to tear the flesh from my wrists so that two might die.'

He held out his arms. Kieron looked at the bloody mess on his wrists and turned away.

'I struck off the chains myself,' said Sholto.

When he had recovered himself, Kieron turned to the stranger. 'I ask your pardon, sir.'

'No offence was given, sir. May the sword you have taken have some further acquaintance with those who brought it.'

'Ludd be willing,' said Sholto.

Kieron gathered his wits and looked round the clearing. There were perhaps a hundred men, women and children gathered there. Some wore their night clothes, some were injured, some sat silently or wept, some carried arms and strolled about nervously, unable to keep still.

'Are these all who have lived through it?' asked Kieron.

'No, boy, there are many more. Our numbers grow, as you see.' He pointed to a group of five people who had just arrived. 'Most of the downs folk were untouched. We have sent messengers, telling them to rally here at the Misery.'

Suddenly, Kieron recollected where he was. The Misery was a high stretch of woodland about five kilometres from Arundel. As children, he and Petrina had played in the Misery, marvelling at its name, marvelling at its huge beech trees. There was a day, long ago, when they had lain under a beech and listened to the song of the bees, when Petrina had told him of the predictions of the astrologer Marcus, and when he had confessed to her his desire to fly.

But all that was far away in a world of children, a world long dead.

'Why do you send for people to rally here?'

'Why else,' said Sholto, 'except that when our numbers are strong we should venture down to the sea at Little Hampton, where the invaders now lie, and give them a taste of their own physic.'

Kieron left Sholto and Petrina, and sought out the stranger with bloody wrists.

'How many ships have they?'

'Ten, perhaps twelve now. More will be coming.'

'How many men?'

The stranger shrugged. 'Eight hundred, a thousand. More will be coming.'

'How many more?'

'Who can say? They are a nation which thrives upon the misfortunes of other nations. They are the people of the sea. They have no home. They settle like locusts. And, like locusts, when the food is gone, they go elsewhere.'

'You say they are a nation. How can they be a nation? I have seen some of their dead. They are of different colours, different races.'

'They have one thing in common. They are all men without a country. Each has forfeited the right to live at peace in the land of his birth. They are all the more dangerous because they have put themselves beyond the acceptance of civilised men. They have little to lose. They call themselves the Brotherhood of Death.'

Petrina tugged at Kieron's arm. 'Come and take some food, Kieron. You must need it. When did you last eat?'

He tried to remember. Yesterday, he must have eaten. But yesterday was more than a few hours ago. Yesterday was a lost world. He tried to remember when he had eaten and what he had eaten. He could not.

Petrina led him near to a fire over which a large cauldron bubbled. She gave him a platter filled with stew. He sat down cross-legged, and ate mechanically. His brain told him that the stew contained rabbit and parsnips and carrots and potatoes and herbs. It tasted like wet sand.

People continued to arrive at the Misery. One of them was Aylwin. He was in a poor condition, half fainting. He had been supported on the journey by his mother, Lilias. When she had seen him safely received, she went away from the Misery and plunged a dagger into her heart. Her husband was dead, and she had received much attention from the Brotherhood of Death. She no longer wished to live.

'Aylwin!' said Kieron. 'I am glad to see you alive.'

Aylwin held out his right arm. 'Be not too glad, Kieron. The world we knew has gone for ever.' There was a tight rope round his wrist, where the hand had been severed. 'I will paint no more.'

'You will paint again,' said Kieron. 'This I swear.'

Brothers Hildebrand and Lemuel came to attend to Aylwin.

Kieron looked at them scornfully. 'You seek a hot-air balloon, brothers? I have not had time to construct another. And where is Brother Sebastian, that devout scourge of heretics?'

'Brother Sebastian is dead,' said Lemuel mildly.

'Aha. The Divine Boy was impatient for his company.'

Hildebrand held out his hand. 'Peace, Kieron. What is past is past. Brother Sebastian was, perhaps, over-zealous. There will be no reckoning.'

'Peace, you say! A strange word when the seigneur and his family lie horribly dead, and half the towns folk with them. By the hammer of Ludd, there will be a reckoning, Brother. But it will not be for a hot-air balloon.'

Petrina scolded him. 'Speak no more, Kieron. Bitter words are not needed on this day of grief. The brothers have used their skills upon the sick and wounded, also they have hazarded their lives more than once.' She put her arm round Aylwin who was near to fainting. 'Would you make speeches while Aylwin bleeds to death?'

'Forgive me,' said Kieron. 'As always, I am a fool. I will not unsay what I have said, but let us wipe the slate.'

'Kieron,' said Hildebrand, 'you speak plain. The slate is clean. All of us now need each other. Perhaps that is the divine purpose.'

The neddies took Aylwin away and made a rough couch for him of grass and bracken. Presently, Kieron heard him moaning; and then the moaning rose to a screaming. Kieron stood up and tried to go to his friend. But there was no strength in his legs, and the world had begun to spin crazily, and Petrina was saying words that he could not hear.

And then there was nothing but nightmares. And when he woke he could still hear screaming, but the voice was his own.

3

For hundreds of years in the island of Britain there had been no monarchy, no parliament, no central authority. The country had been divided into seigneuries, each held and governed feudally. The grand seigneurs, the largest land-owners, occasionally held counsel in London. Their concerns were largely with matters of agriculture and trade. They were not empowered to raise taxes, establish armies, or decide matters of national policy. Each seigneur was responsible for the security of his own domain. He could, and frequently did, seek alliance one way or another with his neighbours; and by means of intermarriage, many seigneuries were enlarged or united with others. It had been the intent of Fitzalan of Arundel to bring his seigneurie and that of Talbot of Chichester together by marriage. Besides, since Talbot was unlikely to last, the seigneuries might have united in a manner most satisfactory to the Fitzalans. But Fate had put paid to that; and the dream of an enlarged and prosperous seigneurie had perished with the deaths of Fitzalan and his daughter.

Though there was no centre of temporal authority in Britain, there was yet a centre of spiritual authority: the Luddite Church. The First and Second Men having been destroyed, as it were, by their own hands in the manner of their indiscriminate use of machines, Luddism developed from an almost forgotten philosophy of untutored men into a flourishing creed. Ned Ludd, the idiot boy, who took a hammer to destroy weaving machines at the beginning of the Industrial Revolution, slowly assumed the mantle of divinity.

As Christianity declined, so Luddism rose. It was a more appropriate philosophy. Jesus of Nazareth, or Joshua ben David, to give him his proper Hebrew name, had never had to consider the moral problems involved in the use of machines. Chiefly, he had spoken for universal brotherhood, and he had spoken against oppression. His philosophies were outmoded. More important than universal brotherhood and oppression was the question of survival of the human race. Twice the human race had attempted to destroy itself by the use of machines. In retrospect, it was seen that the one person who had opposed machines was the true saviour of mankind. Ned Ludd, the idiot boy of Leicestershire, acquired in retrospect divine power. It was discovered that he had broken small loaves and fed thousands. It was discovered that he had walked upon the river Trent without sinking. It was discovered that he had changed water into beer, on the eve of his crucifixion.

So, in Britain, the Luddite Church waxed strong; and anti-machinism grew into a religion powerful enough to inhibit all forms of invention. Powerful enough to compel the seigneurs to accept that any unauthorised machinery was evil.

The Luddite Church was peculiar to Britain; but the revulsion for machines was universal. Throughout the world, as men struggled to emerge from the centuries of barbarism that had followed the destruction of the second machine-based civilisation, there lingered an almost racial dread of the power of machines. In some races and in some countries it was stronger than in others. In Russia and China and Africa and India, where a machine-based way of living had never been fully accepted by the mass of the people, the people had, for the most part, returned to the ways of their long dead ancestors. They ploughed the land with wooden ploughs drawn by oxen, mules, horses. They threshed their corn or rice with flails. They killed game with spears or arrows. They used spinning-wheels and wove cloth laboriously by hand.

But in Japan, where the dread of machines was accompanied by a fatal fascination, the steam-engine had been developed once more, and men were already experimenting with its use to propel vehicles and small boats. The Japanese, however, had turned once more to their historic philosophy of isolation; and Japanese steam-engines were retained only for the domestic use of the Japanese.

The steam-engine had also been reintroduced to the continent of North America; but there it was being used primarily in the tremendous task of re-establishing transcontinental communication. It would be many years yet before American ships, powered by steam, proved more efficient in crossing the Atlantic Ocean than the great windjammers.

Meanwhile, the Luddite Church of Britain, an island which had once been the cradle of a great Industrial Revolution, authoritatively maintained that all unnecessary machines – that is, machines considered by the Church to be unnecessary – were evil. And so Britain was condemned to remain one of the most backward countries of Europe.

But the coming of the freebooters, who had attacked along the south coast not only near Arundel but in many other places, eventually provided Kieron with the opportunity to weaken the hold that the Luddite Church had over the minds of men, and to demonstrate that machines, which had enabled two civilisations to be destroyed, were also necessary for the survival and advancement of a third.

4

Kieron slept throughout the rest of the day and the following night, while downs folk and people from the farther parts of the seigneurie continued to arrive at the Misery, alerted by messengers who rode the downs on horseback. Fortunately, the weather remained mild and dry. The able-bodied men set about building rough huts and tents; some of them hunted for deer, rabbit, pheasant; the women prepared food and attended to the injured.

Kieron did not return to consciousness when Sholto lifted him bodily and carried him to a small shelter made of spruce branches and bracken. Nor was he aware that Petrina sat with him through the night, soothing him, cooling his hot forehead, murmuring words of tenderness when he cried out.

In the early morning, he awoke refreshed, his head marvellously clear. He ate pheasant breast and drank goat's milk at sunrise, and he began to feel a new man. Apart from posted watchmen, hardly anyone in the camp was stirring. They were all tired from shock, or wounds or various exertions. When he had breakfasted, he drew Petrina back into the shelter. She was exhausted from a night of sleeplessness, but Kieron did not know this. He unbuttoned her blouse and fondled her breasts. Petrina moaned with pleasure, her fatigue forgotten. The sound of her voice and the feel of her breasts excited him beyond endurance. He lay with her. It was a necessity. He lay with her. It was the first time he had lain with a woman.

He wondered why it had been so necessary. It was more than simple desire, he thought hazily. It was, he supposed, an affirmation of love and life. He had seen much death and much horror. Now he had sought refuge from it in physical and emotional union. He remembered Alyx. He remembered Alyx with love. It was no disloyalty to Petrina. He remembered the Alyx of *Mistress Fitzalan's Leap*. That was best way to remember her. The rest was nightmare …

Afterwards, he and Petrina lay close, whispering, sharing. Someday, he would tell her about Alyx; and someday, she, too, would share the mourning. And together they would pick flowers in remembrance …

Presently, the camp in the Misery – so appropriately named – became alive with activity. Women prepared hot food. Men looked to their weapons, consulted with each other, enquired of the latest news. Kentigern, Seigneur Fitzalan's bailiff, had somehow managed to escape the destruction at the castle with nothing more than flesh-wounds in the leg and shoulder. In the absence of higher authority, Kentigern was considered by common consent to be the leader of the survivors. He was a capable man. Already, he had sent messengers to London to acquaint the Grand Council with the state of affairs. And he had sent men both east and west to ascertain the extent of the free-booters' invasion.

The stranger who had sailed with the freebooters was called Isidor. Once he had been mate on a four-masted barque plying along the European coast for the wine trade. His vessel had been taken by the freebooters off the coast of Spain with many casks of wine on board. The captain was hanged and the crew enslaved. Many of them had subsequently died of fevers and poor rations. Isidor was one of the last survivors.

While Kentigern awaited the results of his communications, and while more people congregated in the Misery, Kieron sought information from Isidor. He wanted to know more about the freebooters.

For more than a hundred years, so Isidor told him, the freebooters had been a pestilence in the Mediterranean Ocean. Though they were drawn from many countries and many creeds, they had these things in common: that each had put himself outside the law in the land of his birth, and that each had little liking for honest toil. For many years, though their acts of violence and theft had been terrible to those who had to endure them, the freebooters had not constituted a serious threat to the security of nations. They had sailed only in small groups consisting of two, perhaps three or four, vessels, despoiling only isolated communities and occupying captured territory only for so long as it took to organise a force sufficient to repel them. Frequently, when their strength was challenged, they would put to sea without giving battle. Their strength had lain in their very elusiveness.

But, of recent years, their numbers had grown, and their strength had increased in an alarming fashion. They had become unified under the absolute command of a man who styled himself Admiral Death. No one knew his real name. No one knew from which country he came, for he spoke many languages, as if to the manner born.

Admiral Death, according to Isidor, was still a young man, perhaps not yet thirty years old. Yet he had natural authority, the gift of commanding. In the space of a few years he had unified the numerous small groups of Mediterra-nean freebooters. He had transformed them into a seaborne nation, subject to its own laws, acknowledging the sovereignty of no other nation upon earth. Every man and woman in the freebooters had sworn absolute alle-giance to him. His word was life or death.

He held some curious notions. He would not tolerate children or pregnant women. Children, wherever he found them, were put to the sword. Women who were demonstrably pregnant when captured were likewise put to the sword. If they became pregnant later, they were thrown overboard. Clearly, Admiral Death had little interest in man's greatest hope of immortality.

His flag ship, from which Isidor had escaped, now lay anchored off Little Hampton. It was Admiral Death who had personally led the thrust inland to Arundel. It was Admiral Death who had devised the concerted attacks along the south coast of Britain.

According to Isidor, it was Admiral Death's intention to establish a semi-permanent colony on the shores of Britain, from which he would be able to conduct his attacks along the northern coasts of Europe. Ironically, he had chosen Britain because of the strength of the Luddite Church. He knew that the Luddites held machines to be anathema. Consequently, he knew also that the ability of the people on the island of Britain to defend themselves would be severely restricted. Admiral Death was a great believer in machines. He had much experience of their usefulness – in a purely destructive sense. He had the use of gunpowder and cannon; and his engineers had devised siege engines – ballistae and the like – capable of hurling explosive bombs against fortified positions. Admiral Death did not despise swords, bows, axes and crossbows; but he knew from experience that they were no match for bomb-shell and cannon. The god of war smiled not upon the righteous but upon superiority of weapons.

Admiral Death, however, had one major weakness. It was a weakness common to all seafaring men. He was afraid of fire. But he was more than ordinarily afraid. He was unreasonably afraid. It was said that some years ago he had been plundering a Mediterranean French city and had been acciden-tally trapped in a waterfront warehouse when one of his men put it to the torch. It was said that, though Admiral Death eventually managed to escape, he had been severely burned, particularly about his legs, and that his man-hood was gone from him for ever.

Kieron, who had been listening to Isidor gloomily, brightened at this latest intelligence.

'You have spoken with Kentigern of these matters?'

'Ay, that I have. He has heard what you have heard and more.'

'Then our task is clear. We must prey upon this madman's fears. We must fire his ships and inflict such damage that, to his dying day – which, Ludd permitting, may be soon – he will have cause to regret that he came to these shores.'

Isidor smiled. 'Easily said, my friend. Because of his fear, the Admiral is doubly cautious. Such vessels as now lie tied up at Little Hampton are well protected. Other vessels lie out at anchor. Strict watch is kept. It will be hard to surprise them.'

'We shall find a way,' said Kieron. 'We shall find a way. To know the ene-my's true weakness is surely half the battle.'

5

Kentigern had been a good bailiff, but he was not a good general. Now that Seigneur Fitzalan and his family were dead, Kentigern was regarded as the temporary leader of those who had survived, until Seigneur Fitzalan's closest surviving relative laid claim to the lands and properties of the seigneurie. It therefore fell to Kentigern to determine how and when and if the forces of Admiral Death should be attacked and repulsed.

Several hundred people had now rallied to the Misery. There were many women and children; but also there were two hundred or more men capable of bearing arms. Kentigern's first thought was to send a sortie into Arundel to discover if the invaders had maintained any presence there and also to list the extent of the damage suffered by the town.

He did not wish to risk many of his fighting force. So he called for twenty volunteers. Among those who stood forward and received his approval were Kieron, Sholto and Isidor.

The twenty men approached Arundel with great caution. They carried swords, bows, crossbows, clubs. Their caution was unjustified. They found Arundel as Kieron had last seen it – deserted, except by the dead. Evidently, Admiral Death's men had retired to Little Hampton, there to consolidate their defences.

The party was led by Kentigern's second-in-command, a man called Liam who had once been a captain of foot soldiers and had some skill in the art of fighting. When Liam had assured himself that none living remained in Arundel, he was of a mind to return to the Misery and report his findings to Kentigern. But Kieron spoke with him.

It was a fine, bright day, but chilly. Sea birds had come inland. They pecked at corpses in the streets, and scratched and squabbled amid the desolation.

'Master Liam, should we not bury our dead?' asked Kieron.

Liam gazed about him hopelessly. 'I am commanded to report upon the state of the town and the castle, Kieron. Besides, we are but twenty men. It would take us more than two days to bury those who have fallen.'

'Must we leave them to the sea birds and the weather?' demanded Sholto. 'I think not, captain. These were our folk. I will dig all day and all night, if need be. I am a strong man, and I will undertake to dig deep enough to bury twenty myself.'

Kieron thought for a moment. 'Liam is right, Sholto. We would exhaust ourselves trying to bury all the dead. We shall need our strength to avenge them … But suppose we collected the bodies. Suppose we burned them, perhaps in the castle yard. At least, we would save them from the sea birds; and there are enough of us to make our farewells to them in a civilised fashion.'

'The invaders would see the smoke,' objected Liam. 'They might think that we have returned to our homes, and be tempted to make a second attack.'

'It would take them more than an hour to march inland from the coast,' Kieron pointed out. 'When they first came, we were unprepared, expecting no attack. Men, women and children were butchered defenceless in the night. But if they came again, though there are not many of us, we are armed and ready. We know this country, and they do not. If we light the funeral pyre in the late afternoon, and if these freebooters march upon us, we can inflict much damage before we retire. It would be something to dispatch a score or two of murderers at the funeral of our friends.'

'That is good reasoning,' commented Isidor. 'If they do not come, we have no difficulties. If they do come, we can kill a few before we retreat into the darkness.'

Liam scratched his head. 'Kentigern asked only for news. He gave no instruction as to the dead.'

'Kentigern has much on his mind,' observed Kieron mildly. 'His concern is rightly with the living. But he is not a hard man. If he were here, I believe he would allow us to take care of our dead. He would not wish to see them reduced to carrion.'

Liam made up his mind. 'By the hammer, you are right, boy. Therefore, let us prepare a large bed of wood, which is all we can now offer these who were our friends.'

There was plenty of wood available. Large stocks of logs were always in store at the castle. Also much half-burned timber lay around for the picking up. Presently, a very large platform of wood had been established in the castle yard. It was broad enough and long enough to support many bodies; and it rose almost the height of a man's shoulders from the ground.

Now came the more arduous and less pleasant task: the collecting of the bodies. Kieron, Sholto and two other men elected to gather the dead from the castle and its grounds. The remaining men split themselves into three groups and took hand carts to scour the town.

There was one body that Kieron wished to deal with himself, alone; though he knew that it would break his heart.

Alyx lay as he had left her, undisturbed. But she now bore little resemblance to the Alyx Fitzalan who had once been so full of life and love and sheer grace. The body was a pale, shrunken thing, grotesque, doll-like.

The tears coursed down Kieron's face. He forced himself to look so that the manner of her death would be burned into his brain for ever. There were the lips he had kissed. There were the breasts that had been held warmly against him.

'Alyx, dear and lovely Alyx,' he sobbed. 'I will kill for you. If need be, I will spend my life killing for you, until the last of the animals who brought you to this has perished horribly, and the earth is clean.'

He found some torn brocade hanging by a window, and wrapped her carefully. It was Indian cloth of gold and silver, a fitting shroud for a child of sunlight and movement.

And when she was covered, all of her, he held her close for the last time. And as held her, he saw the picture: *Mistress Fitzalan's Leap*. He marvelled that he had not noticed it before his first and last painting. It hung crazily from the wall, and had been slashed by a sword. But the damage was not irreparable. The canvas could be sewn, and fresh pigments would conceal the joining.

Kieron knew that he could never paint like that again. It did not matter. The Alyx who lay in his arms was dead. But the Alyx of the portrait was alive in all the bloom and exuberance of youth. That was how she must now live, he told himself bitterly, caught like a fly in amber. When there was time, he would attend to the portrait; and a hundred years hence men would marvel at her grace and beauty.

He lifted his burden and carried it out to the funeral pyre. The men had worked hard at their grim task. Already, the bodies were piled high. Kieron climbed on to the pyre, treading carefully so that he would not disturb the dead, and laid Alyx as near as he could to the body of her father.

When he came down, Sholto and the others spoke to him, but he did not hear what they were saying.

Men were sprinkling whale oil on the timbers. Presently all was ready.

'Will someone say something?' asked Liam.

'I will say something.' Kieron suddenly recollected what was happening. 'I will say something. Before the torch is put to this pyre which will consume the remains of our loved ones and friends, I ask that all here will swear to take ten lives for one or to die in their efforts. We deal not with people but with animals. We deal with the instruments of death.'

'It is a beautiful oath,' said Isidor. 'I swear.'

'I also,' said Sholto, 'though Ludd knows we are not a fighting people.'

The fire leaped high, and the men drew back from the heat, staring as if in a trance as the logs and timbers spit and cracked, and the flames roared like living creatures in the light wind.

Liam had sent a man up to the watch tower to keep an eye on the river and the road to the sea and the flat coastal land; but the rest of the men stayed in the castle yard, held almost magically by the great wall of fire that now rose up to surround and consume the dead.

The heat grew intense, and the men had to stand farther and farther back, while their faces became red and the sweat dried as it was formed.

Great gouts of black smoke rose to the sky, sparks showered; and the fire of death roared with its own self-consuming life.

'Farewell for ever,' said Kieron silently. 'If there is a life hereafter, as the neddies swear, may you again ride a fine horse, Alyx, on a June morning. And presently I will join you and paint such a picture of you held between earth and sky that all the ghosts of all the men who ever lived will marvel. But, forgive me, I think that life is only for the living; and so your final refuge is in the memories of those who have known and loved you.'

The man who had been in the watch tower was speaking excitedly to Liam. Kieron emerged from his private thoughts to learn that, in the fading light, the watch man had seen a column of men marching from Little Hampton. He estimated that they would reach the castle within the half-hour.

'If we are prudent,' said Liam, 'we will shortly depart from this place. We have fulfilled our task and more. We have seen to our dead, and we may retire with honour.'

'Not I!' shouted Kieron wildly. 'I mourn my dead, and I am anxious to demand a reckoning.'

Liam, a strong man, seized him by the shoulders and shook him. 'Boy, your spirit is great, but you are half crazed with grief. We are twenty men. I am told a hundred or more march against us. They have weapons at the very least equal to ours and possibly superior. Now is not the time to fulfil your oath. Be patient. The time will come when we may strike.'

Kieron broke his hold. 'Sir, you are a good man, and you lead us. As you say, I am half crazed with grief. But grief sharpens my wits. These who march against us will have to come up the hill to the castle, will they not?'

'So?'

'So, we have burned our dead. May we not offer a similar accommodation to the freebooters? I am told that Admiral Death has little liking for fire.'

'You speak in riddles, Kieron. Speak plain before we depart, taking you forcibly, if need be.'

Kieron tried to accommodate his thoughts. 'They come against us, these freebooters, drawn by the sight of the funeral pyre. In the castle cellars there will doubtless still be many barrels of whale oil, along with logs and kindling. If we were to load four-wheel carts with the whale oil and with any substance that will burn, and if we were to wait until the freebooters were coming up the hill—'

Liam grasped the idea instantly. 'Kieron, your thoughts have some greatness.' He turned to the rest. 'Sholto, take what men you need and find three four-wheel carts quickly. Mangan, take the rest of the men into the castle, bring out what is left of the whale oil and any substance that will burn quickly.'

Presently, the carts were loaded with barrels of oil, small wood, cloth and straw, and anything that would burn quickly. Then they were hauled out of the castle gate to the top of the hill, and were ready for launching down the road to the sea.

The watch man reported that the freebooters were already crossing the bridge over the river Arun. Twilight came rapidly. It was hard to see down the length of the hill from the castle gate.

'If the ruse does not work,' said Liam, 'we shall have to run for our lives. We cannot stand against so many.'

'It will work,' said Kieron with utter confidence. 'The darkness comes fast, but that is no matter. Indeed it is to our advantage. We know their numbers, they do not know ours. In the darkness, and with chariots of fire bursting upon them, they will panic. Such as escape burning, we may easily put to the sword. Let us listen for their feet and their voices before we launch the attack. Let us hear their breathing.'

Liam looked at him with respect. 'Some day, you may be a great general, Kieron.'

Kieron laughed. 'Some day, I shall be a general of the clouds.'

The freebooters began to ascend the hill. The darkness made the shape of their column indistinct; but their voices and the clatter of their arms could be heard clearly. They marched without any attempt at concealment, without any sign of fear. What was there to be afraid of? The inhabitants of this town were largely dead or taken prisoner. The survivors could only be a cowed and desperate few.

Now they were less than a hundred paces from the castle gate. Now they were no more than sixty or seventy paces away. Their faces began to show ruddily in the reflected glow of the funeral pyre.

'Now!' shouted Liam.

Three men flung torches on to heaps of cloth and straw soaked in whale oil. The rest pushed at the wheels and sent the carts careering down the hill.

Within moments, the flames rose high. Burning whale oil slopped from the barrels and on to the wheels, turning the carts truly into chariots of fire. The freebooters were confronted with a fearsome sight. The fire-carts bearing down upon them took up most of the width of the narrow street. In the terrible moments as the carts gathered speed, the column of freebooters pan-icked, became an unreasoning mob. The front ranks turned to flee, elbowing and kicking their fellows out of the way, trampling some of them. But the fire-carts were already moving faster than a man could run.

Four or five of the freebooters retained cool heads and pressed themselves against the castle walls to allow the fire-carts to run past. It availed them little. They fell to arrows from bows or bolts from crossbows, their positions being made wonderfully clear by the light from the flames.

Two of the carts collided and careened crazily. Their flaming barrels of whale oil shattered upon the street, creating a terrible river of fire. Men danced dreadfully in it as their legs burned, or fell into it and were destroyed with merciful speed.

The carnage was horrible, but it lasted no more than two minutes. The carts reached the bottom of the steep hill and fell to pieces in great bursts of fire.

'We have worked a great destruction,' said Liam. 'Now let us go. This will be something to gladden the hearts of our people.'

'Not I, captain. Not yet!' Kieron brandished the sword he had plucked from the body of Alyx. 'There are those who still live. They are burned, but if we do not destroy them they will crawl back to their ships and they will live.'

'Kieron reasons well, captain,' said Sholto. 'Let us—' He gave a great cough and looked at his chest in surprise. An arrow had buried itself deep. He sank to his knees. 'Look after her,' he said to Kieron. 'But remember that a woman is—' He fell. Kieron knelt and lifted Sholto's head. But the smith's spirit had already departed his body.

'Well, then,' said Kieron, standing up. 'Who is for Sholto and those we have set upon the pyre this day?'

There was a great roar of approval. Liam sensed that it were better to go with the tide.

'Forward, then,' said Kieron. 'Kill without mercy.' Nineteen men, armed with bows, swords and axes went down the hill.

The freebooters, such as survived, were in a pitiful condition. The river of fire had passed by them, round them, over them. They lay in the road, some dead, some still in great anguish, beating feebly at their smouldering clothes.

Kieron, dreadful to look at, his face distorted with anger, a torch in one hand and his sword in the other, leaped skilfully among the fiery rivulets of oil, the flaming wisps of straw and crackling fragments of timber.

He found one man, barely recognisable as a man, writhing. 'One for Alyx!' The sword plunged into the freebooter's chest. He coughed, choked and lay still.

Another man, though badly burned, could still hold his sword. Pitifully, he tried to defend himself. But retribution was upon him.

'Another for Alyx!' Kieron was possessed.

He took joy in the killing. He leaped across islands of fire to seek out fresh victims.

'One more for Alyx!'

'A fourth for Alyx!'

One freebooter was not so badly burned that he could not go down on his knees and hold out his hands in an obvious appeal for mercy. He babbled in a tongue Kieron could not understand.

Kieron savoured the moment, dreadfully enjoying his power of life and death. 'Mercy, you shall have, fellow. Better than your people gave.' With a terrible sweep of the sword, he sliced through the freebooter's throat. The man fell, gurgling.

'Another for Alyx!' One small part of Kieron's mind remained shocked at the pleasure he could take in the death agony of a human being. The rest of him exulted in blood lust, goaded on by the vision of a girl who had been violated and brutally murdered.

He continued his deadly journey down the hill. With mindless fury, he struck at those who were already dying, even at some who were already dead. Presently he stopped, drained, exhausted. There was no one left to kill.

He stared about him, as if in a trance. The flames were dying now. The battle, such as it had been, was over. More than a hundred corpses lay on the hill. The stench of burnt flesh was terrible and sweet.

He was aware that someone was shaking his shoulders. It was Liam.

'Kieron, are you well?'

Kieron looked at him vacantly. 'Yes, captain, I am well.'

'Listen, then. Your stratagem was wonderfully successful. But while you have been doing your bloody work, I have taken prisoners. They are not to be killed, Kieron. You understand? They are not to be killed.'

'Why are they not to be killed?'

'Because they speak English. They will tell us more about Admiral Death, and his intentions.'

'And when they have spoken?' asked Kieron.

'I do not know. It will be for Kentigern to decide.'

'I have already decided,' said Kieron, swaying. 'It was my stratagem. They are my prisoners. The sentence is—' Suddenly, he fell, senseless. Liam picked him up and carried him back up the hill.

6

Within three or four days, the encampment in the Misery had become itself a small fortified village. Men had cut trees to build a stockade and to build kitchens and sleeping huts. Though the freebooters had evidently chosen not to occupy Arundel, Kentigern did not deem it safe to attempt to return to the town until his forces were stronger. He had barely two hundred men who could bear arms. Against the reputed strength of the forces of Admiral Death, they would have stood little chance in pitched battle.

Also Kentigern awaited news and instructions from the Grand Council of seigneurs in London, and from the east and the west concerning the extent of Admiral Death's invasion. The news was slow in coming; and when it came it was not overly encouraging. The grand seigneurs had had requests for help and guidance from the survivors in several seigneuries on or near the southern coast. But the grand seigneurs, besides being fortunate for the most part to hold lands at a reasonable distance from the coast, were prudent men. The forces of Admiral Death were highly mobile: the forces of the seigneuries were not. If sufficient men were committed to the south to repulse or defeat Admiral Death, what was to prevent him putting out to sea to strike at another vulnerable area of the coast? His ships could sail much faster than men could march or ride. If it were his pleasure, he could harry the entire coastline of the island of Britain, leaving its defenders to exhaust themselves marching to and fro in futile attempts to meet his invasions with strength.

So the Grand Council cautiously committed itself to raising a force of five hundred armed men within the month to march south, provided that the southern seigneuries affected by the invasion could establish a unified army which at least doubled the strength of the Grand Council's auxiliaries. It was a diplomatic way of saying that the southern seigneuries must look to their own salvation.

The news from the east and the west was no less discouraging. A flotilla of Admiral Death's ships had struck with immense success as far east as the seigneurie of Brighton. Another had struck as far west as the seigneurie of Portsmouth. Each had advanced not inland but west and east respectively to join with the central assault at Little Hampton. Apparently, they were content to hold a long but narrow strip of coast.

The prisoners taken by Liam confirmed this interpretation – after they were put to the torture. The torture was not entirely barbaric. It consisted of tightening ropes about the arms and legs of the prisoners until pain loosened their tongues.

The most reliable informant was one Jethro, a favoured lieutenant of Admiral Death. His legs and arms had been already severely burned by Kieron's stratagem. The application of ropes served only to magnify a pain that already existed.

Jethro enlarged upon the information already received. Admiral Death had a grand design. He wished not only to establish a well-defended colony on the southern coast of Britain, but he wished also to use the island as a recruiting ground. If he was mad, he was also well-informed and concluded that many adventurous young men, tired of the restrictions and authoritarianism of the Luddites, would join his forces, attracted by the military and other machines that were denied them in the seigneuries. And if enough young malcontents did not come to him voluntarily, it would be easy to impress the men he needed by making punitive raids inland. He well knew that it would take the seigneurs a long time to unite in their common defence. Admiral Death did not require a long time for any of his operations. He was impatient of time. Soon he would be overwhelmingly strong, and whatever the seigneurs did then would not matter. Having consolidated his base, Admiral Death would then send ships to conduct similar operations along the coasts of Norway, Denmark, Germany and the Netherlands. Eventually he hoped to control the seaboard of Europe. When he had achieved this, he would be in a position to starve and weaken all who opposed him. And then he would be able to fulfil his great ambition – to make himself master of Europe.

Having disclosed his master's plans, Jethro pleaded movingly for his life, swearing that, upon recovery, he would willingly bear arms against the man to whom he had sworn loyalty. Kentigern, though short of seasoned fighters, reasoned that a man who broke fealty once might well do so again. He pronounced sentence of death.

Jethro was hanged on a fine morning when the birds sang and deer leaped through the woods. Kieron, present and assisting at the execution, saw the look in the fellow's eyes – the look of one who gazes upon the world for the last time and realises for the last time how beautiful it is. Briefly he felt pity; but then the pity dissolved in a dreadful vision of Alyx.

Because of his stratagem with the fire-carts, Kieron had become a hero among the survivors at the Misery. Men almost twice his age looked upon him with respect and listened to his ideas and opinions. He was no longer regarded as a heretic, one who had come close to the stake. All that seemed to belong to a world that had gone for ever. But his new status meant little to Kieron. He remained cold inside, cold with memories of cruelty and horror and death, cold with the knowledge of his own dreadful desire to seek vengeance.

Petrina noticed the change in him more than anyone. On their fifth day at the Misery, they asked Brother Hildebrand to marry them. Their parents were dead, and they had no one left but each other. It seemed to Kieron a logical thing to do. He and Petrina would now be able to share the same bed and seek consolation in each other's arms without idle tongues wagging and without the censure of the neddies. Kieron went through the ceremony mechanically, his thoughts seeming to be far away. A special little hut had been prepared for them by friends, and a small and sadly gay feast had been arranged. But when Kieron and his bride retired to bed that night, he took no joy in her ample breasts and rounded belly. He performed his duty with the same remote efficiency he had displayed at the wedding. And Petrina was left to weep silently in the dark.

On the following day, Kentigern held a council of war. He was tired of waiting for help that did not come, he was tired of living in the woods like an outcast, he was tired of seeing people look to him for decisions and miracles.

Kieron, though young, was invited to attend the council because of his undoubted talent for destruction.

Kentigern spoke first. 'Friends, you know what answer we have received from the grand seigneurs. They will help us, but it will take time; and they require us to establish an army consisting of all capable of bearing arms in the seigneuries that have already been attacked. That, too, will take time. I for one am unwilling to wait and see our people rot while such armies are gathered. Since the freebooters have shown no inclination to hold Arundel, it is possible for us to return to our homes and attempt to rebuild them. But, if we did, it is certain that our activities would be observed. Admiral Death, as we know, maintains a careful watch. At the first sign of our presence, no doubt he would send a force against us. We were not strong enough to resist the first attack. We would hardly be strong enough to resist a second. I propose, therefore, that we ourselves mount an attack upon his vessels at Little Hampton. It will hardly be expected, and the element of surprise will surely afford us some advantage. I ask your opinions on these thoughts, my friends.'

Some spoke for an attack, arguing that there was little to be lost and much to be gained. Some spoke against an attack, arguing that there was much to be lost and little to be gained. Kieron listened to all the speakers attentively, but did not himself offer an opinion.

Finally, Kentigern addressed him directly. 'Well, Kieron, as I have observed, you have listened hard and said nothing. You have already proved yourself a man of some inspiration in the matter of inflicting losses upon the enemy. Have you nothing to say?'

Kieron smiled. 'I am, as you know, one who desires to annihilate the freebooters utterly. My own plans would take time to put into action, assuming that you would be agreeable to them, which I doubt.'

'Tell us of your plans, then, that we may judge.'

'You know that I have experimented with a hot-air balloon?'

Kentigern shuffled uncomfortably. 'Surely it is a thing best forgotten.'

'No, Kentigern, it is a thing to remember. These facts are also things to remember. Admiral Death is afraid of fire. He commands the sea and he commands the land. He does not command the air. I desire to build a hot-air balloon capable of carrying two men. When the wind is right, this hot-air balloon would drift over the fleet at Little Hampton, raining fire upon the ships. Wooden ships will burn. If Admiral Death is deprived of his ships, he is also deprived of a means of supply and a means of retreat. Then would be the time to attack by land.'

There were murmurs of shock and disapproval. Kieron's recent exploits had made him into a hero. Men did not wish to be reminded of matters that had brought him close to the stake.

Brother Hildebrand was among those present. 'Kieron, my brother,' he said mildly, 'Ludd moves in mysterious ways, and has enabled you to redeem yourself in heroic action, of which Holy Church will take great notice. Do not, I beg of you, relapse into previous heresy.'

'Will Holy Church send us one thousand soldiers?' demanded Kieron caustically. 'Will the Divine Boy smash the ships of the freebooters with his divine hammer?'

'Peace,' said Kentigern anxiously. 'We are not gathered here to discuss doctrine or heresy. We are here to devise a means of ridding us of those who have fallen upon us like locusts. Will anyone else advise us?'

'Let us make use of Kieron's stratagem at the castle,' said someone. 'Let us by dead of night take small boats down the Arun. Let us take small boats loaded with casks of whale oil, straw and other combustibles. Let us tie them "beneath the sterns of the freebooters" vessels and put them to the torch. Thus shall we inflict much damage.'

'It will not work,' said Kieron. 'Their sentinels will be ready for us by sea, by river or by land. They cannot be ready for us by air.'

'Nevertheless,' said Kentigern, 'the suggestion is a good one, and the best I have heard this day. I propose to commit one hundred men and ten fire-boats to this enterprise. It is my task now to seek volunteers, for I will not command men who have little enthusiasm for the venture.'

Kieron was among the first to volunteer. Not because he had any faith in the venture, but because it might offer him another opportunity to kill freebooters.

The boats were launched into the Arun at night on the ebb. The Arun flowed swiftly, carrying the attacking party towards Little Hampton at better than five knots. For the major part of the journey, the men sat in the boats; but when they neared Little Hampton they slipped over the side and held on to the gunwales.

The water was icy cold, and many men had to bite hard on cloth or leather to stop their teeth chattering. Kentigern planned to let the boats drift, with the men hanging on to them, guiding them to the centre of the river. When Little Hampton was reached, swimmers would attach the fire-boats to their target vessels and fuses would be ignited so that the boats would not burst into flame until the men had had at least some chance to make their escape.

The plan, as Kieron had foreseen, depended too heavily on an element of surprise which it would be hard to obtain. The drifting fire-boats were dis-covered before they reached Little Hampton. They were discovered by a small patrol of freebooters, equipped with lanterns, and marching along the bank of the river.

The boats were plainly visible by lantern light; and besides, one of Kenti-gern's men had sneezed. The freebooters began to use bows and muskets with terrible effect. The men in the water were too numbed with cold, too hampered by wet clothes and too disheartened to attempt any effective coun-ter-attack. They scrambled for the farther bank, where they were picked off by bowmen and musketeers as they dragged themselves out of the river mud.

One sharp-witted freebooter, guessing the purpose of the boats, tossed his lantern into one of them. It burst mightily into flame; and the survivors of Kentigern's unhappy band were now exposed as if by daylight. Some men did manage to struggle up the muddy bank and into the darkness; but many were killed in the water, and a few drowned, lacking the strength to swim.

Kieron, as soon as he had grasped what was happening, had the wit to lower his head for a while below water and drift on with his boat. Luckily it was not the one that was fired. Downstream, and away from the glare of the flames, he managed to scramble to the bank.

Though he was numb with cold and almost exhausted, he forced himself to run through the darkness, falling down many times, but always managing to pick himself up, somehow. His limbs ached and his skin froze. Running, he knew, would be the only way he could keep himself alive. There were times when he wished to lie down and rest, even to sleep; but he would not allow himself to do so, realising that if he did, he might never rise.

He arrived back at the Misery in a pitiable condition just after daylight. He was not the first survivor to be lucky enough to make his way back. Several had preceded him. Several would come after.

He did not recognize Petrina. He did not seem to recognize anyone or anything. His eyes were vacant; and it was as if blind instinct had kept him going and had made him seek the security of his own folk.

Someone was holding him, someone was talking to him. He did not know who, nor did he understand the words. He must be among friends, he told himself vaguely, otherwise he would likely have been killed. But in case he had fallen into some kind of trap, he tried to raise the sword that he held, the sword that had not left his hand throughout that terrible journey down the river Arun.

He tried to raise the sword, and fell soundlessly. Petrina knelt by him, stroking him, weeping. She attempted to take the sword from his half-frozen fingers; but she could not.

He had a fever, and she nursed him for several days. At one time, the neddies thought him like to die. But he was young and strong; and Petrina warmed him with her body when the fever left him and he was held by a deathly chill. Presently, the chill faded and he became conscious and reasonable. He drank nourishing soup and felt a faint surge of strength in his limbs. He discovered, with some surprise, that he was destined to live.

One morning, he desired to wash himself and make himself presentable. Petrina brought him a mirror. He looked in it and was shocked to see the face of a stranger. A man with gaunt cheeks and deep lines on his face and forehead. A man with hair turning white.

It was a fine thing to have white hair when one was eighteen years old. How would he look when he was thirty? He shrugged. No matter. There was work to be done. Much, much work. What mattered was not how a man looked but what he had achieved.

Of the hundred men who set out on the ill-starred venture, but twenty-three returned, the rest being killed or taken. Kentigern was a broken man, his ability to make decisions seemingly paralysed by the magnitude of the disaster.

7

In various ways, the other seigneuries along the southern coast had fared quite as badly as the seigneurie of Arundel. Like the survivors of Arundel, the others had taken to the woods and to the downs, establishing temporary camps from which they made costly and at times disastrous counter-attacks upon the freebooters. The seigneuries had for so long been autonomous and self-sufficient that they had developed a fatal aversion to co-operating with each other and acting in unity. Their prejudices sprang from an almost racial fear of the evils of central government. For as far back as people could remember, seigneuries were united either by blood ties or by conquest; and it was a long time since any seigneur had been rash enough to attempt to subdue his neighbour by force of arms. Loose marital alliance had been both the strength and the weakness of the seigneurs. Now, confronted by invaders under a unified command, they were at a disadvantage.

It would be a considerable time, reasoned Kieron, before the people were able to abandon their traditional attitudes. A man from the next seigneurie was still regarded as a foreigner and treated with caution. How much more destruction would it take to make people realise that their only hope lay in working together? By the time people had come to their senses and the Grand Council had sent auxiliaries to aid them, Admiral Death would have an iron grip on the land he had conquered. And the people of Arundel, for whom he had the greatest concern, would remain fugitives, people of the woods, relapsing eventually into barbarism.

He had much time to reflect while he regained his strength and recovered from his illness. He began to take pleasure in Petrina once more, rejoicing in the sweet yielding of her body, giving her the seed of his loins and the love of his spirit. He did not need her to tell him when she had conceived. He knew. He had felt her body, relaxed yet taut, quivering joyfully beneath his. He had felt his seed leap joyfully into her womb, like salmon returning to the source of a known river.

One day he went to Kentigern. Now that he had hope of immortality, there was even more to fight for and to live for.

'I am going to build a hot-air balloon, Kentigern. A very large hot-air balloon. I am going to float it over the ships of Admiral Death and rain fire upon them from the sky. I need help. I need you to command men to help me.'

Kentigern sat on a chair with a shawl round his shoulders, like Master Hobart. And, like Master Hobart, he coughed much and drank such strong spirits as were available to him.

'A hot-air balloon is heresy,' he said thickly. 'Holy Church will burn you, and possibly me also.'

'We are all dying,' said Kieron. 'No man lives for ever. And what help has Holy Church given us in this time of disaster?'

Kentigern hiccuped. 'The neddies have prayed for us.'

'Has their prayer destroyed one of the freebooters?' demanded Kieron angrily.

'Who can say?'

'I can say. I would rather have one sword in my hand than the prayers of a hundred neddies behind me.'

'You were right about the fire-boats ... Kieron, forgive me. My mind is not too clear. Construct the hot-air balloon, if you must. My judgment is fled.'

'And I can have the men?'

'You shall have the men.'

'And women to sew canvas and paper?'

'Those also.'

'And you will allow me to choose my time and place?'

'I will allow you all these things,' said Kentigern. 'There is only one thing I will not allow you.'

'What is that?'

'Failure. There has been too much failure. We cannot stand more. So, Kieron, my boy, understand that you stake your life upon this enterprise. If you fail I, poor thing that I am, will personally disembowel you for having persuaded me to damn my immortal soul for nothing.'

'You ask much, Kentigern.'

'I demand success. Kieron. That is all. When news of your enterprise goes forth – as it will – Holy Church will send to investigate. I hope I shall burn more tranquilly if the freebooters burn also.' He gave a dreadful laugh. 'I have seen much in my time. I have seen my master murdered and his women endure unspeakable things. Now we who live must entrust ourselves to a young man's madness.'

Kieron gave a grim smile. 'I would have more respect for Holy Church if it provided arms and men.'

'The Church preaches peace and simplicity. In its wisdom it cares for our souls.'

'Have you heard of anyone achieving peace at the stake, Kentigern?'

'Enough, boy! Destroy the freebooters, if you can, and I will gladly stand beside you when the reckoning comes.'

'I shall need your words, on paper, sir. I shall need words and your signature, commanding men to assist me. Without such a paper, I cannot proceed.'

'Then bring me ink, and I will commit my sin to writing … Do not fail, Kieron. That is all … They say you loved Mistress Alyx. Is that true?'

Kieron was too surprised to dissimulate. 'It is true. We loved each other.'

Again Kentigern laughed. 'Forgive me. I laugh only at myself. I, too, loved her, do you see. But she was far above me. That is amusing, is it not? I would have given my life and honour to hold her, willingly, in my arms.'

'I loved her and I held her,' said Kieron evenly. 'And it was sweet … That is all I care to say.'

'It is enough. But why you, Kieron? Why the prentice painter?'

Kieron shrugged. 'I do not know. Perhaps fortune favours him who dares.'

8

It was many days before Kieron was ready to begin construction of the hot-air balloon; but they were not days spent in idleness. First, he had to design the balloon and experiment with a model of it, and then he had also to assemble the materials for construction and train the people who would help him build it. Half the people at the Misery thought him mad, and the other half thought Kentigern mad. But, until a better authority were set over them, they would obey Kentigern; and he had put his name to a paper calling upon all able-bodied men and women to assist Kieron as needed.

Brothers Lemuel and Hildebrand were filled with horror. They remonstrated both with Kentigern and Kieron. Kentigern offered to countermand his orders if or when Holy Church mustered enough fighting men to push the freebooters into the sea. On being told that his immortal soul was endangered, he observed that he was presently more concerned with mortality than immortality. He even made so bold as to observe that the Divine Boy had accomplished little as yet to justify the devotion of the neddies and the obedience of the common people.

'Where was the protection of Ludd when my master was murdered and my mistress violated?' he demanded. 'Nay, brothers, I understand your concern. But it cannot have escaped your notice that we live now in a disordered world. The days of peace and the seasons of prosperity are gone from us. Desperate men seek desperate remedies. Likely Kieron is mad and I am in my dotage; and you, good brothers, must do what you must. But plague me no more. If Kieron fails, he will die; and, doubtless, I also. But if he succeeds, let there be a reckoning.'

'There will be a reckoning,' promised Brother Lemuel. 'Boyish pranks are one thing; but a deliberate attack upon doctrine is another. Make no mistake. Holy Church is patient. There will be a reckoning.'

Kentigern gave him a twisted smile and took a deep draught of spirit. 'I did not see you at the boats, brothers, when we drifted half-frozen down the Arun.'

'It was not our place to be at the boats, Kentigern,' retorted Brother Hildebrand. 'We were at our devotions, praying for the success of your venture.'

'Perhaps your prayers were not loud enough. Or perhaps the Divine Boy is deaf.' Kentigern was quite pleased with himself. It was the first time he had ever blasphemed.

From Kieron, they got even shorter shrift.

'For the sake of a toy, Brother Sebastian wanted me to burn,' he said grimly. 'But Ludd, it seems, moves in mysterious ways. Sebastian is dead, while I live. An interesting thought … And now I am free to construct a sky machine for the benefit of our people.' He lifted his sword, which he now carried with him always. 'So I say to you, brothers, do not interfere with me or with those who help me, either by word or by deed. Else you may join Brother Sebastian in his perpetual slumber.'

The brothers were horrified. No lay man had ever spoken to them like this before. Truly the world had changed.

'You threaten us?' said Brother Lemuel.

'I warn you, that is all. It is my first and final warning. Now leave me. I am busy.'

The brothers retired in a state of shock. When they had recovered somewhat, they made plans. Brother Lemuel would go to London, to the office of the Inquisitor General. Brother Hildebrand would stay in the Misery and keep a record of all heretical acts. Then, when the Inquisitor General sent forces to re-establish the authority of the Church, Brother Hildebrand would be able to bear witness against all those who had gone against the teachings of the Divine Boy.

There were no horses available – Kentigern saw to that – so Brother Lemuel would have to travel on foot. London was at least three day's march away. The brothers made no secret of their plans, and Kieron was fully informed of their intentions.

Petrina was horrified.

'Kieron, this time they will really burn you. Holy Church cannot ignore a direct challenge. Abandon the hot-air balloon, I beg you. Let us be patient. In time, the grand seigneurs will assemble forces sufficient to defeat the freebooters. Then we shall take up our ordinary lives once more.'

Kieron held her close. 'Rest easy, my love. You know, as I do, that with each day that passes, Admiral Death has a stronger hold upon our land. I will not wait for soldiers that may never come, or may come only to meet their doom. The only way to defeat the invader is in an element he cannot use. I will strike from the air. His soldiers do not have wings. He cannot elevate his cannon. I will strike from the air with fire. Holy Church will have little support if the ships of the freebooters are burning.'

'In six days, Brother Lemuel could return with sufficient men to destroy you.'

'Six days!' He laughed. 'Brother Lemuel is not used to walking. He will have many blisters upon his feet. And will the Holy Office immediately despatch troops upon the word of a poor brother? No matter. In six days I shall be invulnerable.'

'My love, I fear for you.'

'Dear Petrina, I fear for us all.'

9

Having obtained authority from Kentigern, Kieron was now confronted with the formidable task of translating a cherished dream into a practical reality. But a short time ago, he would have been saddened by the knowledge that the first use to which an aerial machine would be put would be as an instrument of destruction. If he had paused to reflect, he would have realised that the doctrine of the Luddite Church was not entirely spurious. Historically, the development of machines had amplified man's ability to destroy. The First and Second Men had destroyed their civilisation with their own ingenuity. From the standpoint of Holy Church there was no reason to suppose that men had now developed a greater wisdom that would sustain them in the creation of a third machine-based civilisation.

Kieron had no time to reflect upon such philosophical problems. Brother Lemuel was bound for London, and Admiral Death was consolidating his hold upon the southern coast. Kieron knew that he would have to produce a quick justification for his enterprise or pay the penalty of failure – either to Kentigern or Holy Church. It made little difference.

The first problem was one of design. In order to rain fire upon the ships of Admiral Death, Kieron would have to wait for a light offshore breeze, which would carry his hot-air balloon from its place of launching, over the freebooters' ships and then out to sea. Eventually, the hot-air balloon would come down in the ocean – it being unlikely that it could reach the coast of France, even if the wind held – and therefore whoever took to the skies with it would drown.

Unless the balloon carried something that could survive in the sea. A boat. A small boat. That would be the carriage in which the crew of the balloon would ride. It would have to be a very small boat and a very small crew. Otherwise, the size of the balloon would be huge beyond the ability of the people of Arundel to construct.

Kieron did much thinking, made sketches, made models. The balloon must not be in the shape of a sphere: it must be in the shape of a tapering sausage, corresponding roughly to the shape of the small boat that would be suspended from it.

Armed with Kentigern's authority, he sent men into Arundel to bring back all the linen, all the paper and needles and thread they could find. While they were gone, he spoke with Aylwin who, though pale and weak, was recovering from the loss of his hand.

'Aylwin, how do you fare?'

'I shall live,' said Aylwin. 'I shall live to be useless at my trade and a mockery to my fellows.'

'How would you like to live for ever?'

'Kieron, I have no taste for jests.'

'The bond between us still holds?'

'You know it does.'

'To the death?'

'To the death … What do you require, Kieron?'

'I require you to journey with me suspended from a hot-air balloon. I require you to rain fire upon the freebooters.'

'You would take a one-armed man on such a venture?' He thrust out the stump of his wrist, now mercifully hidden under clean bindings.

'I would take a friend,' said Kieron. 'I would take a man I trust. I would take one whose hatred of the freebooters passes beyond fear.'

'Kieron, I am your man, as well you know. I am not brave, and this you also know. But I would dangle from the talons of an eagle if I could cause destruction to fall on those who have despoiled our peaceful seigneurie.'

'We may not return from the venture.'

Aylwin gave a faint smile. 'I do not expect to. I have little reason for remaining alive … Why, then, did you ask if I would like to live for ever?'

'Because our venture is one that men will remember. We shall begin anew the conquest of the skies and we shall strike terribly at those who have injured us.'

'I require only one promise, Kieron. Give it, and I shall be happy.'

'What is that?'

'I require to know that many shall die with us and because of us.'

Kieron thought for a moment. 'I cannot control the winds, Aylwin. And we must be sure, when all is ready, that the wind is our ally. But if we can take the hot-air balloon over the vessels at Little Hampton, I swear to you that men will perish in tens and hundreds. Is that enough?'

'It is enough.' Aylwin laughed. 'The dead freebooters in Arundel are your witnesses.'

'So, then. Rest as much as you can. I have work to do. The time will be upon us sooner than you imagine.'

10

Kieron paid little attention to the passing of day and night. He worked by daylight. He worked by the light of whale-oil lamps and torches. He drew plans, made calculations, used models. He was distressed to find that the hot-air balloon would have to be far larger than he had anticipated. It would have to be fully fifteen metres long and two and a half metres in diameter; otherwise it would not carry the load he required. He instructed men in the construction of delicate frames from slender willow shoots. He showed women how they must sew linen and paper together to make a great envelope of the size he required. He set two prentice smiths to construct four braziers. He set woodmen to make charcoal, and others to make a small, light boat. He set boys to make ropes, and girls to fashion the ropes into a great net that would harness the hot-air balloon to the boat.

Kieron knew that the hot-air balloon must eventually come down to the sea, therefore its carriage must be in the form of a boat which could be quickly set loose upon the waves, so that the aeronauts would have some small hope of regaining land.

The Misery, which had been a refuge for despondent and beaten people, became transformed by Kieron's fanatical devotion to the hot-air balloon. Folk who would formerly have scoffed at the crazed notions of Kieron-head-in-the-air became infected by his enthusiasm. Desperation was stronger than prejudice. They looked to him for hope. They looked to him and his fantastic project to inflict great losses upon the invaders. They recalled that already his fire-carts had inflicted more damage than all their fighting men combined. He had promised that, if they gave of their best to the construction of his aerial machine, he would rain fire upon the ships of Admiral Death. Kieron, though clearly mad, had already proved his talent for destruction. Therefore, they worked hard, not questioning his instructions or requirements. They would have followed a daemon if he had promised to burn the freebooters' ships.

Kieron slept little and ate little. He ate only when Petrina could find friends sufficiently courageous to drag him forcibly from his work, while she ladled out a helping of nourishing stew and swore that he would not be allowed to move until he had cleaned the platter. Sometimes, he would fling the platter away and shout obscenities. Sometimes, he would eat docilely, recalling that without food a man is weakened.

He no longer looked like a man of eighteen. His white hair had added years. The lines on his forehead and the hollowness of his cheeks had added character and power. He looked now like a man of thirty, a born leader. People became afraid of him, held him in awe. His sword rarely left his hand. He used it to measure linen and paper, to scratch diagrams in the ground. He used it to point, to threaten, to illustrate a command.

Kentigern was amazed at the changes that had taken place. Men and women who had formerly been listless went about their tasks with speed and energy. Because Kieron required of them as much as they were able to give. In return he promised vengeance.

There came a day when all the main constructions were finished. The envelope had been sewn, the net had been woven, the light boat had been built, the braziers had been worked. It was a day of caulking and seaming. The seams of the balloon and of the light boat were caulked by precious pitch taken from coal tar.

The pitch was hot and pungent. All those who came close to the iron pots in which it simmered coughed with the fumes and dabbed at their streaming eyes.

Kentigern, himself coughing and cursing somewhat, came to look at the fabric of the great balloon, spread out on the grass while the pitch that sealed the joinings of fabric and paper lining cooled in the morning air.

'It is finished, Kieron?'

'It is finished.'

'And it will fly?'

'If some fool does not tear the skin or set fire to it when we are heating the air, it will fly.'

'You have worked hard.'

Kieron shrugged. 'Many have worked hard.'

'You more than most. When did you last sleep?'

Kieron scratched his head and looked puzzled. 'I forget. Does it matter? Yesterday, perhaps, or the day before.'

Kentigern put a hand on his shoulder. 'I confess, I did not believe you would achieve this much. Rest, now, boy. You are tired.'

Kieron looked at him strangely. 'Boy no more, Kentigern. Have I not done a man's work, here and elsewhere?'

'Ay, that you have. You are indeed a man, and I offered no offence.'

Petrina had heard the exchange. 'Make him rest, Kentigern. Command him to stop work. He kills himself.'

Kentigern smiled. 'Petrina, I command your man only to destroy free-booters. In all else, he commands himself.'

Tears were running down Petrina's face. Kentigern supposed it was the smell of the pitch. But it was not the smell of the pitch. She wept when she looked at Kieron's white hair, at his dark eyes and hollow cheeks. She wept when she saw the sword that rarely left his hand. She wept when she saw the feverish brightness come upon him, a brightness and an energy not generated by good food and sound sleep. A daemonic power that compelled him to drive himself and others.

Suddenly, Kieron looked at her. He put his hands on her shoulders and looked at her. It was the first time he seemed to have seen her, or even been aware of her, in days.

'Fret not, my love. Presently, all shall be as you wish ... Do you remember when we were children? We came here to the Misery one hot afternoon in late summer, and we lay under the great beech tree, and I told you I wanted to fly.'

The anxiety on Petrina's face softened. 'I remember. Plums and apples. I ate too many and had much pain.'

Kieron laughed. 'Plums and apples and the bright world of childhood.'

Kentigern coughed noisily. 'I am an intruder. I will go. When will you test the balloon, Kieron?'

Kieron did not look at him. 'This afternoon, when I have eaten and held converse with my wife. This afternoon, Kentigern, you shall see history made.'

Kentigern retired, coughing and muttering to himself.

'Plums and apples,' said Kieron. 'We both ate too many ... Do you remember what else we talked about?'

Petrina smiled. 'I told you that my mother had consulted the astrologer Marcus. He said that you would be a grand master of your art and that I should bear three children.' She sighed. 'So much for the hopes and visions of childhood. We live now in a world where these things cannot come to pass.'

'Do we?' asked Kieron excitedly. 'Do we indeed? What else did Marcus say? Can you remember?'

Petrina's forehead crinkled. 'He said ... He said that your greatest painting would be of a terrible fish that destroys folk by burning them. I can recollect no more.'

'Then let us redeem the astrologer's reputation,' said Kieron. He turned from her and snatched a large brush that had been used for daubing hot pitch upon the seams of the balloon. He dipped it into one of the iron pots and then approached the laid out fabric.

Skilfully and quickly, he painted a great staring eye at the head of the balloon. Then he dipped the brush again and painted below the eye a huge cavernous mouth, with rows of sharp teeth. His strokes were swift and sure. At the far end of the balloon, he painted a great black tail.

'Here is my greatest painting Petrina. The shark that swims through the air and devours men ... Now let us go and eat, then let us lie together. For this afternoon the great fish of death takes to the sky.'

11

Kieron saw to the braziers, made sure that the charcoal was glowing but not spitting out sparks or flames. Then he made sure that the men and women who were to hold the balloon while it filled with hot air knew exactly what to do. Then he tested the net that harnessed the balloon to the boat it would raise. Finally, he gave the signal for the orifices in its underbelly to be held over the braziers so that hot air would enter inside the fabric.

The flat envelope began to swell. Presently, it lifted from the grass. Presently it hung suspended over the boat, with the braziers forcing in more and yet more hot air.

Kieron and Aylwin climbed into the boat.

'Well, Aylwin?'

'Well, Kieron?'

'Shortly we shall be airborne. If you have no stomach for the venture, now is the time to speak.'

'I have already spoken. So have you.'

'Enough, then. Let us see how the fish of death takes to the sky.' He signalled to the men holding ropes attached to the bow and the stern of the small boat.

They paid out. Slowly the balloon began to rise.

'More heat to number one brazier,' called Kieron. 'We are not on an even keel.'

Aylwin took the bellows and, resting them on the arm that lacked a hand, pumped away at number one. The charcoals glowed brightly and the heat balance was maintained.

The small boat, in which Kieron crouched at one end and Aylwin at the other with the metal tray supporting the four braziers swaying a little between them, had risen above the heads of the people below. Kieron signalled for more rope to be paid out, then used hand bellows to make the charcoal glow more brightly in the two braziers he tended. Aylwin also used his bellows. Kieron felt the extra lift.

'Airborne!' he exclaimed triumphantly. 'Airborne at last!' It was as if the clumsy balloon swelled with life, straining impatiently at the ropes that held the small boat, at stem and stern, suspended from it.

There was a great cheer from below. Aylwin looked over the side and stared down at the group of upturned faces. Kieron signalled for more rope to be paid out. Slowly, majestically the balloon rose above the tree-tops of the Misery. It was as if, now that it was truly in the element for which it was designed, the balloon had mysteriously gained physical grace.

Kieron signalled for yet more rope to be loosed. The balloon was now more than fifty metres above the Misery, swaying and riding upon air currents like a boat on a mild sea swell.

Aylwin, white-faced, looked anxiously at Kieron. 'Are we not high enough, Kieron? Truly it is awesome.'

The wind seemed to swallow his words. Ropes and timbers creaked, the charcoal in the braziers glowed golden.

'Look south,' called Kieron. 'Look south. There lies the enemy.'

The air was clear, and the Misery was no more than nine or ten kilometres from the sea. Aylwin followed Kieron's gaze. He could see the ocean. He could see the far horizon. He could see sunlight upon water. And, at Little Hampton, he could see the masts of ships, huddled together like toy boats on a great pond. He laughed nervously. 'They do not look so fearsome from this distance, Kieron.'

'Nor will they seem fearsome when we pass over them and drop fire bombs upon their decks. We shall cause such destruction, Aylwin, that men will speak of it in wonder in the years to come.'

Aylwin shuddered. 'How can you be so sure? How can you be so sure that we shall succeed, that we shall aim well, that the fires will not be put out, that the balloon will not be destroyed, that we shall even pass close enough to the ships?'

Kieron gave a terrible smile. 'Of late, I have given much thought to the problem of how to inflict death and destruction. It is a new trade I have learned, and one for which, as you know, I have some talent. The secret of this trade of dealing in death is to pay great attention to detail. While I have been building this shark of the sky, this formidable monster filled only with hot air, I have also given thought to our means of delivering fire. Rest easy, Aylwin. If we die – and we may – we shall give an excellent accounting.'

He was aware of voices, shouts from below. He looked down at the people in the Misery and saw that two of the men who held the ropes attached to the small boat had been pulled clear of the ground. They hung on to their ropes perilously, shouting, imploring.

Again Kieron smiled. 'We have excellent lift, I see. More than I had hoped for. Therefore we shall carry more weight than I had hoped. But now let us return to earth. Quench number one brazier, Aylwin, and I will quench number four. Thus shall we return gently to our friends.'

Aylwin and Kieron took small flasks of water and poured them very slowly over the glowing charcoals. There was much sizzling, and hot steam rose, giving the balloon more temporary lift. The men hanging on the ropes cried out with alarm.

But as the heat faded, the shark of the sky began to lose height. Smoothly and slowly it sank down to earth. Kieron gave a great sigh of regret as he found himself below the tree-tops of the Misery once more. Presently, there was a slight jolt as the boat grounded.

Kentigern was the first to greet him. 'Well, Kieron, are you satisfied?'

'I am satisfied.'

'And you still believe that you can carry fire to the freebooters' ships?'

'I know that I can. More even than I had calculated.'

Kentigern gave a sigh of relief. 'Well, then, we shall not be damned in vain. While you have been labouring upon the construction of this monstrous thing, others have been engaged in more civilised pursuits. Beer has been brewed. Come, let us drink to the success of the venture.'

'You drink,' said Kieron. 'I have work to do.'

'What work? The balloon is finished.'

'I wish to experiment with the best means of delivering fire. When you have drunk your toasts, Kentigern, send men to seek barrels of whale oil, flasks, goat-skin bottles, bales of straw, lard, pitch – anything that will burn fiercely.'

'You are a dedicated man, Kieron.'

Kieron laughed dreadfully. 'Yes. I am dedicated to destruction.'

12

Two days later, the wind blew gently but steadily from the north. The sky was clear, blue as a heron's egg, and the downs were bathed in a quiet autumnal beauty.

A strange caravan left the Misery. Preceded by a column of foot soldiers headed by Liam, Kentigern and Isidor rode side by side on horseback, the two horses harnessed together by a reversed yoke passing under their bellies. In the centre of the yoke was a stout iron ring. Through it passed a rope. The rope rose tautly upwards to be hooked on the stem and stern of the boat that hung from Kieron's hot-air balloon ten metres above.

Kieron had painted a name on the slender craft. The name was: *Mistress Fitzalan's Revenge*. Petrina wept when she saw it. But she took care not to let Kieron see her weeping.

They had made their goodbyes but an hour before – while Aylwin was confessing his sins to Brother Hildebrand, who, though he had faithfully recorded all heretical acts, saw no reason why he should not give absolution to a mutilated boy who was going to almost certain death.

'I will love you always,' Petrina had said, dry-eyed at the last so that her man should not be weakened.

'And I will love you always.'

'More than you loved Alyx Fitzalan?' As soon as the words were out, Petrina could have cut off her tongue. This was no time for barbs. Kieron was about to put himself in peril of his life.

He was not angry. He held her close; and, in the sight of many men and women, placed his hand upon her breast.

'More fully than I ever loved Alyx.' He smiled, glancing at the balloon that was already filled with hot air and swayed as if impatient at its mooring. 'I have already accommodated the astrologer Marcus by painting a fish that will destroy men by fire. There will be time, will there not, for you to do your part and bear three children?'

She kissed him. 'Please Ludd, there will be time. Come back, Kieron. That is all.'

Then he and Aylwin had seated themselves in *Mistress Fitzalan's Revenge* and had checked all the strange equipment that littered the craft and even hung suspended from hooks over its side. After satisfying himself that supplies of charcoal, flasks of water, goatskins of whale oil, ropes and grapnels and the small tightly packed bales of straw that had soaked overnight in oil were all in position, Kieron applied more fuel to the braziers and used the bellows. *Mistress Fitzalan's Revenge* lifted slowly from her mooring, and was manhandled into position above the two restive horses. The rope was passed through the ring on the yoke and made fast; and the fantastic caravan moved off, the horses snorting and whinnying nervously as they sustained a load, an upward pull, that was against nature.

Kieron's plan was that Kentigern and Isidor should draw the hot-air balloon as near as possible to the windward side of the vessels at Little Hampton. When he judged that he was in position where the offshore wind would carry him over the freebooters' ships, he would release the rope that held *Mistress Fitzalan's Revenge* to the yoke between the horses. After that, all depended upon luck, skill, destiny. Kentigern, Isidor and the foot soldiers would stay to observe, if they were not attacked. If they were to be attacked, they would endeavour to retreat to Arundel and observe matters with a spy-glass.

The strange cavalcade passed through the town of Arundel without hindrance, disturbing only the rats and sea birds attending to the rotting corpses of freebooters who had perished in the path of the fire-carts.

As *Mistress Fitzalan's Revenge* passed the castle, Kieron and Aylwin found that they were high enough to look over the walls. The funeral pyre was now no more than a great heap of ash, disturbed occasionally by gusts of wind.

'Rest easy, my love,' said Kieron softly. 'This day there will be a reckoning.'

Unmolested, the column marched down the hill, across the bridge over the river Arun and took the road to the sea.

It was a beautiful day; a day for strolling among the downs and marvelling at the secrets of nature. It was a day for riding, or for painting, or for grinding corn, or for beating a ploughshare in a forge. It was a day for creation, not for destruction. And yet … And yet there were times when it was necessary to destroy before one could create …

'How do you feel, Aylwin? Are you warm enough?' Kieron had made him put on a sheepskin coat, realising that it would be cold work when they rose a hundred or more metres into the sky.

'I am warm, Kieron. And you?'

'I also. This day we shall strike a great blow.'

Aylwin shivered. 'It is that thought which makes my heart cold, though my flesh be warm. Shall we succeed?'

'You have my word. If Kentigern and Isidor can get us to true windward, you have my word.'

'And if they can not?'

'We shall strike another day.'

But things went well. Things went well until they came within two kilometres of Little Hampton. It was there that they encountered the first of Admiral Death's outposts. It was not greatly manned – a dozen men, no more.

The foot soldiers advanced and attacked the outpost. Bows and crossbows against muskets and crossbows. Seventeen men of Arundel fell in destroying twelve of the freebooters. And they could not destroy them before a fire signal was sent.

Kieron called down to Kentigern. 'We have not much time. Leave the road and strike west. We must be to true windward.'

'We must attend to our wounded,' called Kentigern.

'No time. Leave the road. Leave a few men if you must, but ride west.'

'Damn you, Kieron. You do not have a bolt in your body. Can you hear their cries?'

'I can. Ride west. Waste no time.'

'I will not.'

'Then you are a fool,' said Kieron. 'If you do not ride west, I will rain the fire on you that I hoped to rain upon the freebooters.' He lighted a torch from a brazier and held it close to one of the oil-soaked bales that hung from the side of *Mistress Fitzalan's Revenge*. 'Do you hear me?'

'I hear you. Damn you for ever, there will be a reckoning.'

'There will indeed,' said Kieron tranquilly. 'Ride west.'

Kentigern shouted a command. The remainder of the foot soldiers – no more than seven or eight – stayed with their fallen comrades. Kentigern and Isidor turned their horses and cantered across a field of burnt stubble. There was a high hedge at the end of it.

'Leap it!' called Kieron. 'The balloon will give you lift!' He signalled to Aylwin to pump bellows at number one while he pumped bellows at number four. The charcoals glowed, the balloon strained. The horses that Isidor and Kentigern rode took a leap of nearly two metres height almost simultaneously. Both landed fair.

Aylwin and Kieron had braced themselves. The balloon, and the boat suspended under it, had begun to sway rhythmically as Kentigern and Isidor took to the fields; but the movement was not jerky, the ropes tightening and then slacking somewhat to accommodate the motion of the horses. Even when they took the two-metre leap, the only sensation experienced by the aeronauts was one of smooth rise and smooth fall.

Kieron kept his eyes on the vessels at Little Hampton, now plainly in view but still about two kilometres away, since Kentigern and Isidor were riding parallel with the coast. He saw also that a group of horsemen were already coming at speed towards the outpost that had been destroyed.

'Hurry,' he called down. 'The freebooters send horsemen. Hurry and take us to true windward.'

Kentigern, red-faced and angry, looked up. 'How much farther, madman?'

'Stop about the middle of the next field. I will test the wind.'

The next hedge was not so high. The horses took it easily.

It must be, thought Kieron with elation, the strangest sight ever seen in Britain: two horsemen drawing a hot-air balloon above and behind them like a monstrous kite. Two horsemen drawing a hot-air balloon from which was suspended a boat containing two young men and their weaponry – all that the seigneurie of Arundel could put against the might of Admiral Death.

He laughed aloud.

Aylwin regarded him anxiously. 'What is it, Kieron? If there is something at which I may laugh, tell me. I would greatly value the ability to laugh now.'

'Look at those ships.'

'I have looked. They are formidable.'

'Now look at us.'

Aylwin looked. At the balloon, at Kieron, at the boat and its contents, at the horsemen below. Miraculously, he, too, began to laugh.

'Kieron, my friend, you were insane for conceiving this venture, and I for consenting to it. You are right to laugh. We are absurd.'

'Not absurd, sublime.'

Aylwin sighed. 'It is a great day for dying.'

'No, my friend, not for us. It is a great day for destroying.'

'I read death.'

'I read destruction.'

'Well, babblers,' called Kentigern, bringing the horses to a halt. 'Are we to windward?'

Kieron let a fragment of paper fall from the boat. It drifted towards Little Hampton as it fell. It drifted towards the cluster of vessels, but not to dead centre.

'To the edge of the field, Kentigern.'

Kentigern swore and spurred his horse. Isidor kept perfect pace with him.

Again Kieron let a fragment of paper fall. It drifted true before it reached the ground. Only let the wind hold, he prayed. Only let it hold steady for a half-hour, no more.

He called down to Kentigern: 'We have arrived at the spot, Kentigern. Thank you. Thank you for giving me this day.'

Kentigern looked up, shielding his eyes against the sun. 'You are a fool, Kieron, but a brave one. I know not if you are touched with greatness or with madness. Farewell.'

'See to Petrina, if—'

Kentigern held up a hand. 'Fear not, boy.' Then he said with a strange formality: 'She shall be as my daughter, and I will spill blood in her defence. This I swear.'

'Then I am in your debt for ever.' Kieron signalled to Aylwin. Together they unhooked the rope. The balloon rose.

Isidor put his hands to his mouth. 'Good hunting, shark of the sky. Eat many freebooters this day.'

The balloon rose, stretching and straining almost like a living thing. For the last time, Kieron looked at the horsemen below and waved. They seemed tiny men sitting upon tiny animals. They seemed like strange insects, earthbound.

Then he gave his attention to the vessels at Little Hampton. The vessels towards which *Mistress Fitzalan's Revenge* slowly drifted, in an eerie, wind-washed silence.

13

For a moment or two, it seemed as if the entire world was a frozen tableau, the only movement being that of the hot-air balloon as it continued to drift and rise slowly. Toy ships lay ahead, toy horsemen were held to the earth below. Kieron experienced a great surge of confidence and power, rejoicing in the silence, the smooth and beautiful movement, rejoicing that he was now free in the element for which he had been born.

Aylwin broke the spell. 'More charcoals, Kieron?' he called anxiously.

Kieron's mind returned to matters practical. The balloon, he calculated, was already at topsail height and still rising, the drift was slow – no more than a fast walking pace. If the breeze did not stiffen, the balloon would reach Admiral Death's flotilla in ten or fifteen minutes.

'No, Aylwin. The heat balance is good. Let us put our main set of grapnel ropes overboard. Pay out about twenty metres of rope and make fast. Then check that your fire-bales are ready for casting off.'

Four grapnels, two from the stem and two from the stern, were lowered. The ropes swayed in the breeze. The iron claws of the grapnels glinted in the sunlight. Kieron hoped to engage the grapnels in the rigging of the ships, using them as a temporary anchor.

'My fire-bales are ready, Kieron.'

'Mine also: Is your torch to hand?'

'It lies at my feet … Are you afraid?'

'Yes, I am afraid. But I am also happy. No, happy is not the right word. Eager – perhaps that is the word.'

'I am greatly afraid. You should have chosen a braver man.'

Kieron smiled. 'I chose well … They cut off your hand, Aylwin. They did unspeakable things to those we love. Remember that.'

'You give me strength.'

'You have your own strength. This day we two shall give a great accounting. Does that make you feel better?'

'It makes me feel like a god.'

Kieron laughed. 'Truly, then, we are as gods. Only men strike from the land or the sea. We strike from the air.'

The balloon drifted inexorably closer to the vessels at Little Hampton. Kieron saw much activity upon their decks. Puffs of smoke appeared at their gun ports; but the guns could not be elevated high enough for their cannon balls to come near the balloon.

'See,' said Kieron, 'they panic, they waste black powder.'

'Soon we shall be in musket range.'

'Then let us have more height. Let us see their musketeers shoot into the sun.'

More charcoals were fed into the braziers. Kieron and Aylwin used their bellows. The balloon climbed.

Now the cluster of vessels was no more than a hundred metres away. Again, Kieron estimated the rate of rise, the the rate of drift.

'Lower the grapnel ropes another fifteen metres.'

'Ay, ay.'

'Make ready to engage.'

'Kieron?'

'Yes, Aylwin?'

'Ludd bless you for giving me this chance.'

'Say no more. Act only on my command. We are about to burn vermin.'

Two of the grapnels caught in the rigging of a vessel lying close between two others. But the pull of the wind took *Mistress Fitzalan's Revenge* away from the vertical, so that directly beneath Kieron there was nothing but water.

'Haul in the grapnel ropes,' he shouted. 'We must be above the deck.'

Aylwin tried to haul in. So did Kieron. But the lift was too strong.

'Quench a fourth part of number one brazier, and I will quench a fourth part of number four.'

They took flasks of water and poured sparingly round the charcoals. Again, there was the temporary lift as the hot steam rose. But after a few seconds they were able to haul in the grapnel ropes. Meanwhile, freebooters had begun to climb the rigging, and musketeers on deck were shooting at the shark of the sky.

Kieron looked down and saw the men climbing the rigging to free the grapnels and the men on deck shooting with their muskets. He did not care. *Mistress Fitzalan's Revenge* was now directly above the vessel she had attacked.

'Two fire-bales!' shouted Kieron hoarsely. 'Two from me also.'

He and Aylwin lighted their torches from the braziers and put fire to two oil-soaked bales as they released them from their hooks.

In a great shower of sparks and flames and oil, the bales fell down to the deck, one of Aylwin's fiery missiles carrying two freebooters from the rigging with it. Their screams died with two dull thuds as they hit the deck, one of them falling directly into the flames.

The binding of the bales broke upon impact and the burning remnants scattered upon the deck. The smoke billowed high, and the freebooters drew back in panic; but there were those also who had already begun to organise a bucket chain to quench the flames. Kieron sent two goatskins of whale oil after the bales. His aim was good. One of the goatskins burst on top of an already substantial blaze, rivulets of fire running across the wooden deck. Two or three of the freebooters, caught by the fierce heat, jumped overboard. The other goatskin exploded upon an open hatchway, leading a trail of fire deep into the ship.

There was pandemonium below. No longer did any of the freebooters attempt to bring down the shark of the sky with musket fire. They were too busy trying to extinguish the raging flames, or trying to save themselves. More and more men jumped overboard.

Kieron, looking down, was satisfied that the vessel was doomed. Now was the time to see to the safety of *Mistress Fitzalan's Revenge*. The heat was so intense that burning fragments of straw were whirled aloft in a fierce up-draught. It would be absurd if the hot-air balloon were destroyed by its own weapons.

'Release the grapnel ropes!' he shouted to Aylwin. 'When we are free, lower the next set. The wind will give us one more vessel.'

The grapnel ropes were released, and the hot-air balloon rose suddenly. The lightening of the load in *Mistress Fitzalan's Revenge* had given it great buoyancy. It soared up from the stricken vessel, like a bird set free. It was necessary for Kieron and Aylwin to completely extinguish two braziers to bring the balloon down to the level of the next vessel's rigging.

They had only two grapnel ropes left. The next vessel was a hundred metres away, direct to windward. It was the largest vessel in the flotilla. It carried a flag on which was the gilded emblem of a death's head. Kieron felt a brief surge of pleasure. This second vessel, the only other ship he could hope to attack, was the flag ship. He prayed that Admiral Death would be aboard.

The hot-air balloon drifted towards it, amid a hail of musket fire. Musket balls penetrated *Mistress Fitzalan's Revenge* and the still taut fabric of the shark of the sky. But neither Aylwin nor Kieron was hit. The two grapnel ropes swayed ominously in the breeze. One of the grapnels caught in the rigging. *Mistress Fitzalan's Revenge* swung crazily.

The crew of the flag ship had learned much from what had happened to the other vessel. Many armed men were already in the rigging. Some paused in their ascent to fire hand guns, but with little hope of hitting the two attackers swinging in their frail craft thirty metres higher than any freebooters could climb; while others, more intelligently, sought to reach the grapnel and cut it loose before any more could be attached.

Kieron saw that there was little time left. 'The bales! Drop all the bales.' He shouted. 'Aim for the highest men.'

Aylwin saw the danger, and understood. He and Kieron put torch to the remaining six bales and sent them hurtling down. Aylwin's aim was good. He seemed to have the knack of it. His first bale slithered and bounced down the rigging, leaving burning straw and burning rope in its path, causing two men to jump into the sea to avoid it. His second bale carried away a man who had almost reached the grapnel rope. Man and bale fell to the deck together in a starburst of death and fire. Kieron's first two bales were less successful, one missing the vessel completely as *Mistress Fitzalan's Revenge* swung in the wind. The other falling clear to the deck, but where it fell there was no fire to be seen, the flames, perhaps, having been extinguished in the manner of its descent.

Aylwin sent down his third bale and was gratified to see it enlarge the fire caused by his first. He laughed aloud with pleasure. As with the first vessel attacked, some weak hearts were already beginning to abandon ship.

Kieron also sent down his third bale. It fell truly, but he was mystified to see no burst of fire as it hit the deck. Perhaps the clouds of smoke obscured it, or perhaps it had passed clean into the depths of the ship through an open hold or hatchway.

Aylwin was fairly jumping with excitement. Kieron saw that the rigging was now burning and that soon the grapnel that held them to the vessel would be burnt loose.

'The goatskins!' he called. 'Drop the goatskins of oil!' There were not many left. Kieron began to drop his supply over the side as fast as he could reach them, not pausing to see where they fell.

The deck of the vessel was now a blazing inferno. Aylwin either had not heard Kieron's command about the goatskins, or he did not care. He stood up in the small craft – a perilous thing to do – and hung on to one of the ropes that held it to the net harness over the shark of of the sky.

'Sit down!' Kieron called.

Aylwin did not respond. His face was alive with immense pleasure. He waved the stump of his wrist proudly and shouted words that Kieron could not comprehend down at the freebooters.

Suddenly Kieron felt a sharp lift as the grapnel came free from the burning rigging. The balloon soared. At almost the same instant, there was a great explosion below as the ship blew itself apart. Evidently, fire had reached a supply of black powder.

The balloon's own buoyancy, relieved as it was of the weight of the bales and the goatskins of whale oil, together with the force of the explosion, shot it upwards like a cork from a shaken bottle of sparkling wine.

Aylwin uttered a great cry, and seemed to leap from the craft into the air. Kieron caught a brief glimpse of him, apparently motionless, spreadeagled in the sky, a look of great contentment on his face. Then Aylwin fell; and Kieron lost his balance as *Mistress Fitzalan's Revenge* rose. And the miller's apprentice was seen no more.

Somehow, as he sprawled in the bottom of his frail craft and hung on for dear life, Kieron managed to keep his wits about him. He looked up and saw that the force of the explosion had blown various small holes in the fabric of the balloon. But, as yet, the rents were small.

Presently, the balloon became steady. Kieron picked himself up and glanced cautiously over the side of his small boat. The sight took his breath away. He had never been so awed, so exhilarated. He must be at least five hundred metres above the ocean.

There below, like tiny toy boats at the edge of a great mill-pond, lay the freebooters' ships. He counted eleven all together – and four were burning! The explosion must have spread the fire to the two nearest ships. The pall of smoke was heavy; but it was clear that three of the burning vessels were certainly beyond saving.

From the height he had attained, everything that was happening below seemed to be in slow motion. Regardless of his own safety and the trim of the balloon, he studied the effects of his attack carefully. It would be something to remember always – no matter how long or how short a time he had left to live.

After a few moments he noticed that the most devastated ship, almost a burning hulk and probably the one that had suffered the explosion, was moving, drifting with the current. Evidently it had been torn free from its moorings by the blast. And now, no doubt assisted by the current of the river Arun in its sea reach, the vessel was bearing down upon two of its fellows, as yet undamaged.

Even from this great height – the balloon was still rising – Kieron could see the flurry of activity on the decks and in the rigging of the threatened ships as seamen desperately weighed anchor and made sail in their attempts to escape a fiery doom.

As Kieron watched, his heart swelling with pride at the destruction that had been wrought, there was a huge puff of smoke from one of the other burning ships. Spars and fragments of timber flew out from it. The sound of the explosion came afterwards, dulled by distance, but still sounding as sweet music.

For a moment, Kieron forgot his plight. 'See, Aylwin!' he called. 'Have I not more than kept my promise?' But even as he spoke, he realised that there was no Aylwin to witness. 'No matter, my friend, my brother. I saw the look upon your face, and you were content. Rest easy. It has been a great accounting. Likely, I will join you soon.'

One of the vessels in the path of the fiery hulk could not get under way fast enough. In its death frenzy the burning ship struck the other vessel amidships. 'See, Aylwin,' said Kieron stupidly, knowing full well that Aylwin was not there to hear, but still feeling an overwhelming need to speak. 'The destruction multiplies. Of eleven ships, we have now accounted for five. We two poor prentices have accomplished more than could be achieved by a thousand armed men on land. Did I not offer you the chance to live for ever?'

And then the tears came. Alone in the sky, Kieron was not ashamed to weep as a child. It was a private luxury. No one would ever know. Presently, no doubt, he would drown – he knew nothing of the skill of handling a small boat far out to sea – but it was a good day on which to die, as Aylwin had already discovered.

'Kristen, my mother,' he sobbed, 'Gerard, my father. I am sorry that I could not become a great painter as you required … Master Hobart, you who gave me great love, sorrow not that I forsook the brush and pigments. *Mistress Fitzalan's Leap* was truly your painting. I was but an extended hand, a youthful eye … Alyx, my dear one, I would have defended you, if I could. But you, whom I loved and who are now dead, if there be an afterlife, which I being perhaps purblind, doubt, look upon what I have done … Petrina, my wife, my seed has entered your womb, and I pray that a child may be born. I hope you will remember this day with pride.'

Kieron was exhausted both in the body and in the spirit. Days and nights of hard work and hard thought, the elation he had felt while fire was being rained upon the freebooters, the sadness of Aylwin's death – all these things had drained him of emotion. He was too tired to think clearly, too tired to act. He lay back in *Mistress Fitzalan's Revenge* and closed his eyes. At the best, he thought drowsily, life was but a short journey from darkness to darkness. He had been lucky, very lucky, to know the love of fair women, to paint a great portrait, to construct a hot-air balloon and sail the skies like a god, bringing death to those who trafficked in death. Yes, he had been very lucky for a poor young man barely turned eighteen. A look of great peace came over his face as he slept.

14

Two braziers still burned; and the shark of the, sky, lightened of the greater part of its burden, continued to rise. Kieron, still profoundly asleep or unconscious, was not aware that the balloon had climbed to nearly two thousand metres above the level of the sea. It passed through a tenuous cloud layer; and dew formed upon his face and hands and hair. Then it rose once more into the gold of sunlight.

The dew made Kieron shiver, and he awoke. He awoke to find himself above gold-capped clouds, drifting, in realms of infinite beauty. He looked down at the islands of cloud. They seemed substantial enough to step upon.

He marvelled at the splendour of the sight. 'Perhaps no man has seen this from an aerial machine for centuries,' he said aloud. 'Likely I am the first of the Third Men to look down upon such clouds and behold their glory. Truly, I am fulfilled.'

But the charcoals in the braziers were burning low and the rents in the balloon were releasing hot air. Kieron was granted only a minute or two of ecstasy before the balloon began to fall through the cloud layer.

He watched, fascinated, as the white mist closed about him and the moisture of the clouds caused the dying charcoals to sizzle and spit. The balloon descended slowly, as if it were reluctant to end this its final flight. The fabric, now slack, was flapping noisily, and the holes in it grew larger. Kieron gazed gloomily down at the sea. There was a light swell; but it was not enough, he thought, to swamp the boat. He looked all round for land, but could see none. Perhaps Aylwin had had the better end after all – a quick clean death. Kieron was no seaman and, despite the quietness of the water, held his prospects to be poor.

Mistress Fitzalan's Revenge hit the water quite hard. For a moment or two, the fabric of the balloon was billowing all about him as if it intended to claim yet one more victim in its death throes. He felt hot charcoals against his legs and tried to cry out with the pain; hot linen and scorched paper pressed about his face as if to smother him.

But presently, relieved of its burden, the tattered shark of the sky tried to rise once more. Hastily, Kieron unhooked the harness ropes. Flapping noisily and self-destructively, the balloon lifted itself like a doomed beast, hovered uncertainly, then rolled over on its side and fell to the sea. Before it sank beneath the water Kieron saw once again the baleful eyes and toothy open mouth he had painted. He smiled, remembering once more the astrologer's prediction, remembering that day long ago when all the world, it seemed, was young.

And now he was alone on a wide sea; and he had no strength and no food, and little hope. It was odd that he should have neglected to stock the vessel with food, particularly so since he had not forgotten a pair of light oars. A man could not row far on an empty belly. Perhaps he had known all along that he did not intend to row far.

He felt even more weary now that all was over. I will rest, he thought. I will close my eyes and rest and think on all that has happened, and try to make my peace. Sooner or later, the sea will receive me. And that will be the end of Kieron-head-in-the-air.

He lay down in the boat, making himself as comfortable as possible, drawing his clothes about him. The motion of the boat was gentle and soothing. It reminded him of a long-lost summer when his father had made a small hammock for him and had hung it between two apple-trees. Kieron had lain on the hammock with his eyes closed, making it sway gently, and pretending that he was a mysterious and magical lord of the air.

'Well, for a short time I became a lord of the air,' he murmured. 'That much, at least, was achieved.'

15

'*Comment vous appelez-vous?*' Kieron felt a sword point at his chest. He tried to reach for his own sword, which had lain all the while by his side in the small boat. He could not find it. The sword at his chest pricked him, and he lay still, trying to gather his wits.

'*Je m'appelle Kieron. Je suis anglais.*' His small knowledge of French had been gained from the occasional matelot who bad ventured inland to Arundel. He realised that it would not stretch far.

'*Alors … Vous connaissez l'amiral mort?*'

'*Oui. Je le connais.*'

'*Vous êtes ami ou ennemi?*'

Now there was a life or death question! Kieron did not care greatly which way it went.

'*Je suis l'ennemi d'Amiral mort. Parlez-vouz anglais?*'

There was a laugh in the semi-darkness. Kieron looked away from the swaying lantern that dazzled him and saw that the sky, dominated by a bright full moon, was rich with stars. The lantern waved high above his head, but he looked past it and concentrated on the beauty of the night sky. If he were to be killed, the stroke would not be long in coming.

'*Un petit peu,*' said the stranger. 'I speak the little English … You can stand?'

'I think so.'

'*Bon.* You will please to follow aboard my ship. You see the rope ladder?'

'Yes.'

'You can climb it?'

'Yes. What about my sword?'

'Rest easy. I have it. Come now. Your boat is made fast.'

Kieron climbed up on to the deck of what looked like a small fishing vessel. The lantern had been held almost directly above him by one of the crew. Now that he was no longer dazzled by it, and now that he had fully regained his senses, he was able to see quite clearly in the moonlight. Yes, perhaps a fishing vessel – or one of Admiral Death's supply tenders. It was odd that the Frenchman had immediately mentioned Admiral Death …

'You are fishermen?'

'*Comment?*'

'Fishermen. You take fish from the sea?'

'*Ah, pêcheurs!*' Again there was a laugh. 'Yes, Monsieur Kieron, you shall say we are fishermen. It is a joke. It is good.'

Kieron glanced round him. It really was a very small vessel, carrying, perhaps, a crew of four or five at most. One man was at the wheel, one man had held the lantern, and there was the stranger who now confronted him. He spoke with authority and carried himself with authority. Very likely, he was the master.

Kieron gazed at him in the moonlight. He was heavily bearded, but he seemed like a young man. He spoke like a young man also.

Kieron wished he had his sword in his hand. But it was in the hand of the French captain. The thought was irritating.

'If you are going to kill me, strike now. I will not play games. The day has been good, and I am content.'

'Monsieur Kieron. Who speaks of killing? We find you – *heureusement*, luckily, because Etienne sees well in the dark – we find you, I say, drifting in a small boat. You were already bound for death, *monsieur*.'

That was something Kieron could not answer.

'It is we who must make the questions, monsieur. For what we know, you may be – how I say it? – *un homme dangereux, un felon, un pirate, peut-être*.'

'*Monsieur*, I do not understand,' said Kieron wearily. 'My name is Kieron Joinerson and I am a man of the seigneurie of Arundel on the island of Britain. You find me adrift in a small boat because I have this day inflicted much damage on the vessels of Admiral Death. I struck at him from the air, having constructed a hot-air balloon. It is something he will remember. Now, do with me what you will.'

'*Un ballon!*' exclaimed the Frenchman excitedly. '*Vous êtes l'homme du balloon? Magnifique! Monsieur*, forgive me. I am *Jean-Baptiste Girod, Capitaine* of the *Marie-France* of *Arromanches*. Today I am make – make is right? – the reconnaissance of the forces of Admiral Death. We in France know that this is bad man, very bad man. We know he hold some British coast. We wish to understand his plan. Today we see marvellous thing. We stand off, you understand. But we use *télescope* – glass, glass! We see this thing *dans le ciel*. It gives *feu* – fire? *Quatre ou cinq vaisseaux sont finis. Merveilleux! Henri, Claude, void l'homme du balloon! Où est le vin?*'

Kieron was dazed. Suddenly, men were shaking him by the hand, clapping him on the back.

'Monsieur Kieron,' said Captain Girod, 'forgive me. I return the sword of a brave man. We are honoured by your presence on the *Marie-France*.'

Kieron took the sword. It felt good in his hand.

'*Messieurs*,' said Captain Girod, '*je vous présente un homme de vaillance. A votre santé, Monsieur Kieron*.'

Miraculously wine and glasses had appeared, brought by a fourth man from below. The Frenchmen raised their glasses and drank deep.

Then Kieron also raised his glass. '*Monsieur le capitaine,* I thank you for saving my life.'

'Monsieur Kieron, it was – I say it right?– my pleasure. I am speak of this in years to come.'

The wine tasted good. No sooner was Kieron's glass empty than it was refilled. He swallowed the good red wine of France and felt a tingling in his limbs.

'Captain Girod,' he said thickly, 'can you set me upon the coast of Britain?'

'Monsieur Kieron, name your destination.' He laughed. 'For you, my friend, I will sail the *Marie-France* even under the guns of *l'Amiral Mort.*'

Kieron smiled faintly. 'I wish only to land two or three kilometres east of Little Hampton.'

'Come below, *monsieur,* where it is warm and light. You shall drink more wine while I look at the charts … We are many kilometres from land, you see. It will take time. I do not think you may put ashore much before daylight. It will be *dangereux* – dangerous.'

'I am familiar with danger.'

'*Pardon. Je suis un fou. Monsieur,* come below. Rest.'

'Captain, I would like to stay on deck a while. I would like to look at the stars.'

'*Ah, les étoiles!*' Captain Girod shook his head uncomprehendingly. 'My ship is yours, *monsieur. Excusez-moi.*'

Kieron stayed on deck for a time and gazed at the night sky. Truly, it was very beautiful. Truly, he had never before realised quite how beautiful those remote points of light were in the mystery that men called the firmament.

Suddenly he began to laugh. He began to laugh because he had just discovered that he was longer indifferent to his own fate. But a short time ago, he had not cared whether he lived or died. Now he knew that he greatly wished to live. To look at the sky on other nights such as this. To construct more balloons and other machines of the air. To hold Petrina close in love and desire. To see his son grow tall … To live … To create and to remember … To suffer and take joy … To live!

He laughed loud and helplessly. Perhaps it is the wine, he told himself, feeling fire in his limbs. I am unused to French wine. But he knew it was not the wine. It was – it was … What was it? The life force! That was a good phrase. He felt he had just invented it. The life force. The force that draws flowers and crops out of the earth, that makes women beautiful and causes men – some men – to lift up their eyes to the stars.

'Some day,' said Kieron, gazing at Sirius, the brightest star of all, 'my children's children will reach out towards you. Think not, bright star, that you are beyond the reach of men.'

Again he laughed, thinking how a small French ship had found him, on a great ocean, thinking how chance had brought him back from the dead. 'By the hammer,' he laughed, 'the astrologer Marcus will yet confound all disbelievers.'

Down below, as Captain Girod consulted his charts, he heard the mad bursts of laughter. He shrugged. It was known that the English had always been a little mad. Clearly this one, who had himself challenged the might of an armed fleet, was much afflicted.

16

Captain Girod was as good as his word. He took the *Marie-France* close in to the south coast of Britain almost exactly three kilometres east of Little Hampton. The stars were fading and the sky was turning grey as Kieron clambered over the side of the French ship and prepared to row ashore in his small boat.

'*Monsieur*,' said Captain Girod, 'we have been honoured by your company. Please accept this small gift and remember us with affection.' He handed Kieron a flask of *eau de vie*. 'Some day, I think, our nations will again work together. You will drink to that?'

'I will drink to that. Captain Girod, you have saved my life, but I have no gift to offer.'

'Monsieur Kieron, we already have your gift. *Merde, alors.* It was *formidable. Un homme du del contre les bateaux de l'Amiral Mort*. Please, we shall tell our children's children of this thing. We have your gift. *Soyez tranquille.* Rest easy.'

'I beg one more favour, Captain. Give me oil. Give me the means of making fire.'

'Pourquoi? You cannot make the attack from this small boat.'

'No, Monsieur. I wish to burn my boat when I have landed. It has served me well. No other shall use it.'

'Monsieur Kieron, I comprehend.'

A member of the crew brought a large bottle of oil, some waste cloth and a lighted candle-cup. Kieron stored the candle-cup carefully in his boat so that the breeze would not extinguish the flame.

'Goodbye, Captain, and thank you. May you have a safe voyage home.'

'*Bonne chance, Monsieur.* We salute your audacity. It will be remembered.'

Kieron pulled for the shore. He could only see it dimly, but it seemed to be deserted. There was little swell, but the tide was with him. As he rowed, the *Marie-France* swung slowly round and faded slowly like a ghost in the pre-dawn light.

By the time he had beached, the red rim of the sun had risen above the horizon. Kieron hauled his boat clear of the water. The soft sand felt good beneath his feet. He was amazed at how good it felt. But perhaps that was because he had not expected to walk on dry land again.

He looked along the shore both ways. It was totally deserted. He sat down for a while, picking up handfuls of sand and letting it trickle between his fingers. A sense of desolation grew oddly upon him. He felt that he was the last man alive.

After a time, his mind returned to practicalities. The candle-cup was still burning. He made a small pile of the waste cloth he had been given, then he searched for fragments of flotsam. He found a few splintered pieces of ships' timber, not large, but enough to make a small bonfire with the waste cloth. He poured oil over it and placed the candle-cup beneath a strip of the soaked rag. The flames leaped high. For a moment or two he stood warming himself, realising that he had felt very cold.

Then he recollected the purpose of the bonfire. He turned *Mistress Fitzalan's Revenge* upside down and kicked repeatedly at the thin strips of wood until they were stove in. Then he lifted the wreckage of the boat and let it fall upon the bonfire.

Sparks rose mightily. The wet timbers sizzled and crackled and steamed and smoked. Finally, they burst into flame; and *Mistress Fitzalan's Revenge* was at last consumed by the very element she had carried to destroy the vessels of Admiral Death.

Kieron waited until all the wood of the small boat had been reduced to embers. By which time, the sun was well clear of the horizon. He looked at the glowing ashes and the fragments of charred wood. Soon the incoming tide would reach them, and all traces of the boat would be washed away for ever … This, too, had been a funeral pyre.

Now it was time to return to the living. The sky was blue and it was going to be another fine day. Kieron judged it time to strike quickly inland, lest he encounter any of the freebooters abroad early. He gazed westward, along the beach and out to sea; but he could see no sign of them or their vessels. Which was of no great significance, since the coast curved, and Little Hampton was out of sight.

Kieron left the shore and took to the fields and moorland, passing near the ruins of several abandoned cottages. There was still the smell of smoke and death about them. No doubt they had recently suffered the ministrations of the freebooters.

Although it would have been easier to head directly for Arundel, Kieron judged this not to be a wise course. After the onslaught from the air, Admiral Death may well have decided to march inland, exacting retribution from any who had been so bold as to attempt to reoccupy their damaged towns and villages. Better by far to make a wearisome detour through fields and woodland, perhaps eventually coming to the Misery from the east or the north.

If Kieron had not been persuaded to sleep aboard the *Marie-France*, at least he had been persuaded to eat. Captain Girod had given him good bread, and sliced meat, and Normandy cheese. But that was hours ago; and now he felt hungry once more. He had nothing to eat, but he did have the flask of *eau de vie*. He took out its stopper and drank. The fluid set his limbs on fire and took away the pains of hunger; but it did not seem to cloud his mind. Rather, it appeared to bring clarity of thought and to supply energy.

Kieron strode rapidly across the long stretches of grassland, sword in one hand, flask in the other. Occasionally, he sang songs, occasionally he drank. Always he looked for signs of men. But the world, it seemed, was deserted. Perhaps it was no sad jest to imagine himself as the last man alive.

Now he could see the towers and battlements of Arundel castle. There was no obvious sign of activity. But he stayed well to the east of the castle and travelled north. He felt desperately tired and very thirsty. Even the *eau de vie* could no longer stave off the hunger pains.

It seemed to be a warm morning. The weather was kind. How pleasant it would be to sit down and rest a while. He was greatly tempted; but then he recollected that the only safe place to rest would be the Misery, and prefer- ably in the arms of Petrina.

Somehow he managed to keep himself moving. With luck, and if he used his remaining energy carefully, he would reach the Misery in less than two hours, perhaps even in little more than one.

The sun had already passed its zenith by the time he reached the encamp- ment. He approached it from the north and wondered why he was not challenged by sentinels or watch men. Kentigern, it seemed, was getting careless.

Kieron felt weak. He could not see very clearly, he could not now think very clearly, and his gait was none too steady. For want of food, he had emp- tied the flask of *eau de vie* given him by Captain Girod. But his wits still functioned, if slowly. When he entered the clearing, he stood swaying and taking in the scene with much amazement. Not many people remained, and there were several faces he did not recognise. Everyone seemed to be fran- tically busy making bundles of their belongings and loading them upon horse-drawn or hand-drawn carts.

Kentigern was there, he saw, supervising the loading of the carts. Petrina was there also. They were so busy that they did not notice him at first. He staggered forward. Petrina was the first to turn her head.

'Kieron! Kieron, my beloved! I knew you were not dead!' She ran to him, held him close, supported him, kissed his face and hair. 'I knew you would come. They said you had fallen into the sea from a great height. But I knew you would come.'

'Forgive me, I'm drunk,' was all he could say. 'No food. Much *eau de vie*. Forgive me.'

Great shouts went up from the people. 'Kieron!' 'The Cloud Walker has returned!' 'Kieron is here!' 'Ludd protect us, he has risen from the dead!'

Kentigern came forward. Kieron felt his knees giving way but Petrina held him, strangely poured strength back into him.

'What is this?' he said thickly. 'Where are the rest of our people? Who are these I do not know? What is happening?' He raised the sword he still held, the sword that seemed now a part of himself.

Kentigern said: 'Rest easy, Kieron. Put your sword down. The battle is over. These are slaves escaped from the shattered vessels of Admiral Death. They help us to return to our homes, that is all ... I did not think that you would live. Through the glass, you were seen to fall into the sea from a great height.' He shrugged. 'But you, I think, are a man to confound the Devil.'

'It was not I, but Aylwin who fell.'

'So. Aylwin, who was your friend, was also touched by greatness ... Kieron, you destroyed five vessels, so the escaped slaves tell us, and blew a leg off Admiral Death who is now near to that condition signified by his name. The freebooters have departed from Little Hampton. Perchance, they did not know that there was only one shark of the sky ... So we return to our homes, Kieron. We shall rebuild the town and take some precautions against a repetition of recent disasters. This meets with your approval?'

'I am content,' Kieron managed to say. 'I will live in Master Hobart's house, and, to please a certain astrologer, I will beget three sons.'

Then, despite Petrina's support, he fell unconscious.

The people in the Misery drew close, watched Petrina lift his head, press it to her breast.

'Look upon this man,' said Kentigern. 'He is but eighteen years old, and he was known as a fool. Yet he has delivered us. I, Kentigern, kneel before him. Let no one stand at this time unless he presumes to be a better man.'

The people in the Misery knelt before Kieron. Then, after a space, they made a bed for him on one of the carts. Petrina lay beside him, stroking his white hair. Then they loosed the horses from the cart, and ten men drew him to Master Hobart's house.

17

For the next few days, every man, woman and child who had returned to the town of Arundel worked throughout every hour of daylight and through many of the hours of darkness, also. Walls, doors, windows, even roofs were to be mended, new furniture and furnishings had to be sought or constructed; food had to be got; tools and weapons had to be fashioned; the sick and wounded had to be cared for; and a start had to be made on repairing the damage done at the castle.

Kentigern, in the absence of other authority, assumed responsibility for the seigneurie. He sent messengers east and west to discover if Admiral Death's entire fleet had quit the southern coast of England or had only sought refuge farther from the source of the fire-balloon. He sent messengers with the news of the result of Kieron's attack to the grand seigneurs at London. He organised companies of men to clear the streets of the stinking corpses of freebooters, to mend fences and walk, to round up stray cattle, to scythe the last few fields of corn, to hunt for deer, pheasants, rabbits.

During the first day of the return, Kieron was the only man in the seigneurie who rested. Master Hobart's house had been little damaged and needed little attention. Men fitted a new door and a new window quietly while he slept. Women brought rich brocade for curtains – sent by Kentigern from the castle – and children laid bundles of wild flowers by the doorstep, as if at a shrine.

Kieron slept entirely throughout the first day and the first night. He awoke refreshed on the following morning – refreshed and very hungry, and filled with the unquenchable vigour of youth. He breakfasted greedily; and the breakfast he was given was fit for a seigneur: oatmeal porridge with cream and honey, cold pheasants' breast with pickle and new baked bread, preserve of strawberries and a bottle of golden wine called hock, sent from the castle cellars with the compliments of Kentigern.

Kieron ate all the porridge, disposed of the breasts of two fine cock pheasants, and drank half the bottle of wine. Then he held Petrina close to him and stroked her hair.

'I am alive,' he said wonderingly. 'I am still alive.'

'And you must remain alive for some time,' said Petrina, 'if you are to fulfil your promise.'

'What did I promise?'

'To beget three sons.' She laughed. 'If only to make an honest man of the astrologer Marcus.'

'I will keep my promise,' he asserted. 'I have need of sons. To reconquer the air will take more strength than I possess.'

Petrina's face became grave.

'You do not smile?' he asked. 'You used to be amused by the strange notions of Kieron-head-in-the-air.'

'I thought they were idle fancies. I did not then know the terrible reality.'

He kissed her. 'Be of good cheer, Petrina. I came back, did I not?'

'Yes.'

'And I will always come back. Even though the sky is my true home.'

She gave him a sad smile. 'Your true home … You must know that it is a frightening thought for me … Ah, well, I must make the best of it. I am lucky to have you … No one calls you Kieron-head-in-the-air any more. Did you know that?'

'What do they call me, then?'

'The Cloud Walker. Since your foolish dream became a terrible reality, they laugh no more. They are proud of you. They ask after your health. They ask what the Cloud Walker will do next.'

Kieron laughed. 'That is easy to answer. Having rested and eaten well and known the comfort of his wife, he will go forth to help restore life to our little town.'

'Be not surprised at how men receive you,' Petrina called after him. 'There are some, even, who think you have risen from the dead.'

It was a dull, overcast morning, but the air was warm. Kieron found much activity in the High Street. Carpenters and plasterers were at work. Women cleaned steps with chalk stone and swilled pavements with water. Everywhere there was much bustle as people strove to make their town look as if the freebooters had never been.

Kieron found himself greeted with great deference. Men twice his age, who would formerly have dismissed him with a shrug or a condescending smile, touched their hats or hair and addressed him as Master or Sir. Young men of his own age, with whom he had been wont to exchange insults or jokes, looked upon him with awe, vied for his attention. No one seemed inclined to let him help at menial tasks. Kieron felt alone and uncomfortable. He was greatly relieved when he saw Kentigern approach, presumably upon his round of inspection.

'Well, Kentigern. The town recovers rapidly, I see. Do you have news of the freebooters?'

'Ay, Master Kieron, I have news. Better news, perhaps than we dared hope for. Admiral Death survived your attentions but briefly. He perished, I am told, in much agony in a freebooter's vessel anchored off the Isle of Wight.

With his passing, the command of the freebooters disintegrated. They quar-relled among themselves. Slave crews rebelled. Some freebooter ships fired upon each other. But, more important, they have all left these shores.' He grinned. 'No doubt the story of the attack of the shark of the sky grew with the telling. They had no means of knowing that the same dreadful assault would not be made again.'

'Well, then,' said Kieron, 'Mistress Fitzalan's Revenge has justified her name.'

'More than that,' said Kentigern. 'Sir, I envy you. Mistress Alyx Fitzalan has been avenged mightily.'

Kieron was at a loss. 'It was not for her alone, you understand.'

'Master Kieron, let us not speak any more of these things. There are words best left unsaid ... Now to more immediate matters. I have inspected the records of lineage, mercifully untouched by the freebooters. Somewhere in the Ameri-cas, there is a Seigneur Howard who will undoubtedly inherit from Seigneur Fitzalan. But until and if Seigneur Howard returns to this island, do I have your consent to remain as bailiff of the castle and steward of the seigneurie?'

Kieron was confused. 'You do not need my consent.'

Kentigern laughed. 'Master Kieron, forgive me, in matters practical you are still a fool. I did not save the seigneurie. You did. The people will follow you to the death. If you wish to assume the duties of administration, you are welcome. They are heavy enough, and the burden does not please me.'

'I know nothing of such matters,' said Kieron hurriedly. 'Do not confuse me. You are the bailiff of Arundel. You have my allegiance.'

'I am truly relieved to know it,' confessed Kentigern. 'If men did not know that you accepted my authority, there would doubtless be trouble. A true seigneur they would not question, but a bailiff ...'He shrugged.

'Here is my hand on it, then.'

'I take it in friendship.' Kentigern held out his own. 'What will you do now that the freebooters have gone? Until Seigneur Howard reveals himself, or until the Grand Council appoints a surrogate seigneur, there will be little work for a master artist.'

'I do not wish to paint, except for my own pleasure.'

Kentigern stroked his chin thoughtfully. 'So. Then my task is easier ... By the authority I hold until relieved, as bailiff of the seigneurie of Arundel for the late Seigneur Fitzalan and his heirs or assigns, I now appoint you, Master Kieron Joinerson, Warden of the Coast and Captain of Aerial Warfare. These posts to bring in fee one thousand schilling each per year, payable in portions on the quarter days ... Can you and your family live upon two thousand schilling, Kieron?'

Two thousand schilling! It was far more money than he had ever seen. It seemed a princely fee. Kieron's father had never earned more than two hun-dred schilling a year in all his life.

Kieron was overwhelmed. 'Two thousand schilling is more than enough,' he managed to say. 'But what am I to do for all this money?'

'Why, man, you are to construct hot-air balloons. What else? You are to make sure that never again shall we be so punished by the scum of the oceans. You are to defend us from neighbouring seigneuries; for it is certain that, with the death of Seigneur Fitzalan, there will be those who cast greedy eyes upon Arundel. Possession, you will recall, is nine points of the law. Well, Kieron, will you defend us?'

'To the best of my ability.'

Kentigern laughed heartily. 'That is more than a guarantee. For years to come, Kieron, your name alone will be worth more than a hundred well-armed horsemen ... Of course, the seigneurie will pay for all the arms, materials and supplies you require. Also, men will be trained according to your instructions. Does this meet with your approval?'

'It meets with my approval,' said Kieron weakly.

'Well, then, my friend. Go home and devise plans. Send me a reckoning of what you require in men and materials. Make us invincible, that is all.'

18

For the second time, Kieron was awakened with a sword-point at his chest. Petrina, lying by his side, opened her eyes and screamed at what she saw by the light of a lantern and the pre-dawn greyness that crept through the window. She saw two armoured men, wearing tabards on which were blazoned the device of the Inquisitor General of the Luddite Church. One man held the lantern, the other held the sword.

'You are Kieron Joinerson, lately apprenticed to Master Hobart, the painter?'

'He is the one,' said a dark, cowled figure standing by the doorway.

Kieron recognised the voice of Brother Lemuel.

'Silence, brother,' said the man with the sword. 'You have done your work. Let him speak for himself.'

Petrina desperately covered her nakedness. The night had been one of passion and desire. Kieron tried to clear his head and concentrate. He gazed at the heraldic device upon the tabards: a golden hammer upon a field of azure above symbolic flames worked in thread of gold.

'You are Kieron Joinerson? Speak, fellow. Else I loosen your tongue.'

'I am Kieron Joinerson.'

'Then dress quickly. Your presence is required in the great hall of the castle.'

'My wife?'

'We have no instructions concerning your wife. Hurry, man! The Holy Office does not brook delay.'

'What is the cause of this intrusion?'

'You will know soon enough, if you do not know already. Hurry man!'

Kieron kissed Petrina. 'Rest easy, my love. Do not offend them. Kentigern will deal with this nonsense. That I swear.'

He climbed out of bed and put on his clothes. Petrina lay under the sheets and blankets, shaking and trying to stifle her weeping, cursing her nakedness.

When Kieron was dressed, the sword was held towards his belly while his arms were tied behind his back.

'Petrina, my sister,' said Brother Lemuel with a gentle voice, 'in this time of trial, do you require the consolations of Holy Church?'

Petrina raised her head from the blankets. 'Get from my presence!' she hissed. 'Go elsewhere and corrupt children. After this day's work no woman in the seigneurie will look upon you but to spit.'

Kieron laughed. He laughed with joy to find that his wife had such spirit. He was rewarded by a buffet in the mouth from the lantern-holder. His lip bled, and he savoured the salt taste.

'Sir, I will remember that you struck a bound man. There will be a reckoning.'

The man with the lantern laughed. 'Ay, there will be a reckoning, Master Kieron. When the flames leap high, there will be a reckoning. March!'

Kieron was led out into the street. More armed men were waiting. They surrounded him, as if fearful that the townsfolk might move to release him. But the sun had not yet shown itself, and the people of Arundel still slept after their heavy labours. Whoever had planned this event had planned well.

But as Kieron was marched to the castle, his spirits rose. Kentigern would surely have enough authority to stop this idiocy.

At the castle, the strength of the Inquisitor General's forces was made more apparent. Kieron saw foot soldiers guarding the castle gate; and in the yard there were ten or more horses showing signs of recent and hard travel

Kieron was taken into the great hall, where lamps and a fire burned, and where Brother Hildebrand awaited him together with officers of the Inquisitor General. There also stood Kentigern. Kieron was amazed to note that his hands were bound also.

'Good morning, Kieron,' said Brother Hildebrand. 'You see now to what a condition your persistent heresy has brought you.'

'Good morning, brother,' said Kieron caustically. 'Your task being what it is, I do not wonder that you come like a thief in the night.'

The soldier who had struck him in the bedroom struck him once more. Kieron reeled from the blow. 'I will remember your bravery, fellow,' Kieron grated. 'Pray that I am never unbound.'

He turned to Kentigern. 'Did you not set watch men?'

Kentigern gave a mirthless smile. 'They were not instructed to guard us against the Luddite Church, Kieron. I truly regret the error. The freebooters at least struck as our enemies. These presume to be our friends.'

'We shall pray greatly for you,' said Brother Hildebrand. 'Ludd's will be done. Whatever may befall, rest assured that we shall save your immortal souls.'

'With such friends,' said Kieron, 'we have no need of enemies.'

'Silence, fellow!'

A man stood forward. He wore the habit of a neddy; but round his neck there hung a silver chain, and from the chain a small golden hammer was suspended. He carried a scroll which he opened and from which he then read.

'To Kieron, apprentice of Master Hobart, painter, and to Kentigern, bailiff of Seigneur Fitzalan of the seigneurie of Arundel, greetings. I. Xavier, Inquisitor General of the Holy Luddite Church, commend your souls to Ludd, and require the servants of the Church to convey you to the Sacred College of Nedd Ludd in the city of London where you shall be tried for diverse heresies and sundry treasons. It is my wish that my beloved brother Constant, Steward of the Inquisition, shall have regard for your comfort and safety upon the journey and shall bring you in safety to judgment, which shall be given by the Inquisitor General upon the advice of ten High Stewards and such persons as may speak in your favour.'

Kentigern laughed. 'They mean to burn us, Kieron. It is humorous, is it not? You destroyed the freebooters with your hot-air balloon, and I gave you some small assistance. They mean to burn us. That is droll – if not unexpected.'

'By the hammer, I would like to see them try to burn us if the trial were held in this seigneurie.'

'By the hammer, Kieron, you have the truth of it!' shouted Kentigern. He turned to the Steward Constant, who had just read from the scroll. 'It is an ancient right, Steward, granted to all men, that, if accused of any crime, including heresy, they may choose to be tried in their own seigneurie and in the presence of their people.'

Constant gave an unpleasant laugh. 'It is true, fellow, that a man may choose to be tried in his own seigneurie; but first he must plead such choice in the presence of his seigneur. You have no seigneur. Holy Church, as always, acts within the law and maintains the law … Now, it is a long ride to London. Do you go peaceably, or do my officers knock you on the head and draw you like meat in a cart?'

Kieron and Kentigern looked at each other in dismay.

'It is better to go peaceably,' said Kieron. 'A man with his wits about him still has the dignity of a man.'

'Bind their mouths,' said Constant. 'We must be away before sunrise, else this confused and misguided citizenry may note and dispute our passage.'

Cloths were placed over the mouths of Kieron and Kentigern. Then, with armed men escorting them, they were led out into the castle yard, where saddled horses were now waiting.

Kieron glanced hopefully at the sty. But there was much low cloud, and light would be slow in coming. By the time that people were abroad and the situation made known to them, a troop of horsemen could be many kilometres to the north. He thought of Petrina. When he had been hustled out of his bed chamber, Brother Lemuel had remained. Guards also had been left at the door of Hobart's house. He hoped no harm would come to her. But it would be a terrible thing for her to live the rest of her life as the widow of a man burned for heresy. And there was the child … How would the son of the Cloud Walker feel when he was old enough to understand the fate of his father?

'Have the prisoners well mounted,' said Constant. 'We ride hard. I am entrusted with their safety. I have no wish to explain a broken neck to the Inquisitor General. Also,' he laughed, 'they may yet prove innocence.'

A soldier, helping Kieron to mount his horse, grunted, coughed, opened his eyes wide with surprise and fell to the ground. In the half-light, Kieron saw an arrow shaft protruding from his back.

'Let no one move,' said a voice, 'unless he wishes to follow this one rapidly to eternity.'

'Mount!' shouted Constant. 'Mount, everyone! Let us away!'

Two more men tried to force Kieron into the saddle. Both died.

The Steward Constant stood quite still, peering in the half-light, seeing no one. So did the rest of his party.

'You who are hidden,' called Constant, 'know that I am a Steward of the office of the Inquisitor General and that I lawfully take these men to give account of themselves in his presence. Justice shall be done.'

'You who are not hidden,' answered the voice, 'rest easy. Do not move. Justice shall indeed be done. I will count three. Upon the count of three, all men bearing weapons will let them fall, or they will die. One … Two … Three.'

There was a great clatter as swords, daggers, crossbows and bolts fell to the ground. Kieron looked joyfully about him. The light was gaining strength. He could now vaguely discern figures on the battlements, men crouched by the stables, men standing shoulder to shoulder with drawn bows in the castle gateway.

'That is most sensible,' said the voice. 'Now we may talk.' A man stepped out of the shadows to be revealed as Isidor. Two more men followed him, cutting the ropes that bound Kieron and Kentigern and tearing the cloth bindings from their mouths.

'You come opportunely,' said Kentigern.

'You must thank Mistress Petrina for that,' said Isidor solemnly. 'I am told she broke a chamber pot over the head of a prating neddy; and then, disguised in his habit, left the guarded house to raise the alarm.'

Kieron burst out laughing. 'Miracles come aplenty. Two boys and a hot-air balloon rout the freebooters, and the power of the Luddite Church is broken by a chamber pot. Ludd, it seems, does not always favour the big battalions.'

Kentigern rubbed his wrists and looked at the Steward Constant. 'This creature was about to take us to London for a burning.'

'We knew their plans,' said Isidor. 'We found one who talked with much enthusiasm and a dagger at his throat … I decided not to lead men into the castle, not knowing if they would kill you in the mêlée.'

'An excellent decision. But they would not have killed. Such tricksters need to have their crimes approved in writing.' He turned to the Luddite officers and soldiers, who had now been lined up by more of Isidor's followers. 'Well, fellows, you came not openly to perform your task but under cover of darkness like common rogues. You did not bring your arms when we needed them to drive out the invader. It seems your masters were not overly concerned with the fate of our women and children, having more important matters to consider – such as the dreadful crime of conspiring to construct a hot-air balloon. I have ever shown respect for the Church and its teachings, even when I thought them severe. But now that I have seen how the Luddite Church cares for its flock, I say we have no need of such madness in this seigneurie.'

His words were followed by a great roar of approval. Kieron looked round. The light was gaining strength. It seemed now that all the grown men and many of the women of Arundel were assembled in the castle yard. He saw Petrina and smiled at her.

Kentigern confronted the Steward. He snapped the silver chain that hung round Constant's neck and let the small golden hammer drop at his feet. He put his foot upon it and ground it with his heel. He took the scroll from Constant's hand and slowly tore in into pieces. The Steward stood pale, motionless, surmising perhaps that his last hour had come.

'So, master champion of Holy Writ, you have heard the voice of the people – the free people of Arundel. Many have lost wives, husbands, sons, daughters, while such as you meditated upon the wickedness of heretical acts. I doubt that any man or woman present would shed a tear if we hanged a dozen Luddites before breaking our fast.'

Again there was a great roar of approval.

'But do not tremble, sir Steward. We are civilised folk – until we are greatly wronged. So you may return to your Inquisitor General in London and give him our thanks for the fine horses he has sent us and for the arms. Say they arrived late, but no matter. Say also that Kentigern sends his regrets, but chooses to remain bailiff of the seigneurie of Arundel until an inheritor is recognised. Say also that Master Kieron Joinerson is too busy to attend his trial for heresy, having been appointed Warden of the Coast, Captain of Aerial Defence and – most recently – Master of Machines. Say finally that, if any force be raised against us, if any Luddite mission again enters this seigneurie, we shall reply most dreadfully with fire from the air and with machines of destruction beyond the imaginings of such as you … You will remember these words?'

'I – I will remember them,' Constant managed to say, though his voice was very small.

'Go, then, Six hours from now, dogs and men on horseback shall be sent after you. It will go ill if they find you upon the lands of the seigneurie.' Kentigern turned to the crowd. 'Do I speak for you?'

'By the hammer—' shouted someone, then changed his mind. 'By the reach of the Cloud Walker, you speak for us.' There were cheers and much laughter.

'A last reckoning,' called Kentigern. 'Where are they who brought vermin in our midst?'

The two neddies, Lemuel and Hildebrand, were pushed forward. Lemuel wore only his stockings and a long undershirt. There was blood upon his head and an expression of great mortification upon his face. Hildebrand had the look of one who expected sudden death.

Kentigern stared hard at them both. 'You, I cannot find it in my heart to forgive nor your deeds to forget. You were of our people, your parents, whom you dishonour, raised you in the seigneurie, you saw the terrible destruction we endured. And yet, with pious words, you sought to work more mischief. It is my judgment that chains shall be set upon your hands and legs for a twelve-month. You shall sleep on straw in the stables, and you shall be any man's labourers. If you attempt to escape we shall hunt you with dogs. Be thankful that you live, fellows. Our justice is more gentle than yours would have been.'

Kentigern faced his people. 'My friends, I am not your seigneur; and likely it will be many years before one sits in the castle once more. But I will do my best for the seigneurie. That is all I can say.'

'It is enough!' someone shouted. 'We will have no strangers now. You know us and we know you. Raise hands those who accept Kentigern.'

There was much shouting and cheering, as a forest of hands rose high.

'Well, then,' said Kentigern gaily, 'I am overwhelmed, being too much of a coward to challenge the will of the people … Not many days ago I was in a sad humour, being half convinced that the world was ending. Then the Cloud Walker came to me with wild talk of a hot-air balloon with which he would attack our enemies. He was mad, of course.'

The crowd roared with laughter.

'But his madness was infectious, it seems … And, my friends, was it not an inspired madness? The world we knew has ended, a world in which it was a mortal sin for a man to devise something that would help his fellow men. But the Cloud Walker has given us the opportunity to build a new world. Shall we build that new world, or shall we return to the old ways?'

'The new!' they shouted. 'Let us build the new!'

'I hear your answer,' said Kentigern. 'Well, my friends, set these creatures who came against us back on the road to London. Then go to your homes and eat well, for there is much hard work ahead for all.'

As the crowd dispersed, and the officers of the Inquisitor General were jeered on their way, Petrina came to Kieron's side. He put his arm round her shoulders. 'It was a heavy chamber pot?' he asked.

'It was a satisfyingly heavy chamber pot.' She laughed. 'I had no time to remove the contents.'

Kieron turned to Kentigern. 'I did not know you had such eloquent words in you.'

'Nor did I,' confessed Kentigern. 'Kieron, I am in your debt. I greatly fear that your strange ideas have made a man of me.'

'A man,' observed Kieron, 'must either fall or rise in adversity.'

'Well said. But now we have many problems. Likely, the Luddite Church will try to reassert its authority. How much time do you need to construct hot-air balloons?'

'How many?'

'Let us say five.'

Kieron was aghast 'Five? You want me to make five?'

'Let us hope for the best and prepare for the worst,' said Kentigern.

'Can you give me a hundred men?'

'Yes.'

'And a thousand square metres of linen and paper?'

'Yes – if I have to send riders abroad, and strip every woman in the seigneurie of her petticoats.'

'Well, then, in five days you shall have five hot-air balloons, armed and ready to defend the seigneurie.'

'That is better than I hoped. I think it will take the Luddites at least eight days to raise a force against us – if they have the stomach for it.'

Petrina shivered and said: 'Kieron, come. The sun has risen. We must eat.'

'My love, I am too busy. There is much to think about, much to do.'

Kentigern cleared his throat. 'Cloud Walker, I command you in little. But it is necessary that you remain alive and in good health. Must I send men to hold you while you are fed?'

Kieron laughed. 'You are a hard master, Kentigern. But I have a sterner mistress. I live, now, in fear of chamber pots. I will eat.'

19

By the time he was twenty-eight years old, Kieron had become a legend and had achieved the reputation of being immortal. He had broken both legs, both arms and had sustained other injuries that would have consigned many lesser men to the grave. He had endured all this because of his obsession with the conquest of the air. Hot-air balloons he had left behind him. These were now the province of his less-gifted apprentices and craftsmen. His present obsession was with sailplanes, machines that would glide through the air like birds.

The Luddite Church had never again challenged the seigneurie of Arundel. The Luddite Church was in decline. As the news of Kieron's successful attack upon the forces of Admiral Death had spread quickly through neighbouring seigneuries and more slowly through the rest of the island's seigneuries, followed hard by the news that the Luddite Church had been proscribed in Arundel, men of intelligence everywhere began to think about these matters. The Church had been made to look ridiculous by its furtive attempt to capture the Cloud Walker – the only man who had known how to deal with the freebooters – and charge him with heresy. More, the Church had not only been made to look ridiculous, it had become ridiculous – showing plainly that it was concerned more with dogma than with the welfare of the people.

For centuries the Luddites, drawing their inspiration from the fates that had overtaken the First Men and the Second Men, had maintained their power by fear, authoritarianism, and punishment. They had attempted, as it were, to freeze history, to maintain a society that neither declined nor improved. They had attempted to imprison the spirit of man like a fly in amber. Countless ingenious, inventive and creative people, attempting to improve their own lot and that of their fellow creatures, had been imprisoned, tortured, burned in order to maintain the doctrine that machines were anathema. But a strange and wonderful machine had been necessary to defeat Admiral Death; and the people of the seigneurie of Arundel had delivered their verdict upon the teachings of the Church.

Men of intelligence dwelt upon these matters. Young men – ambitious and imaginative young men – throughout the country regarded the Cloud Walker with as much awe and reverence as their fathers and forefathers had regarded the Divine Boy. Many of the adventurous ones – young men with strange ideas and fanciful notions – broke their apprenticeships, left home and kith and kin, and journeyed to Arundel to seek service with the man who seemed to them to have opened the door to a new golden age. Some were recaptured by their masters or parents and were punished by their seigneurs or by the Church. But enough reached the Free Seigneurie, as they called it, to provide the Cloud Walker with an élite corps of young men with ideas.

He received them joyfully as brothers, sons, companions of the spirit. The best of them lived in his house, ate at his table, having free access to their beloved Cloud Walker. Kieron had long since fulfilled the prediction of the astrologer Marcus and had begotten three sturdy sons. Master Hobart's house had been considerably extended to accommodate wife, sons, and chosen apprentices in comfort. It was no longer just a house. It was a small university.

Petrina had grown beautiful with the years, even more opulent in her body, and immensely proud of her husband and her sons. She presided over her extensive household like a queen. Students competed for her smile and approval. No one but Kieron aspired to her love. Each time he experimented with a new flying machine, she held her breast tightly and tried vainly not to weep. When he was brought home in pain, she soothed him and ministered to him and gave him hope for the future.

Sometimes, she looked at the painting of *Mistress Fitzalan's Leap* that he had lovingly restored, his last act as a master painter. Sometimes she hated that slender, bright-eyed girl, sitting a horse so wonderfully between earth and sky. Sometimes she wept for her. Alyx Fitzalan had never known the joy of lying with her love, had never borne three sons.

Always, Petrina gave herself freely to Kieron – her mind, her spirit, her body. To her alone he was not the Cloud Walker. To her only he was a man who drove himself too hard, a lonely man whose tears and anguish and desire could only be released in the anonymity of darkness.

One day, when the wind was right, blowing steadily from the east, Kieron sat in the aeronaut's cage of his seventh sailplane. It lay upon the beach at Little Hampton, attached to a rope that would be drawn at his signal by eight good horses, the best that Kentigern could supply.

He sat thinking, waiting for the wind to stiffen. He was thinking of the six preceding sailplanes. The first one – no more than a pair of imitation bird wings with a central harness for a man – had actually left the ground but had turned over in flight. Kieron had been lucky to escape with a broken arm only. The second one, having two wings, one set above the other, had not even left the ground, having been shaken to pieces as it was drawn along the beach by a team of horses. The third one, shaped like a gull in gliding flight and made cunningly of wood and canvas, had risen beautifully, only to have its wings broken by the fierce pressure of air, so that Kieron had fallen like a stone into the sea and, having broken a leg, had only been saved from drowning by a devoted apprentice who was a great swimmer. The fourth and fifth sailplanes had been subtle variations upon the gull design. There was a gifted apprentice, Bruno of York, who had travelled on foot across the length and breadth of England to reach the Free Seigneurie. Bruno, like his master, was obsessed by flight and had greatly studied the aerial movements of such birds as the swift and the swallow. He spoke convincingly of air resistance and the importance of what he called smooth or streamed lines. He, though not yet twenty, unlike the other apprentices, did not fear to openly challenge the notions of his beloved master – for which Kieron held him in great affection.

According to Bruno, the ideal form of an aerial machine would be obtained by combining all that was vital in the wing pattern of a gliding bird with a streamlined body derived from the shape of one of the fast swimming fishes. He had even persuaded Kieron to spend half a day by the banks of the Arun, watching trout glide through the water, controlling their movements with a flicker of the tail.

So the design of the fourth and fifth sailplanes had been changed according to Bruno's requirements for streamed lines. The fourth sailplane had risen well from the beach, but had proved impossible to control. After a flight of perhaps two hundred metres, it had buried its fish-nose in the sand and had thrown Kieron head over heels through the air to land most painfully upon his back.

But, with Bruno's assistance, he had made the best heavier-than-air flight so far. Together, they laboured on the design of the fifth sailplane. Longer, more slender wings. Smoother, streamed lines. A fish-tail, which could be moved a little from side to side by the aeronaut pulling ropes.

This one flew almost a kilometre, till the fabric was ripped from one of its wings and once more Kieron broke a limb.

The sixth sailplane was an even more ambitious version of the fifth. It was almost entirely Bruno's own design. Besides a moving tail-fin, he had devised thin, moveable flaps on the wings, and had so arranged matters that the aeronaut could control the movements of the wing-flaps or tail-fin by pushing and pulling wooden bars.

It was a beautiful machine, long tapering wings; slender rounded body. Sleek as a fish, light as a great bird. Bruno pleaded to be allowed to make the first flight. The other apprentices were awed by his temerity. Hitherto, the Cloud Walker had always been the first.

But, thought Kieron, why should not Bruno enjoy his own triumph if, indeed, there were a triumph to enjoy?

So, on a bright morning, Bruno sat in the tiny aeronaut's basket built between the wings, tested his controls, glanced nervously back at the small tail-wings and the tail-fin, upon the design of which he had lavished much thought and care, smiled at Kieron, and gave the signal to the horsemen who would draw the sailplane on its wooden wheels along the beach, until it gained enough speed to rise.

The sailplane rose from the beach much faster than Kieron had anticipated. It rose beautifully, smoothly, confidently, the rope that held it to the horses dropping cleanly from the iron hook in the machine's nose. Bruno seemed to know instinctively how to handle the sailplane. It was more than fifty metres high when a sudden gust of wind seemed to snatch at it with nimble fingers and fling it aloft. The sudden lift caught Bruno unawares, he was thrown out of his small basket; and, with a long despairing cry, he fell to earth, being killed instantly.

Now as Kieron sat in the cage of the seventh sailplane – substantially the same as Bruno's design but with larger tailplanes and with straps to fasten the aeronaut to his machine – he thought of the heavier-than-air machines that had failed and also of the brilliant young man who had given his life in the struggle to reconquer the air. Bruno had looked somewhat as Aylwin had looked many years ago; though Bruno's wits were much sharper than Aylwin's had been, and his passions were much stronger.

I have killed many enemies and only two friends, mused Kieron as he sat in his aeronaut's cage. I have been lucky.

The wind was good. The men on horseback seventy metres ahead of the sailplane, looked round expectantly, awaiting the signal. Let them wait, let them mutter and curse, thought Kieron complacently. The wind will get better.

His mind turned to his other apprentices ... To Lachlan of Edinburgh, who had marched south with a tattered fragment of a book containing the precious knowledge of how to prepare a gas that was lighter than air. Lachlan swore that one day he would produce this gas in such quantities as to raise many balloons and allow them to remain aloft for ever ... To Torben, who had come from Norwich, determined to learn about hot-air balloons, and then determined to construct better ones than the Cloud Walker had made. He had succeeded, too. Torben of the quiet ways, the small voice and the great ambition. He had even constructed a hot-air balloon that had carried three men across the sea to the Nether Lands ... And then there was Levis of Colchester – Levis, the wild one, who made his own black powder and designed his own rockets and fired them into the sky as if he were taking part in a religious ceremony. Levis had already blown three fingers off one hand and made himself blind in an eye by premature explosions; and his aerial rockets, though spectacular, leaving trails of smoke and fire across the sky, were fit only for use as weapons to terrify and confound the enemy. Though, so far, the Free Seigneurie had encountered no other enemy, being perhaps too powerful, too resolute, and possessing many ingenious minds. Levis, the dreamer, disliked his rockets being taken for weapons. He dreamed always of a rocket that would one day reach out towards the stars ...

Kieron smiled, thinking of these young men and others. People called them, affectionately, the Cloud Walker's Fledglings. But would not such fledglings one day command the skies?

The sailplane quivered. The wind had strengthened. Boys holding the wing-tips shivered. The waiting men on horseback swore at their restive mounts and glanced frequently at Kieron; but none was brave enough to question the judgment of the Cloud Walker.

Kieron sighed, gave a last look around him, and raised his hand. Perhaps he would die, as Bruno had done. Perhaps not. But this day belonged to Bruno himself. Whatever happened, others would continue the work.

The horsemen saw the raised hand. The sailplane lurched forward, boun-cing somewhat over uneven patches of sand. Once the left wing-tip came down nearly touching. That would have brought disaster. But Kieron moved a wing-flap and the sailplane righted itself. As the horsemen gathered speed, the machine became more stable. Kieron saw sand and sea rushing past him. Then suddenly there was no more bumping. Majestically, steeply, the sail-plane rose. Not too steep, not too steep, thought Kieron, easing his tail-flap to turn a little from the wind. The sailplane began to swing smoothly in a wide arc. Kieron glanced down and saw that he must be fifty, perhaps sixty metres above the ground. He felt a slight jerk as the tow rope disengaged smoothly from its hook.

'Bruno,' he said aloud into the wind, 'we are airborne. You are right, boy, this is better than balloons. With craft such as these, we shall not drift with the wind. We shall truly sail the sky.'

He brought the sailplane round in a great circle, knowing that he was already losing height and that he must endeavour to land smoothly on the beach. As the wings swung, he glimpsed the seigneurie of Arundel – a toy castle and a toy town in the morning sunlight. He thought of Petrina and his sons – and then the castle was lost to view, and he concentrated anxiously on the problems of flight.

He had practised the wing controls on models and with the sailplane teth-ered in a high wind. He had the feel of his craft. It seemed even to be an extension of his own body.

Slowly, patiently, he eased the descending sailplane until it pointed along the beach, its tail and nose at the right attitude. Then he centred his controls.

Down below the horsemen sat like statues. If they did not move he would crash into them. They scattered – one man falling from his mount and being dragged somewhat by it.

The air whistled about Kieron's face. The sea and the shore seemed to rush towards him. There was a sickening bump as the wheels hit the sand, then the sailplane bounced a few metres into the air once more and came down sedately. As the speed lessened, one wing-tip touched the sand; and the sailplane swung violently round. But for his harness, Kieron would have been thrown out with some force. That was one important thing that had been learned from the death of Bruno.

The machine had stopped and all was well. Men and boys were running towards it. For a moment or two, he sat in silence, wishing that Bruno were with him.

'We have done it,' he said softly. 'Bruno, we have done it. We have flown more than a kilometre in a heavier-than-air machine. This is the beginning.'

Suddenly he was aware of shouts, exclamations, cheers. And the world was about him once more.

POSTSCRIPTUM

Kieron leaned back in his wheeled chair, knowing that he would rise from it no more, and was content. They had brought doctors to tend him and fuss about him; doctors who said that he must have no more excitement, that he must rest a while. He knew better than the doctors. He knew that soon he would rest eternally. He was content.

It was late spring. He leaned back in his chair in the castle rose garden, and sniffed the sweet scents that drifted to him on a light breeze. There was a bed of damask roses, gloriously golden in colour. A master gardener in France had bred the rose and, seeking to please the Cloud Walker, had called it *Madame Petrina.* There was also a bed of tiny white roses, bred by the castle's own master gardener and called simply *Alyx.*

Between the small white roses of *Alyx* and the full golden roses of *Madame Petrina,* Kieron, Seigneur of Arundel by consent of the people, First Holder of the Eagle's Wings by unanimous vote of the International Guild of Aeronauts, sat contentedly and remembered all that an old man should remember.

Kentigern was long dead. Kentigern who had been a good seigneur and a true friend for more than thirty years. Petrina was dead – dear warm Petrina. She had been dead how long? Not long. He could still feel the pain. Two of her sons also. The first – inevitably called Marcus – burned to death on his first voyage as navigator of a hydrogen airship. And the second, Aylwin, had died when his sailplane had been caught in a storm. Kieron was glad that hydrogen airships were finished. They were too dangerous. They had destroyed many good men. Now helium was the great lifter. He was glad also that the Germans and the French and the Americans and the Japanese were developing petroleum engines to power the sailplanes.

But such discoveries and inventions had come too late to save two of his sons. Not too late to save Jason, though. Jason was master of electrics on a helium-lifted dirigible capable of carrying two hundred people. Jason was safely airborne, flying about the world to places like Tokyo, Lima, New York, Johannesburg with all the assurance and confidence of a generation that accepted mastery of the air.

A great shadow passed over the rose garden. Without looking up, Kieron knew what it was. It was the daily, helium-filled airship from London to Rome. It always came over at this time. You could set a clock by it. Its propellers were powered by steam engines. Perhaps in a few years the petroleum engines would drive the great airships also.

Kieron fingered the red and white ribbon that hung round his neck and the Eagle's Wings, worked in iron from a meteorite, that was suspended from it. He was proud of the Eagle's Wings. They had been given to him by men of many nations.

The International Guild of Aeronauts had its meeting place in the city of Geneva in Switzerland. Kieron had never been further abroad from the seigneurie of Arundel than the *Marie-France* had carried him. But he knew where Switzerland was. He had looked at the maps.

Once, long ago, the newly-formed Guild of Aeronauts had sent men to him, he being the first one to reconquer the air, asking him to set down the articles of their Guild.

He had thought the matter over and had been able to define only one article. He had written it for them in his own poor hand.

'The clouds and the winds are free, passing over all countries, belonging to all men. Let no man take to the skies with malice in his heart or hatred of his fellow men. On earth there are frontiers, in the sky there are none. Let those who have the good fortune to become airborne remember that the blood of all men is of one colour.'

It was the first and only article required by the International Guild of Aeronauts. Any who wished to fly for other purposes than peaceful commerce were denied the lore of flight, the facilities of the airborne.

Recently, the Guild had requested Kieron to visit Geneva to receive the Eagle's Wings. Being old, he replied that he no longer felt equal to the journey, but he thanked them for their kindness, none the less.

If the Cloud Walker was unable to visit Geneva, the International Guild of Aeronauts was not unable to visit Arundel. They came, two thousand of them, in ten helium airships. They came, bearing gifts, speaking many languages.

There were Indians, Africans, Frenchmen, Germans, Russians, Americans, Chinese and many nationalities of which Kieron had not even heard. The numbers swelled as men journeyed from all parts of Britain.

In the end, four thousand men stood with bared heads in pouring rain, while the Cloud Walker sat in his wheeled chair under canvas and listened to speeches in many languages.

He understood from the British and American speeches what all these young men were saying. He was overwhelmed by their honour. The Cloud Walker had become more than a man: he had become a symbol.

When he had his first weakness of the heart, the doctors whisked him away from the conference and prescribed complete rest.

So now here he was in the rose garden, luxuriating in the scent of *Madame*

Petrina, gazing with the fondness of memory at the small white roses called *Alyx*.

Kieron Joinerson, no longer known by that name, but known simply as Seigneur Kieron or the Cloud Walker, was content.

The Rome dirigible had passed over the rose garden. Somewhere above the Pacific Ocean, heading for Japan, Jason, son of Kieron and Petrina, was attending to his duties.

A doctor came from the castle to take one of his periodic checks on his illustrious patient. As he approached the wheeled chair, he heard a great sigh. Then he saw the body slacken.

The Cloud Walker was seventy-eight years old. In his last moments he had remembered many things. The sound of bees in childhood, the thin voice of a master painter, *Mistress Fitzalan's Leap,* the touch of Petrina, the first cry of a first child.

And he remembered Aylwin also, and the shark of the sky, and Capitaine Girod, and Kentigern, and Bruno, with his obsession of streamed lines. And he remembered the floating dandelion seeds, the whirling leaves of autumn, and all the butterflies of childhood.

Whatever, as the doctor confirmed, he died peacefully. The Cloud Walker had believed only that life was for the living. But who shall say that his spirit has not reached out to the stars?

ALL FOOLS' DAY

ONE

7 July 1971. Two-thirty a.m. The air warm, clear patches of sky loaded with stars, and the Thames rippling quietly through the subdued noises of London like a jet and silver snake.

Two-thirty a.m. A car whispering sweetly, as cars do in the moist hours of darkness. A car, a man and a woman, routed for Chelsea from Kingston. A man and a woman journeying from the good life to the good life. A man with a bellyful of misery and loneliness and some precious dregs of self-respect – driving in top gear to a centrally-heated, sound-proofed limbo with an original Picasso and the latest Scandinavian furniture …

Matthew Greville, aged twenty-seven, ex-human being and adman of this city had been drunk and was now sober. As he drove, he glanced occasionally at his wife, Pauline, wondering if such sobriety could be contagious. Evidently not.

Where did sobriety begin and intoxication end? Perhaps it began about eight miles back with a cat. The cat was black, fat, old and – as Pauline had remarked with comfortable assurance – obviously filled with the death-wish. It had come streaking across the road like a wild thing in pursuit of sex, rats or possibly nothing more substantial than visions.

There had been a moment of choice when Greville could have put on the brakes and sent up a hurried prayer to the Cats' God. He had had the time and he wanted to stamp on the brake pedal. The odd thing was that his foot wouldn't move.

The cat passed under the car. There was a bump. Finally, Greville managed to move his foot. The car screeched reproachfully to a stop.

'What, may I ask, is this in aid of?' said Pauline gently.

'I hit a cat.'

'So?'

'So I'd better see whether the poor wretch is dead.'

'There are too many cats,' remarked Pauline. 'Does it matter? I'm rather tired.'

'There are too many cats,' agreed Greville, 'but oddly it matters, and I'm tired, too.'

'Darling, don't be lugubrious. It was such a nice party. I'm not in the mood for suicidal cats.'

Greville was suddenly disgusted – with himself. 'I won't be a minute.' He got out of the car and slammed the door.

He found the cat about thirty yards back. It was not dead. It had rolled into the gutter and its back was horribly twisted, but there was no sign of blood.

'Die, please die,' murmured Greville. Ashamed, he knelt down and stroked the cat's head. It shuddered a little, then nuzzled him, leaving blood upon his hands. It seemed pathetically grateful for his attention.

'Pussy, please, *please* die,' he coaxed.

But the cat clung obstinately to life. Then the pain came, bringing with it thin, bubbling screams.

Greville could stand it no longer. He eased his hand under the animal and suddenly lifted it up. There was a final cry of anguish before the edge of his other hand came down with all the strength he could muster. The force of the blow took the cat from his grasp and returned it heavily to the gutter. But its neck was broken, and after one or two twitches there was only stillness.

He stood there shaking for a few moments. Then he went back to the car.

'I presume you found the beast?' said Pauline coldly.

'It was rather badly messed up. I – I had to kill it.'

'Did you, indeed! Then, for goodness' sake don't touch me until you've had a bath … You have to make a production of every damn thing, don't you, darling?'

He said nothing. He settled himself in the driver's seat and turned on the ignition. After a few minutes he was surprised to notice that he was dawdling along at less than forty miles an hour. But perhaps that was because he was already becoming sober.

Or drowning …

People are traditionally expected to review their lives when drowning. Therefore, concluded Greville, he was drowning. For the memories were coming thick and fast.

Life (was it really life?) began with Pauline. Five years ago when one of her stiletto heels got stuck in a metal grating in the Strand. It was an evening in late autumn. He rescued the shoe and made so bold as to buy her some hot and deliciously aromatic chestnuts. They talked. He took her home to a surprisingly comfortable three-girl flat in Notting Hill Gate.

There were other meetings. Regular meetings. She was in advertising and ambitious. He was in an oil company and frustrated. They both thought he had talent. Greville thought he could write poetry and was even prepared to accept the prostitution of novels. Pauline thought he could write copy. High-class copy for high-class ads. Temptation for Top People.

Before he knew what had happened, he had a job at twice the salary and half the work. The great and glorious mantle of the adman had wrapped itself comfortably round his shoulders. He still thought it was because he had talent. He did not discover until much later – after they were married – that it was because Pauline also had talent.

Hers was more formidable. It consisted of an easy manner with executives and clients, an affinity for bedrooms, a body that seemed somehow to carry a written guarantee, and a mind like a digital computer.

Greville climbed fast. And the funny thing was that for two years he didn't know who was holding the ladder.

He discovered it in the most conventional of ways – quite by accident when he returned from a Paris conference one night too soon. By that time, Greville and Pauline had a flat in a new block in Holland Park. It was a nice flat, high up, with views over London and two bedrooms.

Greville had arrived at London Airport just after eleven o'clock. He let himself quietly into the flat just before midnight. He had made the stealthy approach in case Pauline was asleep. There were the remains of drinks in the living-room – two glasses – and a blue haze of cigarette smoke.

At first he was glad that Pauline had had company. He thought he must have just missed the visitor. Then Pauline's voice coming muffled from the bedroom – excited and inarticulate – told him that he had not quite missed the visitor. Logically enough, the second voice belonged to the man who had given him the opportunity of rubbing shoulders with the great at the European Project conference in Paris.

Indecision. Masochism. Cowardice.

Greville listened to the sounds in the bedroom. He sentenced himself to listen, taking a terrible satisfaction in his own humiliation. Then, when all was quiet, he simply went away.

He found himself a hotel at Marble Arch, spent the rest of the night drinking duty-free cognac, and returned to Pauline at the appointed time. He never told her about it, and he never again returned from a trip unexpectedly. But thereafter he kept the score. He let her see that he was keeping the score just so that she would not get too careless. She never did.

Accounts came Greville's way, all kinds of accounts from steel to lingerie. So did private commissions. And consultancies.

No longer an ordinary account executive – let other people do the work – he concerned himself with policy and strategy. And the money kept on rolling.

Holland Park, Portman Square, Victoria, and now eighteen thousand pounds-worth of status residence in Chelsea. A Picasso and Scandinavian furniture. Success. Success. Success …

'Darling,' said Pauline bisecting his reverie with her number one conciliatory voice. 'I was talking to Wally Heffert while you were laying it on for the Evans girl.'

'That must have been nice for you.'

'Oh, well, he's quite a cheery old stick.'

Dull, divorced and loaded, thought Greville. Wally Heffert, king of Hef-

167

fert, McCall and Co. Lord High Custodian of three frozen foods, a dozen cigarette brands, Trans-Orient Air Lines and the Junior Joy contraceptive pill. Therefore by definition a 'cheery old stick'. Pauline's natural prey.

'He thinks a lot of your work,' she went on. 'He'd like to talk to you about a retainer. Heffert McCall are getting more than they can handle ... It would be quite a big slice, I imagine.'

'How long have you been sleeping with him?' asked Greville conversationally, keeping his eyes on the road.

'Please don't be immature, darling. That stupid cat must have upset you.'

For Pauline, 'immature' was a multi-purpose word. It could equal obscene, petulant, idealistic, depraved, old-fashioned, naïve or honest – depending upon the occasion and the context.

In the present instance, it clearly equalled obscene plus petulant.

Greville turned the car towards Chelsea Bridge. The speedometer needle crept high once more. He did not know it, but he had just made a decision.

He turned to Pauline. 'Do you know, darling, I think I'm actually sober.'

Suddenly, she sensed that something was wrong – badly wrong.

'What the hell are you talking about, Matthew?'

Chelsea Bridge was before them. A slightly arched ribbon of road. There was nothing else on the road. There was nothing but the sky and the river.

'Being alive, that's all. My God, it hurts!'

Sixty-five, seventy, seventy-five, eighty ...

'Stop the car! Do you hear? Stop the car!'

He turned and smiled at her. There was affection in his voice. Even compassion. Because at last he felt that he could afford to forgive.

'Dear Pauline,' he said. 'It's no good only one of us being sober. Why don't we stop the world?'

They both tore at the wheel. The car skipped crazily against the steelwork of the bridge. Then it somersaulted twice and landed on its side.

Greville, still alive, found that he was lying almost on top of Pauline. Her eyes were open, reminding him of the cat. But this time there was no problem ... She still looked beautiful; and, for a moment, he was sure he could smell roasting chestnuts ...

Then he tried to move. And the tears in his eyes mingled with his own blood.

A few minutes later, another car began to cross Chelsea Bridge. And a little after that an ambulance and a police car came.

TWO

Until early July the summer had been a typically English summer – that is to say, despite manned weather satellites and computer-based long-range forecasts, it had remained as unpredictable as ever, confounding scientists, prophets, farmers and tourists alike. One day the sky would be clear and the sun hot; and the next day torrential downpours would reduce the temperature to a level plainly indicating warmer underwear.

But by the middle of July it began to look as if the summer might possibly settle down into one of those vintage seasons that everybody remembers from childhood, though nobody can actually pin down the year. Each day, after early mists, the sky became abnormally clear. The heat was not too intense, and light breezes made life pleasant enough for those who still had to go to work.

July passed, August came – and still the good weather persisted. It was not confined to the British Isles or even to Europe. Most of the countries in the Northern Hemisphere basked in what was truly a golden season. Later, it would be the turn of the Southern Hemisphere to enjoy the fantastic run of weather. But no one was yet to know that, for the next ten years throughout the world, summertime was going to break all known records.

Matthew Greville, however, was among the minority who remained quite uninterested in the weather; and, in fact, he was largely unaffected by it during the next three years. The crash that killed Pauline merely dealt him multiple head injuries. He remained in hospital until September, while the surgeons made a thoroughly efficient job of saving the sight of his left eye and restoring muscular control of the left side of his body. At the same time, the psychiatrists were busy persuading him that life could still be worth living. As it turned out, their task was rather more difficult than that of the surgeons. But eventually they at least got him to a state in which he was fit to plead.

The police had taken considerable interest in the 'accident', since there had been no other cars on the bridge at the time. They measured the tyre marks, interviewed people who had been at the party in Kingston – including one Walter Heffert of Heffert, McCall and Co. – and took statements from Greville himself. The result of all this activity crystallised into two charges. Manslaughter and Dangerous Driving. Greville collected sentences totalling three years, which he found monstrously unjust. He would have preferred the death penalty.

It was not until the first week in October, about the time that Greville was being transferred to one of the better-class English prisons for better-class English criminals, that the long and utterly glorious summer came to its end. Though there had been enough nocturnal rainfall and light daytime showers to keep the crops healthy, there had been ten weeks of virtually uninterrupted sunshine. It was followed by a month of intermittent rain – and floods.

Some curious facts began to emerge about the summer. There had been roughly three times the average amount of sunshine for the period. There had also been about five times the average number of suicides. This was spectacular enough to make the front pages of most of the newspapers. Prominence was also given to the discovery that new sun-spots had appeared and had been emitting a new type of radiation. The facts that the radiation possessed properties hitherto unknown to science and that the surplus suicides exhibited symptoms hitherto unknown to psychiatry gave rise to considerable speculation.

The name given to the waves (or were they particles?) emitted from the sun-spots was Omega radiation – chiefly because the scientists were baffled and because every fruitful investigation seemed destined to be a long-term project. The name eventually given to the five-fold increase in self-destruction (by a journalist who drowned himself a few weeks later) was the Radiant Suicide.

It was the popular press that had first suggested a 'statistical relationship' between Omega radiation and what everyone now called the Radiant Suicide. The idea triggered off a chain reaction among scientists, religious leaders, psychologists and plain cranks.

One so-called scientist 'borrowed' two groups of children from a well-meaning if mentally retarded headmaster with a proper respect for Scientific Method. The scientist kept one lot of children in a cellar for long spells while the other lot were compelled to spend most of their time in the open air exposed to sunlight. Not surprisingly, he found that after a day or two of this kind of treatment the open-air group could do sums much faster and more accurately than the cellar group. From this he appeared to conclude (a) that Omega radiation stimulated intellectual activity and could therefore induce nervous exhaustion, and (b) that anybody who wanted to avoid nervous exhaustion and, therefore, suicide would be well advised to live underground. Having the courage of his convictions, he himself took to a subterranean existence – and committed suicide two months later.

The psychologists and psychiatrists were rather more reluctant to link the increase in the suicide rate with Omega radiation – chiefly because radiation was outside their province. They took a more esoteric approach and began to fling about such phrases as 'thyroidal displacement', 'societal emotional imbalance', 'liberation of the collective death-wish', 'induced hyper-mysticism' and 'cathartic destruction'. The Radiant Suicide, apparently, was quite explicable. In a world in which the idea of war was rapidly becoming absurd, it was modern man's neurotic simulation of the consequences of tribal conflict. Eventually the psychologists and psychiatrists produced so many plausible explanations of the Radiant Suicide as to convey the impression that they had almost invented it.

However, for the most part the religious fanatics took a simpler view. It was merely an Awful Warning sent by God. We would have to mend our ways or else …

But while the cranks of various persuasions were airing their pet philosophies and producing equally useless panaceas, a few intelligent people were busy collating the facts.

And the facts that emerged were these:

1. Until shortly before the detection of Omega radiation, the suicide rate was approximately normal.

2. The incidence of suicide increased with the incidence of radiation.

3. Cloudy weather tended to slow down the rate of increase perceptibly but not significantly.

4. Though there had been tremendous increases in the suicide rate throughout the world, the increases in the Northern Hemisphere had so far been slightly larger than in the Southern Hemisphere.

5. The types of people affected were those who, under normal conditions, would be considered the least prone to suicidal impulses.

6. Many people who had either failed in their attempts to commit suicide or had been rescued by others reported that, shortly before the urge to self-destruction, they had experienced tremendous sensations of peacefulness and of identification with something greater than self. A common element of their reports was the widespread conviction that death would render the experience absolute or permanent.

7. The intensity of the Omega radiation was still increasing, and many astronomers expressed the view that the new sun-spots could be expected to remain 'active' for a considerable period of time.

These were the facts. And they were responsible for sending the sales of sedatives, tranquillisers, alcoholic drinks and Bibles soaring to unprecedented heights.

By the end of 1971, thirty-four thousand people in the United Kingdom had taken their own lives – yet the statistical expectation was only six thousand five hundred. The Home Secretary, woolly-minded as ever, recommended that suicide be treated as a criminal offence once more. It was anti-social, he said, and definitely bad for the country's economy. So a bill was rapidly pushed through Parliament. It came to be briefly immortalised as the 'Do Yourself In Deterrent'. For one of its provisions was that one-third of the estate of any suicide (after death duty) *could* be claimed in forfeit by the State. Another provision was that attempted suicide *could* be punished by a maximum of ten years' imprisonment. The bill, needless to say, was totally ineffective – but it contributed somewhat to the government being overthrown six months later.

Meanwhile Matthew Greville was adapting himself to the routines of prison life. It was far more comfortable than he had imagined; and this, in itself, proved a major frustration because he believed that he ought to be made to suffer – not only for Pauline, but for the very uselessness and pointlessness of his life. For all the minor deceits he had ever practised, for all the little vanities he had ever developed, for the talent he had wasted, the ideals he had abandoned, and for every cliché-ridden perverted ethic he had ever subscribed to in admanland. Suicide would appear to have been the perfect answer – perhaps it might have been on 7 July 1971. But he had spent months trying to analyse his intentions and motives, and he was no wiser. Did he really intend to kill himself on Chelsea Bridge? Or Pauline, or both of them? Or was he only indulging in a melodramatic gesture that got out of control?

If he hadn't killed the cat … If Pauline hadn't grabbed at the wheel … If … If … If …

There was no satisfactory solution – not even suicide. For that was now only a sort of luxury. He wanted to be punished, he wanted to be hurt, he wanted to feel again the strange anguish of being alive …

During his entire stay in prison seven warders and fifty-four prisoners committed suicide. As a penance for existing and a reward for not killing himself, Greville became the self-appointed gravedigger-in-chief.

Throughout the short and fairly dry winter of 1972, the Omega radiation intensified. So did the Radiant Suicide. And the pessimists were already predicting a warm dry summer.

Science and human ingenuity came up with a remarkable number of solutions – none of them satisfactory and some of them dangerous. One of the many new 'tranquil stimulants' coming out of the laboratories of the manufacturing chemists in hysterical haste (this particular drug was marketed as Positive Pep) was responsible for more than a hundred thousand miscarriages or premature births, and therefore contributed quite significantly to the increase in the suicide rate. Another one was more effective in preventing suicide – but one of its side effects was to produce delusions of grandeur. A third was equally effective in preventing people from killing themselves: the problem was that it tended to create addiction, and addiction overloaded the heart.

Thousands of 'mental hygiene' groups were formed, an organisation called Death-Wish Anonymous sprang into existence, dozens of different sects, disciplines and esoteric societies mushroomed. And religious revival became a major industry.

But, despite everything, by the end of 1972 (again there had been an utterly glorious summer) more than a hundred and twenty thousand people in the United Kingdom alone had taken their own lives. The proportional increase was similar in most other countries.

Meanwile, the Omega radiation – the most elusive and enigmatic form of radiant energy ever discovered – intensified. And while researchers into its nature remained baffled, researchers into its effects came up with more interesting data.

It had been discovered that Omega-proof shields could be devised. All you needed was a wall of lead sixteen feet thick, or a thicker wall of less dense material. But even this was no good unless the people to be shielded by it remained permanently shielded. Anyone prone to what was abbreviated to Radiant-S, or simply R.S., needed only a few minutes exposure to trigger off the reaction. The only variable was the time factor. It could be months before the R.S. impulse manifested itself, or merely a matter of hours.

Another interesting discovery was that all children were 'R.S.-proof' until the age of puberty. And, in fact, from puberty until about the age of twenty-five (the presumed end of growth and adolescence) the risk of R.S. was only about half as great as for the rest of the population.

But, most curious of all, was the emerging classification of R.S. types. During the first two years the information gathered from more than a hundred and fifty thousand victims indicated that, in terms of professions and vocations, the most susceptible types were bank clerks, accountants, scientists, executives and managers of all kinds, shopkeepers, typists, dons (but not teachers!), pilots, sea captains, bus drivers, engine drivers, mathematicians, professional gamblers and bookmakers, *minor* politicians, watchmakers and civil servants. Spinsters, or – more accurately – virgins over the age of twenty-five were a very heavy risk: so were bachelors similarly.

The least likely R.S. subjects were creative artists of all kinds, lunatics, political and religious fanatics, actors, dancers and entertainers, cranks, homosexuals, prostitutes, eccentrics, doctors and nurses, teachers, sportsmen, sadists, masochists and pathological animal lovers.

Clearly, it was now a case of, '*Do* send your daughter on the stage, Mrs Worthington.' But stratagems of this kind were not much good if the person concerned happened to have a repressed flair for, say, mathematics.

1973 came. And went – after another brilliant summer. The final reckoning in Britain was just under half a million R.S. victims. Added to which a secondary reaction was now apparent. The birth rate was falling, for obvious reasons; and the natural death rate was rising, for equally obvious reasons. People were beginning to be afraid to have children and, ironically, they were also indirectly killing themselves with worry. Towards the end of the year Parliament reintroduced conscription – which had been out of favour for more than a decade. However, the need this time was not for soldiers but for burial squads, bus drivers and clerical workers.

In the autumn of 1974, having served his full term after contriving to avoid remission for good conduct by deliberately assaulting a prison officer, Matthew Greville was released from prison. He was given a rail ticket to London and the sum of eighteen pounds nine shillings and sixpence, which he had earned in his capacity as gravedigger.

He had no home to go to, since he had long ago instructed his solicitor to sell the Chelsea residence and all it contained. There had been quite a large mortgage to pay off. Nevertheless, when all assets (including the Picasso) had been realised, the solicitor was able to deposit just over eleven thousand pounds in Greville's account. Greville had promptly disposed of the entire amount to various charities.

When he arrived in London, he hired a taxi and toured the city, savouring its richness and its bustle (for despite the Radiant Suicide London still managed to put on a brave face), noting the changes, the new skyscraper blocks that were still going up – and the new churches that were being built. Then he told the taxi driver to take him to Chelsea Bridge, where he got out, paid off the taxi and began to walk across.

The dents were still there in the steelwork. He had to look carefully for them, but they were still there. They had been painted over, and two or three badly twisted metal sections had been renewed, but the hidden hieroglyphs still proclaimed the final result of life with Pauline – and, perhaps the result also of an encounter with an unknown cat.

He stared for a while at the message that none but he could decipher. The sky was misty blue, and the sun covered all of England with the gold and ripening light of autumn. It was a perfect day. But the weather was entirely lost upon Greville. After reliving yet again the strange drive from Kingston (only three years ago, but in another kind of time) he headed for the nearest bar and proceeded to get drunk.

He stayed drunk for three days, at the end of which time he woke up early in the morning in Hyde Park – shaking with the effects of drink and nervous tension, and remembering little of what had passed since his visit to the bridge.

He pulled himself together and inquired the way to the nearest army recruitment centre. He had to wait an hour for it to open. The military gentlemen in charge were not filled with joy at the prospect of enlisting a jailbird and an obvious tramp. However, after some deliberation they magnanimously allowed him to volunteer for the Emergency Burial Corps. He was pathetically grateful. This was the kind of work he wanted – just as in prison. It was a public service.

By the end of 1974, one million two hundred thousand British subjects had committed suicide.

The first large holes in the fabric of society were becoming apparent. Transport was strained to breakdown point. It began to take as long as a week for a letter to get from London to the cities of the Industrial North. Rationing of food and fuel was reintroduced. The gas supplies were still unaffected; but shortage of coal and fuel oil and irregular deliveries was responsible for domestic electricity only being available between fixed hours. A bill for the Direction of Labour was quickly pushed through the House. It provided powers by which every male between eighteen and sixty-five could be re-directed to more vital work at a week's notice. The Direction bill helped a little – that is to say, it delayed the inevitable and ultimate breakdown – but its main function seemed to be to enable the government, and the society it represented, to make a fairly orderly withdrawal ... A withdrawal from the more complex functions of a civilised community ...

And still the Omega radiation poured invisibly, painlessly and madden-ingly from the remote face of the sun. And still the scientists (now heavily depleted) struggled to find some kind of efficient protection or even immu-nisation. And still the R.S. rate climbed.

In 1975 it passed the three million mark. Matthew Greville, private in the E.B.C., no longer dug graves by hand. He used a mechanical excavator. Then he operated a bulldozer to push the piles of thin plastic coffins into long com-munal graves.

At the end of 1976, the year's death roll touched ten million. Three separate emergency governments were operating autonomously in the North, the Midlands and the South. Coffins were obsolete. All manufactured materials were needed by the living.

1977. Another glorious summer. The emergency governments had now disintegrated into eleven regional councils. Rail travel was suspended indef-initely except for fuel and food between some major cities. Typhoid fever raged in London; rioting in Edinburgh, York and Birmingham; starvation in South Lancashire and North Cheshire. Stealing, 'desertion' and withholding of labour became punishable by death in seven of the eleven regions ... Total death roll: fifteen and a half million.

Matthew Greville, temporary major in the London Emergency Burial Corps, was captured by slavers from the Midlands. Heavy chains were fas-tened round his ankles, and together with a group of other 'foreign recruits' he was sent down a mine in the Province of Nottingham to hew coal. Like the pit ponies with which they worked and died, the foreign recruits were kept permanently below the surface. The rations sent down to them varied accord-ing to the coal they sent up. Needless to say, the mortality rate was high.

1978. The total death roll in what had formerly been known as the United

Kingdom was estimated by the statistics section of the Second London Commune to be in the region of eight million.

Towards the end of 1978 Matthew Greville escaped from the mine by feigning death and contriving to accept in silence a routine bayonet thrust. This was the method by which tired inspectors normally contrived to discover such attempts in their examination of the twice weekly burial cart. Greville's wound, three inches deep, surprisingly did not pierce any vital organs. After a period of hiding, during which he endured mild fever and some starvation, he escaped from the Province of Nottingham and was almost immediately recruited by the Leicester City Volunteer Force as an unskilled farm labourer. The work was considerably easier than mining; but the food was not so good in quantity or quality. He lost weight, his hair began to turn grey, then white. But he remained alive and remarkably healthy.

In 1979 the Second London Commune disintegrated. So did practically all similar organisations throughout the British Isles, Europe and the entire world. Matthew Greville, one of the hundred and fifty thousand people still occupying the off-shore islands once literally described as Great Britain was a free man again – living on a hand-to-mouth basis.

The Radiant Suicide – less selective as a result of the three preceding years of very intense Omega radiation – had taken the high and the low, the intelligent and the intellectually subnormal, the strong and the weak, the old and the young. In the end, all it had left as custodians of the future of mankind were the emotionally disturbed – the cranks, the misfits, the fanatics, the obsessionals, the geniuses, the idiots, the harmless eccentrics, the homicidal maniacs, the saints and sinners extraordinary who had never found peace or happiness or understanding in an ordinary world.

Now there was no longer an ordinary world. The ordinary, the average, the normal – as a way of existence, as a standard of behaviour – was obsolete. There was no accepted ethic left – apart from personal survival – to which anyone could be expected to conform. All that remained was … transnormal …

In 1980, the Omega radiation became very slightly less intense. But there were no scientists left to measure its intensity, or even to verify that the sunspots producing it were still active.

1980 was chaos.

THREE

7 July 1981 (perhaps). Two-thirty a.m. – Greville mean time. For now that the world was dying, now that there were no more calendars, newspapers, or work days, time was wonderfully subjective. You could declare every day to be Sunday, thought Greville, and every night to be New Year's Eve … He was drunk, and he knew he was drunk, and he didn't care a damn …

Besides, there was an anniversary to celebrate. The liberation of Matthew Greville, sometime adman of this city. No, a double anniversary! For one must not forget the quietus of Pauline.

Dear, dead Pauline. Likewise a prostitute, but more honest. Likewise a fellow-traveller to eternity. But some bastard had made a reservation for her on the doomsday express.

Who was that bastard?

Answer: Matthew Greville, the poet of the four-colour ad., the ex-extraordinary crap-shitting conman of the stockbroker belt. The Shakespeare of the glossy mag., the Goethe of the *Sunday Times* colour section, the da Vinci of *Woman's Own*.

But where now were the *Sunday Times* and *Woman's Own* and the glory that was *House and Garden?*

All gone into the dark …

O dark, dark, dark, amid the blaze of noon …

The air was warm, and the sky was a bowl of darkness leaking with a thou-sand stars, and the Thames still rippled like a fat serpent through the steel and concrete bones of London.

Matthew Greville was sitting in a station wagon on Chelsea Bridge. The car's bumper was just touching the metalwork where another car had struck it ten years before at something like eighty miles an hour. For a couple of hours now he had been indulging in the society of ghosts – and in brandy, *Salignac* '71, a very fine year …

'Did I ever love you, Pauline?' he demanded loudly. 'Did I ever give-all-ask-nothing flaming well love you?'

The silence was an answer, accurate and immediate.

'I lusted, my dear,' he went on. 'I lusted, you lusted, he, she and it lusted … Ashes to ashes and lust to lust the basic philosophy of a world where we needed under-arm deodorants, breath-sweeteners, gin and rubber goods before we could sweat together in fashionable democratic joy.'

He hiccupped. 'Know what I've been doing since I gave you the final orgasm, darling?' He lifted the bottle of brandy, tried to see how much it still contained by the dashboard light, then took another swig. 'Promise not to laugh, and I'll tell you.'

The silence was not a laughing silence. The ghost was definitely sober and not at all like the living, fleshly ghost of Pauline.

'I'll tell you,' he echoed, finishing off the *Salignac* and flinging the bottle through the open car window. 'I've been digging graves – by special appointment ... You know what I was like, darling. I always had to be best. And, by God, I turned out to be the best bloody gravedigger in history. Immortality at last ... And do you know how I became the biggest little gravedigger of them all? I'll tell you. I buried mankind, that's how. I buried mankind.' His voice broke. 'And I want you to know, you poor dead little bitch, that killing you hurt me more than cutting coal, pulling ploughs or shoving a million bodies into the wretched earth ... That's how much you mean to me, Pauline, because you were the one that stopped me from living. And, goddammit, as if that wasn't enough, you even stopped me from dying ... Bitch ... Bitch ... Dear, lovely bitch!'

Tears were rolling down his face. But Greville did not know that he was crying. For the *Salignac* and the darkness and the memories were too much. He had already fallen asleep. Somewhere, a dog howled; and the sound caused his hand to tighten on the shotgun that still rested across his knees. The dog howled again and was answered by a chorus of howls. Greville stirred uneasily and groaned, but he did not open his eyes. In the London of 1981 there were not many people who would have dared – drunk or sober – to go to sleep in a car with the window open.

The passing of normal man and the emergence of transnormal man represented either a grotesque end of human development or a new and grotesque beginning. Nobody knew which. The normals, along with their normal processes of evaluation were extinct; and the transnormals didn't seem to care about ends or beginnings – unless they were personal ends and personal beginnings.

All the cities had stopped – like run-down clocks or mechanical toys or deserted hives. Deserted? No, not entirely deserted. For there were the transnormals – so few haunting the great urban graveyards of so many. Like children wandering round an empty mansion ...

But the transnormals were not entirely alone, for when normal man passed into history his very passing created an imbalance in the animal ecology of the planet. The death of three thousand million human beings left not only a great silence but also – as it were – a partial vacuum among living things. And the vacuum was beginning to be filled.

In the cities the wild dogs now roamed – dogs who had survived starvation, disease, cannibalism. Dogs whose wits had been sharpened by hunger, whose civilised conditioning had evaporated almost instantly with the knowledge that man no longer existed as a dog's best friend.

The fancy dogs, the lap dogs, the soft dogs and all the carefully bred triumphs of canine splendour had disappeared. They were the first to die – the poodles, the pekes, the dachshunds, the Yorkshire toys. They were just not tough enough to compete. So they starved or died of grief – or were eaten by the rest.

The sturdy and quick-witted mongrels, the big dogs, the Alsatians, the Great Danes, the boxers, the bulldogs – they survived. They survived to challenge each other. Some of them lived and hunted alone. Some of them hunted and died alone. Many of them learned to trade individualism for the security of the pack. The leaders of the pack maintained the pack law. The only reward was food: the only punishment was death.

It was the same with cats. Except that cats found it harder to shed their individualism. Many of them continued to hunt alone. A few of them formed small groups. They were greatly outnumbered by the dogs, but they were also more ferocious, more unpredictable.

The most numerous of all were the rats. With the withdrawal of normal man, their numbers increased phenomenally. They tended not to hunt in groups or in packs but in swarms. And a swarm of rats was enough to make dogs turn and cats retreat ingloriously to a spitting-point of safety.

The law of the city-jungle was almost a closed circle. Almost but not quite. For the dogs hunted cats, rats and – reluctantly – each other; the cats hunted dogs, rats and – less reluctantly – each other; the rats hunted dogs, cats and – most happily – each other. But all of them hunted man. Especially at night-time when, instinctively, the animals knew they had the advantage.

The rats were to be feared most; for, indifferent to their own losses, their swarms would attack anyone or any living thing at any time. A determined man with a shotgun had a reasonable chance of shooting his way out of an attack by cats or dogs. But if he was cornered by a rat swarm, his best policy was to turn the gun upon himself.

But, surprisingly, groups of transnormals – or even individuals – still continued to live and move about in the cities. Their numbers were being reduced as the numbers of predators increased. But for many transnormals, the cities were the only places they had truly known. The towers of concrete and steel, the silent streets, the vacant windows and smokeless chimneys of a once normal environment still continued to provide an illusion of security. Until the food ran out, until the water supply failed, or until the rats came …

In the countryside the change was no less dramatic, but different. Despite the fact that Britain had been a highly industrialised country, four-fifths of the land had still been used for farming – even up till the early 1970s. But by the time the Radiant Suicide had taken its full toll, the English countryside had begun to revert rapidly.

The wind blew fences down, and there was no one to repair them; low-lying fields became flooded, and no one cleared the ditches for drainage. Animals trampled the hedges, winter ice split and buckled the secondary roads; nettles and ferns, convolvulus and wild hops straddled the rough tracks; sturdy young trees began the slow process of converting pasture into woodland; and in the farmhouses, chimney stacks toppled, roofs caved in and ivy groped whisperingly for a hold on dusty window-panes.

Most of the dairy cows – mild and stupid milk-producing machines – were unable to survive without the symbiotic attention of their masters. But bulls everywhere – unless, being chained up, they were condemned to perish miserably – rejoiced and flourished in their new-found freedom. They crashed through the remaining hedges and competed mightily to woo the surviving cows. Presently some of the cows calved down, and their offspring provided the nucleus of a new yet infinitely older strain. A survival strain.

Pigs were well placed in the survival stakes. When they were hungry enough, they would eat anything that was even vaguely edible – from carrion to the bark of trees. They were lean and hungry brutes, vicious and nimble. Some of them became cannibals, learning craftily to squash or stamp their opponents to death and then trample the corpses until they yielded the life-giving sweetness inside.

Hens – and cocks – also learned to survive. Their minds, narrow and dim and semi-mechanical, only vaguely perceived that something was wrong with the world. Many of the survivors provided satisfactory meals for wea-sels, dogs, foxes, rats, cats, hawks, eagles and even owls. But the cunning ones took to the trees, made secluded nests for themselves, brought forth young more adaptable and survival-conscious than their parents.

Rabbits multiplied with joyous abandon. So did stoats and weasels and foxes. So did otters and coypus.

And so did the red deer of old England. Small herds of them had been kept in parks here and there over the country. They were among the first of the animals to sense the new freedom conferred on them by the activity of sun-spots nearly a hundred million miles away. They exulted in it. The herds became large. They were not afraid of rats or cats, and they could outrun dogs. They began to spread, reclaiming the land that was once their kingdom.

And there were the horses. Not draught horses or racehorses. Now there was a wilder breed – wild as any slaves that ever survived the years of bond-age. There were quick horses, heavy horses, killer horses. They thundered across the land that had once been farmland. Their numbers were still small, but they were growing. They, too, were reclaiming a kingdom.

And on the moors, on Exmoor and Dartmoor and in the New Forest the wild ponies ran. There were no more tourists left to tempt them with sugar. There was only the wind and the rain and the sky, and the rolling pattern of seasons. For normal man, the self-appointed master of all living things, was obsolete. And most of the remaining members of the human race were – for the first time, and in their own way – running wild …

Greville awoke with a start.

It was the sound of dogs that woke him. The sound of dogs with a quarry in view. The sound of dogs and the sound of rifle or pistol shots.

The grey pre-dawn light was rolling softly up the Thames. Shapes were vague and unfamiliar. The air was still, and there was nothing to suggest that London was not a dead city – nothing except gun shots and the sound of dogs.

Greville yawned and stirred. There was an ache in his back, an ache in his legs, an ache in his head. His tongue felt like the pitted surface of a dirt road. He yawned, cleared his throat, peered through the car window, then looked at his hands. They were fairly steady. He was surprised.

The barking of the dogs came nearer. And now there was another sound. The muted put-put-put of a two-stroke engine.

Greville was curious. Dogs hunting somebody on a bike or scooter at dawn. Somebody, evidently, had quite a taste for living dangerously.

He checked that the shotgun was loaded – both barrels – then got out of the car. He sniffed the clean air appreciatively, and listened.

The two-stroke was getting much nearer. Somebody on the South Bank seemed to be heading for Chelsea Bridge – somebody and a retinue of dogs.

He looked along the bridge, but the light was still poor enough to shroud the other end of it in a dark grey obscurity. He breathed deeply and stood there with the shotgun cradled in his arms. The aches were fading. He was beginning to feel reasonably human.

Suddenly there was a muffled thud, a doggy howl of anguish followed by a barking chorus of triumph. The put-put-put of the two-stroke stopped. It was followed by two shots in rapid succession.

There was movement at the other end of the bridge. Greville could see a figure running towards him. Behind the figure there was a tide of low moving shapes. Hungry and relentless shadows on four legs.

The figure turned and fired once more into the dark carnivorous tide. The fugitive managed to gain a few yards while some of the dogs turned upon their wounded comrade and the others were momentarily checked by renewed fear of the gun. But hunger was greater than fear. The fugitive wasn't going to make it.

The running figure evidently realised that escape was now impossible, for he or she had begun to head from the centre of the bridge to its side. Death by drowning was certainly preferable to death by dogs.

It was at that point that Greville ceased being an interested spectator.

'Over here!' he bellowed. 'This way!'

Then he, too, began to run.

He was about forty yards from the still indistinct shape of the fugitive. The dogs were nearer, and they were overhauling fast.

'Drop flat!' shouted Greville.

The fugitive didn't seem to hear or understand.

'Drop flat!' he roared again, brandishing his shotgun.

This time the command was obeyed.

The figure fell in a sprawling, rolling, untidy heap.

The leaders of the pack were less than a dozen yards from it when Greville let them have the first barrel. One dog collapsed, screaming and writhing, another yelped and turned tail. Three dogs fastened upon their fallen companion.

With a mighty shout, Greville ran towards them. Altogether there were about twenty dogs on the bridge. Their advance was momentarily checked while they considered this new factor.

Greville, still running, was about ten yards from the figure on the ground. He stopped, fired the second barrel at the dogs, broke open his shotgun, felt in his pocket for two fresh shells and simultaneously shouted: 'Crawl here and get behind me, damn you!'

He didn't even look at the person who silently obeyed his command. His attention was taken entirely by the ragged and menacing line of dogs across the bridge.

The light was getting better. They gazed at him malevolently. They knew the power of the thing in his hand, and knew also that its power was not infinite. They snarled and slavered and got ready for the final charge.

He fired again at a dog that seemed to be one of the leaders. Then he swung his gun round and brought down an Alsatian that was trying to outflank him. He knew that he would not get another chance to reload and with a wild and savage cry, he did the impossible, the totally unexpected. He charged the remaining dogs, swinging his shotgun like a club.

This, itself, was totally outside the experience of the pack. They had seen many humans running – but always away, never towards. They were confounded. And their inability to appreciate Greville's act as an act of desperation led to their undoing.

For a second or two they froze and a lean mongrel fell with a broken neck beneath the butt of Greville's gun. He gave another terrible cry, raised the gun again and brought down a terrier leaping for his stomach. There was a frightful hanging moment of uncertainty, then the rest fled.

With trembling fingers, Greville felt in his pocket for two more shells. He loaded, then began to retreat cautiously backwards towards the car. At the far end of the bridge the dogs were gathering themselves for yet another attack. But they had missed their chance. The crisis was passed.

The figure on the bridge – the fugitive that had crawled behind him like a frightened child – was now hobbling towards the car. Greville glanced at it in amazement.

On the bridge where, just ten years before, he had accidentally(?) killed a woman, he had now accidentally(?) saved one.

He began to laugh. The irony seemed to be of a quality to justify laughter …

FOUR

The girl's name was Liz. Elizabeth Hopper, age twenty-two, nationality – transnormal. She had escaped on a motor-scooter, she said, from a kind of brothel/hospital/fort in Richmond and she had wildly optimistic hopes of finding her twin sister, recently 'liberated' from the same brothel/hospital/fort by a bunch of pirates whose accents had proclaimed their Northern origin. Liz and Jane Hopper, it seemed, were more than just twins: they were super-twins. The degree of empathy or *einfühlung* that existed between them might have provided any normal psychologist of the abnormal with five years of study and a reputation-making monograph on empathetic modes of communication and experience between complemental psychic patterns.

All of this Greville learned in the first ten minutes. All of this and a great deal more.

He had got back to the car to find that the girl had arranged herself comfortably on the passenger seat. Her left leg was troubling her. Evidently she had hurt it when, after running down a particularly enterprising dog, the impact of the collision had thrown her off the scooter.

Greville slammed the door and started the engine. The dogs at the other end of Chelsea Bridge had remembered that breakfast was still in the vicinity. Their numbers had increased – doubtless the commotion had served to recruit all available forces within a radius of a quarter of a mile on the South Bank. They began to pour across the bridge in a solid, bloodthirsty phalanx.

Greville slipped the car into second gear, kept the clutch pedal depressed, and let the engine idle. He waited until the dogs were about twenty yards away. Then his foot came down on the accelerator pedal and the car shot forward with a sharp jerk. He kept the accelerator pedal flat and drove straight at the dogs. They tried to scatter, but they were packed too close together.

His impact speed was about thirty miles an hour. He stayed in second gear, ploughing a bumpy lurching path right through the pack of dogs. The barking, the howls of pain and frustration rose high enough to drown the noise of the engine.

He carried right on to the end of the bridge. Then he did a quick U-turn and came back again. The crushed bodies of half a dozen dogs lay in the roadway. The rest were utterly confused. Some of them tore at their mangled comrades, but most of them stood on the bridge, barking as if the sheer volume of noise would resolve their bewilderment.

Greville drove the station wagon murderously and mercilessly at them. His second pass scored four more victims. At the North Bank he did another U-turn and came thundering back. But the surviving dogs had lost all stomach for the fight. They fled howling. Later, no doubt, they would return to devour the corpses of the fallen. But for the time being breakfast was less important than survival.

Greville turned once more and took the car back to the North Bank, away from the horrible sound of the dogs that had not been killed outright.

He switched off the engine and turned to examine his companion. 'Well, that's that,' he said calmly. 'Let's have a cigarette.'

'No, thanks. I don't smoke.' Her voice was pleasant. She seemed remarkably self-possessed for one who had so recently avoided a terrible kind of death.

'I'm delighted to hear it. Cigarettes aren't going to last much longer. One of the most significant tragedies resulting from depopulation.' He inspected her without any effort to disguise the fact that he was doing so.

She was wearing a short sheepskin jacket, a faded blue shirt and a pair of men's trousers tucked into calf-length boots. Her hair was short, black and untidy. Her face was pale and bruised. She had the body of a woman and the oddly innocent face of a child. Her eyes were blue and unafraid. She did not seem to mind his inspection at all.

'How is your leg, now?' he asked abruptly.

'Feeling better. It got rather a nasty knock when I came off the scooter. I think it will be all right for walking … Would you like me to go, now?'

'Don't be stupid. You'd be dog-meat before you'd done a couple of hundred yards. Where's your gun?'

'I lost it on the bridge.'

Greville let out an exasperated sigh. 'You're not very interested in surviving, are you?'

She smiled. 'I was so busy trying to survive when I saw you that I just forgot all about the gun. Anyway, it was empty.'

'Didn't you have any spare ammunition?'

'No.'

'Jesus! You're a case, you are. What the hell were you trying to do?'

Then she told him.

He did not find her story hard to believe. In a fantastic world, the fantastic had become merely ordinary.

'So you were setting off with a toy pistol and a motor-scooter to scour the length and breadth of England for sister Jane,' he remarked drily when she had finished. 'What made you think you were going to live long enough even to get clear of London?'

'I didn't really know what things were going to be like,' she confessed. 'I haven't been out a great deal in the last two years. They kept us pretty busy, you know.'

'Who did?'

'The Richmond Lot.'

The Richmond Lot, it transpired, were a group of nearly a hundred men who shared some fifteen to twenty women and were attempting to organise themselves into a tribal group. Their chief was a Canadian ex-wrestler who called himself Johnny Blue Fur – a great hulk of a man whose intelligence-to-weight ratio was possibly an improvement on that of the dinosaur, but not a startling one.

However, surprisingly enough, the Eskimo and French Canadian ancestry of Johnny Blue Fur had produced a mountainous human being who was not only a kindly person but one with a sense of justice. Also, not being in the slightest interested in women, he could remain – as it were – above party conflict.

The reign of Johnny Blue Fur seemed destined to be quite a long and remarkably peaceful one – until the arrival of about thirty well-armed men from the north. They came in a couple of ancient army trucks, and they did not come as enemies but simply as a band of men 'on the scrounge'. After having made it clear that there was nothing to be scrounged in Richmond – a fact which he gently underlined by assembling his own scroungers, complete with rifles, sub-machine guns and pistols – Johnny Blue Fur hospitably invited them to stay the night at The House.

The House was one of those large, rambling Victorian mansions that had been built on the banks of the Thames for the greater glory of nineteenth-century industrialists. Now, at the beginning of the last two decades of the twentieth century it had been transformed into a combined brothel, hospital, headquarters, chief's residence and storehouse for the Richmond Lot.

Johnny Blue Fur was simple enough, despite the anxious warnings of his lieutenants, to believe that the visitors would not abuse his hospitality – particularly in view of his numerical superiority in arms and men. But the Northerners (who were rather vague about their origin and would say no more than that they had 'a little place in Lancashire') were resolute, avaricious and very well organised. Far better organised than the Richmond Lot.

They were tough, they were short of weapons and women, and they had no intention of going away empty-handed.

Johnny Blue Fur laid on a lavish party for their benefit. The wine was passed around freely, and so were the women – among them Liz and Jane who, being twins, seemed to be especially favoured. The party did not break up until about a couple of hours before dawn.

An hour later, when most of the Richmond Lot were deep in their boozy slumbers and even The House guard was dozing, the Northerners came very much to life. Evidently they had only appeared to drink a lot, or else their capacity was quite remarkable.

There was very little shooting. In the dark it was difficult to tell friend from enemy, and there was neither the time nor the opportunity to light oil lamps.

For about five minutes sheer pandemonium existed. Johnny Blue Fur distinguished himself by throwing three men (one of them his own) through a second-storey window before he was felled by a rifle butt. And one of the guards in the grounds managed to cut down four of the raiders with a burst from his sub-machine gun as they ran to their trucks. Then he himself was shot.

But the Northerners managed to get away with six of the women (some of whom were probably too drunk or too exhausted to care), eight rifles and about two hundred rounds of ammunition. Liz might also have been taken as well as Jane, for she had had to spend what was left of the night with one of the visitors. But when he snatched her up, she began to scream and struggle. Then he panicked and tried to strangle her into submission, but somehow she managed to kick him in the stomach; and while he was recovering from that, she crawled away and was lost in the darkness and confusion.

Apparently she and Jane had been almost literally inseparable. They had been 'requisitioned' by the Richmond Lot – and saved from probable death by starvation or transnormal causes – in the summer of 1979. Prostitution, defined grandly by Johnny Blue Fur as free love, turned out not to be quite as repulsive as either of them had feared. At least they had enough food and were relatively safe. And when things could be shared, they did not seem quite so bad. But with Jane's forced departure – which had taken place several days ago – a curious feeling of deadness came over Liz. It was as if she had been given a tremendous dosage of local anaesthetic in mind and body. Nothing mattered any more. Nothing, that is, except finding Jane somehow and finding a way of being together again. She decided to escape from the Richmond Lot at the first opportunity.

Greville had listened to the rest of her recital for the most part in silence. It did not surprise him. There was very little that could surprise him these days.

When she had finished, he said: 'So now you are my problem.'

'Not if you don't want me to be,' said Liz simply.

'I saved your life, didn't I?'

'Yes.'

'Then it seems reasonable for me to have a controlling interest in it.'

'Have you got a woman?' she asked bluntly.

'No.'

'Do you want one?'

'I don't know. I hadn't thought about it.'

'Well, you'd better think about it,' she said practically. 'But if you just want a good screw, make up your mind and let's get it over with. Then we can go our own ways.'

Her calmness annoyed him. Once more Greville inspected her critically – this time as if he was mentally undressing her. She remained unembarrassed.

'I never make love before noon,' he remarked humourlessly.

'Who said anything about love?' she retorted. 'It's something people like me have to do to stay alive.'

Greville refused to let himself show any pity, because pity was nothing more than placing a weapon in the hands of an opponent. 'I suppose even people like you develop a taste for it.'

'Especially people like me,' said Liz. 'And especially if we get screwed about twice a day for a year or two. We either jump in the river or develop a taste for it.' She returned his critical inspection with interest. 'Mind you,' she added, 'there are times when it's repulsive anyway, but I've learned to put up with them.'

Greville slapped her. It was not a very hard blow, but surprisingly she began to cry.

Despite the implications of her last remark, he didn't know why he had slapped her – just as he didn't know why he was now putting his arm round her shoulder and trying to comfort her.

'It wasn't you. It wasn't you,' she sobbed. 'It was those horrible dogs … Oh, hell, I want to be sick.'

Greville opened the car door and helped her out. She retched, but very little came up. When she had finished, she began to shiver violently. With the shotgun in his hand and keeping an alert eye for dogs, he made her walk up and down until the shivering stopped.

'Thanks,' she said at last. 'I seem to be thanking you for everything, don't I?'

'It's a habit you'll grow out of.'

'Yes … I don't even know your name.'

'Call me Greville.'

'Is that all of it?'

'It's enough.'

Liz sighed. 'Well, what are you going to do with me, Greville?'

'I don't know. I shall have to think about it.'

'Don't think too long. If you don't want your pound of flesh, I'm going to try and get a bit nearer Jane.'

He laughed. 'You've got about as much chance of finding Jane as of finding a needle in the proverbial but now obsolete haystack.'

'What's that to you?' demanded Liz wearily. 'We're all nut-cases together.

Besides, I have a sort of built-in direction-finding apparatus. And, anyway, it doesn't matter how I waste my time, does it?'

'It matters to me,' said Greville. And suddenly he was amazed to realise that it did. 'It's quite a long time since I talked to anybody,' he said, as if that explained everything. 'I think I might take you home with me. You might even be useful.'

'I'm no good for anything but screwing,' said Liz flatly.

'For all I know you might not even be any good at that. Incidentally, while we're on the subject, try to find another word for it.'

'Does it offend your modesty?'

'No,' he said evenly. 'Only my aesthetic sense. Now, if you have got over having the vapours, let's think in terms of breakfast.'

FIVE

Breakfast consisted of very salty ham, coarse home-made bread and bottled beer. They ate it near Cleopatra's Needle, on the Embankment. It was a long time since Liz had been in London, and she wanted to see what time, transnormals, and the reign of cats and dogs had done to it. She was not haunted by ghosts as Greville was, and she was fifteen years younger. Also she had never really known the normal world, for all her growing and most of her exploring had been done during the terrible decade of Omega radiation. So she could not experience the perspective of sadness that Greville experienced, nor could she be aware as he was aware of the immense tragedy in the passing of a great city. If she did not seem to notice the desolation so much it was simply because experience had taught her that this kind of desolation was natural: it was just a part of life.

They ate their meal sitting in the car and watched the sun climb slowly with the bright golden promise of another warm day. The food was part of the rations Greville had brought with him on his obsessional anniversary visit to Chelsea Bridge. There had, of course, been a practical excuse for the long – and hazardous – expedition from his cottage in Norfolk to the great city. He was on the scrounge – for guns, ammunition, shoes, clothing, tools, books, and almost anything.

He had been living in East Anglia for about eighteen months. He had drifted there and found the cottage that he had made into his private lair purely by chance. When the Leicester Volunteer Force disintegrated in 1979 – along with practically every other quasi-social organisation in the country – he had almost instinctively made his way south. On his wanderings he had become entangled, and rapidly disentangled, with several small groups of one kind or another. But he had not attached himself or allowed himself to become personally involved for the very simple reason that he knew that most of the groups he had encountered were doomed. Some of them had been no more than amateur brigands, others were small tribes based loosely on the family and recognising only the ties of real or symbolic kinship, yet others were fanatical do-gooders trying with a few dozen hands to resurrect the body and spirit of an entire civilisation. But none of them had staying power because they were either living on the past or trying to rebuild it. They could not understand that, in the broad sense, they were nothing more than grave-robbers – like Egyptian peasants looting from the Valley of the Tombs of Kings.

Greville was disgusted with failure, his own and everyone else's. So he recoiled from membership of a group – any group – and determined to lead a fairly solitary existence. Above all, he needed time to think, time to come to terms with a mad world, time to come to terms with his own private madness.

He had discovered the cottage in Norfolk as he struggled vaguely towards London. It was more than a cottage: it was a citadel, for it stood on an island less than an acre in size in Ambergreave Lake, about twenty miles south of Norwich. There had once been an Ambergreave Manor, a rambling sixteenth-century mansion, that had been burned down in 1976 when the owner poured two gallons of petrol over himself and struck a match. The cottage on the island had originally been built as a folly at a time when such architectural extravagances were popular attractions in the grounds of large English country houses. But a nineteenth-century Lord of Ambergreave, who took a serious and considerably optimistic view of his qualities as a poet, had the folly converted to a retreat where he could live in splendid isolation for weeks at a time while churning out an abundance of sonnets that would surely establish a considerable niche for him in English literary history.

Unfortunately, it did not occur to him that English Literature itself was subject to mortality. Nor could he have possibly entertained the notion that within five years of his death his poems would be forgotten by everyone but the printer to whom he had paid in the course of time more than a thousand guineas for the publication of various slim volumes.

Such, however, proved to be the case. Greville had discovered his effigy in marble above a substantial-looking vault in the churchyard of the village of Ambergreave, which was about three miles away from the remains of the manor house. The grave – and, in fact, the entire churchyard – was rapidly disappearing under a mass of weeds and shrubs. But he had been sufficiently interested in the man who had provided his ideal retreat to find out something about him. The inscription below the statue read: *To the undying memory of Augustus Rowley, visionary, philosopher and man of letters. Born 1833: died 1873 of languishment and a profound melancholy. He here awaits the vindication of time and circumstance, secure in the belief that he accurately interpreted the call of his Maker.*

Greville had been amused by the wordy epitaph, which he suspected had been written by Augustus Rowley himself. And, indeed, he had reason to be grateful to that obscure and pathetic dilettante, for the cottage on the island in a lake that was itself the creation of some previous Rowley had proved to be an ideal lair for a solitary transnormal in the transnormal world of the late twentieth century.

Indulging a whim, Greville had cut down the weeds that were scrambling vigorously round the grave of Augustus. Occasionally he would visit the churchyard and indulge in one-sided conversations with the extinct vision-ary, philosopher and man of letters. He took especial pleasure in trying to explain to the mute and invisible Augustus the present state of a world that, in the nineteenth century, must then have seemed to be the still point, the fixed centre of a turning universe. He had a happy feeling that if Augustus could really have appreciated the catastrophe that had overtaken his secure and well-ordered cosmos, it would have been quite enough to make that man of letters turn from the exquisite sculpture of his deathless sonnets to the quarry-like blastings of free verse.

Now, as Greville sat in the car with Liz and gazed at the battered lines of Waterloo Bridge, one span of which had been almost demolished by unknown causes and about which there lay a wreckage of small craft, and some quite sizeable pleasure boats, he was reminded of Augustus Rowley's certain conviction of immortality. *Sic transit gloria mundi* … This is the way the world ends, not with a bang but a whimper.

'You are miles away,' said Liz. 'Where the hell are you?'

He looked at her with a start and realised that she had finished eating. She had also emptied her bottle of beer.

'Sorry,' said Greville. He lifted his own bottle to his lips and drank from it gratefully. He suddenly felt very thirsty. 'Would you like another bottle? There's a crate in the back of the car.'

'No, thank you … What were you thinking about? Were you wondering what to do with me?'

'No. That problem's settled, at least. I'm taking you back to Norfolk. If you make yourself agreeable, I might even eventually let you go chasing off after your sister Jane.'

'And if I don't make myself agreeable?'

'Then I might toss you back to the dogs.'

'Oh, well,' said Liz equably and obscurely, 'while there's a choice, life is not without interest … Now, what were you thinking about? You had a sort of sad, faraway look in your eyes.'

'Augustus Rowley,' he said, 'and mortality.'

Then he told her about the cottage on the island and about Augustus Row-ley's grave and the tiny ghost-like village of Ambergreave.

'It sounds all right,' remarked Liz noncommittally, when he had finished, 'and Norfolk's on the way to Lancashire, so maybe I'm not doing too badly.'

'You could have done considerably worse about an hour ago,' Greville reminded her. 'So don't take anything too much for granted.'

'When are we going back?' she asked.

'Today. Now, in fact.'

'I thought you were on the scrounge.'

He pointed to the untidy heap of assorted goods in the back of the station wagon. 'I did quite a bit of scrounging yesterday. I've got enough to be going on with.'

'Oh.' She seemed disappointed.

'What's the matter?'

'I wanted to see a bit of London. The last time I was here I was hardly more than a kid.'

'There's nothing much to see,' he said flatly. 'Nothing but death and destruction, dogs, rats and a million broken windows.'

'If we looked around a bit, you might find something you needed,' said Liz hopefully.

Greville smiled. She was as eager and as pathetic as a child trying to talk an adult into giving it an outing.

'All right,' he capitulated. 'You can have a couple of hours. Then it's back to Norfolk. I can't risk any night driving.'

'Greville, you're my kind of transie,' she said gleefully. 'And any time you feel like a good screw—' she pulled a face '—I mean, any time you wish to engage in carnal distraction, just make a noise.'

He laughed. 'Where do you want to go to first?'

'The Festival Hall. About ten centuries ago, I was taken to a concert there – a piano recital by a Hungarian called Georgia Sniffles, or something like that. He was marvellous. I always remembered it.'

'Waterloo Bridge doesn't look too healthy,' Greville pointed out.

'Aren't there any other bridges?'

He started the car, turned it round and went back to Westminster Bridge. Presently, after having made various detours round blocked streets, he pulled up outside the Festival Hall. Liz jumped out happily.

'Careful,' he warned. 'There may be a brigade of livestock lurking inside.'

'Nonsense,' said Liz. 'There's nothing to eat here, except maybe a few hundredweight of sheet music.'

Nevertheless, Greville loaded his shotgun and then rummaged in the back of the station wagon until he found a single-barrel four-ten, which he gave to Liz with a handful of cartridges. He also gave her a battery powered torch.

'It's going to be dark inside,' he said. 'But don't use the torch more than you need. Dry cells that still work are hard to come by these days.'

The Festival Hall seemed like a great derelict barn. Broken glass lay around in profusion. As they passed through the main doorway, they left the bright morning sunlight behind and entered a deep necropolitan gloom. The thin pencil beam of the torch probed a scene of desolation. Much of the wood panelling had been ripped away – presumably for fuel – and even the banisters of the main staircase had been hacked to pieces.

Liz, determined not to be oppressed by the destruction, began to hum tunelessly to herself. She led the way up the stairs, hesitating only moment- arily when she had to step over a clean-picked skeleton still wearing the tattered remains of a printed dress like a grotesquely gay shroud.

'Rats,' said Greville, as the torch beam hovered briefly over the sad heap of bones.

'Where?' whispered Liz apprehensively.

'I don't mean here and now. But *that's* the work of rats. Dogs would have crunched the bones. So would the kind of cats that have managed to sur- vive … Let's get out. This place is too depressing.'

'I want to see the hall,' protested Liz. 'I want to see where Georgie Sniffles had his grand piano, and I want to imagine all the people – the fat old ladies, the men in dinner jackets, the boys in brown corduroy, and all those girls in silk and taffeta rustling like a million grasshoppers.'

'If you hear any rustling,' retorted Greville, 'shoot first and have visions afterwards. Rats don't make allowances for nostalgia.'

Eventually they groped their way into the auditorium, a vault so black and so still that it seemed as if no sound at all – and certainly not music – could have disturbed its slumber for a thousand years. Strangely, there was not much damage. Here and there seats had been slashed, or clawed; and there was an overwhelming mustiness. But apart from cobwebs and mildew, the hall was structurally intact.

Liz shone the torch on the stage – and gave a small cry of wonder; for the last performance ever given in the Festival Hall had been The Nutcracker ballet. And the backcloth, frayed and tattered, was still miraculously hang- ing. Great faded Russian fir trees still loomed magically in the crystal forests dreamed of by Tchaikovsky. A few scatterings of paper snow – or rat leavings – lay carelessly on the bare boards; and it seemed for a moment as if the lights might go up, the music begin, and the bright figure of the Snow Queen float gracefully from behind black velvet drapes.

'Oh! Isn't that absolutely wonderful!' breathed Liz. 'You can almost feel it – after all these terrible years.'

Suddenly, she dropped the torch and began to sob.

'Come on,' said Greville in a voice that was purposefully harsh. 'You've seen enough. We're getting out of here.'

He picked up the torch and guided the still sobbing Liz away from the fir trees and the pathetic and enduring snow. As they went down the stairs he wondered if, before the rats came, the skeleton lying bleakly under its cover- ing of printed cotton had also seen Tchaikovsky's fir trees and the paper snow of history. Perhaps the sad little skeleton had even danced upon that very stage. Perhaps it had once been a prima ballerina. Perhaps … He cut off the thoughts before they could develop further. He did not want to know about the past any more. All he wanted – and all Liz wanted – was the blessed sunlight.

As they returned to it, the summer morning seemed incredibly sweet. They could not have been inside the Festival Hall more than about ten minutes. But to Greville it had seemed more like ten years. Slowly, Liz was recovering herself.

'Maybe it would be better if we cut out the sight-seeing and headed for Norfolk,' said Greville gently. 'There's not very much left in London now – apart from ghosts and scavengers.'

However, despite her recent tears, Liz was not to be deterred. 'I may never come here again,' she said. 'I may get myself killed or swallowed up in the north ... London was such a lovely exciting city, wasn't it? I want to store up a few memories to tell all the grandchildren I'll most likely never have ... Besides, you promised. You promised me a couple of hours. You wouldn't go back on your promise, would you?'

Greville sighed. 'I suppose you wouldn't be a transie if you didn't like banging your head on a wall. Where to next?'

'The centre of the universe,' said Liz, suddenly gay. 'Piccadilly Circus. We'll sit in the Lyon's Corner House, and drink coffee and watch all the people going to work.'

Greville drove the car back over Westminster Bridge, along the Embankment and up Northumberland Avenue. When they reached Trafalgar Square, it seemed momentarily like the day after a stupendous carnival or an orgy on the grand scale. There were two or three buses – one of them overturned – a cluster of taxis straddling the entry to the Strand, and an assortment of private cars large and small. Also there were people, lying about with careless abandon as if they were too drunk to move, as if they might have been celebrating some momentous occasion – such as the end of a war to end all wars.

The only trouble was, nothing moved. Nothing except the pigeons. For the pigeons were still there. With the conditioning of decades behind them, they would probably continue to haunt Trafalgar Square long after the last Londoner was dead.

Even as Liz and Greville glanced at the scene, the aftermath of the carnival resolved itself into a sunlit nightmare. The buses were rusty hulks, the taxis had been cannibalised for spare parts – even wheels and radiators – and some of the cars had been riddled with small-arms fire. The drunks – men, women and a few children – were no more than tattered rag-doll skeletons, lying where they had fallen, some of them with rusty guns cradled like strange talismans in arms that were only whitened bones.

And only the pigeons moved. They had been feeding (even pigeons had adapted to the new order – and a new diet) or basking or squabbling or merely strutting importantly among the buses. But the sound of the car had disturbed them; and they rose angrily and noisily up into the morning sun-light, whirling past the high effigy of Nelson, who still stood on his column and stared serenely ahead with his wide blind eyes.

A shot rang out. A chip of roadway sprang up in front of the station wagon.

'I thought there might be one or two about!' snapped Greville obscurely. He slammed the car into first gear and accelerated. Another bullet ricocheted plaintively where a moment ago the station wagon had been standing.

Greville drove skilfully round the overturned bus, zigzagged among the wrecked small cars and then found a clear run through Cockspur Street and the Haymarket.

Piccadilly Circus presented much the same kind of petrified desolation as Trafalgar Square, except that two massive army tanks blocked the entry to Regent Street, and Eros – the frail statue which had once seemed like an irre-sistible magnet for hundreds of thousands of Londoners – had been blown to glory.

Piccadilly Circus had obviously been the scene of a pitched battle. The carnage was heavier than in Trafalgar Square, and tattered remnants of uni-forms still hung over the disorderly heaps of bones. The front of the London Pavilion had been shot to pieces and so had Swan and Edgars. The main entrance to the Piccadilly Tube Station was merely a pile of rubble; and large pieces of masonry lay scattered among the bones and wrecked cars that blocked the entrances to Piccadilly and Shaftesbury Avenue.

'Satisfied?' demanded Greville harshly.

Liz nodded, her face white.

'Right. Now we can get the hell out of here and go to a place where it's still relatively pleasant to live.'

'Please,' she said. 'There's just one thing more I'd like to see … It – it means quite a lot. I want to go to the British Museum. It's all tied up with being a little girl and feeling safe and secure in a fairly normal world … My father used to go there a lot. He took me once or twice when I was about nine … Do you think we could take a quick look?'

'If we don't get ambushed on the way,' retorted Greville grimly. 'But that's the last stop. After that, we're off to Norfolk.'

'Yes,' sighed Liz. 'That's the last stop.'

Greville took the car along Coventry Street. He drove slowly. There were what looked like several miniature shell-holes in the scarred roadway, and the passing of the station wagon raised clouds of fine dust from the rubble.

SIX

So far, they had not encountered any human being – unless one could include the brief sniping in Trafalgar Square – but it was still quite early in the morning; and the 'normal' transnormal would give the rats and cats and other nocturnal scroungers plenty of time to disperse before he ventured forth. However, as the car turned up Charing Cross Road, Liz and Greville saw their first transie of the day – an old man almost bent double under the weight of an obviously heavy sack over his shoulder.

He took one glance at the car, dropped the sack and scuttled like a frightened rabbit. Out of curiosity, Greville pulled up by the sack and inspected its contents.

'What is it?' asked Liz.

'Tinned goods.' Greville looked along the road, but the old man was nowhere to be seen. He might still be lurking in a doorway or he might have decided to abandon his spoils rather than risk being shot. There was no way of knowing.

Greville opened the rear door of the station wagon and lifted the sack. 'It would be a pity to leave this lot, wouldn't it?'

'What if he comes back?' asked Liz.

'What if he doesn't?'

Finally they compromised by taking half the tins – mostly fruit juices, but there was also a tin of sausages and beans – and leaving the rest in the sack on the roadway.

'I'm surprised the rats haven't chewed the labels off,' said Greville. 'The old boy must have found them in a rat-proof cellar, somewhere.'

'Or maybe,' said Liz, 'they were just tucked away in an old fridge.'

Having stowed away the dozen or so tins they had acquired, they set off once more towards the British Museum. Unlike Piccadilly Circus and Trafalgar Square, St.Giles's Circus was hardly damaged, and they crossed Oxford Street without any difficulty. Even in Great Russell Street, there was nothing to impede their progress but a very few old skeletons without even a rag of clothing in the vicinity. In life, thought Greville as he drove past the pathetic remains, they might well have been a bunch of crackpot nudists. Anything was possible in a transnormal world. But what was more probable was that the corpses had been stripped to provide clothing for the living.

Outside, the British Museum seemed completely unchanged – as if it still proposed to endure for ever. But inside, the massive building was a ruin.

In the library, the works of Shakespeare, Dostoevsky, Jung and Einstein – along with obscure medieval chronicles, twentieth-century text-books of nuclear physics, histories of witchcraft and political philosophies – all had been converted into a vast cosmopolis of nests for vermin. Fortunately, the nests were old, the vermin had departed to make new conquests. But their half-digested droppings of Dante and Ouida, Homer and Silas K. Hocking remained.

The British Museum stank. And the stench was of decay and death, and blind and bloody futility. But, also, there were piles of charred books and smoke blackened ceilings. Testimony, perhaps, to the empty revenge of a few transnormals on the culture that had formerly rejected them. Or perhaps merely the work of homeless and starving children who had made fires to ward off evil spirits, emboldened animals and the bitter cold of darkness – until the rats took over.

But the devastation was not confined to the library. In the Egyptian Room the massive stone statue of Rameses still stood, defying rats, beetles, transnormals and time itself. But elsewhere the destructibles had been destroyed, the combustibles had been burnt, the eatables had been eaten.

As Greville surveyed the gloomy immensity of halls and galleries, he was surprised at how much of history could be eaten – and probably not only by insects and animals. But then, he reflected grimly, life was essentially cannibalistic. Cultures and societies consumed each other, as well as animals and men …

Liz had been silent. Unnaturally silent. She merely held his hand tightly like a small child. A frightened child. No father now to reassure her, no discreet whispers of ordinary people patronising the relics of the centuries with tepid and sophisticated curiosity. Only gothic halls of desolation and the almost tangible silence of the dead that have been made to die yet again.

In the dull light, Greville suddenly noticed that Liz seemed very pale and withdrawn. For a while he had been so absorbed in the mute tragedy around him, that he had barely given her a thought. But now he suddenly realised that it would be a good thing to get her outside as quickly as possible – out into the morning sunlight.

'Come on,' he said. 'You've already seen too much.'

She seemed only to be able to stop herself from running with a tremendous effort. Out in the blessed sunlight once more, she heaved a great sigh of relief. And fainted on the steps.

Greville caught her. After a minute or two her colour came back, and he gave her a bottle of beer.

ALL FOOLS' DAY

'Well, you got what you wanted. You've seen the sights,' he said drily. 'Shall we put a few miles behind us?'

She nodded. 'I'm sorry. I thought – I thought ...'

'You thought it was all going to be sad and terribly romantic,' he interrupted roughly. 'Well, it isn't. It's mean and it's dirty and it's downright ugly ... Now, if you aren't going to be sick or anything like that, let's get in the car and start moving.'

After half an hour's driving, involving several small detours, Greville took the station wagon cautiously along Old Street and into Shoreditch, where he hit the A10. Then he picked up speed. Driving along the trunk road was easier but more dangerous, for trunk-road districts were the main hunting grounds of most 'foreign' scroungers.

Liz still remained withdrawn. She slumped in the passenger seat and stared listlessly at the road ahead. Greville had been a little surprised by her reactions both at the Festival Hall and at the British Museum. From what he knew of her recent existence, he would have thought that she would be able to take the disintegration of London landmarks in her stride. But then, he reflected, the city she remembered would have been a bright, imaginary city of childhood. Despite her 'cloistered' life in Richmond – perhaps even because of it – she had probably cherished the happy illusion that things could not be quite so bad in what was once one of the great cities of the world.

Apart from the old man who had dropped his sack and fled, they did not encounter any other transnormals in the journey across London. Greville was agreeably surprised. He did not harbour many illusions about his fellow transnormals, and knew that a well-laden car complete with provisions, guns and ammunition would be regarded by a lot of people as a prize worth taking risks for. He drove with a pistol handy and a loaded shotgun across his knees. If he could help it, he was not going to be taken by surprise.

But it was still quite early in the day and, apart from thoughts of plunder, there was no reason why any transnormals should bestir themselves. Later, no doubt, probably towards noon, London's dwindling inhabitants would waken up and venture abroad. But by that time he would be clear of the city and on the relatively easy road to Cambridge.

As the car passed without much difficulty through Hackney, Stoke Newington and Tottenham, Greville's spirits rose. It was a fine summer morning and, despite his alcoholic rendezvous on Chelsea Bridge the night before, he was feeling good. Soon he would be back in Ambergreave; and with Liz – well, at least he would have someone to talk to. And, if required – to use her own description – someone to screw. However, sex was a problem that had not really bothered him for some time. In a detached sort of way, he wondered if it still mattered.

'How old are you?' asked Liz suddenly. Her colour was coming back, and she looked as if she was beginning to revive.

Greville had to think for a moment. 'Thirty-seven,' he said at last. 'Why?'

Liz smiled. 'I wondered about the white hair.'

'It turned overnight,' said Greville solemnly, 'with the shock of discovering that I had reached puberty.'

They both laughed, and the laughter seemed to disperse much of the tension that had been building up.

The ambush did not come until they had almost reached the small town of Ware, thirty miles north of London.

It came on a dull, dead suburban road where most of the gardens and privet hedges of semi-detached houses were so overgrown that the houses themselves were nearly lost to view.

It came in the shape of an old truck that suddenly hurtled out of a side-road and blocked Greville's path. He braked, swerved and tried to drive round it. But the ambushers had chosen their spot well. The road was too narrow.

To avoid a collision, Greville stamped on the brake pedal and brought his station wagon to a halt with the front wings just touching the rear of the truck. Before he could reach for his gun, the privet hedges on either side of the road parted, displaying at least four rifles or shotguns already covering him.

A figure stepped out of the hedge on the near side. It was brandishing an old army-type revolver.

'Don't do anything neurotic,' piped a thin voice, 'unless you feel like having your face spread all over the windscreen.'

Greville kept his hands on the wheel and let out an audible sigh. Then he gazed through the open side window at the cheerfully lethal expression on the face of a boy of perhaps sixteen.

SEVEN

The ambushers came out from behind the hedges that had concealed them and stood warily round the car. The driver of the truck jumped down and joined them. Somebody lit a cigarette, somebody laughed. They seemed extraordinarily pleased with themselves. Altogether there were half a dozen of them; and none of them looked to be more than about eighteen.

The boy with the revolver was not laughing. There were tiny beads of sweat on his face, and he seemed to have trouble containing a tremendous and subtle excitement. Greville looked at his eyes – blue, piercing and at the same time oddly remote – and knew that they were the eyes of a killer.

The revolver waved negligently. 'All right, Uncle,' said the thin, high-pitched voice, 'get out of the car very slowly because we're all terribly nervous, and our fingers have a habit of twitching when we get the least bit upset.'

This injunction was met with a guffaw by one of the other boys. 'Good old Nibs! He's a real way-out Charlie!'

Nibs glanced at the speaker. 'Shove it, Smiler. My sense of humour has a low sugar content.'

The words were spoken very quietly, but as he got out of the car Greville noticed that Smiler seemed to shrink visibly.

'And now let us observe your esteemed lady companion in all her glory,' said Nibs. He waved the revolver towards Liz. 'Come on, now, move your hot little bottom.'

Liz and Greville exchanged glances. Neither of them could read anything at all in the other's eyes. Liz seemed unnaturally calm. Thank God for that, thought Greville. One little wrong thing and these kids would start shooting just for the hell of it.

Liz got out of the car very slowly.

Greville turned to Nibs. 'What do you want?' he said evenly.

Nibs lifted the revolver fractionally until it was pointing at Greville's stomach. 'Say sir.'

'Sir.'

Suddenly Nibs leaned forward, put out his free hand and slapped Greville's face hard. 'Say thank you.'

Greville immediately suppressed the impulse that rose in him. He knew that Nibs wanted to kill him. He thought he could get the gun, and he thought it would take all of ten seconds to break the boy in two. But there were other guns. And there was Liz.

'Thank you – sir.'

'That's better, Uncle. Now go down on your knees and beg my forgiveness for asking tiresome questions.'

Greville got down on his knees, not daring to look at Liz. One of the boys sniggered. 'That Nibs. He has style, man. Real style.'

'I beg your forgiveness, sir,' said Greville quietly. He was thinking: so long as this kid can show them how big he is by using me as a door-mat, he'll let me stay alive.

'That's better, Uncle. We begin to understand each other. You may kiss my shoes.'

Greville kissed his shoes. Nibs lightly kicked his face for the privilege. The rest of the gang found this excruciatingly funny.

'Stand up, Uncle. You're overdoing it.'

Greville stood up. Nibs spat in his face.

'Thank you, sir.'

'Uncle,' said Nibs, 'you're bright. But don't let it go to your head.'

'No, sir.'

'Now what kind of treasures have you got in your nice little motor-car?'

'Guns, ammunition, some shirts, woodworking tools, a crate of beer and a few books.'

Nibs slapped him again. 'You forgot to say sir.'

'Sorry, sir.'

'It looks to me, Uncle,' said Nibs pleasantly, 'as if you might have come by your little haul somewhat dishonestly. That is not nice, is it?'

'No, sir.'

Nibs glanced at his companions and sighed. 'My dears! What is the older generation coming to?' There was a gust of laughter. Nibs turned to Greville once more.

'I hope you are bitterly sorry for your sins.'

'Yes, sir.'

'Repeat after me: I am filled with remorse and penitence.'

'I am filled with remorse and penitence, sir.'

'I am very distressed by your recent lack of honesty, Uncle,' said Nibs solemnly. 'I know the temptations are great in this wicked world, but you should try to be strong. You didn't try hard enough, did you?'

'No, sir.'

'Then you must try much harder in future – if you have a future. Meanwhile purely in the interests of justice, we shall have to confiscate this little lot. Firearms are particularly dangerous in the hands of inexperienced persons.'

Greville was beginning to understand how Nibs had become the leader of a gang of boys most of whom were older and stronger than he was. The boy, despite his weak face and effeminate voice, had brains and a literally striking personality. He also had a sure feeling for his audience. At the moment, the other boys were hanging on his every word and enjoying themselves hugely. Through Nibs, no doubt, and on the person of Greville they were wreaking vengeance for the lost security of a world that had simply gone from bad to worse throughout the major part of their young lives.

Most of them had probably been orphaned years ago, and they could only have survived by good luck and sheer singlemindedness. Greville could imagine the kind of terrifying problems with which they would have had to cope. Objectively, he could be sorry for them all. Subjectively, he felt like killing them – particularly Nibs – with his bare hands.

So far, Liz had done nothing except watch Greville make his bid for survival by passively accepting whatever form of abasement the boys cared to thrust on him. In the bright sunshine she thought his face looked tired and old. A good deal older than thirty-seven. She felt sorry for him. She felt sorry for herself too. She thought he was underestimating Nibs and his confederates. She thought they were both going to be killed anyway. She thought it would be a good idea to try to take one or two of these nasty little transies with them. All she needed from Greville was a sign. But there was no sign. Nothing at all.

Then Nibs was talking again. 'Now, Uncle, having satisfactorily disposed of the burden of your worldly possessions, let us consider your only remaining problem. What about hot bottom, here?' He gave Liz a look of moist malevolence.

'She's my woman – sir.'

'Your wife?'

Greville thought quickly about that one. 'No.' He collected another slap. 'No, sir.'

Nibs was really enjoying himself. 'Uncle, you distress me. Not content with stealing, you also have an unwholesome taste for fornication … That is very naughty. Repeat after me: I am a dirty old man.'

'I am a dirty old man, sir.'

'Do you repent of this sordid fornication?'

Greville hesitated, and the gun barrel rose again. 'Yes, sir.'

'I'm pleased to hear it. We shall remove the temptation.' He turned to Liz. 'Take off your clothes, dearest. We wish to inspect the charms that have turned poor Uncle here into a sinful old gentleman.'

Liz did not move. She looked past him, trying not to think.

'Big Ears,' said Nibs, addressing a dullish youth who was at least as tall as Greville and probably about twenty pounds heavier, 'help the lady to disrobe.'

Big Ears grinned, laid down his shotgun and took hold of Liz. She kicked him. Big Ears laughed and hit her in the stomach. Liz groaned and doubled up. Big ears pushed her to the ground and rolled her on her back. Then he tore her blue shirt open from neck to waist.

Liz kicked him again, and again he hit her in the stomach. Then he ripped the shirt off over her head, leaving her panting and groaning.

'All right?' said Big Ears, looking at Nibs.

'For the moment.' Nibs was watching Greville and relishing the situation.

'She's a proper little playmate,' said Big Ears. He scooped Liz up almost fondly and set her on her feet. 'There's still quite a bit of mileage left in her, I shouldn't wonder.'

'Yes,' said Nibs, still looking at Greville. 'I imagine Uncle, here, hasn't ever tried her in top gear.'

'She looks a pretty fair shag,' said one of the other youths. 'How about it, Nibs?'

'Let's have a go,' added Big Ears almost pleadingly. 'There's nothing else to do before we send 'em.'

Nibs smiled. 'Boys, whatever are you thinking of? Here am I trying to re-educate Uncle. Do you want to set him a bad example?'

There was a burst of laughter. Nibs turned to Greville with a sigh, and shrugged. 'Boys will be boys, Uncle … I do hope you will forgive their gay high spirits.'

Greville said nothing. Nibs hit him and he still said nothing. He knew he wasn't going to be killed now until they had finished raping Liz. That gave him a little more time. What use it would be, he did not know. Probably they were both going to be killed anyway. He wondered cynically whether Liz would really prefer to die before or after. But he didn't look at her. He hadn't the courage.

'Uncle is sulking,' said Nibs. 'Let's see what we can do to cheer him up … Smiler, you and Big Ears and Mumbles can play with darlingest on the lawn for a few minutes – and don't make it longer than five each because Jim-Jim and Lookers won't be very happy if there isn't much left … Jim-Jim, move the truck in case we have visitors. Lookers, you can help me entertain Uncle until Smiler and Co. have got rid of their problems.'

Liz began to fight, but she could do nothing at all against Smiler, Big Ears and Mumbles. They lifted her bodily and took her behind one of the over-grown privet hedges where nothing more exciting than a weekly mowing and a spring planting had happened for nearly half a century. They dumped Liz in the now long grass. Mumbles held her arms, Smiler pulled her trousers down and Big Ears prepared himself to take the first ride.

Liz suddenly stopped struggling. What the hell was the use? But she didn't close her eyes. As Big Ears lay on top of her, forcing her legs apart and rhythmically exciting himself by noting her pain reaction as he pinched and pulled the nipple of her left breast, she tried to will her body not to respond, tried to pretend the pain belonged to someone else. He bit her lip, forcing her mouth open against his. But still she did not close her eyes. She gazed into his, clouded and vacant with lust, hating him, willing him to die. He didn't. He just worked stolidly and mindlessly towards a crude mechanical climax.

Meanwhile, Jim-Jim got back into the truck and backed it into the side road, while Lookers sat on the edge of the pavement and cradled his two-two rifle with the barrel pointing generally in Greville's direction. And Greville did nothing.

Now that his active force had been temporarily reduced, Nibs handled his revolver carefully. He stood two paces back from Greville. He was taking no chances.

Nibs listened eagerly to the subdued noises behind the hedge. Occasionally, there was a grunt. Occasionally, Liz could not avoid letting out a low animal moan. Nibs smiled. The beads of sweat became larger on his downy upper lip. He was getting more sensual pleasure out of the situation than if he had been on top of Liz himself.

Much more, thought Greville. For besides being a killer Nibs was a sadist. God alone knew what had happened to him to turn him into what he was. It must have been something pretty ghastly. Or a whole lot of things that were pretty ghastly … He tried not to think about Liz … He tried only to think of a way of getting a gun before he himself was shot.

Still keeping his revolver trained on Greville, Nibs took a quick look over the hedge. 'Big Ears has finished,' he said conversationally. 'Your dear lady looks as if she's enjoying it, Uncle. You must have been starving her. Never mind, she ought to have a pretty full belly by the time old Mumbles has finished with her. Mumbles doesn't say much, but he's got talent.'

Jim-Jim, gun in hand, had returned from parking the truck. 'I can hear something,' he said.

Nibs laughed. 'It's only hot bottom having fun. Smiler's on the job.'

'No. I mean a car engine. Listen.'

They listened.

'It's a car all right,' said Lookers, rising briefly into eloquence. 'Shall we let it through, Nibs? We got a nice enough haul for one day.'

But Nibs was drunk with power. 'Not on your nelly.' He peered over the hedge. 'Let Smiler finish his ride by himself. She isn't going to stand up and cheer. The rest of us are going into routine. There's another one coming.' He turned back to Greville. 'Come across the road, Uncle, and lie down – unless you want to have it now.'

Greville walked obediently across the road and lay down in a gateway, while Nibs stood behind him. Jim-Jim had disappeared and was already gunning the truck's engine. As far as a casual observer was concerned, the road was deserted – except for a station wagon apparently parked at a crazy angle to the kerb.

Greville permitted himself to hope a little. Not too much, but a little. If only the car that was coming contained two or three well-armed men!

For about a hundred yards the road was straight. Then there was a slight bend. Nibs had chosen his spot carefully. It was not the kind of road where you would expect trouble. It was suburban, dead, uninteresting.

Suddenly the oncoming car appeared round the bend. It was an ancient Land Rover with tarpaulin covers over the back. Nibs raised an arm. Someone on the other side of the road repeated the signal. Jim-Jim brought the truck roaring out of the side road. There was a screeching of brakes as the Land Rover pulled up.

It's now or never, thought Greville. But Nibs had anticipated him. Even as he leaped to his feet the revolver came crashing on to the back of his head. He blacked out and went down again. By the time he returned to consciousness, the driver of the Land Rover was already out of his car and being interrogated by Nibs and Big Ears. Mumbles was standing beside Greville, his rifle ready and a benign expression on his face.

Greville's hopes faded rapidly. The driver of the Land Rover wore the long black habit of a priest.

EIGHT

In almost any other situation the priest would have been a comic figure. As it was, he seemed pathetic and grotesque. He was a plump, bald man of about fifty. He faced the four homicidal youths who barred his path with an odd mixture of bewilderment and self-confidence.

However, his reactions must be reasonably fast, thought Greville, for he had managed to stop his car much quicker than Greville had done. The Land Rover now lay about ten yards behind Greville's station wagon; and the fat priest had come ambling towards the boys almost eagerly, as if he simply could not see the guns that were pointed at him. So eager did he seem to be that he literally fell over himself and appeared to twist an ankle – to the intense amusement of Nibs, Big Ears, Jim-Jim and Lookers.

Smiler was still behind the hedge with Liz, working steadily to his appointed end and at the same time trying to make up his mind whether she had really fainted or was just shamming. Mumbles, despite the diversion in the roadway, kept his eyes on Greville. He wasn't taking any chances at all.

The priest got to his feet, winced with pain, limped a couple of steps and then sat down again. He looked up at Nibs, squinting against the sunlight.

'Good morning, father,' said Nibs. 'God be with you.'

'My son, what on earth are you playing silly tricks for? If I hadn't managed to brake quickly I might have suffered a very serious injury. I might even have been killed … As it is, I doubt very much whether I shall be able to do any more driving today. My leg hurts abominably, and my nerves are quite shaken.'

This little speech was greeted by a gale of laughter.

'Be consoled, father,' said Nibs. 'I shouldn't be at all surprised if you haven't just been granted a Sign. God moves mysteriously, I believe. He may even have decided to terminate your driving career altogether.'

Nibs was clearly at the top of his form. His remarks provoked more laughter, and Big Ears seemed to be on the point of having a convulsion.

'My son,' said the priest indignantly, 'it does not do to mock the cloth.'

'I stand reproved,' said Nibs. 'Now, fat arse, what have you got in the back of your agony wagon?'

The priest blinked. 'Nothing, I'm afraid, but two poor children … Please don't frighten them. They're rather sensitive.'

Nibs turned to Lookers. 'Go and get an eyeful. Fat arse may be playing games.'

'Please!' said the priest. He seemed to be trying to stand up again. But Lookers had almost reached the Land Rover.

Then miracles began to happen thick and fast.

In a loud voice, the priest shouted, 'Now!' At the same time, he simultaneously launched himself at Nibs, grabbing him round the knees and bringing him down, revolver and all.

While that was happening, Mumbles momentarily took his eyes away from Greville. It wasn't much of a chance, thought Greville, but it was the best he was likely to get. He rolled over, grabbed the nearest foot and threw Mumbles off balance. The boy tried to bring his rifle round, but Greville held the barrel; and a bullet ricocheted peevishly along the road. Then Mumbles was down. All Greville's pent up fury broke loose. With one hand, he grabbed the boy's throat, lifted him bodily and brought his head crashing back against the hard pavement. Mumbles sighed and lay still.

Meanwhile, from somewhere in the back of the Land Rover, a sub-machine gun chattered loudly and briefly. Lookers clutched his stomach, spun like a top and fell. The same burst swept by to include Jim-Jim and Big Ears. Jim-Jim ran three paces then doubled up and lay twitching and screaming. Big Ears just stared – a look of utter disbelief on his face – as blood spurted from his neck and chest. Then he slumped soundlessly forward.

'Enough!' shouted the priest. He was lying on top of Nibs, whose arm was twisted behind his back and whose face was pressed into the roadway. The priest had his revolver. He was pointing it at Smiler's white startled face which had just appeared over the top of the hedge.

Greville raised his own arms quickly. He didn't want to get shot by mistake. 'That's all of them,' he called. 'You've got the lot.'

The priest's eyes – no longer weak or comic – flickered briefly towards him. 'Keep your hands up,' he said. 'We don't want any silly mistakes, do we? He turned to Smiler once more. 'Now, smart boy, come through that hedge very slowly – if you want to live a little longer.'

Smiler forced his way through the hedge. His trousers were hanging round his ankles. He made a move to pull them up, but the priest said: 'Dress will be informal. Stay still!'

Smiler stayed still.

'Look,' said Greville, 'they've been raping my girl. She's behind the hedge. Can I go to her?'

'Charming,' said the priest. 'Stay still. What about the one you got?'

'I belted his head,' said Greville. 'He's still breathing.'

The priest called towards the Land Rover: 'All right, children, come out.'

The tail gate was lowered and two girls – neither of whom could have been

more than twenty – got out. One carried a shotgun, and the other an automatic rifle.

'Are you all right, Father Jack?' asked the girl with the shotgun.

'Quite all right, my dear,' said Father Jack, standing up. He turned to Greville once more. 'Collect all the hardware,' he indicated the weapons lying by
Smiler, Jim-Jim, Big Ears and Lookers, 'and don't be clever. Put them in the
middle of the road. Then you can see whether your girl is still with us.'

Greville did as he was told. Then he went into the tiny little garden where
Liz had been taken.

She lay as Smiler had left her, in the long grass. She was completely naked
and looked as if she had taken a hell of a beating; but she was still conscious.
One of her eyes was badly bruised and almost closed up. There was blood
running from a swollen lip and teeth marks all over her shoulders and
breasts. There were two wide yellowish-blue patches on her belly.

She recognised Greville, tried to smile and couldn't. 'I told you I wasn't
much good for anything but screwing,' she whispered hoarsely, so low that he
could hardly hear. Then suddenly, she rolled over and was violently sick.

Greville knelt and supported her shivering retching body. 'Oh, Liz! I
brought you into a real dose of trouble, didn't I?' He wanted to comfort
her and murmur stupid tender things, but all the words were frozen inside
him.

Presently, she stopped vomiting. He gathered her torn shirt and trousers
and helped her to put them on. Then he hunted for her shoes and found that
they had been thrown under the hedge.

She tried to stand up. She could get to her feet, but she couldn't stand
upright. Nor could she move. Greville picked her up gently and carried her
out of the garden. He took her to the station wagon and laid her on the passenger seat. Tears were trickling down her face, but the crying was soundless
and without any movement. He found some brandy and offered it to her, but
she just turned her head away.

Greville closed the car door and went towards Father Jack. Despite the
cassock, Father Jack did not look at all like a priest now. He seemed to have
grown visibly thinner and taller. No longer a comic figure, he looked tough
and purposeful.

Mumbles had returned to consciousness, and Father Jack had lined him
up with Nibs and Smiler, whose trousers were still round his ankles. The
three youths had their hands on top of their heads.

As Greville left Liz one of Father Jack's 'children' went to her. The other
kept her automatic rifle pointing at the three boys. With the revolver that he
had acquired from Nibs, Father Jack administered the *coup de grace* to Jim-
Jim, who had not stopped screaming from the moment he was hit. The shot
rang out and Jim-Jim's screams ended abruptly.

The silence that followed seemed extraordinary – something far more subtle than a mere absence of sound.

'Well, now,' said Father Jack, 'we live in exciting times, don't we? How did you come to get mixed up with these bad lads?'

'The same way as you,' said Greville and told him what had happened.

When he had finished, Father Jack looked at Nibs thoughtfully. 'I'm beginning to think that you are a shade anti-social, my son.'

'Shove the crap,' said Nibs. 'You were lucky, but that's the way it goes. Today, you, tomorrow somebody else. Nobody gives a damn about anything. Why should they? We're all bleeding nuts.' Nibs was pale but his voice was steady.

Suddenly, Greville felt bitterly sorry for him. Suddenly, Nibs was not just a boy psychopath: he was all of mankind. He was the human tragedy writ small … He was also a homicidal sadist …

At that moment, Mumbles rose to a brief eloquence. He had been standing there with a dazed expression on his face and blood trickling steadily down his neck from the head wound he had gained when Greville slammed him against the stone pavement.

'I want to say something,' said Mumbles. 'You're going to kill us, I know that. But I want to say something. I want to say I'm sorry. Not just for this. Not for trying to get you, or screwing the girl or anything like that … I don't know what I want to say really … I just want to say I'm sorry … Maybe I'm sorry because it's such a bloody rotten world … Maybe I'm sorry because this is the one we lost.' His voice broke. 'I don't know. I'm just sorry, that's all. There's nothing else to it.'

Father Jack gazed at him intently. 'That's a very interesting speech, my son. Kindly turn round. Your face saddens me a little.'

Mumbles turned round obediently, presenting the back of his head to Father Jack. With a rapid movement, the priest lifted his revolver and hit Mumbles with it just below the base of the skull. Mumbles fell without uttering a sound.

'Now,' said Father Jack, turning to Smiler and studying his partial nudity, 'you appear to have been surprised *in flagrante delicto*. Have you any observations to make?'

'Go stuff yourself,' retorted Smiler bravely.

Father Jack sighed. '*Ego te absolvo*, my son.' He shot Smiler neatly through the forehead.

Nibs looked at the body, then he looked at Greville and finally at Father Jack. He licked his lips. 'Father, can I confess before …' He looked at the gun and left the sentence unfinished.

'Confess away, my son.'

'It's not that I believe any of the crap your lot hands out, you understand,' went on Nibs calmly. 'But my family was Catholic, see? It – it sort of brings us together a bit.' He glanced once more at Greville. 'If it's not too much trouble, I'd like it a bit private.'

'Go down on your knees,' said Father Jack. He turned to Greville. 'Perhaps you will excuse us?'

Greville said nothing. He went back to the car and spoke to Liz. She even managed to smile at him. Then she closed her eyes and leaned back as if she wanted to do nothing at all but sleep.

Greville watched Father Jack and Nibs. The boy was on his knees in the roadway. He was talking quickly and quietly. Evidently, thought Greville, he had quite a lot to confess.

It lasted about five minutes. Then Father Jack laid his hand on the boy's forehead, and Nibs made the sign of the cross.

And almost immediately, he lunged at Father Jack's legs. The priest went down heavily, with Nibs scrabbling for the gun. He didn't get it.

'*Ego to absolvo*, my son,' said Father Jack in a loud voice. The gun could not be seen. The sound of the shot was flat and muffled.

But Nibs was suddenly transformed from a killer making his last attempt at killing into a small and oddly pathetic heap. He rolled convulsively on to his back and lay still in the roadway. Just another dead boy. A late and indirect casualty of ten years of Omega radiation.

Father Jack picked himself up and shook the dust off. His limp had completely disappeared. 'Well, now,' he said, 'perhaps we ought to look to the lady.'

NINE

Father Jack was not a Catholic priest – in fact, he had not been ordained as any kind of priest. For nearly twenty years he had been head gardener at the Convent of the Sacred Heart, near Newmarket. Before that he had been a convict and before that he had been an unambitious and reasonably successful burglar. Before he became a burglar, he had served for five years as a paratrooper.

But now, as an almost natural result of all the years of Omega radiation and the Radiant Suicide, he had become simply Father Jack. 'Father' in the literal sense of the word, for he had polygamously married four of the oldest surviving girls at the convent and had already begotten half a dozen children.

At the beginning of the Radiant Suicide, the Convent of the Sacred Heart had a complement of one mother superior, eight teaching and working nuns, fifty girls, a head gardener, an assistant gardener and a general handyman. In the first two years, the assistant gardener, the handyman and two of the nuns committed suicide. Everyone else was enjoined to carry on as if nothing abnormal was happening; for there was still God's work to be done. A few of the girls were taken away by their parents, but most remained and were rapidly orphaned.

For many years the convent had been growing most of its own food; and so its occupants were able to keep going in a reasonably normal fashion until early in 1977. The trouble came one day when Father Jack – who was then still plain Jack Rowbottom – was out hunting for meat. It came, as trouble usually came, in the shape of a truckload of men out on the scrounge.

Jack Rowbottom had already taken the precaution of acquiring firearms and instructing the nuns in their use; so that, despite the fact that they were outnumbered by an enemy with superior firepower, the nuns gave a fairly good account of themselves. Meanwhile most of the girls took advantage of the escape route that had been thoughtfully provided for such an occasion at the cost of much sustained labour by the head gardener. It was an incredibly small tunnel which he had dug from the cellars of the convent to the outer wall of the kitchen garden. Immediately outside the wall there was a few acres of shrubs and woodland. The girls were supposed to scatter and hide among the trees until any trouble that arose had either passed by or been dealt with effectively.

Jack Rowbottom did not get back from his hunting expedition until the attack on the convent had ended and the attackers had gone away laden with spoils. The nuns were all dead of either bullet wounds or knife-wounds gained in the hand-to-hand fighting. The mother superior had been hanged from a banister, although judging from what had already happened to her the hanging could have no more than a symbolic value. A few of the girls were unlucky enough to go back to the convent too soon. A few more had been caught. They were raped and/or abducted or killed.

So Jack Rowbottom, left by himself with more than thirty adolescent girls and an odd sense of responsibility, inescapably became Father Jack – father extraordinary of the Convent of the Sacred Heart.

Provided they were left in peace, he thought he could train the girls to be reasonably self-sufficient. For most of them had already learned to help in the kitchen gardens and they could look after pigs and poultry. Some could weave, some were passing fair at carpentry and some could even cure bacon.

But obviously they were not going to be left alone. So Father Jack set about training them for survival. First he selected the six strongest and least nervous of the girls and formed them into a commando. Then he took them out raiding for weapons. The girls, though young, made rather good fighters since they had been accustomed to a rigorous discipline. Father Jack underlined the lesson of discipline and added to it the training in surprise attack and hand-to-hand combat that he himself had acquired as a paratrooper. Before he had finished, the girls could shoot, bayonet, throw knives, garrotte, kick and gouge as good as most young soldiers and better than many.

They got their weapons. Then they set about converting the Convent of the Sacred Heart into a citadel. Then the commando was split up to train other commandos. And eventually Father Jack had nearly thirty girls, deceptively young, deceptively helpless, who were all trained fighters.

Occasionally he left the convent to go on scrounging expeditions, taking two or three of the girls with him. He was returning from one of these expeditions when Jim-Jim had blocked the road with his truck and had thus precipitated the fracas that had certainly saved Greville and Liz from being ultimately killed.

Greville learned all this about an hour after Nibs had been despatched and while they were taking a late lunch outside a solitary and deserted pub about half way between Ware and Royston. In return, he gave Father Jack a succinct account of his own activities during the last ten years. But for some reason he could not understand, he translated Pauline's death into the death of a stranger. She became simply the driver of another fictitious car into which he had crashed while he was drunk. Father Jack accepted this version easily enough. There was no reason why he shouldn't.

There was nothing on either side of the pub at which they had stopped except a long rolling ribbon of road, carpeted here and there with patches of dandelion, nettles and convolvulus. There was nothing behind the pub except a wide vacancy of overgrown fields and sprawling hedges. That was why they had chosen it – because it was free from the possibility of surprise attack.

After Greville had collected up all the spare guns, and had then made Liz as comfortable as he could, they had driven away from the scene of the ambush slowly and in convoy, with Father Jack's battered Land Rover leading the way. Surprisingly, Liz did not appear to have suffered any lasting physical injury; but she was sore, pitifully sore and especially between her legs. Marilyn, the elder of Father Jack's 'children', had examined Liz to the best of her limited ability. She arrived at the sensible conclusion that what Liz needed more than anything was a good hot bath and a long, lazy soak.

So here they were at the pub, whose cracked but still hanging signboard proclaimed it to be *The Angler's Rest*. Somewhere in its interior, the girls had found an old zinc bath full of the dusty and accumulated household debris of years. They had cleaned it up while Greville used a spanner to make one of the taps in the kitchen work. Eventually he managed to turn it, and out came a trickle of red, muddy water that presently grew into quite a fast flow and became relatively clear.

Meanwhile, Father Jack had taken a couple of portable paraffin stoves from his Land Rover and began to heat the water in a large jamming pan and an old five-gallon oil drum that had been discovered in the pub.

While all these preparations were going on Liz lay slumped in her seat in the station wagon. She looked even worse than she had done when Greville took her out of the garden after she had endured the attentions of Big Ears and Smiler; but her spirits had improved. She managed to smile a little and even say a few words.

Liz took her bath in the pub's best room. She couldn't walk to it. Greville had to carry her. Father Jack, who seemed to be supplied with an amazing variety of goods, had given her a bar of soap and a bottle of baby cream. Then, while Liz tried to take the aches out of her body, the rest of them settled down to their late lunch. Occasionally one of the girls would take her some more hot water, and they even tried to get her to have some food. But Liz was not hungry.

Lunch consisted of cold chicken and warm champagne. The chicken had come from the Convent of the Sacred Heart: the champagne had come from a doctor's house in Bayswater. Four bottles had been wrapped in rags and hidden in the cellar under a pile of coal and junk. But Father Jack was an indefatigable scrounger. When he searched a house he searched it thoroughly.

'Try her with some of the champers,' said Father Jack, regarding the small heap of chicken bones in front of him with some satisfaction. 'It can't do any harm.' He grinned. 'Tell her I blessed it.'

There was still some left in the second bottle they had opened. Greville took it in to Liz. She had rubbed soap all over her body in a desperate and futile attempt to reduce the bruises and teeth-marks. But the heat of the water only served to accentuate them.

Greville thought it would do no harm to try a light-hearted touch. 'I hope it isn't catching,' he said. 'You look as if you've suddenly developed measles or something all round your breasts and shoulders.'

Surprisingly, Liz giggled. 'It's not a disease, it's an allergy,' she retorted. 'My doctor warned me, it was likely to develop if I had any intimate contact with members of the opposite sex.'

'Father Jack has sent you some holy water. You're supposed to drink it and say to yourself: "Whatever happens to me is for the best in this best of all possible worlds".'

'You know,' said Liz, taking the bottle, 'there are times when I could almost believe that – like now.' She set the champagne bottle to her lips and drank greedily.

In one long draught, Greville noted with satisfaction, she drank nearly half a pint.

Liz hiccupped. 'It's a lovely feeling,' she said, 'when it's all over. It's like when you stop banging your head on the wall. It's like waking up from a bad dream. You can see the sunlight, and you know it wasn't for real, after all.'

'You were thirsty,' said Greville, eyeing the empty bottle. 'I'll get you some more.'

'No, stay with me. Getting tight isn't the answer … I'm all right, really, you know. I'm quite used to that sort of thing, but it's usually less strenuous … I've wasted enough time in here. You can help me get out.' She giggled again. 'Then you can put some of that baby cream between my legs. I don't think I can bend far enough myself.'

Greville dried her, then he applied the baby lotion. Then he helped her to dress. While he was putting her shoes and socks on, they heard the sound of a car starting. Greville dashed out of the pub just in time to see the Land Rover pulling away. One of the girls in the back waved cheerily to him, then the car picked up speed, carving a smooth double track through dandelions, foxgloves and the long high nettles of midsummer.

Greville stood there for a few moments, scratching his head and feeling perplexed and watching the Land Rover dwindling in the distance. The sound died: and then there was nothing but the sky and fields that had grown wild as the prairie and were rippling like a green inland sea under the light touch of a breeze.

Liz hobbled out of the pub. 'See. I'm O.K. for walking … What happened?'

215

'Father Jack took off,' said Greville. 'He seems to be in a hell of a hurry.'

When they went to the station wagon, they found one possible reason for Father Jack's hurried departure. It had been stripped of everything – all the goods that Greville had scrounged in London, and the rifles and ammunition that he had taken from the late Nibs and his confederates – everything except two shotguns and twenty cartridges.

On the driver's seat there was a slip of paper on which had been scribbled a short message:

For services rendered. I'm sure you wouldn't have objected, but why risk disagreement? Kindest regards to your good lady. The Lord will provide.

Greville felt simultaneously extremely foolish and extremely angry. But Liz began to laugh.

'Christ!' she said helplessly. 'Never trust the clergy … You know what, Greville? I think he's my kind of transie.'

And suddenly Greville was laughing, too.

TEN

The delay caused by the encounter with the late Nibs and his companions together with the extra time needed to give Liz her bath made it impossible for Greville to get back to Ambergreave Lake and his cottage on the island before it was dark. After they had both recovered from Father Jack's rapid departure, Greville made Liz comfortable in the station wagon, settled himself in the driver's seat and started the engine.

'No more stops,' he said grimly. 'Not for anyone or anything.'

'What if someone else has the same idea as those other clever little bastards?'

'We don't stop. We drive round it or through it. If we can't do either, we've had it anyway. A couple of shotguns aren't much of an arsenal.' He started the car, took a last vague glance at *The Angler's Rest*, and then set off in the tracks that had been carved by Father Jack's Land Rover along the weed-covered road. He thought that if he put his foot down he stood a very good chance of overtaking the Land Rover before long. But he had no desire to overtake it. Whatever Father Jack had taken, he had earned.

So Greville let the station wagon roll along at a reasonable pace, profoundly thankful that he and Liz were still alive. After a time, he was pleased to see that Liz was dozing. She lay huddled in her seat like a small child tired out after a big party.

Some party! thought Greville. It had been hilarious. He began to sweat as he recalled how near they had both been to a particularly stupid – and sordid – form of death. But then, he reflected, all death was sordid. You could die of cancer, accidents, old age, overeating, alcoholism (if you were lucky), hunger, appendicitis, rats, cats, dogs, disease and bullets. Whatever it was, it was stupid and sordid – about as stupid and sordid as staying alive.

The road slipped by. The sun began to sink low towards the western edge of the world. The station wagon passed unmolested through small, ribbon-like villages. Greville was past caring about precautions. He had been near enough to total disaster not to worry too much about what might happen next. Goddammit, if anything was going to happen it bloody well would! So why frighten hell out of one's self by worrying about it. *Que sera, sera* …

Presently Liz woke.

'I'm sorry,' she said.

'Don't be. A bit of rest was what you needed.'

'Not about that. About landing you with me. I'm more trouble than I'm worth. If I hadn't wanted to see the Festival Hall and the British Museum everything might still have gone all right for you.'

'If you hadn't got yourself into a mess on Chelsea Bridge,' pointed out Greville drily, 'the day might have been a hell of a lot duller. On the other hand, I might be dead by now. Who the devil knows?'

'Nevertheless,' said Liz, stretching herself and wincing, 'I want you to know that I'm sorry.'

'Your sorrow is noted.' He smiled. 'It will probably be held against you.'

'Where are we?'

'About forty miles from salvation. There are a few more villages to get through and a small town called Thetford. If we survive those, we stand a reasonable chance of living till morning.'

'I don't even know whether I want to live till morning.'

'You do. That's the trouble. We all bloody well do. It's part of the old genetic programming. When God created the world he filled it full of cretins and said: "Now look, chaps, the great thing is not to write great poetry, create symphonies or produce paintings that make people want to cry." The great thing is to live till morning. And if you are still alive when morning comes, why then you must do your best to increase the odds against some other poor bastard. For if you don't do unto him, as sure as I knocked together this old firmament out of nothing he'll do his damnedest to do unto you.'

Liz began to laugh. 'Greville,' she said, 'I think you're practically the greatest. You pinched me from the dogs, you lick somebody's shoes to give me a chance of living, you put baby lotion on my legs – and lose half your possessions while you're doing it – and you still let me ride in your car and try to keep me happy. You realise you're destroying my faith in human nature?'

'That is the aim,' retorted Greville. 'Essentially, I'm a sadist.'

The sun slipped smoothly over the horizon. The twilight that followed was hardly light enough to drive by, but it suited Greville's programme. He did not switch the car's headlamps on. Instead he dropped speed to little more than twenty miles an hour and stayed in third gear. He was hoping to slip through Thetford – the last real danger point before Ambergreave – in as inconspicuous a manner as possible.

By the time they reached the outskirts of the town stars were pricking the now turquoise eggshell of the sky. Greville's eyes were tired with peering through the windscreen; but they were not too tired to notice the flickering of an oil lamp about a hundred yards along the road.

It was a typical night prowlers' set-up, he thought. Someone would be listening for cars, someone else would be organising the block and, no doubt, a small posse of transnormal citizenry would be ready to pounce if they thought the attack could be carried through without much loss.

'Poke a shotgun through the side window,' said Greville. 'Don't shoot until I tell you, and don't shoot at anything but lights.'

At the same time as they swung the searchlight on him, Greville switched on his own headlamps. The road block was a poor one – it was only a farm trailer. Furthermore, there was a wide grass verge on the right; and if he drove straight at the three men who were standing on it in the glare of his headlamps, he stood a good chance of getting through.

'Now!' he shouted.

The first barrel accomplished nothing except a vaguely human scream; but Liz had better luck with her second try. The searchlight went out.

Greville put his foot down and headed straight for the three men. They began shooting, but the car's headlamps must have ruined their aim. The station wagon lurched sickeningly as it hit the grass verge. Then there was a heavy thud and a bump as it hit at least one of them. Then it was through.

For good measure, Liz fired a couple of backward parting shots, but they probably accomplished nothing. For now there was only darkness once more. Greville switched his lights off immediately, and almost by instinct found his way back to the road.

'Not long, now,' he said. 'Providing we get through the town in one piece. Things aren't quite tough enough yet in this part of the world to make people really desperate. The real danger is not from the locals but from nomads.'

'That road block seemed like a local affair,' observed Liz.

'It was. But they weren't really trying, and they hadn't had much experience. Otherwise we wouldn't be here.'

Liz yawned. 'You almost fill me with optimism.'

He laughed grimly. 'Sometimes I even convince myself.'

They passed through Thetford without any more difficulty. Greville was on home territory and knew his way sufficiently to take the narrow streets at a speed high enough to dismiss all danger of spontaneous attacks. The only thing to be feared was a well prepared block; but fortunately they didn't encounter any.

When they were clear of the town, he switched on his headlamps once more, and Liz saw that the car was running along a smooth straight road flanked on either side by tall trees.

'Thetford Chase,' said Greville. 'It used to be a national park or something like that. Plenty of deer. I'll bring you hunting some time.'

'Cheers for the rustic life.'

'It has its moments.'

A few minutes later they came to the village of Ambergreave. Greville gave a long blast on the car's horn. It startled Liz out of a semi-doze.

'What the hell did you do that for?'

'A local signal,' explained Greville. 'No sense in running the risk of collecting unnecessary pot-shots. Just possibly somebody might be tempted.'

Liz was surprised. 'You mean they won't attack just because you live round here?'

'It's not an infallible rule. But as I told you, we're not entirely down to cannibalism in these parts yet.'

Ambergreave was a long straggly village with most of the houses and cottages set well apart. It took longer to drive through than the town of Thetford and it seemed totally deserted. Presently the station wagon turned off the hard road. Greville changed down into second gear, nursing the car along a narrow bumpy track. Presently the track widened then sloped gently down to the edge of Ambergreave Lake, a broad expanse of water, still as a mirror, reflecting the large low moon like an orange lantern.

Greville drove along the edge of the lake to a small jetty, then pulled the car up and switched off the engine. But he left the headlamps on, and Liz saw that they were illuminating the shape of a small rowing dinghy.

She got out of the car, stretched herself cautiously and watched Greville go down to the boat. He lay down on his stomach on the jetty and put his arms into the water, evidently feeling for something round the side of the dinghy.

'What are you doing?'

'De-fusing the transport,' he retorted laconically.

Presently he stood up and held out his hands towards her. There was a grenade in each, with a long trailing piece of wire linking them both.

'If anyone wants to come visiting,' he explained, 'they have to use the boat. In which case they blow themselves to glory.'

Liz gazed across the stretch of water at the vaguely outlined patch of land on which Greville's cottage stood.

'How nice to live on an island,' she said.

'Don't we all?' said Greville. 'There was once a character called John Donne who used to write poetry and think otherwise. But he was a nut-case. A real nut-case. He had delusions of grandeur ... Yes, poor old Donne was up the spout – a regular transie.' He stowed the grenades in the car, switched off the headlamps and locked the doors. 'The trouble is, everybody lives on islands and nobody knows how to build rowing-boats ... Now come and sit at the back here, and I'll ferry you home – just like they used to do in the romantic movies.'

Liz stepped into the boat and sat down. 'It would be nice to be able to go to the pictures,' she said wistfully.

Greville took the oars and pushed off. Suddenly he began to laugh.

'What's so funny?'

'It's just occurred to me,' said Greville, 'that at least ninety per cent of all the film-stars must have survived – for a time at least. Which just goes to show that God – if there is a god – must have a nice sense of humour.'

ELEVEN

On the outside and by moonlight Greville's retreat looked like an uneasy hybrid of miniature pagan temple and Victorian public convenience. It had a broad flight of steps leading up to a small portico flanked by Lilliputian marble columns. The whole of its front was faced with large blocks of some kind of stone; but, as Liz later discovered, the sides and back were of Suffolk brick and with ordinary cottage windows. The steeply sloping roof was covered with pantiles, adding a vague suggestion of the Japanese to its mixed ancestry.

Greville tied up the dinghy and led Liz up the steps to the massive double-front door – a thing of oak and studs and wrought iron. He pushed it open, felt on the inside wall and pressed a switch. An electric light came on, and somewhere there was the subdued noise of a generator starting automatically.

'It's marvellous,' said Liz, surveying the electric light and the untidy but comfortable room that it illuminated.

'It's what happens when an English country gentleman gets an acropolis complex with pagoda complications,' remarked Greville drily. 'Let's get to bed for Christ's sake. It's been somewhat of a day ... Do you want anything to eat first?'

'All I want,' said Liz, 'is unconsciousness.'

'You can have that for free.'

The bedroom was a small poky room leading off the far end of the living room. It looked like an afterthought – as indeed it was, along with the tiny kitchen. It contained nothing but a large bed, a chest of drawers and a thick rug that lent a touch of luxury and decadence to the dull brick floor.

'If you want to pee or have a shit,' said Greville, 'you'll have to go outside. There's a lavatory of sorts just through the kitchen door.'

'I don't want to do anything,' yawned Liz, 'except sleep. I've just about had my lot for today ... Are we sleeping together?'

'There's only one bed,' Greville pointed out. 'If you prefer the floor you can have it.'

'I don't, but on the other hand I don't think I could face a good screw tonight ... Not,' she hastened to add, 'that I'm suggesting anything. It's just that I'm still sore enough not to want it.'

'You disappoint me,' said Greville. 'I was just getting myself in the mood for an all-night sex orgy. Now shut up and get into bed.'

He went out of the bedroom and bolted the outer door, then he came back and bolted the bedroom door. Liz took off her few clothes. So did Greville. He did not look at her.

'Get into bed. I'll switch off the light.'

She got into bed and waited for him. Greville kicked off his shoes, switched out the light and joined her. There was a sudden silence as the generator ceased producing electricity.

For a while they lay side by side, not touching, each of them naked and each of them conscious of the other's nearness. The darkness and the silence were absolute. They were two children alone in the cosmos, with no one to comfort them but each other.

Greville, tired though he was, found that he could not sleep. So did Liz. They were too close to each other for comfort – too close and yet too far away.

'Greville,' whispered Liz at last, 'if you want it, I think I can face it.'

'Shut up and go to sleep. I don't want any damn thing.'

Liz smiled in the darkness. 'Everybody wants something. If they didn't they'd just die … What do you want?'

'Peace,' said Greville.

'You can't get it alone.'

'How do you know?'

'I've tried. If I thought I could get it alone I wouldn't have worried about Jane.'

'I don't give a tinker's cuss for Jane.'

'I know.'

'I don't give a tinker's cuss for you, either.'

'Liar! Not for me as a person, maybe. But you want me to depend on you.'

'Don't be stupid. You are just a bloody complication.'

Liz rolled herself against him. 'I expect that's what you need. I bet you've been looking for a bloody complication for quite a while.'

In the darkness Greville hit her. 'You're madder than most,' he said heavily. 'You like to press your luck.'

Her face stung, but Liz didn't turn away. The tears trickled silently down her cheek, and she kept her voice steady so that Greville would not know about them.

'So I'm right, then,' she murmured. 'Does it frighten you that somebody else knows?'

Greville hit her again. 'Now shut up and go to sleep. Remember you can't dial 999 anymore. I can do what the hell I like with you.'

'Good night,' said Liz.

'Good night.'

Neither of them slept. For an hour or more, Greville tossed and turned, trying, as he thought, to find a comfortable position. Liz just lay there in the dark, wide-eyed and waiting.

Presently, he grabbed hold of her roughly. There were no preliminaries.

'Serves you right, doesn't it?' he shouted. 'All you want to do is be flat on your back with your legs wide open.'

But he had to turn her on her back and open her legs himself.

Liz said nothing. There was nothing to say. Besides, it was very painful and she felt that if she used her voice at all she would scream or cry out.

Mercifully, Greville didn't take long to reach a climax. And when he had finished, when his body became slack and relaxed, when Liz knew that she had conquered the impulse to scream, she cradled him, holding his head to her breast as if he were a small child. She soothed him and whispered meaningless words to him. And so they lay together – each feeling tired and lonely and lost – until daybreak.

TWELVE

The day was a most unusual one: it rained from before dawn till after dusk. Greville found later that he could not recall whether it was months or years ago when it had last rained all day. He lay on his back in bed with Liz at his side – doubtless pretending to be asleep – and gazed in delight at the rain-drops running down the grey dawn window.

He concentrated and tried to remember what he had been doing during the last downpour. The memory wouldn't come, and because it wouldn't come it annoyed him. It continued to annoy him throughout the rest of the day; for as the rain showed no signs of ceasing, he realised that it was a rather special occasion. There must have been other similar occasions, but they were lost in the fuzz of transnormal happenings in a wholly transnormal world. It was the fact that he couldn't remember the last time it rained all day that caused him, in the end, to start a diary.

But meanwhile he lay in bed and watched the rain make patterns on the window, and wondered for perhaps the ten thousandth time why he was still alive.

He looked at Liz and saw her face in the grey light – a face without cares or wrinkles, frozen by time. The face of a child. A dead child … There was something in him that wanted to cry …

Liz stirred. The child was resurrected as a woman.

'I'm sorry about last night,' he said. 'It must have hurt you.'

'Not much. Besides, I belong to you for the time being. You can do what you like, can't you?' The words were hard but the voice was soft. Liz felt she was only stating the fact.

But the statement triggered off an internal explosion for Greville. 'Nobody belongs to anybody,' he snapped. 'And especially you don't belong to me. Now if you can divest yourself of the puppy mentality, we'll get up and see about breakfast.'

Liz was not perturbed. 'What's that scar on your stomach?'

'An old bayonet wound. The only way I could get out of a coal mine was to play dead. Somebody prodded me just to make sure. It didn't work … Now, breakfast.'

Breakfast was a lavish affair. Greville managed to produce ham, eggs and home-made bread. He even had a bottle of coffee extract.

Liz was delighted. 'Where did you get all this stuff?'

'I have connections,' he said briefly. 'I told you things weren't too hard yet in this part of the world.'

Much to his surprise the rain was still coming down when breakfast was over.

'What would you like to do today?' he asked.

'Nothing much.'

'That suits me fine. There are one or two things I have to do, but they won't take long. While I'm doing them, you can tidy this place up.'

He put on oil-skins and went out into the rain to feed the half-dozen hens that he had caught and partially tamed. When he had done that he poured some petrol with miserly care into the fuel tank of his petrol-paraffin powered generator. Then he topped up the car batteries that provided his illumination. By the time he got back to the folly, the bed was made and the pots had been washed. Liz had found out how to work the two-stroke pump in the kitchen.

'Go easy with the detergent,' warned Greville, noticing the legacy of suds in the sink. 'That is one of the things that is very hard to come by.'

The rain continued, and he didn't know what to do. If he had been by himself the answer would have been simple. He would have settled down with a book and would probably have lost himself in it till hunger called. Greville was a great one for books. Other people's books. Books he would like to have written himself. He read them with enthusiasm, delight, disgust, guilt, ecstasy, impatience and envy. But whether they were good, bad or indifferent he always read them with envy. For they were the children that he had never had.

Chiefly he read novels – stories of a world that no longer existed and that almost seemed now as if it could never have existed. His favourite dislike was an old-fashioned novel called *Room At The Top*. He felt somehow that it was a kind of photographic negative of certain aspects of his own early life. A negative because, basically, he had never wanted to occupy room at the top. But Pauline had wanted it, and so he had masqueraded for a while as an ambitious go-getter.

Greville collected and hoarded books the way some transies still collected and hoarded money. Neither were going to be much use, he thought, in a transnormal world. But the compulsion was obsessional. Besides, books were almost as good as brandy. They provided an avenue of escape, and the hangover was less noticeable. Also they were considerably easier to come by than brandy. Pretty soon the supply of brandy would give out. But the supply of books would last for a long time yet. Only the rats ate them; and although they were good for lighting fires they were not satisfactory as a basic fuel ...

Greville was tempted to ignore Liz, settle himself with a book, and treat her as if she didn't exist. The only flaw in the proposition was the last bit. He couldn't treat her as if she didn't exist. He had lived alone too long not to be acutely and painfully conscious of someone else's presence. Besides, he had virtually added to her quota of the previous day's rapes.

'I'd better show you where things are,' he said at length. 'Then you won't need to keep running to me for every little thing you want.'

Liz had already discovered the larder, which was surprisingly well stocked with tinned food, bacon, eggs and even fresh butter. Greville took her into the living-room, threw back a rug, and lifted a trap-door.

'The wine cellar of one Augustus Rowley, visionary, philosopher and man of letters,' he announced.

Liz laughed. 'Who died of languishment and a profound melancholy.'

Greville was surprised. 'Who told you that?'

'You did – yesterday morning when we were having breakfast by Cleopatra's Needle … It's funny. It already seems about a year ago.'

Oddly Greville didn't remember. But he was pleased that she had remembered. 'Time is subjective,' he announced drily. 'I thought you would have defined it as several screws ago.'

'I thought you didn't like me to talk about screwing.'

'Touché. Now come and see what the cellar holds.'

The cellar held an incongruous store of goods that Greville had collected patiently and sometimes at great risk over a long period. There were piles of canned goods – mostly soup, vegetables and fruit. But there were also some tins of corned beef.

And there were two .45 revolvers, a small .38 and an ancient .303 rifle together with boxes of ammunition. There were also several hand-grenades and a stack of perhaps thirty five-gallon cans of petrol together with a very large drum of paraffin. There were also trousers and jackets of varying shapes and sizes, shirts, shoes, socks, bottles of beer, wine and spirits, rat traps, a tin of strychnine, a small astronomical telescope, reels of cotton, balls of wool, a few bales of printed cloth, more books, a first-aid kit and a bottle of chloroform, a sack of potatoes (some of which were sprouting), two violins, a box of soap tablets and a few tins of cigarettes.

'It's wonderful,' breathed Liz, surveying the treasures. 'You must have had a hard job getting this lot together.'

'The squirrel mentality,' said Greville. 'You won't believe it, but the only thing I had to shoot anybody for was the telescope. I took it from what was left of a junk-shop in Norwich. An old man saw me and started popping off with a shotgun. I couldn't get out of the place unless I shot back. He peppered me and it hurt so much and I got so mad that I damn near blew his head off … People die for the oddest things, you know. And the joke is I didn't really want the telescope anyway. It was just something to carry.'

'Have you ever used it?' she asked.

'No.'

'Then we shall use it some night when the sky is clear. And you'll set it up and I can look at the moon.'

'What the hell for?'

'To give an old man in Norwich a reason for dying,' she said simply.

It did not take long to complete the tour of inspection of Greville's cottage. Liz looked at his books and at his large collection of records and at the twelve-volt record player that had been a major prize of an early scrounging expedition.

'Will it really work?' she asked, fingering it in obvious delight.

'Try it and see.'

Liz chose a Strauss record – the Emperor Waltz – and the music seemed to fill the cottage, briefly shutting out time, transnormality and all the bitter memories of recent years. After the Strauss she tried another record, a song, this time, which she remembered having heard as a child. The name of the singer, Marlene Dietrich, meant nothing to Liz; but the song, *Where Have All The Flowers Gone*, brought tears to her eyes.

Greville remained unmoved – or gave the appearance of remaining unmoved. He did not want Liz to think that he was a push-over for such sentimental nonsense.

The morning wore on. They both became hungry. Because it was too wet to go out shooting and because there was no fresh meat or vegetables in the larder, Greville permitted himself the luxury of opening cans.

For lunch they had soup and baked beans and pineapple. And because it was somehow a special sort of day, Greville went really reckless and opened one of his three remaining bottles of *Asti Spumante*.

The wine relaxed them. Greville yawned and looked through the window at the low grey sky and the smooth curtain of rain. It fascinated him.

'A raindrop,' he said suddenly and disconcertingly, 'is like a glass cathedral. It's a place for worship. One ought to be small enough to walk inside and drown in liquid prayer.'

'Raindrops fall,' Liz pointed out. 'They get destroyed.'

Greville hiccupped and shook his head. 'They change, that's all. Then somehow or other they get back to the ocean and back again into the sky ... Perpetual motion ... Perpetual prayer ... Let's go to bed. I'm tired.'

A flicker of apprehension passed over Liz's face. She was remembering the soreness between her legs, and she was also remembering the previous night.

Greville laughed. 'Not for that,' he said. 'Enough is as good as a feast. We'll be chaste little children taking our after-lunch naps. Hell, what else is there to do? We can't bloody well go out and save the world.'

'I'll clear the table first,' said Liz.

'You'll come to bed. Suburban efficiency doesn't suit you.'

'Do I strip?'

'Do what the hell you like. I'm stripping. I feel better that way.'

'Can we listen to some music?'

'No. I want to sleep.'

'Oh, well,' said Liz, eyeing the record player. 'I suppose there's plenty of time.'

Greville pretended to be irritated. 'Put some bloody music on, then, if that's what you want. But turn the volume down.'

Liz looked through the records as she took off her clothes. She found the Italian Symphony and put it on. Then she went into the bedroom. Greville had already closed his eyes. But when she got into bed he put his hand on her breast and let it lie there lightly.

'Maybe it's as well I didn't let the dogs have you,' he murmured drowsily. 'Just possibly you might teach me how to become human.'

Liz said nothing. She was lost in the strangely sad gaiety of Mendelssohn. She didn't so much listen to the music as inhale it, each breath drawing her deeper into a sea of unbeing with the insistence of an anaesthetic.

She was asleep long before the record ended. So was Greville. Despite the rain and the proximity of each other, they both slept profoundly. Greville was the first to wake, by which time it was already growing dark. He looked at Liz in the dim light and was suddenly and unaccountably afraid. He wanted to kill her or run away from her – or both. His hand was still on her breast; but the impulse to let it slide up and fasten tightly round her neck was sudden and fierce.

He tried to control it and couldn't.

Of its own volition, apparently, the hand started to move.

Liz woke. She looked at him. The hand had already reached her neck.

'It doesn't matter,' she said softly. 'You can do what you like.' There was no fear in her voice.

Greville laughed shakily. The spell was broken. 'It's still raining,' he said. 'Damned if I can remember when it last rained as long as this … Let's get up.'

THIRTEEN

The first entry in Greville's diary was written late that evening when the rain had stopped and when Liz, having satiated herself with an orgy of music, was indulging in such domestic activities as remaking the bed and clearing away the remains of a late meal. The diary itself was an old school exercise book that Greville had found in a deserted cottage. The uneven and faded writing on the cover proclaimed it to be the English Book of one Robert Andrew Cherry, age 11. Robert Andrew Cherry, who was doubtless long since dead, had also obligingly supplied the date on which he had received his English Book: 30 April 1972.

Whatever had happened to the boy must have happened soon afterwards for he had only managed to do three short pieces of work. One of these was an essay entitled *What I want to be when I grow up*. It was the essay that had made Greville want to keep the book.

'When I grow up,' Robert Cherry had written, 'I want to be a man who writes stories. I would write good stories. I would not write children's stories. I would write stories that would be read by lots of grown-ups. Then I would be famous. I would have a red car and a big house and my wife would be very proud because I was famous. I would write stories about spaceships and distant planets. Some of my stories would be made into films. Then I would be rich and would not have to work anymore. I would let my father live with me and look after the garden. Then he would be too busy to be unhappy because my mother is dead. I would give my father a red car, too, but he cannot drive.'

Greville had kept the book because Robert Cherry, doubtless a victim – direct or indirect – of the Radiant Suicide, was also the ghost of Greville's own childhood. That was how it had once been …

Now the unused pages of Robert Cherry's English Book were to be put to use at last. Greville considered tearing out the essay and the two spelling exercises that followed it. Then he decided against it. Instead he turned the book upside down so that it was back to front.

He found a pencil and, after a few moments' thought, he wrote at the top of the pages: 'For Robert – who would have known better.'

Then he made the first entry:

'8 July 1981 (give or take a little). Day Two for certain. Yesterday I kept a rendezvous – dead drunk – with Pauline on Chelsea Bridge. I also cheated the dogs of a breakfast called Liz.

'The girl is good for nothing, as she puts it, but screwing. And she's had plenty of that. But somehow she's still oddly innocent. She wants to go looking for a twin sister; and I have an idea that I'll do my damnedest to stop her … What was it that overrated poet once said? "Teach us to care and not to care. Teach us to sit still".

'I don't know about sitting still, but I'd like to have the first bit. Last night I "screwed" Liz – the first in a long time. Tonight I almost killed her. Liz has life, and maybe I'm envious of life. Whatever happens to her there's always the cheap little consolation that but for me she would have been dead anyway …

'It's been raining all day. I can't remember when it last rained all day. And because of that I have a crazy thought at the back of my mind that history is being lost. My history. The rain has made me realise that I still have the greatest vanity. I don't want my history to be lost. This is my bid for immortality – by courtesy of the rain and Robert Cherry. And so to bed.'

But Greville didn't immediately go to bed. The rain had stopped, the sky had cleared and Liz had finished her work. She wanted to go out for a breath of air. So he took her round the tiny island. And they gazed at the lake and the faint patina of stars in a high washed sky. And before they came back to the cottage he kissed her. He had screwed her already. Already he had wanted to kill her. But this was the first time he had kissed her. He was surprised to find that, oddly, it hurt like a knife.

They went to bed chastely and lay close together with an oddly impersonal tenderness. For a time they made desultory conversation in subdued voices, almost as if they were afraid of being overheard. Greville had been troubled by that kiss. He was still troubled – so, experimentally, he tried again. And again it hurt.

It was not so much a pain as a terrible tightness. The tightness started in his chest and seemed to wind round his body until his breathing became shallow and he could feel a faint dampness of perspiration on his head. In the darkness his thoughts began to turn to Pauline. He did not want to think of Pauline. But the struggle was a hard and conscious one; and the tightness spread from his body into the muscles of his legs and arms.

Liz was aware of his tension but she did not remark upon it. She had been with many men who had betrayed their stresses in various ways. She prided herself on being able to take things as they came; and for the time being she had found comfort, security and companionship. There was, she felt, nothing more that one could hope for – except that whenever death came, as it inevitably would, it would be a quick and easy one.

Presently, still holding each other, they each fell into an uneasy sleep. Liz had nightmares, and once she woke up screaming. She dreamt that she was in a cage, naked, in a large and rather foul-smelling room. She dreamt that tit-bits of food were being thrown to her between the bars and that she was given a bowl from which to drink. But when she drank the liquid burned her throat. Presently the door opened and men came into the cage. They were large and coarse and hot with lust. They began to do things to her, and the dreadful thing was that she could not struggle. And the even more dreadful thing was that she began to like it. She hated the foul breath, the grunts, the weight, the sudden spasms of pain. She hated the way her limbs were responding, the way her mouth opened, the way her breasts began to work against her like independent saboteurs. She loathed the whole horrible situation; but somehow she did not want it to end.

And it was the feeling that there were forces making her like what she hated that caused her to scream.

Greville shook her and slapped her. The screams dissolved into moans, and the moans became translated into an uncontrollable sobbing. Presently she felt exhausted and empty. Presently she slept once more – with Greville holding her so tight that his arms began to ache. Morning was a long time coming.

When it came, it was as if – apart from a lingering freshness – the deluge of the previous day might never have been. The sun rose into a clear blue sky. And Day Three, as Greville later recorded in his diary, was the happiest time he had ever known in his life. Despite the years of transnormality and hardship, despite the multi-megadeath of normal man, despite the recent excursion into a London of the dead and dying, despite homicidal teenagers, humiliation and ambush, Greville felt as if he did not have a care in the world.

After breakfast – and, as he told himself, simply to cheer Liz up – he proposed a picnic. A further extravagant onslaught was made on the wine and tinned goods. Then they rowed ashore while the sun was still low in the sky, and Greville showed Liz the churchyard where Augustus Rowley was buried.

Together they read the inscription below the marble statue:

To the undying memory of Augustus Rowley, visionary, philosopher and man of letters. Born 1833: died 1873 of languishment and a profound melancholy. He here awaits the vindication of time and circumstance, secure in the belief that he accurately interpreted the call of his Maker.

Liz uncorked the wine. 'To Augustus Rowley, guardian and patron saint of all good transies.' She drank from the bottle and handed it to Greville.

'To Augustus,' he said, 'without whose vision and philosophy two transies at least would have been considerably the poorer.'

They spent the whole day in the churchyard. They read some more epitaphs and then made love in the long grasses of high summer between a tablet commemorating the interment of Abigail Sarah Busterd, gathered unto her Lord in 1909, and James Jolly, called from on high in 1923.

Afterwards they slept peacefully and tranquilly though Greville's hand remained at all times on his shot-gun. Then they woke, read some more epitaphs and drank some more wine. They were not disturbed, and in the heat of the afternoon they bathed in the hypnotic glare of the sun and talked happily and freely of a world that each of them found difficult to remember. Finally, and as if to celebrate the continued absence of disaster, they made love yet again in the late afternoon before making their way back to the lake and its island citadel.

It was a golden day. They saw no one. They were threatened by no predators, human or animal. They could have been alone in the country in an entirely normal world – except that there were no planes to cut the blue sky into slices with their vapour trails and penetrating wedges of noise. Nor were there any cars to transform the weed-covered roads into battlegrounds. Nor were there any sane specimens of officialdom to object to the joyful and carefree desecration of holy ground.

Before they left the churchyard, Liz made a garland of buttercups and daisies to hang round the marble neck of Augustus Rowley; and Greville carefully balanced the empty wine bottle on the surprisingly flat top of the statue's head.

FOURTEEN

The weather remained fine. The days blended gently into each other. July seemed to have expended its total rainfall in that single downpour. Optimistically, Greville began to think that Liz would eventually lose the silly notion of going off into the deep blue yonder to look for her twin sister. But he reckoned without the nightmares. They came fairly frequently – about every two or three days.

The girl in the cage, Liz had explained to him in a matter-of-fact way, was not really herself but Jane. Somewhere, the northerners who had stolen her from the Richmond Lot were keeping Jane and treating her on the level of an animal – an animal that was useful for entertainment only. Greville neither believed nor disbelieved in telepathy or telepathic dreams; but he displayed strong scepticism simply in order to counter the sudden fits of restlessness and depression that Liz began to experience. He had found a kind of contentment and a kind of satisfaction that he had not thought could exist. It would come to an end, as all things would come to an end, but he wanted it to last as long as possible.

Liz was a mass of conflicts. She was becoming accustomed to Greville. He treated her far better than she had been treated in Richmond; and she was beginning to learn how to deal with his black moods. But there was still the pull of Jane. And there were the nightmares, when, in effect and for a briefly horrible time, she *became* Jane, experiencing her degradation and the hopelessness of her plight.

Greville began to devise distractions. There were only ten or twelve people still living in the village of Ambergreave, and only two who were actually dangerous. The rest, by unspoken and common consent, seemed to live on a *laissez-faire* basis – recognising still a basic pattern of interdependence that the disintegration of society had not wholly destroyed. Greville introduced Liz to the few people with whom he had any dealings and taught her to avoid the cottage where Big Willie Crutchley lived incestuously with his mother and on principle attempted to kill almost anything that moved.

Big Willie was half-idiot and half-genius. Half-idiot because he only wanted to destroy, and half-genius because he had adapted almost perfectly to the new conditions. Realising that eventually there would be an end to guns and ammunition, Big Willie had taught himself to survive independent of them. He reverted to the primitive approach. For hunting and for personal defence he became expert in the use of sling and crossbow – both devised and manufactured by himself without reference to humanity's previous experience, for Big Willie could neither read nor write. In the old days he had been inferior; but ten years of Omega radiation had placed him among the surviving élite. For large semi-wild animals such as deer, pigs and bulls, he dug pits and planted sharpened stakes in them. For small creatures such as dogs and cats he devised cunning snares.

Big Willie and his mother would eat anything – including, so it was said, human beings. But they, too, at least partially accepted the principle of *laissez-faire* for they had never been known to eat anyone who lived in Ambergreave. And he only fired warning shafts from his crossbow if anybody was so careless as to come too near his pits and traps. Of course, if the warning shafts were ignored …

Big Willie and Greville conscientiously avoided crossing each other's path. Greville realised that Big Willie was probably waiting until he ran out of ammunition. But, Greville promised himself, when that time drew close, he would remember to deal with Big Willie first.

Perhaps the most useful and most efficient member of the small community – if it could be so described – was Miss Worrall.

Miss Worrall lived in a derelict windmill. At least the windmill, an old tower mill, had been derelict for half a century until Miss Worrall installed herself. That was in the early days of the Radiant Suicide before normal man realised that his number was up. Miss Worrall was an ex-music teacher of indeterminate age who had developed a passion for dogs and the simple life.

She came to Ambergreave with two Alsatians, and she adopted the derelict mill as her home. The Alsatians multiplied, and were very carefully and strictly trained. At the same time, Miss Worrall (no one ever discovered her Christian name) perhaps with a flash of insight or clairvoyance, began to renovate the windmill. The surviving villagers claimed it was impossible; there were those who could remember the 1914 war but could not remember the tower mill ever having sails. Nevertheless, Miss Worrall constructed sails, doing all the carpentering herself and only soliciting help to get the new sails into position. Then she found a mason who still retained enough skill to fashion a tolerable pair of millstones – and, lo, the windmill was a going concern once more.

Miss Worrall began to grind corn. As the years of Omega radiation wrought havoc with the outside world, she continued to grind corn; and, for a time, her business throve as all the powered mechanical mills came to a stop. But then the farms began to disintegrate, and there was less corn to grind. Prudently, Miss Worrall allowed her pack of Alsatians to increase to eight. Once, and because it was known that she always kept a good supply of flour, the mill was attacked by a dozen or so armed, determined and hungry men. They did not get any flour; and several of them had their throats torn out by the Alsatians. Since then, Miss Worrall had lived in peace. There was still a little wheat to grind, for the surviving villagers grew patches of it here and there; and Miss Worrall never took more than a tenth of the harvest for her services. She lived alone with her dogs, an old piano and about twenty faded photographs of the same man. Greville liked her. He had good reason to; for she had once saved him when he was starving.

So he introduced Liz to Miss Worrall, and he introduced her to the Cuthbert family – Charles Cuthbert, a large florid man with two wives and two half-grown children, was the local blacksmith and machine fixer – and to Alaric Newton, R.A., who lived in a tree house and painted in oils and had once been one of the best marksmen with a rifle in England.

Liz got on well with Miss Worrall and would occasionally pay a social visit on her own. Presently she had almost the same degree of control over the Alsatians as their owner.

Now and then Greville would take Liz hunting with him. It was not necessary to travel far to go hunting for, with the exception of a few small patches of land close to the villages, the countryside had reverted to a degree of wildness that was surprising in view of the fact that it was only a few years since society had relinquished its control. On these occasions Greville would arm himself with a rifle and a pistol, while Liz carried one of the shotguns. Between them, he felt, they had quite enough fire-power to deal with everything except rats … And possibly humans …

Greville's favourite quarry was pig, the semi-wild and surprisingly dangerous variety that had adapted so well to the new-found freedom. Of all the domesticated creatures, the pig had done best since the passing of normal man; and, in fact, the pig population of Britain now exceeded the population of transies.

The strength of the pigs lay in their ability to eat practically everything – including, if necessary, each other. Greville was rapidly becoming an expert in pigs. He could tell the carnivorous ones at a glance. And, whenever possible, he avoided them; for there was a strong and most un-piggy flavour to their flesh. They did not make good pork and they did not make good bacon. All that they were fit for was stew – and they had to be very well cooked at that.

One afternoon, when Greville and Liz were out hunting a few miles from Ambergreave, they witnessed an astounding sight. They were in a small patch of woodland, and it was one of those still summer days when sound carries tremendously and when it seems almost possible to shout and be heard from one end of the land to the other.

Having disposed of a light lunch, Greville and Liz were resting under a large and obviously ancient oak whose low leafy branches spread out to make a wide green and brown umbrella, obliterating the blue sky. Greville was half-dozing when suddenly he became aware of a faint and distant whisper. It seemed to be growing in volume. Greville had heard such a whisper before. He looked at Liz, but she was totally unconcerned and had probably not heard it.

The whisper grew, and then a new sound was added – a muffled throbbing that shook the earth and that came from a different direction. The throbbing was not so easily identifiable. It could be pigs, horses or deer.

Greville stirred uncomfortably. As the throbbing increased, the whispering seemed to disperse until it was all around them. He looked at the oak tree and then he looked at Liz.

'I think it's time to do a bit of climbing,' he said. 'We're going to have visitors.'

Liz was getting familiar with country noises. 'It's a pretty large herd – whatever they are. Sounds heavy enough for horses … What's the other sound?'

'If it's what I think it is,' retorted Greville, 'we shall very likely wish it wasn't. Come on, there's no time to waste. I'll give you a leg up.'

Liz slung her shotgun round her shoulder and began to climb the tree. Greville hauled himself after her.

The throbbing stopped, then started again, then stopped and started once more. Horses, pigs or deer – they were drawing closer. But the whispering, now much louder, seemed to be everywhere.

Greville and Liz were perched on each side of a thick forked branch about fifteen feet above the ground. Greville wedged himself into a reasonably good shooting position. He took the shotgun from Liz and gave her the pistol. In the circumstances the shotgun seemed likely to be their best guarantee of salvation.

From the forked branch their view of the ground below was restricted to a small irregular patch of a few square yards. This was not a great drawback, reflected Greville, for if they could not see much, neither also could they be seen.

Presently a pig passed below him. Then another and another. Although it was high summer, they had the look of very hungry carnivorous pigs. Greville was surprised. But he was less surprised when he realised how many there were, for the grunting and snorting he heard seemed to indicate that the wood was full of them.

But above and around all the pig-like noises there was the ubiquitous whispering. Even the pigs were scared. They milled to and fro as if trying to decide on a direction.

Then the first wave of rats came.

A brown tide seemed to surge over the grass and even over the squealing pigs. Suddenly there were rats everywhere. Greville had never seen so many before. At times there was the crazy illusion that the brown tide was three or four rats deep. The stench was nauseating.

The rats, evidently, had been driving the pigs and had now managed to surround them. They were coming in for the kill.

But, as victims, the carnivorous pigs were less than obliging. The rats leaped at their ears, snouts, legs, tails. and many of the pigs seemed at times to be totally covered in rats. But they careered about, trampling the rats in their hundreds. They rolled on them, snapping at them and even screamed at them. But still the rats came on.

It was a contest in which neither side could claim decisive victory, for eventually the surviving pigs broke through the thinned-out cordon of their attackers. In the matter of escape, their speed proved decisive. Presently, there was nothing left below the oak tree but a couple of dead pigs covered totally in rats.

Liz was sick.

She clung to the oak tree for dear life, but the remains of her lunch fell steaming to the ground. The rats looked up. Bright beady eyes registered movement. Some of them began to desert the carcasses of the pigs and make for the tree-trunk.

Greville waited until a dozen or so had started to climb. Then he let them have a blast from the twelve-bore shotgun. Most of the rats fell back dead or mortally wounded. The rest scampered away. But in a few seconds they were trying again.

It cost Greville ten cartridges – more than half the shotgun ammunition he was carrying – before the rats gave up. Then he and Liz had to stay in their tree for half the afternoon while the surviving rats stripped the dead pigs. Eventually they moved away. Eventually there was silence

'I think it's safe for us to go down now,' said Greville at length.

'Oh, God!' said Liz, white-faced and shaking. 'Get me home quick, then I can have my hysterics in peace.'

Greville climbed down first and scouted around to see if any of the rats were left. He did not find a single one – living. The pigs had been reduced almost to skeletons and so had the dead rats. The tide of destruction had passed, leaving behind it only the warm, foul and obscenely intimate smell of death.

As they made their way hurriedly back to the lake, Greville dwelt with silent and obscure satisfaction on the fact that Liz, in a moment of stress, had used the word 'home'.

FIFTEEN

Extracts from Greville's diary:

'August. Day thirty-one, I think. Hell, I've lost track. The stars are pursuing their appointed courses, the sun is slowly burning itself to a celestial cinder, the moon still continues to go round the earth – and humanity is lying in little bits all over the planet, like the tiny parts of a vast and horribly broken clock.

'But where is the mainspring? What made us go? What was it that took us gibbering out of the trees and planted us in chromium-plated cities? What was the great sane tick-tock of civilisation all about? And why did it all explode pitifully like a home-made bomb when some fiery little pot-hole on the sun set up a ham radio station and started beaming: "Time, gentlemen, please"?

'Christ, I can't even ask questions that are worth asking. The gods have an odd sense of humour. So I'll abolish them. There are no more gods, by order, Matthew Greville, transnormal and illiterate, hereditary custodian of one million years of evolution, great ape of the second coming ...

'I love Liz. The thought terrifies me. I love Liz. It's a sickness. It's the sickest transnormal joke that any transie could possibly play on himself. What place is there for love in this best of all possible worlds? Love only thyself, brother, for the great day of spiritual masturbation is at hand. Love only the quick screw and the sudden violence and the sleep that sometimes passeth without dreams.

'But, sweet Christ, I love Liz – and it hurts like mad and it makes me afraid and sometimes it even gives me the illusion of no longer being alone.

'What is she? A hot little bitch who sold her body for a meal or two a day and anybody's bed at night. But let him that is without sin throw the first fit.

'My God! There are times when she's beautiful. She stands there in a torn shirt and a patched-up pair of jeans, skinning a rabbit and looking as if she could launch a thousand ships. And sometimes she lies down with nothing on at all and her legs wide open, and you'd think there was nothing to it but a sweet ten minutes of erection and demolition work.

'But suddenly the sex doesn't seem to matter. I look into her eyes and find that there's something there that's farther away than the stars and brighter than the sun. Something that sings and cries and dreams and mourns. Something that's so close it suffocates and so remote that I'll never touch it.

'She's a witch. No broomstick. Only nightmares about a twin sister and compulsions to find a rainbow that leads to shimmering little heaps of fool's gold.

'She ran away. Three days ago she ran away, having stolen one shotgun, ten cartridges, half a dozen cans of soup and two of Miss Worrall's Alsatians. I wondered why she had been ingratiating herself so much with the dogs. She had been quietly planning the whole little venture.

'We went to bed around midnight and made some love that was quite worth the making, and then we slept. By dawn the bitch had gone. She'd taken the boat, of course, so I had to swim ashore. Then I had to row myself back to get a few things.

I don't suppose I'd have found her except that I knew she'd head north. And, serve her right, the dogs gave her away. She should have realised that their occasional barking was going to be a first-class advertisement. But, thank the Lord, she didn't. And so I came up with them a little before sunset.

'She was wild enough and determined enough. She set the dogs on me, and I had to blow them both to glory – good dogs they were, too – before she'd call it a day.

'I hit her. Christ, how I hit her! I'd had about twelve hours of hell, thinking I'd never see her again. So she had to pay for it. I closed one of her eyes and smashed up her lips and did things to her that must have made her wish she'd never been born. And then I cried like a child and asked her to shoot me.

'How transnormal can you get? She didn't, of course. She could hardly move, but she just took her trousers off, maybe thinking that was the remedy for everything, or maybe thinking that was all I really wanted.

'I didn't want it at all. I told her I loved her, and then she began to cry, too. It was a fine night with a large harvest moon – if anybody was bothering to gather a harvest – and we slept rough at the bottom of a big tree with a couple of dead dogs to keep us company. We didn't make love at all. We just wanted to touch each other and know that we were alive.

'In the morning we were both stiff as boards, and poor Liz looked as if she had had the beating of a lifetime. She could hardly walk, and the way back was endless. We didn't get home till the early hours of the following morning. Then, if you please, instead of collapsing she had to have music.

'So it was *Rhapsody in Blue*, then bacon and red wine for breakfast. Finally, we went to bed.

'So here we are again, demented desert islanders, sharing a love idyll complete with black eyes, nightmares, blisters on our feet, aching loins and the knowledge that every day of joint survival, every moment of happiness (and who in his wrong mind would dare to use the word?) is stacking up the odds on the cosmic roulette wheel.

'It can't last. We know it can't last. Who can afford such delusions of grandeur in the world in which we live now? I know it's a sort of psychic hire-purchase – but, hell, we're going to have to pay later, anyway.'

SIXTEEN

Day drifted into day, August drifted into September, and the brown and gold mantle of an Indian summer fell smokily over the land. Greville was surprised and only vaguely disturbed to find that life with Liz was evolving into a routine – or, possibly, a ritual. They went scrounging only when it was vitally necessary, when one of them needed clothes or shoes, or when the food supply began to dwindle seriously. For the most part they lived simply as 'desert islanders'. Liz still had her nightmares, still cherished hopes of finding Jane; but she seemed willing to accept Greville's claim upon her, and she seemed willing enough to share the dangerous illusion of love.

Inevitably, scrounging was getting more and more difficult, more and more dangerous. The towns and cities were still the best bets; but because sheer necessity was forcing the surviving transies to organise themselves into groups of one kind or another, the chance of freelance scroungers falling into traps was increasing rapidly.

On one occasion Greville took Liz as far afield as Ipswich. They were looking primarily for clothes. In normal times the journey by car from Ambergreave would have taken about an hour; but because of the state of the roads and the detours it was necessary to make, the trip took the best part of a day.

The centre of Ipswich had been picked as clean as a whistle; but the suburbs still held the promise of plunder, for, having looted the centre of the city, the town transies began to move progressively outwards. It was while Liz and Greville were exploring the possibilities of a large deserted suburban house standing in about two acres of garden jungle that they first encountered organised transnormality.

Greville had managed to force his station wagon up the weed-choked drive and it was standing in front of the house while he and Liz explored the upper storeys. The house was a solid nineteenth-century three-decker, complete with attic and trap door leading to a tiny fenced-in roof area. While Liz was trying on some rather old-fashioned clothes (chiefly evening-gowns and cocktail dresses) that she had found, Greville amused himself by going out on to the roof.

It was fortunate he did so, for he was able to observe the approach of about fifteen men. They did not approach haphazardly or with stealth as he would have expected ordinary transies to do. They marched three abreast behind a leader. Some of them carried shotguns, one or two had rifles and there were even a couple of spear men. The leader carried a sword and a pistol and looked for all the world like something that belonged more properly to the pages of *All Quiet On The Western Front*.

The entire troop was obviously well drilled for they marched briskly in step along the tracks left by Greville's car. Clearly they were proposing to investigate the intruders in their bailiwick.

Greville might have considered trying to talk himself out of trouble but he was not prepared to take risks with Liz. If there was a shortage of women in the area – and even if there wasn't – her prospects with a bunch of transnormal pseudo-soldiery would not be particularly rosy.

Fortunately Greville was well-armed. It was suicide to go on a scrounging expedition without being well-armed. So he was carrying rifle, pistol and grenades. Liz, still no doubt trying dresses on in front of a cracked mirror in one of the bedrooms, had a pistol and a shotgun.

Greville gazed down at the approaching men below with an odd air of Olympian detachment. No doubt they had women and, perhaps, children dependent upon them. But in the transnormal world of the 1980s it was simply a question of *sauve qui peut*.

He flattened himself against a chimney-stack so that he would be hard to see, and took the pin out of one of his precious grenades. There was no time to warn Liz; and in any case, she would be aware of the situation quite soon enough.

He waited until the little group was about thirty yards from the car. Then he tossed the first grenade. He did not wait to see its effect but immediately withdrew the pin from a second grenade and dropped that, too. Luck – or whatever powers there were – was on his side. The first grenade dropped a little behind the men: the second grenade dropped a little ahead. There was hardly more than a second between the two explosions. Eight or nine of the men appeared to be killed instantly, a couple lay screaming and writhing and three who were only lightly wounded or mildly concussed picked themselves up and fled.

Greville thought their leader had been killed; but evidently he hadn't. He lay on the grass fumbling with his sword. Presently he raised it, displaying an off-white handkerchief knotted hastily on the end. Then he stood up. At the same time, Greville stood away from the chimney stack and called out to him. However, even as he shouted there was a flat, muffled crack. The man with the sword spun round and fell down. Liz had shot him from a bedroom window.

Greville went down to her. She was half in and half out of a green velvet cocktail dress.

'Come on,' said Greville. 'Grab your things. Our friends may have more friends. We'd better get out as fast as we can.'

Liz grabbed a few of the dresses that lay at her feet and followed him downstairs, still trying vainly to zip up the green dress.

Outside, in the late sunlight, Greville briefly inspected the dead and dying. He gave the *coup de grace* quickly to two of the wounded, and hustled Liz into the car. Then he reversed the station wagon, drove at a recklessly high speed to the open road and headed back to Ambergreave.

They did not get home until very late, but Liz insisted on trying on all her new dresses for his approval before they went to bed. Greville was tired and nervous and depressed with his reaction to the afternoon's encounter. Luck would not be with them always. Sooner or later they, too, would be on the receiving end. He found to his surprise that he could contemplate his own death but he could not bear to think of Liz being killed.

'I hope you are satisfied with the dresses,' he said brutally. 'I hope they fit. And I hope you like the bloody colours. Dresses are getting quite expensive these days. That little lot cost a dozen men. Do you think they were worth the price?'

'Nothing is ever worth the price,' retorted Liz calmly, 'but it always has to be paid … Let's go to bed. After all, there's a price on that, too, isn't there?'

Greville didn't answer. He wanted to take her in his arms; but he was chilled by the knowledge that every day gave him more to lose.

SEVENTEEN

It was the night of the first really heavy autumn fog, as Greville later recorded in his diary. It was a night for sitting by a log fire, reading, talking, listening to music, mending clothes, making impossible plans and finally dissolving the said plans in a deep and luxuriously warm sea of sleep. During the course of the night Liz and Greville managed to do all these things with a quiet satisfaction that might almost have amounted to happiness. And during the same night what was left of the village of Ambergreave began to die – violently and in a fashion bizarre even for the world of transnormality.

Greville had three clocks and no means of knowing the time. The second clock was always an hour ahead of the first clock, and the third clock was always an hour ahead of the second clock. When one stopped it could be reset by the others, when one gained or lost it could also be reset by the others. Thus, he argued, it was possible to maintain an arbitrary standard – and it was also possible to adjust the concept of time to one's personal convenience. If he got up late, he could look at the first clock and cherish the illusion that he had risen early. If he felt like going to bed early, he could look at the third clock and demonstrate that it was late. Actually he had long ago lost interest in clock time; though he still liked to feel it was available if he needed it. That was why he took care to wind the clocks regularly. It was a private joke that Liz could never understand.

Clock number three (Greville was in a going-to-bed early mood) struck midnight just as the shooting started. Greville stared at Liz; Liz stared at Greville. They were not particularly worried – merely interested, for the shooting sounded quite far away. And anyway they were separated from it by more than a hundred yards of water. Anyone who wanted to attack them would first of all have to find himself a boat.

'What the hell?' said Liz unconcernedly, as she endeavoured to thread a needle in order to sew a button on her shirt.

'Dogs,' said Greville. 'Just possibly rats, but dogs most likely. The fog has probably drawn them into the village. They'll be looking for easy pickings. They don't need vision as much as human beings do.'

Liz shuddered, remembering her own encounter with dogs on Chelsea Bridge. 'I hope they are in for a nasty surprise. To be eaten by dogs is bad enough, but to be eaten by dogs in a pea-soup – that's the absolute end.'

Greville laughed. 'The female mind never ceases to surprise me. If you're going to die, what does it matter whether you die in summer or winter, in sunlight or in fog?'

'A hell of a lot,' retorted Liz. 'When I die I want to be able to have a last look at something worth seeing … We'll have to go scrounging again pretty soon. I've got three working shirts and they're all dropping to pieces.'

'I'm not going to risk a bullet in the belly just for shirts,' said Greville. 'We'll wait until there's a longer shopping list. Now stop making like the extinct suburban housewife and come to bed. We'll go and find out who has been eaten by the dogs tomorrow morning.'

'Let's have some more music first,' suggested Liz. Her appetite for music was beginning to be insatiable. They had already listened to Tchaikovsky's 1812 and the Rachmaninov Second Piano Concerto.

'Balls to music. We've had a surfeit. I want sex.'

She smiled. 'I'm hungry. It's a long time since we ate.'

'Well, go and cut yourself a slice of ham while you're taking your knickers off. I'm tired.'

'If you're tired, you won't want it.'

'I'm not that tired.'

There were more shots. They sounded farther away.

'Definitely dogs,' said Greville. 'If they meet the dogs at the windmill it should be quite an interesting duel. The baddies won't know the goodies, but the goodies will have very strong ideas about the baddies … I wonder if Miss Worrall has forgiven you for stealing two of her Alsatians yet?'

'It was you who killed them,' Liz pointed out.

'And it was you who tried to get them to kill me, you little bitch.'

Greville stretched and yawned. The shooting seemed to have died away. 'Now. You either come to bed or I drag you there. Which is it to be?'

Liz giggled. 'A bit of both,' she said.

But by the time Liz had eaten her fill of ham, the mood for making love had deserted him. It had given way to a disquieting tenderness. He simply wanted to hold Liz in his arms and abolish the world. In the end that was effectively what he did – for a few hours.

The fog was still there in the morning. There was nothing to do and nowhere to go, so they stayed in bed until hunger made them rise. Then they had a lazy breakfast and went back to bed again. This time they made love, for it was as if the fog had effectively and permanently cut them off from all humankind. It was as if they were entirely alone on the planet – so much alone that it was possible to entertain visions of unending isolation, of immortality and a closeness and interdependence so satisfying that it was almost painful.

There had been no more sounds of shooting to disturb their night. There were none to disturb the drugged sensual limbo of their morning. But by mid-afternoon the fog had cleared. Liz was prepared to declare the entire day a sexual holiday, but Greville was beginning to feel restless.

When the sun broke through, he had a sudden desire to get up and find out what had been happening in the outside world. He had a desire to see other people, to look at a world broader than that bounded by four bedroom walls.

Presently, he and Liz rowed away from their enchanted island. Now that the fog had cleared, the day was perfect in its autumn glory. There was not a breath of wind, and the leaves of all the trees round Ambergreave Lake – brown and bronze, orange and deep crimson – looked as if they might have been somehow riveted to the still air.

The landscape was motionless. In the low golden sunlight it seemed petrified – a fantastic and lovely vista of still life.

In the village of Ambergreave there were aspects of still-life also; but they contained nothing beautiful – only the hanging terror of violence, the obscene degradation of pain, the musty flavour of wanton destruction.

The first bizarre object Liz and Greville encountered was a body, a male, clothed in what was apparently a monk's habit. It lay untidily in the middle of the village street. The man's throat had been torn out. There was also a bullet wound in his chest.

Liz and Greville stared at each other. Instinctively they stepped back from the body and gazed warily at the nearby cottages. They saw nothing but the vacant eyes of windows. There was not a sound to trouble the still air.

Greville fingered his shotgun nervously. He was surprised to find that his hands were wet with sweat. Death itself was not strange to him, nor was violence. But this was something absurd, something utterly grotesque.

'My God!' whispered Liz. 'What a horrible mess!'

'Shut up and listen,' snapped Greville. 'And keep your gun handy.'

But there was nothing to listen to – only a dreadful stillness, the frightening nullity of silence. They waited, motionless, expecting attack, expecting noise, expecting anything. There was nothing.

'All right,' said Greville at length. 'It won't come to us, so let's go and look for it. Keep about five paces behind me and watch the left-hand side of the street. I'll take the right. Something pretty bloody crazy has been going on.'

They advanced cautiously along the street. Cottage after cottage spewed forth nothing but silence. It was as if, thought Greville, the whole village was transformed into a vacant film set.

Then they saw a head stuck on the end of a pole which had been fastened to a cottage gate. The head was Big Willie's head, grinning in death as it had often grinned in life. A message had been painted crudely in white on the roadway. Greville had the briefly hysterical illusion that Big Willie was trying to read it.

There were only four words: *Despair! The Lord commandeth.*

Greville muttered an obscenity and turned to Liz. She stared back at him, white-faced.

'Let's take a look inside the house,' said Greville grimly, 'and see if Big Willie's mother has also repented.'

They went up to the cottage door. Greville kicked it open and rushed inside, shot-gun ready. He need not have worried.

Whether Big Willie's mother had repented of incest and probable cannibalism was now a point only of academic interest. She lay on the floor, her knees drawn up, her skirt thrown back, her ankles tied to her wrists, and with a wooden stake driven through her chest. She had not been a very old woman – probably, thought Greville, only in her late forties – and she had been quite handsome in a gipsy sort of way; with big dark eyes and prominent cheek bones.

Like Big Willie, her eyes were still open. But they did not register either amusement or pain. Only a horrible comic expression of infinite surprise.

There were two dead 'monks' in the room. One had a knife in his back, the other had what presumably was a hatchet wound in his head, since a blood-stained hatchet lay nearby.

Liz had followed Greville into the cottage. He pushed her out again almost immediately. The scene, he felt, was not one to linger over.

'The hell with all this,' he said roughly. 'Let's see what has happened at the windmill.'

Neither Big Willie nor his mother was an insupportable loss to the community. But Miss Worrall came under the heading of key personnel. Without her services as a grinder of corn it would be virtually impossible to make bread. Besides, Greville rather liked her. She seemed to him the kind of transie who was almost eccentrically normal.

The mill was on the far side of the village. Liz and Greville had to go down the entire length of the main street to get to it. They passed more corpses, including that of Charles Cuthbert the blacksmith, and three more pseudo-monks. Cuthbert had evidently had his throat cut. The 'monks' appeared to have died variously of gun-shot wounds and dogs.

But the windmill itself was the scene of greatest devastation. It also presented the remains of what must have been quite a battle. Miss Worrall's Alsatians – Greville counted five of their bodies – had done phenomenal service, for they appeared to have accounted for at least twice their number of 'monks'.

The Alsatians had died of gun-shot wounds, knife wounds and sheer bludgeoning. The 'monks' had died mostly of throat and facial wounds. In death, dogs and men seemed to be mingling almost affectionately – as if each was now regretting the excesses to which they had been driven by fear, blood-lust, pain and plain savagery.

The tower of the mill was of solid stone which Miss Worrall had covered with pitch a long time ago. The 'monks' – at least, the survivors – evidently found such a permanent surface irresistible: they had painted more choice slogans upon it.

Only God washes whiter than white … Heaven has fewer vacancies … and, with final simplicity, *Transies go home …*

Neither Greville nor Liz paid much attention to the slogans, however. Their eyes were drawn to the windmill sails, now slowly and creakingly rotating in a barely perceptible breeze.

The sails had been used as a makeshift cross. Where they joined the hub and the hub joined the main spindle in the windmill cap, Miss Worrall hung. She had been crucified in the traditional manner.

Liz tried to be sick – but nothing would come. Greville wanted to find something – anything – and smash it to pieces.

It was fortunate he had his shotgun ready, for as they gazed at the appalling sight he heard a low growl. A surviving Alsatian, dripping blood, seemed to drag itself in slow motion from inside the windmill. It summoned up its strength for a last onslaught – doubtless so crazed by pain it no longer knew or cared who was friend and who was enemy. It was as well that the Alsatian's reactions had been slowed down, for so had Greville's. He only just managed to shoot it in mid-air. The close range blast from the twelve-bore almost tore the dog in two. It was dead before it touched the ground.

Liz stopped trying to be sick and began to cry.

'Shut up!' said Greville. 'Save it till later. This isn't the bloody time for luxuries.'

Liz looked at him and shut up. As she did so, both of them became aware of another sound. It was like a long low animal moan that subsided in a fit of coughing. It seemed to come from inside the windmill. There was silence for a moment or two. Then it came again. This time it sounded human.

'There's one of the bastards left,' cried Greville exultantly. 'Maybe we can trade an eye for an eye.'

Throwing caution aside, he ran to the open windmill door and scrambled up the wooden steps. Fearfully, Liz followed him.

There was nothing on the ground floor – nothing but a couple of sacks of corn, half a sack of flour and Miss Worrall's old piano. Greville ran upstairs to the second storey – Miss Worrall's bedroom and the sleeping quarters of her two favourite dogs. There was nothing there either.

The third storey was the grinding room. It contained the millstones, a pile of empty sacks – and the source of the noise that Liz and Greville had heard.

One of the 'monks' lay on the pile of sacks. There was blood on his face and – symbolically enough – blood on his hands.

Greville felt a sudden surge of satisfaction. Here, at least, was something that could be made to suffer for all that other suffering.

He raised his shotgun. The man on the pile of sacks smiled faintly.

'Vengeance may prove somewhat inadequate,' he said apologetically. 'I rather think I'm already dying.'

Greville was surprised as much by the voice as by its owner. He was no less surprised by the words.

'Maybe we can persuade you to put off that happy event for a little longer,' snapped Greville. 'Now who the hell are you and what were all the fun and games in aid of? And talk quickly and sensibly or I shall have the pleasure of blowing your hands and feet off one by one.'

The man on the sacks did not appear to be greatly perturbed by the threat.

'I'd like some water,' he said. 'I'd never have believed I could feel so damned dry.'

Greville turned to Liz who was standing behind him. 'Get him some water. There's a pump just outside.'

She went back down the stairs and returned a few moments later with an earthenware jug. The man on the sacks licked his lips.

Greville took the jug and went close to him. 'Now, let's talk.'

'The water first, please.'

Greville poured some of the water on the floor at his feet.

'I said: Let's talk.'

The wounded man half-stifled a moan. 'Much good may it do you,' he said weakly. 'But as a point of what once might literally have been academic interest, you are being uncharitable to one Professor Francis Watkins, sometime holder of the chair of psychology at the late and not entirely lamented University of East Anglia … Oh God! For Christ's sake kill me.' The last words rose into a scream, and the scream brought a fresh trickle of blood from his lips.

Sadistically, Greville poured more water at the feet of Professor Francis Watkins. 'Now tell us all about your religious persuasion,' he said pleasantly. 'If it sounds interesting, we might even give you a drink of water. If you can convince us that it's rather jolly to chop people up and crucify them, we might even be kind enough to finish you off. But don't bore us. We don't like to be bored.'

Despite his ghastly appearance, and despite the pain, the man on the sacks managed to smile. 'Anything is a fair trade for water,' he murmured. 'Sir, you are addressing a conscript lay member of the quite extraordinary order of the Brothers of Iniquity. I was starving and they fed me. I was useful and they let me live … The great joke is that I once had the effrontery to consider myself an authority on abnormal psychology.' He began to laugh, but the laughter died into a thin, bubbly scream.

Suddenly Liz took the jug out of Greville's hand. She bent down, and cradled Professor Francis Watkins in her arms like an overgrown child. Then she gave him some water.

'Thank you, my dear. It hurts, you know. It hurts even to discover that there is compassion left in England today.'

EIGHTEEN

Despite his optimism – and in the circumstances it must have been justifiably described as such – Professor Francis Watkins, authority on abnormal psychology and temporary Brother of Iniquity, was not mortally wounded. A bullet had passed through his shoulder, another had ploughed through the top of his leg, and his arms and hands had been bitten by dogs. But with reasonable care, he would live.

That much Liz discovered when, regardless of Greville's obvious disgust, she ripped away the 'monk's' habit and began to clean up the wounds as well as she could. The blood coming from Professor Francis Watkins's mouth was simply due to the fact that he had bitten his tongue rather badly when the wounds were still fresh and giving him quite a lot of pain.

Greville resented the man on the pile of sacks. He resented him because his own blood-lust was dying, because, caught between pity and hatred and revulsion, he was no longer sure of himself. Professor Francis Watkins was not a young man. He was fat and sixtyish and pathetic. He was the kind of transie to whom things were destined to happen simply because he completely lacked the art of avoiding anything. As some people are accident prone, this man was disaster prone. That, thought Greville, you could tell at a glance. If anything terrible was going to occur, he was the kind of man who would be naturally drawn to it as to a magnet.

The water revived him a little, and so did Liz with her inexpert ministrations. While she cleaned him up the tears streamed down his face in gratitude; and when he had got over the crying he began to pour out his story – regardless of the pain it caused his tongue – in a spontaneous act of confession.

While civilisation was collapsing upon itself, Professor Francis Watkins, whose own psychology turned out to be more abnormal than he had formerly supposed, retired to his library with stocks of food as large as he could muster, prepared to sit out what he had first regarded as only a temporary and rather interesting return to the Dark Ages.

But the Dark Ages got darker instead of lighter, the food store dwindled slowly away; and in the end he was forced to go out and risk his life – and, more important, the future of his library – for such delicacies as potatoes, turnips and, in the end, even carrion. He was no cook, but he had discovered that you could eat practically anything if you boiled it long enough.

The trouble was he was not much good at finding food. Sooner or later he would have to quit his beloved library or die in it of starvation. He could not drive a car, he could not fight and he could only just manage to pull the trigger of a gun. The wonder was that he had managed to survive it all.

Finally, when he had gone two days without food, an idea came to him. Civilisation had collapsed, but surely small centres of culture and learning must be flourishing somewhere? He just could not imagine a world in which all that he regarded of value had disappeared.

Granting, then, the existence of intelligent groups of people more fortunate than himself – people, doubtless whose primary concern would be the preservation of all that was worthwhile (to him, this only meant books) until the return of sane social organisation – it merely remained for him to find one of these groups, attach himself to it and wait patiently until the world was ready to appreciate the significance of Freud and Jung, of Adler and Pavlov, of Yevtushenko and Eysenck once more.

That was the theory. It seemed a good theory. There was only one problem. Professor Francis Watkins had acquired one of the best private libraries on psychology in the whole of England. He did not want to abandon it. Indeed, it was his duty not to abandon it. Therefore he could either remain with it and die or take the best books with him. Unfortunately he had no means of transport.

But he was nothing if not a resourceful man. Hunger had sharpened his wits. He could not drive a car, but he could certainly push a small cart. If he could find a cart.

He couldn't. However, he found a substitute – or to be strictly accurate, he found three substitutes. They were perambulators that he discovered in a derelict baby-wear shop. They were the only forms of transport that he could lay his hands on.

So he filled them full of books. The choice was heartbreaking. Even loaded to overflowing, the perambulators could only carry about twenty per cent of the books that he considered essential for the foundation of a decent library in psychology.

And having filled the perambulators with his best books – the task of selection alone took him the best part of three days – he set off into the bright blue yonder. He didn't know where to go, but he felt that if he journeyed long enough in almost any direction sooner or later he would find sanctuary.

His method of progress was simple. He would push the first perambulator about a hundred yards, then he would come back for the second, and then for the third. Assuming that he could get enough food to keep body and soul together, he calculated that he would be able to cover five miles a day. At that rate, he told himself, it ought not to take longer than a month before he came across people who were similarly dedicated to keeping the intellectual achievements of the world alive.

There were only two flaws in the grand design. He didn't really know where he was going; and even if he did, he certainly couldn't find enough food to sustain him while he was getting there.

On the strength provided by about six pounds of very old potatoes and the rancid remains of a two-pound tin of butter, he wandered about for eight or nine days, meticulously pushing the first perambulator, going back for the second and then for the third. It was a miracle that be avoided being eaten by dogs or rats. And perhaps in doing so he had used up his entire ration of miracles.

For, having consumed the last of his potatoes and the last of his butter, he suddenly realised that he was not going anywhere at all, and lay down to die. It was then that the Brothers of Iniquity found him.

If he had been more than half alive, they would have killed him. As he was obviously more than half dead, they did their best to save him. Their best consisted simply of giving him food and keeping him warm. For a day or two he raved, believing that, surrounded as he was by tonsured heads and robes of Hessian and even sack-cloth, he had truly arrived back in the Dark Ages. But then he grew lucid and began to get better.

So the Brothers of Iniquity shaved his head, provided him with a monk's habit and initiated him as a compulsory novice. The initiation rites of the Brothers of Iniquity were simple and exceedingly effective; the novice was forced to do what he most disliked doing. Men who were physical cowards were forced to fight against veterans of the Order with knives, razors or bottles. Men who were naturally courageous were made to endure all kinds of indignities without the means of retaliation. Men who were normally sexed were handed over to a group of homosexuals. Men who could not swim were thrown into a river. Men who could not bear to be alone were given a period of solitary confinement. And so on. Every man had his Achilles' heel, and every man was subject to public exposure and degradation.

Professor Francis Watkins was not greatly interested in women, so the Brothers of Iniquity produced for him a half-starved nymphomaniac whom they had acquired in their travels and neglected to rape or kill only because she would have welcomed both or either.

The nymphomaniac, a gaunt and physically strong woman who looked about twice her actual age, was given a bottle of whisky and the promise of solid food for every successful completion of the sexual act that she could achieve with Professor Francis Watkins. The two of them were locked in a cellar for a day and a night – at the end of which time Professor Francis Watkins was hysterical and the woman had earned a credit of three meals. The degradation was witnessed by a senior Brother, who kept a long but somewhat entertaining vigil for the purpose.

This, however, was only the first part of the initiation. The Brothers had noted that, above all, Professor Francis Watkins wished to preserve his books. So they made him burn them. It was the only occasion on which he attempted to display courage. He refused to light the bonfire and told them that they could kill him first.

The Brothers of Iniquity had no intention of killing him. They merely offered him the choice of burning the books or spending an unspecified time locked up with the nymphomaniac. He decided to burn his books. Anything seemed preferable to the kind of rape that had not, to the best of his knowledge, been documented or even suggested in the books he was about to destroy.

It was only afterwards, when his spirit was broken, that he realised there were compensations in belonging to the Brothers of Iniquity. The Order, though not unique in history, was certainly unique in modern times. It embodied a form of mania that was in itself fascinating. For the Brothers of Iniquity were dedicated to the propositions that God was mad, cruel and utterly absurd.

God, they believed (or, at least, the fanatics among them believed), had brought about Omega radiation and the Radiant Suicide simply because man was in danger of developing a rational, healthy and flourishing society. Further, they believed that God had purposely left the process of destruction incomplete because he wished to offer redemption to the chosen. The chosen were, of course, the Brothers of Iniquity. It was their mission to complete God's work among the lesser mortals; and when they had completed the task of cleansing the planet they would then be able to enjoy the ultimate privilege of destroying themselves. At which point, according to their theologians, they were destined for immortal madness in some indescribably psychotic heaven until God should choose to have more interesting nightmares and clothe them with substance in some far and infinitely absurd anti-Eden.

The surprising thing was not that transnormals should develop such ideas but that so many transnormals should be capable of organising themselves so effectively; for the Brothers of Iniquity were numbered now in hundreds. Their mortality rate was high; but so was their rate of recruitment. And their leader, who called himself Brother Lucifer, had the kind of demagogic quality that earlier tyrants might have envied.

Adopting the proposition that life, being God-given, was absurd, he sought to magnify its absurdity by pursuing absolute frustration along a path of random acts. He permitted the Order to indulge in ritual cannibalism because of its absurdity; but death by torture was the fate of anyone who dared to eat pork because he decreed that pigs, being almost perfectly absurd, were therefore sublime and possibly the purest manifestation of God's will. On one occasion he had even sacrificed about a hundred of the brethren in a forlorn attempt to save half a dozen pigs from a very large pack of dogs.

After a time, and humiliated though he was by the constant indignities.

heaped upon him in accordance with the precept of absolute frustration, Professor Watkins began almost to enjoy his experiences in a masochistic sort of way. He was in a unique position for field-work, he felt. He had still not abandoned hope that sooner or later the nightmare would end and that somehow he would once again find his way into a world of academic peace and security; but meanwhile he, the trained observer, would record the basic, naked manifestations of human madness and depravity. Some day he would be able to write about it. Some day he would be able to evaluate what had happened and perhaps use his knowledge to do what no one else had ever been able to do before – to evaluate, by negative reference, the basic criteria of sanity.

But then he was overtaken by the random consequences of Iniquitism. The Brothers, lost in a fog, discovered Ambergreave and decided to sanctify it by their attentions. It was the first time Professor Francis Watkins had seen the philosophy of the Brothers of Iniquity put into practice on a large scale. He was terrified by what he saw. He was also badly bitten; and, in a state of moral and physical collapse, had hidden himself in the windmill, hoping that the Brothers would go away and leave him. But one of them found him before the company departed. When he would not move, and because he seemed to be wounded, he was shot twice for good measure and left to die in his own time.

This was the story he told Greville and Liz, while taking grateful sips of water and easing himself into a comfortable position. Greville had thought that nothing could surprise him anymore. He was wrong. Professor Francis Watkins could and did surprise him. Give or take a little, thought Greville, there but for the grace of sheer chance go most of us.

'I would add,' said Professor Francis Watkins, smiling wanly, 'that despite the care of your good lady, my own stupid constitution and your commendable patience, I would be much obliged if you would discharge that instrument of destruction in such a way as to provide me with the minimum of pain and a fairly rapid demise … I – I rather fear I have seen a little too much.'

'Where are the Brothers of Iniquity now?' asked Greville.

The old man shrugged. 'Who knows. They went to the south – that is, I believe, towards Thetford – but sheer whim could take them anywhere.' He shuddered. 'It could even bring them back here … Now, if you would be so kind as to aim carefully and press the trigger … I really think I would be much obliged, you know.'

If he had pleaded for life, Greville would probably have shot him. But he was pleading for death and, perhaps affected by a philosophy of absurdity himself, Greville refused to grant the final luxury.

He save Liz an inquiring look. She nodded.

'We're taking you home,' said Greville. He laughed grimly. 'After all, we have our own standards of iniquity to consider.'

Professor Francis Watkins started crying again.

NINETEEN

Francis – for so they came to call him – took quite a long time to recover from his wounds. Being an oldish man, unused to exertion or privation, he did not have much stamina. Nor did he have any will to live. Because of this, and out of sheer perversity, Greville determined that he should live. What was to be done with an ex-professor of psychology, Greville did not know; nor did he care to look very much into the future, for he had a presentiment that, somehow, time was running out.

The trouble was that he, who had managed alone and had been aloof for so long, had allowed himself to become emotionally involved with mankind once more in the person of Liz. He loved her as he had never loved Pauline. He loved her enough to be more afraid for her than for himself. They had got over the stage of wanting to take from each other and had learned to give to each other. It was a delicious, agonising, heady sort of feeling. It was a mad honeymoon in a nightmare world. Above all, it was a relationship that was utterly vulnerable ... And now there was Francis ... And suddenly the cottage on the island that was big enough for two was overcrowded. The citadel had become an open city. The hard world of reality, disguised as an old man with bullet wounds and dog bites, had entered by insane invitation through the back door.

They had carried Francis from the windmill to the edge of the lake in a wheelbarrow. They had ferried him across to the island, taken him into the cottage and dumped him on the bed that had so recently been a bed of love. That, thought Greville, as he levered the old man on to sheets that still bore the imprint and even the warmth of recent love and tenderness, was symbolically the end of the honeymoon. There would, with luck, be other times; but they would never again be like the times that had gone.

It was still daylight, though the sun was already sinking through a quiet sky. Greville told Liz that he was going to go back to Ambergreave and explore a bit more systematically.

'But what if those bloody maniacs come back?' protested Liz.

'That's one of the things I want to find out,' said Greville. 'My guess is that the fog saved us last night. If they'd known there was an island in the lake, an island with a house on it, very likely they'd have had a go. According to our friend, they have pushed off towards Thetford. He may be right, but it would be damn stupid not to check on it. I'll take the car and drive a little way along the Thetford road. I just want to make sure they aren't going to double back.'

'You'll be careful?'

'Of course, I'll be careful. What the hell! Do you think I want to get myself hammered?' Greville's irritability served to disguise his anxiety.

'I don't know,' retorted Liz. 'Transies do stupid things, don't they?'

Greville held her to him for a moment, then went out of the cottage. Life, he thought, was a crazy affair. You could spend years teaching yourself not to care about any damn thing in the world. You could witness suicide, murder, mayhem, starvation, disease and massacre and remain reasonably detached. Then suddenly you were flung head first into a mud-bath of emotion. You struggled in it, you wallowed in it and finally you ended up drowning in it – and caring like hell about every god damned inconsequential tragedy in an inconsequential world.

He rowed ashore, checked his guns and started the car. Then he drove slowly through Ambergreave, gazing at the horror and desolation that surrounded him in the now fading light, and feeling like a lone survivor in a world irrevocably committed to putrefaction and death.

It was some time since he had felt so lonely. The day was still quite warm, but it was some time since he had felt so cold. The sails of the windmill were still rotating slowly, and what was left of Miss Worrall was rotating with them. Suddenly he could not bear the sight. He stopped the car and got out.

After a few minutes of searching, he discovered Miss Worrall's carefully hoarded store of paraffin. She had about thirty gallons left. He poured three-quarters of it on the ground floor of the mill and took the rest outside to splash on the sails as they came round. Then he used one of his precious matches to light the funeral pyre. It blazed up quickly and the sails began to burn like some monstrous Catherine wheel, flinging off sparks and bits of timber. The stone shell of the windmill acted like a chimney and drew the fire inside until the roaring and the heat made Greville stand well back.

Setting fire to the mill was a fool thing to do, he decided. But he felt better for having done it. He waited until the sails came crashing down, bringing what was left of Miss Worrall to be incinerated in their midst, then he started the car once more and drove cautiously along the Thetford road.

He drove about five miles and discovered only two wounded Brothers of Iniquity resting by the roadside. Doubtless they were hoping to overtake the main body by nightfall.

Neither of them had weapons and, in fact, it would probably not have made a great deal of difference if they had. They were both weakened by pain and loss of blood. They were lying on a thick patch of grass round a bend, and Greville was already driving past before he noticed them. He stopped the car about fifty yards further on, and hurled himself out on the theory that he might have walked into an ambush.

He waited, but nothing happened. Then he picked himself up and, shotgun in hand, walked back towards the two men. They saw him coming. One of them tried to crawl away, but the other was too weak or too stiff to move.

Greville felt inclined to indulge himself in melodrama. He stopped about five yards from them. The man who was trying to crawl gave up the attempt and turned to face him.

'Stand up,' said Greville.

They both tried, but neither of them could make it.

'The sentence of this court,' said Greville, 'is that you shall have a little time for reflection.'

He shot each of them at close range in the stomach. Then, unmoved by the resulting screams, he turned the car round and drove slowly back in the direction of Ambergreave.

TWENTY

Each day for a few days after the massacre at Ambergreave Greville made probing sorties in different directions – chosen more or less at random. On two occasions he discovered small villages through which the Brothers had obviously and recently passed, leaving behind them a swathe of destruction similar to the one they had left at Ambergreave; but he did not encounter any more of them alive. They seemed to be heading generally south, perhaps making for London. Greville rather hoped that this was the case, because he felt that in London or its environs they stood a reasonable chance of encountering opposition that would prove too big for them to handle. The worst fate he could wish upon them was not that they should encounter a larger and better armed group of humans but simply that they should receive the attention of a horde of rats – preferably very hungry rats, and preferably at night.

Meanwhile, despite his age and lack of stamina, Francis continued to improve. Among his treasures in the cellar, Greville had a large store of exceedingly old and quite useless penicillin tablets. These he fed to Francis like sweets, and the old man developed a liking for them since they had the vestiges of a synthetic orange flavour. They didn't appear to do him any harm and just possibly may have done him a little good.

Greville allowed Francis to continue to occupy the bed in which he and Liz had created their private world of ecstasy. The bedroom became Francis's private territory. Greville had found a massive four-poster in one of the derelict houses of Ambergreave. Section by section he hauled it down to the lake and floated it across to the island. Further scrounging provided him with a foam rubber mattress.

The four-poster was magnificent, hand-carved and obviously very ancient. When it was assembled in the living room Liz was so delighted with it that she made a canopy and curtains for it. The bed completely dominated the room, and in the evenings when Francis had tactfully retired to his own territory, Liz and Greville, feeling mildly sinful, would build up a large fire and retire to bed content simply to talk and look at the flames. Then, after a time, Greville would draw the curtains and effectively reduce the cosmos to a cube enclosing one man and one woman.

But despite a sufficiency of food and the double luxury of sex that had generated love, the outside world could not wholly be ignored. The autumn was deepening, the days were growing shorter, Liz was getting more frequent nightmares about Jane, the odds against survival were steadily lengthening, and across a few yards of water the village of Ambergreave lay mute, stinking and desolate – a constant reminder that what had happened yesterday would probably be repeated with variations tomorrow. Mankind, or what was left of it, had turned cannibal just as much as the pigs and the rats. The surviving transies were living off the past and off each other. And because of this they were clearly doomed. Sooner or later their numbers would become critically low; and then, no doubt, man would join the dodo and the phoenix to become a legend in a world where there was no one to take any notice of legends.

Left to his own devices, Greville might have been content to live from day to day, taking each day as it came, merely thankful for another twenty-four hours of grace. But there was Francis. And if Greville had been tempted ever to regard his island as a kind of shabby Eden, Francis would most certainly have been cast for the role of serpent.

'You know,' said Francis one afternoon when they were sitting out of doors, enjoying an hour of late sunlight, 'what saddens me most is that there probably aren't enough people left to care.'

'To care about what?' asked Greville. He was watching Liz pluck a chicken – one that had signed its own death warrant by refusing to lay – and he was marvelling that it was possible to turn such a mundane act as plucking a chicken into a sequence of movements that had grace, charm and an oddly symbolic kind of promise.

'About the future of man,' said Francis sombrely. 'It's easy to care about individual futures, easiest of all to care about our own. But it's damned diffi-cult to care about an abstraction ... It's such a pity, really. We spent about half a million years growing self-consciousness, language and conceptual thought. Then we spent another half million years learning what to do with them. Then the sun gets an itch in its belly, the irritation gets radiated across a hun-dred million miles of space and triggers off the death-wish in three thousand million creatures, each of whom is potentially greater than the sun simply because the sun can neither laugh nor cry.'

Greville, absorbed in Liz, who was absorbed in the chicken, had only been listening vaguely.

'There are still a few people left who can laugh and cry,' he said.

Francis sighed. 'Yes, but can any of them care? Can any of them really care? Do any of them want to care? I'm just a tired old man full of worn out paranoia and I would like to feel that somewhere somebody cared.'

'Why?' asked Greville.

'So that an ape with a soul that gibbered for the moon and died with a tool in its hand will not have died in vain. I'm a romantic, I know, but this is an ignominious way for mankind to go out. Better to have had the sun turn into a nova, better to have died to a man of some insidious and unconquerable disease. Better even to have blown ourselves to glory for the sake of, ideas … But not like this. It's so futile, so untidy.'

'Yes,' said Greville bitterly. 'We had a great civilisation. We had nuclear weapons, bacteriological warfare and brain-washing. One-third of us developed heart diseases from overeating and two thirds of us developed other diseases from malnutrition. It was a hell of a civilisation! We had hot lines from Washington and London to Moscow and Peking. But there weren't any hot lines from the slums of Bombay to New York. You could have your nose reshaped or your double chin removed for a mere five hundred pounds at the London Clinic, but in Central Africa we let them die of beriberi, malaria, leprosy and plain hunger for free.'

Francis smiled. 'Dear lad, for a transie you are beginning to sound abnormally normal … Of course there was injustice. Of course there was tyranny and fear and tremendous waste. And what do you think the answer could have been? Communism, Utopianism, humanism or any other -ism? Well I can tell you that -isms never got anybody anywhere. The moment you have an -ism you begin to freeze ideas. Orthodoxy evolves into tyranny, and then you are back to – what was the phrase? – square one. No, Greville, my friend; what humanity needed was simply time. Another ten thousand years of it. Not much to ask, really, from a cosmic point of view. But the sun had indigestion, and here we are. I suppose it's funny, in a way, but my sense of humour isn't what it was.'

Greville was enjoying the argument. He knew it was going nowhere, because there was nowhere for it to go. But he was enjoying it. He had not endeavoured to solve the problems of the world for nearly twenty years, and now that they were past solving he felt he could almost achieve an Olympian detachment. There were no problems to solve now – apart from the ordinary personal ones. All that remained was to render a verdict.

'Humanity,' he said, 'wasn't worth another ten thousand years. It was rotten.'

Francis, too, was enjoying himself. It was a long time since he had held a tutorial. 'So Beethoven was rotten? And Buddha and Leonardo da Vinci, and Socrates, and – coming a bit nearer home – Dag Hammarskjold and Albert Schweitzer?'

Greville laughed. 'Transies,' he said, 'crazy mixed-up transies. They suffered from delusions of grandeur – and so did Attila, Genghis Khan, Julius Caesar, Napoleon, Hitler, Stalin … And even Jesus Christ … Transies all … Exceedingly dangerous specimens in a world of latterday apes.'

Francis permitted himself a display of indignation that he did not actually feel. 'The trouble with you is that you are afraid to admit what has been lost. You are afraid of admitting anything because if you did it would move you to tears … Yes, we butchered people in the twentieth century as we butchered them throughout history. We butchered their minds and bodies. But at the same time sight was being restored to the blind, hearing to the deaf, limbs to the disfigured or the malformed. We could make one voice heard across the planet, one orchestra could play to three continents. We could set down thinking machines on the face of the moon. What we lost when the sun decided to have celestial hiccoughs was not so much a few thousand million people as a vision of greatness … We could have been great, you know. In time we could even have been great enough to enter the mind of God.'

'Now I know why you survived,' retorted Greville. 'You're just another frustrated bloody saviour. You lived in a little academic world and did crosswords with the Almighty and didn't have erections because you thought they were just a shade uncouth. You're just an ape with a computer complex. You think that because you've got a few million grey cells sitting on top of your spine you're more special than a tree. How the hell do you know that a tree isn't more perfectly designed to enter what you grandly call the mind of God?'

'Because,' said Francis, 'a tree is never more than a tree. But there have been moments when men have been greater than man … The perennial ape I grant you. Grant me in return a few concepts that could have justified the existence of life on this burnt-out cinder whirling stupidly round a dyspeptic star.'

'Hot or cold?' inquired Liz. She had finished plucking the chicken, and it was her first contribution to the conversation.

'I beg your pardon?' said Francis.

'I said: hot or cold?'

'We are temporarily deserting the mind of God to consider the future of a dead chicken,' explained Greville drily. 'Liz is less intellectual than practical. You and I may discuss the now theoretical potential of mankind, but she will see that our bellies are filled while we are doing it. She is also good for sexual solace, and that, more than anything, keeps away the eternal cold.'

Liz surveyed them both. 'A woman gave birth to each of you,' she said. 'I expect it was a pretty energetic process. Let's hope the original screw was more satisfying than the end product … Now, hot or cold?'

'Hot,' said Francs.

'Cold,' said Greville.

Liz grinned. 'You're both a couple of liars.' She picked up the chicken and took it into the house.

Greville watched her go, and felt his heart ache.

Francis watched Greville. 'She's right, you know. We are a couple of liars. You don't believe what you say any more than I do.' Then he could not resist adding a trifle maliciously, 'On the other hand, it appears there are still a few things that have not been lost.'

TWENTY-ONE

Extract from Greville's diary:

'October. Day ninety – a piece of precision I allow myself as a slight luxury. It's not accurate, of course. I never stick at any damn thing, even the memoirs of a semi-retired grave-digger.

'Francis is dead. He wasn't with us long enough to matter. And yet he mattered. What was it about him? He was just another sad, lonely creature, an absurd old man with a headful of abstractions and three-syllable words. He wasn't programmed for survival. He was even too stupid to look after himself properly. He would go for days without washing. If Liz hadn't forced a minimum routine of hygiene on him he would have worn all his clothes until they stank – or fell off in rags. He was lazy, he was impractical, he was pompous. And yet … And yet I liked him. Why the hell should I feel so affectionate for somebody who was so absurd? My trouble is that I'm learning how to care. It's dangerous.

'Francis was absurd enough to die absurdly for an absurd reason. Or maybe there were two reasons. Because I shall never know whether he died for the Concise Oxford Dictionary or for a half-starved boy in cat skins. I suppose it was my fault, really. I shouldn't have indulged him. After all, what was he? Nothing more than a piece of human wreckage that Liz persuaded me to save against my better judgement.

'All right, Greville, my lad! Make like God! Offer your divine verdict on one more machine that failed!

'The truth is there is no verdict to be offered upon Francis, except the customary open verdict. I liked him, that's all.

'It happened on a scrounging expedition. Liz and I had the usual kind of shopping list – food, clothes, guns, ammunition, petrol, paraffin. But all Francis wanted was books. I told him there would probably be no time left to look for books, but he wanted to come anyway. He probably had a theory he could persuade me to make time. He succeeded – and died.

'We'd had quite a bit of luck, really, The car was running well, the roads we chose (or what was left of them) didn't have any nasty surprises, and the weather was fine. I determined to avoid towns and villages as much as possible. Isolated houses, preferably large ones – and preferably uninhabited – were the main targets. We didn't want to fight anybody. We just wanted loot. But if it came to fighting, we were as prepared as we could be: one rifle, one revolver and two shotguns. We weren't too badly off for ammunition, since I'd found a little in what the Brothers of Iniquity had left of Ambergreave.

'The first couple of houses that we tried had been picked clean as a bone. The third one was inhabited, and we were lucky enough to be able to reverse the car and get the hell out of it before the shooting became accurate. But the fourth house was a gold mine. It was difficult to understand why someone had not cleaned it out before us. Maybe it was too secluded. We only discovered it by accident. Liz spotted what looked like a narrow track leading into a wood; and there at the end of it was the house.

'Our total haul was three pairs of trousers, five shirts, several blankets, a couple of evening gowns (circa 1960), a dozen or so unlabelled tins (later we found they all contained fruit juice), a couple of oil lamps, various wood-working tools and about six or seven gallons of paraffin at the bottom of a forty-gallon drum. Fortunately we had brought a couple of empty five-gallon cans with us.

'The next house we found was even better. It was nearby and had probably once been a gamekeeper's cottage. There we got a rusty shotgun, a box of candles, a large jar of pickled onions, two small jars of jam, three boxes of matches (damp, but they were all right when we dried them out), an old sheepskin jacket and about a hundred pounds of flour. The flour had been stored in earthenware jars – God knows how long – but it was still fresh and dry. It was the jackpot.

'Francis helped us load all our spoils in the station wagon and said casu-ally: "How about going back by Bury St. Edmunds? It's the shorter route."

'"Too dangerous," I said. "I don't like towns, these days. We'll go back the way we came. Then we'll have no trouble."

'"There's a public library in Bury," said Francis diffidently. "There may still be a few interesting books left."

'"Fuck the books. You can't eat them."

'Francis sighed. "Metaphorically, one can, of course. That's what books are for."

'Surprisingly, Liz supported Francis. But I overruled the pair of them. We set off back the way we came. We weren't so lucky on the way back. We hit a road block.

'Maybe the people who manned it had heard us go through the first time and guessed that we were on a scrounging expedition. Or maybe they just set up blocks at random intervals.

'The block in this case was nothing more than a very old tractor that more or less filled the narrow lane. Whoever set it up had chosen a bad place because although it was round a bend, I still had about twenty-five yards' warning. Enough to stop the car, reverse it round the bend and make a turn of sorts. We got away even before the shooting started.

'But, to the delight of Francis, the only alternative route back to Amber-greave that I knew led through Bury St. Edmunds. It was late afternoon. Soon it would be dusk. I thought the risk was worth taking.

'There was no trouble in the outskirts of Bury. It seemed like a ghost town. We drove on until we came to the market square. Still no trouble.

'And there was the public library, and here was Francis in the car, pining for a few miserable books.

'"Give me five minutes – only five minutes," he pleaded. "Man does not live by bread alone. Besides, the whole place is deserted. Who in their right minds would want to live here?"

'I was inclined to agree with him. "Look," I said. "I'm going to park in the middle of the square so that if anybody wants to shoot they'll have to shoot from a distance. I'm not going to get out of the car and neither is Liz. We'll cover you as well as we can, but you'd better make it quick."

'"Greville, my friend," said Francis, nearly falling over himself in his eager-ness to get out of the car, "you are almost a civilised transnormal. One should not allow an educated mind to starve. It's the worst kind of vandalism."

'"Three minutes," I said. "You talk too much."

'Beaming all over his face, Francis ran across the square like a child of another age heading for the school tuck-shop.

'Liz and I sat side by side, each with a shotgun ready to poke out of either window. There's a special art in shooting from a car. By then, even Liz was getting good at it. But there was nothing to shoot at. Night was coming down, the world was quiet and, for all we could tell, we were the only people in the vicinity.

'I was glad of the fading light. The car seemed horribly exposed, standing in the middle of the square. But that was the best place to be. Anyone who wanted to investigate would have to cover about forty yards of open ground: anyone who wanted to shoot from the cover of the nearest building could barely see his target.

'Liz shivered. "We're not alone," she said.

'"How do you know?"

'"I can feel it."

'"Does your extra-sensory perception extend to knowing where the opposition is?"

'"No."

'"Then concentrate on it."

'Francis had taken a small rechargeable electric torch with him. We could see the dancing glow it cast on the inside walls of the library. Many of the windows were broken. I had a feeling he would be a bit disappointed. Rats would have disposed of most of the books.

'It seemed a long time, but it was probably only two or three minutes, before he returned, staggering, with a pile of books. He dumped them in the back of the station wagon, piling them untidily on the rest of our treasures.

'"There's not much left," he said, puffing from his exertions. "The *Britannica* seems to be reasonably untouched, though. Another couple of trips and I'll have the rest of the volumes."

'"What the devil do you want an encyclopaedia for?" I asked irritably.

'"What the devil do you want to go on living for?" retorted Francis.

'"You'd better be quick, then. Liz seems to think we are not alone."

'"Good," said Francis equably. "Loneliness is not conducive to happiness." He trotted back to the library.

'The second trip did not take so long.

'"I heard noises," he said unconcernedly, as he dumped his load of books. He chuckled. "Maybe it's a late borrower in the fiction department."

'"Get in. We're pulling out."

'"Not until I have the rest of *Britannica*." And off he went again.

'The minutes passed. He was a long time coming back. I was just about to go and haul him out when I saw his unmistakable, book-laden bulk in the semidarkness.

'He pushed the books among the rest of our loot. "Guess what!" he said excitedly. "I've found a boy dressed in skins."

'"That's nice," I said. "Now get in. We've been here far too long."

'"No," said Francis. "I've just remembered. I need a good dictionary ... The boy's starving. Do you think –"

'"No, I don't bloody well think. Now get in the car before I shoot you."

'Francis laughed. "Never make a threat you don't propose to carry out. Just one more minute. I know exactly where the dictionary is ... About the boy. Perhaps we might just –"

'"We might just nothing!" I snapped angrily and pointed the shotgun at him. "Now get in before I blow you to glory."

'Francis sighed. "Sorry to be a nuisance. I'll just get the dictionary." And off he went.

'I felt like shooting him. I felt like beating his silly brains out with a gun butt. I did nothing but sit and wait and fume.

'Liz attempted to soothe me in an odd sort of way. "What does it matter? What does anything matter? Don't get worked up about him, love. He's got to have something to take to bed at nights." She giggled. "Even if it is only a dictionary."

'And suddenly I felt sorry for anyone and everyone who did not have his Liz.

'Presently Francis emerged from the library. He was carrying more than the dictionary. There was an indistinct but vaguely human shape in his arms. He staggered a little, and I would have got out to help him – except that I was feeling too damned angry again. Hell, I'd saved the man's life, and he didn't give a damn about what I thought or felt or wanted. I let him struggle across the square with his armful of skin and bones. I couldn't see the child very well, and I was thinking that pretty soon I might just as well turn my little cottage into a combined vagrancy hostel and orphanage.

'Francis had almost reached the car when somebody – by luck or good management – did an excellent bit of shooting.

'At the same time, Liz thought she saw a movement on the far side of the square and banged away with her shotgun. So did I. Both barrels. Somebody screamed.

'Then I turned to look at Francis. He had dropped to his knees, still clutching his sad little bundle of humanity. He looked as if he was staying upright by sheer will-power. I jumped out of the car and ran to him. Liz was still shooting.

'Francis had a boy of perhaps nine or ten in his arms. The dictionary had fallen to the ground.

' "Sorry, dear lad," said Francis. *"Deus ex machina.* Very fitting … The boy's all right?"

' "The boy's fine," I assured him, and took the little heap out of his arms.

' "I've had it," said Francis. "Keep our Neanderthal friend as a souvenir … The poor child couldn't move … I found him with a home-made bow and two arrows, if you please." He sank down on his haunches and grinned. "He was trying to read *Grimm's Fairy Tales* by candlelight."

' "I'll get you back to the car," I said.

' "No good … Take the boy … And, Greville –"

' "Yes?"

' "Love somebody … Build something." Francis made a low and terrible kind of growling noise. Then he flopped back in an untidy heap.

'I looked at the child I was holding. The bullet had passed right through Francis and struck him in the back of the head.

'He could have been about ten, I suppose. He was wearing a single garment made of cat skins, and he looked as if he'd been starving for months. Probably he wouldn't have lived long anyway.

'I looked at Francis, then I looked at the child once more. Oddly, the child's face seemed much older. It looked as if it had already endured all the miseries of man.

'Francis was dead and the child was dead, and Liz was banging away with her shotgun as if it was the glorious twelfth.

' "The boy's fine," I babbled, as I laid him down by the side of Francis. "He'd like to stay with you a while, just to keep you company."

'Then I came to my senses, and dashed back to the car. And I started the engine and got the hell out of it quick. Liz never saw what she was shooting at. Maybe they never saw what they were shooting at, either.'

TWENTY-TWO

The frosts came, bringing with them the sharp and antiseptic flavour of winter. The landscape died in hoary splendour. Leaves drifted into bleak, undisturbed mountains, dead wood fell, and the November world hung grey with loneliness.

In an odd way the death of Francis sobered Greville and Liz. It frightened them more than the destruction of Ambergreave had done, more than any of the bizarre or pointless killings they had witnessed – or brought about – since they came together. It frightened them because Francis had come to belong to them, because, having accepted him in their intimate world, they had unconsciously bestowed upon him their own unconscious assumptions of immortality.

True, they lived in the shadow of violence and had some experience of the art of murder; true also that they were conscious – Greville particularly so – that each day of continued existence was a welcome and possibly unmerited bonus. But none of this really compelled them to accept the fact of their own mortality.

The death of Francis did. For, in the short time that they had known him, Francis had become a part of them; and a part of them had died.

It was impossible now to retire to their little cottage on the island and shut out the world. It was impossible because the world entered in the form of a ghost. Invisibly, Francis listened to their music. Silently, he took issue with Greville's more dogmatic statements. And there was even mute laughter when Liz uttered one of her habitual *non sequiturs*. Greville would not have believed it possible that one who was dead could be so insistently and negatively alive.

The gaiety was gone, the fantasy could no longer be maintained. Even in the act of love there was only desolation. Skeletons seemed to be rattling inside the passionate flesh: intimations of oblivion defied Beethoven, alcohol, food and orgasm.

Greville could not understand why an old man whom they had only known briefly should affect them so much. He could not understand why an invisible sentinel should bar all the familiar avenues of escape.

'Love somebody,' Francis had exhorted, dying. 'Build something.'

Well, there was someone to love – though love itself was a most painful luxury. But what was there to build? What could you create in a world that

267

was dying, that was surrendering all its illusions of greatness to the primal law?

You could build nothing but a pyramid of memories – the glory that was supermarkets, the grandeur that was launderettes. Physically and emptily potent, Greville became despondent with awareness of his spiritual impotence. And the despondence was infectious.

The nightmares that had plagued Liz returned with greater intensity. Jane was another ghost, inhabiting the colourful drowned world of darkness. Jane was Liz, and Liz was Jane; and together they endured the twilight terrors of being alone in a nocturnal madhouse where lust and cruelty were the only signs of human companionship.

One morning Liz could stand it no longer. She gave Greville his breakfast then pointed a loaded pistol at him.

'I'm going away,' she said calmly. 'You can come with me, but you can't stop me. If you think you'll humour me by conning and then bring me back at the first opportunity, you'll probably succeed. But then I shall just have to kill you and start out again … I tried once before. You stopped me, and I was glad you stopped me. But not this time.' Her voice faltered a little. 'I'm playing it for real.'

Greville looked at the pistol, then proceeded to finish his meal without hurrying. Liz had become a passing fair cook. The 'bacon' tasted like vintage bacon, the free-range egg was far more acceptable than any egg he had ever bought in a shop.

While he was eating, he tried to think; but all the normal processes of thought seemed to be blocked.

Reluctantly, he put down his knife and fork and gave his attention to Liz. The pistol was still pointing steadily at him. 'Chances are I could kick the table over and snatch the pistol,' he thought. 'She'd be too surprised to shoot.'

But he didn't kick the table over or attempt to do anything. He was saddened by the pistol. He was saddened by Liz. He was saddened by the sudden inescapable knowledge that his tiny island was no longer big enough.

'Jane?' he asked unemotionally.

'Jane,' confirmed Liz.

'How long have we been together? It seems quite a long time.'

Liz thought for a moment. 'Three months, I suppose … You lose track.'

'Four months,' corrected Greville. 'Four months and about two weeks. The way things are, it's practically a lifetime.'

'It's over,' said Liz flatly. 'It was nice, but it's over. I'm going to look for Jane. I should have gone a long time ago. You shouldn't have stopped me. That way we'd have still remembered the happiness.'

'I love you,' said Greville. 'That means something?'

'Yes.' She hesitated. 'But not enough.'

'I saved you from the dogs.'

'I'm glad about that.' She smiled impishly. 'But you also saved yourself, didn't you?'

'From the dogs?'

'No. From dying … It's no good. I've made up my mind. I'm going. I've got to find Jane or I shan't get any peace.'

Greville surveyed her sombrely. 'I'll tell you something. I'm not sure I believe in Jane.'

Liz tightened her grip on the pistol. Her knuckle showed white where her finger had taken the first pressure on the trigger. 'What the hell do you mean?'

'I'm not sure I believe in Jane,' repeated Greville calmly. 'I think she may be a figment of your warped imagination. I think she may be nothing more than an excuse for you to do whatever comes into your little transie mind. I think she may be a carefully cooked up excuse that you've given yourself for continuing to stay alive.'

For a moment or two, he thought she was going to shoot him; then suddenly she began to laugh. It was high, hysterical laughter. The kind of laughter, thought Greville, that you might indulge in if you were shocked, hurt or afraid.

'You big, stupid bastard,' said Liz. 'Do you think I could spend months needling myself with nightmares about somebody who doesn't exist?'

'Yes. We're all slightly nuts or we wouldn't be here. It may suit you to have an imaginary sister. For all I know, you may have a bloody great dose of schizophrenia. Jane could be your private piece of therapy – enduring all possible ills and degradation just because you feel guilty because you are still alive. Maybe you even had a twin sister. Maybe she died. What proof have you got that you're not just playing psychological games?'

'I don't need to prove anything to anybody,' said Liz simply. 'Jane is real enough for me. That's all that matters. And I've got to find her … You remember that morning on Chelsea Bridge? Hell, you don't think I was taking risks like that just for kicks, do you?'

'Why not?' retorted Greville. 'I had a damn silly reason myself for being on Chelsea Bridge. Why shouldn't you be just as crazy as I am?'

Liz laughed. 'This is getting us nowhere. The only problem to be solved is whether I have to put a bullet in you or whether I go peacefully … You can stop me, as I said. But then there'd be a next time; and I wouldn't let you stop me then.'

Greville looked at her and thought of all the good times they had had, remembering the love-makings, the insatiable appetite for music, the shared dangers and discoveries.

'Where is this alleged Jane?' he asked at length. 'Did your nightmares, imaginings or whatever give you a convenient map reference?

'She's in a kind of brothel near Manchester,' answered Liz evenly. 'It's a kind of cellar – I think it's underneath a town hall, or something like that. They keep her in a cage, and she gets screwed about four times a day, and if she's lucky she gets just about enough to eat. But they never let her out of the cellar. She doesn't know whether it's summer or winter. She thinks she's been there about a million years … She's ill.'

'That's bloody marvellous,' exploded Greville. 'Assuming it's not all a product of your sick mind, what do you expect to do – home in on the psychic emanations like a guided missile? And even if you do that, what the hell can you do when you get there? Shoot up the place single-handed? God dammit! If you want to commit suicide, why don't you just walk into the lake?'

'Thanks for the encouragement. If there's nothing to be done, at least I can join her. That way we'll share the load … Now, if you haven't got any further illuminating observations, I'll get my bits and pieces together – assuming, of course, you prefer not to be shot first. I'll need the car, I think. But you shouldn't have much difficulty picking up another one that still works … So the only question that remains to be answered is whether I pull the trigger or not.'

'You crazy little bitch,' said Greville quietly. 'You bloody little screwing machine.' He got up from the table, turned his back on her and walked through the doorway.

'Where do you think you're going?' snapped Liz.

'To look for a bleeding map,' he called over his shoulder. 'I've got one somewhere. If we're going to bust up the happy home and go to Manchester – which is one of the most elaborate ways of dying that I can think of – then we'll need to choose a route that combines the maximum safety with the maximum speed. To think I've been hoarding petrol for a half-cock trip like this!'

Liz stared after him, wide-eyed. Then she dropped the pistol and began to cry. Greville pretended to take no notice. He found the map – an ancient Esso road map, badly torn and with two sections missing – and spread it over the bed. Then he found a pencil and began to draw an intricate series of lines that crisscrossed the trunk-roads and avoided all towns.

He was still absorbed in plotting a route that would add up to less than two hundred miles – he had cautiously allowed twenty-five miles to the gallon – when Liz followed him into the bedroom.

She had discarded the pistol. She had also discarded her clothes. She was shivering a little. She lifted the map off the still unmade bed and scrambled between the sheets.

'I haven't got anything else,' she said with a grin. 'Besides, what else can you expect from a screwing machine?'

Greville began to take his shirt off. 'We'll start tomorrow morning,' he said, 'early. I don't much care whether Jane is real or not. I don't much care whether we get to Manchester or not. But I'll do my best ... One way or another, it had to come.'

'Yes,' murmured Liz. 'It had to come.'

Oddly enough, and despite the promptings of sheer physical desire, they did not make love. There were too many ghosts. There was Jane and there was Francis. And above all, there was the sadly overwhelming ghost of a tiny refuge that was about to cease to exist.

Until this moment, thought Greville, he had never properly appreciated his cottage on the island at Ambergreave. It was the only place where he had learned what it was to be alive. It was the only place he had ever loved because it was the only place where he had dared to place his entire self in bondage.

He lay there with Liz in his arms, touching her for the sheer delight of touching. It didn't matter that Francis and Jane were standing at the foot of the bed. It didn't matter that mankind had gone down the drain and that personal death was lurking round the corner.

It mattered only that two people could come close enough to look at each other and, though they could never really touch each other or understand each other, not be afraid. Man, he reflected, was doomed to perpetual loneliness though he had never been programmed for it. Man – every man – was a skilled impersonator. But just occasionally there was no need to impersonate anyone or anything. It was enough to exist.

He looked at Liz, lying quietly by his side, and felt as if he were seeing her for the first and last time. He looked at the subtle curves of her breasts, the enigmatic roundness of her belly, the small brown forest that grew between her legs.

Here, he thought, is life. Here is the ancient song. Here is the non-verbal answer to all the verbal sophistications that men have used to demolish themselves and each other since time began.

Then he looked through the window at the grey November light, at the motionless leaves rimmed with a myriad crystals, at the sleeping branches of the apple trees, and back again to the sad long light of impunity.

He didn't want to make love. He just wanted to hold close and pray.

The only trouble was he was too proud, too empty and too lonely for prayer.

TWENTY-THREE

It had taken them the best part of three days to get within ten miles of Leicester. Greville had optimistically calculated that they could get to Leicester, which was slightly past the half-way mark, with about a hundred and twenty miles of driving. Instead, it had taken nearly two hundred miles of driving; and at that rate, unless he could indulge in a bit of successful scrounging, he would only have enough petrol for a one-way journey. But probably, he reflected with bitter consolation, it was only going to be a one-way journey, anyway. What Liz hoped to accomplish when and if they got as far as Manchester, he had no idea. It was a crazy expedition undertaken for the craziest of reasons in a crazy world by two crazy people. Its chances of success – even if success were only to be defined as mere survival – were just about zero.

They had made a late start from Ambergreave, for there was more work to be done than he had thought. They might have made an earlier start if Liz had not spent half the night screaming. The nightmares had begun a little after midnight. When the screaming started, he had slapped her; but she didn't even open her eyes. It was as if she were in a trance, lost without recall in the terrors of a private world. The first fit didn't last much more than an hour. When Liz came out of it, she refused to talk. She just looked at him, wild-eyed, as if he were a total stranger. Greville got up and made a warm drink for them both. Then they got a little sleep – until the next session. That didn't last quite so long; but there were two more bursts of the same trance-like hysteria before dawn; and when they finally got up they were both bleary-eyed and already worn out.

After a hurried and rather sumptuous breakfast – they had far more food than they could take with them on the journey – Greville had rowed ashore and checked the car, while Liz busied herself collecting guns, ammunition and provisions.

There had been a hard frost and the windows of the station wagon were iced up. It took Greville the best part of an hour to clear them, check the tyres, oil, petrol and battery, and get the engine warmed up. At first he thought it wasn't going to start – the battery didn't seem to have enough juice in it to turn the engine over. Eventually, after about twenty minutes of cranking, he managed to get it to fire. He raced it for a while until the whole engine was warm, then switched off and rowed back to the island.

Liz had got most of their treasures out of the cellar and had dumped them in a pile on the floor. There was far too much to carry, and more time was lost over the selection process.

By the time they were ready to move, both of them were feeling hungry again; so they sat down amid the wreckage of their little citadel to eat a final meal.

Greville surveyed what had been his private, secure and very comfortable retreat gloomily. Once it had felt and looked like home. He didn't think he would ever see it again. Whatever else happened on the fantastic expedition which they were about to undertake, he did not think there would ever be any absolute turning back. The shade of Augustus Rowley could now rest in peace – until the next plague of locusts.

By the time they eventually got started, a red, wintry sun was peeping through the cloud-laden sky. To Greville, it seemed to be the colour of blood – a discouraging omen. Nevertheless, he gave Liz a cheery grin and started the car. They were on their way.

Then everything began to go wrong. Greville had not realised how rapidly the world in which he lived was deteriorating. Two of the roads he had chosen for the first day's run were blocked – one by a large tree that had fallen across it, and the other by a large hole so camouflaged by grass and weeds that he nearly drove into it.

Greville was impressed by the hole. He got out of the car and inspected it. The grass that covered it had the air of grass that had been established for quite a long time: the dead and dying weeds – convolvulus, nettles, ground-sel and bistort – looked as if they had been there since the beginning of the world. He came to the conclusion that the hole had been caused by high explosive. Quite a lot of it. He wondered why such a quiet country lane should have received such attention. He was wondering about it for a long time. But after a couple of days of hard driving, during which he had encountered several such holes, he thought he had the answer.

The roads he had chosen led only through small villages; and if anyone still lived in those villages they might reasonably be expected to protect themselves as best they could against scroungers – particularly well-armed and motorised scroungers, and most particularly against scroungers in convoy who might be able to overwhelm any local resistance and take whatever they wanted.

Greville had a sudden mental vision of all the roads of England – why stop at England? All the roads of the world – being steadily choked by weeds and grass and trees or being deliberately destroyed by man. In the end, with radio and telephone gone, with travel reduced to what a man could accomplish by walking, the world would contain nothing but groups of desert islanders. Strangers would be feared not because they might be dangerous but simply because they were strangers. Then tabu would raise its indestructible head once more; and anyone who did not belong to the family, sect, clan or tribe would be destroyed for the very clear and logical reason that he did not belong.

Greville had to make two major and several minor detours before darkness on the first day. When darkness came, he tried driving on his headlamps; but the effort was too tiring. There was always the risk that every clump of grass concealed a hazard, and even if it was only a pot-hole large enough to break a half-shaft, it was still large enough not only to wreck the expedition but to completely ruin the chances of its survival. For Greville and Liz were already a long way from any known sanctuary; and while it was still possible to attempt to get back to Ambergreave on foot, the possibility was not such as to inspire optimism.

They drove off the road and spent the first night in a little clearing that had once been part of a large field. Liz had brought a paraffin stove; and so they were able to heat some of their tinned food and have a reasonably satisfying meal.

They slept uneasily and uncomfortably in the car with the windows up. It was just as well that Greville, despite protestations from Liz, had refused to allow any ventilation.

Huddled together in contortions which they would regret bitterly next day, they had not been dozing long when there was a pattering all over the car that sounded like heavy rainfall. However, it was not heavy rainfall, as Greville discovered when he switched on the interior lighting. It was rats – hundreds or more probably thousands of them – trying to get in.

They could smell meat; and the meat they could smell was filled with terror. Liz gazed at the phalanx of vicious little faces on the bonnet and began to shake uncontrollably. With a curse, Greville leaned forward and pressed the horn. The rats disappeared almost instantly; but within a second or two they were back.

Greville switched on the headlights and illuminated an entire mobile carpet of rats. The clearing was alive with them. They seemed to ebb and flow, an evil hungry tide that looked as if it was about to engulf the entire car.

He started the engine. The noise drove them back briefly. But they became accustomed to it and came on once more.

In a fit equally compounded of anger and fear and plain irritability, Greville slipped the car into first gear and began to drive round the clearing in a tight circle. The rats fell away from the bonnet. Those already on the roof were thrown clear by the motion. Dozens of them, hypnotised by the headlights, passed beneath the wheels. They were immediately torn to pieces by those who perished next time round.

Eventually, it dawned upon the rats that they were on a no-win basis. The survivors – and that included the vast majority – took their leave. But they left behind them a stench; and the stench was so bad that Greville had to move the car back to the relatively exposed road.

Again they tried to settle down to sleep; but sleep would not come. And it was with relief that they took up the journey once more at first light.

It was another jewelled morning. The flat East Anglian landscape, unfettered now, free from the tidy patterns of agriculture, the greedy attentions of man, was reverting to its own primal mystery. Fen and woodland marched towards each other; and the rolling brown acres of ploughed land were no more.

The frost was a heavy one; but the car started easily. While it was warming up Greville and Liz stretched themselves and stamped about to get warm. Liz wanted to make a hot drink, but Greville decided to drive for a while first. As far as human beings – and animals – were concerned, early morning was probably a good time for travelling. Very few of either were at their aggressive best until the day had properly started. Frost translated the petrified landscape into the kind of pictures that were used to illustrate old-fashioned children's books. Any moment, thought Greville as he chugged along cautiously at twenty-five miles an hour, one might be confronted by the inevitable knight on a white charger. Or possibly dragons.

But neither knights nor dragons presumed to materialise in the desolate, white-edged world. He and Liz were alone with a car-load of junk and desperation.

They were driving from nowhere to nowhere, from oblivion to oblivion, through frozen avenues of time on a winter morning that any sensitive person would have recognised as the naked manifestation of eternity.

In a couple of hours, they had covered nearly thirty miles, which, allowing for the usual stops, map consultations (virtually useless because sign-posts were more or less non-existent) and three small detours, was pretty good going.

Greville felt pleased with himself. He felt entitled to enjoy his breakfast. It consisted of eggs and homemade bread and some precious coffee. Taken by the roadside, with the eggs cooked in bacon fat and the bread used to polish the pan clean and the black coffee stinging his throat like some deliciously painful nectar, he could almost feel happy. He looked at Liz, and his spirits rose. Whatever happened, he told himself firmly, they would stay together.

During the rest of the day they made good progress. Huntingdon had been by-passed without incident. There remained Kettering and Market Harborough as the only towns of appreciable size before Leicester. If he exercised a little bit of ingenuity, it should be possible to get round both of them without too much difficulty.

But whatever route was taken, they could not avoid villages. The two that they passed through during the morning were as silent as the grave. No smoke rose from the chimney-stacks. Cottage windows, glassless, stared blank-eyed and mute. In the third village, passed shortly after midday, a pack of dogs seemed to have used the houses as a temporary refuge. At the sound of the car they came hurling out of doorways and even first-storey windows, eager for something to kill and eat. Watching them lunge futilely at the wheels and the bodywork, Greville was almost sorry for the half-starved brutes. After all, they had been deserted by those to whom traditionally they were supposed to be the best of friends; and like man, they just didn't know what had hit them.

A more pleasing sight occurred later in the afternoon when Liz and Greville caught sight of a huge herd of deer. They were passing through relatively open country at the time; and the herd of deer were bounding across the plain – almost parallel with the road – in joyous exultation, glorying in life, freedom, the sharp air of late autumn, and the marvellous absence of the restraining and frequently lethal hand of man.

Being of a practical turn of mind, Liz suggested that they stop the car and drop one of the deer for meat. Greville vetoed the idea. He said he didn't want to waste time skinning and cutting; but secretly he was too moved by the obvious *joie de vivre* of the herd to want to do anything to spoil it. Besides, they had plenty of food for the time being. The time to shoot deer was when one really needed to.

They had covered nearly seventy miles by nightfall. It wasn't a bad start. It wasn't bad at all. This time Greville chose a small hill on which to spend the night – a hill that, according to the map, was miles from anywhere. He kept the car on the roadside, partly on the theory that any predatory animals would be more likely to haunt the nearby woodland and partly on the theory that it would be easier to move away if he had to.

There were no incidents, however – at least, none apart from Liz. The nightmares seemed to be taking an even tighter hold on her. She did not scream this time, she just moaned and shivered and cried softly. Nothing Greville could do would rouse her; and she remained curled up in her seat, sleeping at times, but for most of the time emitting sad and inhuman little noises until well after daybreak.

When, at last, she came to her senses, she did not seem to recognise Greville for a time; and she was strangely uncommunicative throughout most of the morning. She had cooked breakfast like an automaton, programmed for the task. And, in the same way, she had eaten it.

Greville humoured her and tried not to intrude too much upon her private thoughts. It seemed to him that as the morning wore on her spirits were raised slightly. He assumed it was because they were near to Leicester and because she felt that the worst part of the journey was behind them.

But it had nothing to do with how far they were from Leicester or Manchester.

While they were driving along a monotonously straight and relatively clear piece of roadway, Liz said abruptly: 'Jane's dead. She died last night … I'm going to have a baby.'

Greville stopped the car and gazed at her in wonderment. 'Say it all again – slowly. Maybe I'm further round than I thought.'

'Jane's dead,' repeated Liz. 'She died last night. It was some kind of fever … Hell, I don't really know what it was. Maybe it was just starvation and misery, or maybe she just couldn't stand the screwing any more … Anyway, she said to thank you. She said you were all right … So now we don't need to go to Manchester any more, do we? She really is dead, you know … I've been … I've been cut off. It's an odd sensation … A long time ago I read in a book somewhere about people that had to have limbs amputated. Afterwards, some of them could still feel the fingers and arms that weren't there … Phantom limbs, I think they were called … Now I've got a phantom limb … It's funny, really.'

Greville looked at her. She was dry-eyed and almost abnormally calm. There was not even a tremor in her voice.

'So Jane's dead,' he managed to say finally. 'I'm sorry … I really am sorry … You're sure she's dead?'

'I'm sure.'

Greville was silent for a minute or two. 'You said something else,' he prompted at length. 'It didn't seem to be connected with Jane.'

'That's right. I'm going to have a baby.'

He was silent again a for a while. Then: 'How long have you known?'

'Three months,' said Liz unconcernedly. 'Maybe four … You begin to lose track of time.'

'And why the bloody hell didn't you tell me before?' he exploded violently.

Liz smiled. 'It will be a little girl … I expect I shall call her Jane.'

'I said why the hell didn't you tell me before?'

'You might have chucked me out. You might have told me to go and have my bloody baby in a field … Besides, you should have known. You saw I was getting fatter, didn't you?'

'You were skin and bone when I found you. I thought you were just putting on weight because you were eating reasonably well for a change.'

Liz laughed. 'That's a good one! It's the best excuse for blindness I've heard yet.'

'Why didn't you tell me!' he raged.

'Because,' she said quietly, 'I don't even know if you are the father. It could be one of the Richmond Lot. It could be one of the Northerners. It could even be one of those wretched kids that screwed me on the way out of London … I was afraid to tell you. But now I'm not afraid any more, because I know that everything is going to be all right … It will be a little girl and I shall call her Jane.'

Greville stared at her helplessly. He felt as if someone had just hit him with a block of wood – about fifteen times.

'Let's try to get some grip on reality,' he said in a carefully controlled voice. 'Always assuming, of course, that there's a bit of reality to get a grip on … You say Jane's dead. All right, I accept that. I was never sure she was alive, so I can't much quibble about her dying … But this baby … Goddammit, you can't be that woolly-headed. You must have some idea.'

'No idea,' retorted Liz flatly. 'That time I ran away – it wasn't just for Jane, you know. I thought I'd find her and then we could go somewhere quiet and then I could have my baby, and you never need know … I've got to say this. I can't really care who the father is.' She patted her stomach protectively. 'After all, she's mine.'

'Jesus Christ!' said Greville helplessly. 'What in the world do we do now?'

Liz seemed to be in command of the situation. 'Turn back,' she said. 'We'll go back to the cottage and you can screw me as much as you like – except for a little time before baby comes and a little time afterwards … Then we shall all be happy.'

'Shall we indeed,' snapped Greville. 'Shall we indeed!'

He raced the car's engine, went into first gear viciously and tore away with a jerk. Throwing caution to the winds, he began to cruise along at nearly forty miles an hour, his spirit numbed, oblivious of everything. The road began to twist and turn, but he did not slow down.

He did not see the sign: *Beware trespassers. You are approaching manorial territory*. It was a big sign, newly painted, at the side of the road. But he didn't see it.

He didn't even see the road-block until it was too late. Anyway, it was a damn silly road-block – a few bales of hay manned (if that was the right word) by a couple of tweedy-looking gents with shotguns.

Seeing that he had left it too late to reverse, he slowed down a little as if he proposed to stop. Then when he was about twenty yards from the bales of hay, he changed down in to second gear and accelerated like the devil.

The engine screamed, the gear-box whined, and the station wagon leapt forward, scattering men and bales with reckless abandon. Greville saw one of the men bowled head over heels, his shotgun going off as it pointed to the sky. It gave him a savage delight. He hoped the man was hurt – badly hurt. He hoped he would live quite a long time to nurse his pain.

The other man had disappeared completely from view, but he was evidently shooting, for the car was rattling as if it had been hit by a volley of hail-stones. Then they were through the tumbling barrier of bales and away.

Greville gave a cry of triumph. The road-block had occurred at a good time. It had occurred when he badly needed to do something and smash somebody.

He was still accelerating, still filled with a bubbling boiling mixture of anger and violence and hatred and love when suddenly there was a sound like the end of the world. The roadway seemed to drift up towards him in slow motion like a snapped ribbon. Then the car slewed over sideways and began to roll.

The last thing he heard was Liz shouting.

The last word he heard was: 'Jane!'

Then suddenly, inexplicably, there was nothing but fog. And the fog became a black enveloping river.

TWENTY-FOUR

There was a cage. He couldn't get in, and Liz couldn't get out. She was naked, and she wasn't alone in the cage. There was a ring of male faces. Greedy faces, vacant faces – slack with lust and anticipation.

Francis stood by Greville's side, dressed like a circus ring-master. 'Walk up! Walk up!' he shouted jovially. 'See the greatest little show on earth. See the beautiful lady ridden bareback by the most intrepid erection and demolition experts in the world … Walk up! Walk up!'

'Stop!' screamed Greville, his voice making no sound. 'That's Liz. You can't let them do that to Liz.'

'Walk up! Walk up!' said Francis, oblivious. 'See the Turn of the Screw in three dimensions and natural colour.'

Big Ears was in the cage. 'Let's have a go,' he pleaded. 'There's nothing else to do.'

Nibs was also present. 'By all means,' he said grandly, 'provided you repent afterwards of such sordid fornication. Let us trust this is a lesson to poor Uncle. I am afraid that at times he harbours indelicate thoughts.'

'Stop it!' screamed Greville silently. 'She's mine. Liz belongs to me.'

Francis took off his top-hat and put on a mortarboard and gown. 'Gentlemen,' he said, 'we have here a most interesting example of paranoia. The patient has delusions of considerable grandeur. Note the simple phrasing: Liz belongs to me. Apparently, gentlemen, the patient genuinely believes that he is capable of possessing another human being. Extrapolating further, I think it is only fair to adduce his belief in the concept of romantic love.'

'I love her,' said Grenville mechanically. 'She belongs to me.'

'Go stuff yourself,' retorted Smiler.

Francis dissolved into Father Jack. He regarded Greville benevolently. '*Ego te absolvo*, my son.'

Liz waved at Greville cheerily. 'I'm no good at anything but screwing,' she said.

Father Jack shot her neatly through the forehead.

And Greville woke up screaming.

'Steady, lad! Steady there! You're with friends.'

The room came into focus; and with it a man's face. It was large, round and ruddy. It had a thick, grey moustache and on top a thin, receding line of hair.

The lips were smiling but the eyes were cold and remote. The head was attached to a body. The body wore a check shirt and a tweed jacket.

Greville stopped screaming. 'Where's Liz?' The words were no more than an exhausted whisper.

'Ah yes, the woman.' Cold Eyes paused. 'It's no good beating about the bush, laddie. Take it on the chin, there's a good fellow. Best in the end, what? She's dead, d'you know.'

'Dead?' Greville felt suddenly numb.

'Dead,' repeated Cold Eyes. 'Mean to say: you can't go driving cars all over land-mines without making a bit of an omelette, what?'

'Dead,' repeated Greville stupidly. 'Dead.'

'After all,' went on Cold Eyes. 'It was a bit naughty, wasn't it? My men asked you very decently to heave to. But off you go like a mad thing without so much as a civil "by your leave". It's a wonder you aren't dead, too, laddie. The car is pretty much a write-off.' He laughed heartily. 'Still, what the hell. There's no need to worry about your no-claim bonus, eh? Main thing is to get you up and about … No bones broken. Would you believe it! The devil takes care of his own.'

'Who – who are you?' asked Greville.

'Name of Oldknow laddie. Sir James Oldknow – not that it matters these days … My boys seem to like to call me Squire.'

'Where the hell am I?'

'Ah, the classic question,' said Cold Eyes jovially. 'You are in Brabynes House, laddie, in the village of Upper Brabyns, in the manor of Brabyns, Leicestershire … And now it's my turn. What's your name?'

'Greville.'

'Christian or Surname?'

'Both.'

'Don't play games, laddie. I'm a busy man.' Cold Eyes made a sign, and another face came into Greville's field of vision. It was attached to a massive body.

The newcomer slapped Greville's face twice – hard. As he tried to avoid the second blow, he realised that he was in a bed.

'Be good,' said the burly man, 'and answer the Squire's questions. He doesn't like people who don't co-operate.'

'Now,' said Sir James Oldknow. 'Christian or Surname?'

'Surname.'

'And your Christian name is –?'

'Matthew.'

Sir James smiled once more with his lips only. 'How nice. We already have Mark, Luke and John … How old are you?'

Greville had to think about that one. 'Thirty-seven.'

'You look ten years older … The white hair, I suppose.'

'I feel ten years older.'

The burly one slapped him again. 'The Squire doesn't like cheekiness,' he said.

'What was your profession?' asked Sir James.

'Grave-digger.'

'Naughty,' said Sir James. 'Very naughty.' He gave a sign, and the burly man advanced on Greville once more.

'You're a slow learner.' The burly man hit Greville in the throat. He was too weak to avoid the blow. Sir James waited patiently until he had finished coughing and gasping.

'Profession?' he repeated. 'That is, before the solar eruptions, of course.'

'Adman.'

'I beg your pardon'

'Advertising man … I was a copywriter.'

'Splendid,' said Sir James, rubbing his hands. 'Absolutely splendid. I have just the job for you. In a way, I suppose it's promotion … No doubt you will be happy to learn, Mr Greville, that you will shortly enter the field of Public Relations.'

Greville felt a hysterical urge to laugh bubbling dangerously inside him. He fought it down. Sir James – Oldknow did not look as if he would approve of laughter – unless it was his own.

'Public Relations?' echoed Greville blankly.

'You heard me the first time, laddie. Try to keep a grip on things. It'll be an advantage – to you … Now, are you going to take a sensible interest in life?'

'Yes.' The burly man was out of sight once more, but not out of mind.

'Then I'll put you in the picture.' Sir James Oldknow settled himself on the side of the bed. 'My family has had a few thousand acres in this part of the world for about three centuries … Not that that's important in itself, d'you know. But it gives a man roots. It gives him his bearings … D'you see what I'm driving at?'

'I think so.'

'Well, now. Here I am in this topsy-turvy world, a man with land, a know-ledge of how to deal with men, a sense of position and – though I say it myself – a bit of a flair for leadership … It begins to add up, doesn't it?'

'Yes,' agreed Greville carefully, 'it begins to add up'

'The point is,' continued Sir James, 'when the sun gets a bit off-colour and people start kicking the bucket, it makes for a nasty spot of anarchy – unless you're lucky enough to have somebody who knows what's what.'

'I imagine you know what's what,' supplied Greville.

'That's it, laddie, that's it. I know what's what … Incidentally, while I think of it, have you got any Negro blood in you?'

The impulse to laughter bubbled once more, but Greville managed to suppress it. 'I don't think so.'

'Good. Good … You don't look as if you have. But what about Jewish blood? That's a bit more insidious, isn't it?'

'I'm afraid I haven't got any Jewish blood either. Is that bad?'

'No, laddie. It's excellent. Depending on how you shape, I might even consider you for breeding purposes. We're a bit thin on intellectuals … Now where was I?'

'What's what,' prompted Greville.

'Ah, yes. Well, that's me. The point is, laddie, I represent order in chaos. Stability. Permanence. Some chap once wrote about the rich enduring qualities of the English tradition. Well, there you have it. You see, with the world as it is we've got to take a sensible approach. And that brings us back to the feudal system, doesn't it?'

'Inescapably,' agreed Greville. Soon, he was thinking, soon I shall be able to cry for Liz. If I humour him, maybe this clown will go away; and then I shall be able to think about her. I shall be able to build up a picture of what she was like. I shall be able to see the look on her face when I kissed her – and the look there was when she told me about the child … Oh, Liz! Dear, warm Liz!

'Basically,' said Sir James, 'it's a mutual security pact. I look after you: you look after me. You swear fealty: I swear to protect you. Damn simple. Damn fine arrangement. I've got two hundred and forty-seven men, seventy-four women and about two thousand acres. You've got yourself. We strike a bargain. You give me energy and loyalty. I give you security and protection. What could be neater?'

'Nothing at all,' said Greville tactfully. 'Nothing at all.'

'Good. Then you're in the Public Relations business … Very properly, my people are a bit afraid of me. That's good. That's very good. But it's important that they should understand me – that's where you come in. And when they understand me, it's important that they should like me – that's where you come in again … I'm a bluff old type. No finesse. Never had time for it. That's where you come in once more. Understanding, liking, finesse. Your department. People have to know that what I tell 'em to do is for their own good … Now, how does it sound to you?'

'A definite challenge,' said Greville.

'Think you can meet the challenge?'

'I hope so.'

'Good. There'll be speeches, news sheets – that sort of thing. You see, I want my people psychologically prepared for war.'

Greville was weak and aching, and he was beginning to feel light-headed. 'For war?' he repeated dully.

'For war,' said Sir James emphatically. 'The age-old struggle has never been – as friend Marx would have us believe – between the haves and the have-nots. That was just a damn big socialist-communist red herring. The real struggle is between order and anarchy. Order as represented by established authority, and anarchy as represented by the long-haired decadents who gibber about equality and all that rot … Point of fact, there's a rather nasty bunch of annies about five miles away. Their presence is, to say the least, disturbing. Not only do they give sanctuary to a few of my runaway serfs – in every society there are bound to be a few malcontents – but they attempt to undermine me with subversive propaganda. Incidentally, that'll be another of your jobs – counter-propaganda … Anyway, as I see it, the trick is to deal with the annies before they outnumber us … So my people have got to be made to see what a rotten lot of decadent bastards they are. D'you follow me?'

Greville's head was aching, his limbs were aching and his throat was aching. More than anything he wanted to be alone. 'The lucidity of your argument is admirable, Sir James,' he said. 'You may count on me to do whatever I can.' For a sickening moment, he was afraid he had overplayed it. In fact, he knew he had overplayed it. But Sir James Oldknow was impervious to irony.

'Splendid,' he said. 'Absolutely splendid. Tomorrow we must get you out of bed. Then you can have the regulation two weeks' basic training, and then you shall swear the oath of fealty. After that, my dear fellow, you're in business. Do a good job and you will not find me ungrateful.'

'What is the basic training about?'

'Oh, lots of things,' said Sir James, airily. 'Husbandry, unarmed combat, the use of the longbow.'

'I see … I'm already a pretty fair shot with a rifle.'

Sir James Oldknow laughed. 'Firearms,' he said, 'are strictly for the use of the Praetorian guard … You have quite a lot to learn, laddie. I hope you benefit by it.'

TWENTY-FIVE

It was nine days before Greville managed to make his escape from Sir James Oldknow and his latter-day feudal system. But for two men – known respectively as Nosey and Big Tom – he might not have attempted to escape at all, or, at least, not until it was too late; for he was haunted by memories of Liz. The thought that he would never see her again sapped his energy and even his self-respect. For a while he was not really sure whether he wanted to live or die. Memories of Chelsea Bridge rose disturbingly in his mind – not of the day when he saved Liz from the dogs but of the night he killed Pauline.

He had killed her, he thought, because he was trying to kill himself. Maybe he had killed Liz for the same reason and, oddly, in a similar way. Maybe both episodes constituted one of the odd little jokes of history. Maybe the possibility that someone else's child lay cradled in Liz's belly was somehow a sequel to the fact that other men than he had lain between Pauline's legs. And maybe Liz and Pauline were the same person in a different world …

Fortunately he didn't have much time for introspection. Come to that, he didn't have much time for anything. Sir James Oldknow was as good as his word. Weak though he was, Greville was hauled out of his bed early on the following day by Big Tom – the heavy individual who had been present at his interview with Sir James.

It was barely after dawn when Big Tom arrived. Greville was still uneasily asleep. Big Tom picked him up like a child and set him on his feet. Then he threw his clothes at him.

'The Squire says for you to get basic training,' he announced happily. 'I'm basic training.' He laughed. 'By the time I've finished with you, you'll think there's nothing more basic in the world. I'm going to toughen you up. Even a bloody clerk has to be able to stand on his own two feet.'

After he had dressed, Greville was taken out of Brabyns House, through two wooden gates in two wire fences that he later learned were electrified, and to a kind of mess hall where about twenty men were eating breakfast.

Breakfast consisted of porridge, some rather grey bread, a slice of bacon and a hot drink that was obviously meant to be a coffee substitute and tasted like burnt toast mixed with water. Greville was allowed ten minutes for eating; then training began.

Along with the other men, whom Big Tom was attempting to forge into a commando unit for the coming war against the annies, Greville was put through all the acute miseries of an assault course. He was too weak to resist. In fact he was still too weak even to last out the morning. After physical exercises, there was archery and knifemanship; and after that there were more exercises. Greville collapsed long before the midday break. Big Tom had a bucket of water thrown over him, then he was carried to a large wooden hut with straw-filled mattresses on the floor and left there to dry off and meditate. He was too exhausted to do either. He fell asleep wet and woke up wet and shivering.

It was almost dark and somebody was shaking him. It was a man who introduced himself as Nosey.

'Wake up, mate,' said Nosey. 'I've got a ration of stew here for you. Better get it down. There's nowt else till tomorrow.'

The stew was in an old tin can. It smelt nauseating; but Greville was suddenly and dreadfully hungry.

'Stewed cat,' said Nosey. 'It's better than dog – more like rabbit. Except that the bleeding cook doesn't know what to do with decent meat … Here, I've got a bit of news for you. She's alive.'

'Alive?' repeated Greville blankly.

'Your old woman, mate. The Squire had her put in the pen – that's the place where he keeps women that are not for the likes of you and me … She's got a duck in the oven, I hear. So nobody gets her until she's foaled down. The Squire's very proper about things like that.'

During the ten minutes or so that passed before the rest of the men returned to the barracks, Greville learned quite a lot about the Squire and his little community. But the thought that dominated him was that Liz was still alive. It was an elixir. It seemed to pump the will to live back into his veins.

When the other men came, Nosey immediately switched his conversation to obviously safe subjects – food, women and Big Tom. Food and women, it appeared, were strictly rationed. Big Tom, on the other hand, was completely unrationed. He was also universally disliked. Not hated, just disliked. For though he had fought and beaten every man in the barracks – it was all part of the basic training – he had enough sense to be magnanimous in victory. He respected men who could fight well; and anyone who was fortunate enough to give almost as good as he got could be sure of the occasional extra ration of both food and sex. Big Tom could lift a hundredweight sack of corn in each hand simultaneously. He offered every recruit the choice of fighting him or lifting the corn. If they chose to lift the corn and failed he would beat them until they were unconscious. Big Tom was a third-generation Liverpool-Irishman. He was also a devout Catholic. The Squire had given him a woman, and he had given the woman three children. Every Sunday he walked with her to Brabyns Church where the Squire, also a Catholic, officiated as part-time priest.

Conversation in the barracks was of brief duration, for the men were tired out. Nosey took a palliasse next to Greville's. Presently they were both surrounded by snores and heavy breathing. But Nosey remained awake.

'Hey, Greville,' he whispered at length 'Think you'll stick it?'

'Stick what?'

'This here feudal lark. The Squire's dead keen on it. Gives us history lessons. Says we've got to go backwards before we can go forwards ... Maybe he's got something. But I shouldn't like to be one of his villains, or whatever he calls 'em. He has 'em branded, you know. A big V stuck right in the middle of the forehead. Keeps 'em in the old stables ... Mind you he only makes villains out of blokes that give a bit of sauce ... Think you'll stick it?'

'No,' said Greville. 'I don't think I'll stick it. I think I'll get my girl back and take off.'

Nosey smothered a laugh. 'You'll be lucky. You'll be bloody lucky, mate. The Squire may be a bit weak in his nut, but he's got this whole place sewn up tight. The last bloke that tried it was hunted down like a fox ... Tally-ho, and all that. The old Squire still keeps a pack of hounds. Would you believe it – dogs all over the damn country, and he keeps a pack of hounds ... They made a right mess of this bloke I'm telling you about. All that was left was his shoes.'

'Then why the hell did you ask me whether I was going to stick it?' demanded Greville irritably.

Nosey laughed quietly. ' 'Cos I ain't going to stick it, neither, mate. My old bag wasn't much, but he didn't have no call to put her in the bawdy house.'

Greville remained silent.

'Know why he put her in the bawdy house?' demanded Nosey rhetorically. ' 'Cos she wouldn't wash his bleeding feet ... Anyway, sleep on it mate – and thank some bastard or other that you ain't dead yet.'

'I'll sleep on it,' agreed Greville. 'Thanks for the stew – and other things.'

'Pleasure,' whispered Nosey. 'Sweet dreams.'

Oddly enough, Greville's dreams were extraordinarily sweet. He dreamt about Liz. She was still alive, and that was all that mattered.

The next morning, after a breakfast that was a replica of the previous day's, there was Big Tom and basic training once more. Part of the basic training appeared to consist of felling trees to make a clearing all round what Big Tom called the defence 'perry-meter'. In between spells with seven-pound axes and two-handed saws there were more archery sessions. Greville could not get the hang of the longbow. It made his wrists ache. The arrows either fell short or went gloriously wide. His ineptitude seemed to please Big Tom enormously.

'No wonder you got white hair,' he boomed jovially. 'You think too much. You're a bloomin' intellectual. Now stop holding the bow like you was trying to play a one-string harp. Fit the arrow, draw it back – and give us a bit of time to get in front of the target, so we'll be safe.'

The men rose to Big Tom's unsubtle humour with Pavlovian reflexes. Pretty soon Greville was the butt of the entire group. He accepted the role with equanimity. He felt it might be useful to establish a reputation for being unable to do anything satisfactorily that required skill or sustained physical effort.

The day passed without incident. By the time they returned to the barracks after the evening meal, Greville was worn out. Most of his companions were younger men and had adjusted more easily to the rigorous training. Also none of them had been recently blown up by a land-mine.

Greville felt that his aches and pains were not entirely futile, however. He had acquired quite a knowledge of the topography of the Squire's dominion; and such knowledge was going to come in useful sooner or later.

That night Nosey again found a palliasse that was next to Greville's. 'Have you had any bright thoughts yet?' he asked, when it was apparent that the others were asleep.

'Not yet,' Greville admitted.

'Not to worry, mate.' Nosey chuckled grimly. 'We got all the time in the world … Me, I'm no good at working out what to do, so you'll have to be the brains. But when you've sorted out what's necessary, I reckon I'll be as useful as the next man.'

'We need guns,' said Greville, 'not bows and arrows.'

Nosey laughed. 'You'll be lucky. Think again, mate. The only gun you're likely to get near to is the one Big Tom wears – unless the Squire decides he can trust you, or unless they send us out to mop up the annies.'

Greville fell asleep trying to devise ways of getting at Big Tom's revolver – not that it would be of much use, because as far as he could make out the rest of the men in his group were sufficiently frightened or sufficiently stupid to be loyal. Some of them were already excellent longbowmen. And whereas a rifle might hold off archers, a revolver was worse than useless.

The next day was pretty much the same as the day before, except that in the afternoon, while he was recovering from a session of unarmed combat, Greville saw a team of six of the Squire's villeins drawing a single-furrow plough. Since the Squire had a number of horses, the sight puzzled him – until Nosey explained that it was a punishment detail. The villeins were supervised by a couple of louts with rifles and truncheons – presumably members of Sir James Oldknow's Praetorian Guard. Greville watched, fascinated, as the men strained to draw the plough through the half-frozen soil. He felt as if the centuries were being stripped away, as if indeed it was possible to make a literal return to the Dark Ages.

Days followed each other. Greville's muscles and spirit toughened. At night, in the blissful few minutes when he was relaxed before sleep came, he thought alternately about Liz – he had already discovered which of the manor house buildings was the pen – and methods of escape. But first, he must find a means of communicating with her. It would be stupid to start anything until he was certain of success. After all, as Nosey had said, there was all the time in the world.

As it turned out, Nosey was wrong. There was very little time left for either of them; and certainly not enough time to establish communications with Liz.

It was on the eighth day of his basic training that Greville was given the choice of lifting two one-hundredweight sacks of corn or fighting Big Tom. In his own peculiar way, Big Tom was fair-minded. He had waited patiently until he judged that Greville was fully recovered. Then he decided to have his bit of fun.

Big Tom was about eighteen stone and Greville was about twelve stone. He chose to lift the corn. Big Tom laughed aloud. He sent two men for the sacks, then lifted them himself and dumped them at Greville's feet. 'There you are, me boy. And the saints help you if you can't move the dear little darlings.'

Greville had already considered the problem and thought he had an answer. He laid both sacks on their sides, about two feet apart, and pushed most of the corn to the top and the bottom of the sacks, so that each was rather slack in the middle. Then he crouched down, put an arm securely round each sack, and attempted to stand up. He managed to lift both sacks about a foot off the ground before he fell flat on his face.

Some of the group who had been watching applauded, being of the opinion that he had succeeded in the terms of the challenge. But Big Tom was angry. No one else had ever lifted both sacks simultaneously clear of the ground. He felt that Greville had somehow deceived him. He was also determined not to be deprived of his simple pleasure.

'A good try, me boy. But you didn't quite make it.' Then to demonstrate what he meant, he hoisted both sacks shoulder high. 'So now you'll have to be spanked for being too clever by half.'

Whereupon he seized Greville as if he were a child, lifted him horizontally and then dropped him heavily, face down, so that his stomach hit the knee that Big Tom had extended.

Big Tom did not let him go; and while Greville hung there winded and retching, Big Tom brought the flat of his free hand down humiliatingly and heavily on Greville's bottom. The spanking did not last long. It was simply a demonstration of overwhelming superiority.

During the rest of the afternoon, Greville was taciturn and submissive. He wore the aspect of a beaten man – beaten spiritually as well as physically – and because of that Big Tom did not indulge in his customary horseplay.

Indeed he seemed to go out of his way to make sure that Greville did not have any strenuous tasks. It was his way of showing that the encounter was past and done with, and that now that Greville knew his place he could be accepted as one of Big Tom's happy family. Oddly enough, a few of the other men were fairly subdued, too. Some of them felt that Big Tom had overdone it. Because Greville's hair was white, they assumed he was quite old; and it seemed to them that Big Tom had deliberately taken advantage of his age.

That night in the barracks men whom Greville did not know by name dropped by to exchange a few words with him. No one mentioned the incident of the sacks of corn; but their very avoidance of the subject made it an unspoken topic for which they were offering unspoken sympathy.

'Don't let it get you,' said Nosey, sitting on his palliasse. 'From what I can gather, that big bastard didn't do his self no good. He just lost friends and influenced people, like.'

'I'm not crying about it, Nosey,' remarked Greville evenly. In the dim light he was examining his boots. They were good, solid boots, ex-W.D., with studs in the thick leather soles. 'It's all in the day's work.'

'You're still going to bust loose?'

'When the time comes.' Greville had no idea when the time would come. He was too tired to make plans. He could only hope that after he had done Big Tom's basic training and become the Squire's P.R.O. an opportunity would present itself.

But Greville reckoned without spontaneity, impulse and his own emotions. If anyone had asked him why he was examining his boots in the barracks just before he went to sleep, he could not have given a satisfactory answer. But something deep inside him knew; and something deep inside him was merely waiting for the opportunity.

It came just before midday on the ninth day. Another new recruit had been added to the group – a big, strapping boy of perhaps eighteen. Big Tom had switched his attentions from Greville to the youngster who, becoming bored with his lot as a pig-keeper, had been so rash as to volunteer for special training. He was already regretting the decision; for Big Tom had presented him with the traditional choice, and he had elected to fight. Now he lay on his back, a bruised and bleeding mass, feeling very sorry for himself.

Brief though it was, Greville had watched the fight carefully. Big Tom, he noted, liked to rush in and finish things as quickly as possible. He was an aggressive fighter whose only instinct – fortunately supported by great strength – was to charge and destroy.

Greville chose his position carefully. He was standing on a slight rise in the ground. Then, while Big Tom was preening himself on the easy victory, Greville said in a loud voice: 'Nobody but a loud-mouthed overweight idiot could get any glory from beating old men and boys.'

Big Tom gazed at him in amazement. 'Say that again, me boyo,' he grated. 'You must be very tired of living.'

'Take off that gun,' said Greville, glancing at Big Tom's revolver, 'and you'll take off half your courage. Liverpool Irishmen were never much good in a fair match.'

Big Tom took the revolver out of its holster. For a moment, Greville thought he had overdone it. For a moment, he thought he was going to collect a bullet for his pains.

But Big Tom laid the revolver carefully down on the grass. 'Nobody touch that mind,' he warned the now silent group of men who were gazing at Greville in awe. 'Nobody touch that. It's going to take me just thirty seconds to break the spine of yon fellow with the sharp tongue – enough time for him to make his peace with God.'

Greville did not move. 'Your mother must have been a worn-out old cow,' he called encouragingly. 'You have that sort of face.'

With a roar of rage Big Tom charged. Tank-like, he charged up the slight rise at Greville, who waited until he was less than three yards away. Then Greville jumped, drew up his feet, half-twisted sideways and simultaneously straightened both legs as if they had been bent spring steel.

Both boots hit Big Tom full in the face. He catapulted backwards and fell flat on his back with a sickening thud. He did not move.

Greville picked himself up, saw that Nosey had got the revolver, and went to inspect Big Tom. So did one or two of the other men. The rest seemed dazed by the speed of it all.

Big Tom's face was a mess. But that wasn't going to worry him at all. He was dead. In falling, his head had struck a fairly large stone and the stone had smashed his skull.

Someone lifted Big Tom's head, and then there were angry murmurs. But Greville heard Nosey's voice.

'The first man that tries anything gets a bullet in his guts. I've only got six, so that'll leave quite a few of you. But who wants to be one of the six?'

No one answered. Suddenly Greville felt an icy calmness coming over him. It was not working out as he had planned. He had been going to wait; but it was no use waiting now. He had been going to wait until he could get Liz – but now she would have to be abandoned. For a time ... His mind began to work like a computer.

'Give me the gun, Nosey,' he said.

Nosey handed it over cautiously.

'Now break all their longbows. We don't want—'

Someone started to run. Greville shot him in the back. 'We don't want anybody popping off at us when we push off, do we?' he said imperturbably.

Two deaths in less than five minutes were quite sufficient to demoralise twenty men. They stared hypnotically at Greville as if he were holding a magic wand.

It took Nosey an incredibly long time to break twenty longbows.

'What next, mate?' he asked.

'Next,' said Greville, 'you use the string to tie these gentlemen's hands together.'

That took even longer. One man grabbed Nosey while he was busying himself with the bow-strings and tried to use him as a shield. But Nosey had the good sense to drop to the ground, and Greville managed to shoot the offender through the shoulder. That left four bullets.

Greville looked back across the fields to the manor house, less than four hundred yards away. He thought that when they left the hue and cry would be raised pretty quickly. Ahead, about the same distance from them, lay the line of trees that marked Brabyns Wood. The wood, he had learned from previous talks with Nosey, was about half a mile across. On the other side was more open country, and beyond that was the village of Lower Brabyns where the Squire's so-called anarchists lived.

Nosey, at least, had recovered from the shock and speed of events. 'Everybody trussed something beautiful, mate,' he reported with a grin. 'We're doing a great job.'

'Now,' said Greville, eyeing the sullen line of men with their hands tied behind their backs, 'now, we all play ring-a-roses and lie downs.'

Nobody moved. So another bullet crashed into the leg of the nearest man. He fell down. The rest lay down.

'Well?' said Nosey. 'You've dropped us into the shit, proper, haven't you?'

For the first time Greville smiled. 'I think it's about time we joined the annies,' he said. 'Are you any good at running?'

TWENTY-SIX

When they heard the dogs behind them, Greville decided that he and Nosey would have a better chance if they separated. The dogs, presumably, had picked up the scent. Doubtless they would continue to follow only one scent; but even if they split up and followed both, the chances of individual survival were still surely better.

Nosey was not in very good shape. Neither, come to that, was Greville. He knew that he had set too hot a pace at the beginning. Altogether, they must have covered at least three miles by now. Brabyns Wood lay far behind them. That had been the easiest part of the flight. Since then they had been floundering through patches of half-frozen mud and the seemingly interminable and deceptive carpet of long dead grasses and weeds that covered what was once good farming land. Now they were shambling unsteadily up a long and gentle rise; and they could hear the excited barking of the dogs behind them. They were exhausted.

The village of Lower Brabyns could not be far ahead; but it was much farther from them than the dogs were. Greville turned and looked at Nosey's tortured face.

'Stop a minute!' The luxury of not having to push one leg in front of the other was so great that Greville didn't think he could start moving again.

'We've had it, mate,' groaned Nosey. 'We're outnumbered. Them fucking dogs has got four legs. We've only got two.'

'So we separate,' panted Greville. 'Give them something to think about … You go that way. I go this way … Half a mile detour for each of us. Then we close on the village … Here, take the gun.'

Nosey still had some spirit left. 'Keep it. You'll need it just as much as me.'

'No time for arguing. Take the bloody gun. I'm tired of carrying it anyway … And – good luck, Nosey.'

Nosey took the gun and held out his other hand. 'And the best of British luck to you, too, mate. We ain't going to make it, but what the hell.' He managed a grin. 'It was worth it just for Big Tom. So long.'

'We'll make it,' said Greville. 'Get moving.'

Greville sent a mental priority telegram to his legs. He stared down in amazement as one came out in front of the other. The movement developed into an unsteady walk. The walk broke into a tottering run. He didn't look back, which was perhaps fortunate. For Nosey did not move at all. He just

293

sank gratefully down on the grass and stretched his aching limbs. Then he examined the revolver. Three bullets. Which left two for the dogs …

Greville had covered more than three-quarters of a mile before he heard the shots. Mechanically he counted them. One … A long pause … Two … A longer pause … Three …

Greville kept moving. He was too tired even to think about Nosey. He knew that when he next stopped he would stop for good. So he kept moving. He had crested the hill and was coming down the far side. Consequently the dogs sounded a little farther away. He looked ahead, straining to catch a glimpse of Lower Brabyns. He thought he saw something that looked like a village in the distance; but odd patches of fog seemed to be obscuring his vision.

He wondered vaguely why the fog should be tinted with crimson, and why in the middle of the fog there should be strange little flashes of lightning. But he managed to keep moving. There was nothing else to do.

Presently he began to fall down. It was a frightening sensation because he seemed to be falling from a high building. It was frightening also because the temptation to lie where he had fallen was tremendous; and the energy required to pick himself up seemed to be more than mortal man could supply. Nevertheless, he did manage to pick himself up. Cursing at first, then groaning, then crying, then whimpering.

The world had become dark. He didn't know where he was going and he didn't even know where he had been. All he knew was that he had to keep moving.

Eventually there was no strength left to keep moving. He fell over something that seemed to cut into both legs. As he went down he thought he could hear bells ringing. Not church bells. Little bells. Oddly, he thought of James Elroy Flecker:

> When those long caravans that cross the plain
> With dauntless feet and sound of silver bells
> Put forth no more for glory or for gain,
> Take no more solace from the palm-girt wells …

And then he thought of palm-girt wells. And a hot sun pulsing energy out of an azure sky. He thought of sweaty camels and sweaty men with brown, lined faces. He thought of palm trees and water and music. And of the Samarkand that had existed only in a man's mind.

The vision was beautiful. Too beautiful to let go. But he was too tired to hold on to it. The sound of silver bells dissolved into silence. The sun was eclipsed. The oasis became dazzlingly black pools. And all that was left was night …

When Greville finally opened his eyes, he found that he was sitting in an easy chair. The first thing he saw was a log-fire spitting and crackling in an open hearth. The second thing he saw was a group of people – two men and a woman. The third thing he saw was a naked female torso. No arms. No legs. Only breasts like overripe melons and a belly that was so smoothly round that it surely contained all the fecundity of the cosmos. It was made of stone. Beyond the torso was another block of stone, roughly and vaguely carved, with two holes in it. Beyond that was a thing of iron. It might have been a twisted skeleton; it might have been a twisted bedstead; it might even have been a joke of a cage for an oddly mutated parrot. There was something about it that made Greville want to laugh.

He laughed.

One of the men spoke. 'Well, well. Another bleeding philistine. Just my bleeding luck … Now that you've joined the party, brother, you'd better tell us who issued the invitation.'

TWENTY-SEVEN

Having told his story, Greville sank back in the easy chair, gazed hypnotically at the log fire and gratefully sipped the drink that had been given him – a very generous measure of good Scotch. Once he had begun to talk, he found – to his amazement – that it was difficult to stop. He had told them not only about Big Tom and Sir James Oldknow's military ambitions but about Liz and Francis, the cottage at Ambergreave and even about Pauline. He had talked for quite a long time, and at the end of it he was surprised to find that it all amounted to a public confession. At the end, he realised that he had simply been trying to justify himself – but for what and to whom he did not know. He felt empty and light-headed. The Scotch and the warmth of the room had eased the pain in his limbs and transmuted it into an almost delicious aching. He was curiously uncertain whether he was dreaming or had just awakened from a dream.

But at least he was alive … I ache, therefore I exist …

The three people regarded him intently. The two men – one weather-beaten and rock-like, the other tall and angular – were standing. The woman, full-figured, attractively faded and in her mid-forties, sat on the chair opposite Greville.

'We're not really anarchists, you know,' she said. 'That's just the Squire being two-dimensional. Actually, we're nothing but cranks, misfits and loafers. There's about a hundred and fifty of us; and we came together simply for security … I'm Meg, by the way. The tall and rather intellectual-looking gentleman is Joseph. He fancies himself as a historian. The rugged individual is Paul. This is his studio. He's responsible for the sculpture that seemed to amuse you.'

'We're an unholy trinity,' remarked Paul drily. 'Meg lives with both of us. That's how we keep power in the family.'

Joseph said: 'They're just trying to confuse you. Actually, we're a sort of hereditary triumvirate. We were in at the beginning and so we got saddled with the decision-making. It works quite well, really. You see, there's only one basic commandment: try to do as little damage as possible. It amounts to a rather negative philosophy, I'm afraid, but the odd thing is it seems to work.'

'Shit,' observed Paul. 'We've got a community that's holding its own simply because most people aren't too loopy to see where their own interests lie. We don't give a damn whether people are homosexual or Hungarian. We don't give a damn whether they are sex-crazed or schizophrenic. So long as they do their whack and don't bust up the furniture. We've got two prophets, one messiah and an eighteen-stone bitch of a spiritualist. We've got demented mechanics and phallic sculptors – that's me. We've got prostitutes – precious few of those, I'm afraid – and even bleeding saints, if there was anybody to canonize 'em. But they are all with it enough not to interfere with each other. Now, we picked you up more dead than alive on a telephone-wire Maginot Line devised by a black-hearted Negro called Alexander the Great. We're so damn crazy we'd think anybody normal – if there was anybody normal – was a hundred octane nuts. So are you in or out? If it's out, we'll give you a pack of food and boot you out of the village in the nicest possible way. If it's in, you don't say "sir" to anyone, but you bloody well do what you're told until you find your feet. Now, what do you want?'

Greville liked Paul. He liked his aggressive honesty. He had a feeling that this was the kind of community in which he might possibly find a place. But before he could contemplate any kind of future, there was a problem to be solved.

'What the hell do you want?' demanded Paul.

Greville looked at him. 'First of all, I want Liz.'

Paul sighed. 'How romantic! Sir James Oldknow has acquired her for breeding purposes. So what do you propose to do about it – go and ask him politely to send her down here, complete with trousseau and layette?'

'I thought you might help me.'

'Did you now! And we're supposed to get ourselves chopped up just because you lost your woman? Think again.'

Greville began to get angry. 'If you sit on your backsides long enough, you'll find you've all been volunteered into the feudal system.'

'I doubt it,' said Meg. 'Alexander, our little Negro friend, is so crazy he's worth two battalions. If Sir James Oldknow starts empire-building, he may live to regret it.'

'Actually,' said Joseph, 'Sir James has already been kind enough to send us a deputation. They arrived about half an hour after you did. Sir James says he wants you back. He also says that though you've been rather naughty, he's pre-pared to forgive and forget. However, until your go back, Liz isn't going to get any more food … Rather primitive, I thought, but doubtless quite effective.'

'What are you going to do?' asked Greville.

'Nothing,' said Meg calmly. 'This isn't our problem. As Paul says, we don't propose to risk our people for someone we've never seen.'

Greville was silent for a moment or two. 'Can you give me any weapons?' he asked at length

Paul laughed. 'Sir Lancelot rides again! What the hell do you think you can do?'

'Not much,' said Greville simply. 'But I can try … Will you give me any weapons?'

'We'll have to talk to Alexander,' said Joseph. 'He has acquired quite an armoury, so I expect something can be arranged.' He gave Greville a thin smile. 'I hope you don't know what you are doing … Incidentally, and just to observe protocol, you'll have to steal whatever you need and leave us – in the best tradition – stealthily and by night.'

Greville managed to raise a smile. 'Oddly enough,' he said, 'that is exactly what I thought of doing.'

TWENTY-EIGHT

The night was cold; but Greville had been given a couple of sweaters and a thick pair of corduroy trousers. There had even been two volunteers to go with him – hoping, doubtless, to acquire women of their own. But Paul had vetoed that idea. He had pointed out, somewhat drily, that if on the morrow any other bodies than Greville's were discovered, Sir James Old-know would have a legitimate tailor-made reason for marching into battle. The one thing that was likely to bring unity to his mixed bag of followers was woman-stealing.

So Greville was entirely on his own. Alexander, the Negro, a pint-sized Napoleon who insisted on styling himself General of the Anarchists had been most kind. He had let Greville have an ancient but workable sten-gun, half a dozen magazines, two grenades, a knife and a suicide pill. Greville had not been particularly interested in the suicide pill, but Alexander had insisted. He claimed it was *de rigeur*.

As Greville made his way across the five miles of no-man's-land that lay between the two villages, he was thankful that the night was moonless and rather misty. He did not, however, harbour a great deal of optimism for his expedition. He knew that he needed more than darkness and the element of surprise. He needed about ten good men or about ten successive miracles.

He realised there was very little hope of being able to get anywhere near Liz. Probably Sir James had moved her out of the pen, anyway. But there was just a slender chance, thought Greville, that if he created enough diversions and raised enough hell he might get within shooting range of Sir James Old-know himself. And even if he couldn't retrieve Liz, at least there was the possibility of scoring an eye for an eye ...

Alexander himself had escorted Greville through what Paul had called his telephone-wire Maginot Line. It did indeed consist of stretched telephone wires. They had been threaded through empty tin cans and fixed at intervals to knee-high wooden posts. Between the wires small pits had been dug in the earth at random so that any force attempting a night-time invasion would make quite a lot of noise and probably collect a few sprained ankles in the process. It was on Alexander's Maginot Line that Greville had foundered that very morning.

Before Alexander turned back to the village, he gave Greville one final piece of advice. 'Now, boy,' he whispered, 'remember there ain't no hurry in this thing. Take your time – you got all night. Move a little, then stop and listen like you was a goddam big microphone. When you find something moving, use the knife like I showed. And don't let the poor bastard have any chance to give you the playback. *Bon soir*, old chappie, *bon chance* and *bon* bloody *appetit.*'

With muted chuckles, Alexander retreated into the darkness; and Greville was alone.

As the Negro had said, he had plenty of time – there were still two or three hours to go until midnight – but Greville was eager to get the whole thing over and done with. At least, he told himself grimly, when you are dead you no longer have to worry about being afraid or getting hurt.

So he pushed or through the winter night with a speed and lack of caution that would have made Alexander throw up his hands in despair. For a while, luck was with him, however. After half an hour and without incident he had reached Brabyns Wood.

He had also reached the end of his one-man assault upon the feudal system. For, as he soon discovered, Brabyns Wood was alive with men.

At first Greville thought they were Sir James Oldknow's private army. massing for a surprise attack upon the anarchists. But there were too many of them. And, by the light of several fires that had probably been used for warmth and cooking, he discovered an even more convincing reason why they could not be Sir James Oldknow's men. Each of them wore a monk's habit.

The sight was incongruous, fantastic, absurd – and terrible. Each of the 'monks' carried a weapon of some kind. Several had rifles or shotguns, but most were armed with spears or longbows.

At first Greville wondered why they advertised their presence so openly. But then, he reflected, there was no reason why they shouldn't. The Brothers of Iniquity were too numerous to be attacked by wandering bands of scroungers.

And that led to a torrent of questions. Why were they there? What did they intend to do? Which way did they intend to go? Would they turn south and obliterate the feudal system? Or would they travel north and devote their attentions to anarchism?

Greville's first impulse was to turn back and attempt to warn Alexander. But while he was doing that, the Brothers of Iniquity might well decide to tackle the nearer community of Upper Brabyns. The only thing to do, he decided, was to wait and find out.

He did not have to wait long.

As he crept cautiously nearer to Brabyns Wood, the fires began to be extinguished, one by one.

Then, to his immense surprise, he literally walked into one of the brothers –

posted, presumably, as a sentry. Both men fell over. Even as he went down, Greville remembered Alexander's final piece of advice. The knife seemed to jump into his hand of its own volition. He struck once, and hit nothing but the earth. He struck again with the same result.

The man he had walked into evidently had better eyesight, for he managed to fling himself on top of Greville. But Greville still had the knife. Alexander had told him to aim either for the throat or below the rib cage and to strike upwards. But he didn't know where his assailant's throat was and he didn't know which way was upwards. He just plunged the knife in again and again, wherever the opportunity seemed to present itself. He expected screams, but there were no screams. And, uncontrollably, he kept on striking with the knife long after the man was dead.

Eventually, Greville rolled from under the body and picked himself up. No fires were visible now. There was nothing but utter blackness – and the sound of many men moving.

They were moving towards him. And that must mean that they had decided on Lower Brabyns.

Without thinking, Greville lay down once more by the side of the man he had just killed. There was a warm wetness over his hands and face. Salty fluid trickled into his mouth. He didn't know whether it was his blood or the dead man's. He didn't care.

Columns of men passed on either side of him, not more than two or three yards away. He heard voices and occasional laughter. He waited until there was nothing more to hear at all.

Then he got up, and turned back in the wake of the Brothers of Iniquity. He was thinking of Francis and of the destruction that had been wrought at Ambergreave. He felt physically and spiritually numbed.

Theoretically, Alexander's Maginot Line would give warning of the attackers. But suppose it didn't? Suppose the Brothers of Iniquity had inspected it in daylight and were planning a detour? Or suppose that Alexander's sentries were not as alert as they should be? If this band of sadistic psychopaths got as far as the village they would soon make short work of anarchism and would leave behind them the same trail of desolation that they had left at Ambergreave.

Greville unslung his sten gun. He judged he was about fifty yards behind the rearguard. He judged also that in about ten minutes, unless the Brothers of Iniquity changed direction, they would be among the telephone wires and tin cans. That, no doubt, would be the time to signal the start of the party.

But the Brothers of Iniquity were nearer to Lower Brabyns than Greville had calculated. About two hundred yards ahead he heard what, less than twelve hours ago, he had interpreted as the sound of silver bells.

He quickened his pace. The need for silence was over. After about ten seconds he actually ran into one of the rearguard columns.

And then everything began to happen at once.

Greville emptied his first magazine into the darkness ahead. Screams and shouts told him that he had found targets. At the same time, a small searchlight was switched on somewhere in the village. It swept over the telephone wires, picking out the columns of advancing men.

Greville dropped to the ground, tore out the empty magazine and slipped another one into the sten. Then he rose to one knee, firing at the same time, spraying the black lines that were negotiating the telephone wires to the sound of old tin cans.

Fifteen or twenty men fell as if they had been scythed. The rest evidently could not understand that the firing could be coming from behind them. With savage cries they forged ahead, eager to get to grips with the defenders.

Greville changed magazines once more and began to cut into another line of the advancing men. At the same time the Brothers themselves started shooting. And then there was a blinding flash, and another, and then an entire dazzling barrage of light.

Greville stood amid the Brothers of Iniquity, temporarily blinded. Arrows whistled. Rifles and light machine-guns began to chatter away. Bedlam reigned.

Suddenly, he felt a smashing blow in his shoulder. Then there was another one in his leg. He spun like a top, still firing the sten gun blindly. Then the whole hullabaloo seemed to be fading away. Overcome by a curious lethargy, he decided to sit down. The lethargy persisted. So he decided to lie down.

He didn't know it, but his finger was still crooked tightly round the trigger of the sten gun. He lay on his back, shooting blindly at the hidden stars until his magazine was empty.

The vibration stopped, and he knew that there was nothing left to worry about.

He had had a hard day, he thought dimly, and now it was time to go to sleep.

TWENTY-NINE

Greville opened his eyes. He was in a comfortable bed between clean, sweet-smelling sheets. He became fascinated by specks of dust dancing in a shaft of sunlight. Their movements were lazy and random – like tiny stars, he thought vaguely, dancing from nowhere to nowhere in a miniature cosmos.

He felt a dull pain that seemed to stretch down the left side of his body; but against the overwhelming fatigue that came down like a curtain, the pain didn't matter too much.

Beyond the shaft of sunlight, half-hidden by shadow, there was a woman's face. It looked a bit like Liz; but then it obviously wasn't Liz. The effect of concentration became too much for him.

'Hello,' he mumbled thickly. 'You're someone else, aren't you?'

Then he gave a great sigh and went back to sleep.

Six hours later, when the sunlight had given way to twilight, he woke up bathed in sweat and screaming: 'Liz! Liz! Oh, Liz!'

Somebody lit an oil lamp; and there was Liz, standing by the bed, holding his hand, wiping the sweat from his forehead. He looked at her and could have sworn that she was real.

'See what happens when I'm not there to look after you,' said Liz. 'You made a fine bloody mess of yourself, didn't you?'

'I thought … I thought …' he babbled. 'Goddammit, what's happened?'

'Not to worry. Everything's all right, love. Now go back to sleep. You'll live.'

He tried to sit up, and the effort made him groan. Great knives of pain sawed away at the muscles of his shoulder. He collapsed sobbing.

'Here,' said Liz. 'drink this. They haven't got any pain-killers left.'

Brandy slopped over his chin, but most of it found its way into his mouth. The burning sensation was utterly beautiful. The room got dark, and he found a nice warm whirlpool. The trick was to dive clean into the centre of it.

'Sleep,' commanded Liz. 'You've been pressing your luck. I'll be here when you wake up.'

Once more he slept. And awoke before daylight. Thirsty but cool. The pain had gone away.

Liz was still there. The lamp was still burning.

'My love,' said Greville. 'Oh, my love!'

Liz smiled. 'So you're still delirious, then?' She leaned over the bed and kissed him on the lips. 'Didn't you know bad pennies always turn up?' she whispered. 'Now go back to sleep till morning.'

'I want a drink.'

'Brandy?'

'No, water.'

Liz gave him a glass. 'You must be someone else,' she said happily. 'The man I knew wouldn't have touched it.'

Greville drank greedily, then closed his eyes.

Morning came. He opened his eyes, and Liz was still there. She lay curled up in a big chair, sleeping.

As the lamplight lost its battle with the increasing daylight, Greville studied her. Her nose was shining, her lips had fallen open. She was wearing a drab brown dress that fitted her like a potato sack.

Greville felt on top of the world.

He didn't say anything because he didn't want to waken her. If he had been a praying man, he would have said: 'Thank you, Lord, for miracles gratefully received.'

But he was not a praying man. He was simply glad to be alive, and glad that life included Liz once more. He looked at the swelling of her belly. Beneath the potato sack, beneath the flesh there was the absolute testament – a busy little colony of cells that would one day have the effrontery to call itself human.

What the hell did it matter who the father was? For he could only ever be the father in an empty biological sense. Whatever the stupid facts, no matter who provided the mechanics of the act, the child would belong to Greville and Liz. At the beginning, he thought half-cynically, it would be nothing more than a tiny blue-eyed computer. And he and Liz would jointly programme it. Perhaps they would make of it something that could look at the night sky and be moved to tears. Or perhaps it would turn into a twentieth-century Caligula. But whatever happened, it would belong to them alone. For they would make out of the clay a statue that would at least dance and take pleasure in the illusions of life …

He drifted into dreams again. It was quite late in the day when he next awoke. There were other people in the room besides Liz. Meg and Joseph.

'Congratulations,' said Meg. 'We didn't really have any doubts. Both bullets passed clean through. But congratulations. Another week or so, and you'll be bouncing around with the best of us.'

'How the devil did you get hold of Liz?'

'We bought her,' said Joseph. 'It seemed the easiest way. After the Brothers of Iniquity had departed, we were in no position to take her by force – even if we had wanted to.' He gave a tight smile. 'However, our visitors themselves donated the price. It was, I recall, ten rifles and two hundred rounds of ammunition.'

Greville was silent for a moment or two. 'They'll use the rifles against you,' he said at length. 'Sooner or later, Sir James Oldknow will come charging down here with the Brigade of Guards and the Household Cavalry.'

Joseph shrugged. 'We hope it will be later rather than sooner. In order to teach him the facts of life, we invited him to see what had happened to the Brothers of Iniquity. The final count, I believe, was a hundred and fourteen dead. Of which, I may say, you appear to have accounted for at least thirty … He was duly impressed.'

'But not for long,' observed Greville. 'I doubt whether anything impresses the Squire quite so much as his own delusions of grandeur.'

'Which is where you come in,' said Meg. 'Or where we hope you will come in. We lost about fifteen per cent of our strength, including Paul and Alexander. Since you are such an aggressive character, we rather hope that you might take up where dear little Alexander – rest his soul – left off.'

Greville gave her a wan smile. 'I'm not sure I'm community-minded enough for you people,' he said. 'I'm not even sure I have any faith in democracy.'

Meg snorted. 'Poof! Who wants democracy. You can't have democracy with a colony of nut-cases. What we need are benevolent despots.'

'What he needs,' said Liz pointedly, 'is a bit of peace and quiet. Give him a chance to get some strength before you start filling his head with nonsense.'

'You're quite right, my dear,' said Joseph primly. He turned to Greville. 'We'll come and see you again tomorrow. I'm rather afraid we need someone like you. But enough of that. I'll have some food sent up. Your bandages have already been changed, and I expect Liz can attend to your bodily needs … Anyway, thanks for helping us. You were the best investment we have made for a long time.'

When Meg and Joseph had gone, Liz said impishly: 'I like that bit about attending to your bodily needs. Have you got any?'

'Jump into bed and find out.'

'Not today, thank you,' she retorted. 'I'm blowed if I'll have you passing out on me before I reach a climax.'

Presently there was a timid knock at the door, and a child of about ten, a girl, brought in a tray on which there was a bottle of red wine, two glasses and two steaming plates.

'Venison and two veg,' announced the child in awe. 'Meg said you was to eat it all … But she said if there was any left over, I could have it.'

Greville regarded her benevolently. 'I'm almost certain there's going to be quite a lot left over. Stay and find out.'

The child sat at the foot of the bed and watched greedily while Liz and Greville ate. There was indeed a lot left over. Neither of them were very hungry. They were too excited at being together again.

By the time they had finished the meal, it was almost dark once more. Liz lit the oil lamp. Greville kept the bottle of wine and the glasses, and sent the child scuttling away with several large slices of venison.

'Chateau-neuf du Pape,' he read the label on the bottle incredulously. 'Where the hell did they get it?' He poured another glass for Liz and himself. 'Had any good screws lately?' he asked casually.

'Dear love, as far as the Squire was concerned I was just a mare in foal. Three meals a day – until you became naughty – and nothing to do. The welfare state. I never had it so boring.'

'Come into bed,' said Greville, relaxing. 'I can't do a bloody thing, but I just want you close.'

'Amen,' said Liz. She took off her dress and displayed the roundness of her belly. 'You've got over it?'

'I've got over it.'

She smiled. 'I think I was crazier than usual … It's going to be our child isn't it?'

'It's going to be our child,' said Greville positively.

It was very difficult for them to touch each other without giving Greville a certain amount of pain; but after a time they learned the trick. Liz lay on his right side with their legs touching from hip to toe. To Greville it was like a benediction. He wanted to stay awake and savour the situation, but presently he was fast asleep.

When they woke up in the morning they were both stiff – Greville from his bullet wounds and Liz because she had hardly dared to move. They kissed each other in the grey, early light. They kissed each other and mumbled words that were nonsensical and profound, words that could have little meaning for anyone who overheard them, words whose only value was as the sound effects of pleasure …

At length, Greville said: 'I've been thinking.'

'Why? I'm sure it's not good for you just now.'

He patted her affectionately. 'Because of that lump in your belly, I suppose … We've got to live somewhere, haven't we?'

'Yes.'

'We've got to have as much security as we can get.'

'I suppose so.'

'Then,' said Greville, 'we might as well join the Band of Hope – but only on our terms.'

'Fine,' said Liz equably. 'What are our terms?'

'Ridiculous,' said Greville. 'Absolute dictatorship masquerading as sweetly reasonable co-operation … They'll never wear it, of course. But at least I've got an ace to play … Everybody is short of women. I think I know where I can lay my hands on about thirty.'

'Where?' demanded Liz, wide-eyed. 'Although,' she added, thoughtfully, 'I'm not sure that I want to know.'

'The Convent of the Sacred Heart,' said Greville. 'Now you'd better make me presentable so that I can do a bit of hard bargaining with Meg and Joseph.'

Meg and Joseph appeared shortly after breakfast.

Liz was still in bed, naked; but neither of the visitors seemed disturbed or embarrassed.

'I trust you slept well?' said Joseph.

Greville glanced at Liz and smiled. 'Adequately, bearing all things in mind.'

'Have you thought about our proposition?' asked Meg.

'I have. And I'm going to make a little speech. After which, it's in your hands.'

'Go ahead,' invited Joseph. 'Speeches are as yet unrationed.'

'Well, mine goes like this. You people are trying to get together a community that works and will survive. As things are at present, you haven't got a chance. You survived the Brothers of Iniquity by the skin of your teeth. Your next problem is Sir James Oldknow with a fanfare of trumpets. And after him – if you survive again – there will be someone or something else. If it isn't people it will be dogs or rats or something like that. You're too exposed. You're too free and easy. And you're not growing. In fact, with every challenge that comes along, no matter what happens you can only continue losing … Am I overstating the case?'

'Possibly,' said Joseph, 'but not so that one notices it. Proceed.'

'Well, then, if you – or in fact anybody – wants to build a community that will last and expand you've got to go back to fundamentals. You've got to find a piece of land that's suitable and be prepared to hold it against all comers – human, animal or vegetable. Then you've got to get recruits. Then you've got to be able to expand as you need to expand … You could try an island, of course – something like the Isle of Man or Guernsey or even the Isle of Wight. But all islands are at the same time too big and too small. They're too big when you start and too small when you really want to grow bigger. One thing is sure, you can't sit here in the middle of England indefinitely and hope it will all turn out for the best.'

'So far,' said Meg, 'you've done nothing but state the problem. What about the solution?'

Greville's shoulder was beginning to throb, but he ignored it. 'The solution is to find a piece of land which you can defend, on which you can expand and from which you can't retreat. Then you start recruiting. And you don't recruit by inviting people to join you for tea and cakes. You recruit by taking the offensive against any nearby community that is either decadent – in the sense that it's going nowhere – or failing. In short, you steal people. You guarantee them food and a certain amount of freedom: in turn they give you a certain amount of "co-operation" – no more, in both cases, than is strictly necessary. As time goes by, the amount of co-operation that's required will become less – we hope. As time goes by the amount of freedom that can be allowed will be more – we hope. But expanding will have to be the order of the day. That way you can grow. Any other way, and you've had it.'

'That's all very well,' said Joseph, wrinkling his nose, 'if one wants to found a new society.'

'What else is there to found?' demanded Greville calmly. 'We've already got enough bloody chaos to last us for a thousand years. Liz has a child inside her. I'd like to think it's got some sort of bearable future. I'd like to think it's not going to have to spend the best part of its life just avoiding being killed by rats, cats, dogs or humans. I'd like to think it will get a chance to live.'

Meg was getting exasperated. 'Fine talk,' she said icily. 'You're still up in the air. Come down to earth and tell us what it's all about. Tell us what you'd like to do.'

'I'd like you to give me absolute power for a year. Failing that I'd like you to leave me alone until I get well. Then Liz and I will push off after saying thank you very much.'

' "Absolute power", ' quoted Joseph, ' "corrupts absolutely". '

'I'm corrupt already.'

'To hell with that,' snapped Meg. 'What would you do?'

Greville smiled. 'First of all, I'd get my strength back. Then I'd make arrangements to collect enough women to give us a decent chance of biological survival. Then I'd start a mass migration. I'd wait till the decent weather comes, then I'd take the whole community down to the tip of Cornwall. There might be somebody there already, of course. But in that case we'd either lick 'em or make 'em join us. If, on the other hand, they licked us, the problem would be solved anyway … But if they didn't lick us, or if there was no one there in the first place, we could begin to build. We'd start with a couple of square miles of territory – backs to the sea and all that stuff. We'd clear it of all the livestock we didn't want and erect fences, barricades, ditches – anything to keep the rest out. Then as we grew we'd gobble up a bit more territory each year.' He laughed. 'A couple of generations from now, who knows, we might even get as far as Devon. Ten generations from now – providing we don't get another good dose of solar radiation – we would very likely get as far as holding a general election and filling the Houses of Parliament with people who couldn't do any real harm … Now tell me I'm too far gone.'

'You're far gone,' said Meg. 'But aren't we all … You said something about collecting women, I believe. We need women very badly.'

'Unless something drastic has happened,' said Greville, 'and we can't rule that out of course, there's a remarkable character called Father Jack who has about thirty women at the Convent of the Sacred Heart in Newmarket ... I think if we put the proposition to him in the right way, he might join us. But that we wouldn't know until and unless we sent someone to tell him all about the idea ... I think he'd join us if only because one man can't hope to survive a lot of bloody females for ever. He's quite a character, is Father Jack. He saved our lives once – on a purely commercial basis, of course.'

Greville felt exhausted. He was amazed at himself. He was amazed at the unfounded optimism, the glib talk, the unreasonable assumptions. He was amazed even that Meg and Joseph had heard him out. Most of all he was amazed that they did not laugh.

The scheme was hair-brained, impractical and doomed. It was nothing more than a sick man's fancy, a wish-fulfilment for a man so traumatised at the prospect of becoming a daddy that he was busy building new Jerusalems out of daydreams and a high temperature.

There was quite a long silence.

'It's mad enough to have a chance of working,' muttered Joseph almost as if to himself.

'He's stupid enough and dangerous enough to make it work,' said Meg grimly. She turned to Greville. 'I suppose we'll have to make you emperor, as well.'

Greville smiled. 'No. I've just thought of a nice democratic safeguard. We'll have a monarchy but no king. I'll be simply the king's general ... If you ever get a king, he'll be able to sack me.'

'Where did you say this convent of the whatnot was?'

'Newmarket.'

'You think your Father Jack would agree?'

'If he doesn't, we could always beg, borrow or steal ... But he will.'

'You know,' said Meg thoughtfully, 'I'm beginning to think that any direction is better than no direction ... How would you propose to open up negotiations with Father Jack?'

'I'd write him a letter.'

'So all we need now,' said Joseph drily, 'is faith and a gentleman with a cleft stick ... You're a fool, Greville. An absolute fool. But then history was made by fools ... I'm very much afraid we're going to have to make you the king's general, after all.'

Liz joined in the conversation for the first time. She threw joined the bed clothes and gazed at her stomach in amazement. 'It's quickened,' she exclaimed. 'I feel as if I've just swallowed a squirrel with a big bushy tail.'

THIRTY

It was spring – a riotous and intoxicating spring that, coming after a fairly mild and wet February, had covered the land with a carpet of green and the trees with a thick powdering of buds almost a month earlier than it should have done.

Greville was riding with three other heavily armed men in a jeep along a weed-covered road where bumps and pot-holes were giving him considerable anxiety; for Liz, travelling with some of the women in a large truck about a hundred yards behind him, was in the last month of her pregnancy. The baby could arrive any time. But he did not want it to arrive on the road to Newmarket. The entire company – a hundred and twenty-three people – would rest up for a few days at the Convent of the Sacred Heart before they took the road once more to Cornwall. That would be the ideal time for Liz to have her baby. Then she could get a bit of strength back before they started on the last leg of the journey.

The jeep stopped, and the column of vehicles behind it stopped, as they had stopped once every half-mile or so all the way from Leicestershire. Presently the two motor-cycle outriders who had been forging ahead roared back into view and waved them on, signifying that the next half-mile of road was clear and navigable.

The jeep jerked forward once more and continued at the leisurely speed of fifteen miles an hour. The odd assortment of cars, vans, trucks and station wagons behind it dutifully kept the regulation convoy distance of fifty yards between each vehicle.

Looking back over the last few months, Greville was still surprised at the speed with which his ideas had been accepted by Meg and Joseph and the group of people they represented. He was even more surprised at the speed and ease with which he had assumed the role of 'king's general'. At first he had taken his office lightly, seeing it as no more than a temporary expedient for getting things done. At first the title itself had been no more than a joke, invented on the spur of the moment. But the joke had a hidden subtlety; and the title had stuck. It had amused everyone. It had provided a necessary focus for their sense of the absurd.

Only a monarch could depose the king's general. But there was no monarch. And if ever the group got tired of Greville's autocracy they would have to create a greater autocrat to bring it to an end. For the present, however, they were content. Greville had offered them something more than mere personal survival: he had offered purpose and direction. The odd thing was, he reflected, that even transies needed something in which to believe, some concept of a future that it was possible to build.

The joke, Greville realised, was on himself. He had never imagined that he really possessed qualities of leadership. He had never imagined that he could accept responsibility for the fate of an entire community. Yet here he was, a white-haired if rather juvenile Moses, leading a small tribe of crazy and credulous human beings to a promised Land's End.

Land's End … The finality of the title itself was symbolic. For if one was going to make a new beginning where better to start than at Land's End.

Greville moved his arm and felt a dull stab in his shoulder. The wound had healed beautifully; but there was always a stiffness when it was going to rain. He looked at the sky – clear blue with a few puffy white clouds. But he knew it was going to rain. The shoulder never lied.

The jeep stopped once more. One of the motor-cycle outriders, a boy of perhaps eighteen, roared back to it, pulled up with a flourish and a screech of brakes, and saluted Greville. 'The convent is just over a mile ahead, sir.' He grinned. 'We made contact with their day-guard … Dead smashing!'

'Go back and tell Father Jack we'll be with him in ten minutes,' said Greville. 'Tell him not to worry about food or sleeping arrangements. All we'll need will be a bit of space.'

'Yes, sir.' The boy saluted again and slapped the butt of the rifle that was slung over his shoulder. Then he roared off again.

It was funny, thought Greville, how so many of the young ones had developed a sudden enthusiasm for military etiquette. They stood to attention at the drop of a hat. They saluted like mad. And they seemed to compete with each other in every possible way to obtain the favour of the king's general. He hoped it wasn't an omen. He had no intention of founding a military state.

Poor Joseph! Poor Meg! Nobody seemed to pay much attention to them these days. And how they hated the efficiency and discipline that Greville had imposed. Perhaps they saw him as an anachronism – a sort of fascist dinosaur that wouldn't lie down.

And yet whenever Greville talked with them in public, he made a great point of being deferential. He wanted everyone to know that the king's general existed only on sufferance. Oddly enough nobody seemed convinced. The prevailing attitude seemed to be that Meg and Joseph – the remains of an ineffectual triumvirate – existed on sufferance, and it amused Greville to make them feel they were necessary as advisers.

The jeep was moving again. The road had given way to a narrow and overgrown track. The Convent of the Sacred Heart was only two or three hundred yards ahead.

Greville began to relax. The first part of the journey was over without a single casualty. It was, he felt, a major triumph. What was more important, Liz had not given birth en route. And that was an even greater triumph.

The jeep pulled up at the convent gates. Greville glanced round quickly. The jeep was covered, he was pleased to note, by two groups of Father Jack's young ladies, complete with rifles, sten-guns and machine pistols. Somewhere in the background he caught a glimpse of a bazooka team.

Father Jack himself, unchanged, still wearing the long black habit of a priest, came out through the convent gates and greeted him. 'Forgive the welcome committee, but one doesn't take unnecessary chances … I trust you had a reasonable journey, my son.'

'Much better than I thought,' said Greville. 'Incidentally, how many girls have you got? My messengers said you had thirty-five?'

Father Jack sighed. 'We were rather inconvenienced in January. A very bad month. The number is now twenty-seven … How many men have you got?'

'Eighty-three.'

'My, my,' said Father Jack. 'What lucky girls they are … You realise, of course, that the whole expedition is ludicrous.'

'Certainly. Life itself has become ludicrous. What have we got to lose?'

Father Jack smiled. 'I don't know about you. But I personally have a great deal to lose – I'm happy to say … I trust, my dear fellow, for the sake of your sanity, that you never have to be responsible for a body of women.'

At that point, a small boy ran forward to the jeep. 'Please, general,' he said breathlessly, 'it's Liz. I was told to say she had been taken short. They reckon the baby is going to come pretty soon. They said I was to tell you because you said you wanted to be there.'

Father Jack beamed. 'Well, well. An auspicious omen. Needless to say, we have our own maternity ward. Some of the girls are a trifle adventurous at times. Perhaps you had better bring your dear lady inside.'

Greville's shoulder began to ache once more.

He looked at the sky.

It started to rain.

EPILOGUE

7 July 2011. Shortly after dawn.

A servant carrying a tray entered the tent of the Kaygee of the Army of the Western Republic. The servant coughed deferentially and set the tray down by the white-haired old man in the sleeping bag.

Greville was awake, but he pretended to be asleep. He thought the servant might decide to go away. He would have liked a few more minutes to savour his private thoughts.

But the man just stood there uncertainly, coughing and making discreet little noises, hoping to rouse his master without appearing to have actually done so.

Greville sighed. It wasn't the man's fault, of course. He had standing orders for the expedition: to deliver early morning tea every day fifteen minutes after dawn.

The man coughed again, louder. Greville sat up.

'Good morning, Kaygee. I hope you slept well.'

'Well enough. What's the weather like?'

'It's going to be another fine day. A little early mist, but it will be gone by the time you have finished breakfast. Shall I pour, sir?'

'Yes.'

Greville watched the level of hot, steaming tea rise in his cup. It was going to taste wonderful. It always did. He still had not accustomed himself to the luxury. It was only a year ago that some adventurous young captain had taken his windjammer as far as Ceylon and brought back the first cargo of tea for over thirty years.

As yet, thought Greville, sipping the delicious liquid gratefully, tea was only for the rich and the powerful. But soon other windjammers would follow the first; and then everyone in the Republic would be able to have his morning cup. Which would prove that God was in his heaven once more and all was right with the world.

'Another cup, Kaygee?' The servant held the pot expectantly.

'No thank you. That's quite enough.'

The servant smiled, put the cup and saucer (fine bone china) back on the tray and went out of the tent. Greville amended his list of tea-drinkers to the rich and the powerful – and their servants. He knew that the pot would be drained and a pinch of carbonate of soda added to the tea-leaves to make them yield a second brew before they were thrown away.

He got out of the sleeping bag and stretched. Then he began to put on his clothes slowly, cautiously, methodically. At sixty-seven one did everything slowly, cautiously and methodically, he reflected. It was not an age at which one could easily afford sudden movements. Nor was it an age at which one could easily make lightning decisions … Or, having made them, understand why …

He stepped out of the tent, and sniffed the morning air. The sentry brought his rifle to the present and slapped its butt so hard that Greville winced. The man's hand must be tingling with pain, yet he stared ahead blankly.

'Way for the Kaygee!' he shouted ceremoniously, though there was no one in the immediate vicinity to obstruct the passage of the Kaygee.

'Good morning,' said Greville.

'Morning – sir!' shouted the sentry, as if he were addressing a multitude.

'Dismiss.'

The sentry slapped his rifle again and went ostentatiously through the ritual of dismissal.

Greville was alone. Except for the fact that if he so much as sneezed half a dozen men would appear from nowhere to protect the Kaygee against disaster.

He had marched a column of two hundred men all the way from Truro to London. And he still didn't know why.

There had been reasons, of course. There had to be reasons – otherwise Father Jack, the first President of the Republic, would not have given his official blessing. Greville would have come just the same; but for political purposes it was necessary for the Kaygee and the President to be in complete harmony.

The reasons he had given Father Jack were quite convincing: it was necessary – now that the Republic was thriving – to find out the state of the country, to explore the possibility of further recruitment, to look for various scientific and technical instruments that could not at present be manufactured by the Republic's resources, and to seek out any other organised communities with which the Republic might develop mutually profitable relations.

But Father Jack was not easily deluded.

'Greville, my son,' he had said, 'we have nearly seven thousand citizens, the economy is sound and I don't give a damn if the clever lads at Truro University need an electron microscope or whatever. As far as I can see, what they need first of all is a change of nappies … But if you have set your heart on this expedition, then I'll have to give the official say-so, in which case it's just as well that you've got some nice official reasons. They don't mean anything to me but I suppose they'll keep the Council of Electors happy. Just don't get yourself killed, that's all.'

And so, after a leisurely march across southern England, Greville's column was encamped in what had once been Battersea Park on the South Bank of the Thames. Today, they would enter what was left of the City of London. But that was not important to Greville. All that mattered at the moment was that he was about to keep a sentimental rendezvous.

It was almost eleven years since Liz had died. She had given him two sons and a daughter. Then all had been set for them to share a decade or two of contentment and relative peace. Except that she had developed cancer of the womb. When it got too bad, Greville himself had delivered the *coup de grace*. That was the way Liz had wanted it.

Two sons and a daughter. Conrad, twenty-nine, and – so they said – a brilliant biologist. But Greville was never really sure that Conrad was his own son; and, oddly, because of that he loved him more than the others. Then there was Jason, twenty-three, a born trouble-maker who thought that everybody who had ever lived had been crazy except, perhaps, Joe Stalin and Mao-tse-tung. And after Jason there was Jane, nineteen, and probably the most beautiful woman in the Republic. Jane was a born actress, as was evinced by the packed houses of Truro Theatre. She didn't look at all like Liz. She didn't look at all like Greville. Only Jason looked like Liz – which was, perhaps, why Greville couldn't carry out his duty and execute him when he had led the rebellion. About three hundred citizens had been killed before it was over. The death penalty was obvious and inevitable.

But, in the end, Father Jack had saved the day with his decree of lifelong exile. Jason had been packed off to Ireland to see if he could convert the savages to neo-Marxism.

Greville looked at the remains of Battersea Park in the early light. It was nothing more than a piece of wilderness – primeval, as if man had just set foot in it for the first time …

'Kaygee, will you breakfast now?'

Greville was snapped out of his reverie by the appearance of a bright young man with one star on his shoulder.

'I rather think I will not breakfast at all, thank you.'

'But, Kaygee, the President himself instructed us to—'

'The President is over-anxious,' said Greville. 'Dismiss.'

'Yes, sir.'

'Wait a moment.' Greville had a sudden thought. 'The scouts have been across to the other side?'

'Yes, Kaygee.'

'Did they establish any contact?'

'No, sir.'

'Then we may take it that the bridge is clear and open?'

'Yes, sir.'

'Good, I think I'll take a little walk. Give me two men and tell the Second that I'll be back in half an hour.'

'But, Kaygee,' protested the young man helplessly, 'we have explicit instructions from the President not to let you—'

'Bugger the President,' interrupted Greville calmly. 'In the nicest possible way, of course. Now do what I said.'

'Yes, Kaygee,' said the young man miserably. 'Will you confirm it in writing?'

'I'll confirm your arse if you don't move.'

The lieutenant almost literally evaporated. He was replaced by two of Greville's bodyguard, armed with automatic rifles and grenades.

'Follow me at twenty paces, and don't let me know you're there unless it's a matter of life and death.'

'Yes, Kaygee,' they said simultaneously.

Pretending that he was entirely alone, Greville strode briskly forward, making his way out of the Battersea Park and towards the road that led to Chelsea Bridge.

I wonder, he thought, how many of them know what Kaygee stands for? Probably they think it's some mystical title that goes back to antiquity. A few of the older ones will know. But to the young ones, Kaygee is nothing more than an incantation. It's a word that means everything and nothing. It's not even something they can still make jokes about ... The trouble with people nowadays is that they take everything too seriously. Goddammit, there isn't a decent transie left!

He laughed aloud at the notion; and the men following him fingered their guns nervously. They had not heard the Kaygee laugh for a long time. They couldn't decide whether it augured well or badly.

The morning mist had already cleared. Greville stood on the grass and moss-covered roadway and gazed at Chelsea Bridge, twenty yards ahead. Then he turned to the two men who had been following him.

'You will stay here. I am going to take a short walk along the bridge. I'll be back in a few minutes.'

'Sir. Permission to speak.'

'Granted.' There was a touch of annoyance in Greville's tone that boded ill for the man who had spoken.

'Sir, we are supposed to protect you,' he continued desperately. 'We cannot fulfil our duty if we have to remain here.'

'You will not need to protect me on the bridge, and I shall not cross to the other side.'

Greville turned away to avoid further argument. Really! They were treating him as if he were a baby. Something would have to be done about discipline. He could hardly move these days without stumbling over some well-meaning idiot armed to the teeth.

He walked slowly on to the bridge.

He looked over the side.

He was filled with childish delight.

The Thames was blue.

A blue river! He had seen plenty of blue rivers in the last twenty years. But somehow he had never expected that the Thames could turn blue once more. But having been free from industrial pollution for nearly forty years, what other colour could it be?

He was amazed and enchanted.

Greville turned his attention to the bridge. It was falling to pieces.

The suspension cables were coated with rust. So were the vertical wires. He doubted very much whether it would last another decade …

A voice, familiar but unrecognised, came from nowhere and whispered in his ear: 'Love somebody … Build something.'

Then suddenly the past came rushing back.

He remembered that night with Pauline. The cat that he had killed; and then the growing tension between them, resolved finally in the crash. He remembered Liz in the thin dawn light – a girl in a faded blue shirt and a pair of men's trousers that was two sizes too big for her. He remembered the dogs …

But most of all he remembered two faces. Pauline's face, dead and beautiful: Liz's face, alive and innocent, pale and bruised.

It was all so long ago. So very long ago. Pauline belonged to another world; but Liz only belonged to another time.

And yet … And yet they had both belonged to that other world.

So much had happened …

So much that was strange and terrible. So much that was warm and intimate …

Now, a new world was being born – a world in which the older people, the transies, were treated with a mixture of amusement and affection and fear; while the younger people, convinced of their own sanity and general soundness, were busy with dreams of new civilisations, new empires, new systems, new golden ages.

It was all, thought Greville, so sadly amusing. It was like Tchaikovsky's 1812 Overture – full of sound and fury, signifying nothing.

I am an old man, he thought. I have lived sixty-seven years and I am in my dotage. It appears that I have brought two hundred men all the way to London just so that I can keep a rendezvous with memories. I ought to be shot …

When the bullet hit him, he thought it was the greatest joke of all time. He couldn't really believe it; but nevertheless it was very funny. He watched the blood make a mess of his nice clean uniform with amazement.

The first bullet slammed into his stomach.

The second bullet smashed his wrist.

The third bullet broke his leg.

He fell down.

There was a sound of automatic rifle fire as his two bodyguards rushed towards him, firing blindly across the bridge. They never reached him. For the enemy had automatic rifles also.

Greville was still conscious. He lay slumped by the metal parapet, staring at dents in the rusty ironwork. He felt a great surge of satisfaction. This was the very place.

He thought of Pauline. He thought of Liz. The two faces became blurred and indistinguishable.

'*Love somebody … Build something*,' whispered that familiar but still unrecognised voice.

'I knew what it was to love,' he said aloud. The thought surprised him. It also hurt him – more than the bullets had done.

'Goddammit I knew what it was to love!'

Things were happening at both ends of the bridge. Greville's column had brought up their horse-drawn tank. The horses were released, and the tank roared forward under its own power and on the four gallons of precious diesel fuel that it still contained. Meanwhile, at the other end of the bridge, a bazooka came into operation. The first shot blew the turret off the tank, but it still continued on its way. The occupants were determined to get to their beloved Kaygee at all costs.

The second shot missed and hit one of the bridge suspension cables. It snapped like cotton. The bridge swayed and began to slant dangerously sideways. But the tank still came on.

Greville felt entirely happy. He had been hit by three bullets but he felt entirely happy. Or perhaps 'satisfied' would be the better word. London was still alive.

'We've got a new civilisation going, Pauline,' he babbled. 'We're back to square one. Everybody wants to kill everybody else. It's quite exciting, really.'

The second suspension cable snapped, and the bridge rested perilously on a single I beam. The tank came on: the bazooka continued firing.

Greville looked once more at Pauline's dead face. It dissolved. Then he saw Liz. 'I'm sorry,' she murmured, 'I'm only good for screwing.'

Greville reached out a hand to touch her. The pain was hitting him now and he found it hard to speak.

'I never really told you,' he whispered with difficulty. 'There weren't the words for it. You gave me much more than screwing. Much more even than love. You gave me—'

There was a great tearing. The bridge sagged for a moment like crumpled cardboard. Then, taking Greville and the tank with it, it fell into the river.

The blue waters of the Thames foamed and clouded, turned grey, then dark brown. But presently they cleared as fragments of debris and a dead body, held up by a little air still trapped in its clothes, drifted slowly down the river, under the city's remaining bridges and out towards the sea.

It was a fine summer morning, promising a long warm day.

A FAR SUNSET

Human kind
Cannot bear very much reality.

T. S. Eliot

ONE

The star ship blew itself to glory, as the three of them knew it would, on the thirty-fifth day of their imprisonment in the donjons of Baya Nor. If they had shared the same cell, they might have been able to help each other; but since the day of their capture they had been kept separate. Their only contacts had been the noia who lived with each of them and the guards who brought their food.

The explosion was like an earthquake. It shook the very foundations of Baya Nor. The god-king consulted his council, the council consulted the oracle; and the oracle consulted the sacred bones, shivered, went into a trance and emerged from it a considerable time later to announce that this was the signal of Oruri, that Oruri had marked Baya Nor down for greatness, and that the coming of the strangers was a favourable omen.

The strangers themselves, however, knew nothing of these deliberations. They were incarcerated with their noias until they were rational enough – which meant until they had learned the language – to be admitted to the presence of the god-king.

Unfortunately the god-king, Enka Ne the 609th, was not destined to make the acquaintance of all of them; for the destruction of the star ship was a very traumatic experience. Each of the strangers wore an electronic watch, each of them had been able to keep a very accurate calendar. And each of them knew to the minute when the main computer would finally admit to itself that the crew had either abandoned the ship or were unable to return. At which point the main computer – for reasons obvious to the people who had built the vessel – was programmed to programme destruction. Which meant simply that the controls were lifted from the atomic generator. The rest would take care of itself.

Each of the strangers in his cell began a private countdown, at the same time hoping that one or more of the other nine members of the crew would return in time. None of them did. And so the star ship was transformed into a mushroom cloud, a circle of fire burnt itself out in the northern forests of Baya Nor, and a small glass-lined crater remained to commemorate the event.

In the donjons of Baya Nor, the second engineer went insane. He curled himself up into a tight foetal ball. But since he was not occupying a uterus, and since there was no umbilical cord to supply him with sustenance, and since the noia who was his only companion knew nothing at all about intravenous feeding, he eventually starved himself to death.

The chief navigator reacted with violence. He strangled his noia and then contrived to hang himself.

Oddly enough, the only member of the crew who managed to remain sane and survive was the star ship's psychiatrist. Being temperamentally inclined to pessimism, he had spent the last fifteen days of his captivity psychologically conditioning himself.

And so, when the donjons trembled, when his noia cowered under the bed and when in his mind's eye he saw the beautiful shape of the star ship convulsed instantly into a great ball of fire, he repeated to himself hypnotically: 'My name is Poul Mer Lo. I am an alien. But this planet will be my home. This is where I must live and die. This is where I must now belong … My name is Poul Mer Lo. I am an alien. But this planet will be my home. This is where I must live and die. This is where I must now belong …'

Despite the tears that were running unnoticed down his cheeks, Poul Mer Lo felt extraordinarily calm. He looked at his noia, crouching under the bed. Though he did not yet perfectly understand the language, he realized that she was muttering incantations to ward off evil spirits.

Suddenly, he felt a strange and tremendous sense of pity.

'Mylai Tui,' he said, addressing her formally. 'There is nothing to fear. What you have heard and felt is not the wrath of Oruri. It is something that I can understand, although I cannot explain it to you. It is something very sad, but without danger for you or your people.'

Mylai Tui came out from under the bed. In thirty-five days and nights she had learned a great deal about Poul Mer Lo. She had given him her body, she had given him her thoughts, she had taught him the tongue of Baya Nor. She had laughed at his awkwardness and his stupidity. She had been surprised by his tenderness, and amazed by his friendship. Nobody – but nobody – ever acknowledged friendship for a simple noia.

Except the stranger, Poul Mer Lo.

'My lord weeps,' she said uncertainly. 'I take courage from the words of Poul Mer Lo. But his sadness is my sadness. Therefore I, too, must weep.'

The psychiatrist looked at her, wondering how it would be possible to express himself in a language that did not appear to consist of more than a few hundred different words. He touched his face and was surprised to find tears.

'I weep,' he said calmly, 'because of the death of a great and beautiful bird. I weep because I am far from the land of my people, and I do not think that I shall ever return …' He hesitated. 'But I rejoice, Mylai Tui, that I have known you. And I rejoice that I have discovered the people of Baya Nor.'

The girl looked at him. 'My lord has the gift of greatness,' she said simply. 'Surely the god-king will look on you and be wise.'

TWO

That evening, when at last he managed to get to sleep, Poul Mer Lo had nightmares. He dreamed that he was encased in a transparent tube. He dreamed that there was a heavy hoar frost all over his frozen body, covering even his eyes, choking his nostrils, sealing his stiff immovable lips. He dreamed also that he dreamed.

And in the dream within a dream there were rolling cornfields, rippling towards the horizon as far as the eye could see. There was a blue sky in which puffy white clouds drifted like fat good-natured animals browsing lazily on blue pastures.

There was a dwelling – a house with walls of whitened mud and crooked timbers and a roof of smoky yellow reeds. Suddenly he was inside the house. There was a table. His shoulder was just about as high as the table. He could see delicious mountains of food – all the things that he liked to eat best.

There were toys. One of them was a star ship on a launching pad. You set the ship on the launcher, cranked the little handle as far back as you could, then pressed the Go button. And off went the star ship like a silver bird.

The good giant, his father, said: 'Happy birthday, my son.'

The wicked witch, his mother, said: 'Happy birthday, darling.'

And suddenly he was back in the transparent tube, with the hoar frost sealing his lips so that he could neither laugh nor cry.

There was terror and coldness and loneliness.

The universe was nothing but a great ball of nothing, punctured by burning needle points, shot through with the all-embracing mirage of stillness and motion, of purpose and irrelevance.

He had never known that silence could be so profound, that darkness could be so deep, that starlight could be so cold.

The universe dissolved.

There was a city, and in the city a restaurant, and in the restaurant a specimen of that vertical biped, the laughing mammal. She had hair the colour of the cornfields he remembered from childhood. She had eyes that were as blue as the skies of childhood. She had beautiful lips, and the sounds that came from them were like nothing at all in his childhood. Above all, she emanated warmth. She was the richness of high summer, the promise of a great sweet harvest.

She said: 'So the world is not enough?' It was a question to which she already knew the answer.

He smiled. 'You are enough, but the world is too small.'

She toyed with her drink. 'One last question, the classic question, and then we'll forget everything except this night … Why do you really have to go out to the stars?'

He was still smiling, but the smile was now mechanical. He didn't know. 'There is the classic answer,' he said evenly. 'Because they are there.'

'The moon is there. The planets are there. Isn't that enough?'

'People have been to the moon and the planets before me,' he explained patiently. 'That's why it's not enough.'

'I think I could give you happiness,' she whispered.

He took her hand. 'I know you could.'

'There could be children. Don't you want children?'

'I would like your children.'

'Then have them. They're yours for the begetting.'

'My love … Oh, my love … The trouble is I want something more.'

She could not understand. She looked at him with bewilderment. 'What is it? What is this thing that means more than love and happiness and children?'

He gazed at her, disconcerted. How to find the truth! How to find the words! And how to believe that the words could have anything at all to do with the truth.

'I want,' he said with difficulty, and groping for the right images, 'I want to be one of those who take the first steps. I want to leave a footprint on the farther shore.' He laughed. 'I even want to steal for myself a tiny fragment of history. Now tell me I'm paranoid. I'll believe you.'

She stood up. 'I've had my answer, and I'll tell you nothing,' she said, 'except that they're playing the Emperor Waltz … Do you want it?'

He wanted it.

They danced together in a lost bubble of time …

He wanted to cry. But how could you cry with frozen lips and frozen eyes and a frozen heart? How could you feel when you were locked in the bleak grip of eternity?

He woke up screaming.

The donjons of Baya Nor had not changed. The black-haired, wide-eyed noia by his side had not changed. Only he had changed because the conditioning – thank God – had failed. Because men were men and not machines. Because the grief inside him was so deep and so desolate that he, who had always considered himself to be nothing more than a blue-eyed computer, at last knew what it was to be a terrified animal.

He sat up in bed, eyes staring, the hairs at the nape of his neck twitching and stiffening.

'My name is Paul Marlowe,' he babbled in words that his noia could not understand. 'I am a native of Earth and I have aged four years in the last twenty years. I have sinned against the laws of life.' He held his head in his hands, rocking to and fro. 'Oh God! Punish me with pain that I can bear. Chastise me! Strip the flesh from my back. Only give me back the world I threw away!'

Then he collapsed, sobbing.

The noia cradled his head upon her breast.

'My lord has many visions,' she murmured. 'Visions are hard to bear, but they are the gift of Oruri and so must be borne. Know then, Poul Mer Lo, my lord, that your servant would ease the burden if Oruri so decrees.'

Poul Mer Lo raised his head and looked at her. He pulled himself together. 'Do not sorrow,' he said in passable Bayani. 'I have been troubled by dreams. I grieve only for the death of a child long ago.'

Mylai Tui was puzzled. 'My lord, first there was the death of a great bird, and now there is the death of a child. Surely there is too much of dying in your heart?'

Poul Mer Lo smiled. 'You are right. There is too much dying. It seems that I must learn to live again.'

THREE

In the year AD 2012 (local time) three star ships left Sol Three, known more familiarly to its inhabitants as Earth. The first star ship to venture out into the deep black yonder was – inevitably – the American vessel *Mayflower*. It was (and in this even the Russian and European inspection engineers agreed) the most ambitious, the largest and possibly the most beautiful machine ever devised by man. It had taken ten years, thirty billion new dollars and nine hundred and fourteen lives to assemble in the two-hour orbit. It was built to contain forty-five pairs of human beings and its destination was the Sirius system.

The second star ship to leave Sol Three was the Russian vessel *Red October*. Though not as large as the American ship it was (so the American and European inspection engineers concluded) somewhat faster. It, too, was expensive and beautiful. It, too, had cost many lives. The Russians, despite everyone's scepticism, had managed to assemble it in the three-hour orbit in a mere six years. It was built to contain twenty-seven men and twenty-seven women (unpaired), and its destination was Procyon.

The third ship to leave was the *Gloria Mundi*. It had been built on a relative shoe-string in the ninety-minute orbit by the new United States of Europe. It was called the *Gloria Mundi* because the Germans would not agree to an English name, the French would not agree to a German name, the English would not agree to a French name and the Italians could not even agree among themselves on a name. So a name drawn from the words of a dead language was the obvious answer. And because the ship was the smallest of the vessels, its chief architect – an Englishman with a very English sense of humour – had suggested calling it The Glory of the World. It was designed to carry six pairs of human beings: one German pair, one French pair, one British pair, one Italian pair, one Swedish pair and one Dutch pair. It was smaller than the Russian ship and slower than the American ship. Inevitably its target star was farther away than either the American or the Russian target stars. It was bound for Altair – a matter of sixteen light-years or nearly twenty-one years, ship's time.

In the twenty-first century the British sense of propriety was still a force to be reckoned with. That is why, on the morning of April 3rd, AD 2012. Paul Marlowe, wearing a red rose in the button-hole of his morning coat, appeared punctually at Caxton Hall registry office at 10.30 a.m. At 10.35 a.m.

Ann Victoria Watkins appeared. By 10.50 a.m. the couple had been pro-nounced man and wife. It was estimated that three hundred million people witnessed the ceremony over Eurovision.

Paul and Ann did not like each other particularly: nor did they dislike each other. But as the British contribution to the crew of the *Gloria Mundi* they accepted their pairing with good grace. Paul, a trained space-hand, pos-sessed the skills of psychiatry and teaching and was also fluent in French and German. Ann's dowry was medicine and surgery, a working knowledge of Swedish and Italian and enough Dutch to make conversation under pressure.

After the ceremony they took a taxi to Victoria, a hover train to Gatwick, a strato-rocket to Woomera and then a ferry capsule to the ninety-minute orbit. They spent their honeymoon working through the pre-jump routines aboard the *Gloria Mundi*.

Despite many differences in size, design and accommodation, the Ameri-can, Russian and European space ships all had one thing in common. They all contained sleeper units for the crews. None of the ships could travel faster than light – though the Russians claimed that given theoretically ideal condi-tions *Red October* could just pass the barrier – so their occupants were doomed to many years of star travel; during which it was a statistical cer-tainty that some would die, go mad, mutiny or find even more ingenious ways of becoming useless. Unless they had sleeper units.

Suspended animation had been developed years before in the closing dec-ades of the twentieth century. At first it had been used in a very limited way for heart transplants. Then someone had discovered that the simple process of freezing a neurotic for a period of days or weeks, depending on the degree of neurosis, could produce an almost complete cure. Then someone else hit upon the idea of using suspended animation for the insane, the incurable or the dying. Such people, it was argued, could be frozen for decades if neces-sary until an answer was found for their particular malady.

By the beginning of the twenty-first century, suspended animation had become an integral part of the way of life of every civilized community. Not only the seriously ill and the seriously mad were frozen. Criminals were frozen, suspended animation sentences ranging from one to fifty years, depending on the seriousness of the crime. And rich citizens, who had lived most of their lives and exhausted all the conventional rejuvenation tech-niques would go voluntarily into indefinite suspended animation in the sublime hope that one day somebody would discover the secret of immortal-ity. Even the dead, if they were important enough and if they could be obtained soon after the point of clinical death, were frozen – on the theory that a few more decades would bring great advances in resurrection techniques.

But whatever the value of suspended animation was for those who hoped to cheat death, the asylum, the executioner or the normal laws of existence, it was certainly the ideal form of travelling for those who were destined to venture into deep space.

It was estimated that the *Gloria Mundi* could not possibly reach Altair in less than twenty years of subjective time. Therefore a programme of rotational suspended animation had been worked out for the crew. For the first three months of the voyage all crew members would be live and operational. For the rest of the voyage, with the exception of the last three months, each pair would, in turn, remain live for one month (terrestrial time) and then be suspended for five. In case of an emergency all five frozen pairs (or any individual whose special skill was required) could be defrozen in ten hours.

During the course of the long and uneventful voyage to Altair, Paul Marlowe spent a total of nearly four working years in the company of his 'wife'. He never got to know her. As a psychiatrist, he would have thought that the absolute isolation of a long space voyage would have been bound to bring two people intimately together. But he never got to know her.

She had dark hair, an attractive face and a pleasant enough body. They made love quite a lot of times during their waking months. They shared jokes, they discussed books, they watched old films together. But somehow she was too dedicated, too remote. And he never really got to know her.

That, perhaps, was why he could summon no tears, could feel no personal sense of loss when she finally disappeared on Altair Five.

FOUR

Morning sunlight poured through four of the sixteen small glassless windows of the donjon. Poul Mer Lo was sleeping. The noia did not waken him. Clearly he had been touched by Oruri. He needed to sleep.

As always she marvelled at the stature and appearance of the outlander. He was half as high again as Mylai Tui, who was reckoned exceedingly tall – and therefore ugly – by her own people. His skin was interestingly pale, whereas hers was brown and almost, indeed, the prized black of the Bayani of ancient lineage. His eyes, when they were open, were light blue – a wondrous colour, since all Bayani eyes were either brown or ochre. The muscles in his arms and legs were like the muscles of a powerful animal. Which was strange since, though he was clearly a barbarian, he was a man of some sensibility. He was also very much a man; for she, who had experienced many vigorous Bayani as a priestess in the Temple of Gaiety, had found to her surprise that she could only accommodate his thanu with difficulty. The effort was at times painful: but also, at times, it produced joy greater even than the condescension of Oruri.

She shrank back from the mental blasphemy, shutting it out. Nevertheless she took joy in the remembered frenzies of Poul Mer Lo. Apart from the facts that his nose was rather sharp and his ears seemed to be imperfectly joined to his head his only serious malformation was that he had too many fingers.

Poul Mer Lo stirred and yawned. Then he opened his eyes.

'Greetings, my lord,' said Mylai Tui formally. 'Oruri has bestowed upon us the blessing of another day.'

'Greetings, Mylai Tui.' He was getting familiar with the customs as well as with the language. 'The blessing is ill deserved.'

But the words were mechanical and the look in his eyes was blank. Or far away. Far, far away …

'Soon we shall eat and drink,' she went on, hoping to bring him back to reality. 'Soon we shall walk in the garden.'

'Yes.' Poul Mer Lo did not move. He lay on his back despondently, staring at the ceiling.

'My lord,' said Mylai Tui desperately, 'tell me again the story of the silver bird. It is one that is most beautiful to hear.'

'You already know the story of the silver bird.' He did not look at her, but laughed bitterly. 'You probably know it better than I do.'

'Nevertheless, I would hear it once more … If my ears are still worthy.'

Poul Mer Lo sighed and raised himself on one arm, but still he did not look at her.

'There is a land beyond the sky,' he began. 'It is a land filled with many people who are skilled in the working of metal. It is a land where men do not know the laws of Oruri. It is a land where people may talk to each other and see each other at a great distance. It is truly a land of miracles. Among the people of this land there are some who are very wise and also very skilled and very ambitious. They have looked at the night sky and said to themselves: "Truly the stars are far from us, yet they tempt us. Shall we not seek ways of reaching them so that we may know what they are like?"'

Mylai Tui shivered and, as always at this point, interrupted. 'Such men,' she pronounced, 'must not only be brave and mad. They must also be most eager to accept the embrace of Oruri.'

'They do not know the laws of Oruri,' pointed out Poul Mer Lo patiently. 'They hunger only for knowledge and power … So it was that they dreamed of building a flock of silver birds whereon their young men and women might ride out to the stars.'

'It was the old ones who should have made the journey, for their time was near.'

'Nevertheless, it was the young ones who were chosen. For it was known that the stars were far away and that the flight of the silver birds would last many seasons.'

'Then the young ones would grow old on the journey.'

'No. The young ones did not grow old. For the wise men had found ways of making them sleep for the greater part of the journey.'

'My lord,' said Mylai Tui, 'those who sleep too much also starve.'

'These did not starve,' retorted Poul Mer Lo, 'for their sleep was deeper than any living sleep that is known in Baya Nor … You have asked for the story, noia, so let me tell it; otherwise neither of us will be content.'

Mylai Tui was saddened. He only addressed her as noia – knowing that it was incorrect – when he was angry.

'I am reproved by Poul Mer Lo,' she said gravely. 'It is just.'

'Well, then. Three silver birds left the land beyond the sky, each of them bound upon a different journey. I and eleven companions were chosen to ride the last and smallest of the birds. We were bound for the star that you know as the sun of Baya Nor. The wise men told us that the flight would take twenty or more cool seasons … We journeyed, most of us sleeping, but some always watching. As we came near to this star we saw that it shone brightly on a fair world, the world of Baya Nor. To us who had ridden upon the silver bird through a great darkness for so many seasons, the land of Baya Nor seemed very beautiful. We directed the bird to set us down so that we might see what manner of people lived here. Nine of our party set out to wander through your forests and did not return. After many days, we who were left decided to look for them. We did not find them. We found only the darts of your hunters and the donjons of Baya Nor ... Because no one returned to set the bird upon its homeward journey, it destroyed itself by fire.' Poul Mer Lo suddenly looked at her and smiled. 'And so, Mylai Tui, I am here and you are here; and together we must make the best of it.'

The noia let out a deep breath. 'It is a sweet and sad story,' she said simply. 'And I am glad, my lord, that you came. I am glad that I have known you.'

Outside there were sounds of marching feet. Presently the bars were taken from the door. Two slaves, watched by two guards, entered the donjon with platters of food and pitchers of water.

But Poul Mer Lo was not hungry.

FIVE

The *Gloria Mundi* had gone into the thousand-kilometre orbit round Altair Five. Farther out in solar space other satellites were detected; but they had been rotating round the planet somewhat longer than the terrestrial vessel and they were untenanted. They were nothing more than great dead lumps of rock – the nine moons of Altair Five that had once, perhaps, been a single moon. To the naked eye they were large enough to reveal themselves as a flock of large and apparently mobile stars.

The planet itself was a miracle. Statistically it was the jackpot, for the occupants of the *Gloria Mundi* could not bring themselves to believe that – in a cosmos so empty, yet whose material content was so diverse – either of the other terrestrial vessels could have encountered an earth-type planet. The odds were greater, as the Swedish physicist succinctly put it, than the chance of dealing four consecutive suits from a shuffled pack of playing cards.

Altair Five was not only earth-type; it was oddly symmetrical and – to people who had conditioned themselves to expect nothing but barren worlds or, at best, planets inhabited by life forms that were low in the biological series – quite beautiful. It was slightly smaller than Mars and nine-tenths of it was ocean, spotted here and there by a few small colonies of islands. But there was quite a large north polar continent and an almost identical south polar continent. But, most interesting of all, there was a broad horseshoe of a continent stretching round the equatorial region, one end of it separated from the other by a few hundred kilometres of water.

The polar continents were covered for the most part by eternal snows and ice; but the great mass of equatorial land displayed nearly all the features that might be observed on the terrestrial continent of Africa from a similar altitude.

There were mountains and deserts, great lakes, bush and tropical rain forests. Under the heat of the sun, the deserts burned with fiery, iridescent hues of yellow and orange and red; the mountains were brown, freckled with blue and white; the bush was a scorched amber; and the rain forests seemed to glow with a subtle pot-pourri of greens and turquoises.

The planet rotated on its own axis once every twenty-eight hours and seventeen minutes terrestrial time. Calculations showed that it would complete one orbit round Altair, its sun, in four hundred and two local days.

The life of the planet was clearly based upon the carbon cycle; and an analysis of its atmosphere showed only that there was a slightly higher pro-portion of nitrogen than in that of Sol Three.

The *Gloria Mundi* stayed in the thousand-kilometre orbit for four hun-dred and ten revolutions or approximately twenty terrestrial days. During that time every aspect of the planet was photographed and telephotographed. In one section of the equatorial continent, the photographs revealed the classic sign of occupation by intelligent beings – irrigation or, just possibly, transport canals.

The occupants of the *Gloria Mundi* experienced sensations akin to ecstasy. They had endured confinement, synthetic hibernation and the black star-pricked monotony of a deep space voyage; they had crossed sixteen light-years in sixteen years of suspended animation and over four years of waking and ageing. And at the end of it their privation and endurance had been rewarded by the best of all possible finds – a world in which people lived. Whether they were people with four eyes and six legs did not matter. What mattered was that they were intelligent and creative. With beings of such calibre it would surely be possible to establish fruitful communication.

The *Gloria Mundi* touched down within twenty kilometres of the nearest canals. With such a large ship – and bearing in mind that the German pilot had only experienced planetary manoeuvres of the vessel in simulation – it was a feat of considerable skill. The vessel burned a ten-kilometre swathe through the luxuriant forest then sat neatly on its tail while the four stability shoes groped gently through the smouldering earth for bedrock. They found it less than five metres down.

For the first three planetary days, nobody went outside the vessel. Vicinity tests were conducted. At the end of three days the airlock was opened and two armoured volunteers descended by nylon ladder into a forest that was already beginning to cover the scars of its great burning. The volunteers stayed outside for three hours, collecting samples but never straying more than a few metres from the base of the ship. One of them shot and killed a large snake that seemed to exhibit the characteristics of a terrestrial boa.

On the ninth day of planetfall an exploration team consisting of the Swed-ish pair, the French pair and the Dutch pair set out. Each of the members of the team wore thigh-length boots, plastic body armour and a light plastic visor. The temperature was far too high for them to wear more – other than fully armoured and insulated and altogether restricting space suits.

The women carried automatic sweeper rifles: the men carried nitro-pistols and atomic grenade throwers. All of them carried transceivers. Between them they had enough fire-power to dispose of a twentieth-century armoured corps.

Their instructions were to complete a semicircular traverse in the planetary east at a radius of five kilometres, to maintain radio contact every fifteen ter-restrial minutes and to return within three planetary days.

All went well for the first planetary day and night. They encountered and reported many interesting animals and birds, but no sign of intelligent beings. In the middle of the second planetary day, radio communication ceased. At the end of the third day, the team did not return.

Six people, tormented by anxiety, were left aboard the *Gloria Mundi*. At the end of the fifteenth day of planetfall, a rescue team consisting of the three remaining women set out. They, too, carried nitro-pistols and grenade throwers.

The fact that it was the women who went and not the men was not fortuitous. Of the men who remained, two were vital to the running of the ship (assuming no success in rescue) if it was ever to return to Earth; and the third, Paul Marlowe, was suffering from a form of acute dysentry.

He said goodbye to Dr Ann Victoria Marlowe, *née* Watkins, without emotion. He was too ill to care: she was too clinical to be involved. After she had gone, he lay back on his bed, tried to forget his own exhausting symptoms and the world of Altair Five and to lose himself in a microfilm of one of the novels of Charles Dickens.

The rescue team maintained radio contact for no more than seven hours. Then it, too, became silent.

After four days, Paul Marlowe was over the worst of his dysentery; and he and his two companions were in a state of extreme depression.

They considered waiting in the citadel of the *Gloria Mundi* indefinitely; they considered pulling back into orbit; they even considered heading out of the system and back to Sol Three. For clearly there was something badly wrong on Altair Five.

In the end they did none of those things. In the end they decided to become a death-or-glory squad.

It was Paul Marlowe, the psychiatrist, who worked the problem out logically. Three people were necessary to manage the ship. Therefore there was no point in sending one or two men out if he or they failed to return. For the vessel would still be grounded. So they must either all go or all stay. If they stayed in the *Gloria Mundi* and eventually returned to Sol Three, they would lose their self-respect – in much the same manner as mountaineers who have been forced to cut the rope. If, on the other hand, they formed themselves into a second search party and failed, they would have betrayed the trust vested in them by all the people of the United States of Europe.

But the United States of Europe was sixteen light-years away and under the present circumstances, their duty to such a remote concept was itself a remote abstraction. What mattered more were the people with whom they had shared danger and monotony and triumph – and now disaster.

So, really, there was no choice. They had to go.

By this time the ship's armoury was sadly depleted; but there were still enough weapons left for the three men to give a respectable account of them-selves if they were challenged by a visible enemy. On the twentieth day of planetfall they emerged from the womb-like security of the *Gloria Mundi* to be born again – as Paul Marlowe saw it imaginatively – into an unknown but thoroughly hostile environment.

The designers of the *Gloria Mundi* had tried to foresee every possible emergency that could occur – including the death, disappearance, defection or defeat of the entire crew. If by any remote possibility, it was argued, such types of catastrophe occurred on a planet with sophisticated inhabitants, it would theoretically be possible for the said inhabitants to take over the ship, check the star maps, track back on the log and the computer programmes and – defying all laws of probability, but subscribing to the more obtuse laws of absurdity – return the *Gloria Mundi* to Earth.

That, in itself, might be a good and charitable act. Or, depending on the nature, the potential and the intentions of the aliens who accomplished it, it might by some remote chance be the worst thing that could possibly happen to the human race. Whatever the result of such highly theoretical specula-tions could turn out to be, the designers, were of the opinion – wholeheartedly endorsed by their respective governments – that they could not afford to take chances.

Consequently the *Gloria Mundi* had been programmed to destroy herself on the thirty-fifth day of her abandonment – if that disastrous event ever took place. Thirty-five days, it was argued ought to be long enough to resolve whatever crisis confronted the crew. If it wasn't, then the *Gloria Mundi* and all who travelled in her would have to be a write-off.

The designers were very logical people. Some had argued for a twenty-day limit and some had argued for a ninety-day limit. Absorbed as they were in abstractions, few of them had paid much attention to the human element, and none of them could have foreseen the situation on Altair Five.

By the evening of the twentieth day of planetfall, the three remaining crew members had covered about seven kilometres of their search through the barely penetrable forests and had found not the slightest trace of their com-panions. They had just set up a circle of small but powerful electric lamps and an inner perimeter of electrified alarm wire behind which they proposed to bivouac for the night when Paul Marlowe felt a stinging sensation in his knee.

He turned to speak to his two companions, but before he could do so he fell unconscious to the ground.

Later he woke up in what was, though he did not then know it, one of the donjons of Baya Nor.

Much later, in fact thirty-three days later, the *Gloria Mundi* turned into a high and briefly terrible mushroom of flame and radiant energy.

SIX

It was mid-morning; and Poul Mer Lo, surrounded by small dancing rainbows, drenched by a fine water mist, was kneeling with his arms tied behind his back. Behind him stood two Bayani warriors, each armed with a short trident, each trident poised above his neck for a finishing stroke. Before him lay the sad heap of his personal possessions: one electronic wrist-watch, one miniature transceiver, one vest, one shirt, one pair of shorts, one plastic visor, a set of body armour, a pair of boots and an automatic sweeper rifle.

Poul Mer Lo was naked. The mist formed into refreshing droplets on his body, the droplets ran down his face and chest and back. The Bayani warriors stood motionless. There was nothing to be heard but the hypnotic sound of the fountains. There was nothing to do but wait patiently for his audience with the god-king.

He looked at the sweeper rifle and smiled. It was a formidable weapon. With it – and providing he could choose his ground – he could annihilate a thousand Bayani armed with tridents. But he had not been able to choose his ground. And here he was – at the mercy of two small brown men, awaiting the pleasure of the god-king of Baya Nor.

He wanted to laugh. He badly wanted to laugh. But he repressed the laughter because his motivation might have been misunderstood. The two sombre guards could hardly be expected to appreciate the irony of the situation. To them he was simply a stranger, a captive. That he could be an emissary from a technological civilization on another world would be utterly beyond their comprehension.

In the country of the blind, thought Poul Mer Lo, recalling a legend that belonged to another time and space, the one-eyed man is king.

Again he wanted to laugh. For, as in the legend, the blind man – with all their obvious limitations – had turned out to be more formidable than the man with one eye.

'You are smiling,' said an oddly immature voice. 'There are not many who dare to smile in the presence. Nor are there many who do not even notice the presence.'

Poul Mer Lo blinked the droplets from his eyes and looked up. At first he thought he saw a great bird, covered in brilliant plumage, with iridescent feathers of blue and red and green and gold; and with brilliant yellow eyes and a hooked black beak. But the feathers clothed a man, and the great bird's head was set like a helmet above a recognizable face. The face of Enka Ne, god-king of Baya Nor.

It was also the face of a boy – or of a very young man.

'Lord,' said Poul Mer Lo, struggling now with the language that had seemed so easy when he practised it with the noia, 'I ask pardon. My thoughts were far away.'

'Riding, perhaps, on the wings of a silver bird,' suggested Enka Ne, 'to a land beyond the sky … Yes, I have spoken with the noia. You have told her a strange story … It is the truth?'

'Yes, Lord, it is the truth.'

Enka Ne smiled. 'Here we have a story about a beast called a tlamyn. It is supposed to be a beast of the night, living in caves and dark places, never showing itself by day. It is said that once long ago six of our wise men ventured into the lair of a tlamyn – not, indeed, knowing of the presence or even the existence of such a creature. One of the wise men chanced upon the tlamyn's face. It was tusked and hard and hairy like the dongoir that we hunt for sport. Therefore, feeling it in the darkness, he concluded that he had encountered a dongoir. Another touched the soft underbelly. It had two enormous breasts. Therefore, he concluded that he had come upon a great sleeping woman. A third touched the beast's legs. They had scales and claws. Naturally, he thought he had found a nesting bird. A fourth touched the tlamyn's tail. It was long and muscular and cold. So he decided that he had stumbled across a great serpent. A fifth found a pair of soft ears and deduced that he was lucky enough to discover one of the domasi whose meat we prize. And the sixth, sniffing the scent of the tlamyn, thought that he must be in the Temple of Gaiety. Each of the wise men made his discovery known to his comrades. Each insisted that his interpretation was the truth. The noise of their disputation, which was prolonged and energetic, eventually woke the sleeping tlamyn. And it, being very hungry, promptly ate them all … I should add that none of my people have ever seen a tlamyn and lived.'

Poul Mer Lo looked at the god-king, surprised by his intelligence. 'Lord, that was a good story. There is one like it, concerning a creature called an elephant, that is told in my own country.'

'In the land beyond the sky?'

'In the land beyond the sky.'

Enka Ne laughed. 'What is truth?' he demanded. 'Beyond the world in which we live there is nothing but Oruri. And even I am but a passing shadow in his endless dreams.'

Poul Mer Lo decided to take a gamble. 'Yet who can say what and what does not belong to the dreams of Oruri. Might not Oruri dream of a strange country wherein there are such things as silver birds?'

Enka Ne was silent. He folded his arms, and gazed thoughtfully down at his prisoner. The feathers rustled. Water ran from them and made little pools on the stone floor.

At last the god-king spoke. 'The oracle has said that you are a teacher – a great teacher. Is that so?'

'Lord, I have skills that were prized among my own people. I have a little of the knowledge of my people. I do not know if I am a great teacher. I do not yet know what I can teach.'

The answer seemed to please Enka Ne. 'Perhaps you speak honestly … Why did your comrades die?'

Until then, Poul Mer Lo had not known that he was the last survivor. He felt an intense desolation. He felt a sense of loneliness that made him cry out, as in pain.

'You suffer?' enquired the god-king. He looked puzzled.

Poul Mer Lo spoke with difficulty. 'I did not know that my comrades were dead.'

Again there was a silence. Enka Ne gazed disconcertingly at the pale giant kneeling before him. He moved from side to side as if inspecting the phenomenon from all possible angles. The feathers rustled. The noise of the fountains became loud, like thunder.

Eventually, the god-king seemed to have made up his mind.

'What would you do,' asked Enka Ne, 'if I were to grant you freedom?'

'I should have to find somewhere to stay.'

'What would you do, then, if you found somewhere to stay?'

'I should have to find someone to cook for me. I do not even know what is good and what is not good to eat.'

'And having found a home and a woman, what then?'

'Then, Lord, I should have to decide how I could repay the people of Baya Nor who have given me these things.'

Enka Ne stretched out a hand. 'Live,' he said simply.

Poul Mer Lo felt a sharp jerk. Then his arms were free. The two silent Bayani warriors lifted him to his feet. He fell down because, having kneeled so long, the blood was not flowing in his legs.

Again they lifted him and supported him.

Enka Ne gazed at him without expression. Then he turned and walked away. After three or four paces he stopped and turned again.

He glanced at Poul Mer Lo and spoke to the guards. 'This man has too many fingers,' he said. 'It is offensive to Oruri. Strike one from each hand.'

SEVEN

Poul Mer Lo was given a small thatched house that stood on short stilts just outside the sacred city, the noia with whom he had spent his imprisonment, and sixty-four copper rings. He did not know the value of the ring money; but Mylai Tui calculated that if he did not receive any further benefits from the god-king he could still live for nearly three hundred days without having to hunt or work for himself.

Poul Mer Lo thought the god-king had been more than generous, for he had provided the stranger with enough money to last his own lifetime. Wisely, perhaps, Enka Ne had not shown too much favour. He had made sure that Enka Ne the 610th would not be embarrassed by the munificence of his predecessor.

The little finger on each hand had been struck off expertly, the scars had healed and the only pain that remained was from tiny fragments of bone working their way slowly to the surface. Sometimes, when the weather was heavy, Poul Mer Lo was conscious of a throbbing. But, for the most part he had adjusted to the loss very well. It was quite remarkable how easily one could perform with only four fingers the tasks that had formerly required five.

For many days after he had received what amounted to the royal pardon, Poul Mer Lo spent his time doing nothing but learning. He walked abroad in the streets of Baya Nor and was surprised to find that he was, for the most part, ignored by the ordinary citizens. When he engaged them in conversation, his questions were answered politely; but none asked questions in return. The fate of a pygmy in the streets of London, he reflected, would very likely have been somewhat different. The fate of an extraterrestrial in the streets of any terrestrial city would have been markedly different. Police would have been required to control the crowds – and, perhaps, disperse the lynch mobs. The more he learned, the more, he realized, he had to learn.

The population of Baya Nor, a city set in the midst of the forest, consisted of less than twenty thousand people. Of these nearly a third were farmers and craftsmen and rather more than a third were hunters and soldiers. Of the remainder, about five thousand priests maintained the temples and the waterways and about one thousand priest/lawyer/civil servants ran the city's administration. The god-king, Enka Ne, supported by a city council and an hereditary female oracle, reigned with all the powers of a despot for one year of four hundred days – at the end of which time he was sacrificed in the Temple of the Weeping Sun while the new god-king was simultaneously ordained.

Baya Nor itself was a city of water and stone – like a great Gothic lido, thought Poul Mer Lo, dropped crazily in the middle of the wilderness. The Bayani worshipped water, perhaps because water was the very fluid of life. There were reservoirs, pools and fountains everywhere. The main thoroughfares were broad waterways, so broad that they must have taken generations to construct. In each of the four main reservoirs, temples shaped curiously like pyramids rose hazily behind a wall of fountains to the blue sky. The temples, too, were not such as could have been raised by a population of twenty thousand in less than a century. They looked very old, and they looked also as if they would endure longer than the race that built them.

In a literal and a symbolic sense Baya Nor was two cities – one within the other. The sacred city occupied a large island in the lake that was called the Mirror of Oruri. It was connected to the outer city by four narrow causeways, on each side of which were identical carvings representing all the god-kings since time immemorial.

If Baya Nor was not strong in science, it was certainly strong in art; for the generations of sculptors and masons who had carved the city out of dark warm sandstone had left behind them monuments of grandeur and classic line. Disdaining a written language, they had composed their common testament eloquently in a language of form and composition. They had married water to stone and had produced a living mobile poetry of fountains and sunlight and shadow and sandstone that was a song of joy to the greater glory of Oruri.

Poul Mer Lo knew little of the religion of the Bayani. But as he surveyed its outward forms, he could feel himself coming under its spell, could sense the mystery that bound a people together in the undoubted knowledge that their ideas, their philosophy and their way of life were the most perfect expression of the mystery of existence.

At times, Poul Mer Lo was frightened; knowing that if he were to live and remain sane he would have to assume to some extent the role of serpent in this sophisticated yet oddly static Eden. He would have to be himself – no longer an Earth man, and not a man of Baya Nor. But a man poised dreadfully between two worlds. A man chastened by light-years, whipped by memories, haunted by knowledge. A man pinned by circumstances to a speck of cosmic dust from that other speck he had once called home. A man who, above all, needed to talk, to make confession. A man with a dual purpose – to create and to destroy.

At times he revelled in his purpose. At times he was ashamed. At times, also, he remembered someone who had once been called Paul Marlowe. He remembered the prejudices and convictions and compulsions that this

strange person had held. He remembered his arrogance and his certainty –
his burning ambition to journey out to the stars.

Paul Marlowe had fulfilled that ambition, but in fulfilling it he had died.
Alas for Paul Marlowe, who had never realized that it was possible to pay a
greater price for private luxuries than either death or pain.

Paul Marlowe, native of Earth, had accomplished more than Eric the Red,
Marco Polo, Columbus or even Darwin. But it was Poul Mer Lo, grace and
favour subject of Enka Ne, who paid the price for his achievement.

And the price was absolute loneliness.

EIGHT

The half-starved youth, clad in a threadbare samu, who climbed up the steps as Poul Mer Lo watched from his verandah, seemed vaguely familiar. But though there were not many beggars in Baya Nor, their faces all looked the same – like those of the proverbial Chinamen to people on the other side of a world on the other side of the sky …

'Oruri greets you,' said the youth, neglecting to hold out his begging bowl.

'The greeting is a blessing,' retorted Poul Mer Lo automatically. After two fifty-day Bayani months, he found ritual conversation quite easy. According to form, the youth should now tell of the nobility of his grandfather, the virility of his father, the selfless devotion of his mother and the disaster that Oruri had inflicted upon them all to bring joy through penitence.

But the boy did not launch into the expected formula. He said: 'Blessed also are they who have known many wonders. I may speak with you?'

Suddenly, Poul Mer Lo, who had been sitting cross-legged with Mylai Tui, enjoying the light evening breeze, recognized the voice. He sprang to his feet.

'Lord, I did not—'

'Do not recognize me!' The words shot out imperiously. Then the boy relaxed, and carried on almost apologetically: 'I am Shah Shan, of late a waterman. I may speak with you?'

'Yes, Shah Shan, you may speak with me. I am Poul Mer Lo, a stranger now and always.'

The boy smiled and held out his begging bowl. 'Oruri has seen fit to grace me with a slight hunger. Perhaps he foresaw our meeting.'

Silently, Mylai Tui rose to her feet, took the bowl and disappeared into the house. Poul Mer Lo watched her curiously.

She had seemed almost not to see Shah Shan at all.

'Poul Mer Lo is gracious,' said the boy. 'It is permitted to sit?'

'It is permitted to sit,' returned Poul Mer Lo gravely.

The two of them sat cross-legged on the verandah, and there was silence. Presently Mylai Tui returned with the bowl. It contained a small quantity of kappa, the cereal that was the staple diet of the poor and that the prosperous only ate with meat and vegetables.

Shah Shan took the kappa and ate it greedily with his fingers. When he had finished, he belched politely.

'I have a friend,' he said, 'whose head has been troubled with dreams and strange thoughts. I think that you may help him.'

'I am sorry for your friend. I do not know that I can help him, but if he comes to me, I will try.'

'The kappa is still green,' said Shah Shan.

Poul Mer Lo was familiar enough with idiomatic Bayani to understand that the time was not ripe.

'My friend is of some importance,' went on the boy. 'He has much to occupy him. Nevertheless, he is troubled … See, I will show you something that he has shown me.'

Shah Shan rose to his feet, went down the verandah steps and found a small stick. He proceeded to draw in the dust.

Poul Mer Lo watched him, astounded.

Shah Shan had drawn the outline of the *Gloria Mundi*.

'My friend calls this a silver bird,' he explained. 'But it does not look like a bird. Can you explain this?'

'It is truly a silver bird. It is a – a—' Poul Mer Lo floundered. There was no Bayani word for machine, or none that he knew. 'It was fashioned by men in metal,' he said at last, 'as a sculptor fashions in stone. It brought me to your world.'

'There is another thing,' continued Shah Shan. 'My friend has seen the silver bird passing swiftly round a great ball. The ball was very strange. It was not a ball of yarn such as the children play with. It was a ball of water. And there was some land on which forests grew. And in the forests there were waterways. Also there was a city with many temples and four great reservoirs … My friend was disturbed.'

Poul Mer Lo was even more amazed. 'Your friend need not be disturbed,' he said at length. 'He saw truly what has happened. The great ball is your world. The reservoirs are those of Baya Nor … Your friend has had a very wonderful dream.'

Shah Shan shook his head. 'My friend has a sickness. The world is flat – flat as the face of water when there is no wind. It is known that if a man journeys far – if he is mad enough to journey far – from Baya Nor, he will fall off the edge of the world. Perhaps if he is worthy, he will fall on to the bosom of Oruri. Otherwise there can be no end to his falling.'

Poul Mer Lo was silent for a moment or two. Then he said hesitantly: 'Shah Shan, I, too, have a friend who seems wise though he is still very young. He told me a story about six men who found a sleeping tlamyn. Each of the men thought the tlamyn was something else. Eventually, they argued so much that it woke up and ate them.'

'I have heard the story,' said Shah Shan gravely. 'It is amusing.'

'The tlamyn is truth. It is not given to men to understand truth completely.

However wise they are, they are only permitted to see a little of the truth. But may not some see more than others?'

Shah Shan's forehead wrinkled. 'It is possible,' he said presently, 'that a stranger to this land may see a different countenance of the truth ... A stranger who has journeyed far and therefore witnessed many happenings.'

Poul Mer Lo was encouraged. 'You speak wisely. Listen then, to the strange thoughts of a stranger. Time is divided into day and night, is it not? And in the day there is a great fire in the sky which ripens the kappa, rouses the animals and gives the light by which men see ... What is the name of this great fire?'

'It is called the sun.'

'And what is the name of all the land whereon the sun shines?'

'It is called the earth.'

'But the sun does not shine on the earth by night. At night there are many tiny points of light when the sky is clear, but they do not give warmth. What is the Bayani word for these cold, bright points of light?'

'Stars.'

'Shah Shan, I have journeyed among the stars and I swear to you that they seem small and cold only because they are very far away. In reality they are as hot and bright and big as the sun that shines over Baya Nor. Many of them shine on worlds such as this, and their number is greater than all the hairs on all the heads of your people ... My own home is on a world that is also called Earth. It, too, is warmed by a sun. But it is so far away that a silver bird is needed to make the journey. And now that the silver bird on which I came is dead, I do not think I shall return again.'

Shah Shan was watching him intently. 'There are cities like Baya Nor on your earth?'

'There are cities greater than Baya Nor. Cities where men accomplish wonderful things with metal and other substances.'

'Is Oruri worshipped in your cities?'

'For my people, Oruri has many different names.'

'And you have god-kings?'

'Yes, but again they are known by different names.'

'I have heard,' said Shah Shan, smiling, 'that Enka Ne permitted you to keep all that was found with you. They were things which the god-king found interesting but of no practical value. Is there anything among these things that would lend weight to the wonders of which you speak?'

Poul Mer Lo hesitated. There was the atomic powered miniature transceiver – the most he could raise on it would be static. There was the electronic wristwatch, a beautiful instrument but lacking, perhaps, the dramatic quality he needed to convince Shah Shan that he spoke the truth.

And there was the sweeper rifle. The ace that he had sworn only to use in extremity.

Should he risk throwing the ace away? He looked at Shah Shan, a boy filled with curiosity and a turmoil of strange new notions. Poul Mer Lo made his decision.

'Stay here,' he said. 'I will bring you something that is both wonderful and terrible.'

He went into the house, took the sweeper rifle from the niche he had made for it and returned to the verandah.

'This,' he said, 'is a weapon that, if it is used properly, could kill half your people.'

Shah Shan looked at the small plastic and metal object uncomprehendingly.

'Observe,' said Poul Mer Lo. He stood on the verandah, raised the rifle to his shoulder, pushed the breeder button and sighted at the base of a large tree about a hundred metres away. He pressed the trigger.

There was a faint whine, and the rifle vibrated almost imperceptibly. At the base of the tree, a plume of smoke began to rise. Then the tree toppled over.

'Observe,' said Poul Mer Lo. He switched his aim to a clear stretch of water on a waterway that was about two hundred metres away. He pressed the trigger. The water began to stream, then boil, then produce a miniature waterspout.

'Observe,' said Poul Mer Lo. He aimed at the ground not far from the verandah and blasted a small crater in which the lava hissed and bubbled long after he had put the rifle down.

Shah Shan put out a hand and touched the weapon gingerly. 'Truly, it is the work of gods,' he said at last. 'How many have you destroyed with it?'

Poul Mer Lo smiled. 'None. There has been no cause.'

'It shall be remembered,' said Shah Shan. Then he, too, smiled. 'But it did not save you from the darts of the hunters, did it?'

'No, it did not save me from the darts of the hunters.'

'That, too, must be remembered,' said Shah Shan. He rose. 'My lord, you have given me kappa, you have nourished my spirit, you have shown, perhaps, that my friend is not entirely mad. Oruri is our witness ... I will go now, for time runs swifter than water. And for many there is much thinking to be done. Live in peace, friend of my friend ... The fingers did not cause too much pain?'

'It is over,' said Poul Mer Lo briefly. 'It was a small price.'

Shah Shan formally touched his lips and his eyes, then turned and went down the verandah steps.

Poul Mer Lo watched him make his way towards the sacred city.

Without speaking, Mylai Tui picked up the empty kappa bowl and the sweeper rifle and took them away.

NINE

There had been many discussions aboard the *Gloria Mundi* about the possibility, probability and variety of extraterrestrial life. During the first three months of the voyage, before any of the twelve crew members had been suspended, the discussions tended to take place on the mess deck after dinner, or in the library. During the last three months of the voyage they tended to take place in the astrodome. But during more than nineteen years of starflight, when only one pair was operational at a time, the favourite place for discussion was the navigation deck. It was there that the ship's log was kept up to date. It was there that diaries were written and letters 'posted' for successive pairs so that the month-long vigil would not be too lonely.

It was there that in the seventeenth year of star time, Paul and Ann Marlowe held a champagne and chicken supper to celebrate their successful triumph over the first meteor perforation of the entire voyage. It had not been a very big meteor – less than an inch in diameter – but it had passed with a musical ping clean through the hold of the *Gloria Mundi*, leaving what looked like two neat large calibre bullet holes on each side of the ship's hull.

As soon as the air pressure dropped the alarm bells began to ring. Paul and Ann, mindful of basic training, immediately dashed to the nearest pressure suits and were fully encased long before they were in any danger of explosive decompression. It took them barely five minutes to trace the leaks and another fifteen minutes to process the self-sealer strips and make a chemical weld. Then Paul covered the emergency plugs with two slabs of half-inch titanium, and the crisis was over. It had not been a big crisis really, but it was a good excuse to open one of the bottles of champagne. After he had made a brief statement in the log, Paul scribbled a note to the French pair, who were next on watch. It read: *Since we saved you from a fate worse than freezing, we feel entitled to broach a bottle of the Moet et Chandon '11. I believe it was a very fine year … Don't be too envious. We really had to work for it. Paul.*

And so it came about that he and Ann were sitting at table on the navigation deck with the *Moet et Chandon* in a makeshift ice bucket and Altair on the other side of the paraplex window, more than two light years away and looking like a fiery marble.

'Suppose,' said Paul, after his second glass, 'we came upon a world that was nothing but water. Not a bit of land anywhere. What the hell would we do?'

Ann shook her dark hair and giggled. She had never been much given to alcohol, and the champagne had gone to her head. She hiccupped gravely. 'That's easy. Go into low orbit and drop a couple of skin divers complete with aqualungs to look for intelligent sponges.'

There was a brief silence. Then Paul said tangentially: 'It's an odd thing, but I've never been quite sure whether or not I believe in God.'

'What is God?' demanded Ann. 'What is God but an extension of the ego – a sort of megalomania by proxy?'

Paul laughed. 'Don't mix it with me, dear, in the field of psychological jargon. You're only a gifted amateur. I'm a hardened professional.'

'Well, what the hell has God got to do with intelligent sponges?' demanded Ann belligerently.

'Nothing at all … Except that if God exists he might just possibly have a sense of humour far more subtle than we bargain for. He might have created intelligent sponges, moronic supermen, parthenogenetic pygmies, immortal sloths or sex-crazed centipedes just for kicks – or just to see what them crazy mixed-up human beings would do when they encountered them.'

Ann giggled once more. 'If there is a God, and I don't think there is, I'll bet that human beings are His *pièce de* godlike *resistance*. They are so damn complicated He would have got Himself confused if He'd tried to dream up anything more complicated … Anyway, if Altair has inhabitable planets, my money is on sex-crazed centipedes … At least it would be amusing. Just think what they could do with all those legs.'

Paul filled their champagne glasses again and in doing so emptied the bottle. He gazed at it regretfully. 'There are further complications … Predestination. Kismet. What if our little venture is not a shot in the dark? What if the whole thing is fully programmed? What if we are all just shoving back the light-years to keep an appointment in Samara.'

'You talk a lot of twaddle,' said Ann. 'Causation is quite nice and cosy – if you don't let it get out of hand. An infinitely variable universe must be filled with infinitely variable possibilities … But if you want to know what I think, I think we're going to find no planets at all – or else a stack of bloody burnt out cinders. The one thing we are not going to find is intelligent life.'

'Why?'

'Finagle's Second Law.'

'And what, pray, is that?'

Ann was incredulous. 'You mean to say you've never heard of Finagle's Second Law?'

'I haven't even heard of the first.'

Ann hiccupped. 'Pardon me. That's the point. There is no first. There is no third, either. Only a second.'

'All right, I get the message. I won't even ask who Finagle was. But what the hell is his Second Law?'

'It states that if in any given circumstances anything can possibly go wrong, it invariably will.'

'So you think we'll either score three lemons or come unstuck?'

'It's safer to think that,' said Ann darkly. 'Nobody in their right mind would tangle with Finagle. The great trick, the ultimate discipline, is always to expect the worst. Then whatever else happens, you're bound to be pleasantly surprised.'

Paul was silent for a minute or two. Then he said: 'I think I'll go right out on a limb and set myself up as a clairvoyant.'

Ann turned to the paraplex window and gazed sombrely at Altair. 'Well, there's your crystal, gypsy mine. What do you see?'

Paul followed her gaze, staring at Altair intently. 'I see the jackpot. We shall find an earth-type life-bearing planet. There might even be intelligent beings on it.'

'Christ, you're pushing the odds, aren't you?'

'To blazes with the odds,' said Paul. 'Yes, I'll go all the way. We shall find intelligent beings on it … And I rather think we shall keep that appointment in Samara.'

Ann smiled. 'And what, pray, is that?'

'You mean to say you've never heard of an appointment in Samara?'

'*Touché. Prosit. Grüss Gott* … That champagne was terrific.'

'It's an oriental tale,' said Paul, 'And the story goes that the servant of a rich man in Baghdad or Basra, or some place like that, went out to do a day's shopping. But in the market place he met Death, who gave him a strange sort of look … Well the servant chased off home and said to his master: "Lord, in the market place I met Death, who looked as if he were about to claim me. Lend me your fastest horse that I may ride to Samara, which I can reach before nightfall, and so escape him."'

'Pretty sensible,' said Ann. 'Give the servant eight out of ten for initiative.'

'Ah,' said Paul. 'That's the point. The servant displayed too much initiative. The rich man lent the servant his horse, and he duly set off for Samara at a great rate of knots. But when he had gone, the rich man thought: "This is a bit of a bore. My servant is a jolly good servant. I shall miss him. Death had no right to give him the twitches. I think I'll pop down to the market place and give the old fellow a piece of my mind."'

'*Noblesse oblige*,' said Ann. 'A very fine sentiment.'

'So the rich man went to the market place and buttonholed Death. "Look here," he said, or words to that effect, "what do you mean by giving my servant the shakes?" Death was amused. He said: "Lord, I merely looked at the fellow in surprise." "Why so?" asked the rich man. "He is just an ordinary servant." "I looked at him in surprise," explained Death, "because I did not expect to find him here. You see, I have an appointment with him this evening – in Samara."'

Ann was silent for a while. 'Champagne is schizophrenic,' she said at length. 'One minute it lifts you up, and then it drops you flat on your face ... Anyway, we didn't see Death in the market place, did we?'

'Didn't we?' asked Paul. 'Didn't we see Death when we went up in orbit? Didn't we see him when we blasted off on the long shot? Don't we make a rude gesture to him every time we pop ourselves back in the cooler?'

'I'm not afraid of dying,' said Ann. 'I'm only afraid of pain – and of being afraid.'

'Poor dear,' said Paul. 'I'm the spectre at the feast. Dammit, Death just chucked a meteor at us; and it did hardly any damage at all. So he can't be too interested in us, can he?'

'I'm cold,' said Ann, 'but at the same time just a trifle lascivious. Let's go to bed.'

Paul stood up, smiling. 'Lasciviousness is all,' he said. 'Thank God we don't have to keep the house tidy. It's another ten days, I think, before we have to slide ourselves into the freezer.'

Ann took his hand. 'That's the thought that makes me cold. Meanwhile, come and keep me warm.'

There was only one double berth on the *Gloria Mundi*. The crew called it the honeymoon suite. That was where they went.

But even while Paul Marlowe was engaged in the act of love, even as he reached the climax, he was thinking about an appointment in Samara.

There was still the taste of champagne in his mouth, and in Ann's.

But for both of them the taste was sour.

TEN

He woke up and found that he was trembling. He looked at his surroundings without recognition for a moment or two, but the disorientation was brief. Over in the corner of the room a string of smoke rippled upwards towards the thatch from the tiny flickering oil lamp set on the miniature phallus of Oruri. One or two flies buzzed lazily. By his side, the naked brown girl slept peacefully with one arm thrown carelessly across his stomach.

He looked at the three stubby fingers and flattened thumb on her small hand. He looked at her face – neat and serene. An alien face, yet perhaps it would have raised no eyebrows in central Africa. Her serenity annoyed him. He shook her into consciousness.

Mylai Tui sat up, bleary-eyed. 'What is it, my lord? Surely the nine sisters are still flying?'

'Say it!' he commanded. 'Say my name.'

'Poul Mer Lo.'

He shook her again. 'It is not Poul. Say Paul.'

'Poul.'

'No. Paul.'

'Poel.' Mylai Tui enunciated the syllables carefully.

He slapped her. 'Poel,' he mimicked. 'No, not Poel. Say Paul.'

'Poel.'

He slapped her again. 'Paul! Paul! Paul! Say it!'

'Pole,' sobbed Mylai Tui. 'Pole … My lord, I am trying very hard.'

'Then you are not trying hard enough, Mylai Tui,' he snapped brutally. 'Why should I bother to speak your language when you can't make a decent sound in mine? Say Paul.'

'Pol.'

'That's better … Paul.'

'Paul.'

'That's good. That's very good. Now try Paul Marlowe.'

'Pol Mer Lo.'

Again he hit her. 'Listen carefully. Paul Marlowe.'

'Pol Mah Lo.'

'Paul Marlowe.'

'Paul Mah Lo.'

'Paul Marlowe.'

'Paul ... Marlowe.' By this time Mylai Tui hardly knew what she was saying.

'You've got it!' he exclaimed. 'That's it. That's my name. You are to call me Paul. Understand?'

'Yes, my lord.'

'Yes, Paul.'

'Yes, Paul,' repeated Mylai Tui obediently. She wiped the tears from her face.

'It's important, you understand,' he babbled. 'It's very important. A man has to keep his own name, does he not?'

'Yes, my lord.'

He raised his hand.

'Yes, Paul,' corrected Mylai Tui hastily. Then she added hesitantly: 'My lord is not afflicted by devils?'

He began to laugh. But the laughter disintegrated. And then tears were streaming down his own face. 'Yes, Mylai Tui. I am afflicted by devils. It seems that I shall be afflicted by devils as long as I live.'

Mylai Tui nursed his head on her breast, rocking to and fro, rhythmically. 'There is a great sadness inside you,' she said at length. 'O Paul, my lord, it hisses like water over burning stones. Kill me or send me away; but do not let me witness such pain in one to whom I am not destined to bring the first gift of Oruri.'

'What is the first gift of Oruri?'

'A child,' said Mylai Tui simply.

He sat up with a jerk. 'How do you know that you will not give me a child?'

'Lord – Paul – you have loved me many times.'

'Well?'

'I have not worn the zhivo since I left the Temple of Gaiety and gave up the duties of a noia, Paul. You have loved me many times. If you had been an ordinary Bayani, by now I would have swollen with the fruit of love. I am not swollen. Therefore Oruri withholds his first gift ... My Lord, I have sinned. I know not how, but I have sinned ... Perhaps you will fare better with another noia.'

He was thunderstruck. For in a terrible moment of clarity he saw that Mylai Tui possessed a wisdom greater than he could ever hope to attain. 'It is true,' he said calmly. 'I want a child, but I did not know that I want a child ... There are so many things I do not know ... Yet, there is no sin, Mylai Tui. For I think that my blood and yours will not mingle. I think that I can never get a child save with one of my own people. And so I shall not send you away.'

Mylai Tui sighed and smiled. 'My lord is merciful. If I cannot bear the son of him who came upon a silver bird, I wish to bear the son of no other.'

He took her hands and looked at her silently for a while. 'What is it that binds us?' he asked at length.

Mylai Tui could not understand. 'There is nothing to bind us, Paul,' she said, 'save the purpose of Oruri.'

ELEVEN

Three gilded barges, each propelled by eight pole-men, passed slowly along the Canal of Life under the great green umbrella of the forest. In the first barge, guarded by eight brawny priestesses, there was the small shrouded palanquin that contained the oracle of Baya Nor. In the second barge, guarded by eight male warriors, was the god-king, Enka Ne, the council of three and the stranger, Poul Mer Lo. In the third barge, guarded also by eight warriors, were the three girl children who were destined to die.

Poul Mer Lo sat humbly below the dais on which the god-king reclined, and listened to the words of his master.

'Life and death,' said Enka Ne, in a voice remarkably like that of Shah Shan, the beggar, 'are but two small aspects of the infinite glory of Oruri. Man that is born of woman has but a short time to live, yet Oruri lives both at the beginning of the river of time and at the end. Oruri *is* the river. Oruri is also the people on the river, whose only value is to fulfil his inscrutable purpose. Is this thought not beautiful?'

The bright plumage rustled as Enka Ne took up a more comfortable position. Poul Mer Lo – Paul Marlowe of Earth – found it difficult to believe that, beneath all the iridescent feathers and the imposing bird's head, there was only the flesh and blood of a boy.

'Lord,' he said carefully, 'whatever men truly believe is beautiful. Worship itself is beautiful, because it gives meaning to the act of living … Only pain is ugly, because pain deforms.'

Enka Ne gave him a disapproving stare. 'Pain is the gift of Oruri. It is the pleasure of Oruri that men shall face pain with gladness and acceptance, knowing that the trial shall bring them closer to the ultimate face … See, there is a guyanis! It, too, fulfils the pleasure of Oruri, living for less than a season before it receives the infinite mercy of death.'

Poul Mer Lo gazed at the guyanis – a brilliantly coloured butterfly with a wing span longer than his forearm – as it flapped lazily and erratically along the Canal of Life, just ahead of the barge containing the oracle. As he watched, a great bird with leathery wings dived swiftly from a tree-fern on the banks of the canal and struck the guyanis with its toothed beak. One of the butterfly wings sheared completely and drifted down to the surface of the water: the rest of the creature was held firmly in the long black beak. The bird did not even pause in flight.

Enka Ne clapped his hands. 'Strike!' he said, pointing to the bird. A warrior raised his blow-pipe to his lips. There was a faint whistle as the dart flew from the pipe. Then the leathery bird, more than twenty metres away, seemed to be transfixed in mid-flight. It hovered for a moment, then spiralled noisily down to the water.

Enka Ne pointed to the warrior who had killed the bird. 'Die now,' he said gently, 'and live for ever.'

The man smiled. 'Lord,' he said, 'I am unworthy.' Then he took a dart from his pouch and pushed it calmly into his throat. Without another word, he fell from the barge into the Canal of Life.

Enka Ne looked intently at Poul Mer Lo. 'Thus is the purpose of Oruri fulfilled.'

Poul Mer Lo gazed at the enigmatic waters of the canal. The barge had already left the body of the warrior behind it. Now a butterfly wing floated past and then the still twitching shape of the leathery bird, with the rest of the guyanis still gripped in its beak.

Paul Marlowe, man of Earth, struggled against the dream-like fatalism which had caused him to accept the role of Poul Mer Lo in a dream-like and fatalistic world. But it was hard, because he was still enough of a psychiatrist to realize that two people were inhabiting the same body and were making of it a battleground. Paul would be forever the outcast – technological man, with a headful of sophisticated and synthetic values resisting the stark and simple values of barbarism. Poul was only a man who was trying desperately to belong – a man who wanted nothing more than peace and perhaps a little fulfilment in the world into which he had been thrust.

Was it Paul or was it Poul who was travelling along the Canal of Life with Enka Ne? He did not even know that. He knew only that the great green hypnosis of the forest and the brightly plumed hypnosis of the god-king and the meaning of life and death were all far too much for the would-be fratricides who lived in the same tortured head.

It was a heavy, languorous afternoon. By sunset one of the girl children in the following barge would be sacrificed against the phallus of Oruri in the forest temple of Baya Sur. Poul was fascinated. Paul was shocked. Neither knew what to do.

'Lord,' said Paul – or Poul, 'which was of greater value: the life of the guyanis or the life of your warrior?'

Enka Ne smiled. 'Who can know? No one save Oruri. Was it not Oruri in me that bade the warrior be at one with the guyanis?'

'Who can know?' said the man of Earth. 'It is certain that I do not.'

The god-king's councillors, crouching together, had heard the exchange in silence. But they were plainly unhappy that a stranger should question the act of Enka Ne. Now one of them spoke.

'Lord,' he said diffidently, 'may it not be that Poul Mer Lo, whose life is yours, has a careless voice? The affliction may easily be remedied.'

Enka Ne shook his feathers and stretched. Then he gazed solemnly at the councillor. 'There is no affliction. Know only that the stranger has been touched by Oruri. Whoever would challenge the purpose of Oruri, let him now command the death of Poul Mer Lo.'

The councillors subsided, muttering. Poul Mer Lo was sweating with the heat; but somewhere in a dark dimension Paul Marlowe was shivering.

'See,' said Enka Ne, 'there is the first stone of Baya Sur.' He pointed to an obelisk rising from the smooth water of the canal. 'Soon there will be a sharp glory. Let no man come to this place without tranquillity and love.'

Baya Sur was, unlike Baya Nor, no more than a single stone temple set in the forest and protected from its advance by a high stone wall. At the landing place about forty men – the entire population of Baya Sur – waited to greet the barges. The one containing the oracle was the first to pull in. The palanquin was lifted ashore carefully by the priestesses and carried into the temple. Then Enka Ne gave a signal and his own barge was poled in. He stepped ashore with a great rustling of feathers and with all the arrogance and brightness and mystery of a god. After him came the councillors, and after them came the stranger, Poul Mer Lo. No one stayed to meet the three girl children. Looking over his shoulder as he walked along the paved avenue that led to the temple steps, Poul Mer Lo saw them step ashore and walk gravely after him like tiny clockwork dolls.

Before the sacrifice there was a ritual meal to be undertaken. It was in the great hall of the phallus where the only source of natural light came from the orifice of a symbolic vagina built into the roof. In the bare walls, however, there were niches; and in the niches were smoky oil lamps.

The palanquin had been set near to the stone phallus. Immediately before the phallus there was a large bowl of kappa and several empty small bowls. The three girl children, silent and immobile, sat cross-legged facing the phallus. Behind them sat three priests, each armed with a short knife. Behind the priests sat the councillors, and behind the councillors sat Poul Mer Lo.

Suddenly, there was a wild, desolate bird cry. Enka Ne strutted into the chamber in such a manner that, for a moment, Poul Mer Lo again found it necessary to remind himself that beneath the plumage and under the bright, darting bird's head, there was only a boy. The god-king pecked and scratched. Then he gave his desolate bird cry once more and strutted to the bowl of kappa.

He urinated on it and gave another piercing cry. Then he crouched motionless opposite the palanquin. An answering bird cry came from behind the dark curtains.

One of the priests began to put small handfuls of kappa into the little bowls. The two other priests began to hand the bowls round – first to the girl children, who immediately ate their portions with great relish, then to the councillors, and finally to Poul Mer Lo.

Paul Marlowe wanted to be sick, but Poul Mer Lo forced him to eat. The frugal meal was over in a few moments. Then daylight died, and the room was filled with the flickering shadows cast by the oil lamps.

The god-king rose, strutted to the phallus of Oruri and enfolded it with his wings. Then he whirled and pointed to one of the girl children.

'Come!'

She rose obediently and stepped forward. She turned and leaned back on the phallus, clasping her hands behind it and around it. The god-king suddenly lay at her feet. There was an expression of intense happiness on her face.

One of the priests pressed his arm under her chin, forcing her head back. Another knelt, pressing her stomach so that she was hard against the phallus. The third advanced with knife arm extended and with the other arm ready as if to grasp something.

Enka Ne uttered another bird cry. From the closed palanquin there came an answering bird cry. The knife struck once, then rose and struck again. There was no sound.

The hand plunged into the open chest of the girl and snatched out the still beating heart.

Blood poured from the gaping wound on to the prostrate body of the god-king.

There were two more bird cries – piercing, desolate, triumphant.

Poul Mer Lo fainted.

TWELVE

The expedition, the religious progress, was almost over. So far it had taken eight days and would be completed on the ninth, when the oracle and god-king returned to Baya Nor. The three girl children were now safely in the arms of Oruri. The second had been sacrificed in a manner identical with that of the first at the temple of Baya Ver and the third at the temple of Baya Lys.

Poul Mer Lo had learned not to faint at the spectacle of a living heart being torn from the body of a child. It was, he had been told, at the best rather impolite. At the worst it could be construed as an unfavourable omen.

Now, on the eighth night shortly after the ceremonial death-in-life feast that followed the sacrifice, he lay restlessly on his bed in one of the guest cells of Baya Lys. He was wondering why Enka Ne had invited/commanded his presence on the journey. To accompany the oracle and the god-king on a religious progress was a privilege normally reserved only for those who had distinguished themselves greatly in war or worship.

Suddenly he became aware that someone else was in the cell. He sat up quickly and saw by the light of the small oil lamp a half-starved youth in a tattered samu squatting patiently on the floor. There was a covered bundle by his side.

'Oruri greets you,' said Shah Shan, rising.

'The greeting is a blessing,' answered Poul Mer Lo mechanically.

'I sorrow if I have disturbed your meditations.'

Poul Mer Lo smiled. 'My meditations were such that I welcome one who interrupts them.'

Shah Shan indicated the bundle at his feet. 'My friend, of whom I think you know, bade me bring you some things that were found in the forest. He was of the opinion that they would have some meaning for you.' He untied the piece of cloth and displayed the contents of the bundle.

There was one plastic visor, two atomic grenades and a battered transceiver.

Poul Mer Lo was instantly transformed into Paul Marlowe who, gazing at the odd collection, felt a stinging mistiness in his eyes.

'Who found these things?' he managed to say at last.

'The priests of Baya Lys.'

'They have found nothing else?'

'Nothing … Except …' Shah Shan hesitated. 'My friend told me that it has been reported that a great blackened hole exists in the forest where formerly there was nothing but trees and grass. These objects are certainly very curious. Do they have any significance?'

'They belonged to those who travelled with me in the silver bird.' Paul Marlowe picked up one of the atomic grenades. 'This, for example, is a terrible weapon of destruction. If I were to move these studs in a certain way,' he indicated two tiny recessed levers, 'the whole of Baya Lys would be consumed by fire.'

Shah Shan was unperturbed. 'It is to be hoped,' he remarked, 'that, receiving the guidance of Oruri, you will not cause this thing to happen.'

Paul smiled. 'Be assured that I will not cause it to happen, Shah Shan, for it would encompass my own death also.'

The boy was silent for a while. 'The domain of Baya Nor is bounded by one day's march to the north,' he said at last. 'Beyond that is land occupied by a barbaric people. It may be that your friends have become the friends of these people … Or they may have been killed, or they may have wandered and died in the forest … How many travelled with you?'

'There were twelve of us altogether.'

'And three came to Baya Nor.'

'Three were taken prisoner by the people of Baya Nor.'

The boy shrugged. 'It matters not how we describe the event. Nine still remain shrouded by mystery.'

'These people of the forest – how are they called?'

'They call themselves the Lokh. We call them Lokhali. They speak a strange tongue.'

'Is it possible to meet and talk with the Lokhali?'

Shah Shan smiled. 'Possible, but not advisable. And it is likely that the conversation would be brief. These people live for war.'

'Perhaps if Enka Ne were to send presents, and ask for news …'

Shah Shan stiffened. 'Enka Ne does not treat with the Lokhali. So it has always been. So it will always be. Doubtless in the end Oruri will grant them a terrible affliction … Poul Mer Lo, my friend is puzzled. The oracle has pronounced that you are a great teacher and that because of you greatness shall be bestowed upon Baya Nor.'

'I do not know that I am a great teacher. So far my teaching has been very small.'

'Then, my lord, you must make it big,' said Shah Shan simply, 'for the oracle speaks only the truth … My friend is rich in glory but not rich in time. He wishes to see the fruits of your teaching before he answers the call.'

'Shah Shan, your friend must not expect too much. The essence of teaching is to learn first and then teach afterwards.'

'Permit me to observe, Poul Mer Lo, that the essence of teaching is to be understood … It was many days before you learned to speak Bayani, was it not?'

'Many days indeed.'

'What, then, is the tongue you would speak with your own kind?'

'It is called English.'

'I wish to speak this Ong Lys. For then I might more perfectly understand the thoughts of Poul Mer Lo.'

'Shah Shan, what is the use? There is no one but I who can speak this tongue.'

'Perhaps, my lord, that is why I wish to learn it … I am a poor and insignificant person, having nothing to offer you. But my friend would be greatly pleased.'

Paul Marlowe smiled. 'It shall be as you wish, Shah Shan. Your friend is either very clever or very simple.'

Shah Shan looked at him in surprise. 'You do not know which?' he asked. 'But why cannot my friend be both?'

THIRTEEN

Paul Marlowe banged the calabash hard against the step of the verandah where he was sitting. Silently, Mylai Tui poured some more kappa spirit into it.

He took a long swig and felt a bitter satisfaction as the fiery liquid wrought havoc in his throat and his stomach. He was getting drunk rapidly and he didn't give a damn.

'Big breasted brown-faced bitch,' he muttered in English.

'My lord?' said Mylai Tui uncertainly.

'Say Paul, damn you!' Again in English.

'Paul?' repeated Mylai Tui anxiously. It was the only word she had caught.

'Thank you,' he snapped in Bayani. 'Now be silent. There are times when a man needs to become a fool. This is one of them.'

Mylai Tui bowed her head and sat cross-legged, cradling the pitcher of kappa spirit in her lap, mindful of the future needs of Poul Mer Lo.

It was twilight and the nine moons of Altair Five were pursuing each other across the sky like ... Like what? thought Paul Marlowe ... Like frightened birds ... Nine cosmic cinders on the wing ...

'I am dead,' he said in English. 'I am a corpse with a memory ... What the hell is going on in Piccadilly Circus tonight? Who won the test match, and what sensational scandals will break in the Sunday papers tomorrow? For clearly tonight is Saturday night. Therefore let there be a great rejoicing.'

He emptied the calabash, shuddered, and banged it against the verandah step once more. Silently, Mylai Tui refilled it.

He wanted to listen to Beethoven – any old Beethoven would do. But the nearest stereo was a fair number of light years away. Damn!

'I shall declaim,' said Paul Marlowe to no one in particular. 'Is there not reason to declaim? It was in another country and, besides, the wench is dead.'

'Paul?' said Mylai Tui uncertainly.

'Shut up! Jew of Malta – I think – by kind permission of a bleeding ancestor.'

'Paul?'

'Shut up, or I will gorily garrotte you, you brown-bottomed whore.' He began to laugh at the alliteration, but the laughter degenerated into a fit of coughing. He cleared his throat.

'Only speaking in the tongues of men,' he said.
'What can I make of a broken image,
a single shaft of light,
a white star over winter marshes
when harsh cries of night birds
quiver above unheard voices, and the river
sings like a whip of laughter in the misty twilight?'

'Paul?' said Mylai Tui again, with great temerity.

'Be silent, you bloody ignorant female beast! I speak the words of some goddamned twentieth-century poet whose name temporarily escapes me ... Why do I speak the words of said anon poet? I will tell you, you little Bayani slut. Because there is a hole inside me. A hole, do you hear? A damn big hole, one heart wide and twenty light-years deep ... I am dead, Horatio ... Where the hell is the rest of that rot-gut?'

Mylai Tui said nothing. If it pleased her lord to speak with the voice of a devil, obviously there was nothing to be said. Or done.

'Where the hell is the rest of that rot-gut?' demanded Paul Marlowe, still in English.

Mylai Tui did not move.

He stood up, lurched forwards unsteadily and kicked the pitcher out of her hands. The kappa spirit was spilled all over the verandah. Its sweet smell rose suffocatingly.

Paul Marlowe fell flat on his face and was sick.

Presently, when she had cleaned him up, Mylai Tui managed to drag him inside the house. She tried to lift him up to the bed but was not strong enough.

He lay snoring heavily on the floor.

FOURTEEN

The diabolical machine was finished. It stood outside the small thatched house that was the home of Poul Mer Lo. The two workmen, one a woodcutter and the other a mason, who had built it under the direction of the stranger, stood regarding their achievement, grinning and gibbering like a pair of happy apes. Poul Mer Lo had hired them for the task at a cost of one copper ring each. According to Mylai Tui, it was gross over-payment; but he felt that munificence – if, indeed, it was munificence – was appropriate. It was not often that a man was granted the privilege of devising something that would change the pattern of an entire civilization.

Mylai Tui squatted on the verandah and regarded the machine impassively. She neither understood nor cared that, in the world of Baya Nor, she had just witnessed a technological revolution. If the building of the contraption had given Poul Mer Lo some pleasure, then she was glad for his sake. Nevertheless, she was a little disappointed that a man who was clearly destined for greatness and whose thanu had raised her to ecstasy should dissipate his spirit in the construction of useless toys.

'What do you think of it?' asked Poul Mer Lo.

Mylai Tui smiled. 'It is ingenious, my lord. Who knows, perhaps it is also beautiful. I am not skilled to judge the purpose of this thing it has pleased my lord to create.'

'My name is Paul.'

'Yes, Paul. I am sorry. It is only that it gives me some happiness to call you my lord.'

'Then you must remember, Mylai Tui, that it also gives me some happiness to hear you call me Paul.'

'Yes, Paul. This I know, and this I must remember.'

'Do you know what you are looking at?'

'No, Paul.'

'You are looking at something for which there is no Bayani word. So I must give you a word from my own tongue. This thing is called a cart.'

'A kayurt.'

'No. A cart.'

'A kayrt.'

'That is better. Try it again – cart.'

'Kayrt.'

'This cart runs on wheels. Do you know what wheels are?'

'No, Paul.'

'Say the word – wheels.'

'Wells.'

'That is good. Wheels, Mylai Tui, are what men need to lift the burden from their backs.'

'Yes, Paul.'

'You have seen the poor people hauling logs, carrying water and bending themselves double under heavy loads of kappa and meat.'

'Yes, Paul.'

'The cart,' said Poul Mer Lo, 'will make all this toil no longer necessary. With the cart, one man will be able to carry the burden of many, and because of this many men will be free to do more useful work. Is that not a wonderful thought?'

'Truly, it is a wonderful thought,' responded Mylai Tui obediently.

'Lord,' said one of the workmen, 'now that we have built the kayrt, what is your pleasure?'

'It is my pleasure to visit Enka Ne,' said Poul Mer Lo. 'It is my pleasure to take this gift to the god-king, that in his wisdom, he will cause many carts to be built, thus greatly easing the toil of the people of Baya Nor.'

Suddenly the smile vanished from the face of the small Bayani. 'Lord, to build the kayrt is one thing – indeed, it has given much amusement – but to deliver it to Enka Ne is another.'

'You are afraid?'

'It is proper to be afraid, my lord. It is proper to fear the glory of Enka Ne.'

'It is proper, also,' said Poul Mer Lo, 'to make offerings to the god-king. I am a stranger in this land, and the cart is my offering. Come, let us go … See, I shall ride in the cart and you, taking the shafts, shall draw me. It may be that Enka Ne will have need of men who know how to fit a wheel to an axle. Come.'

Poul Mer Lo perched himself on top of the small cart and waited patiently. The two Bayani muttered briefly to each other and urinated where they stood. He had witnessed such a ritual many times. It was the way in which a low-caste Bayani anticipated sin by giving himself absolution beforehand.

Presently, having touched hands and shoulders, the two men took a shaft each and began to draw the cart slowly along the Road of Travail towards the Third Avenue of the Gods. Poul Mer Lo waved cheerily to Mylai Tui.

'Oruri be with you,' she called, 'at the end as at the beginning.'

'Oruri be with you always,' responded Poul Mer Lo. Then he added informally: 'Let there be the paint of dancing upon you this night. Then shall pleasure visit us both.'

It was a fine morning. The air was clear and warm but not heavy. As Poul

Mer Lo sat on his cart, listening to the squeaky protest of the wooden wheels against the stone axle-tree, he felt at peace with the world.

A light wind was blowing in from the forest. It carried scents that were still strange and intoxicating to him. It carried the incense of mystery, the subtle amalgam of smells that made him feel almost at times that he was the most fortunate man in the universe. Here, indeed, was the farther shore. And his footprints were upon it.

Presently, the cart overtook a group of early morning hunters returning to the city, laden with their kill. They gazed at the vehicle in amazement. Poul Mer Lo smiled at them gaily.

'Oruri greets you,' he said.

'The greeting is a blessing,' they returned.

'Lord,' said one, 'what is the thing upon which you sit and which men may move so easily?'

'It is a cart. It runs on wheels. With the grace of Enka Ne, soon you will be carrying your meat to Baya Nor on carts. Soon the people of Baya Nor will learn to ride on wheels.'

'Lord,' said the hunter, perplexed, 'truly it is a wondrous thing. I pray only that it may be blessed by a sign.'

'What sign?'

'Lord, there is only the sign of Oruri.'

The cart had now reached the end of the Road of Travail, and the broad dirt track gave way to the broader and stone paved Third Avenue of the Gods. The wheels rattled noisily over the cobblestones. There were more people about – city people, sophisticated Bayani, both high and low born, who gazed at Poul Mer Lo with a mixture of what he interpreted as amusement and awe.

He would have been more accurate if he had interpreted the smiling stares as antagonism and awe. But he was not aware of the antagonism until it was too late.

The cart was already half across the causeway leading to the sacred city. By this time it had collected a retinue of more than fifty Bayani. This, in itself, was not unfortunate.

What was unfortunate was that Poul Mer Lo should encounter one of the blind black priests and that the wheels of the cart should pass over his bare toes.

The priest screamed and tore the hood from his face.

His eyes, unaccustomed to daylight, were screwed up painfully for quite a long time before he was able to focus on Poul Mer Lo.

'Oruri will destroy!' he shouted in a loud voice. 'This thing is an affliction to the chosen. Oruri will destroy!'

There was a dreadful silence. Poul Mer Lo gazed at the hoodless priest uncomprehendingly.

Then somebody threw the first stone. It bounced off the cart harmlessly. But it was a signal.

More stones came. The crowd began to rumble. Part of the causeway itself was torn up as ammunition.

'Oruri speaks!' screamed the priest.

And then the stones began to fall like giant hail.

'Stop!' shouted Poul Mer Lo. 'Stop! The cart is a gift for Enka Ne.'

But the woodcutter, holding one of the shafts, had already been struck in the small of the back by a sharp piece of rock. He fell, bleeding. The mason abandoned his shaft and tried to flee. The crowd seized him.

'Stop!' shouted Poul Mer Lo. 'In the name of Enka Ne, I—'

He never finished the sentence. A strangely heavy round pebble, expertly aimed by a child on the fringe of the crowd, caught him on the forehead. He went down with the sound of a great roaring in his ears.

FIFTEEN

Poul Mer Lo was aware of an intense, throbbing pain. He opened his eyes. He was in a room to which there seemed to be no windows. Here and there, smoky oil lamps burned in niches in the stone walls.

He felt cold.

He tried to move, and could not.

He was chained to a stone slab.

A Bayani with a white hood over his face leaned over the slab and peered through narrow eye-slits. 'The spirit has returned,' he announced to someone outside Poul Mer Lo's field of vision. 'Now the stranger will speak.'

'Who – who are you? What am I doing here? What happened?'

'I am Indrui Sa, general of the Order of the Blind Ones. You are Poul Mer Lo, a stranger in this land, quite possibly an instrument of chaos.'

'Where are the two men who were with me?'

'Dead.'

'What happened to them?'

'Oruri crushed them to his bosom. Stranger, they were the victims of chaos. Speak of them no more. Their names are undone. Their fathers had no sons. Their sons had no fathers. They are without meaning … But you, stranger, you Oruri did not take. Oruri looked upon you but he did not take you. This we must understand.'

'I was going to Enka Ne in the sacred city. I was taking him the cart I had caused to be built.'

'Enka Ne had called you?'

'No,' answered Poul Mer Lo.

'Help him,' said the Bayani in the hood.

From out of the gloom another dark shape advanced.

Poul Mer Lo felt the sudden touch of cold metal on his stomach. Then he screamed.

He gazed, horrified, at the pincers gripping a large fold of his flesh.

'I grieve for you,' said Indrui Sa. 'The god-king receives only those who are called … Help him!'

The pincers were tightened and twisted Poul Mer Lo screamed again.

'Thus, perhaps, Oruri hears your sorrow,' said Indrui Sa. 'It may be that your ignorance and presumption will inspire some mercy … Stranger, you rode not upon an animal but upon that which had been built by the hand of man. How call you this thing?'

'It is a cart.'

'Help him!'

Again the pincers were tightened and twisted. Again Poul Mer Lo screamed.

'The kayrt is no more. Oruri saw fit to destroy it. What did you hope to encompass with this kayrt?'

'It was a gift,' sobbed Poul Mer Lo. 'It was a gift to Enka Ne. I thought – I thought that if the god-king saw the use to which the cart could be put, he would cause many of them to be built. Thus would the toil of men be greatly eased.'

'Stranger,' said Indrui Sa, 'human toil is the gift of Oruri. Let no man diminish that gift … Help him.'

Once more the pincers tightened and twisted. Poul Mer Lo screamed and fainted. When he became conscious once more, Indrui Sa was still speaking. He sounded as if he had been speaking a long time.

'And therefore,' said Indrui Sa, 'it is clear, is it not, that you were the uncomprehending instrument of chaos. Two men have been destroyed, the kayrt has been destroyed and the foot of the priest will require much rest. Repent, Poul Mer Lo, of ignorance. Repent also of presumption. Give thanks to Oruri for the blessing of a speedy death which, bearing in mind the degree of chaos you have already inspired is more than—'

Suddenly there was a wild desolate bird cry.

Instantly Indrui Sa stopped speaking and fell upon his face.

Poul Mer Lo heard a rustling and saw a bright, darting bird's head and brilliant plumage that glistened even in the lamplight.

'Who speaks of death?' asked a high, reedy voice.

There was silence.

The god-king gave his piercing cry once more. 'Who speaks of death?'

Indrui Sa picked himself up. 'Lord, the stranger brings chaos.'

'But who speaks of death?'

'Lord, chaos is the product of unbeing, therefore unbeing is the reward of chaos.'

'Oruri hears you, Indrui Sa, most worthy of men and upholder of the law. Oruri hears you and is desirous of your company.'

Indrui Sa stiffened and remained motionless.

Poul Mer Lo was vaguely aware of others coming into the chamber.

Enka Ne uttered his bird cry once more. 'Strike!' he said.

A warrior stepped forward and thrust a short trident into the throat of Indrui Sa. There was a brief whistling noise, then he fell suddenly.

'Release the instrument of chaos,' commanded Enka Ne. Then, without waiting to see if his command was carried out, he turned and left the chamber.

Presently, Poul Mer Lo found himself stumbling up a narrow spiral staircase, stumbling out into the brilliant and painful sunlight.

SIXTEEN

'It is very strange,' said Shah Shan, speaking excellent English, 'this friend-ship that exists between us. We are men of two worlds, Paul. It is strange that Oruri should guide you across the great darkness of space to shed some light in the darkness of my mind.' He laughed. 'One is tempted to look for a pattern.'

'Shah Shan, you have a great talent for learning,' said Paul Marlowe. 'In two hundred days – four Bayani months – you have learned to speak my language better than many people in my own world who have studied it for years.'

'That is because I wish to see into your thoughts.'

'On Earth, we should undoubtedly call you a genius.'

Shah Shan laughed. 'I do not think so. From what you have told me, your planet has many who are more gifted than I.'

'By our reckoning,' said Paul, 'you are nineteen years old – still a boy. Yet you rule a kingdom wisely, and you have assimilated more information in a few months than our most talented young men can assimilate in as many years.'

Shah Shan shrugged. 'Please, Paul, humour me a little. For me the old ways of thinking die hard. Enka Ne rules Baya Nor. Shah Shan is merely his shadow, a simple waterman.'

Paul laughed. 'Ritual schizophrenia.'

'I beg your pardon?'

'I'm sorry. I meant that in a sense you have two excellent minds, both able to perfectly control the same body.'

'Oruri speaks for Enka Ne,' retorted Shah Shan. Then he grinned. 'But Shah Shan is insignificant enough to speak for himself.'

'Paul,' said Mylai Tui in English with an atrocious accent, 'will you dronk some mare kappa spreet?'

'Ask our guest first, love.'

'I am sorry. Shah Shan, police you will dronk?'

Shah Shan held out his calabash. 'Police I will dronk,' he said gravely.

The three of them were taking their ease on the verandah of Paul's little house. It had been a hot day, but though the evening was still warm, the clouded skies had rolled away to reveal a fine, far dusting of stars. Overhead the nine small moons of Altair Five flew raggedly westward like bright migrating birds.

Paul Marlowe looked at the moons and the stars without seeing either. He was thinking of the last few months, of the time since Shah Shan had begun to come to him regularly to learn English. He knew that it was difficult for Enka Ne to make time for Shah Shan, and he had been puzzled as to why the boy should devote so much precious energy and concentration to learning a language that he could only ever hope to speak with one person.

But then he realized that Shah Shan was not so much intent upon learning a language as upon learning all he could of the world that existed on the other side of the sky. Instinctively, the boy knew that the Bayani language was inadequate, that its simple collection of nouns and verbs and qualifying words could only provide a horribly distorted picture of the world that had once belonged to Paul Marlowe.

So Shah Shan, with the typical fanaticism of genius, had applied himself not only to a new language but to the attitudes and philosophy of the one man who spoke that language. He had used Paul like an encyclopaedia; and in four Bayani months he had mastered not only the language but much of the knowledge of the man who spoke it.

'You know, of course,' said Shah Shan, 'that in twenty-three days Enka Ne will return to the bosom of Oruri?'

Paul sighed. 'Yes, I know. But – is it necessary?'

'So it has always been. The god-king reigns for a year. Then Oruri sees fit to renew the form.'

'But is it necessary?'

Shah Shan regarded him calmly. And in the eyes of the boy there seemed to Paul Marlowe to be a wisdom that passed beyond the realm of understanding.

'It is necessary,' said Shah Shan softly. 'The face of a civilization cannot be changed in a single lifetime, Paul. You should know that. If Enka Ne did not offer himself gladly and with great joy, Baya Nor would disintegrate. Factions would arise. Most probably the end would be civil war ... No. Enlightenment must come closely, peacefully. You, the instrument of chaos, are also the instrument of progress. You must plant the seed and hope that others will reap the harvest.'

'Shah Shan, you are the first man to bring tears to my eyes.'

'Let us hope that I am also the last. I know nothing of the new god-king. He has been found already, and is being instructed. But I know nothing of him. It may be that he will be more – what is the word I want?'

'Orthodox?' suggested Paul.

'Yes, more orthodox. Perhaps he will insist on tradition. You will have to be careful.' Shah Shan laughed. 'Remember what happened when you introduced us to the wheel?'

'Three men died,' said Paul. 'But now your citizens are able to use carts, wheelbarrows, rickshaws.'

Shah Shan took a deep draught of the kappa spirit. 'No, Paul, your arithmetic is wrong. I have not told you this before, but Enka Ne was forced to execute one hundred and seventeen priests – mostly of the blind order – in order to preserve your life and to permit the building of carts. It was a high price, was it not?'

Paul Marlowe looked at him, appalled.

SEVENTEEN

It was a grey, cool morning. Winds blew erratically and disturbingly from the forest, filling the city of Baya Nor with strange odours – musky intimations of mortality.

Death had been very much on the mind of Paul Marlowe. It was the prospect of death – and, perhaps, the recent spate of English lessons – that had caused a reversion to type. Poul Mer Lo, the pseudo Bayani, had given way to Paul Marlowe, an Englishman of the twenty-first century of Earth. A man who was depressed and revolted by the fact that his only friend on this alien world would be joyfully going to his death in six more days.

He had grown to love Shah Shan. Love on Earth, reflected Paul bitterly, was suspect if not obsolete. And love for a man was more than obsolete: it was perverted. But here on this other fragment of dust on the other side of the sky, love could be admitted. There need be no justifications, no feelings of guilt, no sense of shame.

But why did he love Shah Shan? Was it because, as Enka Ne, the boy had spared his life when it would have been so much safer, so much easier to have given thumbs down? Was it because, back on that other burnt out particle of fire, he, Paul, had never had a brother? Or a son …

No matter what the reason, the fact remained. Shah Shan was going to die. Or, rather, Enka Ne, the god-king, was drawing close to the bosom of Oruri. And the brightest mind in the whole of Baya Nor was going to be sacrificed to the senseless traditions and superstitions of an ignorant little tribe that had not changed its ways for hundreds of years.

What was that Bayani proverb? He who is alive cannot die. Paul Marlowe laughed. God damn Oruri! Then he laughed again as he realized that he had only called on one god to confound another.

Because of his sadness he had wanted solitude. So he had left the small house and Mylai Tui and had wandered slowly along the bank of the Canal of Life until he came to where the kappa fields met the heavy green perimeter of the forest. And now he was sitting on a small mound, watching the women toiling in the muddy fields as they tended the new crop.

They were singing. The words came to him faintly, intermittently across the indecisive gusts of wind …

A little kappa, a little love.

Oruri listens, waiting above.
A little kappa, a little light.
Oruri brings the gift of night.
A little kappa, a little song.
The day is short, the night is long.'

Yes, thought Paul savagely, God damn Oruri! Oruri was the millstone round these people's necks, the concept that kept them in a static, medieval society with a medieval technology and medieval attitudes that would hold them back for a thousand years.

God damn Oruri!

Suddenly, his silent monologue, his reverie of exasperation was broken by a long-drawn high pitched cry. He had never heard such a cry before. He didn't know whether it was animal or human, whether it was close or distant.

The cry came again, this time ending in a gasp. It was close – so close that he was briefly tempted to believe he had made it himself.

It came from somewhere on the other side of the mound.

He scrambled the few steps to the top of the hillock and looked down. There at the base on the other side a small Bayani woman squatted over a hole in the ground. It looked as if she had scooped the hole out of the rich soft soil with her fingers, for it was arranged in two neat piles on each side of her; and her hands were buried in the fresh, moist earth – presumably supporting her as she squatted.

She had not seen him. Her gaze was fixed directly on the ground ahead of her. As he watched, fascinated, the cry came once more.

It was not a cry of pain, nor was it a cry of fear. For no reason at all, the word keening came into Paul's mind. He had never heard real primitive keening; but this, he supposed, was how it must sound.

Oddly, he felt that he was intruding upon something intensely private. Yet, consumed with curiosity, he wanted to stay and watch. He lay down on the top of the mound, trying to make himself as inconspicuous as possible. For a moment, the woman stretched, raising her head to the sky and sweeping the long hair from her face with a soil-stained hand. Then she fell back into the squatting position and let out another weird cry.

He saw that she was big with child.

And he understood that, for reasons best known to herself, she had come to this desolate spot to give birth.

He witnessed the entire operation. It did not take long. The woman began to pant and bear down rhythmically. Soon the crown of the baby's head had been forced past the lips of the vagina. Presently, its tiny body slid like a small dark fish into the hole that had been prepared for it.

The woman rested for a time – still in the squatting position. Then with a movement that could not have been emulated by any European woman, and probably not by any woman of Earth, she bent expertly down, her head and shoulders low between her knees, and bit through the umbilical cord.

Having done that, she knotted the length that was still attached to the baby's stomach and then lifted the tiny body out of the hole, resting it on one of the piles of soft earth, where it began to cry lustily. It was not long, then, before the afterbirth came. The woman uttered one more cry – softer this time – then stood up and stretched herself. The wind from the forest blew, catching her long hair and streaming it behind her. She looked for a moment like a small black statue, cut from living rock, courageously defying time and the elements.

Then the moment was gone for ever as, with a matter of fact gesture, she scooped up the newborn baby and with her feet swept the soil back into the hole on top of the steaming afterbirth. When the operation was finished, and still clutching the baby possessively to her breast, she stamped the earth flat. Then she sat down cross-legged to examine the child to whom she had just given birth.

Paul Marlowe stared at her, obsessed with the notion that the entire incident was all part of some bizarre dream.

Suddenly, she began to keen once more. This time the sound was shrill and desolate. It was a cry from the soul, a cry of anguish. And he knew that the dream was real.

He stood up. The woman saw him. The sound died in her throat. She held the baby to her apprehensively, almost as if she were trying to deny its existence. For the first time there was fear on her face.

Paul scrambled down the hillock.

'Oruri greets you,' he said gently.

'The greeting is a blessing,' she murmured. But there was a sob in her voice that she did not manage wholly to stifle.

'Forgive me, but I was on the other side of the hill. I heard you and came to see what was happening. I could not help but watch.'

'Lord, there is nothing to forgive.' The tears were streaming down her face. 'Truly, lord, there is nothing to forgive – except that …' she could restrain herself no longer. Sobbing shook her small body; and the child at her breast became silent in the presence, perhaps, of tragedy.

'What is it, my daughter?' Unconsciously Paul lapsed into the vernacular Bayani.

'O, my father, this, before Oruri – for whom I have nothing but love – is my third mortal sin. I weep because the blade of Enka Ne must now pass through my womb and through the fruit of my womb. Unless … Unless …'

Paul Marlowe was perplexed. 'Unless what?'

'Unless my father is graciously able to unsee what he has now seen. Unless the greater purpose of Oruri can only be fulfilled by the departure of myself and this poor fragment of my flesh.'

'My daughter, what is wrong? The child lives and you live. Can more be asked?'

The woman had recovered herself a little. 'Yes, lord,' she said defiantly, 'more can be asked. Much more can be asked. Observe the third sin.' She held out the child.

Paul Marlowe stared at it uncomprehendingly.

'My daughter, you have a fine, strong son. Worse may happen in life than to bear such a child.'

'Observe!' said the woman, almost as a command. She held out the baby's left hand.

Paul Marlowe noted the three tiny fingers and thumb closing and unclosing spasmodically instantly, he felt a slight discomfort and prickling where the small finger had been struck from each of his hands by the orders of Enka Ne a few months ago.

'So, your child is vigorous, my daughter,' he managed to say.

'Observe!' repeated the woman, dully. She held out the baby's right hand. On this one, *four* fingers and a thumb opened and closed spasmodically.

Paul Marlowe was dumbfounded. Four fingers and a thumb!

'Now my father will understand why I must go from this place and not display myself or this mortal sin in Baya Nor.'

He gazed at her blankly.

Suddenly, she fell to her knees and pressed her head against his legs. 'My lord, you are a stranger and therefore, perhaps, Oruri has granted you a greater wisdom. Say only that you will unsee what you have seen. Say only that I may go peacefully from this place. I do not ask more.'

'My daughter, there is much that I do not understand.'

'Lord, there is much that none understands – save Oruri and Enka Ne. Say only that I may go from this place. Say only that you will unsee what you have seen.' She gripped him painfully, beseechingly. He could feel the salt tears from her eyes upon his flesh.

'From me, there is nothing for you to fear,' he said softly.

'Truly, I will unsee what I have seen … But, my daughter, where will you go?'

She pointed to the dark green rim of the forest. 'There, my father, is no sin and no punishment. It is where I and my child will live or die.'

'I hope, then, that you will live,' he managed to say.

The woman rose to her feet, and smiled. 'Pray for me,' she said simply. 'I have much need of it.' She turned away.

As in a trance, Paul Marlowe watched her walk purposefully towards the line of trees and shrubs that swayed in the cool breeze like an emerald sea.

Faintly, the voices of the singers in the kappa fields came to him: '*The day is short, the night is long.*'

EIGHTEEN

After a long day spent in stretching and drying the largest kappa leaves he could find, until they became tough and durable like parchment, Paul Marlowe – feeling oddly, now, more like Poul Mer Lo – occupied his favourite position on the verandah step of his small thatched house. Inside the house, Mylai Tui was cooling kappa spirit by patiently dipping the earthenware jar in a large pitcher of water and allowing the water on the jar to evaporate. Presently, she would bring him a brimming calabash. Presently, he would get drunk.

It was seventeen days since Enka Ne the 609th had returned to the bosom of Oruri. As the sun swung low on the western horizon, Paul Marlowe allowed his gaze to drift across the serene stretch of water that was called the Mirror of Oruri towards the sacred city and the lofty Temple of the Weeping Sun.

He had not been present at the ceremony. Only those of high rank were permitted to be present on such solemn occasions. But Shah Shan had described the ritual to him on his last visit, three days before the event. It was attended, apparently, with all the pomp and ceremony of an ancient terrestrial coronation – with horrific variations.

A coronation in reverse. For as Enka Ne approached the stone phallus against which he would lean joyfully while the living heart was torn from his chest, he would be stripped of all his regalia until nothing remained to be despatched to the bosom of Oruri but Shah Shan, a Bayani waterman with a fine brain and an excellent command of English.

As soon as the blow had been struck and the beating heart removed – to the accompaniment of a great cry of joy from all present – the body would be allowed to fall to the base of the phallus. And then there would be the answering call – a single desolate bird cry; and Enka Ne the 610th would strut from behind the phallus, a bird covered in brilliant plumage, with iridescent feathers of blue and red and green and gold, and with brilliant yellow eyes and a hooked black beak.

The king is dead. Long live the king!

Thus would the enduring glory of Oruri have been reaffirmed.

Paul Marlowe gazed across the water at the Temple of the Weeping Sun. And tears ran down his cheeks, unheeded.

Mylai Tui brought the calabash, full of cooled spirit.

'Thank you, my love,' said Paul in English.

'Think nothing of it,' said Mylai Tui dutifully. It was a phrase she had learned most carefully. She sat patiently, waiting for the further commands of her lord.

Paul took a deep draught of the kappa spirit. Fire coursed through his veins. But his head remained cool and empty.

He was thinking of what Shah Shan had said to him at their last meeting.

'You must not be sad, Paul,' he had said. 'You do not yet understand the ways of my people. But you must not be sad. It may be that Enka Ne will think of you when he is called. It may be that he will wish to send you some small token for the kindness and patience you have shown to an insignificant waterman.'

Sure enough, on the day of the sacrifice, a black Bayani of the god-king's personal guard had brought him one hundred and twenty-eight copper rings and one long green feather from the plumage of Enka Ne. Paul had been about to ask him if Enka Ne had sent any message, when the great cry of sacrifice drifted across the water from the Temple of the Weeping Sun. A look of intense happiness had come over the face of the small Bayani warrior. Without a word, he had reversed his short trident and, with a tremendous thrust, plunged it into his own throat. The death was spectacular and messy, but it was also almost instantaneous.

Paul Marlowe took another drink from the calabash and gazed at Mylai Tui.

'Do you remember a bright lad by the name of Shah Shan,' he said in English thickly, 'a youngster whose eyes were full of fire and whose brain was full of nine million nine hundred and ninety-nine thousand question marks?'

'I do not understand, lord,' answered Mylai Tui in Bayani. She was accustomed to his increasing use of the strange tongue, but rarely accustomed to his meaning.

'Say Paul, blast you.'

'I am sorry, Paul,' she said in English. 'You speak too quickly.'

He switched to Bayani. 'Do you remember Shah Shan – the first time he came to this house?'

'Yes, lord,' she answered in Bayani. 'I remember the first visit of Shah Shan. He was very thin, very hungry.'

Paul took another drink. 'He had bright, searching eyes. He had the gift of greatness … I am sad that he will come no more.'

'Lord,' said Mylai Tui simply, 'I rejoice, having seen the visage of a god upon the face of a man.'

'The god is now dead,' said Paul grimly.

'No, lord, the man is now dead. The god lives. So it has always been. So it will always be.'

'World without end,' he mocked, raising the calabash to his lips. For some time, now, his relationship with Mylai Tui had been strained. Thinking back, he decided that it had begun to show signs of strain when Shah Shan started to come regularly for his English lessons. Until that time, Paul Marlowe, native of Earth had done his best – despite lapses – to become Poul Mer Lo of Baya Nor. He had been very reliant on Mylai Tui and had tried to draw close to her and understand her way of looking at things.

But then Shah Shan with his quick mind and natural curiosity had met him on his own ground and, learning not only the language but the ways of the land on the other side of the sky, had encouraged Paul to remember with some pride that he was a twenty-first century European. Shah Shan had learned English far faster and much more fluently than Mylai Tui. By skilfully stimulating his teacher, he had precipitated Paul into journeying back through space and time to his own world. Shah Shan had a flair for grasping intuitively. With remarkably few words, Paul could create a scene for him – whether in a London street or on a rocket launching pad or on an East Anglian farm – that was both vivid and immediate. Under a joint spell of perception, they could together travel far and recreate much, while Mylai Tui was left hopelessly behind – lost in a welter of complex and meaningless words.

It was then Paul had discovered that, despite her discipline and training as a noia in the Temple of Gaiety, she was inclined to be jealous and possessive. She wanted the stranger for herself. At first her possessiveness amused him. Then it began to annoy him.

Oddly enough, Mylai Tui had displayed another aspect of her strange temper for the first time a few days before Enka Ne – or Shah Shan – was due to die. It had been caused by the incident Paul had witnessed on the morning he had walked along the Canal of Life to sit down and stare idly at the toilers in the kappa fields.

Although he had promised the woman who had given birth to her baby on the other side of the mound where he was sitting that would 'unsee what he had seen', he had taken the promise literally only insofar as not mentioning the place or the time to anyone. He would not betray her, but neither would he attempt in the literal sense to unsee what he had seen. It was, perhaps, his most important discovery in Baya Nor.

Mylai Tui had three fingers and a thumb on each hand. Everyone else he had met had three fingers and a thumb on each hand. And, because of the command of Enka Ne at their first meeting, he himself now conformed, having had each of his little fingers struck off.

Consequently, he had assumed that three fingers was normal – biologically normal. But what if that were not entirely so? The woman on the other side of the mound had given birth to a baby with three fingers on one hand and

381

four fingers on the other. How many more women in Baya Nor bore children with four fingers and a thumb on one of their hands? And, carrying the thought further, how many women bore children with four fingers and a thumb on each of their hands?

That day, after returning home, he had asked Mylai Tui to let him see her hands. It was then he realized that he had never looked at them closely – really closely – before. He inspected them, cursing his rudimentary knowledge of anatomy and bemoaning the fact that he did not have a magnifying glass.

Then he discovered that the bone bump on the side of her left hand was perhaps a little longer and more uneven than the bump on the side of her right hand. He took her left hand again, staring at it intently. Surely, there was the faintest mark of a scar?

'Mylai Tui, did you ever have four fingers on this hand?' he had asked abruptly.

She had snatched the hand away from him as if he had offered her a deadly insult. And she had stood there, shaking and trembling and staring at him with eyes wide with horror.

At first, he thought she had misunderstood him. 'I ask only if you ever had four fingers on this hand,' he had repeated.

'Defiler!' she screamed. 'Outlander! Beast! Savage!'

Then she had fled from the house.

He was completely baffled. Time passed, night came, and he thought that perhaps she had gone for good. She did not return until shortly before dawn of the following day. Then she came back and woke him up peremptorily. She was carrying a long thin korshl – the Whip of Correction that was used on petty criminals.

'Oruri has condescended to give guidance,' she said tonelessly. 'I have offended my lord. The offence cannot remain. Grace me with one blow of the korshl for each of the fingers on my hands.'

He was dumbfounded. 'Mylai Tui, I cannot do this thing.'

'That is my punishment,' she said, 'according to the wisdom of Oruri. Six blows from my lord – or I must leave this house where I have been shamed for ever.'

He saw that she meant it. He did not wish to lose her. Still not understanding, he took the korshl.

'Lay heavy, lord,' said Mylai Tui, presenting her back. 'Oruri frowns upon a light penance.'

He struck, but apparently he did not strike hard enough. For his kindness which, said Mylai Tui, she did not deserve, Oruri would graciously award her two extra blows.

Early in the morning and still heavy with sleep, Paul Marlowe found himself participating in a waking nightmare. Mylai Tui was clearly not to be satisfied until the blood ran down her back. Eventually, in desperation, he did in fact draw blood. The sight of it dropping down to make small thin rivulets on her legs seemed to give Mylai Tui considerable satisfaction.

When the prescribed punishment was over, she fainted. Since that time he had not dared to refer to her fingers again.

Now, as he sat on the verandah step, sipping his kappa spirit, he became suddenly filled with a great and impersonal sadness – not only for himself and Shah Shan and Mylai Tui, but for all living things on all possible worlds scattered throughout the black starlit vault of space. He was sad because of the very predicament of living. Because every living creature – like the guyanis, the brilliantly coloured butterfly that he had seen killed by a leathery bird when he travelled with Enka Ne along the Canal of Life – was doomed to journey from darkness to darkness, with only a brief burst of sunlight and pain between the two long aspects of eternity. The guyanis had died, then the bird who had killed it was struck down by a warrior, then the warrior himself died at the command of Enka Ne. Now Enka Ne was dead and another Enka Ne was alive. And doubtless many more guyanis butterflies had been torn to pieces by toothed beaks. And doubtless many more warriors had gone to the bosom of Oruri.

Multiply these things by a billion billion, square the number and square it again. The resulting figure would still not be big enough to tally all the tragedies, great and small, taking place throughout the universe during one billion billionth part of a second.

Yes, thought Paul, living was indeed a sad situation – only slightly less sad than dying …

The sun had set and the nine moons of Altair Five were swarming silently across the sky. They were not bright enough to cast nine distinct shadows. They merely coated the sadness of the world with a threadbare film of silver.

Suddenly, Paul dropped the calabash and stiffened. Coming along the dusty track leading to his house there was a youth clad in a tattered samu and carrying a begging bowl. There was something about the walk, something about the gaunt moon-silver features … Paul Marlowe realized that he was trembling.

'Oruri greets you,' said the boy.

'The greeting is a blessing,' responded Paul mechanically.

'Blessed also are they who have seen many wonders.' The boy smiled. 'I am Zu Shan, the brother of Shah Shan. I am also the gift of Enka Ne.'

NINETEEN

It was the middle of the night. Mylai Tui was asleep. Paul was awake. Outside the house, Zu Shan was lying half awake and half asleep with three other boys on a rough pile of bedding in the skeleton of the school that he was helping to build for Poul Mer Lo, the teacher.

Almost five Bayani months had passed since Enka Ne the 610th had assumed his spiritual and temporal role. During that time he had consistently ignored Poul Mer Lo. The attitude of Enka Ne passed down through his council, his administration and his religious orders. It was as if those who controlled the destiny of Baya Nor had decided to unsee what they had seen.

All of which, thought Paul, was very strange. For though he had intentionally kept out of the way of the new god-king, he had continued with his innovations. The school was one of them.

It had started really with Zu Shan, who was the first official pupil. Then, as Paul was wandering through the city one morning, he came across a beggar – a small boy of five or six who, even by Bayani standards, seemed exceedingly dull-witted. He did not even know his own name. Looking at him, seeing his ribs sticking out and the tight flesh clinging pathetically to the bones of his misshapen legs, Paul was more than ordinarily moved. He was quite accustomed to the sight of beggars in Baya Nor, for the economy was not prosperous and the organization of labour was atrocious.

But this small child – though there were others like him – appeared to possess a mute eloquence. He did not talk much with his lips. All real communication seemed at first to be made with his eyes. They alone seemed to tell his entire story – a common one. He came of a family that was too large, he was not old enough or strong enough to do useful work, and in desperation his parents had trained him to beg and consigned him to the care of Oruri.

Then the eyes had said: 'Pick me up, take me home. Pick me up, take me home.' Impulsively, Paul had scooped up the bony bundle and had taken it back to Mylai Tui. The boy would never be able to walk properly, for the parents, with practical consideration for the child's career as a beggar, had broken the bones in both legs in several places, and they had knit together in a crazy and grotesque fashion.

Paul called the boy Nemo. He never did need to talk a great deal. It was not until later that Paul discovered he was a natural telepath.

After Zu Shan and Nemo there came Bai Lut, a one-armed youth whose right arm had been struck off for persistent stealing. And after Bai Lut there was Tsong Tsong, who had been fished out of the Mirror of Oruri, more dead than alive and who could not or would not remember anything of his past – though, at the age of perhaps eleven, he could not have had much past to remember.

And that was the entire complement of the Paul Marlowe Extra-Terrestrial Academy for Young Gentlemen.

As he paced up and down the room, while the small night lamp sent up thin desultory spirals of smoke, Paul thought of his school and of his achievements – or lack of them. He thought of the many hours he had spent simply trying to teach that the earth was round and not flat. He thought of the seemingly endless number of dried kappa leaves he had covered with charcoal scrawl, trying to demonstrate that it was possible to record words in the form of writing. He had modified some of the conventional sounds of the letters in the Roman alphabet to accommodate the Bayani tongue and he had stuck to a more or less phonetic form of writing.

But, with the exception of little Nemo, who was just about capable of writing his own name and those of his companions, no one seemed to grasp that it was possible to assign a logical sequence of meanings to a few marks on some dried kappa leaves. Or that even if it were, the operation could have any conceivable use other than the gratification of Poul Mer Lo.

On more practical and amusing levels, however, there had been more successes. Zu Shan had developed a flair for building small gliders, Bai Lut was good at making kites, and Tsong Tsong had – with some help – fashioned a successful model windmill which he used, oddly enough, to power a fan.

The boys seemed fascinated by the idea of harnessing the wind. It was something they could understand. Perhaps in the end, thought Paul, he would achieve a transient immortality by introducing the wheel and the use of wind power to the inhabitants of Baya Nor.

But what else could he do? What else was he equipped to do?

He did not know. Nor did he know whether the new god-king was really ignoring him or merely waiting for the stranger, who had enjoyed the favour of his predecessor, to commit some offence that would justify his permanent removal.

The uncertainty by itself did not worry him too much. What did worry him was his own feeling of inadequacy, his growing mood of futility and, above all, his isolation. He had begun to think more and more of Earth. He had begun to live more and more in the past. He dreamed of Earth, he day dreamed of Earth, he longed to be back on Earth.

If he couldn't develop some kind of mental discipline to shut Earth away in a tiny compartment of his mind, he would presently go quite crazy. And that would be the saddest joke of all – one demented psychiatrist, the sole survivor of the expedition to Altair Five.

Mylai Tui groaned in her sleep. He stopped pacing up and down and decided that he would try to get some sleep himself. He glanced at her in the dim light and noted vaguely that she was getting rather fat. Then he lay down by her side and closed his eyes.

He still could not sleep. Visions of Earth kept drifting into his mind. He tried to concentrate on the school and calculate how long it would take to build with the help of four boys, two of whom were crippled.

Long enough, perhaps, to bring Enka Ne the 610th to the stone of sacrifice. Or Poul Mer Lo to a state of melancholic withdrawal from which there would be no return.

He let his arm rest lightly on Mylai Tui, feeling the soft warm flesh of her breast rise and fall rhythmically. It gave him no comfort. He was still staring blankly at the mud-cemented thatch of the ceiling when dawn came.

TWENTY

Two workmen had just delivered a load of rough-hewn wood for strengthening the framework of the small school. Poul Mer Lo noted with satisfaction that the wood had been brought on a four-wheeled cart complete with a two-man harness. He also noted with even greater satisfaction that the small Bayanis took their cart very much for granted. They might have been accustomed to using such vehicles for years instead of only for a matter of months. Poul Mer Lo – and this was one of the days when he did not think it was such a bad thing to be Poul Mer Lo, the teacher – wondered how long it would be before some Bayani genius decided that the front pair of wheels, their axle linked to a guiding shaft, would be more efficiently employed if they could swing on a vertical pivot.

But perhaps a vertical pivot and guiding mechanism for the front axle-tree was as yet too revolutionary a concept – as revolutionary as differential gears might have been to an eighteenth-century European coach-builder. Perhaps it would require a few more generations before the Bayani themselves added refinements to the new method of transport that had been introduced by the stranger. Certainly, Poul Mer Lo decided, he would not present them with the device himself. It would be a mistake not to let the Bayani do some of their own discovering.

It was a warm, sunny morning. When they had unloaded their wood, the workmen rested a while, wiped the sweat from their foreheads and regarded with obvious amusement the crazy structure that was being built by two boys and two cripples. Poul Mer Lo gave them the copper ring he had promised, and there was much exchange of courtesies.

Then one of them said somewhat diffidently: 'Lord, what is this thing that you cause these lost ones to raise? Is it, perhaps, to be a temple for the gods of your own country?'

'It is not to be a temple,' explained Poul Mer Lo, 'but a school.' There was no word for school in the Bayani language so he simply introduced the English word.

'A sku-ell?'

'That is right,' answered Poul Mer Lo gravely. 'A school.'

'Then for what purpose, lord, is this sku-ell to be raised?'

'It is to be a place where children come to learn new skills.'

The Bayani scratched his head and thought deeply. 'Lord, does not the son of a hunter learn to hunt and the son of a carver learn to carve?'

'That is so.'

'Then, lord, you do not need this sku-ell,' said the Bayani triumphantly, 'for the young learn by watching the old, such is the nature of life.'

'That is true,' said Poul Mer Lo. 'But consider. These are children now without fathers. Also the skills that they shall learn shall be skills such as their fathers have not known.'

The Bayani was puzzled. 'It is known that lost ones are the beloved of Oruri, from whom they will receive that which they are destined to receive ... Also, lord, may not new skills be dangerous?'

'New skills may indeed be dangerous,' agreed Poul Mer Lo, 'but so also may old skills be dangerous. The school is where – with the blessing of Oruri – these lost ones may perhaps gather some small wisdom.'

The Bayani was baffled, but he said politely: 'Wisdom is good to have, lord – but surely Enka Ne is the source of wisdom?'

'Without doubt, Enka Ne is the greatest source of wisdom in Baya Nor,' said Poul Mer Lo carefully, 'but it is good, is it not, that lesser beings should endeavour to achieve wisdom?'

The Bayani urinated on the spot. 'Lord, these matters are too great for poor men to consider ... Oruri be with you.' He signalled to his companion, and they picked up the harness of the cart.

'Oruri be with you always,' responded Poul Mer Lo, 'at the end as at the beginning.'

He watched them as they trundled the cart back along the Road of Travail towards the Third Avenue of the Gods.

For a while he supervised the stacking of the timber. Then, because the day was hot, he sat down to rest in the shadow of the small patch of roofing already on top of the school house.

Presently Nemo scuttled towards him, sideways, legs all twisted and arms used as forelegs, like some pathetic hybrid of crab and baboon. His small wizened face was creased in an expression of perplexity.

'Lord, I may speak with you?' asked the child formally.

'Yes, Nemo, you may speak with me.'

The boy circled in the dust, vainly endeavouring to make himself comfortable.

'Lord, in the night that has passed my head was filled with strange creatures and strange voices. I am troubled. It is said that those who listen to the people of the night go mad.'

Poul Mer Lo gazed at him curiously. 'Tell me first of the creatures.'

'I do not know whether they were animals or men, lord,' said Nemo. 'They were encased in a strange substance that caught the sunlight and became a thing of fire, as sometimes does the surface of water when a man sits by the Mirror of Oruri. They were tall, these beings, and they walked upon two legs. The skin of their head was smooth and hard like ring money. In their heads they carried weapons or tools. Truly they were terrible to behold. Also their god was with them.'

'Their god?' echoed Poul Mer Lo blankly.

'Yes, lord, for such a being could only be a god.'

'Describe this god, then.'

'It was many times the height of many men, lord. It came down from the sky, walking upon a column of fire that scorched the white earth, transforming it into great clouds of steam and a torrent of water. Then, when the steam had subsided and the water was no more, the god opened his belly and brought forth many tall children – those whose skin was as fire in the sunlight.'

Poul Mer Lo was trembling. He was also sweating profusely. And, sweating and trembling, he could visualize the scene almost as clearly as Nemo.

'Tell me more,' he said hoarsely. 'Tell me more of this vision that came to you in the night.'

'Lord there is no more to tell. I saw and was afraid.'

'What of the voices, then?'

Nemo frowned with concentration. 'The voices did not seem to come from the creatures, lord. They came from the god.'

'Try to remember, Nemo, what they said. It is important.'

The boy smiled. 'They, at least, did not frighten me, lord; for they spoke chiefly in riddles.'

Poul Mer Lo wiped the sweat from his forehead and forced himself to be calm. If he could not stay calm he would never get the rest of the story from Nemo. And it was important that he should learn all that the boy knew. It was more important than anything else in his life.

'Tell me these riddles, Nemo, for it may be that I shall understand.'

Nemo looked at him curiously. 'Lord, are you ill or tired? I should not weary you with my unimportant thoughts if you are not well.'

Poul Mer Lo made a great effort to control himself. 'It is nothing, Nemo. I am in good health. Your story interests me ... What were these riddles?'

Nemo laughed. ''All men are brothers,' he said. 'That, surely, is a fine riddle, lord, is it not?'

'Yes, Nemo, it is a very good riddle. What else?'

'There are lands beyond the sky where the seed of man has taken root ... That, too, is very funny.'

'It is indeed funny ... Is that all?'

'No, lord. There is one more riddle – the most amusing. It is that some day the god with the tail of fire will unite all the children of all the lands beyond the sky into a family which will be numberless, as are the drops of water in the Mirror of Oruri.'

'Nemo,' said Poul Mer Lo quietly, 'what you have dreamed is a most wonderful dream. I cannot understand how these things could be made known to you. But I believe that there is much truth in what you have seen and heard. I hope that you will have such dreams again. If that happens – if you should again receive the grace of Oruri – I hope also that you will tell me all that you can remember.'

Nemo seemed relieved. 'Those afflictions will not bring madness, then?'

Poul Mer Lo laughed – and tried vainly to suppress the note of hysteria in his voice. 'No, they will not bring madness, Nemo. Nor are they afflictions. They are the gift of Oruri.'

At that point Mylai Tui came from the house with a calabash and a jug of watered kappa spirit. Seeing her, Nemo scuttled away. He and Mylai Tui hated each other. Their hatred was the product of jealousy.

'Paul,' said Mylai Tui gaily in English. 'I wish you to drink. I wish you to drink as I drink, so that the joy will be shared.'

She poured some of the watered kappa spirit into the calabash then raised it to her own lips and handed it to him. She seemed happier than she had been for many, many days.

'What is this joy of which you speak?' he said haltingly in Bayani. His head was reeling.

'Oruri has looked upon us,' explained Mylai Tui.

'I am no wiser.'

Mylai Tui laughed. 'My lord, you are great with wisdom but not with perception.' She pirouetted. 'Whereas I,' she continued, 'am now indisputably great with child.'

TWENTY-ONE

It was in the seventh month of the reign of Enka Ne the 610th that the forest tribe known to the people of Baya Nor as the Lokhali attacked the temple of Baya Lys. Although Baya Lys was three days' journey from Baya Nor overland, it was only one full day's journey away on the Canal of Life. Apart from the ignominy of having a temple desecrated and its priestly occupants put to death in various dreadful ways, the Bayani felt that this warlike tribe was getting too near to the sacred city for comfort.

Accordingly, Enka Ne declared a holy war. The standing army of Baya Nor was swollen by volunteers; and when the oracle decreed that the time and circumstances were propitious for victory, over two thousand men moved off into the forest along the overland route.

Poul Mer Lo had asked to be allowed to go with them, not because he had any desire to participate in the kind of bloody vengeance that the Bayani were eagerly anticipating, but because he remembered the last evening of the religious progress on which he had been permitted to accompany Enka Ne the 609th.

While he was spending a restless night in one of the guest cells of Baya Lys, Shah Shan had come to him, bringing a bundle that had contained one plastic visor, two atomic grenades and a wrecked transceiver. These, said Shah Shan, had been found by the priests of Baya Lys near a blackened hole in the forest – in territory that was near to the land occupied by the Lokhali.

When Poul Mer Lo had suggested that Enka Ne might treat with the Lokhali to obtain news of any survivors from the *Gloria Mundi*, Shah Shan had rejected the idea instantly. The Lokhali, he had explained, lived for war. Not only was it impossible to have peaceful relations with them, but it was also beneath the dignity of the superior and civilized people of Bay Nor.

There the matter had ended. Since that time, Poul Mer Lo had not pressed his suggestion, knowing that in matters of this nature even Enka Ne, alias Shah Shan, had a closed mind.

But now the Lokhali had broken the uneasy state of peace – or, more accurately, non-war – that had existed between them and the Bayani. It was a golden opportunity for going along with the avenging army and trying to discover if any of the Lokhali had encountered any survivors of the *Gloria Mundi*. Twelve people had travelled in the star ship. Three were accounted for. But of the remaining nine there had been no news whatsoever. The forest might have swallowed them. Or the occupants of the forest. There was no trace of them save the relics that Shah Shan had brought to the guest cell at Baya Lys.

Poul Mer Lo's application was rejected. It was rejected in person by Enka Ne in the Temple of the Weeping Sun.

It was the first and last time Poul Mer Lo had audience with Enka Ne the 610th. Unlike his predecessor, he was an old, old man. The ceremonial plumage lay ill upon him. His bird cry was thin and reedy. He strutted sadly, like one who was too heavily burdened with care and responsibility – which, probably, was the case.

'I am told you are a teacher, Poul Mer Lo,' he had said.

'Yes, lord, that is so.'

'It is the province of a teacher to teach, is it not?'

'Yes, lord.'

'Then teach, Poul Mer Lo, and leave more weighty matters to those who know how best to deal with them. The hunter should remain with his darts, the warrior with his trident, and the teacher with his – what is the word you have given us? – sku-ell.'

Then Enka Ne uttered his desolate bird cry, indicating that the audience was at an end. As Poul Mer Lo withdrew, he heard the god-king vainly trying to stifle a paroxysm of coughing.

The expedition against the Lokhali was brief and successful. After eleven days, the victorious army – minus about four hundred and fifty casualties – returned to Baya Nor with nearly one hundred prisoners.

Enka Ne addressed the prisoners at considerable length in the sacred city, regardless of the fact that they could not understand a word of what he was saying. Then he decreed that every eighth man should be set free, without food or weapons, to make his way back – if he could – to the land of the Lokhali, there to report on the clemency and omnipotence of Enka Ne. The remainder were to be crucified on the Fourth Avenue of the Gods to demonstrate the vengeance of Oruri and the unprofitability of attacking Bayani temples.

On the day of crucifixion, which had been declared a day of celebration and rejoicing, Poul Mer Lo, in common with several thousand Bayani, strolled along the Fourth Avenue of the Gods.

Apart from the fact that nearly ninety men were dying in a slow and altogether gruesome manner, the scene was vaguely reminiscent of a terrestrial fair or carnival. Cheapjacks were offering various delicacies and novelties, jinricksha men – using two-wheeled carriages, by grace of the stranger, Poul Mer Lo – were doing a roaring trade in slow journeys between the rows of wooden crosses. And children were working off their surplus energies by pelting the dying Lokhali with stones, offal and small aromatic missiles compounded of excreta.

Poul Mer Lo, steeling himself against the suffering, passed the dying Lokhali, one by one, and tried to observe them with scientific detachment.

He failed. The stench and the pain and the cries were too much for him. He did not even notice that they were all taller than the Bayani or that most of them possessed four fingers and a thumb.

However, as he passed one who was clearly *in extremis*, he heard a few words – half murmured, half moaned – that stopped him in his tracks and brought back visions of a world that he would never see again.

'*Grüss Gott*,' sobbed the Lokhali, '*Grüss Gott!* Thank you … Thank you … "*chantez de faire votre connaissance*" … Man … Woman … Good morning … Good night. Hello! Hello! Hello!'

'Where are they?' demanded Poul Mer Lo in Bayani.

There was no response.

'Where are they – the strangers?' he repeated in English.

Again there was no response.

'*Ou est les étrangers?*'

Suddenly the Lokhali's body jerked spasmodically. Then he gave a great cry and hung slackly on the wooden cross.

In a fury of frustration, Poul Mer Lo began to shake the corpse.

But there was no miracle of resurrection.

TWENTY-TWO

Paul Marlowe was no longer quite so dissatisfied with his 'Extra-Terrestrial Academy'. In the last few months both Zu Shan and Nemo had made quite remarkable progress. Once Paul had managed to convince them that it was both a privilege and a pleasure for any thinking person to find out as much as possible about the world in which he exists, and that knowledge brought the power to accomplish much that could not be otherwise achieved, the boy and the crippled child became filled with insatiable curiosity.

It was as if something had exploded in their minds, sweeping away all the inhibitions, the closed-thought attitudes, and the deadening traditions of centuries of Bayani culture. The sophisticated savages became primitive scientists. They no longer accepted what they were told. They challenged it, they tried to refute it, they asked awkward questions. By Earth standards, Zu Shan was about fifteen – three or four years younger than his dead brother – and Nemo could not be more than six. Yet hardship and suffering had brought them a premature maturity. So that when they did eventually grasp the importance of learning, they began to learn at a very high speed.

The same could not be said of either the one-armed Bai Lut or Tsong Tsong. They did not have the spark. Their minds would never get into top gear. Temperamentally, they were hewers of wood and drawers of water. They lacked imagination – and that strange ability to take an intuitive leap into the dark. They were content to play with toys, whereas Zu Shan and Nemo, though not above playing with toys, also wished to play with ideas.

Zu Shan, sensing perhaps that there was more to be got from his teacher than could properly be expressed in Bayani, began to learn English. Nemo, not to be outdone, also elected to learn what was for all practical purposes a 'dead tongue'.

But, besides providing the means for expressing new concepts, it gave them a sense of status to be able to talk to Paul in his own language. It gave them, too, a sense of intimacy, and drew the three of them close together.

Zu Shan was never quite as fluent as his brother in speaking the language of the stranger; but he soon learned enough to say all that he needed to say – if he took his time about it. Nemo, though younger, had an advantage. He had already discovered that on occasion he could establish sufficient *en rapport* to read minds.

The three of them were sitting on the verandah step one evening while

Paul sipped his kappa spirit. It had been a hard but pleasant day, for they had completed the building of the school. It contained chairs and tables, a potter's wheel, a small furnace for baking pots, a few kappa leaf charts and some tools that the boys had designed themselves. It also contained four rough beds. It was the first boarding school in Baya Nor.

'You are looking far away, Paul,' said Zu Shan. 'What are you thinking about?'

Nemo smiled. 'He is thinking about many things,' he announced importantly. 'He is thinking about the stars, and about the words of the dying Lokhali soldier, and about the star ship in which he came to Altair Five, and about a white-skinned woman. I have been riding his thoughts, but there are so many different ones that I keep falling off.'

Nemo's favourite description for his telepathic exercise was 'riding thoughts'. To him it seemed a very accurate description; for he had discovered that people do not think tidily, and that their mental processes are frequently disjointed – which was why he could not receive for very long without 'falling off.'

Paul laughed as the tiny crippled Bayani recited the revealing catalogue. 'You will get yourself into trouble one of these days, Nemo,' he observed. 'You will ride a thought which tells you that I am about to drop you into the Canal of Life.'

'Then I shall try to avoid the disaster,' retorted Nemo complacently.

'Have you had any new dreams recently about the god who brought forth strange children from his belly?'

'No, only the old dream. I have it quite frequently now. I'm getting used to it.'

Paul sighed. 'I wish you could arrange to dream in greater detail. I wish, too, that I knew where you got the dream from. It could, I suppose, be something you have picked up out of my dreams.'

Nemo rolled his oddly ancient eyes. 'Lord,' he said in Bayani, 'I would not dare to trespass in your sleeping journeys.'

Suddenly Zu Shan sat upright. 'I have just remembered something that may explain Nemo's dream,' he said. 'Have you ever heard the legend of the coming, Paul?'

'No. Tell me about it.'

'It is a story that mothers tell their children,' went on Zu Shan. 'It must be very, very old ... You know, of course, that Oruri can take many shapes?'

'Yes.'

'The story goes that long ago there were no people at all in the land of Baya Nor – I mean, on Altair Five – but that Oruri looked down on this world and saw that it was good. Therefore he came and stood on a white mountain and looked over the land. And out of his great happiness, many people were born,

395

and they walked down from the mountain to play as children in the new world that Oruri had found. According to the legend, Oruri stands waiting on the white mountain. He is waiting until the people are tired of their play. Then they will go back to him and he will return with them to the world from which he came.'

'It is a good legend,' commented Paul, taking a draught of his kappa spirit. 'The plot thickens, does it not?'

'What do you mean, Paul?'

'Only that I cannot help seeing Oruri as a star ship … I think too much of star ships, these days … And yet … And yet Nemo dreams of creatures in strange metallic clothing. And his god descends on a column of fire as a star ship would. And the god opens his belly …'

'Paul.'

'Yes, Zu Shan?'

'If the hunters are to be believed there is such a mountain – many days' travel to the north. They call it the Temple of the White Darkness. They say it is protected by strange voices, and that a man may approach it but the voices will either turn him back or drive him mad. They say that if he is courageous enough to approach the mountain, he will only stiffen and die.'

Paul Marlowe took another drink of the kappa spirit. 'I am not surprised, Zu Shan. I am not at all surprised … You have never seen snow, have you?'

'No, you have told us about it. But I don't think there is anyone in Baya Nor who has ever seen it.'

Paul felt suddenly elated and happy. Maybe it was the kappa spirit. Or maybe …

'Do you know,' he said, after a brief silence. 'I think you two are going to make history. I think you are going to see snow.' He hiccupped. 'Damn it, I wonder how much ring money I shall need to buy the services of half a dozen really good hunters?'

'Paul,' said Zu Shan, 'I do not think there is enough ring money in Baya Nor to persuade six hunters to go through the Lokhali country towards the Temple of the White Darkness.'

'I have something better than ring money,' said Paul. 'It is about time I showed you my sweeper rifle. Your brother, who permitted me to keep it, is the only Bayani who has ever seen what it can do.'

TWENTY-THREE

Unintentionally, the one-armed Bai Lut, a youth without any great degree of intelligence or initiative, changed the course of history not only on Altair Five but on many worlds about which he would never know. He changed the course of history by building a kite. It was a beautiful kite constructed of slivers of springy yana wood and with the wind-catching surfaces painstakingly woven from musa reed which, when separated into its fibres was used to weave musa loul, the kind of cloth known to the Bayani.

The kite had taken Bai Lut many days to make. It was in the shape of a giant guyanis butterfly. Bai Lut had dreamed of building such a kite for a long time. Having only one arm, he had to work hard with his toes as well as his fingers. When it was finished, he regarded his achievement with awe. It was truly beautiful. He would have been quite content to die after such an achievement – or, at least, after he had seen it fly successfully – for it did not seem possible to do anything greater in life.

He prayed for a smooth, steady wind. His prayer was answered. And, with about two hundred metres of 'string' made from twisted hair – which had taken longer to manufacture than the kite itself – he flew the musawinged guyanis and watched it soar joyously over the Canal of Life and lean high, almost yearningly, over the Mirror of Oruri towards the sacred city.

It may be that Bai Lut had prayed too ardently to Oruri for a wind. Because, when all of Bai Lut's string was extended and the kite was as high as it could go, a great gust came – so suddenly that the string snapped.

It was a tribute to Bai Lut's craftsmanship and intuitive grasp of aerodynamics that the guyanis kite did not immediately spiral down into the Mirror of Oruri. Instead it began to execute graceful curves, losing little altitude, but gliding almost purposefully towards the sacred city. Presently it was no more than a slowly descending speck in the sky. Presently it was out of sight.

And then the wind dropped, and the kite dropped. But Bai Lut did not know where to look for it. He was miserable with the conviction that he would never see it again. And in that he was right. For it had come to rest in the Temple of the Weeping Sun; and, though he fortunately did not know it, the guyanis kite had fallen on the stone phallus of sacrifice.

The following day, Poul Mer Lo was giving a lesson in school to his four pupils on basic mechanics and specifically on the use of the lever. He had demonstrated how a lever could be employed to do work that a man alone could not accomplish and was about to embark on the theory of the calculation of forces when he was interrupted by Nemo.

'Lord,' said the tiny cripple formally in Bayani, 'the warriors of Enka Ne are approaching along the Road of Travail.'

Poul Mer Lo looked at the small boy in surprise. He was surprised not only by the interruption but by the formal method of address.

'The warriors of Enka Ne pass many times along the Road of Travail, Nemo. What has this to do with that which now concerns us?'

'Lord,' said Nemo in some agitation. 'I have been riding the thoughts of the captain. The warriors are coming here. They are in a hurry. I think they will arrive very soon.'

Poul Mer Lo tried not to betray his anxiety. 'In which case, we will pass the time considering how this instrument that I have shown you may be used to ease the burden of man.'

'Paul,' said Nemo desperately, breaking into English, 'there is something very strange in the mind of the captain. He is thinking of a guyanis butterfly and the Temple of the Weeping Sun ... It – it is very close now ... I – I keep falling off.'

'Do not be afraid, Nemo,' said Paul gently. 'No one here has done anything of which he need be afraid.'

But in that he was wrong.

A Bayani warrior, armed with ceremonial trident, appeared in the doorway. His eyes flickered over the children, then came to rest on Paul.

'Oruri greets you,' said the warrior truculently.

'The greeting is a blessing,' responded Paul.

'Lord, I am the voice and hand of Enka Ne. Which of your lost ones fashioned the guyanis that was not a guyanis?'

'I do not know what—' began Paul.

But Bai Lut sprang importantly to his feet. 'I am the maker of the guyanis,' he announced. 'Truly it was a thing of much power. Can it be that Enka Ne has observed—'

'Enka Ne observes all that is worthy of observation,' cut in the warrior. 'The flight of the guyanis was not well omened ... Die now – and live for ever.' Expertly he flung his short trident. The prongs struck deep in Bai Lut's throat. He fell over backwards, gurgled briefly and lay still.

For a moment or two Paul was stunned. He looked helplessly at the three horrified children then at the Bayani. Meanwhile, more warriors had filed into the school.

'Lord,' said the captain, 'it is the will of Enka Ne that you and these lost ones must withdraw from this place.'

'But surely there cannot be any –'

'Lord,' said the Bayani sternly, 'Enka Ne has spoken. Let there be no more dying than the god-king commands.'

Paul looked helplessly at Zu Shan and Nemo and Tsong Tsong, and then at the sad and bloody heap that was once Bai Lut, and finally at the dozen or so warriors waiting patiently behind their captain.

'Come,' he managed to say at length in a voice that was extraordinarily calm, 'what Enka Ne commands, it is fitting that we should obey.'

He led the boys out between ranks of Bayani warriors. About twenty paces away from the school, they stood watching and waiting and listening as the warriors of Enka Ne smashed tables, chairs and all the carefully constructed equipment.

Presently they heard the captain say: 'Make fire.'

And presently the Bayani soldiers trooped out of the school as tell-tale spirals of smoke began to drift from under its eaves.

The dry wood burned quickly and fiercely and noisily. The heat forced everyone back; but the Bayani warriors remained until Bai Lut's funeral pyre was no more than a heap of glowing ashes.

The captain turned to Poul Mer Lo. 'Such is the will of Enka Ne,' he said.

If Bai Lut had not made the guyanis kite, if the wind had not broken his hair string, if the boy had not been so casually killed and the school burned down, Paul Marlowe would probably not have summoned sufficient determination to make the journey to the Temple of the White Darkness.

And it was the journey, and the timing of the journey, that changed the course of history.

TWENTY-FOUR

With the knowledge that she was pregnant, Mylai Tui had become happy; and her happiness had grown in direct proportion to the increase in the size of her belly. Not even the death of Bai Lut and the burning of the school could diminish it greatly; these were things about which she cared only because they were things about which Paul Marlowe cared.

She was happy not only with the simple feminine satisfaction of biological fulfilment. She was happy with the uniqueness of bearing a son – obviously it was to be a son, for a girl would not kick so lustily – for one who had ridden on the wings of a silver bird from a land beyond the sky. Fortunate was she whom Oruri had chosen to be the vessel of the seed of him who had the gift of greatness.

She looked at Paul with pride. He was taller than any in Baya Nor; and though his skin, despite much exposure to the sun, was still sadly pale and far from the desired black of the Bayani of ancient lineage, he was very much a man – as his thanu and vigorous muscles testified. Such a one must surely beget a son in his own image. And then Mylai Tui would be a woman whom all other women could only envy.

Her happiness and her anticipatory daydreams, however, were short-lived. They came to an end on the evening that Paul told her of his determination to make the journey to the Temple of the White Darkness.

'Paul,' she pleaded in bad English, 'you cannot do this thing. Are you so sad that only death will end the sadness?'

'It has nothing to do with sadness,' he explained patiently. 'There are mysteries which I must try to unravel. And it seems that the mountain may at least provide another clue ... I shall go as soon as I can find hunters to go with me.'

'You will not find any,' she said, lapsing into Bayani. 'There are none so foolish in Baya Nor as to wish to venture into the bosom of Oruri before they are called.'

Laughing, he, too, spoke in Bayani: 'Courage, pride and greed – these are the things that will give me the hunters I want. The journey will appeal to their courage. Their pride will be challenged because I, a stranger, am not afraid to make this journey. And the twenty copper rings that I shall offer to each man will be sufficient to overcome any falterings of courage ... Besides, there is the weapon I brought with me and which I was permitted to keep by

Enka Ne. It lies, now, wrapped in musa loul and buried in a box of hard wood. When I show the hunters its power, they will have no doubts.'

'You will have to pass the Lokhali, lord. The people of Baya Nor do not fear the Lokhali – but neither do the Bayani pass through their country, unless it be as an army.'

'Yes, we shall have to pass the Lokhali. But, Mylai Tui, with the weapon I brought from the other side of the sky, we shall be as an army.'

'My lord, the weapon did not prevent you from entering the donjons of Baya Nor.'

'It did not.' Again he laughed. 'But who may question the purpose of Oruri?'

Mylai Tui was silent for a moment or two. Then she said: 'None have ventured to the mountain and returned.'

'There are those who have seen the mountain and returned.'

She gave him a look of sad resignation. 'Lord, I know there is much about you that I cannot understand and much that I will never understand. I am proud to have lain with you, and I am proud to have received at last the gift of your loins. If it pleases my lord to seek Oruri before Oruri does the seeking, then I will endeavour to accept this thing ... But stay, my lord, stay long enough to look upon the face of your son.'

He took her hands. 'Mylai Tui, I know it is hard for you to understand. But my head is sorely troubled by many questions. This thing will not wait. I must go as soon as I may, and I must see what can be seen. But I will return. I will return because I greatly desire to lie with you, as I will lie with you this night. And I will return because I desire greatly to gaze upon the harvest of the joining of our flesh ... Now let there be an end. The decision is made. Zu Shan seeks the hunters, and I doubt not that they will be found.'

Suddenly, she brightened. 'It is possible, is it not, that Enka Ne may learn of this madness and prevent it?'

Paul gave her a penetrating look. 'I respect the power of Enka Ne. Let the god-king respect mine. Otherwise, many in Baya Nor may have cause to grieve.'

Three days later, in the early evening, when the nine moons rode high and swiftly through a cloudless sky, Zu Shan brought four hunters to the house of Poul Mer Lo. The usual courtesies were exchanged, and the men squatted in a semi-circle on the verandah while Mylai Tui supplied them with kappa spirit.

'Paul,' said Zu Shan in English, so that the Bayani would not understand, 'there are the men we should take. There were others attracted by the payment you offered. But these are the best. Two of them I already knew, and the others are known to them. They are among the best hunters in Baya Nor. But more than that, they have much faith in Poul Mer Lo, the teacher. And one of them, Shon Hu, has even seen the mountain. He has hunted very far, and he says he knows the way.'

'Are they afraid?'

Zu Shan gave a thin smile. 'Yes, Paul, they are afraid – as I am.'

'Good. Men who are afraid live longer. You have done very well, Zu Shan – better than I thought.'

He turned to the Bayani, who were politely sipping their kappa spirit as though no one had spoken.

'Hunters,' said Poul Mer Lo in Bayani, 'I journey far. It may be that there will be danger on this journey, for I am told that the Temple of the White Darkness is not a place where men go who wish to count the great number of their grandchildren.'

The hunters laughed, a little self-consciously.

'But I think,' went on Poul Mer Lo, 'that we shall be among those who return; for if men desire something greatly, they can often accomplish it. Also, we shall carry a terrible weapon which I have brought with me for this purpose from the land beyond the sky.'

'Lord,' said the man who had been identified as Shon Hu, 'the journey is one thing but the Lokhali is another.'

Poul Mer Lo rose, went into the house and returned with his sweeper rifle.

'Your darts and blow-pipes, your tridents and clubs are excellent weapons,' he said. 'But how many Lokhali can you stop with them if we are attacked?'

Shon Hu looked at his companions. 'Lord, we are only men – good men, perhaps, but no more than men. Perhaps, *if* Oruri smiled, we would carry three times our own number of Lokhali with us into his bosom.'

Poul Mer Lo pushed the breeder button of his atomic rifle. About two hundred metres away there was a small group of trees looming in the twilight.

'Observe!' said Poul Mer Lo. He sighted, pressed the trigger and swept the tops of the trees with the rifle. After two or three passes, smoke began to rise. After five passes, the trees burst into flame – a noisy, crackling bonfire.

'Lord,' said Shon Hu at length, 'you have shown us a fearful thing.'

'It is,' agreed Poul Mer Lo, 'a most fearful thing. Your job, Shon Hu, will be to protect me. My job will be to use this weapon. If we are attacked by the Lokhali, many of them will need to explain to Oruri why they wished to obstruct the passing of Poul Mer Lo and his companions ...' He gazed round the semi-circle. 'Nevertheless, I know our journey is still a difficult and dangerous one. If any of you feels that he has spoken rashly, let him now stand and go forth. We who remain will pray for the good fortune of his children and his children's children.'

No one moved.

Silently and sadly, Mylai Tui brought more kappa spirit.

TWENTY-FIVE

After much hard bargaining, Shon Hu had obtained a barge for the very reasonable sum of nine rings. Poul Mer Lo, impatient to get the expedition under way now that he had made his decision, would have paid the sixteen rings demanded by the barge builder without question. But, as Shon Hu explained, to have paid such a price without haggling would have excited much interest. The barge builder would have boasted of his achievement, enquiries might then have been made about Shon Hu, the actual purchaser, and the ring money might then have been traced back to Poul Mer Lo. That in itself might well have been sufficient to bring the transaction to the notice of one of the officers of the god-king; and, quite possibly, the whole expedition would have been frustrated before it had begun. For, after the burning of the school, it was obvious that Enka Ne was not so oblivious of the activities of the stranger as Poul Mer Lo had formerly supposed.

So he had to wait patiently for two full days while Shon Hu and a phenomenal quantity of kappa spirit brought the price down to nine rings.

The time was not wholly wasted, however, for there was much to be done. Supplies of fresh water had to be stored in skins, as had quantities of dried kappa and smoked strips of meat; for though the expedition included four hunters, Poul Mer Lo did not propose to waste much time hunting for food. Of his personal possessions, he proposed to take only the transceiver and the sweeper rifle. The atomic grenades that Shah Shan had presented to him at the temple of Baya Lys were not suitable weapons for close range fighting – if, indeed, any close range fighting should occur. To call them weapons was not completely accurate, either, for they were far more use to engineers than soldiers – except, perhaps, where a very long fuse could be used as during a retreat, or for very long range work.

Poul Mer Lo did not really know why he was taking the transceiver. It was in excellent order; and its miniature 'hot' battery would remain efficient for a long time to come. But he well knew that there was no other working transmitter on Altair Five. During the last few months, many times at dead of night he had put the transceiver on full power and swept carefully through the medium and short wave bands. All he could raise was the usual random crackle.

The sweeper rifle gave him some cause for anxiety. There was a visual indicator showing its charge level, and this was now registering well below the half-charge mark; indicating that the rifle was now not good for more than half a dozen full strength discharges. Somehow, it had leaked; and as he did not possess a geiger counter there was no means of telling if the micropile were still intact. For all he knew, thought Poul Mer Lo, both he and the rifle might now be dangerously radioactive – a menace to all and sundry. But there was nothing to be done about it. If such were the will of Oruri ... He was amused at himself for letting the expression creep into his train of thought.

Shon Hu said that it would be possible to travel by barge for two and a half days – one day along the Canal of Life and one and a half days upstream on the great river, which was known, picturesquely enough, as the Watering of Oruri. After that there would be perhaps three days in the forest and a further day, or perhaps two days, on the uplands. Shon Hu was vague about this latter stretch of the journey. All that he seemed certain about was that once the forest was left behind, the Temple of the White Darkness would be clearly visible. How it was to be approached was a matter upon which Oruri would doubtless provide guidance when the time came.

The expedition was to depart from Baya Nor at the first sign of light so that much poling could be done before the sun rose high in the sky. Also, such an early departure would be unlikely to attract the attention of anyone but hunters; for few Bayani cared to move before the sun was clear of the horizon.

The barge was ready, laden with food, water, the blow pipes, darts and tridents of the hunters, the sweeper rifle and the transceiver, and a pile of skins for the use as bedding and then as clothing when the warm forest was left behind. Besides the four hunters, Poul Mer Lo was taking Zu Shan and Nemo with him. Tsong Tsong was to be left behind as company for Mylai Tui, and Poul Mer Lo had given her sufficient money to purchase a girl servant to help in the house if the baby should arrive before he returned from the Temple of the White Darkness.

Nemo was the real problem. With his grotesquely deformed legs he could not possibly walk. Yet Poul Mer Lo did not wish to leave him behind – not only because the oddly ancient child desperately wanted to go with him but because Nemo's telepathic powers might prove useful. It was Nemo, with his visions of a god bringing forth children from his belly, who had triggered the whole thing off. Just possibly there might be something on the slopes of the white mountain. Just possibly Nemo might sense where and what that something was. Yes, he would have to go. And so a sling was made for him so that he could ride on the back of each of the hunters in turn.

The night before departure, the hunters, Nemo and Zu Shan slept on skins on the flat bottom of the barge. Poul Mer Lo did not sleep. Neither did Mylai Tui. They lay close to each other and remote from each other in the small house that, over the months, had begun to acquire for Poul Mer Lo the sweetly subtle smell of home.

Mylai Tui was certain it was the last time they would hold each other.

'Lord,' she said in Bayani, 'I am fat, now, and can no longer pretend to possess some beauty. It is not fitting that a woman should speak thus – but I greatly desire that you should lie with me and try to remember how it once was.'

He kissed her and fondled her. 'Mylai Tui,' he said, also speaking in the high Bayani that he knew she preferred, 'to be with child does not diminish beauty, but changes the shape of beauty. I will remember how it once was. But how it now is is dear to me also. And this, too, I will remember.'

They made love, but though there was great tenderness there was little passion. It had seemed strangely, thought Poul Mer Lo when it was over, more like a solemn ritual, dignifying or celebrating some unique event that had not happened before and would not happen again. He was puzzled and, for the first time, he was afraid.

'Lord,' said Mylai Tui simply, 'the fire is kindled, flourishes and dies. We shall not come to each other again. I wish to humbly thank you, for you have given me much joy ... I do not have the gift of leaping thoughts like Shah Shan, whom I think you loved, and like some others whom, perhaps, you love in a lesser way. But if my thoughts could not leap, lord, my flesh leaped joyously. I am sad now that it will leap no more.'

He held her very close. 'I shall return from the Temple of the White Darkness,' he whispered. 'This I swear.'

'If it is the will of Oruri,' said Mylai Tui, dully. 'My lord has the gift of greatness and can accomplish much.'

'I shall return,' he repeated fiercely.

Mylai Tui sighed. 'But we shall come together no more. This I know. It is written on the water. It is written in the wind ... Lay your hand on my belly, lord.'

He did so, and was rewarded with a kick.

'Is not your son vigorous and mighty of limb like him that presented the seed?'

'Truly, he will be a fine child.'

'Then go now, for the first light is with us. And remember, lord. Such as I am, I gave what I could. I will remember with pride that I carry the child of one who has ridden upon a silver bird. But go now, for the waters sting in my eyes, and I would not have you remember me thus ... Oruri be with you – at the end as at the beginning.'

'Oruri be with you always,' responded Poul Mer Lo. He touched her forehead with his lips. Then he got up and quickly went from the house.

In the pre-dawn light, the world seemed very quiet and very lonely. He walked briskly down to the Canal of Life without looking back, and trying not to think of anything at all. But there was a taste of salt upon his lips, and he was amazed that non-existent tears could hurt so much.

TWENTY-SIX

It was going to be a hot day. The Canal of Life lay placid and steaming with a light mist that held close to its surface, drifting and swirling lazily in the still air. Voices carried. From many paces away, Poul Mer Lo could hear the low murmurings of the hunters and the boys as they made ready for the journey.

Excitement was in the tight atmosphere. Poul Mer Lo felt almost that he could reach out his hands and touch it as he stepped aboard the rough but sturdy barge that was to carry them on the journey. He pushed regret and doubt out of his mind. He locked his last memories of Mylai Tui – knowing now that they were indeed his last memories of her – into some deep compartment of his brain where they would be safe until he needed to take them out and dwell upon them.

'Lord,' said Shon Hu, 'we have eaten and are ready. Speak only the word.'

Poul Mer Lo glanced round the small craft and saw six faces gazing at him expectantly. 'As this journey begins,' he said formally, 'though it be long or short, easy or most hard, let all here know that they are as brothers to help each other in difficulty and to rejoice or suffer with each other according to the will of Oruri ... Let us go, then.'

The hunters turned to the sides of the barge and urinated into the Canal of Life. Then they took up their poles and pushed away from the bank. Presently the barge was gliding smoothly over the still, mist-covered water; and as the sun rose above the edge of the forest, bringing with it new textures and forms, and intensifying colours, Poul Mer Lo began to feel for the first time since his arrival on Altair Five an odd lightness of heart. So far, he thought, he had been chiefly a spectator – despite his introduction of the wheel into the Bayani culture and despite his sporadic efforts to fulfil the prediction of the oracle that he would be a great teacher. But now, he felt, he was really doing something.

Whether the legend of the coming and Nemo's dreams amounted to anything did not really matter. Whether there were any spectacular discoveries to be made at the Temple of the White Darkness did not really matter. What did matter was that he had managed to break through the centuries old Bayani mood of insularity. For so long, they had cultivated the habit of not wanting to know. They had been content with their tiny static society in a small corner of the forests of Altair Five.

406

But now things were different; and whatever happened there could be no permanent return to the *status quo*. The hunters, he realized, were not coming with him for the ring money alone. Nor were they coming because of blind faith in Poul Mer Lo. They were coming basically because their curiosity had been aroused – because they, too, wished to find out what was in the next valley or over the next mountain.

They did not know it, but they were the first genuine Bayani explorers for centuries … All that I have done, thought Poul Mer Lo, and perhaps the most important thing that I have done, is to help make such a mental climate possible.

Which turned his mind automatically to Enka Ne. For hundreds of years the god-kings of Baya Nor had – consciously or otherwise – maintained their absolute authority and absolute power by inhibiting curiosity. This Shah Shan had realized. He had had the wisdom to encourage Poul Mer Lo, whom the councillors and the priests of the blind order regarded as an instrument of chaos because he asked questions that had not previously been asked, and did things that had not previously been done.

But the Enka Ne who came after Shah Shan was of a different temperament altogether. For one thing he was old. Perhaps in his youth, he, too, had possessed an enquiring mind. But if so, it had been crushed by his elders and by the ritualistic Bayani approach to life. Now that he was old, he stood clearly and decisively for orthodoxy.

As the barge left the kappa fields and the cleared land behind, passing under the great green umbra of the forest, Poul Mer Lo wondered idly if Enka Ne knew of his expedition. It was highly probable; for though Zu Shan had been very cautious in his recruitment of hunters, he had talked to several who had rejected the invitation. They, in turn, must have talked to others; and it was quite likely that an embroidered description of the expedition had now reached the ears of the god-king.

But now, thought Poul Mer Lo comfortably, it was too late to prevent the journey; and, in any case, if the god-king were as clever – despite his orthodoxy – as Poul Mer Lo suspected, he would not wish to prevent it. He would be somewhat relieved that the stranger had chosen to seek the bosom of Oruri far from Baya Nor.

Presently the barge passed the forest temple of Baya Sur without incident. There was no one at the landing place to witness its passing, since no one knew of its coming. And so the small craft sped on, deep into the forest to where the Canal of Life joined the Watering of Oruri.

The sun had passed its zenith before the hunters were ready to abandon their poles and take food and rest. They pulled in to the bank of the canal where there was a very small clearing and threw the anchor stone overboard.

Poul Mer Lo was glad of the opportunity to stretch his legs. He had offered to take turns with the poles, as Zu Shan had done; but the hunters had rejected his offer with great politeness. He was Poul Mer Lo, the stranger, unaccustomed to the ways and rhythms of watermen. He was also their employer and captain; and therefore it would be unthinkable to let him do menial tasks except *in extremis*.

When they had eaten, Poul Mer Lo, Zu Shan and two of the hunters dozed. Nemo and the remaining two kept watch against wild animals, for there were many carnivorous beasts that hunted by night and by day in the forest.

As he fell asleep, Poul Mer Lo was transformed once more into Paul Marlowe – the Paul Marlowe who lived and slept and endured suspended animation aboard the *Gloria Mundi*. He was on watch with Ann, and he had just saved the occupants of the star ship from death by explosive decompression after the hull of the ship had been penetrated by small meteors. He tasted champagne once more – *Moet et Chandon '11*, a very fine year. Then there was some vague discussion on the nature of God …

The dream disintegrated as Nemo shook him. For a terrible moment or two Paul did not know where he was or recognize the wizened face of the child.

'Lord,' said Nemo in Bayani, 'a barge follows us. I think it is no more than ten flights of the dart away. I ride the pole-men's thoughts. They are seeking us. They have been offered many rings to overtake us. Enka Ne has sent soldiers. Lord, I do not think we can escape.'

Paul Marlowe pulled himself together. He stood up and looked at the barge. There did not seem to be any way of camouflaging it or hiding it in time. But he refused to accept defeat without doing something. The only hope was to get out into the canal and pull like mad.

'Let us go quickly, then,' he said to the hunters, who were gazing at him anxiously. 'It is said that he who waits for trouble will be found by it most easily.'

Within seconds the anchor stone was hauled up, the barge was in midstream and everyone – including Paul – was poling strenuously. Even Nemo, perched on the end of the barge, had a short pole with which, in the squatting position, he could provide a few extra pounds of thrust.

Unfortunately, the Canal of Life had few bends; and it was not long before the pursuers could see the pursued. Glancing over his shoulder, Paul saw that the following barge was a large one with sixteen pole-men and at least twice that number of warriors. It was gaining rapidly. In less than a minute it would be only the flight of a dart away – and if darts then began to fly, that would be the end of the matter.

'Stop poling!' he commanded, and picked up his sweeper rifle.

'Lord,' said Shon Hu, 'it seems that Oruri does not favour this enterprise. But speak the word and we will fight if we must.'

'There will be no fighting,' said Paul positively. 'Take heart, Shon Hu. Oruri does but test us.'

The pursuers, seeing that the men ahead of them had stopped poling, lifted their own poles and allowed the two craft to drift slowly towards each other.

Paul recognized the Bayani warrior standing in the bows of the following barge. It was the captain who had been sent to execute Bai Lut and burn down the school.

'Oruri greets you!' called the captain.

'The greeting is a blessing,' responded Paul.

'I am the voice and hand of Enka Ne. The god-king commands you to return to Baya Nor, there to give account of this journey.'

'I am grieved that the god-king commands my presence, for this journey is most urgent and cannot wait.'

The captain seemed amused. 'Lord, I am commanded to enforce the command of Enka Ne, and that I will do most willingly.'

Paul rested the sweeper rifle casually on his hip, his finger on the trigger. He had previously pushed the breeder button to full power discharge.

'Captain, listen to me for a moment. I wish you to return to Enka Ne and present my humble greetings, saying that I would that I could return to do his bidding, but that this matter cannot be delayed. If you return thus and in peace, the anger of Oruri will be withheld. I have spoken.'

The captain laughed, his warriors laughed. Even the pole-men permitted themselves to grin.

'Brave words, my lord. But where is the strength behind the courage? You are few, we are many. As you will not come, then we must take you.'

'So be it,' said Paul. He pressed the trigger. The sweeper rifle whined, vibrating imperceptibly. The water immediately ahead of the following barge, which was still drifting slowly onwards, began to hiss and bubble to boiling point. It became turbulent, giving off great clouds of steam, then suddenly it was resolved into a great water spout. The barge, full of petrified soldiers and pole-men, drifted helplessly into the water spout. Immediately the wooden bows burst into flame, and the pressure of the water and steam capsized the heavily laden craft.

With cries of terror men and soldiers floundered in the Canal of Life. Paul had released the trigger as soon as the barge caught fire; but the patch of water continued to hiss and bubble for some moments. One poor wretch drifted near to it and was badly scalded.

'Thus,' said Paul looking down at the captain struggling in the water, 'the anger of Oruri comes to pass. Return now to Enka Ne and report this thing, giving him the words I have spoken.' He turned to his own pole-men: 'Let us continue, then. It seems that the warriors of the god-king will not hinder our passing.'

Mechanically, and with looks of awe on their faces, the hunters took up their poles and got the small barge under way.

Shon Hu wiped the sweat from his face and glanced at the sweeper rifle. 'Lord, with such power in his hands it seems that a man may become as a god.'

Paul smiled. 'No, Shon Hu. With such power in his hands, a man may only become a more powerful man.'

TWENTY-SEVEN

The forest was ancient, overwhelming and oppressive in its great green luxuriance. Amid all the noisy chatter of the wild things it contained, there were strange pockets of silence where it seemed to Paul Marlowe – never a connoisseur of forests, even on Earth – something intangible lay, lurking and brooding.

Perhaps it was the Life Force; for if a Life Force existed, surely the forest – a place teeming with crawly living things – must be its home. Of the large wild creatures, Paul did not see a great deal but he saw enough to make him feel that, in evolutionary terms, Altair Five must be at least a million years behind Earth.

Here and there, on the banks of the far reaches of the Canal of Life, were colonies of large iguana-like animals – spiked, scaly, twice the length of a man and, so the hunters told him, virtually harmless. They were vegetarians. The only time they ever displayed ferocity was during a short mating season – and then only to others of their kind. On the other hand, there were small, delicate crab-like creatures – bright red and remarkably attractive, no larger than a man's fist. These the hunters pointed out with respect as being among the most deadly killers in the forest.

Only once did Paul see a really massive creature during the daytime. It was a creature that the hunters called an ontholyn. It was furry, and fearsome, with tremendous clawed forepaws and a cavernous mouth. Paul watched it rear up on its hind legs to pick carefully of some fruit hanging at the top of a tall tree. It made a strange sound, half roaring and half trumpeting, then it sat back on its haunches to nibble the fruit. The sound, which had reverberated through the forest was, so the hunters said, merely an expression of pleasure. They claimed that the ontholyn was so slow that it was possible for a nimble man to run up to one, climb up its furry sides, tweak its nose and climb down again before the creature realized what was happening.

As the barge sped farther away from Baya Nor along the Canal of Life, it seemed to Paul that he and his companions were making a journey back in time. The clusters of giant ferns, the bright orchidaceous flowers, the stringy lianas that now laced overhead from bank to bank of the canal, the tall, sad and utterly lethal Weeping Trees which leaked a tough, quick bonding and poisonous glue down their trunks to trap and kill small animals that would then putrefy and feed the exposed roots of the tree – all these conspired to make him feel that he was riding down a green tunnel into pre-history.

And, in fact, he was now riding through a green tunnel; for the banks of the Canal of Life had narrowed considerably. The foliage had closed in over-head, and sunlight was visible only as a dazzling maze of thin gold bars through which the barge seemed to cut its way with miraculous and hyp-notic ease.

As the light died, and the green gloom deepened, Shon Hu inspected the banks for a suitable place to moor the barge for the night.

'Lord,' he said, 'we have made good travelling. We are very near now to the Watering of Oruri.'

'Would it not be good to journey on to the great river while we can still see?'

Shon Hu shrugged. 'Who can say, lord? But my comrades like to see where they can plant their poles.'

'That is very wise, Shon Hu. Therefore let us rest.'

They found a small patch of ground near a group of the Weeping Trees. Shon Hu explained that most animals could smell the trees – particularly at night – and took great trouble to avoid them. That was why he had chosen the place. Nevertheless, he advised that everyone should sleep in the barge.

The first night passed without incident. After their evening meal the hunt-ers began to exchange stories, as was their custom. Paul listened drowsily for a while, half drugged by the heavy night scents of the forest and the vapours rising from the water. The next thing he knew, it was daybreak – and a smil-ing Zu Shan was trying to tempt him with a handful of kappa and a strip of smoked meat that tasted like scorched rubber.

'You slept very soundly, Paul. We did not think you would take to the forest so well. How do your bones feel?' Zu Shan spoke in English, proud of the one distinction over the hunters that he possessed.

Paul groaned and tried to stretch. He groaned again – this time with much feeling. 'I feel like an old man,' he complained. 'I feel as if the glue from the Weeping Trees had penetrated all my joints.'

'It is the vapours from the water of the Canal of Life,' explained Zu Shan. 'They cause the bones to ache, but the pain passes away with vigorous move-ment. Poor Nemo feels it worst, I think, because his bones do not have their natural shape.'

Little Nemo was crying like a baby. Paul picked him up and began to gently massage the twisted limbs. 'Lord,' gasped Nemo in Bayani, 'you shame me. I beg of you, put me down.'

Paul ruffled his hair affectionately and set him down in the stern of the barge. 'It shall be as my son commands,' he said gravely, 'for I acknowledge before all present that you are truly my son.'

'Lord,' said Shon Hu, 'there is much poling to be done. Will you speak the word?'

Paul raised his eyes to the steaming green roof overhead. Judging from the already oppressive atmosphere, it was going to be another hot and enervating day.

'Let us go, then,' he said in Bayani, 'with the blessing of Oruri.'

TWENTY-EIGHT

It was on the second night that disaster struck.

The Watering of Oruri was a broad, slow river, fairly shallow but easily navigable. Were it not for the mild current, the pole-men would have had an easier job propelling their craft up the river than along the Canal of Life.

To Paul, it seemed that there could be no end to this strange journey back in time – at least, not until they arrived at the very fount of creation. Baya Nor was less than two days' travel away; yet already it belonged to another world – a world that, fancifully, seemed as if it would not begin to exist until hundreds of millennia had passed.

It was strange, this sense of journeying back in time. He had experienced the same sort of sensations in the donjons of Baya Nor and in the temple when Enka Ne had granted him his life but had commanded that each of his little fingers be struck off.

In a sense, perhaps, he really had journeyed back in time; for he had left the twenty-first century on Earth to travel many light-years and enter a medieval society on the 'far side of the sky'. But now, as he and his companions propelled themselves up a great musky river, flanked by high green walls of overpowering vegetation, even Baya Nor seemed ultra-modern.

The world he was in now seemed as if it had yet to experience the intrusion of man. The voyagers in their frail craft were nothing more than insubstantial dreams of the future, flitting like brief shadows through the long morning of pre-history.

They made camp for the night close by a mossy patch of ground that seemed both incongruous and refreshingly peaceful in the surrounding riot of green.

Life was lived at such a primitive and furious level in the forest through which the Watering of Oruri passed that Paul thought he could actually see plants growing. Oddly enough, although the trees and tree-ferns were much taller here than in the stretches of forest on each side of the Canal of Life, the gloom was not quite so unrelieved. Here and there, broad shafts of dying sunlight broke through the great green roof of foliage to create an odd impression of stained glass illumination in an endless green cathedral.

As he gazed idly at the river bank, tiny flowers closed their petals and almost shrank into the ground as if they were unwilling to witness the dark happenings of the long forest night.

Again the small band of explorers slept in their barge. As on the previous night, the hunters exchanged their stories – which, thought Paul, had much in common with the traditional anecdotes of fishermen back on Earth. He was less sleepy this time and managed to stay awake until one of the hunters took the first spell of the night watch. Then, with the sweeper rifle ready in his hand, he drifted luxuriously into a dark dimension of dreams that seemed strangely attuned to this world of pre-history.

It took several vital seconds for him, when the tragedy happened, to force himself back into consciousness. At first, the cries and the roars and the stench seemed to be part of the dream; but then the barge received a mighty blow and lurched violently. Paul rolled over, realized that he was awake and that the pandemonium was real.

He groped desperately for the sweeper rifle. Fitted along its barrel was a small atomic-powered pencil-beam torch, set parallel with the sights. It was his only source of light. Until he could find it and operate it, he could not possibly discover what was happening. The stench was terrible; but the screams were indescribable.

Frantically, he groped for the rifle. A century seemed to pass before he found it. He felt for the torch button and pressed it as he swung the rifle towards the sound of screaming.

The thin beam of intense light did not illuminate a wide area; but it revealed enough to turn his stomach to jelly.

There, on the bank of the river, was the largest and most terrible creature he had ever seen. As large, perhaps, as the prehistoric *tyrannosaurus rex* of Earth, and certainly no less terrible.

He swung the torch beam up towards the massive and nightmarish head – then almost dropped the rifle in sheer terror. The head, arms and shoulders of one of the hunters protruded from a cavernous mouth.

Instantly, Paul swung the rifle away from the head, down the great curved back to where he judged the creature's belly must be. He pressed the trigger. Blue light shot through the darkness, parallel to the white light of the torch.

Added to the stench of the monster itself there was now the stench of its burning flesh. The fantastic creature seemed to be more surprised than hurt. With a casual and strangely delicate movement, it raised a great forearm and plucked the hunter from its mouth, flinging the body far out into the Watering of Oruri.

Then, with an almost comical calmness, it began to contemplate the unusual phenomenon of the blue and white beams of light. By that time the creature's stomach was burning, with the flesh sizzling and spitting. Gouts of flaming body fat fell to the ground; and smoky yellow flames curled up the high, scaly back.

The beast, thought Paul, hysterically, was already dead – but it just didn't

415

know when to lie down. It stood there, watching itself being consumed by atomic fire as if the event were interesting but not altogether disturbing. Surely the blood must be boiling in its brain!

The whole scene appeared to drift into nightmarish slow motion. Paul, hypnotized, could not take his eyes from the beast to see what his companions were doing. He continued pouring fantastic quantities of energy into the hide of a monster that seemed to have erupted from the very dawn of life.

At last, the terrible creature – almost burnt in two – appeared to realize that it was doomed. It shuddered, and the ground shuddered with it, then it gave a piercing scream – literally breathing fire, as burning flesh and air were expelled from its lungs, and rolled over, taking a tree with it. The thud of its body shook the bank, the barge and even the river. It must have been dead before it hit the ground.

Paul managed to pull himself together sufficiently to take his finger off the trigger of the sweeper rifle. But darkness did not descend, for the corpse of the beast had become a blazing inferno. The smell and the sounds were overpowering.

Shon Hu spoke the first coherent words. 'Lord,' he gasped with difficulty, 'forgive me. I vomit.'

He hung over the side of the barge and was joined within seconds by everyone except Nemo, who had curled himself up into a tight foetal ball and was unconscious.

'Who has died?' whispered Paul, when he could trust himself to speak once more.

'Mien She, lord. He was the one who watched. Perhaps the beast saw him move.'

'Why did he not see the beast move? Or hear it? Such a creature could not move without warning of its coming.'

'Lord, I know not. He is dead now. Let us not question his alertness, for he has suffered much, and it may be that his spirit would be sad to know that we doubted him.'

Paul glanced at the burning corpse once more, and was immediately sick again. When he had recovered, he said 'How call you this monster?'

'Lord, it has no name,' said Shon Hu simply. 'We have not seen its like before. We do not wish to see its like again.'

'Let us go quickly from this place,' said Paul, retching, 'before we vomit ourselves to death. In future, two men will always watch, for it is clear that one may nod. Let us go quickly, now.'

'Lord, it is dark and we do not know the river.'

'Nevertheless, we will go.' He gestured towards the still burning body. 'Here is too much light – and other things. Come. I will take the pole of Mien She.'

TWENTY-NINE

There was not a breath of wind. The forest was immensely quiet. Indeed, but for the dark green smells of night, it would have been possible to imagine that the forest had ceased to exist. Only the river seemed alive, murmuring sleepily as if it, too, wished to sink into a state of unbeing.

It had been a hard and dismal day – hard because the Watering of Oruri had narrowed, making the current more swift, and dismal because the death of Mien She was still very much on everyone's minds.

Nemo had been the worst affected. He had been the worst affected not only because he was a child but because he had experienced telepathically the brief but terrifying agony of Mien She. All day the crippled child had lain curled up at the stern of the barge. He would not eat or even drink; and it was only by patient coaxing that Paul managed to get him to take a few mouthfuls of water at the evening meal.

There had been no cheerful exchange of tall stories when the hunters took their ease after a hard day's poling. When they spoke – if they spoke – it was almost monosyllabically and only because the communication was necessary.

Paul and Shon Hu had taken the first watch. Now they were also taking the last watch. Presently grey wisps of light would filter through the tall trees. Today they would leave the barge behind. Already they were in Lokhali country, and therefore the dangers were doubled. But, thought Paul, after the horror of the previous night, any brush with the Lokhali would seem by contrast to be a form of light relief.

As he sat back to back with Shon Hu, Paul realized that there was something concerning the Lokhali that was trying to surface in his conscious mind. Something important. Something that he had seen but not noticed …

His only encounter so far with the forest tribe had been at the mass crucifixion on the Fourth Avenue of the Gods. His mind flew back to that day and he could see again and hear again the dying Lokhali who, in his extreme agony, had murmured meaningless – and, in the circumstances, bizarre – fragments of German, French and English.

Suddenly, Paul realized what he had seen but not noticed. Four fingers and a thumb! The Lokhali were not only taller than the Bayani, but more perfectly formed. Four fingers and a thumb! Then his mind leaped back to the woman who bore her child near the kappa fields, and then to Mylai Tui, who

417

had been angry at his questions and had then demanded to be chastised for displaying her anger.

And now here he was in the middle of a primeval forest, journeying in search of a legend and with a headful of unanswered questions. He wanted to laugh aloud. He wanted to laugh at the sheer absurdity, the incongruity of it all.

He did laugh aloud.

Shon Hu started. 'You are amused, lord?' he asked reproachfully.

'Not really, Shon Hu. I am sorry to startle you. I was just thinking of some things that Poul Mer Lo, the teacher, finds hard to understand.'

'What manner of things, lord?'

Remembering the reactions of Mylai Tui, Paul thought carefully. 'Shon Hu,' he began, 'we have not known each other long, but this venture joins us. You are my friend and brother.'

'I am proud to be the friend of Poul Mer Lo. To become as his brother would do me too much honour.'

'Nevertheless, my friend and brother, it is so. Therefore I do not wish to offend you.'

Shon Hu was puzzled. 'How can you offend me, lord, who have raised me in my own eyes?'

'By asking questions, Shon Hu. Only by asking questions.'

'Lord, I see you wish to speak. Where no offence is offered, none shall be taken.'

'The questions concern the number of fingers a man should have, Shon Hu.'

Immediately, Paul felt the hunter stiffen.

'Lord,' said Shon Hu at length, 'are there not certain things in your own country of which it is very shameful to speak?'

Paul considered for a moment. 'Yes, my friend, I think there are.'

'So it is also with the Bayani. I tell you this, lord, so that you will understand if I do not find it easy to talk about the number of fingers a man should have. We have a saying: it is a thing that should be heard once and told once … Remember this, lord. Now ask the questions.'

'Shon Hu, were you born with four fingers and a thumb, or with three?'

The hunter held up his hand. 'See, lord.' There were three fingers and a thumb.

Paul held up his own hand. 'You have not answered the question. Look … But I was born with four fingers and a thumb – were you?'

'Lord, I – I do not know,' said Shon Hu desperately.

'Are you sure? Are you sure you do not know?'

Shon Hu gulped. 'Lord, I was told once by my father when he was dying that the left hand had been – defiled … But, it was such a little finger, lord, and the shame was easily remedied … this none living know, save you.'

Paul smiled. 'Be easy, my friend. None living, save me, shall ever know … I wonder how many more Bayani have been born imperfect?'

'I do not know. Not many, I think. The priests take those who are discovered. They are not seen again.'

'Why is it so terrible to have four fingers?'

'Because, lord, those who have four fingers are the forsaken of Oruri. He smiles upon them not.'

'Do you believe this?'

'Lord,' said the hunter in an agitated voice, 'I *must* believe. It is the truth.'

'But why is it the truth?' asked Paul relentlessly.

'Lord, I can tell you only what I know … It is said that many many years ago, before there was a god-king in Baya Nor, the Bayani were not one people. There were those who were tall and lighter of skin, possessing four fingers and a thumb upon each hand. They were not, however, so numerous as the true Bayani, smaller, quicker of mind and body, possessing three fingers and a thumb upon each hand … There was much bloodshed, lord. Always there was much bloodshed. The tall ones with two fives believed themselves to be superior to the small ones with two fours. They ill-used the women of the fours. The fours retaliated and ill-used the women of the fives. Presently, there was a third warring faction – a number of outcasts with three fingers and a thumb on one hand and four fingers and a thumb on the other. Even among these people there was strife, since those with four fingers and a thumb on the right hand believed themselves to be superior to those with four fingers and a thumb on the left. And so the bloodshed became greater and more fierce, as each group reasoned that it alone was of the true blood and therefore most fitted to lead the rest.'

'My friend,' said Paul, 'there is nothing new under the sun. In the story of my own people there has been much needless and futile strife.'

'The war of the fingers reaches to the other side of the sky, then?' asked Shon Hu in surprise.

'No,' said Paul, 'the people of my own race are fortunate enough to possess the same number of fingers. So they found different reasons to inflict death and cruelty. They fought among themselves because some asserted that one particular god was greater than all other gods, or that one particular way of life was greater than all other ways of life, or that a white skin was better than a dark skin.'

Shon Hu laughed. 'Truly, your people, though great in strange skills, must have been very simple of heart.'

'Perhaps no less simple than the Bayani,' retorted Paul gravely. 'Proceed with your story, Shon Hu.'

The hunter seemed, now, to be more relaxed. 'Lord, it came to pass that there was seen more anger among the Bayani than there was love. Also, there was much fear. The crops were not tended because it was dangerous to go alone into the fields. The hunters found more profitable employment as hunters of men. Women prayed that their wombs might bear no fruit, for they were afraid to count the number of fingers on the hands of the babies they might bring forth. Few people died of great age, many died violently. And in time the number of the Bayani shrank, for the number of those who died became greater than the number of those who were born. It was clear that Oruri was displeased and that unless he could be brought to smile again, the people of the Bayani would be no more.'

Paul sighed. 'And all this because of the number of fingers on a man's hand.'

'All this,' repeated Shon Hu, 'because of the number of fingers on a man's hand … But an answer was found, lord. It was found by the first oracle, who fasted unto the point of death, then spoke with the voice of Oruri. And the voice said: "There shall come a man among you, who yet has no power and whose power will be absolute. And because no man may wield such power, the man shall be as a king. And because none may live for ever, the king shall be as a god. Each year the king must die that the god may be reborn." This the priests of Oruri heard, and the words were good. So they approached the oracle and said: "This surely is our salvation. How, then, may we recognize him who will take the form of a god?" To which the oracle replied: "You shall not see his face, but you shall see his beak. You shall not see his hands, but you shall see his plumage. And you shall hear only the cry of a bird that has never flown."'

To Paul Marlowe the story was fascinating, not only because it explained so much but because of its curious similarity in places to some of the ancient myths of Earth. 'How was the first god-king revealed, Shon Hu?' he asked quietly.

'Lord, the priests could not understand the oracle, and the oracle would speak no more. But after many days, the thing came to pass. A priest of the Order of the Blind Ones – who then did not wear a hood, for they had yet to look upon the face of the god-king – was going out to the kappa fields when he saw a great bird covered in brilliant plumage. The bird was uttering the gathering call of the Milanyl birds which, though birds of prey, were nevertheless good to eat … But, lord, this Milanyl bird had the legs of a man. It was a poor hunter named Enka Ne, who, too weak with hunger to hunt as a man, sought to entice game in this manner.'

'And this, then, was the god-king.'

'Yes, lord, Enka Ne was truly the god-king. For he was granted the wisdom of Oruri. On the day that he was shown to the people, he gathered many hunters about him. Then he took off his plumage before the Bayani for the first and last time. He held out his hands. And the people saw that on one there was three fingers and a thumb and on the other four fingers and a thumb. Then, in a loud voice, Enka Ne said: "It is fitting that there should be an end to destruction among us. It is fitting, also, that the hands of a man should be as the hands of his brother. But a man cannot add to the number of his fingers. Therefore let him rejoice that he can yet take away." Then he held out his right hand and commanded a hunter to strike off the small finger. And he said to the people: "Let all who remain in this land number their fingers as is the number of my fingers. Happy are they whose fingers are already thus. Happier still are they who can make a gift of their flesh to Oruri. Wretched are they who do not give when the gift is required. Let them go from the land for ever, for there can be no peace between us." When Enka Ne had spoken, many people held out their hands to the hunters. But there was also much fighting. In the end, those who refused to give were either slaughtered or driven away.'

Patches of light were beginning to show through the tree-tops. The last watch of the night was over. Paul stood up and stretched himself. Suddenly he was pleased with himself. He felt that he had found a missing piece of the puzzle.

'That was a very wonderful story, Shon Hu,' he said at length.

'It is also a terrible story, lord,' said Shon Hu. 'I have spoken it once. I must not speak it again. As you have discovered, the shadow of the fingers still lies over Baya Nor; and blood continues to be spilled even after many years. The god-kings have never loved those with too much knowledge of this thing. Nor do they love those who, contrary to the desire of Oruri, are born with too many fingers.' Shon Hu also stood up and stretched.

'I see … I am grateful that you have told me these things, Shon Hu. Let us speak now of the Lokhali.'

'There is a Lokhali village,' said the hunter, 'perhaps the largest, near the bank of the river no more than a few hours of poling from here. Fortunately, we may leave the Watering of Oruri and strike through the forest before we reach it.'

'Do the Lokhali have barges, Shon Hu?'

'Yes, lord, but their barges are very poor and very small. They only use the river when they are in great need. For they are much afraid of water.'

'Then surely it is safer to voyage past their village in the water than to pass through the forest?'

'Lord, it may be so. But a man does not care to come near to the Lokhali.'

'Nevertheless, I would pass the village … I think I know why the Bayani and the Lokhali have hated and feared each other for many years. The word Lokhali means accursed, wretched, cast out – does it not?'

'That is so, lord.'

'And the Lokhali,' went on Paul relentlessly, 'do not appear to find four fingers and a thumb offensive … It seems to me, Shon Hu, that the Lokhali and the Bayani were once brothers.'

421

THIRTY

Compared to the city of Baya Nor, the Lokhali village was a miserable affair. There was only one great hall, or temple, of stone. The rest of the buildings – though many of them were reasonably large – were of mud bricks, wooden frames and thatch. Many of the bricks were decorated with pieces of flint that had probably been pressed into them while they were still wet.

All this Paul noticed as the barge passed the village, keeping well to the far side of the Watering of Oruri, out of the range of spears and darts.

In fact, if size were any criterion, the village could more properly be called a town; for though the houses were primitive there were many of them and they had been carefully arranged with a certain amount of symmetry.

It was mid-morning, and a great many of the Lokhali were about, including a few dozen womenfolk at the water's edge, some washing and bathing while others were apparently cleaning food, utensils and even children. Those who were actually in the river scrambled rapidly ashore at the approach of the barge. Their cries brought more people down from the village, as well as a party of warriors or hunters. One or two of these roared and shook their weapons ferociously; but none seemed inclined to take to the few small, unstable-looking canoes that lay on the bank.

Paul realized the hopelessness of trying to find out anything of the rest of the crew of the *Gloria Mundi*. From that distance it would have been impossible to distinguish between European and Lokhali – unless the Europeans were wearing their own clothes. And as he himself had, of necessity, long ago taken to Bayani costume, it seemed reasonably certain that any survivors of the star ship would similarly have adopted the brief Lokhali garments.

It was tantalizing to be so near to a possible source of information and yet to be able to do nothing about it. But was there really nothing at all he could do? He thought carefully for a moment or two. Then he picked up his sweeper rifle and aimed at the water about twenty metres from the line of Lokhali on the bank. He pressed the trigger.

The rifle vibrated, producing its faint whine, then a patch of water began to hiss and bubble until it produced a most impressive waterspout. There were cries of awe and consternation from the Lokhali on the bank. Some ran away or drew back, but most seemed almost hypnotized by the phenomenon.

The display would serve two purposes, thought Paul with satisfaction. It would discourage the Lokhali, perhaps, from following the barge along the bank while at the same time the demonstration of such power – or the news of it – would convey to any surviving Europeans that there was yet another survivor.

He put down the rifle then cupped his hands round his mouth and shouted loudly across the water: 'I will come again … *Je reviens … Ich komm wieder.*'

Soon the barge was well past the village. Paul continued to gaze back intently until the river bent slightly and the Lokhali village was out of sight.

Shortly before the sun had reached its zenith, Shon Hu selected a suitable spot on the river bank and guided the barge in towards it.

'We must now pass through the forest, lord,' he said. 'To travel farther along the Watering of Oruri would only increase the journey.'

'Then let us eat and rest,' said Paul. 'Afterwards we will divide that which we have brought into packs that a man may carry.'

When they had eaten and rested, they took the water skins, the dried kappa, the smoked strips of meat, the skins they had brought to protect themselves in the cold uplands, and the sling that had been made for Nemo, out of the barge. Then they deliberately capsized it and weighted it down to the river bed with heavy stones. It was, perhaps, unlikely that the Lokhali would discover the barge, anyway; but if it were submerged, there would be even less chance. The only real problem, thought Paul grimly, would be in finding it themselves when they returned from the Temple of the White Darkness. It was true that they could get back to Baya Nor without the barge, but the journey would be considerably harder – and more dangerous.

As the afternoon shadows lengthened, the group moved away from the Watering of Oruri with Shon Hu in the lead. Paul followed immediately behind him, and after Paul came Zu Shan with Nemo slung like an awkward child from his back. The rearguard consisted of the two remaining hunters.

Remarkably enough, Nemo seemed to have almost completely recovered from the death of Mien She. But Paul noticed that at all times he stayed very close to Zu Shan. The two had come to depend on each other. Though Zu Shan was half a man, he was also still only half a boy. Basically, he found much more satisfaction talking to Nemo than to Paul or the hunters.

The two of them liked to demonstrate their assumed superiority over the Bayani by jabbering away to each other in English; interlaced with a few Bayani words and phrases. The resulting medley was very odd and, at times, amusing. It brought the boys closer and closer together. Originally, the plan had been that everyone should take turns in carrying Nemo. But this neither Nemo nor Zu Shan would permit. Fortunately, Nemo, being hardly more than a small bundle of skin and bone himself, was no heavier – and probably not quite as heavy – as the bundles that the rest, including Paul, were carrying.

Despite the fact that the group had to travel slowly, and somewhat noisily – if the pained expression on Shon Hu's face was any indication – along the perimeter of what was clearly regarded by the Bayani as Lokhali country, the fierce warriors of the forest were never seen. Nor, surprisingly enough, were many wild animals. Perhaps it was as Shon Hu claimed – that the great noise of their passing was sufficient to send any wild things other than belligerent carnivores far out of range of the intruders.

Whatever the reason, they passed two nights and the best part of three days safely in the forest – the only disturbing incident being when a tree-snake fell on Paul. But the small, fearsome-looking creature seemed quite as shaken by the encounter as he was, and rapidly disappeared.

The forest did not end abruptly. It simply began to thin out, so that the leaves of the trees no longer created an interwoven roof that shut out the sky. Paul noticed that the ground became more firm and less damp. The air was growing cooler, and it became obvious that the ground ahead was rising slowly. Presently, large patches of blue became noticeable between the tree-tops. Paul realized then how much he had been missing the open sky.

The forest gave way to savannah – rich grassland where the trees were few and scattered and were often no higher than the grass itself, which frequently came up to the shoulders of the small Bayani. Far ahead, Paul could see the uplands. Beyond them, now and again becoming briefly visible in the haze of late afternoon, there seemed to be a shimmering range of white-tipped mountains. Was it a trick of his imagination or was there really one that stood far higher than the rest? One that he knew instinctively was the Temple of the White Darkness.

Shortly before the sun set, they made camp in the middle of the rolling savannah. Now that the forest was behind, making the death of Mien She seem oddly remote, and now that it was possible to see the stars and the nine sisters – the nine moons of Altair Five – once more, the spirits of the hunters rose. After their evening meal, they wrapped themselves in skins against the cool night air and told stories to each other as before.

Paul had hoped that it would have been possible to make a fire. But to have started a fire in the middle of the savannah would have been very dangerous indeed – besides which, it would have been difficult to find sufficient fuel for one. So he was content to lean against his pillow of skins, himself warmly wrapped, and listen vaguely to the chattering of the Bayani.

As he gazed idly at the stars, he began to think. In the journey through the forest – a timeless journey through time – he had apparently cast off the personality and conditioning of Poul Mer Lo. For some reasons he could not understand, in some way he could not understand, he had become very consciously Paul Marlowe, native of Earth, once more.

And the surprising thing was that it no longer hurt. He was a castaway, far from home, and with no hope of returning. Yet, it no longer hurt …

He was amazed at the discovery.

Presently, the talk of the hunters died down and they made ready for sleep. Zu Shan and Nemo were already asleep, having tired themselves out with the day's journey. Presently, Paul and Shon Hu shared the first watch.

They did not talk. Shon Hu, though satisfied with the day's progress and relieved now that the forest was behind them, was not inclined to be very communicative. This suited Paul who was able – pleasurably for once – to contemplate the night sky and let his thoughts drift among the stars.

When it was time to wake the two hunters for their spell of watch, Paul felt more exhilarated than tired. Perhaps it was the effect of the cooler, bracing air. Or perhaps it was because they were nearing the end of the journey.

Nevertheless he very quickly fell asleep when at last he lay down.

THIRTY-ONE

He was aware of words being spoken loudly and urgently in his head. Vaguely and sleepily he tried to dismiss them as some aspect of a dream that he was not aware of dreaming. But the words would not be dismissed. They were not to be abolished either by sleepiness or willpower. They would not be ignored. They became louder, more insistent.

Until he sat bolt upright, listening to them with a sensation of panic that it was hard to fight down. In the starlight, he could see dimly that the others were also sitting upright. They, too, were listening – motionless, as if the sound that was not a sound had frozen the living flesh. There was also another sound – a real sound – that seemed very far away. With an effort, Paul concentrated on it. With an even greater effort, he managed to analyse it – the sound of Nemo whimpering. Then his thoughts were snapped back by the loud, imperative and utterly soundless message.

> *'Hear, now, the voice of Aru Re!*
> *If you would live to a ripeness, go back!*
> *If you would toil in the fields,*
> *if you would hunt in the forest,*
> *if you would rest in the evening, go back.*
> *If you would look upon women and beget children,*
> *if you would discourse with brothers and fathers,*
> *if you would gather the harvest of living,*
> *if you would pass your days in contentment,*
> *having heard the voice of Aru Re,*
> *go back! Go back! Go back!'*

The words without sound became silent. No one moved. Shon Hu was the first to speak. 'Lord,' he said shakily, 'we have heard the voice of Oruri and still live. This journey is not favoured. Now must we return.'

Paul tried desperately to marshal his racing thoughts. 'The voice spoke to you in Bayani, Shon Hu?'

'Most clearly, lord.'

'And yet it spoke to me in English – the language of my own country.'

'Such is the mystery of Oruri.'

'Not Oruri,' said Paul positively, 'but *Aru Re.*'

426

'Paul,' said Zu Shan, 'the voice spoke to me in both English and Bayani.'

Paul was silent for a moment. Then he said in English: 'That, I suppose, is because you are now able to think in both languages ... What about you, Nemo? Are you all right?'

Nemo's whimpering had stopped. 'I am very much afraid,' he confessed in a thin, high voice. 'I – I cannot remember what language I heard.'

Paul tried to laugh and ease the tension. 'You are not alone, Nemo. We were all very much afraid.'

'We shall go back to Baya Nor, then?' The child's voice was pleading.

Paul considered for a moment, wondering if he had any right to ask his companions to go farther. But how tantalizing, how heartbreaking to be so near and to have to turn back.

At length he spoke in Bayani. 'Already, I have asked too much of my friends and brothers,' he said. 'We have faced danger, one of us has died and there is, doubtless, much danger still to be faced. I cannot ask more of those who have already shown great courage ... Any who wish now to return, having heard what they have heard, will go with my thoughts and prayers. As for me, Shon Hu has fulfilled that which I asked. He has shown me the way. Doubtless, I shall reach the Temple of the White Darkness, if Oruri so desires. I have spoken.'

'Lord,' said Shon Hu, 'truly greatness sits upon you. A man cannot die in better company. This, perhaps, Oruri will consider when the time comes. I will go with you.'

There was a short silence, then one of the two remaining hunters spoke: 'We are ashamed in the presence of Poul Mer Lo and Shon Hu. Formerly, we were brave men. Forgive us, lord ... For some, it seems, there is no end to courage. For others, the end comes quickly.'

'My brothers,' said Paul, 'courage has many faces. I count myself fortunate that I have travelled this far with you ... Go when the first light comes, and a man may see the way ahead. Also, take with you Zu Shan and Nemo; for I rejoice in the knowledge that you will bring them safely to Baya Nor.'

'Lord,' said Zu Shan in Bayani, 'the gift of Enka Ne remains with him to whom the gift was made ... I think, also, the little one may desire to stay.'

Nemo seemed to have recovered himself. 'The little one desires much,' he said, also in Bayani, 'but he will stay in the shadow of Poul Mer Lo.'

Shon Hu laughed grimly. 'Thus are we a formidable company.'

'It is in such company,' retorted Paul enigmatically, 'that men may move mountains ... Now listen to my thoughts. The voice, it seems, spoke to each of us in a different manner. To me it spoke in my tongue, calling itself *Aru Re*. To you, Shon Hu, it spoke in your tongue. And to Zu Shan in a mixture of my tongue and his. But the message was the same for all of us, I think ... Zu Shan, what did you understand by the message?'

'That we should not go forward, otherwise we should die.'

'Ah,' said Paul triumphantly, 'but that was not what the voice said. It advised us, *if we desired certain things*, to go back. It advised, Zu Shan. It did not command. It advised us – if we desired security, long life, contentment, peace of mind – to return the way we came. But the voice did not advise us what to do if we desired knowledge, did it?'

There was a silence. Eventually, Shon Hu said: 'Lord, there is much mystery in your words. I do not understand where your thoughts lead, but I have made my decision and I will follow.'

'What I am trying to say,' explained Paul patiently, 'is that I think the voice meant to turn us back only if we did not have the resolution and the curiosity to go forward.'

'When Oruri speaks,' said Shon Hu with resignation, 'who dare question the meaning?'

'But when *Aru Re* speaks in English,' said Paul, emphasizing the separate words, 'the meaning must be sought more carefully.'

'Lord,' said one of the hunters who were returning to Baya Nor, 'we shall not take the barge. We shall leave it in the hope that Poul Mer Lo – who has wrought many wonders – will require it yet again.'

THIRTY-TWO

There were no more voices in the dark. Nor did Oruri – or *Aru Re* – utter his soundless words in the daytime. After less than a day's travel, Paul noticed that the long savannah grass was getting shorter. Presently it was only as high as his knee. Presently, no higher than his ankle. The air grew colder as they came to the uplands.

And there before them, less than half a day's march away, was the mountain range whose central peak was called the Temple of the White Darkness. All that lay between was a stretch of scrubland, rising into moorland and small patches of coniferous forest.

Suddenly, Paul became depressed. Through the high, clear air, he could see the detail of the jagged rockface of the mountain – capped and scarred by everlasting snow. And sweeping round the base of the mountain was a great glacier – a broad river of ice whose movement could probably be reckoned in metres per year.

As they made their last camp before they came to the mountain, there were distant muted rumbles, as if the mountain were aware of their presence and resented their approach. The three Bayani – the man, the youth and the child – had never heard the sound of avalanches before.

Paul had much difficulty explaining the phenomenon to them. Eventually, he gave it up, seeing that they could not clearly understand. To them, the noise was only one more manifestation of the displeasure of Oruri.

He gazed despairingly at the Temple of the White Darkness, wondering how he could possibly begin his search. He was no mountaineer. Nor was he equipped for mountaineering. And it would be sheer cruelty to drag his companions – children of the forest – across the dangerous slopes of ice and snow. How terrible it was to be so near and yet so helpless. For the first time he was ready to acknowledge to himself the probability of defeat.

Then the sunset came – and with it a sign. Paul Marlowe was not easily moved to prayer. But, on this occasion, prayer was not just the only thing he was able to offer. It seemed strangely appropriate and even inevitable.

There, far above the moorland and the ring of coniferous forest, as the sun sank low, he saw briefly a great curving stem of fire.

He had seen something similar many, many years ago in a world on the other side of the sky. As he watched, and as the sun sank and the stem of the fire dissolved, he remembered how it had been when he first saw sunlight reflected from the polished hull of the *Gloria Mundi*.

THIRTY-THREE

Paul Marlowe was alone. He had left his companions on the far side of the glacier. Shon Hu was partly snow blind, Zu Shan's nose had started to bleed because of the altitude, and little Nemo, wrapped in skins so that he looked like a furry ball, had an almost perpetual aching in his bones.

So Paul had left the three of them on the far side of the glacier and had set off alone shortly after dawn. He had told them that, if he had not returned by noon, they must go without waiting for him. He did not think that they could stand another night on the bare, lower slopes of the mountain.

The glacier had looked much more formidable than it really was. His feet and ankles ached a great deal with the effort of maintaining footholds on the great, tilting ice sheets; and from the way his toes felt it seemed as if sharp slivers of ice might have cut through the tough skins that were his only protection. But on the whole, apart from being bruised by innumerable minor falls, he felt he was in reasonable shape.

And now, here he was, standing near the base of one of the mighty metal shoes that supported the three impossibly slender legs of the great star ship. The shoes rested firmly on a broad flat table of rock in the lee of the mountain, and they were covered to a depth of perhaps three metres by eternal ice. The legs themselves were easily twenty metres tall; and the massive hull of the star ship rose all of two hundred metres above them – like a spire. Like the spire of a vast, buried cathedral.

Paul gazed up at the fantastic shape, shielding his eyes against the glow of its polished surface, and was drunk with wonder.

Then the voice that was no voice spoke in his head.

'I am beautiful, am I not?'

So much had happened that Paul was beyond surprise. He said calmly: 'Yes, you are beautiful.'

'I am *Aru Re* – in your language, Bird of Mars. I have waited here more than fifty thousand planetary years. It may be that I shall wait another ten thousand years before my children are of an age to understand. For I am the custodian of the memory of their race.'

Suddenly, Paul's mind was reeling. Here he was, a man of Earth, having made a hazardous journey on a strange planet, through primeval forests, across wide savannah, into the mountains and over a high glacier to meet a telepathic star ship. A star ship that spoke in English, called itself the Bird of

Mars and claimed to have been in existence for over fifty thousand years. He wanted to laugh and cry and quietly and purposefully go mad. But there was no need of that. Obviously he was already mad. Obviously, the glacier had beaten him and he was lying now – what was left of him – in some shallow crevasse, withdrawn into a world of fantasy, waiting for the great cold to bring down the final curtain on his psychic drama.

'No, you are not mad,' said the silent voice. 'Nor are you injured and dying. You are Paul Marlowe of Earth, and you are the first man resolute enough to discover the truth. Open your mind completely to me, and I will show you much that has been hidden. I am *Aru Re*, Bird of Mars … The truth, also, is beautiful.'

'Nothing but a machine!' shouted Paul, rebelling against the impossible reality. 'You are nothing but a machine – a sky-high lump of steel, wrapped round a computer with built-in paranoia.' He tried to control himself, but could not restrain the sobbing. 'Fraud! Impostor! Bastard lump of tin!'

'Yes, I am a machine,' returned the voice of the *Aru Re*, insistently in his head, 'but I am greater than the sum of my parts. I am a machine that lives. Because I am the custodian and the carrier of the seed, I am immortal. I am greater than the men who conceived me, though they, too, were great.'

'A machine!' babbled Paul desperately. 'A useless bloody machine!'

The voice would not leave him alone. 'And what of Paul Marlowe, voyager in the *Gloria Mundi*, citizen on sufferance of Baya Nor, Poul Mer Lo, the teacher? Is he not a machine – a machine constructed of bone and flesh and dreams?'

'Leave me alone!' sobbed Paul. 'Leave me alone!'

'I cannot leave you alone,' said the *Aru Re*, 'because you chose not to leave me alone. You chose to know. I warned you to go back, but you came on. Therefore, according to the design, you shall know. Open your mind completely.'

Dimly, Paul knew that there was a battle raging in his head. He did not want to lose it. Because he knew instinctively that if he did lose it he would never be quite the same again.

'Open your mind,' repeated the star ship.

With all his strength, Paul fought against the voice and the compulsive power that had invaded his brain.

'Then close your eyes and forget,' murmured the *Aru Re* persuasively. 'It has been a long journey. Close your eyes and forget.'

The change of approach caught Paul Marlowe off guard. Momentarily, he closed his eyes; and for the fraction of a second he allowed the tautness to slacken.

It was enough for the star ship. As great spirals of blackness whirled in upon him, he realized that he was in thrall.

There was no sensation of movement, but he was no longer on the mountain of the White Darkness. He was in a black void – the most warm, the most pleasant, the most comfortable void in the universe.

And suddenly, there was light.

He looked up at (down upon? around?) the most beautiful city he had ever seen. It grew – blossomed would have been a better word – in a desert. The desert was not a terrestrial desert, and the city was not a terrestrial city, and the men and women who occupied it – brown and beautiful and human though they looked – were not of Earth.

'This city of Mars,' said the *Aru Re*, 'grew, withered and died before men walked upon Sol Three or Altair Five. This city, on the fourth planet of your sun, contained twenty million people and lasted longer than the span of the entire civilization of Earth. By your standards it was stable – almost immortal.

'And yet it, too, died. It died as the whole of Mars died, in the Wars of the Great Cities that lasted two hundred and forty Martian years, destroying in the end not only a civilization but the life of the planet that gave it birth.'

The scene changed rapidly. As Paul Marlowe looked, it seemed as if the city were expanding and contracting like some fantastic organism inhaling and exhaling, pulsing with life – and death. In the accelerated portrayal of Martian history that he was now witnessing, buildings and structures more than two kilometres high were raised and destroyed in the fraction of a second. Human beings were no longer visible, not even as a blur. Their time span was too short. And every few seconds the desert and the city would erupt briefly into the bright, blinding shapes that Paul recognized from pictures he had seen long ago – the terrible glory of transient mushrooms of atomic fire.

'Thus,' went on the matter of fact voice of the *Aru Re*, 'did Martian civilization encompass its own suicide … Think of a culture and a technology, Paul Marlowe, as far ahead of yours as yours is ahead of the Bayani. Think of it, and know that such a culture can still be vulnerable as men themselves are always vulnerable … But there were those – men and machines – who foresaw the end. They knew that the civilization of Mars, inherently unstable, would perish. Yet they knew also that, with the resources at their command, three hundred million years of Martian evolution need not be in vain.'

The scene changed, darkened. Without knowing how he knew, Paul realized that he was now gazing at a large subterranean cavern, kilometres below the bleak Martian desert. Here other structures were growing, like strange and beautiful stalagmites, from the floor of living rock. Men and machines scuttled about them, antlike, swarming. Everywhere there was a sense of urgency and purpose and speed.

'And so the star ships were built – the seed cases that would be cast off by a dying planet to carry the seeds of its achievement to the still unravaged soil of distant worlds … Here is the rocky bed where I and six other identical vessels were created. It would have been comparatively easy to build star ships that were no more than star ships. But we were created as guardians – living guardians, fashioned from materials almost impervious to the elements and even time itself. Our task was not only to transport, but to nurture and prepare the seed; and when the seed had again taken root, when the flower of civilization had begun to bloom again, it would be our task to restore the racial memory and reveal the origin of that which could now only achieve maturity on an alien soil. Many died that we might be programmed for life. Many remained behind that we might carry the few – the few who were to become as children, their minds cleansed of all sophistication and personal memories so that they might rediscover a lost innocence, learning once more over the long centuries of reawakening, the nature of their human predicament.'

Again the scene accelerated. The star ships grew towards the roof of the cavern. In a silent, explosive puff, the roof itself was blasted away by some invisible force. Two of the star ships crumpled swiftly and soundlessly to lie like twisted strips of metal foil on the floor of a great rocky basin that was now open to the sky. A tiny, thin, blurred snake – that Paul Marlowe knew was a stream of human beings – rippled to the base of each of the remaining star ships. And was swallowed. Then, one by one, each of the silver vessels became shrouded by blue descending aureoles of light. The rock floor turned to brilliant liquid fire as the star ships lifted gracefully and swiftly into the black reaches of the sky.

'That was how the exodus took place,' continued the *Aru Re*. 'That was how the seedcases carried the seed. Of the five ships that left Mars, one proceeded to Sirius Four, where a great civilization is now maturing; one voyaged to Alpha Centáuri One, where the seed withered before it had taken root; another journeyed to Procyon Two, where the seed remains still only the seed, and where there is yet little distinction between men and animals; the fourth vessel, myself, came here to Altair Five, where, it seems, the flower may yet blossom; and the last vessel made the shortest voyage, to Sol Three, the planet you call Earth. Its seed lived and flourished, though the star ship was destroyed, having settled on land that possessed a deep geological fault. It is now more than nine millennia since the island on which the star ship rested was submerged below the waters you know as the Atlantic Ocean.'

Paul's mind was numbed by revelations, traumatized by knowledge, shattered by incredible possibilities. The Martian scene had faded, and there was now nothing. He floated dreamily and luxuriously in a sea of darkness, an intellectual limbo in which it was only possible to assume 'sanity' by actually believing that these fantastic experiences had been communicated to him by a telepathic star ship.

'Your body grows cold,' said the *Aru Re* incomprehensibly, 'and there is little time left for me to answer the questions that are boiling in your mind. Soon I must allow you to return. But here are some of the answers that you seek. It is true that my mind is a linked series of what you would call computers, but it also stores the implanted patterns of the minds of men long dead. It bears no more relation to what you understand by the term computer than your *Gloria Mundi* bore to its ancestor, the guided missile. You wish to know how I can speak your tongue and converse of the things you have known. I can speak the language used by any intelligent being by exploring its mind and correlating symbols and images. You wish to know also if I can still communicate with the remaining star ships, the guardians that await the maturation of their seed, as I do. We communicate not by any form of wave transmission that you can understand, but by elaborate patterns of empathy that are not subject to the limiting characteristics of space and time.'

It seemed to Paul that, in the black silence of his head, there was a great drum roll of titanic laughter. 'Is it so strange, little one,' said the *Aru Re* softly and with irony, 'that even a machine can grow lonely? Also, we need to share the knowledge when the first of the seed brings forth a truly mature fruit. For then there can be no doubt that the scattering of the seed was not in vain ... I will answer one more question, and then you must return if you are to live. You are puzzled by the variation in the number of fingers of the race you have discovered. There was some small genetic damage during transit, which caused slight mutations. The variations are of no importance. It matters not in the long sweep of history.' Again the titanic roll of laughter. 'In the end, little one, despite their now rigid tabu of the little finger, the far descendants of the Bayani will be as their Martian ancestors were. But perhaps they will have outlived the impulse to self-destruction ... Now, farewell, Paul Marlowe. Your mind flickers and your body grows cold ... *Open your eyes!*'

The darkness dissolved; and once more there was feeling – pain and exhaustion and extreme cold.

Paul opened his eyes. He was still standing at the base of one of the metal shoes of the star ship. Had he ever moved from it? He did not know. Perhaps he would never know. He stared about him, dazed, trance-like, trying to accept the realities of a real world once more.

The ache in his limbs helped to focus his mind on practicalities. His limbs were stiff and painful – as if they had been rigid a very long time, or as if he had just come out of suspended animation.

Shielding his eyes, he gazed up at the polished hull of the great star ship and then down at its supporting shoes embedded in eternal ice. That at least was real. He stood contemplating it for some moments.

Then he said softly: 'Yes, you are truly beautiful.'

He had told Shon Hu and the others not to wait for him after mid-day. The sun was already quite high in the sky. He felt weak and shattered; but there was no time to waste if he were to recross the glacier before they attempted to make their own way back to Baya Nor.

Then, suddenly, there was a curious rippling in his limbs – a glow, a warmth, as if liquid energy were being pumped into his veins. He felt stronger than he had ever felt. He could hardly keep still.

Impulsively, and for no apparent reason, he held out his arm – a strange half-gesture of gratitude and farewell – to the high, sun-bright column of metal that was the *Aru Re*.

Then he turned and set off on the journey back across the glacier.

Zu Shan saw him coming in the distance.

Shon Hu, partly snow blind, could hardly see anything.

Nemo did not need to see. His face wore an expression in which wonder mingled with something very near to ecstasy.

'Lord,' he said in Bayani when Paul was only a few paces away, 'I have been trying to ride your thoughts. There has never been such a strange ride. I fell off, and fell off, and fell off.'

'I, too, fell off,' said Paul, 'perhaps even more than you did.'

'You are all right, Paul?' asked Zu Shan anxiously in English.

'I don't think I have felt better for a long time,' answered Paul honestly.

'Lord,' said Shon Hu, 'I cannot see your face, but I can hear your voice, and that shows me the expression on your face … I am happy that you have found what you have found … The little one told us many strange things, lord, which are much beyond the thinking of such men as I … It is true, then, that you have spoken with Oruri?'

'Yes, Shon Hu. I have spoken with Oruri. Now let us return from the land of gods to the land of men.'

435

THIRTY-FOUR

There were now only two experienced pole-men to control the barge. But by this time Paul himself had acquired some of the tricks and the rhythm of poling, and he was able to relieve Shon Hu and Zu Shan for reasonably long spells; while Nemo continued to nurse his still aching bones in the stern of the small craft. Fortunately, navigation was not too difficult for they were now passing downstream. The poling was necessary as much to guide the barge as to add to its speed.

The journey back from the Temple of the White Darkness to the bank of the river had been easier than Paul had expected. Perhaps it was psychologically easier because they were relieved because the mountain had been reached without any further disasters, and they were now going home. Or perhaps it was because they were already familiar with the hazards of the route and also because Shon Hu's uncanny sense of direction had enabled them to reach the Watering of Oruri less than a kilometre from where they had sunk the barge.

Shon Hu had completely recovered from his snow blindness by the time they had reached the savannah. As soon as they were on the lower ground, they made camp and rested for a day and a night before going back into the forest. They did not hear the voice of the *Aru Re* again – though, out of curiosity, Paul exercised what mental concentration he possessed in an attempt to contact it telepathically. It seemed as if the star ship had now dismissed them altogether from its lofty contemplations.

Though they had found the barge without too much difficulty, it took the three of them the best part of an afternoon to clear it of stones and sediment and refloat it. By that time they were tired out; and though there was still enough light left to pass the Lokhali village before darkness fell, Shon Hu judged it safer to wait until the following morning. By then the barge would have dried out and, with a full day's poling, they could be far from the Lokhali before they had to make a night camp once more.

So it was that shortly after dawn the barge drifted round a slight bend in the Watering of Oruri, and the Lokhali village came in sight. There were few people about this time – probably many of the Lokhali were still at their morning meal – but three or four men were sitting in a little group, desultorily fashioning what looked like spear shafts out of straight, slender pieces of wood. There were also some women bathing or washing. And one who stood apart from the rest and seemed neither to be bathing or washing, but watching.

Paul handed his pole back to Zu Shan and took up his sweeper rifle. At a distance of perhaps a hundred metres, he saw that there was something odd about the solitary woman. She was virtually naked as the rest were; and at that distance her skin seemed quite as dark as that of the others – but she had white hair. Everyone else had black hair. But this one, the solitary one, had white hair.

Paul cast his mind back desperately to the occupants of the *Gloria Mundi*. None of them had white hair. With the exception of the Swedish woman who had been – inevitably – blonde, all of them had been rather dark. And Ann – Ann's hair had been quite black.

But there was something about the solitary woman on the bank, now only sixty or seventy metres away …

Paul had long ago decided on a plan of action if there were any *Gloria Mundi* survivors, able to move freely, in the Lokhali village. It was an extremely simple plan, but his resources were such that it was impossible to risk anything elaborate like a direct assault. For the atomic charge in the sweeper rifle was now ominously low.

However, there were still three factors in his favour: he had some element of surprise, he had a strange and powerful weapon, and he knew that the Lokhali didn't like travelling on water.

Shon Hu and Zu Shan had already been warned to keep the barge steady on command. Now, if only …

The Lokhali had seen the barge; but though the women had come out of the water and the men had picked up their spears, no one seemed inclined to try to do anything about it. They just stood and stared – sullenly and intently. The woman with the white hair seemed to be concentrating her attention on Paul, and on the weapon he held.

With little more than forty metres separating the barge from the bank, Paul judged that now, if at all, he must make the attempt. Probably there were no Europeans left. And even if there were, the chances of being able to contact them, quite apart from rescuing them, would be pretty remote.

And yet … And yet … And yet, the woman with the white hair seemed to be meeting his gaze. That slight movement of the arm – could it be a discreet signal?

'*Gloria Mundi!*' he shouted. '*Gloria Mundi!*' He raised the rifle and waved it. 'Into the water – quick! *Venez ici! Kommen sie hier!* I'll give covering fire!'

Suddenly, the woman with the white hair ran into the water, splashing and wading out to swimming depth. To Paul it seemed as if she were moving in horribly slow motion. But the miraculous thing was nobody looked like stopping her. Then a woman cried out and the spell was broken. A tall Lokhali swung his spear arm back, so did another. Then a third began to run after the woman with white hair. The water was not yet up to her waist, and she still did not have free swimming room.

'Hurry, damn you!' he shouted. 'Hurry!'

He sighted the rifle carefully over her head, fixing on the patch of water between her and the bank. He pressed the trigger.

The rifle whined feebly, faintly; and the water began to hiss and steam. The Lokhali who had tried to follow stopped dead. The two with spears ran towards him. The woman was already able to swim, and the bubbling water behind her had now turned into a water spout – effectively deterring pursuit and partly screening her from the men on the bank.

Then the sweeper rifle died. Its atomic charge had finally reached equilibrium.

The water spout subsided. All that was left to deter the Lokhali was a patch of very warm water – rapidly being carried downstream by the current – and a condensing cloud of steam.

One of the Lokhali hurled a spear. It fell almost exactly between the woman and the barge. By that time, she was less than twenty metres away from it, but she was making very slow progress and seemed curiously tired.

If Paul had stopped to think then, the tragedy might possibly have been averted. It did not occur to him until later that the spear might have been hurled not at the woman but at the barge.

But, without thinking, he flung the useless rifle down and dived into the water, hoping at least to create a diversion. It was not the diversion he had hoped for. Before he hit the water, the Lokhali on the bank had found their voices. By the time he had surfaced, they were being reinforced by other warriors from the village.

Another spear plunged into the river quite near to him, and then another. A few powerful strokes brought him to the woman. There was no time to try to discover who she was.

'Turn on your back!' he yelled. 'I'll tow you!'

Obediently, she turned over. He grasped her under the armpits and with rapid, nervous kicks propelled them both back to the barge. Suddenly, he felt a blow, and the woman shuddered, letting out a great sigh. He paid no attention to it, being intent only on getting them both to the comparative safety of the barge.

Somehow, he got her there.

As Shon Hu hauled her aboard, he saw the short spear that was sticking in her stomach and the dark rivulet of blood that pulsed over her brown flesh.

Then he hauled himself aboard and knelt there, panting with exertion, gazing at the contorted but still recognizable features of Ann.

'Get it out!' she hissed. 'For God's sake get it out!'

Then she fainted.

THIRTY-FIVE

It was Shon Hu who took the spear out. Paul was trembling and crying and useless. And it was Zu Shan and Nemo who, between them, somehow managed to keep the barge on a steady course and pole it safely out of range of the Lokhali spears and away from the village.

Paul managed to pull himself together before she opened her eyes.

'You were right, after all,' she murmured. 'It was an appointment in Samara, wasn't it?'

For a moment, he didn't know what she meant. Then it all came back to him. The *Gloria Mundi*. Champagne on the navigation deck after they had plugged the meteor holes. Philosophizing and speculating about Altair. Then Ann had told him about Finagle's Second Law. And he had told her the legend of an appointment in Samara.

'Ann, my dear … My dear.' He looked at her helplessly. 'You're going to be all right.'

With an effort, she raised herself up from the little pillow of skins that Shon Hu had managed to slip under her head. Paul supported her while she studied the wound in her stomach with professional interest.

'It doesn't hurt much, now,' she said calmly. 'That's not a good sign. Some venous blood, but no arterial blood … That's a bit of help … But I'm afraid I'm going to die … It may take time … You'll have to help me, Paul. I may get terribly thirsty … Normally, I wouldn't prescribe much liquid, but in this case it doesn't matter … Of course, if you can plug it without hurting me too much, you'll slow down the loss of blood.'

She leaned against him, exhausted. Gently, he lowered her to the pillow.

'Any old plug will do,' gasped Ann. 'A piece of cloth, a piece of leather – anything.'

He tore a strip of musa loul, made it into a wad and tried to press it into the gaping wound.

Ann screamed.

Shon Hu made a sign to Zu Shan and drew his pole back into the barge.

He came and squatted by Ann, regarding her objectively. Then he turned to Paul. 'Lord, what does the woman need?'

'I have to press this into her wound,' explained Paul. 'But – but it hurts too much.'

'Lord, this can be accomplished. Do what must be done when I give the sign.'

Expertly, Shon Hu placed his hands on each of Ann's temples and pressed gently but firmly. For a moment or two, she struggled pitifully, not knowing what was happening. Then suddenly her eyes closed and her body became slack.

Shon Hu nodded and took his hands away. Paul pressed the wad firmly into the wound. Presently Ann opened her eyes.

'I thought you must have gone back home, back to Earth,' she murmured faintly. 'It was the one satisfaction I had … Every night, I'd say to myself: Well, at least Paul hasn't come unstuck. He's on his way back home … What happened to the *Gloria Mundi?*'

'It blew itself up, according to the destruction programme, after the three of us left it to go and look for you and the others.'

Ann coughed painfully and held Paul's hand tightly, pressing it to her breast. When the spasm was over, she said: 'So the voyage has ended in complete disaster … What a waste it's all been – what a terrible waste.'

'No, it hasn't,' said Paul, then he looked down at her pain-twisted face and realized the stupidity of his remark. He began to stroke her white hair tenderly. 'Forgive me. I'm a fool. But, Ann, I've discovered something so incredibly wonderful that – that it would seem to make any tragedy worthwhile … That's a damnfool thing to say – but it's true.'

She tried to smile. 'You must tell me about your wonderful discovery … I would like very much to think that it's all been worthwhile.'

'You should rest. Try to sleep … You mustn't talk.'

'I'll be able to sleep quite soon enough,' she said grimly. 'And you can do most of the talking … Now tell me about it.'

As briefly as he could, he told her about his capture by the Bayani and of the friendship that had developed between himself and Enka Ne, otherwise Shah Shan. He told her about Oruri, the ultimate god of the Bayani. Then, passing quickly over much that had happened since the death of Shah Shan, he told her of Nemo's dreams, the legend of the coming, and how he finally made the journey to the Temple of the White Darkness. And, finally, he told her of his discovery of and encounter with the *Aru Re.*

Sometimes, while he was talking, Ann closed her eyes and seemed to drift off into unconsciousness. He was not quite sure how much she heard of his story – or, indeed, whether she could make much sense of it. But he went on talking desperately, because if she were not unconscious but only dozing, she might miss the sound of his voice.

As he talked, everything began to seem utterly unreal to him. He had never found the *Aru Re.* He was not even here on a barge, drifting on a dark river through a primeval forest, talking to a dying woman. He was dreaming.

Probably, he was still in suspended animation aboard the *Gloria Mundi* – and his spirit was rebelling, by creating its own world of fantasy, against that unnatural state that had nothing to do with either living or dying. And presently, he would be defrozen. And then he would become fully alive.

Suddenly, he realized that he had stopped talking and that Ann had opened her eyes and was looking at him.

'Yes, I think you're right,' she said faintly, 'It's been worthwhile … I – I'm not sure I've got it all clearly in my head – my mind isn't working too well. But if the part about the *Aru Re* means what I think, you've made the most wonderful discovery in all the ages … Oh, Paul … I'm so – so …' her voice trailed away.

There were tears running down his face. 'But I've got no one to tell it to,' he burst out desperately, 'no one, but—' He stopped.

'But a dying woman?' Ann smiled. 'Stay alive, Paul. Just stay alive … I'm afraid you've got the harder job.'

He bent and kissed her forehead. Great beads of sweat were forming on it. But the flesh was sadly cold.

'I wish – oh, God, I wish I knew what happened to the others!'

If Ann had survived – at least until his stupid Galahad act – why could not some of the others have survived? If he could find them, no matter what happened afterwards, at least he would have human company. No! That was a bloody silly thing to think. He already had Zu Shan, Nemo, Shon Hu. All good, very good, human company. But still alien. Human but alien. Strangers on the farther shore …

'You have accounted for three,' said Ann in a weak voice. 'I'm … so – so sorry, Paul. But I can account for the rest … It was on that very first night after we left the *Gloria Mundi?*' She laughed faintly, but the laughter degenerated into a fit of coughing that hurt her badly; and it was some time before she could continue. 'You remember we went to look for the Swedish, French and Dutch pairs … It was a long time before I found what happened to them, but I'll tell you about that in a minute … Oh, God, Paul! We were so sure of ourselves – so clever! We were scientists. We had weapons. We had intelligence. The only thing we didn't have was the thing we really needed – forest lore … We were so confident – such easy game … The three of us walked straight into a hunting party of these forest people – they call themselves the Lokh. We didn't even fire a shot. They had us stripped of everything – all that lovely equipment just tossed away by savages – and trussed like turkeys in a matter of seconds … The Italian girl wouldn't stop screaming, so they killed her … They weren't being brutal. It was just their idea of self-preservation. They didn't want to attract our friends, if any, or dangerous animals … Lisa – you remember Lisa? – she was very calm. But for her, I'd have probably gone the same way as Franca. But she made me keep still and quiet – no matter what they did to us … They weren't cruel, just inquisitive … We must have really baffled them … Anyway, they took us back to the village. They kept us prisoners for a while. Then we began to pick up some of the language. We tried to explain to them how we had come to Altair Five. But it was no use. They just refused to believe it … After a time, they let us have our freedom – more or less. After all, there was nowhere to go. We just didn't have enough strength or knowledge … Poor Lisa. She poisoned herself … She just went round eating every damn fruit, flower or root she could find until she got something that did the trick. The Lokh didn't know what she was up to. They thought it was very funny. She was the joke of the village … As for me, it seems ridiculous now, but I still found life very dear. So I just tried to make myself useful about the place … I began playing doctor – treating wounds, setting bones, that sort of thing … I think they got to like me … And that's how it was until you came. The days just ran into one another. And there wasn't any past, and there wasn't any future. At one time, I thought I was going mad … But I wasn't … And that's all … And now it's ending like this.' She smiled. 'Finagle's Second Law – remember?'

Paul lifted her hand and kissed it. 'Oh, my love. My poor love.'

'Oh, yes, I was going to tell you about the others,' she said. 'The Stone Age got them. Isn't that a joke? They had enough fire power to destroy an army, and the Stone Age got them.'

He looked at her, puzzled.

'I'm sorry,' murmured Ann. 'I'm not being very coherent … There are some pretty dreadful beasts in the forest, and the Lokh protect their village by digging a ring of camouflaged pits around it. The camouflage is very good. I've nearly fallen into the damn things myself … They have these pits, with sharpened stakes sticking up in them, in various parts of the forest. Every now and then they go out to inspect them and see what they have caught … They took me out to one of the pits one day. There was some plastic armour, sweeper rifles, transceivers and – and six skeletons at the bottom … The twenty-first century defeated by the Stone Age … The Lokh thought they were being kind showing me what had happened to my companions … That was when I thought I might go mad.'

'Ann,' he said, gently wiping the sweat from her forehead and feeling the terrible coldness again. 'I'm a fool – an absolute fool. I shouldn't have let you talk. Please, *please* rest now.'

'Sooner than you think,' she murmured. 'Much … sooner than you think … Don't reproach yourself, my dear.' Her eyes were half-closed, and there was a faint smile on her lips. 'It was worth it to see … my husband … again … Caxton Hall, ten-thirty … A red rose … You looked rather sweet – and a bit frightened.'

She began to cough, and this time there was some blood. The paroxysm exhausted her, but there didn't seem to be pain any more.

'Not long now,' she said thickly. 'I didn't expect to see it up top so soon ... The blood ... Hold me, Paul. Hold me ... It's such a lonely business ... Afterwards, the river ... It's so lovely to think of everything being washed away ... Washed clean.'

He lifted her body and held it close against him, stroking her hair – the soft white hair – mechanically, while the tears trickled down his face and mingled with the cold sweat on hers.

'My dear, my love,' he sobbed desperately. 'You're not going to die. I'm not going to let you go ... I'm not going to let you ... I must think. God, I must think ... A dressing – that's it. A decent dressing. Then when we get to Baya Nor I'll—' He stopped.

There had been no sound, no sigh. No anything. She just hung slackly in his arms. He was talking to a dead woman.

For some time, he sat there motionless, holding her. Not thinking. Not seeing.

Presently, he was aware of Shon Hu's arm on his shoulder.

'Lord,' said the Bayani gently, 'she travels to the bosom of Oruri. Let her go in peace.'

Presently, they made a shroud of skins for her, and weighted it with stones.

Presently, as she had wished, Ann Victoria Marlowe, *née* Watkins, native of Earth, slipped back into a dark and cleansing river on the far side of the sky.

THIRTY-SIX

Paul Marlowe stared down at the sodden ashes of what had once been his home, and felt nothing but a great emptiness inside him. It was like a cold black void that mysteriously seemed to swell without exerting either pressure or pain. Too much had happened in the last few days, he supposed, for him to feel anything now. Later, no doubt, the numbness would go away and he would be able to assimilate this final tragedy. He wondered, curiously and clinically, if the feeling would be deep enough to move him to tears.

The journey back along the Watering of Oruri and then the Canal of Life had been accomplished safely without any further interference from man or beast – at least, he supposed it had. For after Ann's death, he had been too traumatized to pay much attention to what was going on. He had sat calmly on the barge, staring at and through the impenetrable green walls of the forest, while day merged into night and night merged into day once more. Shon Hu had taken command of the party, deciding when to rest and where to make camp, and Paul had been as obedient and docile as a child.

But as the barge came nearer to Baya Nor the shock began to recede. Slowly he emerged from the deadly lethargy that had gripped him. He began to think once again, realizing that despite privation and tragedy, the journey had been successful, that he had made the most important discovery in the history of mankind, and that he was on his way home. It was the realization of being on his way home that unnerved him a little. Home, originally, had been somewhere on Earth – and he couldn't clearly remember where. It was now on Altair Five – and he could visualize very clearly exactly where it was and what it was.

It was a thatched house, standing on short stilts. It was a small dark woman who was immensely proud of the growing bundle of life in her belly … It was a bowl of cooled kappa spirit on the verandah steps in the evening … It was the sound of bare feet against wood, the smell of cooking, the tranquil movements of a small alien body …

The barge was only a few hours' poling from Baya Nor before Paul had pulled himself together sufficiently to think about Enka Ne. In making his journey to the Temple of the White Darkness, he had not only challenged the authority of the god-king, he had humiliated him. He had humiliated Enka Ne by destroying the pursuing barge and by tipping the god-king's warriors into the Canal of Life.

444

Possibly, for the sake of his prestige, Enka Ne would choose to treat the incident as if it had never happened. But that, thought Paul, was unlikely. It was far more likely that, as soon as he was able, Enka Ne would inflict some punishment or humiliation in return.

That was why Paul had not allowed Shon Hu and Zu Shan to bring the barge back to the city. He had made them stay with it on the Canal of Life, about an hour's walking distance away, while he came on ahead to learn – if he could – something of the situation. If he did not return that day, he had left them with orders to go back into the forest for a while, in the hope that time would diminish the god-king's displeasure and that he, Paul, would be able to establish sole responsibility for his transgression.

It had been raining during the night, but the day was becoming very warm, and the earth was steaming. And now, here he was, staring at an untidy scattering of damp ashes, patiently watched by the child, Tsong Tsong, whom Paul had left as company for Mylai Tui.

Tsong Tsong was as wet and miserable as the ashes. He had never been particularly bright or coherent, and he was now an even more pathetic figure, being half-starved. It had been the desire of his master, Poul Mer Lo, that Tsong Tsong should stay at the house. The child had interpreted the command literally and, even after the house had been burned down and Mylai Tui was dead, Tsong Tsong had kept vigil – patiently waiting for the return of Poul Mer Lo.

If Paul had never come back, he reflected, no doubt Tsong Tsong would have stayed there until he died of starvation.

He patted the small boy's head, looked down with pity at the blank face, the dark uncomprehending eyes, and patiently elicited the story.

'Lord,' said Tsong Tsong in atrociously low Bayani, 'it was perhaps the morning of the day after you went on the great journey … Or the morning of the day after that day … I have been hungry, lord, and I do not greatly remember these things … There were many warriors. They came from the god-king … It was a good morning because I had eaten much meat that the woman, Mylai Tui, could not eat … She was a good cook, lord, though cooking seemed to make her weep. Perhaps the vapours of the food were not good to her eyes … But the meat was excellent.'

'Tsong Tsong,' said Paul gently, 'you were telling me about the warriors.'

'Yes, lord … The warriors came … They made the woman leave the house. She was angry and there were many loud words … I – I stood back, lord, because it is known that the warriors of Enka Ne are impatient men. So, being unworthy of their consideration, and also much afraid, I drew back … My lord understands that it would perhaps not have been good for me to remain?'

'Yes, I understand. Tell me what happened.'

'The warriors said they must burn the house, and this I could not understand, because it is known that Poul Mer Lo is of some importance … It was very strange, lord. When the woman, Mylai Tui, saw them make fire she became as one touched by Oruri. She shook and spoke in a loud voice and wept … She tried to run into the burning house, shouting words that I could not understand. But a warrior held her. It was very frightening, lord … And the house made great noisy flames. And then she seized a trident and wounded the man who held her … And then – and then she died.'

Paul was amazed that he could still find no tears, no pain.

He knelt down and rested his hand on the small boy's shoulder. 'How did she die, Tsong Tsong?' he asked calmly.

The boy seemed surprised at the question. 'A warrior struck her.'

'It was – it was quick?'

'Lord, the warriors of Enka Ne do not need to strike twice … I have been very hungry since then. There was some kappa, but it was black and had the taste of fire about it. My stomach was unhappy … Forgive me, lord, but do you have any food?'

Paul thought for a moment or two. Then he said: 'Listen carefully, Tsong Tsong. There is something that you must do, then you shall have much food … Do you think you can walk?'

'Yes, lord, but it not a thing I greatly desire to do.'

'I am sorry, Tsong Tsong. It is necessary to walk to get to the food. I have left Shon Hu, the hunter, and your comrades Zu Shan and Nemo in the barge some distance from here along the Canal of Life. You must go to them. Tell them what you have told me. Also tell them that Poul Mer Lo desires that they and you shall remain in the forest for as many days as there are fingers on both hands. Can you remember that?'

'Yes, lord … Do they have much food?'

'Enough to fill you up, little one. Shon Hu is a good hunter. You will not starve. Now go – and say to them also that when they leave the forest they must be careful how they come to Baya Nor, and careful how they enquire after me.'

The child stretched his limbs and gave a deep sigh. 'I will remember, Lord … You are not angry with me?'

'No, Tsong Tsong, I am not angry. Go, now, and soon you will eat.'

He watched the small boy trot unsteadily down to the Canal of Life and along its bank. Then he turned to look at the steaming ashes once more.

He thought of Mylai Tui, so proud of the son she would never bear, and of Ann, enduring patiently in the heart of the forest until she could keep an appointment in Samara, and of the *Aru Re*, Bird of Mars, standing in its icy fastness through the passing millennia – a lofty, enigmatic sentinel waiting for the maturation of the seed.

So much had happened that he was drunk with privation and with grief and with wonder. The sun had not yet reached its zenith, but he was desperately tired.

He sat down on the small and relatively dry patch of earth that Tsong Tsong had vacated. For a while, he stared blankly at the ashes as if he expected Mylai Tui, phoenix-wise, to rise from them. But there was nothing but silence and stillness.

After a time, he closed his aching eyes and immediately fell asleep – sitting up. Presently he toppled over, but he did not wake.

He did not wake until shortly before sunset. He was stiff and lonely and still filled with a great emptiness.

He looked around him and blinked. Then he sat up suddenly, oblivious of the throbbing in his head.

He was surrounded by a ring of tridents, and a ring of blank black faces of the warriors of the royal guard.

For a moment or two, unmoving, he tried to collect his thoughts. Obviously the warriors did not mean to kill him, for they could have accomplished that task quite easily while he was still sleeping. They looked, oddly, as if they were waiting for something.

He was debating in his mind what to say to them when he saw, through the descending twilight, a vehicle coming jerkily along the Road of Travail. At first he thought it was a cart. But then he saw that it was a palanquin, carried by eight muscular young girls. The equipage left the Road of Travail and came directly towards the ring of warriors.

Paul stood up, gazing at it in perplexity. He remembered the first time he had seen the shrouded palanquin that contained the oracle of Baya Nor. It had been on a barge on the Canal of Life, when Enka Ne, otherwise Shah Shan, was taking him to the temple of Baya Sur to witness the first of three sacrifices of girl children.

As if at a signal, the girls carrying the palanquin stopped and set it gently down. The curtains shrouding it did not move. But from inside there came a wild bird cry.

Then a thin and withered arm poked out from between the curtains, pointing unwaveringly at Paul. And an incredibly old yet firm voice said clearly: 'He is the one!'

Dazed and exhausted still, Paul was aware of a great roaring in his ears. He felt the hands of the Bayani warriors catch him as he fell.

THIRTY-SEVEN

He was in a darkened room, lit only by a few flickering oil lamps. A man with a white hood over his face peered at him through narrow eye-slits.

'Who are you?' The words came like gun-shot.

'I am Poul Mer Lo,' Paul managed to say, 'a stranger, now and always.'

The man in the white hood stared at him intently. 'Drink this.' He held out a small calabash.

Obediently, Paul took the calabash and raised it to his lips. The liquid was like fire – fire that consumed rather than burned.

Something exploded in his head, and then he felt as if he were being dragged down into a maelstrom. And then he felt as if he were floating freely in space.

When he became conscious again, he realized vaguely that he was being supported by two guards.

'Who are you?' shouted the man in the white hood.

Paul felt an almost Olympian detachment. The situation was curious, but amusing. For all his aggressiveness, the man in the white hood was definitely dull-witted.

'I am Poul Mer Lo,' repeated Paul carefully and with a little difficulty, 'a stranger, now and always.'

'Drink this,' commanded the inquisitor. He held out the calabash.

Once more Paul took it and raised it to his lips. The fire flowed through his body, roaring and all-consuming. His thoughts became tongues of flame. A curtain of flame danced and drifted before his eyes, slowly burning itself away to reveal a great bird, covered in brilliant plumage, with iridescent feathers of blue and red and green and gold.

But the bird did not move. It had no head.

Once more the maelstrom dragged him down. Once more he felt as if he were floating freely in space. This time there were stars. They whirled about him as if he were the still pivot of a turning universe. The stars were whispering, and their message was important, but he could not hear the words. All he could do was to watch the speeding gyrations, the beautiful cosmic merry-go-round, until time itself drowned in the broad black ocean of eternity …

Until he was suddenly aware once more of a darkened room and a few flickering lamps. And a man with a white hood over his face.

The headless bird had disappeared. And yet … and yet he was still aware of its presence.

'*Who are you?*' The words rolled like waves, like thunder.

He did not know what to say, what to do, what to think, what to feel. He did not know what to believe; for identity had been lost and he seemed now to be nothing more than the vaguest thought of a thought.

'*Who are you?*' The waves crashed on the farther shore. The thunder rolled over a distant land.

And then came answering thunder.

And a voice from far, far away said: 'There shall come a man among you, who yet has no power and whose power will be absolute. And because no man may wield such power, the man shall be as a king. And because none may live for ever, the king shall be as a god. Each year the king must die that the god may be reborn … Hear, now, the cry of a bird that has never flown … Behold the living god – whose name is Enka Ne!'

He listened to the voice in wonder, feeling the words beat upon him like hammer blows. He listened to the words and submitted to the voice – knowing at last that it was his. He moved, and there was a strange rustling. He looked down at the blue and gold feathers covering his arms.

From somewhere another voice, old and high and thin, uttered a wild bird cry. 'He is the one!'

Then the man in the white hood cried: 'Behold the living god!' And sank down to prostrate himself at the feet of one who had once been known by the name of Poul Mer Lo.

THIRTY-EIGHT

Afterwards he had rested for a while in an apartment in the Temple of the Weeping Sun, guarded only by a single warrior. The ceremonial plumage had been removed, and the god-king now wore a simple samu, indistinguishable from those worn by thousands of his subjects.

The apartment – whose walls and floor and roof were of highly polished stone, veined, like a rich marble, with streaks of blue and red and green and gold – was not luxuriously furnished. But, compared to the simple furnishings of a thatched house that had stood once near to the Canal of Life, these furnishings were indeed those of a palace.

The foot and head of the couch on which he had rested were of black wood inlaid with copper. The mattress consisted of multi-coloured Milanyl feathers held in a fine net of hair. Large translucent crystals hung from the ceiling, rotating slowly in the slight currents of air, transforming the lamplight emanating from several niches into a soft and mobile pattern.

The god-king yawned and stretched, looking about him for a moment or two. He was hungry. But there were more important matters than food.

He sent for Yurui Sa, general of the Order of the Blind Ones. The man in the white hood.

The warrior on guard heard the instructions of the god-king without either looking at him or making any verbal acknowledgement.

Presently, Yurui Sa entered the room. He stood stiffly, waiting. His gaze, like that of the warrior, remained fixed upon the ceiling.

'Oruri greets you, Yurui Sa.'

'Lord, the greeting is a blessing.'

'Sit down and be with me as with a friend, for there is much that I have to say to you.'

'Lord,' said the man pleadingly, 'be merciful … I – I may not see you!'

'This, surely, needs explanation.'

'So it has always been,' went on Yurui Sa, 'so it must always be. When the plumage has been put aside, the god-king may not be seen by men.'

'So, perhaps, it has always been. But nothing endures for ever. When the plumage has been put aside, the god sleeps but the king still wakes. You may look upon the king, Yurui Sa. I have spoken.'

'Lord, I am not worthy.'

'Nevertheless—' and the voice was regal, the voice of Enka Ne '—nevertheless, it is my wish.'

Slowly, Yurui Sa brought his gaze down from the ceiling. Enka Ne smiled at him, but there was fear on the face of the general of the Order of the Blind Ones.

'There will be some changes,' said Enka Ne.

Yurui Sa let out a great sigh. 'Yes, lord, there will be some changes.'

'Now sit with me and tell me how it came to pass that one who was once Poul Mer Lo is now the god-king of the Bayani, though the time is not yet ripe for rebirth.'

Yurui Sa swallowed uneasily. Then he sat down on the edge of the couch as if he expected the action to bring some terrible disaster.

Apparently, it did not. Thus heartened, he began to explain to Paul Marlowe, native of Earth, how it came about that he was destined to achieve god-head on Altair Five.

'Lord,' said Yurui Sa, 'much that is wonderful has happened, making the will of Oruri clear beyond question … Many days ago, it became known to one who now has no name that the stranger, Poul Mer Lo, intended to make a great journey. The knowledge was not received favourably. Therefore many warriors were despatched to end the journey before it had begun.' Yurui Sa permitted himself a faint smile. 'My lord may himself have some awareness of what happened on that occasion. The warriors failed to fulfil their task – and such warriors do not often fail in their duty. Their captain returned and, before despatching himself to the bosom of Oruri, repeated the message given to him by Poul Mer Lo. That same day, one who now has no name suffered much pain in his chest, coughing greatly, and for a time being unable to speak. Thus was seen the first judgement of Oruri on one who perhaps had misinterpreted his will.'

'You say he coughed greatly?'

'Yes, lord. There were many tears.'

Paul's mind went back to the occasion of his only audience with Enka Ne the 610th. He remembered an old man – an old man weighed down with care and responsibility. An old man who coughed …

'Proceed with your story.'

'Lord, even then there were those in the sacred city who were afflicted by strange thoughts. Some there were – myself among them – who meditated at length upon what had passed. Later, when warriors were sent to destroy the house of Poul Mer Lo, our meditations yielded enlightenment. Also, there was an unmistakable sign of the will of Oruri.'

'What was this sign?'

'Lord, as the house burned, he who has no name was seized by much

451

coughing. As the flames died, so died he who has no name. Thus was seen the second judgement of Oruri ... Then the oracle spoke, saying that fire would awaken from the ashes ... And so, lord, were you revealed to your people.'

Paul Marlowe, formerly known as Poul Mer Lo, now Enka Ne the 611th, was silent for a few moments. He felt weary still – unutterably weary. So much had happened that he could not hope to assimilate – at least, not yet. He smiled grimly to himself. But there would be time. Indeed, there would be time ...

And then, suddenly, he remembered about Shon Hu and the barge.

'When Poul Mer Lo came from the forest, he left certain companions waiting in a barge on the Canal of Life. I desire that these people – and a child who has by now reached them – be brought to Baya Nor unharmed.'

'Lord, forgive me. This thing is already done. Warriors were instructed to watch for the coming of Poul Mer Lo. They have found the barge, its occupants and the boy who was despatched to meet them.'

'None have been harmed?'

'Lord, they have been questioned, but none was harmed.'

'It is well. Yurui Sa, for these are humble people, yet they have a friend who is highly placed.'

The general of the Order of the Blind Ones fidgeted uncomfortably. 'Lord, the hunter, Shon Hu, has said that Poul Mer Lo has held converse with Oruri, also that he has looked upon the form ... Forgive me, lord, but can this be so?'

'It is no more than the truth.'

'Then is my heart filled with much glory, for I have spoken with a great one who has himself spoken with one yet greater ... Permit me to withdraw, lord, that I may dwell upon these wonders.'

'Yurui Sa, the wish is granted. Now send to me these people who journeyed with Poul Mer Lo. Send also much food, for these, my guests, will be hungry ... And remember. There will be some changes.'

The general of the Order of the Blind Ones stood up. Again he sighed deeply. 'These things shall be done. And, lord, I will remember that there will be some changes.'

Enka Ne leaned back upon the couch.

The warrior guarding him continued to stare fixedly at the ceiling.

THIRTY-NINE

It was a warm, clear evening. Paul Marlowe, clad only in a worn samu, sat on the bank of the Canal of Life not far from the Road of Travail; and not far, also, from a patch of ground where ashes had been covered by a green resurgence of grass. Theoretically, he had thirty-seven days left to live.

It was not often these days that he could find time to put aside the *persona* of Enka Ne. There was so much to do, so much to plan. For, since greatness had been thrust upon him, he had become a one-man renaissance. He had seen it as his task to lift the Bayani out of their static, medieval society and to stimulate them into creative thought. Into attitudes that, if they were allowed to flourish, might one day sweep the people of Baya Nor into a golden age where science and technology and tradition and art would be fused into a harmonious and evolving way of life.

The task was great – too great for one man who had absolute power only for a year. Yet, whatever came afterwards – or whoever came afterwards – a start had to be made. And Paul Marlowe's knowledge of human history was such that he could derive comfort from the fact that, once the transformation had begun, it would take some stopping.

And it had certainly begun. There was no doubt about that.

Schools had been established. First, he had had to teach the teachers; but the work was not as difficult as he had anticipated, because he had absolute authority and the unquestioning services of the most intelligent men he could find. They were willing to learn and to pass on what they had learned – not because of burning curiosity and a desire to expand their horizons but simply because it was the wish of Enka Ne. Perhaps the curiosity, the initiative and the enthusiasm would come later, thought Paul. But whether it did or not in this generation, the important fact remained: schools had been established. For the first time in their history, the children of the Bayani were learning to read and write.

Dissatisfied with the broad kappa leaves that he had previously used for paper, Paul had experimented with musa loul and animal parchment. Already he had set up a small 'factory' for the production of paper, various inks, brushes and quill pens. At the same time, he had commanded some of the priests who had become proficient in this strange new art of writing to set down all they could remember of the history of Baya Nor and its god-kings, of its customs, of its songs and legends and of its laws. Presently, there would be a small body of literature on which the children who were now learning to read could exercise their new talent.

In the realm of technology there had been tremendous advances already. The Bayani were skilled craftsmen and once a new principle had been demonstrated to them, they grasped it quickly – and improved upon it. Paul showed them how to reduce friction by 'streamlining' their blunt barges, so that the barges now cut their way through the water instead of pushing their way through it. Then he demonstrated how oars could be used more efficiently than poles, and how a sail could be used to reduce the work of the oarsmen.

Now, many of the craft that travelled along the Bayani canals were rowing boats or sailing dinghies, moving at twice the speed with half the effort.

But perhaps his greatest triumph was the introduction of small windmills, harnessed to water-wheels, for the irrigation of the wide kappa fields. So much manpower – or woman-power – was saved by this innovation, that the Bayani were able to extend the area of the land they cultivated, grow richer crops and so raise the standard of living.

Perhaps the most curious effect of Paul's efforts was that he seemed to have created a national obsession – for kite-flying. It rapidly became the most popular sport in Baya Nor. It attracted all ages, including the very old and the very young.

Once they had grasped the principle, the Bayani developed a positive genius for making elaborate kites. They were far superior to anything that Paul himself could have built. Some of the kites were so large and so skilfully constructed that, given the right kind of wind conditions, they could lift a small Bayani clear of the ground. Indeed, one or two of the more devoted enthusiasts had already been lifted up or blown into the Mirror of Oruri for their pains.

The Bayani seemed to have a natural understanding of the force of the wind as they had of the force of flowing water. Already, a few of the more experimental and adventurous Bayani were building small gliders. It would be rather odd, thought Paul, but not entirely surprising if they developed successful heavier-than-air machines a century or two before they developed engines.

But there were other, more subtle changes that he had brought about and with which he was greatly pleased. Except as a punishment for murder and crimes of violence, he had abolished the death penalty. He had also completely abolished torture. For 'civil' cases and minor offences such as stealing, he had instituted trial by jury. Major offences were still tried by the god-king himself.

The one Bayani institution that he would have liked most to destroy he did not feel secure enough to destroy. It was human sacrifice – of which he himself would presently become a victim.

The Bayani had already seen many of their most ancient customs and tra-ditions either modified or abolished. On the whole, they had reacted to change remarkably well – though Paul was acutely aware of the existence of a group of 'conservative' elements who bitterly resented change simply because things had always been done thus. At present the discontents were disorganized. They muttered among themselves, but still continued to adhere strictly to the principle of absolute loyalty to their absolute ruler.

If, however, they were pushed too far – as, for example, by the abolition of human sacrifice, a concept to them of fundamental religious importance – they could conceivably unite as a 'political' group. The one thing that Paul was determined to avoid was any danger of rebellion or civil war. It would have destroyed much of the progress that had been made so far. If successful, it might even have brought about a 'burning of the books' before books had had time to prove their intrinsic worth.

One thing was sure, because of the intrusion of a stranger who had risen to absolute power the civilization of Baya Nor could never again be static. It must go forward – or back.

So, in order to give his one-man renaissance the best possible chance of flourishing, Paul felt that he would have to leave human sacrifice alone. After all, it did not affect more than twenty people a year – most of them young girls – and the victims were not only willing to accept martyrdom, but com-petitively willing. It was a great distinction. For they, after all, were the beloved of Oruri.

There was, of course, one potential victim who did not have such a com-forting philosophy. And that was Paul himself. He wondered how he would feel about the situation in another thirty-seven days. He hoped – he hoped very much – that he would be able to accept his fate as tranquilly as Shah Shan had done. For, in the Bayani philosophy, it was necessary that one who knew how to live should also know how to die.

As he sat by the bank of the Canal of Life, reviewing the happenings of the last few months, Paul Marlowe was filled with a deep satisfaction. A start had been made. The Bayani were beginning their long and painful march from the twilight world of medieval orthodoxy towards an intellectual and an emotional sunrise. A man's life was not such a high price for the shaping of a new society ...

Paul sat by the Canal of Life for a long time. It was on such an evening as this, when the nine small moons of Altair Five swarmed gaily across the sky, that he had been wont to sit upon the verandah steps drinking cooled kappa spirit and philosophizing in words that Mylai Tui could not understand.

He thought of her now with pleasurable sadness, remembering the baf-fling, almost dog-like devotion of the tiny woman who had once been a temple prostitute, who had taught him the Bayani language and who had

455

become to all intents and purposes his wife. He thought of her and wished that she could have lived to bear the child of whose conception she had been so proud. He wished that she could have known also that Poul Mer Lo, her lord, was destined to become the god-king. Poor Mylai Tui, she would have exploded with self-importance – and love …

Then he thought of Ann, who was already becoming shadowy again in his mind. Dear, remote, elusive Ann – who had once been a familiar stranger. Also, his wife … It was nearly a quarter of a century since they had left Earth together in the *Gloria Mundi* … He had, he supposed, aged physically not much more than about six years in all that time. But already he felt very old, very tired. Perhaps you could not cheat Nature after all, and there was some delayed aftereffect to all the years of suspended animation. Or maybe there was a simpler explanation. Perhaps he had merely travelled too far, seen too much and been too much alone.

The night was suddenly crowded with ghosts. Ann … Mylai Tui … An unborn child … Shah Shan … And a woman with whom he had once danced the Emperor Waltz on the other side of the sky …

He looked up now at this alien sky whose constellations had become more familiar to him than those other constellations of long ago.

He looked up and watched the nine moons of Altair Five swinging purposefully against the dusty backcloth of stars.

And his heart began to beat in his chest like a mad thing.

He counted the moons carefully, while his heart pumped wildly and his arms trembled and his eyes smarted.

He took a deep breath and counted them again.

There were now ten tiny moons – not nine. Surely that could only mean one thing …

Dazed and shaking, he began to run back to the sacred city – back to the private room where he still kept his battered, and so far useless, transceiver.

FORTY

He stood on the small, high balcony of the Temple of the Weeping Sun. His eyes were fixed on the cluster of moons already approaching the horizon. There were still ten.

The transceiver was in his hand, its telescopic aerial extended.

He was still shaking, and sweat made his fingers slip on the tiny studs of the transceiver as he set it for transmission at five hundred metres on the medium wave band. If the tenth moon of Altair Five was indeed a star ship – and what an unlikely *if* that was! – orbiting the planet, surely an automatic continuous watch would be kept on all wave bands. But if it was a star ship, how the devil could it be a terrestrial vessel? It had arrived at Altair Five less than three years after the *Gloria Mundi*. Yet, when the *Gloria Mundi* had left Earth, apart from the American and Russian vessels, no other star ships – so far as Paul knew – had even left the drawing board. On the other hand, if it wasn't a terrestrial vessel, what else could it be? A large meteor that had wandered in from deep space and found an orbital path? A star ship from another system altogether?

Paul's head was a turmoil of possibilities, impossibilities and plain crazy hopes.

'Please, God, let it be a ship from Earth,' he prayed as he pressed the transmit stud on the transceiver. 'Please, God, let it be a ship from Earth – and let this bloody box work!'

Then he said, in as calm a voice as he could manage: 'Altair Five calling orbiting vessel. Altair Five calling orbiting vessel. Come in, please, on five hundred metres. Come in, please, on five hundred metres. Over ... Over to you.'

He switched to receive and waited, his eyes fixed hypnotically on the ten small moons. There was nothing – nothing but the sound of a light breeze that rippled the surface of the Mirror of Oruri. Nothing but the stupid, agitated beating of his heart.

He switched to transmit again. 'Altair Five calling orbiting vessel. Altair Five calling orbiting vessel. Come in, please, on five hundred metres. Come in, please, on five hundred metres. Over to you.'

Still nothing. Presently the moons would be over the horizon, and that would be that. Maybe they were already out of range of the small transceiver. Maybe the damn thing wasn't working, anyway. Maybe it was an extraterrestrial ship and the occupants didn't bother to keep a radio watch because they were

457

all little green men with built-in telepathic antennae. Maybe it was just a bloody great lump of rock – a cold, dead piece of space debris … Maybe … Maybe …

At least the receiving circuits were working. He could now hear the hiss and crackle of static – an inane message, announcing only the presence of an electrical storm somewhere in the atmosphere.

'Say something, you bastard,' he raged. 'Don't just hook yourself on to a flock of moons and go skipping gaily by … I'm alone, do you hear? Alone … Alone with a bloody great family of children, and no one to talk to … Say something, you stupid, tantalizing bastard!'

And then it came.

The miracle.

The voice of man reaching out to man across the black barrier of space.

'This is the *Cristobal Colon* called Altair Five.' The static was getting worse. But the words – the blessed, beautiful words – were unmistakable. 'This is the *Cristobal Colon* calling Altair Five … Greetings from Earth … Identify yourself, please. Over.'

For a dreadful moment or two he couldn't speak. There was a tightness in his chest, and his heart seemed ready to burst. He opened his mouth, and at first there was only a harsh gurgling. Instantly – and curiously – he was ashamed. He clenched his fist until the nails dug into his palms, and then he forced out the words.

'I'm Paul Marlowe,' he managed to say. 'The only survivor—' his voice broke and he had to start again. 'The only survivor of the *Gloria Mundi* … When – when did you leave Earth?'

There was no answer. With a curse, he realized that he had forgotten to switch to receive. He hit the button savagely, and came in on mid-sentence from a different voice.

'—name is Konrad Jurgens, commander of the *Cristobal Colon*,' said the accented voice slowly in English. 'We left Earth under faster than light drive in twenty twenty-nine, four subjective years ago … We are so glad to discover that you are still alive – one of the great pioneers of star flight. What has happened to the *Gloria Mundi* and your companions? We have seen the canals but have not yet made detailed studies. What are the creatures of this planet like. Are they hostile? How shall we find you?'

Paul's eyes were on the moons, now very low in the sky. Somehow, he managed to keep his head.

'Sorry, no time for much explanation,' he answered hurriedly. 'You will soon be passing over my horizon, and I think we'll lose contact. So I'll concentrate on vital information. If you take telephoto detail surveys of the area round the canals, you will see where the *Gloria Mundi* touched down … We burned a swathe through the forest – about ten kilometres long. It's probably visible even to the naked eye from a low orbit … You'll see also the crater where the *Gloria Mundi* programmed its own destruction after being abandoned. Touch down as near to it as possible. I'll send people out to meet you – you'll recognize them. But don't – repeat don't – leave the star ship until they come. There are also people in these parts who are not too friendly … I'll get the reception committee to meet you about two days from now … They are small, dark and quite human.' He laughed, thinking of what he had learned from the *Aru Re*. 'In fact, I think you are going to be amazed at how very human they are. Over to you.'

'Message received. We will follow your instructions. Are you in good health? Over.'

Paul, drunk with excitement, laughed somewhat hysterically and said: 'I've never felt better in my life.'

There was a short silence. Then he heard: '*Cristobal Colon* to Paul Marlowe. We have received your message and will follow your instructions. Are you in good health? Over.'

Paul saw the ten moons disappearing one by one over the horizon. He tried to reach the *Cristobal Colon* again, and failed. He switched back to receive.

'*Cristobal Colon* to Paul Marlowe. We will follow your instructions. We no longer hear you. We will follow your instructions. We no longer hear you … *Cristobal Colon* to Paul Marlowe. We will follow—'

He switched off the transceiver and gave a great sigh.

The impossible seemed oddly inevitable, somehow – after it had happened.

He stood on the balcony of the Temple of the Weeping Sun for a long time, gazing at the night sky, trying not to be swamped by the torrents of thoughts and emotions that stormed inside him.

Faster than light drive … That was what they had said … Faster than light drive … Four subjective years of star flight … The *Cristobal Colon* must have left Earth seventeen years after the *Gloria Mundi* … And now here it was, orbiting Altair Five less than three years after the *Gloria Mundi* had touched down … Probably half the crew of this new ship were still at school when he was spending years in suspended animation on the long leap between stars … No wonder they regarded him as one of the pioneers of star flight … *Cristobal Colon* – a good name for a ship that, like Columbus, had opened up a new route for the voyagings of man … Soon, soon he would be speaking to men who could remember clearly what spring was like in London, or Paris or Rome. Men who still savoured the taste of beer or lager, roast beef and Yorkshire pudding or Frutti del Mare. Men – and, perhaps women – whose very looks and way of speaking would bring back so much to him of all that he had left behind – all that he had missed – on the other side of the sky …

Suddenly, the tumult in his head spent itself. He was desperately tired, exhausted by hope and excitement. He wanted only to sleep.

EPILOGUE

Enka Ne sat pensively on his couch. The single Bayani warrior on guard stared fixedly at the ceiling. The *Cristobal Colon* had touched down successfully and its occupants had been met by a troop of the god-king's personal escort. Besides their tridents they had carried banners bearing the legend: *Bienvenu, Wilkommen, Benvenuto, Welcome*. The troop had been led by a hunter, a boy and a crippled child. It must, thought the god-king, have been quite a carnival … And now men from Earth walked in Baya Nor …

Yurui Sa, general of the Order of the Blind Ones, entered the room and gazed upon the presence, although the god-king wore only his samu.

'Lord, it is as you have commanded. The strangers wait in the place of many fountains … They are tall and powerful, these men, taller even than –' Yurui Sa stopped.

'Taller even,' said the god-king with a faint smile, 'than one who waited in the place of many fountains a long, long time ago.'

During the past months, Yurui Sa and the god-king had developed something approaching friendship – but only in private, and when the plumage had been set aside. They were men of two worlds who had grown to respect each other.

'Lord,' went on Yurui Sa, 'I have seen the silver bird. It is truly a thing of much wonder, and very beautiful.'

'Yes,' said the god-king, 'I do not doubt that it is very beautiful.'

There was a short silence. Yurui Sa allowed his gaze to drift through the archway to the small balcony and the open sky. Soon the light would die and it would be evening.

'I think,' said Yurui Sa tentatively, 'that it would be very wonderful to journey in the silver bird to a land beyond the sky … Especially if one has already known that land, and if the heart has known much pain.'

'Yurui Sa,' said the god-king, 'it seems that you are asking me a question.'

'Forgive me, lord,' answered Yurui Sa humbly, 'I am indeed asking you a question – although the god-king is beyond the judgement of men.'

The god-king sighed. Yurui Sa was asking Enka Ne what, until now, Paul Marlowe had dared not ask himself.

He stood up and walked through the archway, out on to the little balcony. The sun was low and large and red in the sky. It did not look much different from the sun that rose and set on an English landscape sixteen light-years away ... And yet ... And yet ... It was different. Still beautiful. But different.

He thought of many things. He thought of a blue sky and puffy white clouds and cornfields. He thought of a small farmhouse and voices that he could still hear and faces that he could no longer visualize. He thought of a birthday cake and a toy star ship that you could launch by cranking a little handle and pressing the Go button.

And then he thought of Ann Marlowe, dying on a small wooden barge. He thought of Mylai Tui, proud because she was swollen with child. He thought of Bai Lut, who made a kite and brought about his own death, the destruction of a school, and a journey that led to the ironically amazing discovery that all men were truly brothers. And he thought of Shah Shan, with the brightness in his eyes – tranquil in the knowledge that his life belonged to his people ...

The sun began to sink over the horizon. He stayed on the balcony and watched it disappear. Then he came back into the small room.

The god-king looked at Yurui Sa and smiled. 'Once,' he said softly, 'I knew a stranger, Poul Mer Lo, who had ridden on a silver bird. Doubtless, he would have desired greatly to return to his land far beyond the sky ... But – but I no longer know this man, being too concerned with the affairs of my people.'

'Lord,' said Yurui Sa, and his eyes were oddly bright, 'I already knew the answer.'

'Go, now,' said Enka Ne, 'for I must presently greet my guests.'

A slight breeze came into the room, whispering softly through the folds of a garment that hung loosely on a wooden frame. The iridescent feathers shivered for a moment or two, and then became still.

If you've enjoyed these books and would
like to read more, you'll find literally thousands
of classic Science Fiction & Fantasy titles
through the **SF Gateway**

✳

*For the new home of
Science Fiction & Fantasy . . .*

✳

*For the most comprehensive collection
of classic SF on the internet . . .*

✳

Visit the SF Gateway

www.sfgateway.com

Edmund Cooper (1926–1982)

Edmund Cooper was born in Cheshire in 1926. He served in the Merchant Navy towards the end of the Second World War and trained as a teacher after its end. He began to publish SF stories in 1951 and produced a considerable amount of short fiction throughout the '50s, moving on, by the end of that decade, to the novels for which he is chiefly remembered. His works displayed perhaps a bleaker view of the future than many of his contemporaries, frequently utilising post-apocalyptic settings. In addition to writing novels, Edmund Cooper reviewed science fiction for the *Sunday Times* from 1967 until his death in 1982.